The Secret Years

JUDITH LENNOX

The Secret Years

St. Martin's Press
New York

*For my father, Harry Stretch,
and for my grandfather, Thomas Stretch,
who fought in the Great War*

Library of Congress Cataloging-in-Publication Data

Lennox, Judith.
The secret years / Judith Lennox.
p.   cm.
ISBN 0-312-13166-6 (hardcover)
I. Title.
PR6062.E65S4   1995
823'.914—dc20   95-2068   CIP

First published in Great Britain by Hamish Hamilton Ltd.

First U.S. Edition: May 1995
10 9 8 7 6 5 4 3 2 1

PART ONE

1909—1914

Into my heart an air that kills
From yon far country blows:
What are those blue remembered hills,
What spires, what farms are those?

(Alfred E. Housman, 'A Shropshire Lad')

CHAPTER ONE

THE distant hills melted into a coppery sunset. Thomasine, kneeling in the dust, looked up for a moment and was blinded by the sun. The wind traced a ghostly path through the elephant grass; in the valley a few skinny cows pulled yellowed leaves from the trees. The child shaded her eyes with her hand and let her sight blur, so that the hills seemed to dissolve and flatten, the rays of the African sun changing into narrow bands of golden water.

There had been other farms, in other places. Every journey, Daddy said, was to a better place, the right place. Once there had been a whole herd of cows (Thomasine had given them all names), but now there were only a handful.

In a storm the thatched roof blew from the hut, but Daddy and the boy just collected the scattered straw and tied it back on again. The boy explained to Thomasine that the land they had rented from the chief was bad land, ju-ju land, which was why no one had farmed it before. Thomasine asked her mother about the ju-ju land. God created the world in seven days, said Patricia Thorne. How therefore could a single inch of it be evil? But, in exchange for a lock of Thomasine's auburn hair, the boy showed her the caves that the witch-doctor used. The caves were cold and echoing with memories, their entrances doorways into different worlds. Outside in the light again, she sawed off a length of red hair with the boy's knife, and he looked at it with awe and dread before twisting it into a knot and placing it inside the amulet he wore around his neck.

A man and a lady from the Baptist mission visited the Thornes. Daddy had slaughtered one of the skinny cows, so they ate meat that day. The beef was tough and tasteless. The boy and his father dined with them, just as they always did, but when the men went to work and Patricia Thorne was making tea, the missionary lady said, 'But they are dirty, my dear Mrs Thorne. There have been several cases of yellow fever in the past month. And we must surely teach them their place.' Patricia poured the tea, and said, 'But we are all equal, are we not, Miss Kent, in the sight of God?'

One evening, the boy took Thomasine to the village to watch the dancing. The moonlight and the fires illuminated the bodies that swayed like reeds in the wind, that wove stories on the dusty ground. The men wore masks: enlarged and exaggerated distortions of the human face. The beating of the drums echoed through the earth so that Thomasine, too, had to dance. When the music stopped she fell to the ground, overcome with a sense of abandonment. One of the women picked her up and gave her a drink. Another gave her a present of beads and a length of scarlet cloth. A third stroked her long loose hair with blue-black hands, chattering to the other women in a language the child could not understand.

With her mother's help, Thomasine made the scarlet cloth into a skirt. The skies remained blue and empty of clouds. The wheat, that had been up to Thomasine's knees, stopped growing. She questioned her father, pulling at the tails of his shirt as he walked through the blighted field. The rains have not come, and the soil is not right, said Thomas Thorne. Ju-ju land, thought Thomasine, and shivered. A few days later, she picked a stalk of wheat and rubbed it between her fingers, and it crumbled like old paper.

There were only three cows left, and none gave any milk. The sky was hard and metallic, like a brass bowl. Thomasine helped her father carry water from the stream, but the stream was thick and greenish, the mud bed cracked into mosaic. The people left the village, their animals following in a long train behind them, the brightly coloured robes of the women a mere memory in a landcape of dust and ochre. The boy and his father went with them.

Thomasine's father grew thinner, her mother grew fatter. Thomasine couldn't understand why Mama grew fatter, because there never seemed to be much to eat any more. Then one morning there was a little baby on the pillow beside her mother. Thomasine didn't know who had given them the baby, and she dreaded having to give her back. They called her Hilda, after Mama's favourite sister. Mama had shown Thomasine a photograph of her three sisters: Hilda and Rose and Antonia. They lived far away, in England.

Her father was sick one night, and the following morning he set off for the mission hospital to fetch them all medicine. He took the big horse, the bad-tempered one that he would never allow Thomasine to ride. Before he left he bade her take care of her mother and her sister. She waved her handkerchief in farewell, and watched him ride along the valley towards the hills.

She sat beside her mother's bed all day. Patricia Thorne had not risen for six weeks, since Hilda was born. The baby slept and fed, nestled in shawls. Thomasine loved to touch the warm velvety head, loved to watch the little starfish hands. The baby was smaller than her big rag doll.

When Thomas Thorne did not return by nightfall, Thomasine cut up root vegetables and mixed them with maize and made soup. Crouched outside over the fire, stirring the pot, she reminded herself that the mission was eight miles away, that the bad-tempered horse might have thrown a shoe. Yet the sky and the land seemed very dark, very empty.

Her mother swallowed only a mouthful of the soup, Thomasine ate the rest herself. The baby cried a lot, and Mama's cheeks were flushed, her forehead shiny with sweat. Thomas Thorne did not return the next day, nor the next. Mama did not understand when Thomasine asked her whether she should ride out after Daddy, or whether she should stay and look after the baby. Mama's skin was a peculiar yellowish colour, and her eyes seemed to have sunk into her head. Her face looked like one of the masks that Thomasine had seen in the village. Thomasine tried to persuade her to drink water, but the only water she could find was the brackish stuff from the creek. It trickled from Mama's mouth down her chin and neck, on to her nightgown. The baby stopped crying and slept most of the time.

On the third day Thomasine was woken by the silence. When she went over to the bed, she thought at first that Mama was asleep, but when she touched her hand it was cold. She understood that she was quite alone now, except for the baby. She could still feel the gentle tiny rise and fall of the baby's chest. She guessed that little Hilda was hungry too, and knew that she had nothing with which to feed her.

Thomasine dressed in the scarlet skirt, put all their most precious belongings into a bag and saddled the horse. She rode with the baby cradled on her back, African-fashion, towards the mission hospital, and her father.

Southampton wasn't like Port Harcourt at all. It was greyer and colder, and the sky was laced with a fine drizzle. Like walking through the edge of a waterfall, thought Thomasine.

The aunts were waiting for her by the harbour. In the bustle of ships and sailors and passengers she did not think she would ever find them, but Miss Kent, black beady eyes glaring above a sharp nose, dragged her through the crowds and brought her face to face with the three women in Mama's photograph. She was exclaimed over, enveloped in hugs and kisses.

Thomasine heard Miss Kent say, 'We gave a Christian burial to the parents, and to the little baby.'

'*Baby*,' said the red-haired aunt. (Thomasine, unable to remember which name belonged to which, had immediately labelled them the big aunt, the little aunt, and the red-haired aunt.)

'There was an infant,' said Miss Kent.

'She was called Hilda,' said Thomasine.

6

The big aunt blinked and began to polish the rain from her spectacles. One of the ships made an enormous hooting sound, and Thomasine, in her thin black coat and dress, shivered.

'Yellow fever, as I explained in my letter, Miss Harker.'

'This poor child is cold.'

'Miss Kent – we are so inexpressibly grateful. You will dine with us?'

To Thomasine's relief, the missionary lady shook her head. Thomasine was obliged to endure a last violet-scented peck on the cheek, and then she was led away from the dock, her hands tucked around the arms of two of her aunts.

In the tea-shop, while the aunts bickered amiably, she managed to sort out their names. The red-haired one was Antonia, the big one was Hilda, and the little one was Rose.

'A career is so important,' whispered Antonia. 'The poor little mite is an orphan, after all.'

'I am not suggesting, Tony, dear, that Thomasine should not have a career. It is merely the choice of career that I am disputing.'

'Dancing is perfectly respectable, Hilda. All the girls from my school are carefully chaperoned when they work in theatres.'

'I can give Thomasine a thorough grounding in mathematics, literature and geography. So much more choice for a girl, if she can pass her school certificate.'

'She has a dancer's body. Look at her feet – her hands –'

'Surely,' Rose's voice trembled slightly as she poured everyone another cup of tea, 'country air would be so good for Thomasine. And she is only a child . . . only ten . . .'

Aunt Rose passed Thomasine the plate of cakes. She chose one shaped like a cow's horn, full of cream and jam. The ground, after her long sea voyage, was beginning to rock a little less, and she felt very hungry.

'Perhaps,' said Hilda firmly, 'Thomasine should live with Rose and I, but she should have long holidays with Antonia.

We have always loved children, haven't we, Rose? And to look after a child would be difficult for you, Tony, now that you are on your own.'

Antonia looked as though she was about to argue, but then her kid-gloved hand folded over Thomasine's. 'You shall come and stay with me very often, won't you, darling? I shall buy you a pair of slippers and a tunic.'

The countryside, glimpsed through the window of the train, flattened out and became threaded with strips of water. In the weak sunlight everything glittered green and blue and silver. As Hilda and Rose began to pack away thermos flasks and rugs and books into a battered carpet bag, Thomasine exclaimed, 'Do you live in a *lake*?'

Hilda glanced out of the window. Only water was visible, the railway embankment slicing above it. She smiled.

'No, dear. Some of the fields have flooded because of the heavy rain this winter.'

When they disembarked at Ely station, the train hissed and hooted and blew out a great deal of steam. A porter carried their bags outside, and Hilda fumbled in her purse for pennies.

'It is a long walk to Drakesden, dear.'

'I like to walk.' Thomasine had been confined in the ship, in the train, for too long. 'Daddy always said that you had to walk to really know the land.'

Hilda carried both the aunts' bag and Thomasine's. Rose held the child's hand as they followed the narrow paths that led from Ely to the village. The soil was black, and was criss-crossed with water like a chequerboard. Several times they had to walk narrow teetering planks that spanned the swollen ditches. Hilda crossed first, so that Thomasine was safely passed from one aunt to the other. Thomasine's boots were covered with mud, but, walking fast to keep up with Hilda, she began to feel warm for the first time since she had arrived in England.

Drakesden wasn't much bigger than the African village that

the boy had taken her to. The houses were thatched, and made of a yellowish brick. There was a church and a shop, and a few children playing in the street, who stared open-mouthed at Thomasine as she passed.

Hilda went up to the front door of one of the cottages, and put down the bags as she turned the handle. Thomasine read the name painted over the doorway, 'Quince Cottage', and followed her aunt indoors.

She shut Africa and Mama and Daddy and the baby away in a little box of memory. It was easier that way. In the mornings she had lessons with Aunt Hilly, and in the afternoons she explored Drakesden. Sometimes she walked, sometimes she borrowed the rector's pony and rode. The village children still stared at her, especially when she wore the red skirt.

At church, she disgraced herself by walking out of the building first, straight after the rector. Everyone else was just standing still: there was a shuffling ahead in the pews behind the choir stall, but that was all. Desperate to leave the dark dank building, Thomasine picked up her prayer-book and ran outside. She couldn't understand the expression on Mr Fanshawe's face as she said goodbye to him, but later Aunt Rose explained that the Blythes always left church first. Next Sunday, Thomasine noticed that Mr Fanshawe smiled most at the Blythes, and least at those who left church last. She and Aunt Hilly and Aunt Rose were somewhere in the middle.

She asked questions of everyone: Mrs Carter who ran the shop, the tenant farmers, the men and women who worked in the fields. She discussed with Mr Naylor, who worked Chalk Farm, the problems of growing wheat with too little water, and he laughed and told her there was too much water in the Fens. She helped Aunt Rose in the vegetable garden, digging up tiny new potatoes from the dark crumbly earth, and collected warm brown eggs from the hen-house, placing them carefully in a basket of straw.

She rode alongside the dyke one day, and wandered through

a copse of patchy laurel bushes and thorn, and found herself on the edge of a velvety lawn. When she looked up she saw Drakesden Abbey, the Blythes' house. It was huge, bigger than the mission hospital. Then she looked again and saw all the people staring at her: Lady Blythe in a floaty white gown and big flat hat, a dark-haired boy, a fair-haired boy and girl. Mortified, she mumbled her apologies and turned the pony about. Back at the dyke, she met Daniel Gillory, who cackled with laughter when she told him how she had interrupted the Blythes having tea in the Abbey gardens.

It was Daniel who explained to her about the dykes and ditches and windmills and pumps. Daniel was the blacksmith's eldest son. Thomasine had tried to talk to Jack Gillory about how he fixed shoes to the horses' hooves, but he hadn't been a good talker. Daniel was a good talker, though. Daniel, said Aunt Hilly, was an extremely bright boy. He had just won a scholarship for the Grammar School in Ely. Aunt Hilly often lent him books. Daniel was a few months older than Thomasine, and he had fair hair that was halfway between curling and straight, eyes that were halfway between green and hazel. Riding through the fields one afternoon when his father was at The Otter, Daniel explained to Thomasine how the water was pumped from the land into the dykes, and from the dykes into the sea. How both the dykes and the roads were high above the fields because the drained peat had sunk. How, a long time ago, all the Fens had been marsh and lake, an endless watery landscape. Fenmen had webbed feet in those days, Daniel added, his green-gold eyes solemn as he looked at Thomasine. Then laughed uproariously as he admitted the tease, and raced her all the way along the drove, their borrowed ponies' hooves kicking up the dust.

Slowly, she became accustomed to the changing of the seasons. The heat and the cold, the wind and the drought. Her first sight of snow, floating like white blossom from a leaden sky, and in the summer dust devils that briefly reminded her of that other land.

★

She wore the red skirt and an old white blouse of her mother's, too large for her, to have tea with the Dockerills. Thomasine liked the Dockerills: the three-roomed cottage was always busy and noisy.

Mrs Dockerill admired her skirt and her beads. Some of the ten little Dockerills crowded round the scarred table, their elbows all touching, the others perched on stools and boxes and planks. Mrs Dockerill lifted the bacon pudding out of the pot and unwrapped the muslin. She cut it into twelve pieces and placed them on an assortment of plates and bowls. A big piece for Mr Dockerill and Harry and Tom, who worked on the land, middle-sized pieces for Jane and Sal, who were in service but had the afternoon off, and little pieces for the children. The new baby slept in a box in the corner of the room. The smell of the bacon pudding was irresistible.

They had all started eating when there was the sound of footsteps outside. Harry Dockerill opened the door, and Lady Blythe stood there, her son Nicholas and daughter Marjorie behind her. Lady Blythe had brought some old sheets for Mrs Dockerill to cut up for the new baby. Thomasine watched as Lady Blythe came into the cottage and lifted the lids from the pots on the stove one by one, inspecting their contents. The noisy, cheerful Dockerills became suddenly silent. They had put down their knives and spoons and forks, and sat rigidly, uncomfortably upright as their food went cold on their plates. Thomasine, who was aware of feeling cross, but wasn't exactly sure why she felt cross, defiantly stabbed a piece of bacon with her fork.

'White cabbage, Mrs Dockerill?' enquired Lady Blythe, peering into the biggest pot. 'Kale is just as nutritious, and much more economical.'

Then she caught sight of Thomasine. The chill blue eyes met Thomasine's sea-green ones, just at they had outside the church, just as they had when she had trespassed on Drakesden Abbey's lawns.

'Put down your fork, child. Have you no manners? Do you not know how to behave in front of your betters?'

Anger, bubbling and uncontainable, welled up inside her. A memory of her mother pouring out tea for the missionary lady resurfaced.

'All of us are equal in the sight of God, Lady Blythe,' said Thomasine clearly. Her face was hot, but as she looked away her eyes momentarily met those of Lady Blythe's dark-haired son, and she thought she detected not criticism, but amusement.

That time, Daniel Gillory didn't laugh when Thomasine told him what had happened. He stood on the edge of the dyke, bouncing flat stones across the clear cold water.

'The Blythes own most of the cottages in Drakesden,' he explained. 'Most of the land, too. And the farms. So people have to behave themselves. If they don't, they find themselves without a home and without work. That's the way it is round here.'

'*Your* cottage, Daniel?'

'Our cottage – and the land – belongs to my mother. Her grandfather bought it from the Blythes for a bushel of potatoes. It floods badly in spring, so I expect that's why they sold it.' He began to walk along the top of the dyke, Thomasine following after him. 'That's why I want to stay at school. If I can get my School Certificate, then I won't have to work for the Blythes, and I won't have to work for my father.'

'Don't you want to be a blacksmith?' Thomasine was surprised. She rather liked the forge – the horses, the hiss as the hot metal was plunged into water.

'My father belts me,' said Daniel simply.

Thomasine knew that Jack Gillory drank too much – all the village knew that – and she had frequently seen Daniel with a black eye or cut lip. When they had swum together in the millpond the previous summer, she had glimpsed pink weals across his back. Anger welled up in her again.

Daniel said, 'What will you do, Thomasine?'

'Aunt Hilly wants me to be a teacher. She says I'm good at mathematics. Aunt Rose thinks I'll marry.'

And yet neither prospect particularly appealed to her. She could not explain to Daniel Gillory, who had been born in the Fens, how sometimes the landscape trapped and confined her. How the narrowness of the village, with its rigid striations of class, irked her. How, sometimes, she longed for hills and colour and music.

'Or I might go and live with my Aunt Tony,' she said, voicing a secret dream. 'She has a dancing school in London. She took me to a ballet at the Alhambra last year, Daniel. It was wonderful, absolutely wonderful.'

The summer of 1914 was a curious one, when Thomasine seemed to alternate constantly between elation and intense boredom. Her lessons with Hilda, that she had previously enjoyed, became sometimes tiresome, and the evenings when she did not ride or see Daniel seemed painfully long. She had read every book in Quince Cottage and all the interesting books from Ely Lending Library.

Within the small village she was isolated. The village children had never quite rid themselves of their original suspicion of her and, besides, those of her age were now either in service or working on the land. Only Daniel could she describe as a friend, because Daniel too, by winning the scholarship, had marked himself out from his fellows. Although she had grown to love her aunts, their lives, as unmarried women, seemed especially restricted. She found herself arguing with Hilda once, asking why her cleverest aunt had not become a teacher or a nurse, but had immured herself in Drakesden.

'Because my father did not believe that women should work,' said Hilda quietly, 'and as Rose and I did not marry we were obliged to live with him.' Only Patricia and Antonia had escaped, through marriage.

And yet, when she rode or wandered through the fields, or when she lost herself in a really good book, then she was utterly content. At the Whitsun supper, when Thomasine danced with the rest of the villagers in a wide circle, threading in and out of one another like ribbons on a maypole, she was happy.

For Thomasine's fifteenth birthday, at the end of June, Aunt Rose made a pink iced cake and Aunt Hilly gave her a volume of Housman's poems. After Thomasine had finished the household accounts (her regular weekly task for two years now), and after she had watered the vegetable patch and eaten a slice of the pink cake, she walked out of the village and down the drove to where she had arranged to meet Daniel.

She had not asked the rector for the loan of his pony, because she was wearing the new dress that Aunt Rose had helped her sew. The dress was of white muslin with a pale blue sash, and was unsuitable for riding. She had dressed her hair in a new way, caught in at the nape of her neck with a wide blue ribbon, instead of plaits. She trod carefully along the drove, avoiding the worst of the mud.

When she heard horses' hooves she looked up, expecting to see Daniel returning a newly-shod horse to one of the farmers. But it was not Daniel riding pell-mell down the drove, but Nicholas Blythe. She stood aside to let him pass, but he reined in his horse, kicking up bits of grass and mud.

'I say, Miss Thorne. I'm awfully sorry. Didn't see you there. Did I give you a fright?'

Thomasine shook her head. 'Not at all.' She squinted at him. Nicholas Blythe and his elder brother Gerald were usually absent from Drakesden from April to August. 'I thought you were at school, Mr Blythe.'

'I was smitten by the plague. Chicken-pox. I'm supposed to be in quarantine. Gerry had it a couple of years ago, so he's still at Winchester, poor devil. Only it's damned dull at the Abbey just now – Mama and Pa and Marjorie are in London, so there's only Lally and me.'

'What a lovely horse.' Thomasine stroked the black velvety nose.

'He's called Titus. Do you ride, Miss Thorne?'

She nodded, and fished inside her pocket for the sugar-lumps she always carried. The horse's velvety lips nuzzled at her palm.

'Mr Fanshawe lets me borrow his pony.'

'Oh – that old thing. Wouldn't go faster than a trot unless you set off a cannon behind her.'

Thomasine grinned and looked up at him. Nicholas Blythe was dark-haired, dark-eyed, his face a chiselled succession of straight lines and planes. 'Bluebell's a bit of a plodder,' she conceded.

'I say – you should try one of the Abbey nags, Miss Thorne.'

Thomasine had caught sight of Daniel, running towards them down the drove from the blacksmith's cottage.

'Tomorrow evening?' added Nicholas. 'In the meadow by the copse?'

She looked again at him, surprised. It occurred to her that Nicholas Blythe, too, might be bored. The prospect of new company and a ride on one of Drakesden Abbey's superb horses was irresistible. 'That would be lovely. Daniel can come too, can't he, Mr Blythe?'

Daniel had slowed and scuffed his feet as he approached them. Standing slightly apart from them, he bobbed his head almost imperceptibly to Nicholas Blythe.

'Of course. Well, toodle-oo, then,' said Nicholas to Thomasine. 'Till tomorrow.' He kicked the horse into a canter.

'Did you get the boat?' asked Thomasine, when she and Daniel were alone.

For her birthday, Daniel had promised to borrow Mr Naylor's flat-bottomed boat so that they could further explore the river. Daniel's only reply was a grunt and a shrugging of his shoulders. He walked ahead of her, silent, down the drove.

She knew that he was moody, touchy sometimes. She put it down to the long hours that he worked: the five-mile walk to and from school, the hours after school in the blacksmith's shop. She ran to catch up with him. Eventually he said, 'I didn't know you were friendly with Nicholas Blythe.'

'I'm not. I shouldn't think I've exchanged much more than half a dozen words with him before today. He just apologized for nearly riding into me, that's all.'

He had paused at last, and she gave his arm a gentle shake. 'Oh, Daniel, don't be cross. Not *today*.'

Just for a moment then, her eyes met his. Then he fished inside his pocket and drew something out.

'Happy birthday,' he said.

When she unwrapped the fragment of tissue paper, she found a filigree brooch in the shape of a butterfly. 'It's not new,' said Daniel quickly. 'I bought it at Ely market. But it's all right, isn't it?'

It occurred to Thomasine that this was the first time that someone who wasn't related to her had bought her a present. 'It's lovely, Daniel. It's absolutely lovely.' She let him pin the brooch to her blouse.

Nicholas Blythe was already waiting in the meadow when Thomasine and Daniel arrived the following evening. He was astride the huge black stallion he had been riding the previous day, and had another horse on a leading rein beside him.

'I brought the paired blacks,' he said. 'This chap's called Nero. After the Roman emperor, you know,' he added to Daniel.

Daniel's face darkened, but he said nothing.

Nicholas said, 'Shall I give you a leg up, Miss Thorne? I say, you didn't want a side-saddle like Marjie and Mama, did you?'

Thomasine shook her head. 'Of course not. And it's Thomasine, not Miss Thorne.'

From the elevated height of Nero's back she had a new and exciting view of Drakesden. The meadow clung to the lowest slope of the island upon which Drakesden Abbey was built. It was not a real island, of course, just a low hillock of comparatively solid ground in the sea of black peat that made up most of the Fens. Between the meadow and the walls that surrounded Drakesden Abbey was the copse, one of the few pockets of woodland in a landscape where the winter winds discouraged the growth of trees.

Thomasine trotted Nero round the circumference of the meadow and then urged him into a canter. The speed was exhilarating. The trees and the froth of flowers that surrounded the meadow all blurred into one. When, finally, she reined the stallion in, she was laughing.

'That was terrific!'

'*You* were terrific.' Nicholas held out his hand to help Thomasine out of the saddle. Then he handed the reins to Daniel. 'Have a go, won't you, Gillory?'

Daniel climbed into the saddle. Nicholas called out, 'He's a jumper, Gillory!' and Daniel edged the horse back to the furthermost corner of the field, and put his heels to Nero's flanks. The stallion gathered up speed, faster and faster, the noise of the hooves like thunder. Then horse and rider soared into the air, clearing the top of the fence by a foot.

Nicholas rode home through the wood. The trees shut out the pale blue sky. The horse's hooves crushed the wild garlic that bordered the path, and the scent was intoxicating. The sunlight filtering through the trees made chains of gold from the sky to the undergrowth.

He could still feel the touch of Thomasine's hand. It was strange how the sensation had lingered, as though, helping her out of the saddle, her fingers had impressed themselves permanently on his hand. As though his skin remembered her skin. It was not something he had ever experienced before. He knew that some of the fellows at school reacted in a similar way towards the older boys, but Nicholas, reminded of the sins his housemaster vaguely warned him against every term or so, had always rather despised such sentiment.

He heard a rustle in the undergrowth and he looked up. Squinting in the darkness, Nicholas saw two round dark eyes, a small white face, fat black plaits. *'Lally.'*

Reluctantly, his younger sister stood up. Her white blouse was stained with green and the hem of her skirt was dusty.

'What are you doing here?'

'Watching you.'

Nicholas stared at her.

'Watching you,' she repeated, 'and Miss Thorne, and Daniel Gillory.'

Nicholas said, amazed, 'You were there the whole time?'

'I was behind the tree. I saw *everything*. You should have let me come. It isn't nice to leave people alone so much.'

'It isn't nice,' said Nicholas coldly, 'to sneak. To *spy*. Spies are shot in wartime – did you know that, Lally?'

He saw her eyes grow wide, and she glanced fearfully round the wood. Her thumb slammed into her mouth. Even though Lally was almost thirteen, four years younger than Nicholas, Nicholas was sometimes aware that he still thought of his sister as a much younger child. As Baby, the youngest, scarcely out of the nursery. Just for a moment Nicholas wished his mother was back, to bully Lally's sickly governess out of her bed, to deal with Lally's tantrums, to tell her not to suck her thumb. But then he remembered that if Mama was here he certainly would not be allowed to spend his time with Thomasine Thorne. Nicholas was suddenly very glad that Sir William and Lady Blythe remained in London, making the arrangements for his elder sister's wedding.

A week later, they met in the meadow again. This time, Thomasine rode Bluebell, the rector's pony, and Daniel borrowed Nero. The three of them rode out of the meadow and along the drove. They avoided the village and the farms, their instinct for privacy unspoken and mutual.

The drove was badly rutted by cartwheels. They had reached

the edge of Potters' Field when Nicholas said, 'Come on, Gillory. I'll race you to the dyke.'

Then they were gone, hooves beating up the dust, Bluebell clattering plumply along in their wake. The evening sunlight gleamed on the black coats of the stallions and on the boys' uncovered heads. They merged together, two dark shapes blurred into one by the dust storm they had created. Then they reached the dyke and were silhouetted against the sky.

Thomasine caught up with them. 'Well? Who won?'

Daniel grinned, showing white, even teeth. 'I did.'

Nicholas had dismounted from his horse and was sitting on top of the bank. 'Ripping,' he said. 'Absolutely ripping. Beaten by a nose, damn it.'

He lay back, supported by his elbows, his long legs flung out in front of him. 'When you ride like that you forget everything, don't you? Nothing else seems important.' He was looking at neither Daniel nor Thomasine, but at the skyline, cloudless and perfect. 'If the war goes on long enough,' he added, 'I shall join a cavalry regiment. Gerald will be able to join up immediately, the lucky devil. He was nineteen yesterday.'

Thomasine stared at him. She and Aunt Hilly had studied newspapers and atlases only that morning. She said uncertainly, 'Surely it won't be anything to do with us? Surely Great Britain won't be involved?'

Daniel said, 'It depends whether Germany respects Belgian neutrality. If she doesn't . . .'

'If she doesn't,' finished Nicholas, 'then we'll be fighting the Hun. It'll be the most terrific game. Nothing to do with you girls, though.'

He rolled over on to his stomach. 'Don't look so glum, Thomasine. I'm thirsty, aren't you? I should have brought some lemonade. There's pots and pots of it in the kitchens at the Abbey. Tell you what – why don't you come up to the Abbey tomorrow evening? I can show you the gardens. Would you like that?'

She recalled the house that she had only once glimpsed, walled off from the rest of Drakesden. Those secretive windows, the sense that here was something only for the privileged few. She needed change, she needed different places, different people.

'*Like* to? I'd love to, Nicholas.'

Daniel was sitting with his back to them, his legs slung over the edge of the dyke. Thomasine touched Nicholas's hand, and glanced silently at Daniel.

'You too, of course, Gillory,' said Nicholas.

Nicky had gone out and Miss Hamilton was in bed, so Lally Blythe, on her own again, wandered aimlessly around the house. She was, she thought, just now the mistress of Drakesden Abbey. Mama and Papa were in London with Marjorie, Gerald was still at school, Nicky was out, and Miss Hamilton, Lally's governess, was in bed with a sick headache. There was no one to tell Lally what to do.

Freedom was surprisingly dull, though. She didn't like to read, and she didn't like to sew, and she was scared of horses. She ambled out of the library towards her father's study. She was about to turn the doorhandle when she heard voices from inside. A man's voice first, and then a trill of high-pitched laughter. *Robbers*, thought Lally, horrified. The safe was inside Sir William's study, and in the safe were Lady Blythe's jewels and, of course, the Firedrake. Lally liked the Firedrake. Occasionally Papa took it out of the safe and let her hold it. Gathering all her courage, Lally crouched down and peered through the keyhole.

Squinting, she glimpsed the housemaid, Ethel. It was Ethel who was laughing, a thin high giggle that seemed incongruous in the dark sombre study. Ethel was seated on the edge of Sir William's desk, her black button boots swinging slowly backwards and forwards.

Very quietly, Lally turned the handle of the door and peered through the gap. She recognized Francis, the second footman.

He was standing in front of Ethel. Ethel had stopped giggling and was saying, 'No, Frank, you mustn't.' But she didn't sound cross.

It took her a while to work out what they were doing. Then she realized that they were kissing. She had never seen anyone kiss like that before. Their mouths seemed glued together. Ethel was making funny little moaning noises, and her eyes were closed. One of Francis's hands was behind her back, pulling her to him; the other was pushing her skirts up past her knee. Lally could see the top of Ethel's thick black stocking and the band of white skin beyond. Hidden, she continued to watch. She knew that they were all doing something forbidden, she and Francis and Ethel. They in doing that odd sort of kissing in Lally's father's study, and she in watching. Lally knew that she should feel ashamed of herself. But she did not. She only realized, as she watched, that at last she was not bored.

They met Nicholas at the side-gate of Drakesden Abbey. Stepping through the gate, Thomasine knew that she was entering another world. Looking round the orchard, smelling its rich scents, her breath caught for a moment in her throat. As though she was used to air that was thinner, more ordinary; as though Drakesden Abbey's beauty and abundance might sicken her.

The trees were thickly leaved, heavy with fruit. Against the walls of the orchard more fruit trees were shaped into fans, pyramids and espaliers. Butterflies danced in the hot, hazy air.

'There's apples, pears, plums, greengages, medlars and quinces,' said Nicholas carelessly. 'I think that's all.'

'Cherries,' said Daniel.

'Of course. Cherries.' Nicholas walked through the orchard, hitting the swathes of long grass aside with a stick. 'And little sisters –'

Nicholas halted; the stick stilled. Thomasine saw a figure uncurl herself from the perimeter of the orchard. A young girl walked forward.

'Hello, Lally,' said Nicholas irritably.

Both the similarities and the differences between brother and sister were very marked. They were both dark-haired, dark-eyed, even-featured. But Lally's mouth had a downward twist, and her face was a rounder, softer version of her brother's.

'Isn't it your bedtime, Baby?'

'Miss Hamilton's having a nap, and I was so *lonely*.' Lally Blythe's mouth puckered.

Thomasine felt sorry for her. That enormous house; her mother away for weeks at a time. The child's skin was pale, almost translucent, and there were blue circles around her eyes.

'Let me stay, Nicky, *please*.'

Nicholas sighed. 'All right, then, brat. If you behave yourself.'

Lally whooped with joy and clasped Nicholas's arm. They walked through the orchard. The kitchen garden lay before them, its neat rows of cabbages and carrots free of weeds and insects.

Nicholas said, 'Let's show them the Labyrinth, shall we, Lally?'

He led the way. Drakesden Abbey, its walls misted purple by wisteria, lay to one side of them, the slope of the island to the other. The warren of paths was closed off from the rest of the garden by high snaking walls and by tall hedges of lilac, laburnum and privet. The pathways were narrow, carpeted with grass, edged with ferns and meadowsweet. The tread of their feet, their whispered voices, were muffled, and the evening sun was shut away. It felt, thought Thomasine, subterranean, like a real Labyrinth.

Halfway along one of the passageways, Nicholas paused beside a door in the wall and flicked a strand of ivy from the handle. The door creaked open.

'This was my grandfather's favourite garden.'

The three flower-beds inside the walled garden were massed with roses. There was no wind, and the high, weathered brick cut off all sound except the whine of the bees. At the end of the three walkways, set into arched niches in the wall, were three statues. Thomasine glanced at the nearest. A woman and a bird. The woman was naked.

'Leda and the swan,' said Thomasine. Zeus was embracing Leda; their stone feathers and coiled hair were entwined in the shadow of the bricks.

'And there's Daphne,' said Nicholas. Daphne, leaves uncurling from her fingertips, flinched coyly in the furthermost niche.

'Mama doesn't think them respectable girls. A little under-dressed for the English summer, perhaps.' Nicholas waved a careless hand. 'And there, in the middle, is our beloved Firedrake.'

They had walked through the ranks of roses to where the central niche was set into the wall. In the niche was a dragon, water dripping lazily from its stone mouth. Ferns crowded the green stones that trapped the water.

There was a coat of arms above the statue. The same coat of arms was carved into the wall of Drakesden church. 'Our emblem,' said Nicholas. 'We'd have carried pennants bearing Firedrakes into battle, once. Good Queen Bess gave the first Sir Nicholas Blythe the Firedrake to say thank you for a jolly nice weekend. A play on words, you see, Thomasine, because the Blythes owned Drakesden. A firedrake's a sort of dragon. Or a meteor, Pa says.'

'Or a will-o'-the-wisp,' said Daniel.

'Really? Very appropriate, then. Our lowest-lying land's alight with will-o'-the-wisps sometimes. Some sort of gas, my housemaster tells me.'

'Marsh gas,' said Daniel. 'Methane.'

Lally said, 'It's in Father's study, in the safe.'

Thomasine wanted to giggle. Nicholas said wearily, 'What the brat means is not that poor old Pa's study is full of noxious fumes, but that the original Firedrake is there. It's a brooch, or something. It's fairly hideous, so Mama never wears it. Now, infant – run along or Miss Hamilton will be looking for you.'

23

'It isn't *fair*, Nicky.' Lally looked furious, but she began to shuffle back towards the door, her small booted feet dragging along the grass. She pushed feebly at the handle. 'I can't open it.'

Nicholas sighed again. 'Would you . . .?' he asked Daniel.

Daniel held open the door for Lally. When it had shut behind her, Nicholas took something out from behind the lush damp ferns beneath the Firedrake. He held up a wine bottle.

'I haven't any glasses, I'm afraid, but we can pass the bottle round, can't we?'

With the beginning of August the weather grew hotter and closer, the hazy pale blue of the sky lingering long into the evenings. Often they rode: once, to placate Lally, they played hide-and-seek and sardines in Drakesden's gardens. Thomasine, hiding inside the green cave of a box tree, held a finger to her lips to silence Daniel as he moved aside a branch and stepped inside. Ducking his head, he sat beside her on the twisted bough.

'You've torn your skirt.'

Thomasine glanced guiltily down at the long rip in the navy blue serge. 'I caught it on a branch. I'll have to mend it before Aunt Hilly notices.'

The fronds of box tree moved again, revealing Nicholas.

'There you are. I've been looking all over the place.' Nicholas wormed his way inside, too tall to stand upright. There wasn't room for him to sit beside Thomasine and Daniel, so he crouched in an awkward position, dabbing at his forehead with his handkerchief.

'I say! I've had enough of this. Too jolly hot.'

'Where's Lally?' asked Thomasine. 'She's been looking for us for ages.'

There was the sound of dragging feet on the gravel drive.

'Where are you? Do come out! I can't find you.'

Nicholas sighed and rolled his eyes.

'Perhaps we should . . .' Daniel had risen to his feet. 'After all, she's only a kid.'

Lally's complaints grew steadily louder.

Nicholas called out, 'In here, silly!'

Lally's small round face, scarlet with heat and temper, appeared framed by box leaves. 'It's not fair, Nicky. It's too difficult.' Lally's whines began to turn into sobs.

Daniel said quickly, 'A different game, perhaps, d'you think?'

Nicholas sighed again, and pushed his way out of the box tree. Thomasine followed behind him. The glare of the sunlight and the solid wall of heat that seemed to have settled on Drakesden hit her as she left the cool shelter of the leaves. They ambled slowly back to the walled garden, where they collapsed on to the grass. Lally tugged at Nicholas's hand.

'Forfeits, Nicky – do let's play forfeits.'

Nicholas groaned. 'Ghastly Christmas game –'

'Me first,' said Lally. 'Ask me something first, Nicky.'

Nicholas lounged back on the grass. 'Oh ... tell me the names of the Tudor kings and queens, Baby. All of them.'

'Oh, that's mean! I can't do that. You know I'm hopeless at history, Nicky!'

'You've had a governess for years,' said Nicholas unsympathetically.

Lally screwed up her face. 'Elizabeth,' she said. 'And Henry . . .' she glanced uncertainly at Nicholas. 'Eight Henrys –'

Nicholas groaned. Daniel whispered, 'Two.'

'I mean, two Henrys.' Lally gazed at Daniel. 'And ... and . . .'

'Mary and Edward,' muttered Daniel.

'Mary and Edward,' said Lally triumphantly. 'I don't have to do a forfeit, do I?'

'I suppose not. You'd better ask someone else a question. Ask Thomasine, Lally.'

A look of immense concentration settled on Lally's small features. 'You're to tell me the name of Marjorie's fiancé.'

'Oh, for heaven's sake, Lal. How on earth is Thomasine supposed to know that?'

'I haven't a clue. It doesn't matter. Give me a forfeit, Lally.'

There was a long pause. Then Lally said, 'I dare you to climb on to the fountain in the middle of the pond.'

'Don't be ridiculous, Baby. It's quite deep, and she'd get all wet.'

Thomasine had already sprung to her feet. 'I don't mind.'

The fountain, surrounded by a wide pond, was in the centre of the lawn at the back of the house. Looking up to the house as she ran across the lawn, Thomasine saw the curtained windows blink back at her, a multitude of closed eyes.

Nicholas was by her side. 'Which is your room?' she whispered.

'That one.' He pointed. 'Over the conservatory. I say — would you like to see the house?' His voice was casual. 'Come up tomorrow morning. Just you. I'll show you round.'

Lally called, 'Aren't you going to do the dare, then?'

Thomasine kicked off her boots and stockings, and gathered up her skirts in her hands. The water felt delightfully cool. Carp flitted between the lily pads like strands of gold. Soon the water came up past her knees, then it dipped at the raised hem of her skirt, and then lapped halfway up her thighs. The fountain was a baroque excess of cherubs and dolphins, its curved archways of water refracting into rainbows.

Nicholas's voice floated over the pond towards her. 'That'll do, Thomasine! You've done it!'

'No, she hasn't. I said she had to climb on to the fountain. She said she would.'

Thomasine took a deep breath and shut her eyes and walked forward. The spray hit her face, her chest, her shoulders. But she reached out and felt the slippery stone and clambered, bare feet gripping the granite, triumphantly upwards.

Nicholas let out a whoop of triumph, but Daniel leapt into the water and ran towards her, splashing through the goldfish and lilies. With a slip and a slither she tumbled from the fountain into his arms. Just for a moment he bent his head and his lips brushed her forehead, so quickly, she was left uncertain whether the gesture had been accidental. Then, with Thomasine's hands clutched round his neck, Daniel waded back through the pond. They fell, soaked and laughing, on to the grass. Thomasine wrung out her skirt.

Nicholas said coldly, 'I've a dare for you, Gillory. I dare you to walk along the wall by the Labyrinth.'

The laughter stopped quite suddenly. 'You haven't asked Daniel a question,' said Thomasine. 'And the wall's too high and narrow and curvy.'

'It's called a serpentine wall, actually,' said Nicholas supercili- ously. He had already begun to walk away from the pond, back to the Labyrinth.

Daniel ran down the slope after Nicholas. Thomasine scram- bled to her feet. Lally plodded slowly down the slope after the two boys, her thumb locked in her mouth, her eyes dark and hard and secretive.

Daniel was already barefoot; he dumped his boots at one end of the wall. One of the soles had come away, and the leather gaped like an open mouth. The wall was fully eight feet high, a sinuous succession of curves, built from the pale yellow brick of the Fens. When Daniel seized a handful of ivy it ripped away, showering the grass with a fine dusting of powdery cement.

'You'll have to give me a bunk up.'

Nicholas braced his shoulder against the wall and threaded his fingers together. Daniel stepped into his cupped palms, and pulled himself up, his bare feet scrabbling against the brick. Upright, standing on top of the narrow wall, he began to move forward.

'Come on, Gillory,' taunted Nicholas. 'That's crawling – not walking.'

Daniel grinned, and began to run.

In her damp dress, cut off from the heat of the sun by the high wall, Thomasine felt suddenly cold. Shivering, she watched as Nicholas and Lally ran down the winding path beside the wall. She did not follow them; instead she returned to the walled garden.

She took her black lisle stockings from where she had hidden them inside her boots and pulled them back on. They snagged at her damp legs. She had lost her hair-ribbon, and her hair tumbled, wet and tangled, down her back. Her skirt was damp, dirty and torn. She heard Lally's voice at last, and felt a wave of relief.

'You're so clever, Daniel. So brave.'

Nicholas sat down beside Thomasine. 'My turn now.'

'I've thought of a forfeit,' cried Lally. 'I want to ask you a forfeit, Nicky!'

'It's not your turn, Lal. You're breaking the rules. It's Gillory's turn.'

'I don't mind.' Daniel was lacing his boots up.

Lally's face was bright and expectant. 'Well, then. You've to kiss your favourite person, Nicky.'

There was a short silence. Then Nicholas said with a grin, 'Titus isn't here.'

Lally looked cross. 'I meant in the garden. Someone in the garden.'

Nicholas's tanned face went pale, then red. 'Come off it. It's a bit much, asking a chap . . . Not quite the thing . . .'

Daniel said, 'I'll do it.'

A peculiar mixture of emotions crossed Nicholas's face. Anger and resentment and relief. 'If you like,' he muttered.

Daniel walked to the far end of the garden. At the first of the niches, he climbed up, searching for toe-holds in the weathered brick. Then he clasped his arms around Leda's ample body, and kissed her full on the mouth.

It fixed itself like a photograph in Thomasine's mind. Daniel Gillory, in his damp, ragged clothes, his arms embracing the white marble limbs, his mouth caressing those cold, stony lips.

They walked home through the woods, Thomasine treading

behind Daniel through the narrow winding pathway. Daniel beat aside the nettles with a stick, and held the brambles out of her way. The wood glittered, the undergrowth dappled by the light that filtered through the leaves.

Daniel took her hand to help her over the stile. She was aware of the warmth of his skin, the calloused patches at each of his finger-joints. He raised her hand and pressed his lips to the back of it. The gesture was odd, old-fashioned. His hair had fallen over his face; Thomasine smoothed it away with her fingers. His skin was tanned, rough around the chin. Brought up by women, living so much of her life with women, she felt an intense curiosity, mixed with delight. As she slid from the stile, his arms encircled her. His eyes were chips of gold in the darkness of the wood, and his lips touched hers, gently, questingly.

Then the church bell chimed ten times, and a pheasant whirred from the undergrowth, its wings beating through the warm air.

'You're late,' said Daniel. 'Come on.'

Thomasine had told neither Hilda nor Rose about her visits to Drakesden Abbey's gardens. She had not lied — both aunts simply assumed that she spent this summer as she had spent the previous five summers, exploring Drakesden, its fields and droves and streams. Darting through the copse the next morning, Thomasine evaded her suspicion that neither Hilda nor Rose would approve of her spending the day alone with Nicholas Blythe. Yet every now and then guilt resurfaced, boiling and bubbling to the forefront of her mind.

Nicholas met her outside the front steps of Drakesden Abbey. He took her first into the hall, with its great sweeping stairs. The walls were lined with glass cases, each one filled with minutely labelled collections of shells, fossils, stuffed animals and birds. The birds' black glass eyes gazed back at Thomasine dispassionately; the ranks of dead dark creatures did not flinch from the sunlight that poured through the windows.

'When I was a small child they used to frighten me,' said

Nicholas. 'Particularly the wolverine. He's a bit moth-eaten now, poor old thing.'

He led her into the drawing-room. The walls were coral-coloured, clustered with paintings, the ceiling blue, with ornately moulded cornices. The room was filled with the light that poured through the vast windows: so different to the cramped darkness of Quince Cottage.

'Someone brought that back from Venice.' Nicholas pointed to a bureau. 'In the seventeenth – or was it the eighteenth – century . . .?'

'Don't you *know*? I mean, your family . . .'

He shook his head. 'Haven't a clue. Can't tell one thing from the other. All this goes to poor old Gerry, thank God. Come on.'

More rooms, each one a dazzling array of paintings, orna-ments, carpets and well-upholstered furniture.

'The conservatory,' said Nicholas eventually, opening a door.

The conservatory ran the entire length of the back of the house, an elegant structure of glass and wrought-iron, tiled in black and white marble, wreathed in plants. The heat was damp and stifling.

'Sweltering, isn't it?' Nicholas wiped his forehead with his handkerchief.

The vegetation was luxuriant and exotic. The flowers hung, waxy and pendulous, the leaves gleamed a deep dark green. The air in the conservatory was hot and heavy, slightly rank, per-fumed with a sickly scent from the flowers.

Nicholas said anxiously, 'What do you think? Are you enjoy-ing yourself? We'll go outside if you're bored.'

'Oh, *Nicholas*. How could I be bored?' Thomasine looked around her. 'It's simply marvellous. Look at it – it's like – it's like a jungle. Or paradise.'

Nicholas was wearing jodhpurs and riding-boots, and a jacket, shirt and tie. His dark hair clung to his forehead with the heat. 'Shall we have lunch here? No – too hot, don't you think? I say –' he sprang to his feet – 'how about a picnic?'

'A picnic would be lovely. So much cooler outside.'

They went to the kitchen. When Nicholas opened the door some of the chatter died away, to be replaced by the clanging of pots and pans, the purposeful rattling of lids on simmering saucepans.

'Miss Thorne and I would like a picnic prepared, Mrs Blatch. Cold chicken and ham, a little salad and . . . let me see . . . what do you suggest for dessert?'

His voice had altered, his easy friendliness replaced by an arrogance underlaid with nervousness. The servants, many of whom Thomasine recognized, stared at her with curiosity tinged with resentment.

'Come upstairs,' said Nicholas, after they had left the kitchen. 'We've two more floors to see.'

The stairs were wide and winding, lined by portraits of dead Blythes. Lally met them on the landing.

Nicholas said crossly, 'Go back to the nursery, Lally. You're supposed to be doing your lessons.'

Lally's face crumpled and she clutched Nicholas's arm. 'I'm bored, Nicky. I want to come with you. Please, Nicky.'

'Oh, push off, Lally,' said Nicholas. 'Do go away.'

As Lally ran down the stairs, snuffling, Nicholas said, 'Mama should send her to school. Her governess is hopeless with her.'

They went into the library, where heavy curtains and blinds were drawn in an attempt to keep the sunlight from the books. Thomasine wandered from bookcase to bookcase.

'How Aunt Hilly would love it! So many books!'

Nicholas yawned. 'I hate this room. It reminds me of school.'

Next door in Sir William's study, dust sparkled in the rays of light from the gaps between the curtains. Nicholas turned to Thomasine.

'Would you like to see the Firedrake?'

He didn't wait for her answer. Instead, pulling a curtain aside, he began to turn the combination lock of the safe.

'I've seen my father do it,' he explained.

The safe opened and Nicholas peered into the darkness. Thomasine could see papers, rolled and beribboned, and jewel cases. Reaching inside, Nicholas took out something wrapped in a length of velvet.

'Look,' he said, and unfolded the cloth. 'It's rather grotesque, isn't it? The fashion of the times, I suppose. Mama never wears it.'

The Firedrake was a brooch, dragon-shaped, encrusted with semi-precious stones. Thomasine, studying the curved tail, the arched back, the fiery mouth and glittering, baleful eyes, could not decide whether it was ugly or beautiful.

'It's more than three hundred years old. Stand still, Thomasine.'

His hands shook as he unhooked the heavy clasp and pinned it to her dress. He said, 'You look splendid, Thomasine, utterly splendid.' Nicholas's voice sounded odd and his eyes looked as Daniel's had, just before he had kissed her. Catching sight of the clock on the mantelpiece, Thomasine said, 'It's one o'clock, isn't it, Nick? Time for our picnic.'

In the blacksmith's shop the heat was unbearable. Daniel, like his father, was naked from the waist up. Sweat matted his hair and streamed down his back. There was a half-barrel of water in the corner of the workshop, but it was lukewarm and seething with striddlebacks.

Every horse between Cambridge and Ely seemed to have thrown a shoe that day. Daniel fed the fire with turf and held the horses still, while his father hammered and swore. Daniel's arms ached and his tongue was glued to the roof of his mouth. He couldn't bring himself to drink from the barrel, and Harry, his younger brother, was not yet back from The Otter with the ale his father had called for.

Daniel tried to concentrate as he struggled to hold the horse still, but his mind kept drifting. He was in the wood again, and Thomasine was in his arms and he was kissing her. He had kissed girls before. He had even, in the shelter of a barn or the silence of the fields, touched a breast, stroked a thigh. The impulse to go further than that last night, to do what adults did, had been almost overwhelming. But he had come to his senses in time. The church clock had chimed, and she had run home. Yet the heat and hunger still lingered, distracting him.

The mare snorted and kicked, Daniel's damp hands slipped, and the flailing hoof caught Jack Gillory on the chin. Daniel grabbed at the bridle, his father roared, and something hit Daniel hard on the side of his head. Stars danced in the darkness of the blacksmith's workshop, and discordant bells chimed over the snorting of the horse and Jack Gillory's curses.

When his sight cleared, Daniel saw that his father was standing over him, his hand raised to strike again. *Amo, amas, amat,* thought Daniel, sprawled on the floor, testing his brain to see whether it still worked.

Harry's tremulous voice whispered, 'Mr Green wouldn't let me have no more ale, Dad. He says you've got to settle up.'

Somehow Daniel scrambled to his feet. His younger brother Harry was standing in the doorway, an empty bottle in his hand. Harry's face was white and pinched and frightened.

Jack Gillory seized the empty bottle from the child's hand and hurled it to the paving stones. Broken glass sparkled in the heat, and the mare reared again. *'Run,'* whispered Daniel to Harry.

Harry didn't need to be told twice. He wove his way through the allotment, his bare feet pounding up clouds of dust. Something was trickling down the side of Daniel's face, and when he put up his hand to touch his forehead his fingertips came away dotted with scarlet.

There was a bruise on Jack Gillory's chin, curved like a horseshoe. Jack drank a mouthful of water from the half-barrel, and turned to Daniel. Oddly, he was smiling.

'The thing is, boy, that there's work enough for two. I'm not making the money, see.'

The sweat on Daniel's face went cold. He said nothing.

'I reckon this shop needs two of us. All the time, like.'

Daniel blinked. There was a pulse pounding in his temple. 'In the holidays, Dad,' he whispered. 'Before and after school.'

Jack Gillory shook his head. 'Not enough, boy. Can't pay my bills, see? So you'll tell Rector you won't need no more fancy clothes.'

Daniel said, '*No.*'

Jack moved towards him. '*No?* Don't cheek me, lad. I've had enough o' your bloody cheek. You'll bloody do what I tell you.'

His father wasn't the only one with a temper. Something inside Daniel, that he had struggled to hold at bay for weeks, snapped. 'I don't need you, Dad,' he hissed. 'I've got the scholarship, and the rector gives me books and clothes –' Daniel darted round to the other side of the anvil, avoiding a second blow. 'I'm going to be something more than you, Dad! I'm going to have a decent home, and good food, and proper clothes. Not a lousy allotment that only grows weeds, and a mucky house that lets in water in the winter –'

Jack Gillory roared like a bull and lunged at him in the hot, dry darkness.

Daniel yelled, 'I'll not be like you! Stinking drunk every night, grunting like a rutting hog –'

He felt fingers clutching him round the neck, pushing him to his knees. The fire was hot against his face and he saw, as if through a mist, the bent shape of the anvil. Then his face was plunged into water. His father was holding his head in the barrel with the striddlebacks. Daniel tried not to breathe because he was afraid of the worms in his nose, his mouth. He wriggled violently, but the iron grip held him down.

He heard, dimly, just as he was about to stop struggling, a voice cry out, 'Jack! *No!*' And then he was released, and he knelt beside the barrel, sobbing and retching, his head cradled on his arms.

When he could stand, he staggered past his father and mother, grabbing his discarded shirt and scrubbing it against his face. Then he ran out of the workshop and through the allotment, tripping over the straggling cabbages and hardened furrows.

Lady Blythe, her personal maid and elder daughter, arriving back from London nearly a week early, found Drakesden Abbey almost deserted. Hot and dusty from the journey from Ely station, she had little patience with inefficiency and sloppiness. Straight-backed, pulling her kid gloves smartly from her fingers, she issued requests for hot water, a plate of cold salad, some sweet wine. The servants bustled about, trying to look busy, but Gwendoline Blythe was not hoodwinked. She saw the dust on the sills and table-tops, the balls of dirt in the corners of the stairs. She would have to reprimand the housekeeper. The news that Lally's governess had spent most of the last few weeks in her bed made Lady Blythe's mouth tighten in irritation.

When she and Marjorie had eaten and changed, Lady Blythe began herself to look for her children. She had established that they were not in the house, but no one seemed to know much more about Nicholas and Lally's whereabouts. She was longing to see Nicholas again. She thought of her elder son Gerald, who was nineteen, and she shuddered. There would be a war, she thought dully, she must accept that now, and Gerald would join up. There was no question that he would not join up. She thanked God that Nicholas was only seventeen.

Outside, her parasol sheltering her from the rays of the sun, Gwendoline Blythe sent the gardener's boy to the stables. While she waited for him to return, she walked slowly through the gardens. Two white peacocks fanned out their glorious tail-feathers in the heat. Lady Blythe thought that though there were some aspects of marriage that she had always found distasteful, she had never regretted her alliance with Sir William Blythe. Marriage had given her Drakesden.

The boy ran back to her side. 'Mr Nicholas has taken your

bay mare, your ladyship. Mr Dockerill thinks he might be in the paddock.'

As she walked down to the paddock, she thought of her children: Gerald and Marjorie and Nicholas. And Lally, of course. Lally had been an afterthought, an unexpected late addition. She had been convinced that after Nicholas she would have no more children. Two sons and a daughter had seemed the perfect family.

Inside the paddock she saw Nicholas, and she looked for a long moment at her favourite son. Then she saw the girl.

She had thought for a moment that Lally was riding her mare. But Lally was afraid of horses, and besides, only one girl in Drakesden had hair of that dreadful vulgar colour: the Misses Harkers' ill-mannered, impertinent niece. Lady Blythe said her son's name, and Nicholas spun round.

'*Mama!* I thought you were in London . . . it's not time . . .'

'Marjorie and I came back a little early.' Lady Blythe, standing in the shade of the tree, collapsed her parasol. Clouds were filling the sky. There would be a thunderstorm, she thought.

'You should have telegraphed. I'd have met you at the station.' Nicholas's face had turned a dusky pink.

'Of course.' Gwendoline smiled, a small, tight smile. Her sharp eyes caught sight of the remains of the picnic under the tree. 'We took a cab. Gerald is to come back early from OTC camp. Your father has gone to fetch him. They will travel home tomorrow in the motor-car. This wretched war –'

'Has it begun?' said Nicholas eagerly. 'Has war been declared?'

War was unpredictable and threatening. Silently, she reminded herself that war, after all, could not touch Drakesden.

'William says that war will be declared any day now. Germany has insisted that her armies will march through Belgium. I didn't care to remain in London. It seemed – feverish.' She paused, and then asked, 'Have you seen Miss Thorne frequently over the past weeks, Nicholas?'

36

'Oh – not really. Just occasionally.'

She knew he was lying. She had always been close to him, so she could read instantly his moods, his temper. The difficult pregnancy, the premature birth of her second son, had perhaps made his survival seem so much more precious. He had been the only one of the four that she had loved as soon as she had set eyes on him. With her elder son Gerald, love had taken a day or two, but with Nicholas she had just gazed into those slatey dark eyes and known, for the only time in her life, joy. Although all the children had of course been brought up by nannies and nursery maids, that original love had lingered, to be rediscovered and concentrated by time.

'I said she should come up here and ride a decent horse for once.'

The truth, unsaid, shimmered in the air, dividing them. The uncompromising landscape of the Fens seemed to glare back at them, the sunlit fields darkened by the ominous clouds. The thunder rumbled again.

Miss Thorne was riding alongside the dyke. As they watched, she spurred the mare into a canter. The girl wore no hat, and her long, gaudy hair streamed out behind her like a banner. Gwendoline Blythe saw and understood the expression on her son's face. She drew in her breath sharply. The silly boy was in love with the Harkers' niece. The sudden realization that Nicky, too, had begun to know a man's appetites and desires made Gwendoline shiver with anger and disappointment.

'I think that it is time Miss Thorne went home, don't you agree, Nicholas?' said Lady Blythe coldly. 'Perhaps you would see her to the gate.' She turned and left the paddock.

Daniel searched through the orchards, the walled gardens, the Labyrinth. He was careful to keep out of everyone's sight, knowing that without Nicholas he was an intruder at Drakesden Abbey.

When someone did appear, bobbing up in front of him as he

skirted by a laurel hedge, he almost hit them out of his way. He realized, just in time, that it was Lally.

'I'm looking for Thomasine,' he said, trying to keep his voice civil. 'She wasn't at home. Is she here?'

'She's with Nicholas,' said Lally. She gazed up at Daniel with wide dark eyes. 'She likes Nicholas.'

She led him by a circuitous route round the back of the house. She whispered to him as they walked, 'I knew you'd come, Daniel. I was looking for you. I knew you wouldn't leave me on my own. I've got a secret, you see. Shall I tell it you?'

Daniel shook his head wearily. He ached all over. The grinding thunder seemed to reverberate inside his bruised skull.

Lally flinched at the thunder. Lightning forked through a purple sky, and her thumb slammed into her mouth. Looking at her, Daniel said more kindly, 'It's all right, lightning always goes for the highest point. It won't hurt you, Lally. We'll just keep away from the trees.'

Fat drops of water splashed on the dry earth. Lally said nervously, 'I was going to –' and then her words were lost in the clamour of the thunder.

They were beside the cluster of greenhouses and potting-sheds that the gardeners used. The fields and paddocks fell away to the other side.

'Is Thomasine riding?' asked Daniel.

Lally's hands were clamped over her mouth and her eyes were very dark and very bright. Reaching out, she seized one of Daniel's hands.

'In here,' she whispered.

She had opened the door of one of the potting-sheds. Daniel thought that perhaps she wanted to shelter from the rainstorm. He suddenly felt hopeless and exhausted. He knew that he should not have come here. He saw himself clearly for what he was: ragged and dirty, an uncleaned cut on one temple, his hair still matted with water and sweat. No wonder Thomasine preferred the company of Nicholas Blythe.

Inside the potting-shed it was hot and dark, and there was a warm musty smell of peat and roots. Lally stood beside him. She was trembling. She was only a kid, after all, thought Daniel. His sister Nell hid under the table in a thunderstorm.

'You've hurt your head,' said Lally.

She touched the bruised skin on his forehead. Her fingers were small and tapering. Her hot little hand slid down and lay against his cheek. She was only a kid.

When he felt her lips against his, his chief emotion was one of surprise. Daniel gasped. Her small pointed tongue darted into his mouth, licking his teeth, his tongue. Her breath was hot against his face. Thunder crashed overhead.

Lady Blythe had reached the greenhouses. Her parasol was necessary now to keep off the rain. Water hurled from the sky, leaving round black pockmarks on the parched, dusty grass. She heard a sound from the potting-shed. Thinking it was one of the gardeners, she opened the door, intending to ask after Lally. It took a moment for her eyes to become accustomed to the dark.

She couldn't believe what she saw. Her own little daughter, only thirteen years old, in the arms of the blacksmith's son. Lady Blythe screamed.

Her first reaction, on finding them, was to send for the constabulary. To lock up that lout who pushed past her and ran away when she cried out. But to do that, she realized almost immediately, would mean compromising her daughter.

'He didn't make me,' Lally said sullenly. 'I wanted to.'

Even when, dragging her across the lawn back to the house, Lally began to howl and shake and stamp her foot, she still stuck to her story. 'He didn't make me. I wanted to,' she yelled, and Lady Blythe was thankful that the child's hysteria made her words incomprehensible to everyone but her mother. She found some relief in slapping Lally smartly across the face to slow the flow of sobs and screams.

She put Lally to bed herself, unable to risk her babblings

being understood by any of the servants. Undressing Lally and bathing her hot red face, Gwendoline Blythe knew that no one must know what had happened – not even Sir William. She felt physical revulsion when she thought of the incident. It was disgusting and shameful.

Eventually Lally's eyelids drooped and her shudders became less and less frequent. Back in her own bedroom, Lady Blythe let her maid settle her in a comfortable chair. She watched Jardine finish unpacking her bags, and found the witnessing of the routine tasks soothing: the folding of her clothes, the careful placing of lavender bags between the silky layers, the jewel cases put aside on her dressing-table. When the maid had finished, Lady Blythe said, 'Ask Hawkins to unlock the safe for you, Jardine, so that you may put my jewellery away.'

Only when the maid had gone did Gwendoline Blythe allow herself to show her distress. When the door had closed, the trembling, which she had controlled so carefully, began. The thunder crashed overhead, rain battered against the window-panes, but Lady Blythe could still hear the hammering of her teeth. She felt as though they had been violated. As though that dreadful boy, with his filthy clothes and matted hair, had despoiled not only her daughter, but her home as well. As though the dirty stinking waters of the Fen were lapping against the shores of the island.

She would have words with the housekeeper and begin again the weary search to find a suitable governess for Lally. Or a school, perhaps – she had never really approved of schools for girls, but now the idea offered a possible solution. And Nicholas must not be allowed out of sight of his family. A seaside holiday might be a good idea. As for that boy –

There was a knock at the door, and Jardine, looking flustered, came back into the room.

'Mr Hawkins sent me for you, your ladyship. He says, will you come to Sir William's study. It's the safe, your ladyship. It wasn't locked.'

★

That evening Thomasine looked for Daniel. He wasn't in the blacksmith's shop, he wasn't waiting for her by the dyke, and neither was he in the meadow. Mrs Gillory, picking runner beans in her allotment, shook her head when Thomasine asked after her eldest son. There'd been a bit of a set-to earlier on, she explained. Mrs Gillory's face was thin and white, and a dark purple bruise encircled one of her eyes.

Thomasine, disturbed, went for a last hopeless walk around the village. It was still raining, and the sky was full of grey swollen clouds. She could not rid herself of the conviction that something terrible had happened that day: it was there, unspoken, in the rivulets of water that streamed down the drove, in the expression in Nicholas Blythe's eyes after he had escorted her, for what she had known must be the last time, to the gates of Drakesden Abbey.

The following morning, Lady Blythe went to see the rector. Mr Fanshawe's maid showed her into the rectory drawing-room.

'Such an unexpected pleasure, your ladyship,' the rector twittered. 'So much cooler after the thunderstorm –'

'I have come to speak to you about the Gillory boy,' said Lady Blythe. She had another call to make: she did not intend to waste time on platitudes.

'Daniel?' said the rector blankly.

'Yes. Daniel. I believe that you helped him take a place at Ely Grammar School.'

'Daniel himself won the free place, your ladyship – he entered the competition for the scholarship. I provide him with a uniform, and books and pens and pencils. The family is not well-off.'

Lady Blythe said nothing for a moment. Through the open French-windows of the drawing-room, she could see the ranks of dahlias, lilies and snapdragons, still glistening with raindrops from the thunderstorm.

'Isn't it rather a waste, Rector, to provide a boy like that with an education? It only marks him out from his fellows and gives him unsuitable ideas. And when he leaves school – what is there for him? He shall be a blacksmith, like his father. Nothing can alter that.'

The rector said uneasily, 'If Daniel passes his school certificate, your ladyship, it may be possible for him to take up a college place.'

She stood up and went to the French-windows. The rich scents from the garden assailed her. She breathed them in, her eyes half-closed. Into her darkened vision came unwelcomed the memory of Lally, her eyes red with crying, shouting, 'Daniel was with me. Daniel was with me all the time.' She had been obliged to believe Lally. She turned back to the rector. She said gently, 'I don't think that you should assist the Gillory boy any more, Mr Fanshawe.'

Mr Fanshawe said faintly, 'If Daniel hasn't a uniform, your ladyship, he can't go to school.'

'Quite,' said Lady Blythe. 'I'm glad we understand each other.'

His face was bright pink. 'I couldn't do that, your ladyship. Daniel is a bright lad. It would be cruel.'

She glanced through the window to the peaceful garden beyond. 'Do you like it here, Rector?'

He nodded dumbly.

'And Mrs Fanshawe? Is she happy at Drakesden?'

He looked bewildered. 'The quiet of the countryside is beneficial for her nerves, the doctor says.'

'Of course. Mrs Fanshawe would not wish to be obliged to remove to the city.' She added patiently, 'This living is in the gift of Drakesden Abbey. Do you understand me, Rector?'

His pale eyes widened and he whispered, 'But what will Daniel *do*?'

'Oh – he will work for his father. And I daresay we shall find him some labouring at the Abbey.' Lady Blythe found, as she accepted her parasol from the rector's maid, that she was smiling.

A night's broken sleep had not dispersed Thomasine's apprehensiveness. She slipped out of Quince Cottage after breakfast, running down the drove towards the blacksmith's cottage. But Daniel still had not returned home.

Restless and edgy, Thomasine fed the hens, washed up, dusted the parlour and, sitting at the kitchen table, wrote the household accounts in a clear, sloping hand. *Back bacon, 9d; washing soda, 4½d; preserving sugar, 1/6d.* As she wrote, she relived, over and over again, the events of the last two days. The game of forfeits, Daniel's kiss, the splendour of Drakesden Abbey. Her scrambled, humiliating dismount from the borrowed mare, Lady Blythe watching all the while, her eyes like chips of blue ice. The rumour, growing like a living thing in Drakesden's muddy streets, that England was now at war.

There was a knock at the front door. Thomasine's hand shook and a blot of black ink smeared the white paper. Rose's voice called, 'Hilda, dear, come quick. It is Lady Blythe!'

Someone opened the door, and the visitor was shown in. Thomasine put aside her pen and quickly tidied her hair. Her heart was hammering as she opened the door to the parlour.

Aunt Rose looked upset, Aunt Hilda looked furious. Hilda said, 'Thomasine, my dear, there seems to have been a bit of a mix-up. Lady Blythe thinks that you spent yesterday afternoon at Drakesden Abbey.'

She had not lied, but neither, Thomasine knew, had she lived up to Hilda's own unimpeachable standards of honesty and integrity. She had to force the words out.

'Yes, I did, Aunt Hilly.' The flicker of shock in Hilda's eyes hurt her.

Rose whispered, '*Alone*, Thomasine, dearest?'

'With Nicholas. With Mr Blythe, I mean.'

Hilda said hopefully, 'Daniel –?' and Thomasine shook her head.

'Daniel didn't come. I don't know where he is.'

At last, Lady Blythe spoke. 'You see, Miss Harker?'

'I see,' said Hilda angrily, 'that there has been some childish nonsense. I see that your son, Lady Blythe, behaved badly.'

Just for a moment, the anger in Hilda's eyes was reflected in Lady Blythe's. Then the ice returned, and she said, 'I shall come straight to the point, Miss Thorne. A valuable heirloom is missing from Drakesden Abbey. It was taken from the safe. My son saw it at midday, and its loss was discovered in the late afternoon. Nicholas has told me that he opened the safe and showed it to you.'

Thomasine whispered, 'The Firedrake is missing?'

'Just so, Miss Thorne. Do you intend to return it to its rightful owners?'

There was a gasp from Hilda and a small muffled cry from Rose. It took Thomasine, dazed, a moment to understand what Lady Blythe was implying. Then she could hardly get the words out. 'You think that I – you think I *took* it –'

Rose said, 'The servants –'

'I have already spoken to the servants, Miss Harker. Their rooms have been thoroughly searched.'

Hilda's face was white except for two spots of scarlet on her cheekbones. 'A passing stranger, then . . . If your son forgot to close the safe –'

'All the world knows if a stranger comes to Drakesden. You are aware of that, Miss Harker. Miss Thorne had the opportunity – according to my younger daughter she left Nicholas once, ostensibly to tidy her hair.'

'*Ostensibly!*' Hilda had lost her temper. 'Lady Blythe – this is preposterous –'

'Your niece has not denied it, Miss Harker.'

Silently, three faces turned to Thomasine. Tears had gathered in Rose's eyes. Hilda had drawn herself to her full height, her fists clenched. Only Lady Blythe looked untroubled, as though she was unable to conceive that her version of events might possibly be disputed.

'I don't need to deny it,' said Thomasine proudly. 'My aunts know that I would never shame them in such a way.'

Rose's small hand curled round Thomasine's. Hilda said, her

voice cold, 'I think you should go, your ladyship. There really is nothing more to discuss.'

Lady Blythe spoke just once more as she rose to leave.

'You are not welcome at Drakesden Abbey, Miss Thorne. You will never speak to my son again. I would suggest that, if you are capable of it, you find yourself some sort of respectable occupation, as far away from Drakesden as possible. Girls of your type can so easily go to the bad.'

Much later, furiously chopping wood for the stove, Hilda thought through what Thomasine had said after Lady Blythe had gone. 'It was just Nicholas and me, Aunt Hilly. Nicholas showed me round the house and then we had a picnic, and then we rode. That's all.'

That's all. But it was enough, Hilda saw. For a proud, private woman like Lady Blythe to find that her handsome seventeen-year-old son had spent the day alone with a girl from the village must have been both galling and worrying. Which was why Lady Blythe was so angry, of course. Why she had accused Thomasine of doing such a terrible thing.

Hilda stacked the split logs against the outhouse wall. The greatest irony was that in that one matter she and Lady Blythe were entirely in agreement. She, like Gwendoline Blythe, did not think Nicholas suitable company for Thomasine. Their social standing, their birth, their position in the village meant that they were not, and could never be, equals. And yet they were of an age that was ripe for folly. Hilda thought of Nicholas Blythe, of his Byronic good looks, his isolation from the rest of Drakesden. She would have rather trusted Daniel Gillory with Thomasine any day, because Daniel understood the rules.

Daniel went home, eventually, in the late afternoon.

In the downstairs room, Ruth Gillory sent the younger children outside and put a plate of food in front of Daniel. The sound of hammering from the lean-to told him that his father was working.

Even though he had eaten nothing more than a handful of blackberries all day, Daniel picked at the bread and pork dumpling. He felt sick with dread. You didn't get caught kissing Lady Blythe's daughter and expect to get away with it.

His mother sat down opposite him. He realized, after a few mouthfuls, that she was trying to tell him something. Only she couldn't get the words out. Daniel pushed the plate aside, unable to eat any more. His mother was pleating the loose folds of her apron, not looking at him.

'Rector came round,' she said eventually.

Fear thumped him in the stomach, sick and certain. 'And?' he said. He knew what she was going to say next, though.

'He can't help with the clothes and things no more. He said he was very sorry.'

Daniel knew immediately what had happened. She couldn't send him to prison for kissing her daughter, so Lady Blythe had done the next best thing. She had taken away what was most important to him.

He felt his mother's thin, calloused hand touch his. 'It might be for the best, son. It was only causing trouble.'

Daniel scrambled to his feet, knocking over the stool. His anger made his head throb again. He walked out of the cottage into the sunshine, his eyes fixed on the untidy allotment, yet not seeing it.

He wanted to shout aloud at the injustice of it. To curse the entire brood of Blythes who had carelessly entangled him in their lives, and then punished him for that impertinence. He saw what was now his future: the scruffy smallholding, the skinny animals snuffling in the dust, the blacksmith's shop. He began to run, jumping over the fence, zigzagging through the field that separated the Gillorys' land from the dyke. Daniel trod the yellow corn, almost ripened, underfoot, leaving a deep jagged gash through the cornfield to mark his route. It didn't matter: the land belonged to the Blythes.

In the village, people stared at her, whispering. Thomasine knew then that the years in which she had thought she had become part of Drakesden had been illusory. Her acceptance had been only skin-thick, easily broken.

Rumour spread like a peat-fire in the small, isolated village, and too many were willing to give credence to it. Even those whom she had considered to be her friends – Mrs Carter in the shop, Mr Fanshawe, Mr Naylor at Chalk Farm – seemed to look at her in a different, censorious way.

And yet, she could have borne all that if it had not been for Daniel. She had not spoken properly to Daniel since the day they had played forfeits. Since the evening he had kissed her. Now, Daniel worked all day for his father and would not, rumour said, return to school in September. When she tried to speak to him, his answers were monosyllabic and curt to the point of rudeness.

At the end of the week, she wrote the letter. She had realized that she could not remain in Drakesden, that its flat vista and dingy cottages had become intolerable to her. She needed something more. She needed to be free again; she needed a future.

She did not tell Hilda and Rose what she had done, but waited restlessly for Antonia's reply.

London's Liverpool Street Station was covered with recruiting posters. The platform was crowded with men in khaki uniform, their newly cropped hair short and prickly on their reddened necks. Through the milling bodies and the steam hissing from the engines, Thomasine could not at first find Aunt Tony.

Then she saw her – the small, elegant figure, the auburn hair topped by a wide black hat trimmed with feathers. Thomasine, seizing her case, wormed her way through the crowds and showed her ticket to the guard.

'Such a crush!' cried Antonia, running to greet her. 'Darling, let me look at you.'

47

She held Thomasine at arm's length. Thomasine, for what seemed to be the first time in weeks, found that she was smiling.

'Oh, sweetheart, you've still got the hair! Such a funny thing, don't you think, that it should be just you and I? Pat was fair-haired, of course, like Rose. Your eyes are Pat's shape, but my colour. Let me see your feet, Thomasine. Point your toes.'

In the middle of Liverpool Street station, surrounded by soldiers returning to their barracks, Thomasine raised her skirts to her calves and pointed one foot.

'Turn out your ankle,' cried Antonia. '*Yes*, darling! You're a clever girl, you haven't forgotten, have you? Such dreadful boots, though. Hilda never did have the least idea.'

Antonia took Thomasine's hand and pulled her through the crowds. 'I have a class at four o'clock, but if we hurry we shall have time for a cup of tea together.'

An hour later, Thomasine was sitting in the front parlour of Antonia's Teddington villa. Gazing around the room, she found all of the objects still familiar to her from her visit the previous year. No one else had a house like Aunt Tony. Every ornament, every book and every painting had some connection with ballet. And no one else *looked* like Antonia. At just over five foot, she appeared tall and slim and elegant. Her clothes, which she made herself, were exquisite.

Antonia put down her teacup. 'Now – I must dash or I shall be late for my class. You stay here, darling, and have a nice rest. Train journeys are always so exhausting.'

Antonia peered into the mirror, tweaking the plumes of her hat into place. She took Thomasine's hands in hers and kissed her on the cheek.

'You shall start class on Monday afternoon. On Monday morning we shall visit the shops and choose some lengths of material. I expect you could do with a new frock or two.'

Then she was gone. Thomasine watched as, quick and purposeful, Antonia walked out of the front garden and along the street. Thomasine leaned her forehead against the window-pane. She

48

could see the row of similar houses across the other side of the street, differentiated by the colours of their front doors, or the roses or virginia creeper that crawled up their walls. A cat stretched out lazily on top of a nearby wall, and a poster was pasted around the scarlet pillar-box. Thomasine could only see one half of the poster, but she knew it by heart. 'Your King and Country need you', it said. 'A call to arms.'

The houses seemed so high, so crushed together, duplicated so many times against the dusty road and grey sky. Even the trees looked stunted, darkened by the smoke and smog of many winters. She thought, painfully, of Drakesden. Of Daniel and Nicholas, lying in the grass, saying, 'It's going to be the most terrific game.' She shut away those memories, along with the even more painful recollection of the parting from Hilda and Rose. Then she closed her eyes and listened to the sounds of the city.

In September, Daniel was clearing wheelbarrow-loads of windfalls from the orchard when, for the first time in weeks, Nicholas spoke to him.

Lady Blythe's younger son was wearing tennis clothes. He said, pointing to the wheelbarrow, 'You can go back to that later, Gillory. I need someone to collect tennis-balls for me. I have to practise my serve.'

Daniel followed Nicholas to the tennis-courts. Nicholas's perfect white shirt and trousers gleamed in the sunlight.

Drakesden's tennis-court was a grass court, surrounded by lawn on three sides and the Wilderness on the other. Nicholas said, 'Far too hot to run about in this heat,' and aimed, and served.

Daniel had picked up about half a dozen balls when he realized that Nicholas was deliberately serving wide. Three of Nicholas's serves went high over the net, landing in the undergrowth beyond the court. Daniel had to scrabble amongst the nettles and brambles to retrieve the balls.

He knew after the first five minutes or so that he wasn't going to take it. He wasn't going to run about like some damned puppy-dog, allowing Nicholas Blythe to enjoy his humiliation. It wasn't that he had lost his temper: it was that he was aware, still, of an awful injustice, something he could not live with. And after all, he no longer had anything much to lose.

The tennis-ball whirled in the air, *crack* went Nicholas's racquet, and there was a slap of leaves and twigs as the ball landed outside the court. Standing quite still, Daniel folded his arms and waited.

It took Nicholas a couple more shots before he realized what was going on.

'Pick up the balls, Gillory,' he shouted.

'Pick up your own fucking balls,' said Daniel.

The racquet, raised again, was lowered. 'What did you say?'

'I said, pick up your own fucking balls.'

'Why, you little swine –' Nicholas was running towards him. 'So you're foul-mouthed as well as a thief, are you, Gillory? You took it, didn't you? I know you did –'

Nicholas's fists were upraised. Before he hit him, Daniel had just a moment to witness the intensity of the fury and misery in Nicholas Blythe's eyes. Then his fist hit Nicholas's jaw.

Nicholas was two years the elder, but Daniel, his muscles made hard by his work in the blacksmith's shop, was the stronger. And they both had different rules. Or, Nicholas had rules and Daniel didn't. A difference in education, thought Daniel through a red haze of fury, as he seized a clump of Nicholas Blythe's dark hair and battered his head into one of the white lines that marked the edge of the court.

Eventually Nicholas lay curled beside the net, his white clothes ripped and discoloured, sobbing for breath. Daniel's breath hurt in his throat and he could taste blood in his mouth. He knew that his vengeance was hollow and pointless, but all the same he felt better for it.

He said nothing as he turned and walked away from Nicholas. When he reached the blacksmith's cottage and found to his relief that it was empty, he bundled up his few possessions and scrawled a note to his mother, and left it on the kitchen table.

He didn't stop walking that day. At last, when he looked back, he could no longer see Drakesden. It was lost in the natural curve of the earth. The road that he tramped had already begun to lose the absolute flatness of the Fens, to swell and rise.

At the back of a classroom in the Little Snowdrop School of Dancing, Thomasine struggled to copy the twenty other girls in front of her.

'Port de bras,' called Antonia, at the front of the class. 'Your hands, girls, remember your hands! Your fingers, Thomasine! And *smile!*'

Twenty girls, identically dressed, raised their arms to the ceiling, making wide, semi-circular arcs in the air. At the back of the class, Thomasine's arms, slightly late, made the same movement.

She would work very hard to catch up with the other girls. Antonia had told her that in as little as a year's time she could, if she was good enough, audition to work in a theatre. She intended to be good enough; she intended to be the best.

Antonia's voice soared above the distant hum of the street. 'Better, Thomasine, better. Second position, now, girls. And *smile!*'

PART TWO

1918–1920

Hour after hour they ponder the warm field
And the far valley behind, where buttercups
Had blessed with gold their slow boots coming up . . .

(Wilfred Owen, 'Spring Offensive')

CHAPTER TWO

BETWEEN August 1914 and November 1918, the world frag-
mented into chaos. By the spring of 1915, with the sinking of
the *Lusitania* and the dropping of the first bombs on London,
everyone knew that this was a different kind of war. No one
was safe.

On the Front, too, war had changed. Tanks and aeroplanes
replaced red-coated cavalry; phosgene gas ate away at soldiers'
lungs so that, although on dry land, they drowned. Away from
the battlefield, newspapers and posters were used both to keep
the reality of War from those left at home, and to incite anti-
German feelings. When conscription was introduced in 1916,
women were recruited to farms and factories to replace the
absent men. At the battles of Ypres, Arras, the Somme and
Passchendaele hundreds of thousands of young men died attempting to gain a few yards of muddy ground. Casualties among the
junior officers, drawn largely from the public schools, were
particularly heavy. The Great War divided men from women,
soldier from civilian. The twentieth century was born amid a
slither of blood, a howl of agony.

They were in a church hall in Brompton, rehearsing for a
review called *Sunny Days*, when they heard the news. There was
a knock at the door, and the pianist's sister came in. The pianist's
sister whispered to the pianist, and the pianist stopped playing
and whispered to the choreographer.

'The War has ended. The Armistice has been signed.'

There was a chorus of cheers and whistles. Thomasine went
to the window and looked outside at the grey London landscape.

The bands of rain that fell from the sky were almost obscured by fog. Water dripped from the blackened leaves of the trees and gathered in the gutters at the side of the road. The pavements were thick with people, most of them in uniform, all of them hurrying somewhere. The posters (so many posters) on the trees, the letter-boxes, the walls of shops and houses were torn at the edges, their corners curling in the rain.

Thomasine's head ached. *The War has ended, the Armistice has been signed.* Impossible to believe though that the horrors that had taken and shaken their lives so profoundly over the last four years were finished with. She had come to believe the War endless, without hope of resolution, that the food shortages, the dreariness of the unlit streets, the terrible business of searching through lists of casualties in the newspapers for the names of those that you knew, must go on for ever.

'Some of the girls are going down the West End. Are you coming, Thomasine?'

She turned aside from the window, shutting away the view of the streets and the long vista of the past four years, and smiled at her friend, Alice. 'Of course. As soon as I've changed.'

The pianist was packing up her music, the choreographer had already left the room. The dancers changed out of tunics and dancing shoes in the ladies' lavatory: a dozen of them in the cramped, unheated room, elbows jostling, the air thick with sweat and cheap scent. Outside, the fog and drizzle smelt of smoke and dust and fumes from the cars and taxis and horse-drawn vehicles that were making their way through the streets, all heading for the West End.

Alice's arm was linked through Thomasine's. The crowds on the pavements had spilled on to the roads, a mixed and increasingly wild assortment of men and women in a variety of uniforms. Everyone seemed to be carrying flags: Union Jacks, Stars and Stripes, Belgian, French and colonial pennants fluttered in the damp, misty air. Soon the cars had to hoot their horns constantly to get through the press of people; soon every vehicle was top-heavy with men and women, perched on running-boards, bonnets and roofs.

Thomasine's throat was dry and prickly. 'I'm parched,' she said. 'I didn't feel like breakfast this morning. Shall we . . .?'

They were standing outside a tea-shop. Alice nodded. Inside, miraculously, a small corner table was free. The door of the tea-shop closed behind them, shutting out some of the noise.

'Could do with a cup myself.' Alice sat down and scanned the menu. 'And a Chelsea bun.'

She gave their order to the waitress. Thomasine shook her head at the cigarette Alice offered.

'I know,' said Alice, grinning. 'Mother would be shocked. Nice girls don't smoke in public. Well – mother isn't here, and I'm not such a nice girl.' She giggled and lit her cigarette. The fumes made Thomasine cough.

It took them all afternoon to reach Trafalgar Square. They walked most of the way, carried along by swarming crowds of Tommies, sailors, Yankees, Belgians, WAACs, Wrens and munitions girls. Once, they clambered on to a bus, squeezed on the running-board with half a dozen others. But the bus was following no particular route, and somewhere in Piccadilly it ground to a halt, its passage halted by the press of people.

The rain kept falling, the fog did not lift. Thomasine's boots and the hem of her skirt were soon soaked and muddy, and the silk rose on the brim of her hat wilted and collapsed. Every muscle in her body seemed to ache. Too many rehearsals for too many shows, too many hours spent standing in draughty halls, rolling bandages and packing dressings for the Red Cross. The joy and licence that infected the crowd did not take hold of her.

She could not go back to Teddington, though: she could only continue to travel in the direction that the crowd chose to take. Thomasine held her bag closely to her side and clung tightly to Alice's arm. Alice whooped and cheered and sang with the rest of London. At Piccadilly, Thomasine could have walked from one side of the circus to the other on the heads of the crowd. Her feet hardly touched the ground, and elbows dug into her ribs, lifting her and carrying her on the great swaying current of people.

By the time they reached Trafalgar Square, it was almost dark. The summit of Nelson's column was lost in the haze of rain and fog; the base of the column was surrounded by a splintered mass of captured cannon and wooden gun-carriages. People were seizing billboards from the shops and destination boards from the buses, and hurling them on to a makeshift bonfire. Someone threw a match into the wood and flames soared into the air, licking the base of the column, throwing a weird orange light on the faces of the people in the square. The crowd surged backwards to avoid the fire, and Thomasine felt herself crushed between the factory girl in front of her and the tall sailor behind. When the pressure was finally released, she couldn't stop coughing.

'All right, sweetheart?' asked the sailor.

She managed to nod. Beside her, Alice, along with the rest of the crowd, was singing 'Tipperary'. The noise of the singing was overwhelming, the song of a Colossus, cutting out everything else. The sailor behind Thomasine said something to her, but she could not make out the words. He seemed to be mouthing silently, like a moving-picture star. Faces crowded around her, lips apart, miming words. 'It's a long way to Tipperary, it's a long way from home.' There was a smell of beer and cigarettes and smoke from the bonfire.

Impossibly, then, they began to dance. Thousands of people formed themselves into a single entity and, twisting like a python, circled and cavorted around the square. When Thomasine turned and looked, Alice was no longer beside her. The tall sailor held one of her hands, a yellow-faced munitions girl the other. She caught sight once of Alice's blonde head, bobbing in the crowd, and then she was gone. Faces, blurred by the smoke and the rain and the gathering darkness, passed in front of

Thomasine: soldiers, some with crimson scars pitting their skin or distorting their features, others with bandages still around their heads, or their arms in slings. Land-girls and VADs, faces reddened with the heat, their hair plastered to their heads with the rain. Munitions workers, their skin jaundiced with picric acid, made orange by the reflected flames from the centre of the square. The light from the bonfire gouged black shadows into all the faces, ageing them, making them into something grotesque, hardly recognizable as human beings.

The crowd pulled her this way and that. When she looked down, Thomasine saw that her handbag had gone. The silk handles still hung from her wrist, but the bag had disappeared. She looked wildly to left and right, peering amongst the thousand dancing feet, but she could see nothing. Her purse, her dancing shoes and tunic, her doorkey had all been in her bag. Panic rose in her throat. Someone jostled her from behind and she almost fell. Then, her eyes still searching the ground, she began to push her way to the perimeter of the square.

It seemed to take hours. Some people cursed her, others tried to kiss her. She kept on, though, grimly determined to escape the square, refusing to allow herself to be sucked back into the victory dance. Time and again, the crowd rose and squeezed and crushed her, so that she saw stars in the black clouded sky. It was like swimming through flood waters against a strong current.

By the time she reached St Martin's Lane, Thomasine had lost her hat as well as her bag. Leaning against the wall of a shop, she coughed and could not stop coughing. She wanted to curl up on the pavement and sleep, to lie down and never have to get up again. But the noise, the smell and the crush of people was still unbearable. She told herself sternly that she could not sleep here. In spite of the cold rain, she felt hot, so she undid the buttons of her coat and loosened her scarf. Then, taking a deep breath, she made herself begin to walk again, down St Martin's Lane, away from Trafalgar Square.

Her progress was slow and faltering. Several times she was

pushed by the weight of the crowd against the railings, or sucked into the centre of the road. She tripped over couples entwined on the front steps of the houses and stumbled against those locked in each other's arms, swaying, utterly unaware of all that went on around them. Although she knew the centre of London well, tonight the streets seemed unfamiliar, something out of a nightmare. She must find a taxi, she thought. Only – how much would that cost, all the way to Teddington? No – a Tube to the mainline station would be better. She was sure that there was a Tube station not far away. Perhaps on this night, of all nights, no one would notice if she travelled without a ticket.

The sound of gunfire made her jump and look quickly back. A soldier was standing precariously on the railings of a house, firing his revolver into the night. Not far away from him, someone lay on the pavement, curled up in a ball. Two men kicked him in the stomach over and over again. Thomasine ducked to avoid the missiles hurled through the air: a policeman's helmet, beer bottles, onions and brussels sprouts from a green-grocer's stall. One of the sprouts hit her neatly in the centre of the forehead and she staggered and fell, grazing her knee. Her stockings were holed and dirty, her skirt soaking.

When she stood up, she found herself at the entrance of a narrow alleyway. Taking a step or two forward, Thomasine saw that the alleyway seemed deserted, except for the dustbins and rubbish piled in the gutters. It was dark and cool away from the bonfires and torchlights. The high walls of the houses seemed to close in above her, cutting off the clamour of the crowd. The sudden silence was quite shocking. There was a buzzing inside Thomasine's head, and the words of the songs rattled over and over again through her brain. 'Goodbye-ee, goodbye-ee, Wipe the tear, baby dear, from your eye-ee.'

I'm not feeling well, she thought. Leaning against a wall, she closed her eyes and pulled her coat around her. She was cold now, shivering, teeth chattering.

She became aware that she was not alone. Uneven footsteps

crunched on the cobbles and a muffled cough split the sheltered silence of the alleyway. She opened her eyes. A man wearing an officer's greatcoat and cap was standing in the darkness, staring at her. The intensity of his stare disturbed her.

'Are you all right?'

There was something familiar about that voice, but her head ached too much to struggle through the fog of memory to identify it. The fear remained, though, and she began to shake.

'Thomasine? Are you all right?'

When he said her name she pulled her coat tighter about her, and struggled to distinguish his features from out of the darkness. His eyes were darkened by the night, but she knew them to be an uncommon mix of gold and green and hazel.

'Daniel,' she whispered. 'Daniel Gillory.'

She let him help her up. 'You've a bump on your forehead,' Daniel said.

'A brussels sprout,' said Thomasine. 'I was hit by a brussels sprout.'

She giggled, and then the giggle turned into a cough. When, eventually, she managed to stop coughing, Daniel Gillory felt her forehead.

'You've got 'flu, you silly girl,' he said mildly. 'You must be feeling awful.'

She began to cry then. She could not have explained to anyone why she was crying: because she felt ill, because she had lost her purse, because the War was over, because of the waste of it all. Because of a sudden intuition of what the past four years had done to her life, to Daniel's life, to all their lives. Daniel held her while she cried, and when Thomasine had almost finished, he handed her his handkerchief.

'I looked for you,' she said. Her voice was wobbly and uneven. 'I looked for your name in the newspaper. Every single day.'

He looked down at her. 'Just a scratch at Passchendaele. That's all. I was lucky.'

61

Thomasine blew her nose and handed Daniel back his handkerchief. He said, 'I'll see you home. It's late.'

He tucked her hand through his elbow and they began to walk down the alleyway. Daniel's gait was not even; he trod much more heavily on one foot than the other. The scratch, Thomasine realized, must have been a bad one: the battle of Passchendaele had been fought over a year ago. Her own legs felt oddly insubstantial, as though they might buckle under her, or else she might float away, dancing more lightly than she had ever danced before. Their progress was slow and fitful.

They turned out of the alleyway and started down the road. Thomasine said, 'I was trying to find a Tube station.'

'No. Not the Tube.' Daniel glanced from left to right. 'We'll look for a taxi.'

'I haven't any money. Someone cut the handles of my bag.'

He glanced down at her. 'What were you doing here on your own, Thomasine?' His voice was sharp.

Exhausted, she leaned against some park railings and shut her eyes. Even her eyelids seemed to ache. 'I wasn't on my own, I was with a friend, but I lost her in the crowd. I've been living in London with my Aunt Tony for almost four years now. Aunt Rose died of pneumonia just before the Christmas of nineteen-fourteen. It was dreadfully sudden, Daniel. Awful. Aunt Hilly left Drakesden soon after, to become a nurse. I've worked all through the War – I danced at my first concert six months after I came here.'

In the yellow light of the gas-lamp she saw him frown. 'I've hardly been back to Drakesden, Daniel. Not since 1914. Not since the Blythes . . .' Her voice trailed away.

I would suggest that, if you are capable of it, you find yourself some sort of respectable occupation, as far away from Drakesden as possible. Well, she had found a profession, and even if she was uncertain whether Lady Blythe would consider dancing respectable, she was able to recall with defiance the humiliation of that distant and dreadful morning, and know that she had made something of herself.

'*Christ!*' Daniel took her arm again and began to walk along the pavement. He was silent for a long time. Thomasine leaned against him, half-asleep. The noise and clamour of the street had a dreamlike quality now: she felt oddly separated from it, as though she was not really there. She seemed to have walked for a very long time when Daniel whispered, 'God damn the whole race of Blythes.'

In the darkness she could picture, as though it was in front of her, the cutting from the newspaper. 'He did,' she said. 'Gerald Blythe died at the battle of Mons in nineteen-fourteen.'

Daniel said nothing for a while. Then, 'And Nicholas?'

Thomasine shook her head. 'I don't know. He was awarded a medal. He survived, I suppose.'

She began to cough again, her chest hurting with the force of each breath. She heard Daniel say, more gently, 'You look all in. Just sit there a moment,' and she leaned against a door-jamb and closed her eyes.

Thomasine heard Daniel's footsteps growing fainter as he walked away. She knew that it was Daniel because of the heavy alternate tread. For a moment she grieved that he had left her, but then she drifted away, quite pleasantly, to somewhere warm and quiet.

She was woken by a hand shaking her shoulder, a voice saying her name. 'Wake up, Thomasine. I've found a motor. Can you walk?'

She made herself walk, because she wasn't going to let poor, limping Daniel carry her. She thought she had been asleep for hours, but the sky was still black, the distant sounds of revelry unaltered. He led her through a small park fenced with railings. A few couples rolled in the grass, sheltered by the bushes. The moonlight, peeping briefly through the ranks of clouds, delineated the sinuous leafless branches of the trees.

The motor-car was on the far side of the square. 'Where's the driver?' said Thomasine, dazed. She had begun to shiver. Her fingers fumbled as she tried to button her coat.

Daniel shrugged. 'It was probably abandoned this afternoon. Couldn't get through the crowds, I expect. Thought he'd have more joy in the pub.'

He crouched by the front wheels. A twist of the starting handle, and the engine groaned into life. Daniel opened the passenger door from the inside.

'Sit down and tuck my coat around you.' He wiped the windscreen with a cloth. 'Where shall I take you?'

'Teddington. My aunt lives in Teddington.'

The journey was slow and halting. The constant rain, streaming down the windscreen, made it hard to see where they were going. Drops of rain found their way through the open space between the door and the hood. Daniel's greatcoat was soon beaded with raindrops. Every so often they would come up against another band of revellers, and have to stop and hoot the horn. People moved out of the way, Thomasine realized, because Daniel was wearing an officer's uniform. It didn't surprise her at all that Daniel Gillory, the blacksmith's son, had become an officer.

Sometimes she dozed, her dreams exhausting and over-vivid. But the unaccustomed jolting of the motor-car woke her every few minutes, and then she was awake and restless, unable to be comfortable, wriggling her aching limbs. Staring wide-eyed at Daniel, she thought that he had changed a great deal. He drove with easy skill, his watchful eyes studying the road.

'When did you join up, Daniel?'

Daniel glanced sideways at Thomasine. The motor-car jolted on the cobbled road. 'Nineteen-sixteen,' he said. 'I tried earlier, but they wouldn't take me. I was in London for two years before that.'

She made her aching head think back. She knew that Daniel Gillory had been forced to leave school, she knew also that he had run away from home, aged fifteen, to no one knew where. Aunt Hilly had written all that to her.

'Your family . . .?' she said uncertainly.

'My father was killed two years ago, at Arras. Harry died earlier this year. He'd only been in France a couple of weeks, poor little bastard. Sorry, Thomasine. The War hasn't done my vocabulary much good.'

She began to shiver again, and pulled Daniel's greatcoat more tightly round her. 'And your mother, Daniel?'

'Died seven months after I left home. Premature childbirth. I didn't find out until quite a long while later.'

His voice was clipped, expressionless. She might have thought he did not care, had she not noticed the rapid movement of his eyes, and the way his knuckles had whitened as he clenched the steering-wheel.

'Sammy's in an orphanage, and Nell's gone out to service. Quite a nice place, she says. I lost touch with Violet. And the new baby didn't live out the week.'

They drove for a while in silence. They had left the noise and the crowds behind; only the occasional revellers burst into view, a brief flash of light and sound in the darkness. The roads and the houses began to look familiar. The streets were almost empty. In a croaking voice, Thomasine gave directions. Eventually, she pointed out Antonia's house, and Daniel pulled in beside the pavement.

'Just as well. We're almost out of petrol. I'll move it a few streets away, and no doubt the police will find it in the morning.'

She touched his hand. 'You'll come in, won't you, Daniel?'

'If you like.' He sounded doubtful. 'For a few minutes.'

Daniel opened the car door and she climbed out. The cold and the rain hit her with physical force, and she began to cough again. There was a light on in the downstairs window of Antonia's house. Thomasine saw the curtain twitch, and then the door opened.

'Darling! I was so worried! I thought perhaps you'd stayed the night –'

Thomasine used the last of her strength to say, 'This is

Captain Daniel Gillory, Aunt Tony. He was a neighbour of ours in Drakesden. He drove me home.' And then everything blurred and became patched with black and the floor, wobbling, swam up to greet her.

Daniel carried Thomasine up to bed, and then waited, as he had been told to, in the sitting-room. Over the past few years he had become more used to giving orders than to taking them, but he had seen straight away that Thomasine's Aunt Antonia was not the sort of person you argued with.

He sat down and gazed around the room. His leg was aching dreadfully, but he had grown accustomed to that. Both the ache and the limp would lessen in time, the doctors had told him. He glanced from the plain, stylish furniture to the swathe of curtains that hung across the window, and then to the collection of photographs, prints and sketches on the walls and bureau. The room, although small, was both elegant and comfortable. It was, he decided, civilized. It seemed odd to Daniel that such oases of civilization could still exist.

After twenty minutes or so, Antonia returned. Daniel started to struggle to his feet.

'No – no. *Please*. Sit down and rest.'

He collapsed back into the chair as ordered. He said, 'How is she, Mrs . . .?'

'Russell. Antonia Russell.' She frowned. 'Thomasine is sleeping now, but she's not at all well, I'm afraid, Captain Gillory. I shall send for the doctor first thing tomorrow. I'm sure it is the influenza, as you said.'

'Half London has it,' said Daniel. 'I had a dose myself a month ago.'

He saw Antonia make a conscious effort to shake off her worries and smile at him brightly. 'Well, then, Captain Gillory – and how can I thank you for your kindness? You must at least let me feed you. Do you mind eating in the kitchen? So much cosier, I think, when there are just two.'

He followed Antonia into the kitchen. Sitting at the wide pine table he watched her assemble cold gammon, bread, pickles, cake. He noticed that her larder was, like so many people's, almost empty, but he said nothing and did not refuse the food. He had, after all, been ordered to eat. And he was damned hungry.

'I can offer you tea or cocoa, Captain Gillory – or, let me see – there's a bottle of plum brandy somewhere, I believe. My late husband's . . .'

There had been no black-framed photograph in the sitting-room: all the pictures had been of dancers, or of stage sets, or rows of smiling little girls, all identically clad.

'Killed in action?' asked Daniel respectfully.

'Oh! No –' Antonia, her back to him, rummaged in the larder. 'I was widowed long before the War. Here we are, Captain Gillory.'

Triumphantly, she held up the squat, dusty bottle. She was a tiny woman, smaller than Thomasine. Her auburn hair, slightly faded now, was piled elegantly on top of her head. Her stance was very erect, all her movements graceful and controlled.

'I do apologize for the tumbler. I don't seem to have a brandy glass in the house.'

Daniel's fingers folded round his glass. 'You should join me, Mrs Russell. After all . . .'

'Yes. Of course. The War.'

Antonia found a second tumbler and poured a fraction of an inch of plum brandy into the bottom of the glass. She said hesitantly, 'We should drink to Victory, I suppose, but some-how . . .'

He couldn't speak at first. There was a lump in his throat, and images of the past four years flickered like a slide show in front of his eyes. The kitchen was airy and spacious, but just then the awful panic that frequently now overcame him in confined spaces hovered at the edges of his consciousness.

'To Peace,' he managed to say.

67

'To Peace,' repeated Antonia very gently, raising her glass. 'And to good health for us all. For you, Captain, and for Thomasine. And for my sister, and your family.'

He swallowed a mouthful of brandy and the lump in his throat dissolved, and the room became unthreatening again, its walls correctly spaced, its corners properly lit.

Antonia said, 'So you are from Drakesden, Captain Gillory?'

The brandy had warmed his stomach, relaxing him a little. 'My father was the blacksmith, and my mother owned a small-holding. Your sister – the younger Miss Harker – was very kind to me. She lent me books sometimes.'

'Will you go back?'

He finished the last of the brandy and put down his glass. 'I don't know. I hadn't thought. The future – well, it has seemed so improbable, you see, over the last few years. That any of us should have a future, I mean.'

'Of course.' She smiled at him. 'You shall need time to think. Now, Captain Gillory, I must go and sit with Thomasine. You'll stay the night with us, won't you? We haven't a spare room, I'm afraid, but I can make the sitting-room couch very comfortable for you.'

This time, he did not take orders. He rose to his feet, thankful that the brandy had quelled the ache in his leg. 'That's very kind of you, Mrs Russell, but I'd better be going now. Things to do . . .'

He walked out of the room, and took his greatcoat from the stand in the hall.

Antonia said, 'You'll leave an address, Captain Gillory, won't you? I'm sure Thomasine will wish to write and thank you for your kindness when she is well again.'

She held out a notepad and pen to him. He stooped over the sideboard and wrote 'Daniel Gillory' on top of the thick white paper. Then he stopped.

'I can't remember the number of my lodgings,' he lied. 'It's been a year or two. I'll write to you and let you know my address.'

Antonia's eyes met his. They were the same colour as Thomasine's, a dark greenish-blue, and he knew then that he was right not to allow himself to become involved with Thornes, or Russells, or Harkers again.

Antonia opened the front door for him. As he walked down the path, she said, 'If you should ever need us, Captain Gillory – or if you simply need company – then you will always be welcome.'

Daniel drove the motor-car, a Rolls-Royce, a few streets away and left it at the side of the road. It stuttered a little as he pulled over to the pavement, gulping at the last few mouthfuls of petrol.

He knew, as he clambered out and began to walk, that he had only one place to go. He must travel back to Bethnal Green and find the pub in which he had worked between leaving home and joining up. He looked forward to seeing Hattie again; it was just the thought of the East End of London that appalled him. The narrow alleyways, the warrens of cramped overcrowded houses and, worst of all, the Underground.

Here, he was glad of the openness of the streets, the freshness of the air after the rain. In an hour or so, Daniel knew that he would see the first hazy beginnings of dawn touching the roofs of the houses and the ranks of trees that lined the avenues. There were no trees in the East End of London. People lived differently there.

Four years ago, it had taken him three days to travel from East Anglia to London, hitching rides, sleeping at the roadside, scavenging for food. When he had reached the city, he had done the obvious thing, and headed for the first recruiting station. Regular food, clean clothes and paid employment had seemed then an attractive option. But they had laughed at him, a scrawny undernourished fifteen-year-old, and told him to come back in a year or two. He had been mortified, but he had learned since that his experience was common, that those of his class were frequently neither tall enough nor fit enough to enlist as soldiers. It was the public schoolboys who were taken in their thousands, and made officers in charge of their less privileged fellows.

He had found himself, then, in one of the seedier parts of London, possessed by an equal mixture of bravado and fear, determined to survive, resolute that he would not go back to his family. The first fortnight had been awful: little food, no roof over his head. Then he had met Hattie and everything had changed.

Hattie had found him rummaging in the dustbins outside her Bethnal Green public house. She had taken him indoors, given him a plate of pie and mash, and later, hearing a little of his story, offered him work. Washing glasses, hauling ale-barrels, cleaning floors. Hattie was forty and plump and breathless, and her husband had joined up the week before. She wasn't all that well – she needed a boy, she said, for the heavier work. Daniel accepted with enthusiasm and relief.

A week later, he found himself in Hattie's bed. 'Such a pretty face,' she said to him that evening, running her fingers through his curls. Daniel lost his virginity, enveloped in Hattie's acres of warm, white flesh, his head hazy from his first ever tot of whisky, his hands still damp with washing-up water.

After that, they settled into a comfortable and mutually useful sort of life. Gradually, Daniel had taken over more and more of the running of The George and Dragon. He wrote the accounts, ordered the spirits and, at the end of the evening, helped throw out the rowdier patrons. Hattie kept an eye on the barmaids and chatted to the customers. Because Hattie took the trouble to listen to her customers' griefs and joys, the pub was always full.

A year and a half later, at the beginning of 1916, Daniel went to the recruiting office again. This time, no one quibbled. Eighteen months of hauling beer-barrels and eating Hattie's excellent cooking had given him both height and muscles. He was in France by the spring.

By the end of summer, he had become an officer. He could read and write and speak with the right sort of voice, and besides, the swathes of public schoolboys had been mown down at Ypres, at Loos, at Gallipoli. His strong instinct for self-preservation, his impoverished and uncoddled childhood, saw him through the horrors of the Somme with hardly a scratch. He survived, was promoted, was responsible for the welfare and continued existence of sixty men. He was able to get through it all until Passchendaele.

Even now, a year later, he could not think about Passchendaele clearly. It was as though the events of that terrible day had taken him and shaken him up, and left him somehow less than he had been before. The few certainties that he had possessed had been stripped from him so that, waking up in the field hospital after the operation on his leg, he had had to start all over again. Only he hadn't had the energy. It had been months later, convalescing in England, learning to walk again, that he had even begun to pick up the pieces.

The first rays of the early morning sun had begun to sweep over the tidy gardens of Richmond. Daniel knew that he was desperately tired, that he needed to sleep. As the effect of the brandy began to wear off, his leg started to ache again. Reason told him that he should find a room in a cheap lodging house and rest, but he preferred the open spaces and fresh air. Besides, money was short, as always.

He reached Bethnal Green that evening, having hitched lifts in lorries and cars and in donkey-carts. The centre of London still danced and sang in celebration. Litter had begun to accumulate on the pavements, the detritus of victory, tangled flags and bunting and paper hats. Daniel shifted a snoring body out of the doorway of The George and Dragon and went inside.

Somehow, he had expected to find Hattie in the Public Bar, perched on her usual stool, drinking port and lemon and dispensing sympathy. He had a word with one of the barmaids and then, uneasily, hobbled upstairs.

She was in bed, but she woke when he tapped on the door. 'Oh, *Daniel*,' she croaked on seeing him. He sat down beside her on the bed and took her hand in his.

'I thought it'd be longer,' whispered Hattie, 'before they let you home.'

He explained, 'I got back to England the day before yesterday. I'd had the 'flu, you see, Hat. I wasn't a lot of use to them, what with that and the leg. So they gave me my discharge papers, and sent me back home along with the other crocks.'

Hattie nodded. Her brown eyes were luminously bright. 'I've got 'flu, Danny. Mabel Green was in here a few days ago, coughing all over me. I'm sure that's it.'

Daniel smiled, but he didn't believe her. He was horrified at how much weight she had lost since he had last seen her, six months ago. When she coughed, her whole body shook.

Hattie patted the blanket beside her. 'Come and give me a cuddle, Danny. I'm no good for much else, I'm afraid. Ted'll be home soon, so we'll make the most of the time we've got, won't we?'

He lay beside her on the bed, one arm cradled around her shoulders. Exhausted, Daniel closed his eyes, and in the brief span between waking and sleeping a series of images flickered vividly in front of him. Images of battle: mud and cold and barbed wire. The sound of mortars, the whining of bullets. The stench of dead flesh and the scent of violets that presaged a gas attack. The dugout: earth falling on his head, wood splintering around him. The noise of the explosion, and then the appalling silence. Not a chink of light . . . *He couldn't breathe . . .*

Eyes wide open now, Daniel stared at the curtains, the bed, Hattie asleep beside him. He forced himself to breathe regularly, so that the pounding of his heart slowed. Then, when he was sure the nightmare would not recur, he closed his eyes again and dreamed of level fields of green grass and long silver channels of water, pointing towards the sea.

★

The Blythes were in the conservatory at Drakesden Abbey. Sir William was spraying his orchids. Nicholas was sitting in one of the wicker chairs, smoking.

'You should take one of the horses out for a ride, Nicky,' said Lady Blythe, pulling a few dead leaves from a trailing vine.

Nicholas nodded, and stubbed out his cigarette in the ashtray. His fingers, now unoccupied, drummed constantly on the surface of the table beside him: a persistent and irritating habit that he had picked up in the course of the last two years.

'Darling,' Gwendoline reminded him gently, 'that's so bad for your fingernails.'

Nicholas, following her glance, stared at his hand as though it belonged to someone else. Then, very carefully, he lit another cigarette.

Another unfortunate habit, but Lady Blythe held her tongue. She crossed the room to sit beside her son. 'I thought I would write to Marjorie. It's so long since the children were at Drakesden.'

Nicholas inhaled his cigarette. 'Damned difficult place for Edward's wheelchair. All those stairs.'

The years had coarsened his language, but she made allowances. In France, Nicholas must have mixed with all sorts of people.

She smiled at him patiently. 'Edward does not have to come. He can engage a competent nurse. It would be very hard on poor Marjorie if her activities were constantly curtailed by her husband's infirmity.'

'*Christ!*' Nicholas rose to his feet, knocking over the ashtray.

Sir William looked up from the orchids. 'Steady on, old chap.'

'It would be so pleasant, Nicky. We could all be together again.' Gwendoline reached for her handkerchief and dabbed it at the corners of her eyes. 'Except dear Gerald, of course.'

'And Lally,' said Nicholas savagely. 'You've forgotten Lally again, Mother.'

'Lally has only just returned to school.' Gwendoline rang the bell for the servant to clear up the mess from the fallen ashtray. 'It would hardly be sensible to take her away again so soon. You know how difficult she finds it to settle each term.'

Nicholas opened the French doors of the conservatory.

'Keep the heat in, old boy,' said Sir William. 'Tricky little blighters, orchids.'

The doors slammed shut. Lady Blythe watched the maidservant sweep up the ash and then went to her sitting-room to write a note to Marjorie.

Nicholas knew that his sister Marjorie and her two children would come to Drakesden, that Marjorie's crippled husband Edward would be left at home with the competent nurse, and that Lally would remain at boarding-school. Nicholas had known for a long time that his mother always got her own way. The only time, he thought, that she had been thwarted, had been with poor old Gerry. Mother certainly hadn't intended her first-born son to end his days with his guts strewn over a potato field at Mons.

Nicholas's hands started to shake again, so he rammed them into his pockets and began to walk, fast. He was thankful to escape the hot, fetid atmosphere of the conservatory. He breathed great lungfuls of sharp, damp Fen air as he strode past the lawns – now planted with rows of vegetables – past the tennis-court, beside the Wilderness. One of the doctors had said that fresh air and exercise would help. Nicholas had been supposed to tell that doctor everything, but he hadn't, of course, because there were some things you couldn't tell anyone.

A twig cracked not far away as a hare bounded through the undergrowth, and Nicholas threw himself flat, face-down in the bracken and leaf-mould of the Wilderness. Sweat poured down his face; he knew that he smelt of fear. For a moment, when he looked up, he was in Flanders again. He saw it all quite clearly: the mud, the barbed wire, the hot orange star as a mortar exploded. Then in an instant it all dissolved, and he was back in the Wilderness at Drakesden, in a perfect funk, his trousers smeared with mud and dead leaves in his hair. Scrambling to his feet, ashamed of himself, Nicholas's worst fear was that the visions might somehow lock permanently into place, leaving him trapped in the trenches for ever.

He brushed down his clothes, meticulously picking every scrap of soil and leaf from his clothing. He began to walk again, looking round to make sure that no one had seen him behaving like an ass. He passed the greenhouses and the potting-sheds and walked the long line of bays and laurel bushes, resisting the temptation to keep his uncovered head low, to crawl like a serpent on his belly. When he reached the winding paths of the Labyrinth, he felt safer, hidden by the newly-leaved branches overhead and the ferny undergrowth.

At the walled garden, he stopped and tried the door. It opened with a creaking and ripping of ivy tendrils, and then he was inside, surrounded by rose-beds and the statues in their niches. Nicholas walked a step or two forward, letting the door swing shut behind him. It was just the same, he thought wonderingly, it hadn't changed a bit. The walled garden had not, like the lawns and the shrubbery, been dug up to grow vegetables during the War. Perhaps the lawn needed mowing and the roses hadn't been properly pruned, but otherwise it was just the same.

There were no buds on the roses now, but if he looked carefully Nicholas could see the tiny furled green shoots dotted like emeralds along each stem. For once, the scent that over-powered his imagination was not that of rotting corpses or phosgene gas, but that of the roses of Drakesden Abbey.

Nicholas left the walled garden, and wandered towards the orchard. Ducking through the side-gate, he walked down the hill, through the wood. The black branches of the trees knitted together overhead. Rainwater still dripped from the leaves, reminders of the previous night's showers. His feet sank in the soft black mud. He heard the sound of feet shuffling through the leaf-mould and stared, his entire body quivering, into the gloom. A dark figure, rather small, weighed down with a bag, was treading the path through the undergrowth, coming towards him. Nicholas, wide-eyed, said '*Lally!*' and his sister looked up.

She was wearing her school uniform, an unbecoming, shapeless collection of brown garments trimmed with gold. Into the brim of her felt hat she had stuck a collection of leaves, feathers and early spring flowers.

'You look like a Red Indian,' said Nicholas.

'You look a sight,' said Lally, calmly inspecting him. 'I preferred you in your uniform.'

'Talking of uniforms – why aren't you at school?'

'I left.' Lally began to walk towards the orchard gate, leaving Nicholas to carry her bag. 'It was dreadful, Nick, quite impossible. We had to play lacrosse – if I ever caught the ball, which was hardly ever, because no one threw it to me – it would always fall back out of the net. We were in *houses*, and we were supposed to cheer our team. We were supposed to mind if we lost. And the uniform – well, black-haired people shouldn't have to wear brown, should they?'

Nicholas glanced at her judiciously. 'It doesn't do a lot for you, Baby.'

'And I've got so fat. Stodge, stodge and more stodge.'

It was true, she had become rather plump. Lally's small round face, surrounded by two unflatteringly thick plaits, had filled out, and her body, beneath the ugly gymslip and coat, lacked any feminine curves. Yet she was not, Nicholas realized with elder brotherly surprise, unattractive. Her long dark upturned eyes had a feline quality, and her small crimson lips were beautifully shaped.

'You're wearing lipstick!' said Nicholas, shocked.

Lally smiled. 'Isn't it lovely? I tried powder, too, but it was the wrong colour. It made me look like a rice pudding.'

Nicholas grabbed her elbow as she stepped through the gate. 'They'll send you back, you know.'

Lally said smugly, 'No, they won't. I sent a love letter to the art master. I made sure that this awful girl Belinda, who is Head of House, found it. I knew she'd be bound to sneak. He had bad breath and he was a conscientious objector, but still, it did the trick. Besides, I'm almost seventeen now. Even if Mama doesn't give me a single ball, that's it, I'm out. I'm grown-up now.'

Alone in his room at night, the silence of the countryside was filled by Nicholas's worst memories. He tried to shut out the memories by reading, by singing to himself, by rocking himself to and fro, his forehead pressed against his knees. But the memories came flooding back, just as they always did, coloured and scented and with an awful, perfect clarity.

He had joined up in 1916. He'd wanted to join up earlier, but his mother wouldn't let him. Because Nicholas's elder brother Gerald had been blown to bits in the first few months of the War, he hadn't disobeyed her.

He went to the recruiting station with his friend Richardson. Nicholas and Richardson had been pals at Winchester. Richardson was a jolly fine cricketer, better than Nicholas, and Nicholas had always rather admired him, as well as liked him. Richardson had fair hair and blue eyes and a wide smile.

France was different to how Nicholas had thought it would be. There were the rats which ran in great fat swarms over the men as they slept at night, and the lice. After his first few days in France, Nicholas had never again felt clean. The trenches and the shell-craters were awash with cold brown water, and the countryside was not recognizable as countryside, but was a moonscape of thick mud. If a wounded man fell in the mud, he was often unable to climb out of it, and died there.

One morning they were ordered to attack again. It was early September: the battle of the Somme had begun on the first of July. Nicholas and Richardson had been in France since April.

The attack opened at 5 a.m. The ground shook as the guns roared, covering the advance. Someone had blundered, though, and the barrage fell a hundred yards short of its intended target, and Nicholas saw his men mown down by their own side. Some heard the order to retreat, others didn't. Nicholas crouched in a trench with twenty or so survivors. Shells crashed around them. Nicholas wanted to bury himself in the mud and water, to dig into the earth with his fingernails until he was safe.

Eventually they formed up again and made ready to attack the ridge. When they reached the top of the ridge, they found that the barbed wire had been incompletely cut through. Trying to struggle through in single file, they were cut down one at a time. Men became hooked on the wire and died there. Nicholas, who somehow survived to lead his men through the barbed wire, found himself on the wrong side of the ridge, in No Man's Land, hiding in a shell-crater with Holtby and Davis and Crashaw.

It was daylight and although it was raining, the light was still quite good. Holtby, raising his head to look over the perimeter of the crater, was shot in the face, and fell back, screaming with agony. They did what they could for him, which was almost nothing, and Nicholas was relieved when he died a few minutes later.

Then the shelling began. It lasted until darkness fell, about eight hours later. During every moment of that eight hours Nicholas expected to die within the next few seconds. Images of his former life passed before him like a collection of photographs: his childhood, his schooldays, his holidays at Drakesden. The reliving of his previous life terrified him, because he knew that was something that happened before you died. Eventually he found himself almost longing for death, because the tension of waiting was so intolerable.

By evening, he was the only one left. There was no one to give orders to, no one to take orders from. The gunfire had died down now, and the brief patches of silence appalled him. He thought he was the only one left alive, that everyone else on the battlefield, in France, in the world, had died. When he tried to crawl to the edge of the crater, Nicholas found that his limbs would not work properly. He watched his hands move in strange, meaningless circles, grasping at the air. He saw his legs, half-immersed in water, judder. He had lost all sense of time: it seemed to take an eternity to work his way up the muddy bank, to peer out.

No one shot at him, so he heaved his body out of the slime. In the increasing twilight the landscape convinced him of the cessation of the world in which he had grown up. The mud-fields stretched out before him, unending, pitted by craters. This strange country's rivers were channels of mud, its forests tree-stumps sticking out of the mire, bare of leaf and branch. The only colour was the crimson of the blood of wounded men; the rest was monochrome.

Nicholas stayed at the edge of the crater for some time, because he didn't know which way to go. Before, there had always been an officer, or a schoolmaster, or Mama to tell him what to do. At last, when the sporadic rifle-fire began again, he started to crawl. He moved in no particular direction. Sometimes he thought he was moving in circles. His progress was very slow, because neither his legs nor his arms would obey him. Several times he checked himself, wondering whether he had been shot and had somehow not noticed, but he didn't seem to be hurt. He knew that he was in an almighty funk, but he didn't know how to stop himself. His terror seemed to be increasing, rather than decreasing.

He passed many dead and wounded men on his way. Some of them he recognized, some were from other regiments, some were faceless. The wounded men stared at him with anguished eyes and sometimes they moaned and grabbed at him. He used his field dressings up on a man whose arm had been blown off at the elbow, winding the bandage round and round the shattered stump in a fumbling and useless attempt to stem the bleeding.

At last he saw a gap in the barbed wire. Over and over again Nicholas slipped back in the mud as he edged his way up the ridge. It was dark now, and he could only see the outline of the wire when the trench mortars burst overhead. He thought it was the right thing to do, to try and get back through the barbed wire. The metal barbs pulled at him, shrapnel fell around him. His nose and mouth were clogged with mud as he crawled. He muttered to himself out loud, 'Push the wire aside, Nick, move your legs.' He saw the opening in the far side of the wire, and as he hauled himself through, something fell on top of him.

When he pushed it aside, he noticed that the dead man who had tumbled on him was an officer, like himself. The corpse, still partially pinned to the wire, had fallen in a sitting position, its remaining leg stuck out in front, straddled across Nicholas's egress. Very slowly, shuddering, Nicholas climbed over the corpse.

He was forced to look up at the dead man's face. He saw the fair hair, the wide-open blue eyes of his friend. Richardson was not smiling now, though. The lower part of his jaw had been shot away.

Nicholas's scream was a howl of outrage. What he had seen that day was an offence against God and nature and everything he had been taught to respect. His mind refused to accept more horrors, and he found himself longing for, and then reaching out for, physical pain.

CHAPTER THREE

FOR Thomasine, once she had recovered from influenza and the bronchitis that had followed it, the days settled back into a routine. In the mornings she helped Antonia with bills and paperwork, and in the afternoons she taught at the dancing school: tap, ballet and Dalcroze rhythm to chubby infants and gawky adolescents. During the evenings she sewed endless costumes for dancing displays.

Sunny Days had opened and closed during the period of her illness, and there didn't seem to be a great deal of other work around. Every week she scanned the theatre papers. Dancers were requested to audition for a revue in Bournemouth, or a pantomime in Harrogate. She didn't want Bournemouth, she didn't want Harrogate. Thomasine practised hard, convinced that something better would turn up. Post-war London was still dark and dreary, still affected by food shortages. She dreamed of blue skies, of warmth and excitement, of earning enough money to take both Hilda and Antonia on a long, lazy holiday.

One evening, Thomasine and Antonia went to the Alhambra Theatre to see the Ballets Russes. It was a warm evening, and Leicester Square was crowded and muggy. As the orchestra began to play and the curtain was raised, Thomasine forgot her boredom, her restlessness. De Falla's haunting Spanish music filled the theatre, and the dancers made magic on the stage. The costumes, the set – all were so utterly entrancing. *This* was dancing. She was aware of something missing in her life, something unidentifiable, something important. She was almost afraid to blink, to breathe, as she watched Karsavina and Massine on stage: she was afraid to miss even a moment.

The following morning she studied *The Stage* with renewed determination. There was a tiny advertisement tucked away at the foot of a page. 'English dancers,' it said, 'wanted for a revue in Paris.'

For Daniel, the Home fit for Heroes proved something of a let-down. He had left The George and Dragon in the early spring, when the telegram had arrived announcing the imminent return of Hattie's husband. Since then, he had tramped the streets of London looking for work, and finding little. There were, after all, several thousand other ex-officers like himself, also looking for work. The Personal columns in the newspapers were fat with their advertisements: 'Officer, aged 27, four years in command, abstainer, wants work – anything considered.' 'Commander, R.N., aged 39, married, executive officer of ships for duration of war, needs work. Reasonable salary.'

Because he had been an officer, Daniel received no Unemployment Insurance. Officers were gentlemen, and gentlemen had private incomes or had connections, and therefore did not need Unemployment Insurance. He had his severance pay, and that was all. By the middle of 1919, his severance pay was almost spent.

Because he was unable to disguise his limp, he was not considered for the sort of jobs a man of his class might expect to apply for. He was not fit for the docks, the railways, for work on a building site. Neither did he slot neatly into office work. He was too intelligent for a clerk, and had too little education for anything better. If he found himself some clerical work, which he loathed, the job never seemed to last more than a few weeks. He knew that he should complete his disrupted education. He went as far as borrowing a few books from the Public Library, but he fell asleep when he tried to read them. He went once, at the insistence of a friend, to a local Labour Party meeting, and disgraced himself by dozing through half the evening. He still slept badly at night, although the nightmares had begun to be a little less frequent. His lack of reserves, the ache in his leg, infuriated him. He could not yet see his way out of London's cramped streets and dark terraces. He thought, sometimes, of Drakesden, but then he recalled the sort of backbreaking work his father had always done, and he knew that he was not yet capable of that.

He survived, somehow, through a series of odd jobs lasting a day or so, sometimes only a few hours. He wrote letters and filled in forms for men poorer than himself, but hadn't the heart to ask them for more than a penny or two. He still wrote Hattie's accounts and, through her, took on similar work for a couple of other public houses. Hattie would have lent him all the money he needed, but his pride would not let him accept what he saw as charity. Often he knew that, even if he had been able to find it, he was not yet really capable of full-time work.

He was, he sometimes realized, very lonely. He had lost optimism. He was confused, directionless. Until, that is, he met Fay.

Daniel was walking back through Hyde Park one lunch-time, after yet another job interview. He was wearing his uniform, because that sometimes went down well with prospective employers. It hadn't this time, though.

He bought himself something to eat from a stall, and sat down on the banks of the Serpentine. His leg ached and, besides, he had nowhere particular to go. The water was glassy and smooth; clerks and typists, released from their offices for lunchtime, sprawled on the grass. Daniel ate some of his bread roll and threw the rest to the ducks. Not far from him, two girls were sitting. One was plump and dimpled, the other was darkhaired, pale-skinned, red-lipped. It was hot, so Daniel unbuttoned his jacket and lay back on the grass. Through half-closed eyes he watched the dark-haired girl walk towards the water's edge.

She had the sort of figure he had always admired. Slim and

neat, with nicely rounded breasts. Trim ankles and calves (Daniel had no objection to the fact that skirts were getting shorter), and small, slender hands. She wore a white blouse and a dark coloured skirt, and seemed, to Daniel's uneducated eye, to be dressed very elegantly. A scarlet ribbon knotted her long, curling dark brown hair.

She was stooping beside the water's edge, feeding the ducks. When she turned round to speak to her friend, Daniel noticed the lustrousness of her eyes, the smoothness of her white skin. He sat up, uncomfortably aware that he didn't feel like sleeping any more, aware also of a flickering hunger that he had disregarded for months.

A drake mallard, still in search of food, wandered towards him. Daniel flicked a few crumbs from his jacket.

The dark-haired girl laughed. 'He's a greedy one,' she said.

Her accent was good, her voice pleasant. Daniel was not sure whether she was speaking to him, or to her friend.

Then the friend said, 'Come on, Fay. Lawson'll murder us if we're not back in ten minutes.'

The drake waddled off into the water; the two girls stooped to pick up sandwich wrappings, bags, hats. Daniel, rubbing his eyes, looked away, back to the water. He stayed where he was until he heard the two girls move off, their bright chattering voices growing gradually fainter. He stood up, conscious again of the stiffness in his leg.

Then he saw something on the crushed grass where they had sat. Daniel picked it up. It was a handkerchief, neatly folded and ironed. On one corner was embroidered the name, 'Fay'.

Picking up the handkerchief, he looked around. He couldn't see her at first, but then, looking through the crowds, he picked out the white blouse, the dark hair, the scarlet ribbon.

They were heading for the Queen's Gate when he caught up with them. The dark-haired girl, Fay, turned round when he called out her name. He slowed his pace as he drew level with her, trying not to limp. She stopped, and a small, satisfied smile grew on her red lips as Daniel pushed through the crowds towards her.

'Your handkerchief, I believe, miss. You left it by the river.'

She took the handkerchief from him. Her cool, tapering fingertips momentarily touched his palm. 'How sweet of you. My mother stitched that for me – I'd have hated to have lost it.'

'My pleasure,' said Daniel.

'Wasn't that sweet, Phyllis?' She had turned to her friend. 'Thank you so much, Captain –'

'Gillory,' he heard himself say. 'Daniel Gillory.' And then, before he had time to think, 'Do you work near here, Miss . . .?'

'Miss Belman. And this is Miss Grogan.' She tossed back her hair. 'Phyl and I work in a ladies' outfitters in Kensington.'

Daniel took a deep breath. 'Do you often come to Hyde Park? After work, perhaps – we could hire a boat –'

His words were banal, his voice was a croak. But Fay smiled again.

'Friday,' she said. 'Seven o'clock.'

'Paris?' squawked Alice. 'What would my Mum say?'

'Paris isn't *that* far away. Listen, Alice. The show's called *O, Lisette!*, and they're auditioning this Thursday. They're looking for twelve English dancers.'

'English girls are taller and have better legs,' said Alice, knowledgeably.

'We'd be chaperoned,' added Thomasine. 'You could tell your mother that we'd be chaperoned by a respectable English lady.'

'A dragon, I expect,' said Alice gloomily. 'Still, there's always ways . . . if you're clever enough . . .' She giggled.

They were in Alice's untidy bedroom, which she shared with her two younger sisters. The room was small, the floor almost taken up by the three beds. Clothes, combs and toiletries were scattered on every available surface.

Alice's mother had made a Battenberg cake, and they

devoured it hungrily, satisfying their craving for sweet things after more than a year of sugar rationing. 'Have another slice.' Alice pushed the plate towards Thomasine. She patted her stomach. 'Mustn't eat any more if we're auditioning.'

'You'll come, then?' Thomasine could have hugged Alice. She knew that she was far more likely to obtain Antonia's permission to travel abroad if she did not go alone. And besides, apart from an irritating tendency to consider herself more worldly-wise, Alice was good company.

Thomasine peeled the marzipan from her slice of Battenberg cake. For a moment she imagined herself in Paris. Blue skies and pavement cafés, and all around her people speaking in a different tongue. 'Just think of it, Alice. *Paris!*'

'And no more teaching spoilt little brats to pirouette,' said Alice tartly. Alice too helped out with the Little Snowdrops.

'Penny for them, Captain Gillory.'

Daniel looked up, and she was there. Or rather, *they* were there – Fay and Phyllis, identically clad in white blouses and dark blue skirts. Fay's small hand curled round his arm.

'Well, then, Captain Gillory, let's find ourselves a boat.'

They walked to where the rowing-boats were tied up: Fay in the middle, Daniel to one side of her, Phyllis on her other. The park was not as crowded as it had been during the lunch-hour, and faint strains of brass band music wafted through the air along with the cooling breeze.

Some of Daniel's nervousness dissipated with the physical effort of rowing. The two girls sat opposite him in the boat, plump Phyllis and dark-eyed Fay. Today, Fay's hair was pinned into coils around her ears, and her face shaded by a wide-brimmed hat. The hat was trimmed with cloth flowers of scarlet and blue. Daniel thought that beside her friend she looked exotic, gypsy-like.

Daniel just rowed and looked. Phyllis gazed, apparently bored, at the crowds and the scenery. Fay laughed at the antics of the other people on the river.

'There's the dearest little dog in that boat. A poodle, isn't it, Phyl? It has the funniest little face.' She turned to Daniel. '*Such* a day, Captain Gillory. I shall be so glad of my half-day. Every lady in town seems to want a new skirt or tea-gown or whatever. You'd think they'd all have completed their summer wardrobes by now, wouldn't you, Phyl?'

Phyllis grunted. Daniel, steering them round a bend in the river, said, 'Have you always worked in Kensington, Miss Belman?'

'Phyl and I have worked at Chantal's for a year or two, haven't we, Phyl? It's a lovely shop – ever such nice things. I made the trimmings for my hat out of a scrap of Madame Chantal's evening dress material.'

'It looks terrific,' said Daniel. 'You look splendid, Miss Belman. So do you too, of course, Miss Grogan.'

His eyes, though, were fixed on Fay. The wide brim of the hat shadowed her face, so that her eyes seemed darker and larger, the hollows under her cheekbones deeper. It was as though a cool, clean breeze had blown into his life, dispersing the chill winds of war, making him forget, for a while, his bitterness and despair.

Using one oar, he edged them around a boatful of drunken youths straggled across the water. The youths called out to Fay and Phyllis and were ignored. The rowing-boat swayed a little in the back-wash, but Daniel righted it. He was, after all, used to boats. Briefly, the crowded Serpentine reminded him of the silent waterways of the Fens, along which he had travelled for hours, sometimes. Then a party of office-girls shrieked as the stern of Daniel's boat almost touched theirs, and the illusion was gone.

After he had returned the boat to the boatyard, Daniel bought the two girls ices. He didn't buy one for himself because he hadn't the money, and besides, he wasn't hungry. They sat at one of the open-air tables and Daniel watched Fay scoop up the ice-cream from the bowl, and lick the tip of the spoon with her small pointed tongue.

'Ooh – lovely,' she said. 'Now I really must be going. It's past eight o'clock. My landlady will wonder what on earth has happened to me.'

'I'll see you home, Miss Belman.'

She shook her head. 'Not at all. You stay here, Captain Gillory, and enjoy the rest of the evening.' Then she was gone, the high-heels of her shoes clacking on the path, Phyllis scuttling along beside her.

Daniel would have liked to smash the two empty glass dishes to smithereens on the pavement, but he confined himself to cursing under his breath. He had done nothing right, he thought. He had not said the right things, he had not done the right things. He should have bought her flowers, or taken her to a show or a restaurant – if only he had the money for such things. A boat-ride and an ice – God, no wonder she had left before he could suggest that they meet again.

When the auditions were over, they returned to the greenroom. Two of the girls, who knew they had done badly, pulled on their day-dresses and exchanged ballet slippers for shoes, and ran away down the iron stairs, calling out their farewells. The rest of them sat exhausted, the silence interrupted by the occasional nervous giggle or request for a cigarette, or a muttered comment on the events of the past hour.

'*Ghastly* man,' said someone. 'The choreographer, I mean. Such a bully.'

'That Chinese routine. I thought I'd break my neck.'

'The secretary told me that Clara Rose is going to be the star of the show.'

'Lucky thing.' An envious voice. 'Her own dressing-room. Can you imagine?'

Thomasine had to resist the temptation to cross her fingers behind her back. She thought that the audition had gone well, but you never could tell. Sometimes they only wanted blondes, sometimes they wanted every girl to be a particular height. The prospect of Paris had come tantalizingly near, and with it the possibility of truly advancing her career. This would be a real revue, in a real theatre. Most of the shows in which she had taken part during the War had been for charity, to raise money for the Red Cross or for widows and orphans, or to entertain troops recovering from injuries. Even Antonia, when broached tactfully about the subject, had unwillingly admitted that a year spent dancing in a revue in Paris could only further Thomasine's career.

At last the door opened and the secretary peered in. A sudden edgy silence paralysed all the waiting dancers. Thirty anxious faces stared at the piece of paper the secretary clutched.

'This is the list of girls who have been chosen.' She read out the names in a high, whining voice: 'Violet Smith, Edith Hall, Poppy Barrett, Thomasine Thorne, Alice Johnson –'

Thomasine threw her arms round Alice and hugged her.

Daniel applied for another job, in Knightsbridge. He knew, before he was five minutes into the interview, that it was impossible. An infirm elderly gentleman wanted a male companion: someone to write his letters, walk his dog, play him at chess. Daniel knew how much he would hate it, so when his prospective employer asked him which school he had been to, he told the truth.

Outside, it was raining heavily. There wasn't a bus in sight, but the Tube station was just across the road. Angry with his wasted morning, angry with himself, Daniel made himself walk into the black, gaping maw and buy a ticket. The journey down to the trains was like a descent into Hell. He made himself keep on walking, down what seemed like a thousand stairs. People jostled him; his leg ached. When he reached the bottom of the stairs, he climbed into the first train that arrived at the platform, certain that his courage would otherwise desert him.

The train lurched and whined as it started up. It was crowded: that was good, Daniel told himself. No one could imagine themselves buried in a collapsed dugout in Passchendaele when surrounded by fifty sweating clerks and typists. No seats were free, so Daniel grabbed one of the straps. He tried to ignore the pounding of his heart as the train gathered speed. The typists and clerks gazed, bored, at the ceiling, and Daniel made himself concentrate on a woman's hat, the headline in a newspaper. If he could manage this, he told himself, then he could do anything. He would find work, get himself back on his feet again. He'd no longer be the empty, fragile shell the War had made of him.

He managed, for a while. Then the train ground slowly to a halt in the middle of the tunnel, and the lights flickered and went off. The clerks and typists groaned, and Daniel smelt newly-fallen earth and felt the pressure of the broken wood of the dugout, the heavy weight of the soil against his leg. He knew without looking that all of his friends were dead, that he was the only one to survive the explosion of the trench-mortar. When he moved it hurt like hell and dislodged some of the soil. He was afraid to move again, fearing that he would lose the small pocket of air that allowed him to live. He lost track of time. He thought that he had been buried underground for ever. He wanted to die.

When the lights went on, and the train began to move again, Daniel found that he was talking to himself under his breath. His forehead was damp with sweat and he had twisted himself up against the door. A woman was staring at him with disgust, and he realized that she probably thought he was drunk. The train shuddered to a halt, and he half-fell on to the platform, and then ran up the hundreds of stairs.

Outside, it was still raining, but he leaned against a shop doorway, gulping at the air, eyes wide open, rain streaming down his face. He had travelled on the train only for the distance between two stations, Knightsbridge to Kensington. Almost two years now, he thought. He wanted to kill someone, anyone, most of all himself. Almost two bloody years since Passchendaele.

Eventually, he rubbed his eyes and stared across the busy road. The pounding of his heart began to slow, and the London street, crammed with motor-cars and lorries and horses and carts, settled back into place. There was really nothing to be afraid of, what he feared existed only in his own mind. He was crippled in mind and body, he told himself. He was useless. Dully, he read the names of the shops across the road: H.G. Green, High Class Grocer; Laskeys: Everything for the Sportsman; Chantal's Ladies Fashion Emporium.

He crossed the road. It was lunch-time, and everywhere shops and offices were disgorging their staff. Daniel elbowed his way through the crowds, dodging the motor-cars.

When he reached Chantal's, the door opened and Fay came out. She was alone this time; no Phyllis. It seemed like a miracle to Daniel, seeing her again; almost as though his own need had conjured her up, an exotic gypsy spirit flickering out of the dark, hungry places of his mind.

She was no spirit, though. She saw him immediately, and when she turned, her smile was brilliant. 'Why, Captain Gillory. How delightful. Have you been waiting long for me?'

'For ever,' he said, taking her hand and kissing it.

They spent the afternoon together. It was Fay's half-day holiday, so she didn't have to go back to work. They walked in the park, ducking inside shops or museums to escape the frequent showers, and eventually found themselves in the Lyons Corner House in Coventry Street.

'I look like a drowned rat.' Fay, seated at the table, checked her face in a small mirror.

'You look beautiful,' said Daniel.

He spoke only the truth. The rain and their long walk had brought a little colour to her pale cheeks, and her eyes were dark and bright. She didn't blush or quibble at the compliment, which pleased Daniel. Instead, she smiled again, and replaced the mirror inside her handbag.

'How did you hurt your leg?' she said.

He found himself telling her how the dugout in which he and his men had been sheltering had collapsed when a trench-mortar had landed on it, crushing his right leg. He didn't tell her the details, because you didn't tell women things like that. Especially young, pretty women like Fay.

'It must have been frightful,' she said sympathetically. 'And the men you were in charge of – what happened to them?'

'The other officers were all killed. Some of the men in the trenches survived, though.'

Her mouth was a round, red O, her eyes wide. 'How frightful,' she repeated.

The waitress appeared, and Daniel ordered tea and cakes. It had been surprisingly easy, he thought, to talk to Fay about something he had always found impossible to speak of before, even to Hattie.

'You must be awfully brave,' she said.

He shook his head. 'Not at all. In some ways it was easier then – you had no choice except to be brave. You followed orders, you gave orders. It's now that's difficult – fitting in to all this again.'

He glanced round the tea-shop. The noise of it, the crowds and the over-decorated room, he would normally have found oppressive. Somehow, with Fay sitting opposite him, he didn't mind.

'What do you do, Captain Gillory? I mean – you've left the army, haven't you? So what do you do now?'

He laughed. 'Nothing much, I'm afraid. A bit of writing, accounting, that sort of thing. I've been looking for work, but I don't know . . . I can't seem to settle in London again.'

The waitress arrived with the tea and cakes. The milk-jug was only half-full, the cakes small and undecorated. Even their food, Daniel thought with grim humour, had not yet recovered from the War. He watched Fay pour out the milk and stir the teapot. The graceful way she performed the simple, routine actions soothed him.

'I might go home,' he said, surprising himself. 'My family had a smallholding. It's mine now.'

She poured out the tea. 'A smallholding?'

'A little farm. Nothing much. There's a cottage with it, though.'

He found himself describing Drakesden to her. The fields, the dykes and droves and vast, splendid skyscapes. He had not realized, until he spoke of it all to Fay, how much he wanted to go back.

'It sounds marvellous,' she said. 'How lucky you are to come from somewhere like that.'

He realized, ashamed, that she had not eaten, and that he had talked constantly about himself. He offered the plate to her, and she chose an éclair. 'Do you come from London, Miss Belman?'

Her face screwed up disconsolately. 'I've hardly ever been out of it. I went to Margate once, for the day. That was fun.' She took a bite out of the éclair.

It seemed quite natural for Daniel to say, 'We could go for a picnic, if you like. On Sunday.'

Thomasine took the train to the hospital in Sussex where Hilda nursed. From the grounds they could see the sea – the English Channel, thought Thomasine with a rush of excitement. It was ten years since she had last crossed the English Channel.

'I'm sailing in a week's time,' she explained. They were sitting on a bench not far from the edge of the cliff. Although it was midsummer, the sea air was sharp and cold. 'We take the boat-train from Victoria.'

'I hope you are not seasick,' said Hilda. 'The first time I went to France I was terribly seasick. I was so ill I thought I'd never be able to face coming home – I'd have to stay nursing in the field hospital for ever.'

Thomasine had threaded her arm through Hilda's. 'Will you keep on nursing, Aunt Hilly? Now that most of the men have gone home?'

The hospital was a convalescent home. A few ex-soldiers still limped around the garden; some were huddled in wheelchairs, or settled on benches.

Hilda grimaced. '*Nursing!* My dear Thomasine – I am no longer permitted to *nurse*. We have a new matron and, besides, since the end of the War, VADs are considered to be the lowest of the low. I am allowed to scrub floors, to empty vases, to polish bedside tables. Not to *nurse*.'

Thomasine recognized, not for the first time, that Hilda's frustration at the narrowness of the opportunities life offered to her mirrored her own. She squeezed Hilda's hand.

'I won't stay,' said Hilda suddenly, stubbing out her cigarette. 'I had to lie about my age as it was. The falsehood was forgivable, I think. No – I intend to start a school. I have saved a little money, and I will, if you have no objection, my dear Thomasine, sell Quince Cottage. You do not –' she glanced at Thomasine – 'intend to go back to Drakesden?'

Thomasine shook her head. 'I want to travel, Aunt Hilly. I can't seem to settle. A *school?*'

Hilda nodded. 'I have always enjoyed teaching.' She fumbled beneath the folds of her cape for her cigarette packet and grimaced. 'I shall have to give up these, of course. Everyone smoked in France – it was the only way one could keep awake. I tried sucking sweets – and drinking that dreadful coffee – anything – but in the end I succumbed. But a cigarette-smoking headmistress would not be the thing.'

Thomasine laughed. 'Where will you have your school, Aunt Hilly? At Drakesden?'

Hilda shook her head. 'Somewhere else. I would miss Rose so much.'

There was a brief silence. Then Hilda added, 'I shall begin soon to look· for a suitable building to rent. I still have all Father's books, and I know a couple of other ex-VADs who are also interested in teaching. And who are aware that their chances of marriage are now, because of the War, extremely thin. There are a great many women, Thomasine, who must now concentrate their energies on finding a career rather than a husband.' She touched Thomasine's hand. 'So you will go to Paris with my blessing, my dear – I have always approved of women finding something to do with their lives. Not that you will not marry – you are pretty, which I never was.'

They rose from the bench, and began to walk back to the hospital. Thomasine sensed that Hilda was struggling for words. Eventually, she said, 'You will be *careful*, won't you, dearest? These last few years – you have led such a sheltered life –'

Thomasine threaded her arm through Hilda's. 'Don't worry, Aunt Hilly. There's a dreadful English chaperone. And Antonia has already spoken to me.' Antonia's advice had consisted of some rather tantalizing warnings about White Slavers, and impenetrable injunctions to be sensible, which Thomasine had interpreted as remembering to wear a vest.

'Of course.' Hilda breathed out a sigh of relief. 'Tony is much better able to give you advice than I. She has been married.'

They were a few yards from the hospital doors. A wheelchair was parked in the small rose-garden. Hilda paused beside the wheelchair. Its occupant wore a convalescent's uniform. His head was heavily bandaged, his face pitted with angry red scars. There was in the single unbandaged eye no recognition as they approached, no acknowledgement of the presence of other human beings. Not even vacancy, Thomasine realized, only the remains of a sort of primitive fear.

Hilda laid her hand over the soldier's. 'Those poor boys,' she whispered. Thomasine could see the tears in her eyes. 'Those poor boys.'

The summer had not been an easy one for Nicholas, at Drakesden. To begin with there had been various distractions. The arrival of Lally, expelled from her school, had caused all the expected eruptions. But in the end Lally, as she had prophesied, did not return to Lady Mary's or to any other school, but remained at Drakesden, a small and dumpy and rather aimless figure. Although officially 'out', no balls or luncheon parties were planned to celebrate Lally's entrance into the adult world. For one thing, Drakesden Abbey, like so many other medium-sized estates, was struggling financially; for another, none of the Blythes – including Lally herself – seemed to have the necessary enthusiasm.

The quietness of Drakesden seemed to exacerbate his day visions, his nightmares. Nicholas became adept at hiding his sickness. Many times, sitting at the table, or smoking in the billiard-room, he saw – as though it was there in front of him – the trenches, the barbed wire, the mud and horror of it all. He learned to hide his fear from his family, to force himself to continue the conversation or meal almost unbroken. Because of that, his mother released him from the obligation of seeing more doctors. That pleased Nicholas: he had no faith in doctors.

The emptiness of the Fens, the lack of company, gave him time to think. He did not want to think, he could not bear to think. He needed never to be alone, never to be without occupation. The occupations provided by Drakesden – the estate management in which he was expected to take an interest, since he had, by Gerald's death, become heir to Drakesden Abbey – bored him. He had never had any interest in farming. When, after dinner one evening, his father expressed some of his worries about the future of the estate, Nicholas hardly bothered to listen.

'Taxes, old boy. All these damned taxes – saving your presence, Gwennie. Raised during the War, and I'm damned if we'll ever see them go back down again.'

Lally said, 'Perhaps the money was needed to make guns, Daddy.'

Lady Blythe was pouring out coffee. 'Do be quiet if you can't say anything sensible, Lally.' She handed a cup to her husband. 'Surely none of this is of any concern to *us*, William. It is all very irritating, I daresay, but the War is over now, and things must soon return to normal.'

Sir William said, 'We may have to put some land up for sale, Nicholas.'

'If you like.' Nicholas fumbled in his pocket for cigarettes. The light outside was beginning to fade slightly; evenings were always a bad time for him.

'*If you like?*' Lady Blythe had put aside the coffee-pot, and was staring at Nicholas. She was, a surprised Nicholas realized, furious. Her voice quivered. 'Is that all you can say?'

Nicholas shrugged. 'If we need to sell land, then we need to sell land. What more is there to say?'

She picked up the coffee-pot and began to pour again, her mouth set in a rigid line.

Sir William said hastily, 'Only a few acres, Gwennie. Not the best land, of course. A few pockets of low-lying stuff. Some of the Drakesden fields are more trouble than they're worth – always flooding in the winter . . .' His voice trailed away. The corners of Lally's mouth were twitching.

Lady Blythe said stiffly, 'If it is necessary, William, then of course you must sell. I abhor any diminishment of the estate, but it must be done, I suppose.'

'Isn't it funny,' said Lally, stirring her coffee, 'that Daddy and Nicholas, who are Blythes by birth, don't seem to care, yet you, Mama, are so upset? After all, you're only a Blythe by marriage.'

Lady Blythe's face went even whiter. 'What nonsense, Lally. Nicholas loves Drakesden Abbey just as much as I do. Don't you, Nicky?'

He found himself agreeing. He didn't give a damn about a few swampy fields in a backward little village, but he'd have to pretend to, for Mama's sake.

Sir William had risen from his chair, and was mumbling about going outside for a smoke. Lally, stooping beside Nicholas, whispered in his ear.

'We should go out for a drive, Nick. Parsons has mended the puncture, and there's such a sunset.'

'If you have anything to say, Lally,' said Lady Blythe, her composure almost recovered, 'then it should be said to the whole company.'

But Lally just smiled and left the room. Nicholas spent a few minutes placating his mother, and then left too.

When they had motored out of Drakesden, Nicholas said to Lally, 'Why do you do it, Baby? Why do you tease her?'

'Mama?' Lally settled back into her seat. Her dark hair whipped about the brim of her school hat. 'Because she hates me. No – she doesn't *hate* me. She is indifferent to me. I'd rather she hated me.' Her voice was matter-of-fact, not betraying any resentment.

Nicholas, braking to round a corner, said uneasily, 'You just rub each other up the wrong way.'

'Don't be silly, Nick. And do slow down a little.'

She had taken a lipstick and compact out of her pocket, and was carefully applying scarlet to her lips. Nicholas braked gradually, and tried to keep to the more level sections of road.

'Anyway –' Lally snapped the compact shut – 'I was right, wasn't I? You couldn't care less about Drakesden, and Mama wants to keep every inch of it.'

When Lally spoke like this she disturbed him. He almost preferred the other Lally, the Lally who lied and prevaricated to spare herself from doing anything she did not want to do. People should not tell the truth so baldly. The whole world would fall to bits if people started telling the truth.

He let the motor-car gather up speed again. 'It's not quite like that,' he said. 'It's just that it wasn't going to be mine, was it? It should have been Gerry's. It's taking me a while to get used to it. It's not that I don't care.'

Lally glanced at him impatiently. 'Oh, *Nicholas.*'

They had reached a junction. The road led to Ely in one direction, and turned deeper into the Fens in the other. 'Ely?' said Nicholas.

Lally shook her head. 'No. There's a pub the other way. I'd like a drink.'

He didn't bother protesting about her age, sex and general unsuitability for public houses. He knew Lally well enough by now to realize that those sorts of protests were always futile. Instead he swung the car round, away from the dazzling sunset. The road became little more than a drove, rutted and uneven. Nicholas handled the Daimler well, intimate with its idiosyncracies and capabilities.

'Just here,' said Lally eventually.

It was hardly a village, hardly a public house. A few cottagers looked up from their gardens as the car spun round the corner, making clouds of dust billow into the air. Chickens squawked, narrowly escaping the tyres. Ragged children ran towards them as Nicholas slowed the car. He looked doubtfully at the pub. The village was near the Hundred Foot Drain. Between that drain and the Old Bedford River, half a mile away, was the wide expanse of the Hundred Foot Wash, a vast flood-plain, inundated each winter to save the surrounding lands from the waters.

The pub was called The Three Mariners. Inside, there was a wide fireplace, a huge piece of bog-oak protruding from it, and a few stools and benches scattered about. Nicholas ordered beer for himself and Lally (he didn't think they'd run to cocktails), and tried to ignore the interested stares of the locals. Lally drank her beer and looked around calmly. She was the only woman in the pub.

'We'll have to leave,' said Lally thoughtfully. 'It simply won't do.'

Nicholas scooped up his hat and stood, but Lally shook her head.

'Not leave *here*, silly – I haven't finished yet. I mean, leave Drakesden.' She swallowed another mouthful of beer. 'It's quite impossible. Not as bad as Lady Mary's, but not much better. Come on, Nicky – admit it. You hate it, too.'

'It's so quiet.' Nicholas had put aside his glass; his fingers knotted together. 'And so many people have died – or have left –'

He found himself thinking briefly, painfully, of Thomasine Thorne. Thomasine had been different and exciting and strong. She had, in a way, reminded him of his mother – beautiful, and yet so certain, so fearless. Since the War, Nicholas had lost all certainty and, he thought with self-disgust, he now feared almost everything. There were no women of his class in Drakesden other than his mother and sister. As for the young ladies his mother invited for the occasional weekend house-party, Nicholas had been unable to find any feelings greater than mild irritation at their naïvety, their frivolity. He simply had nothing in common with them.

Lally was looking at him. Her dark up-tilted eyes were slightly narrowed. 'It makes you ill, doesn't it?'

He glanced up at her, and his beer slopped over the rim of the tankard.

Lally said, 'No one else notices, silly. There's no need to worry.' She reached out and touched his hand. 'We should go abroad, Nick. Just you and I.'

Nicholas laughed, slightly too loud. All the other men in the pub turned and stared at him. 'Don't be ridiculous, Baby. They'd never let us.'

'*Let* us? It's best just to take what you want. That's what I do.' She had finished her drink. 'Besides, my dear Nicholas, you are twenty-two. Mama couldn't stop you. You've money of your own, haven't you?'

He nodded. He still had his severance pay and a small legacy from an uncle killed in the War. Plus the sum his father had given him on reaching twenty-one. He hadn't touched a penny of it yet – there was nothing to spend it on at Drakesden.

'I was going to buy a motor-car.'

'You can buy a motor-car when we're abroad.' Lally smiled at him coaxingly, and folded her plump little hand over his. 'I'm going to buy clothes – lots of them.'

He almost believed that it was possible. He saw himself in Paris or Monaco, speeding along some narrow cliff-top road or city boulevard, faster and faster and faster.

'And just think how pleased Mama would be to see the back of me,' added Lally smugly.

She rose from the stool and went to the door. Nicholas noticed how the eyes of all the men in the room followed his short, plump sister, with her unfashionable clothes and ugly hat.

On the way back to Drakesden, he put the Daimler into the highest gear, and pressed his foot hard on the accelerator.

The drove was long and straight. Clouds of dust blew up around them. The motor-car bumped and jolted and Nicholas yelled at Lally to hold on to the back of the seat. Fields, dykes and cottages whirled past them, lost in a blur of grey and green. As they gathered up speed (forty, fifty, sixty), Nicholas found that he felt better. Driving was preferable to riding. Even Titus could not gallop so fast.

He remembered Lally at last, and braked. The Daimler skidded in the dust, turning in a half-circle. As it slowed, so Nicholas's anxiety flooded back.

'Are you all right, Baby? Not sick?'

He thought she was crying, at first, but then he realized that she was laughing.

'We could go in an aeroplane, Nicholas,' she said. 'Imagine!'

CHAPTER FOUR

To see in the New Year – and the new decade – the crew and cast of the revue *O, Lisette!* had decorated the café next to the theatre in the hot, jangling colours of the Ballets Russes: orange, shocking pink, lime green, chrome yellow and Lanvin blue. Crêpe streamers spiralled from floor to ceiling, the spindly legs of the tables and chairs were knotted with paper bows. Everybody was there – singers, actors, musicians, dancers and backstage crew. In one corner of the small Montmartre café a jazz band played, the skirl of the saxophone and the pounding of the drums throbbing beneath the shriek of conversation and the tapping, dancing feet.

The twelve dancers of the chorus of *O, Lisette!* were all English, chosen for their height, their long legs, their clear complexions. Chaperoned day and night, they had been permitted to stay out late for this one, extraordinary night.

'One o'clock,' grumbled Alice. 'What use is a New Year's party that you have to leave at one o'clock?'

'Depends how quick you are,' said a tall blonde sitting next to Alice.

Alice followed her neighbour's gaze. Some of the tables and chairs in the centre of the room had been pushed aside for dancing. The music of the saxophone, piano and drum had increased in tempo; people were beating out the rhythm with bells, rattles, bundles of knives and forks.

'Oh, *Poppy*,' said Alice.

Poppy's chin was propped on her hands, and her wide blue gaze rested on a dark-haired man leaning against the wall. His profile was lit by the flickering gaslights; he had a cigarette in one hand, a glass in the other.

'Clive Curran.' Alice poured some water into her Pernod, and shook her head. 'Naughty, naughty Poppy.'

Poppy stuck out her tongue at Alice. 'Well, wouldn't we all, if we had the chance?'

'Not Thomasine. Thomasine's never naughty. Thomasine's a vicar's granddaughter, aren't you, dear?'

Poppy sighed. 'Not that any of us has a hope. Lovely Clive never looks at the chorus-girls. We're moving wallpaper to him.'

Alice was picking up uncoiled streamers from the lid of the piano, the table, the floor. When she had gathered up a dozen or so, she scrambled on to her chair, and then climbed from the chair on to the table-top. The rickety table swayed and wobbled with her weight.

'*Alice* –'

'I'll have a kiss from Clive Curran before the night's out. Bet you.' Alice aimed a streamer. 'The first cocktail of the New Year, Pops – I'll pay if I don't, you pay if I do!'

The first streamer whirled over the heads of the dancers, and struck the lounging dark-haired man neatly on the shoulder. Ringlets of coloured paper uncoiled down his jacket. Alice took aim again and again. Soon, his shoulders, head and back were veined with spirals of pink, orange and yellow.

'He's coming,' said Alice. She watched Clive Curran wind his way through the scattered tables and dancers. As he approached them, he made a great play of brushing streamers out of his eyes. Alice was still standing on the table.

'We don't think you're being very patriotic, Mr Curran. There's three loyal Englishwomen here who haven't had a dance for – oh, at least ten minutes.'

Slowly, Clive Curran's gaze travelled the length of Alice, from her high-heeled shoes, to her short fair hair.

'Most remiss of me. I deserved the bombardment, Miss –?'

'Johnson. And this is Miss Barrett, and this is Miss Thorne.'

'Delighted,' said Clive Curran, smiling at them all.

Thomasine had seen him many times before, but had never spoken to him. Clive Curran was a singer, though he also acted in several sketches in the revue, his French diction as perfect as his English. Sometimes she lingered backstage when he sang, closing her eyes and letting the beauty of his voice fold around her. All twelve of the English dancers were in love with Clive Curran.

He helped Alice down from the table. Alice wobbled a little when she reached the floor, leaning against him. 'Oops – one Pernod too many, I think.'

'Fiendish stuff, Miss Johnson,' said Clive Curran, supporting her with his arm.

The speed of the dance music was growing faster. Under the table, Thomasine's foot tapped in time to the music. Clive Curran surveyed the three girls.

'The thing is – who should I dance with first? I'm spoilt for choice.'

His eyes, a light, sleepy blue, travelled slowly from Alice to Poppy, then to Thomasine, resting on her for a long while. Thomasine's heart began to pound.

Clive smiled. 'I can't choose. It's quite impossible. I'll just have to dance with the three of you.'

He held out a hand, helping Poppy and Thomasine to their feet. They danced together in the middle of the heaving mass of people. The Jog Trot, the Vampire, the Missouri Walk and the Shimmy, taking turns to be held in Clive Curran's arms, to see their own reflections in his eyes. The musicians played the latest dance tunes and songs from the revues and musicals of Paris and London. The cast and crew of *O, Lisette!* bawled out the choruses. If Thomasine had felt tired before – the consequence of more than four months of endless rehearsals and twice-daily performances – all her exhaustion left her as they danced. The pounding beat of the drums, the wild howl of the saxophone, the clang of bells and whistles, drove them all. The room throbbed with the pulse of the dancers' feet. The glasses and bottles on the tables and on the bar shivered in time with the movement. Faces flickered out of the darkness as Thomasine danced: the faces of the dancers with whom she had travelled from England, and now shared a hostel, the faces of the cast and crew with whom she worked. Alice's face, Poppy's face, Clive Curran's face. She liked to look at Clive – his dark, close-cropped hair, his curved lips and heavy-lidded blue eyes. When his eyes met hers she smiled back at him.

Then the music stopped, and glasses of champagne were handed round. They began to count downwards: ten, nine, eight, seven, six. The death-throes of the old decade were chanted by everyone in the room. When they reached zero, some-one shouted, 'To the nineteen-twenties!' and everyone cheered.

'You haven't drunk your champagne.'

Clive Curran was standing opposite her. 'You have to drink your champagne, Miss Thorne.' Gently, he raised her glass to her lips. 'Then you have to kiss me. To see in the New Year, you know.'

She took a mouthful of champagne. Then his lips touched hers. 'Delicious,' said Clive Curran. 'To the nineteen-twenties.'

He danced once more with her that night. It was almost one o'clock, and Thomasine was gathering up her bag and coat, ready to go, when he came to stand beside her, one hand resting on her shoulder.

'You can't go yet, Miss Thorne.'

She was hazy with champagne, with dancing, but she knew the penalty for staying out too late. 'The concierge will report me. I'll lose my job . . . Oh, well . . .' She smiled, and held out her arms to him.

He led her into the centre of the room. The music was slow and mournful. Couples danced, folded into each other, hardly moving.

'Put your head here,' said Clive Curran, indicating the hollow of his shoulder. 'Lovely.'

His arms were surrounding her, his hands stroking her back.

Thomasine could feel his fingertips through the thin materials of her dress and petticoat. To be held by him was warm and exciting and new. She could smell the scent of his skin, feel the heat of his face as it touched against hers. She thought that his lips brushed against the crown of her head, but she wasn't sure.

The music stopped. 'Five to one,' said Clive Curran, looking at his watch. 'I'll walk you home, sugar.'

In the street the air was clear and cold. Alice and Poppy were waiting, bundled up in their coats and scarves, outside the café. Thomasine's hand was tucked through one of Clive's arms, and Alice hooked herself round the other. Poppy walked a little way ahead, swinging her bag, singing to herself.

'Where's the nunnery?' asked Clive.

Alice gave him directions to their *pension*. Thomasine breathed in the icy air and looked at the stars that pinpointed the inky sky. Paris still bore the marks of its bombardment only two years previously, but the crumbling masonry and the craters in the pavements were masked by the people who danced and sang in the streets.

' "I'm for ever blow-ing bubbles" –' sang Poppy.

They had reached their *pension*. Clive looked up at the tall, narrow building with its wrought-iron balconies, its unlit windows and locked doors.

'Not a nunnery. It's a fortress.'

Alice was fitting her key into the lock. 'Just as well we've an escape route then, Mr Curran. There's a nice old vine round the back, and ever such a convenient little porch over the door. You should see me shimmy down that.'

She had turned the key. Thomasine realized that all three of them were waiting for something – she was not sure what – to happen. For Clive Curran to kiss them again, perhaps, or to dance with them in the street, or to tell them that he'd never had such a wonderful evening in his entire life.

But the moment passed, and the door opened, and the concierge, sticking her head out into the cold, glowered at them all.

And Clive Curran raised his hat and walked away.

Paris was colourful and adventurous compared with the grey, foggy London of the War years. The pavement cafés, the elegantly dressed women, the brightly lit buildings all seemed so different. To breakfast on croissants and black coffee instead of toast and tea, to try to adapt to the late nights and the long, sleepy afternoons was exciting. Walking down the Champs-Elysées, window-shopping in the stylish department stores, or investigating the antique shops and booksellers of the Boulevard St-Germain, Thomasine thought, I'm here, I'm free.

Since New Year, though, Clive Curran had not spoken to her. The actors and singers rehearsed separately from the dancers, so she only saw him at the evening or matinée performances. Hiding in the wings, listening to him sing, Thomasine could hardly believe that he had kissed her. Or that the kiss had been in any way special – he had, she reminded herself, kissed Alice and Poppy as well. He had danced with the three of them; he had been unable to choose between them. Poppy had been right: Clive Curran hardly bothered to glance at the chorus-girls. Thomasine knew that she had been stupid to think that he might.

Over endless cups of coffee in small cafés tucked into tree-lined squares, over mugs of cocoa in their bedrooms at night, they talked about him. Whether Clive was in love with Clara Rose, whether Clara Rose was in love with him, whether he should audition for the moving pictures. Poppy was convinced that he should, Thomasine pointed out that then no one would hear his lovely voice. How old he was – twenty-nine, Alice had heard someone say. Whom he would marry. A nice London girl, giggled Alice, patting her curls. A wealthy lady, said Poppy mournfully.

Thomasine had her hair cut one afternoon. The weather was very cold, the gardens and rooftops of Paris glazed with frost. Ice gleamed on the pavements. Poppy twisted her foot running out of the *pension* one morning, and was out of the show for a week. The sky was a hazy pale blue, the Parisian women huddled up to their noses in furs, their hands encased in gloves of pale pastel kid.

She had intended only to have her hair trimmed. But staring in the mirror as the girl unpinned her plaits, she began to dislike her reflection. The pale skin, the schoolgirlish hairstyle, the wide eyes. *Innocent* eyes, thought Thomasine savagely. Her face seemed childish and unformed. The disruptions of her past – the early death of her parents, her leaving of first Africa and then Drakesden, seemed not to have marked her. She knew that the older, more worldly girls like Alice and Poppy still thought of her as a child. She was too proud to ask Alice or Poppy the questions that might relieve her of her ignorance and, besides, she did not know which questions to ask.

The hairdresser had combed out her plaits, and was beginning to trim the ends. *'Non, mademoiselle,'* said Thomasine, in Aunt Hilly's rather rudimentary French. *'Plus. Comme ça, s'il vous plait.'*

She indicated with her hand a level halfway between her cheekbones and her chin. The assistant protested: Mademoiselle had such beautiful hair, and besides the fashion for short hair was a temporary fad. Thomasine scowled and shook her head.

'Comme ça.'

The assistant tutted, but raised her scissors. Great hanks of red hair tumbled to the floor. Beside her, Alice, who was having a manicure, squeaked.

'What will your auntie say?'

Thomasine did not reply. In the looking-glass in front of her, a new reflection was emerging. Her face looked different now, without its heavy Edwardian frame of hair. Her head felt ridiculously light, as though it might float away.

Clive Curran had noticed Miss Thorne at the first rehearsal. She had been the prettiest of a dozen pretty English girls hired to kick their legs and smile, their principal function in the revue to compensate for the lack of any decent songs or sketches. At first, though, Clive had been more interested in the leading lady, Clara Rose, who was reputed to be very wealthy. But Clara had a tongue like a carpenter's chisel, and was conducting an intermittent affair with a Parisian banker.

The bobbed hair suited Miss Thorne, making her look older, more sophisticated. She had bluish-green eyes and a wide, generous mouth. Clive had enjoyed kissing that mouth, wet with champagne. Clive discovered that Miss Thorne's Christian name was Thomasine, which was ridiculous but, he had to admit, suited her. Unusual, unconventional. Clive considered himself to be unconventional – someone who broke the tedious rules that society imposed on one. Thomasine was an excellent dancer, and had nice legs and a lovely smile. As Clive's courtship of the leading lady was, at present, proving largely unsuccessful, he decided that he would get to know Miss Thorne better. One never knew – it might even stir jealousy in that bitch Clara Rose. When the final curtain came down after the evening performance, and they were all shuffling exhausted from the stage, Clive said to Thomasine, 'You've had your hair cut.'

Her smile was quite delightful. 'I've been told off by the chaperone. Are you going to tell me off, Mr Curran?'

He couldn't decide whether she was flirting with him or not. He shook his head. 'Not at all. She looks like a boy, doesn't she, Clara?' Clive turned to the leading lady, standing beside him. 'Especially with the sailor suit.'

For their last number, the chorus-girls wore navy shorts, monkey-jackets and hats, all piped with white. A ludicrous but rather fetching outfit.

'There's clubs in the West End would pay a fortune,' agreed Clara Rose acidly.

Bitch, thought Clive. 'It suits you, sugar,' he said to Thomasine. He reached out a hand and ruffled the gleaming bell of her hair.

She thanked him for the compliment and ran off to the changing-room. Clara Rose, picking up a silk shawl from the wings, followed her. Clive remained on stage, rather amused.

A voice whispered in his ear, 'She was brought up by a collection of maiden aunts and her grandfather was a vicar. Not the girl for you, darling Clive.'

He turned to look at Alice. He had seen Alice quite often over the past few weeks. But there was no mystery, thought Clive, glancing down at her, in Alice. What you saw was what you got. If you liked blonde curls, blue eyes and a nice curvy little figure, then that was fine and dandy. What Clive did not like was to be told his limitations. He did not believe that he had limitations.

'I think I'll be the judge of that, don't you, Miss Johnson?' He was pleased to see the flicker of anger in her eyes.

'You wouldn't get further than a kiss,' she said scornfully.

Alice was becoming just a teeny bit complacent, and just a teeny bit dull. Clive realized that, until now, he hadn't intended to get any further than that single, chaste, champagne-flavoured kiss.

'There's always an attraction in untrodden fields – virgin territories, as it were.'

Alice's flattened palm caught him sharply on the cheek. As she stalked away, Clive raised his fingers to his jaw, checking that she hadn't marked or bruised him. Then he went back to his dressing-room and wrote a note to Thomasine Thorne.

Although this winter had been, for Daniel, a great improvement on the previous winter – and an even greater improvement on the winter before that – he still felt unsettled. He had found work in a small advertising agency in Soho, and for writing untruthful slogans to sell dubious products, he was paid enough to live on. The agency, consisting of a mixture of ex-officers like himself, men who had been unfit for service and clever young women, was congenial enough. London still oppressed him: he was still obliged to take trams or buses instead of using the Underground, and on a bad day even a crowded tram was unbearable. But he got by, because at the end of the day there was Fay.

Or, rather, at the end of some days. Sometimes he saw her twice a week, sometimes only at the weekend, and once three whole weeks went by without their meeting. If she refused to see him, then her refusal was polite and kind and carefully justified, but it was a refusal all the same. When Fay, apparently tentatively, suggested a show or an outing, then Daniel always altered his plans to suit her. He simply could not have done otherwise.

Worse than the infrequency of their meetings was the physical frustration he had to endure. He was permitted to kiss her, to hold her hand, to touch her breasts in the darkness of the cinema or in the privacy of an outing to the countryside around London. He thought she enjoyed his caresses, but he was never quite sure. If he attempted to become more intimate, then she would hurriedly readjust her clothing and push him away. 'Someone will come,' she would whisper, in the uncluttered expanses of Bushey Park. Or, 'No, Daniel – poor Fay's ever so cold.' And then he, guilty and aching, would bundle her back into her coat and rub her small, chilled hands between his, hating himself.

He wished he had a motor-car, he wished he had money. If he had owned a motor-car, then they would have had a private, sheltered place. If he had had money, then they would have been able to go further afield, to somewhere where Fay could not possibly have feared the intrusion of strangers, to where Daniel could see nothing but the wide, open skies, that could not close in on him.

As it was, he managed. He saw her so infrequently, so unreliably, that she seemed quite perfect to him. If he ever felt angry, then he blamed himself for his impatience, for his inability to settle properly to anything. He wondered, sometimes, what she would say if he asked her to marry him. He did not do so, though, because he felt that he had so little to offer her. He regarded his job, his lodgings, his residence in London, as temporary. He had lost the ambition that had fired him before the War, and he had never succeeded in re-accustoming himself to city life. He feared that Fay was temporary too, that she rationed herself because of his own restlessness. Yet he dreamed of her every night: hot, desperate dreams that made him tired and foul-tempered the next day. He tried to see the way forward, yet could not: the pinpoints of light in the darkness seemed to flicker uncertainly.

'You see, sugar – it's not really working out, is it?'

They were in a small café in Montmartre, not far from the theatre. The white icing dome of Sacré-Coeur gleamed on the horizon. For Thomasine, life had seesawed for two months on a fulcrum balanced between delight and despair. When she was with Clive, her delight was almost unbearably intense; when she did not see him, she despaired, certain that she had said the wrong thing the last time they had met, convinced that he had met an older, more sophisticated girl. When he kissed her, she was in heaven. When a fortnight passed and no note was slipped into her hand as she ran off-stage, then she was plunged back into misery.

Clive leant back in his chair and lit a cigarette. 'Don't look at me like that, Toots. After all, it's your decision.'

'*Me? My* decision?'

He inhaled his cigarette and ran a hand through his short dark hair. 'Rehearsals and performances,' he listed. 'That bloody chaperone. The curfew at the fortress. I doubt if we see each other alone for five minutes a week.'

Thomasine touched his hand. 'We're alone now, Clive.'

'Alone?' Clive glared around him impatiently. Several of the fur-clad ladies in the crowded café were staring at him quite openly. 'You call this *alone*?'

'This is lovely. I adore being with you.'

Clive ignored her. 'I mean – properly alone, sugar. You know.' He stubbed out his cigarette and looked up at Thomasine. His voice became cold. 'Or perhaps you don't.'

'Yes, I do.' She thought of the day they had walked together in the Jardin des Tuileries. In the midst of crowded, busy Paris, the trees and walkways and the cold silence of the afternoon had seemed to cut them off from everyone else. Standing on the edge of the wide, circular pond, glimpsing their reflections in the water, Thomasine had felt that only she and he existed.

'You should come back with me to my lodgings,' said Clive. 'Parks – cafés – it's all too bloody juvenile. And it's costing me a fortune. I'd hoped to put a bit by from this ghastly revue.'

Thomasine stared down at her coffee-cup. Her own wages just about covered the rent for the *pension*, meals, clothes and make-up. Even the stamps for the letters to her aunts were a strain on her purse. And Alice's mood seemed to have soured with the oncoming spring, rather than lightened. Thomasine dreaded asking her to cover for her for more than half an hour.

'It's up to you, really, Thomasine. Think about it. But I can't go on like this for ever. Look at me – I'm bloody exhausted.'

She looked at him. He was lounging back in his chair, a cigarette in one hand, his mouth closed in sulky curves. She thought that he looked, as he always did, the most attractive man in the room. When she reached out a hand as if to smooth away the small shadows beneath his blue eyes, he took her fingers in his, and kissed the tips of them one by one. Several of the ladies in the café looked envious.

'It's up to you, sugar,' he repeated. 'I've a free hour on Friday afternoon. If you want, you can come back to my lodgings. I'll leave it to you to make the arrangements. If you don't, then I'll know it's over.'

He waited for her outside the entrance to the Metro. The streets were half-empty, most of the French still sleeping off their lunches. Watching him for a moment unnoticed, as he leaned against the art nouveau curves of the entrance-way, the coat of his collar pulled up in the chill spring wind, she fell in love with him all over again.

Thomasine touched his arm and said his name.

Clive turned to her. 'You're here, Toots. Thank heavens. It's damnably cold.'

He didn't smile, but began to walk quickly down the pavement. Often Thomasine thought herself responsible for Clive's moods, sparking them off by some piece of naïvety that she cringed over later, alone in bed. Now she found it difficult to keep up with him. She loped behind him, her gait uneven on the hilly, cobbled streets. When they reached his lodgings, he fitted the key in the lock and held open the door for her.

'Hurry up, Toots. It's perishing.'

'I've pulled a muscle, Clive. That wretched hornpipe routine.'

He looked at her, and his face softened a little. The concierge glared at Thomasine as they started up the stairs.

'Poor little thing.' Clive slowed his pace. 'I'll rub it for you, when we're in the warm. We're almost there.'

His rooms were at the top of the house: a sitting-room with a small kitchen area, and a separate bedroom. The ceilings were low and sloping, the windows small and dirty-paned. The furniture was sparse; no pictures or photographs softened the harsh angularity of the walls. Thomasine, suddenly edgy, cleaned a patch of grime from the window-pane with her handkerchief and stared out at the rooftops of Paris. Following down the slope of the city she could see the wide, glittering arc of the River Seine.

'How did you manage to escape, sugar?' Clive said sympathetically. 'Alice?'

Thomasine shook her head. 'No, I asked Poppy. I had to give her a pair of stockings and a chocolate bar, though.'

Clive laughed. He had uncorked a bottle of red wine; he poured out two glasses. 'Poor darling. Never mind, I'll buy you stockings. And pounds and pounds of chocolates.'

His kindness touched her. 'I'd get fat. Then I'd be out of a job.'

'We all will be soon,' said Clive.

Thomasine turned aside from the window. 'What do you mean?'

'Oh, come on, sugar.' His voice was quite casual. 'You must have noticed the seats aren't exactly full. I mean, audiences aren't fighting to get in, are they?' He handed her a glass. 'Don't look so worried, Toots. After all, it's a scrubby little thing. No decent songs, and the leading lady's past her best, don't you think?' He swallowed a mouthful of wine. 'Come on – drink up.'

The wine made her less jittery. 'What will you do if the show closes, Clive?'

He shrugged. 'There's a couple of possibilities, but I'm not sure yet. I've had a few offers. It's a question of what's best for my career. I might go back to London ... or there's talk of Italy. Now come and sit beside me, and I'll rub your leg.'

Thomasine sat on the couch, her outstretched legs resting on Clive's lap. She tried not to think of the future, but to enjoy the fact that she was here, with Clive Curran. His long, beautifully shaped hands kneaded her calf muscle, so that the stiffness slowly eased away.

'Lie back,' he said. 'Close your eyes.'

Thomasine lay back on the cushions and closed her eyes. She felt drowsy with wine and happiness. Whatever the future brought, she thought, this was perfect. She was in Paris with the man she loved, she had work she enjoyed, and money enough to keep herself. Her career was progressing well; the choreographer had given her a small solo in the second act.

'Is that better?' he said.

She nodded dreamily. Her leg no longer ached.

He didn't stop, though. Gently, he massaged the arch of her foot, the tips of her toes. Then his hand travelled the distance from her toes, along her shin, to her thighs.

'Don't move,' he said. 'You're enjoying it, aren't you?'

She couldn't speak. The tension had come back, but it was a different sort of tension. He leaned over and kissed her gently on the mouth. His tongue flickered against her lips. Then his kisses began to follow her neck, her throat, her shoulder. His hand slipped inside the curved neckline of her frock.

'Roll over, Toots, and let me undo your buttons.'

She felt her face go scarlet. 'I couldn't Clive. It wouldn't −'
She managed to stop herself just in time. *It wouldn't be proper.*
The old, often-repeated, meaningless words applied at various times by all three aunts to new styles of clothing, to suggested outings, to the company of the opposite sex.

'I just want to see you,' Clive pleaded. His eyes looked anguished. He rubbed at his forehead with his fingers. 'You're so beautiful, Thomasine. I've been feeling rotten all day, and now I feel so much better. *Please.* I just want to see you *properly.*'

Slowly, she shuffled upright, and reached for the back of her dress. Her hands were shaking.

'No,' said Clive. 'Let me.'

She felt him undo her buttons, one by one, and pull her dress over her head. She felt silly, sitting there on the couch in her petticoat. The hungry, urgent feeling had left her.

Then he began to stroke and kiss her again. His head nuzzled between her breasts, and she did not push him away. She looked down at his short, slightly curling dark hair, and kissed the top of his head. She loved the way he smelt, the touch of his skin, the sound of his voice. When he pushed aside the straps of her petticoat so that her breasts were bared, she did not stop him.

'Dear Thomasine,' he said softly. 'Such a lovely skin. Such lovely little breasts.'

His hand stroked her leg from her knee, to her thigh, to her buttock, exploring beneath the skirt of her petticoat. Suddenly defensive again, she caught his fingers.

He looked upset. 'Don't you trust me, Thomasine? Don't you love me?'

'Of course I love you, Clive. It's just that . . .'

'What is it?'

His eyes, sleepy and blue, looked down at her. She could not answer him because she did not know what he wanted, or what she wanted. She did not know what he intended to do. She did not want him to realize the extent of her ignorance.

'Nothing.' She smiled at him. 'Nothing important.'

Afterwards, he found that, just for a while, he disliked himself. She had been, of course, a virgin. He had been as gentle as possible, but he always forgot himself a little at the end. There were limits to how long self-control could last.

She didn't say anything when he turned aside from her. He took a rug from a nearby chair, and flung it over them both. The room was cold, and he hadn't bothered to light the gas-fire. Then he lit himself a cigarette and settled back, and put his arm round her again.

'It's never much good the first time, Toots. Everyone knows that. It'll get better for you.'

He realized, saying it, that he intended to see her again. He was surprised at himself – he found her middle-class naïvety a bit of a bore, and had been on the point of finishing with her. Yet, at the same time, Clive was forced to acknowledge that Thomasine Thorne was terribly attractive, quite the prettiest little thing he had come across for some time. He was tempted to let things run on for a while.

'You should get yourself fixed up.'

She looked at him, and smiled. Her eyes were bright and dark, her skin slightly flushed. Glancing down at her, he knew that she hadn't the least idea what he was talking about. Suddenly Clive was aware of a feeling of irritation – almost resentment. Innocent granddaughters of clergymen, with their need of protection, of unreasonable chivalry, exhausted him.

Daniel received the letter from Nell one Saturday in March. Nell, five years younger than Daniel, had looked after their father after Ruth Gillory's death, and then, at the age of thirteen, when Jack Gillory had joined up, had gone into service. During the latter years of the War, she had written to Daniel – badly spelt, unpunctuated letters in her round, childish hand. Like so many others, he had treasured the letters from home, composing falsely cheerful replies to them, partially because he didn't want to dent Nell's own steadfast good spirits, and partially because he was not yet able to write about what he endured.

When he read her letter, he guessed that her cheerfulness, like his, had always been false. He knew himself remiss in not having visited her since his return to England. The letter was blotched with tears, some of the words unreadable. He threw on his jacket and cap, and took a tram to Liverpool Street station.

He had money for the journey to Ely now, because he had not seen Fay for almost a month. He had no one to buy tickets for in the cinema, no one to ply with flowers or sweets. If it had not been for Nell, he would have been glad of his errand to Ely. It stopped him thinking for a while of his own misery.

The landscape grew more and more familiar the further the train drew away from London. Beyond Cambridge, a flutter of excitement began to grow in his stomach as he looked out of the window. Through the trail of smoke from the train's funnel, he witnessed the flattening of the fields, still painted silver with the spring floodwaters. The sky, grey and lowering, and to Daniel, beautiful, spat rain droplets into the dykes and marshes.

In Ely, he went immediately to the house in which Nell was in service. He had dressed in his uniform, because it still often aroused some sort of respect. The accent which he had adopted in his grammar school days had become habitual to him.

He hardly recognized his sister. She had been a child of ten in 1914; she was a young woman of sixteen now. She had his own golden-brown curling hair, scraped back into an ugly bun, and nice hazel eyes. The eyes were red-rimmed now, the small, thin face swollen and blotchy. Daniel sent her off to pack her bag, and then turned to the butler.

'I want to see the master of the house.'

The butler fluttered and protested, but when Daniel moved one pace closer to him, he scuttled off to find his employer.

The master of the house was a shrivelled man of fifty or so. Daniel said to him, 'You'll write a reference for my sister.'

A sneering refusal.

Daniel added, quite calmly, 'Or I'll have a word with your wife, if you like. Or if that doesn't trouble you, I'll write a nice little letter to the Ely paper.'

'There is a law of libel, Captain Gillory. Or perhaps you have not heard of it?'

'Or,' said Daniel, 'I'll kill you. I don't mind killing you – after all, I've killed people often enough. For King and Country, and all that. I'd quite enjoy it, actually.'

The reference was written, and Nell was escorted out of the house. In a tea-shop in the Cathedral Close, Daniel bought her lunch.

'You look so grown-up, Danny,' said Nell, between mouthfuls of lamb cutlet. 'So *old*.'

'You haven't changed a bit.' Daniel studied his sister. 'Still a troublesome little brat.'

Nell smiled for the first time. 'Oh, Danny.' She reached out and touched his hand. 'It's so good to see you.'

He took her hand in his. She had finished her first course, so he ordered her pudding. He said carefully, when she had almost finished eating, 'You're well, aren't you, Nell? I mean – you're not in trouble?'

She reddened, and shook her head. 'I didn't let him touch me. He tried to, though, often enough.'

He felt a deep sense of relief. When they had finished their lunch, Daniel took his sister round the shops, and bought her a few trinkets. Later, they walked through the cathedral. He had never been religious, but the building was cool and high and vast. It calmed him.

He left Nell at the house of a friend, and walked alone to

Drakesden. There was still no bus service, and he had not the money for a taxi. His leg had begun to ache, but he disregarded it as he tracked the long familiar route across the fields and ditches. The village was all so little changed that he could have been a schoolboy again, his books heavy on his back.

The cottage had altered, though. The back door hung drunkenly from its hinges, and the window-frames were rotted and broken. The lean-to that had been the blacksmith's shop had collapsed, blown down, perhaps, by some long-gone wind. The allotment was overgrown, the outbuildings in poor condition. But, stooping, Daniel picked up a handful of fine dark Fen earth and let it trickle through his fingers to the ground. 'Mine,' he whispered. 'This is mine.' Such soft, fertile earth. Its fertility was due to the frequent flooding – flat, low-lying ground was always at risk of flooding. Lower than sea-level, it was protected only by a complex system of dykes and pumps. The dykes were now higher than the fields because the peat had dried out over the centuries, and shrunk. What ingenuity, thought Daniel, to make something of so hostile an environment. So much to gain, if only you could fight off the seas, the rivers, the winds.

He straightened up then, and he saw it. An estate agent's board, flagging the land between the Gillory allotment and the dyke. Drakesden Abbey land. 'The Blythes' land,' whispered Daniel out loud, walking forward.

'For Sale', said the sign.

On the day that Daniel received the reply to his letter to the estate agent in Ely, he went to visit Hattie in Bethnal Green. Hattie, as he had expected, was happy to help him. They sat in the saloon bar of The George and Dragon together, Daniel with a whisky, Hattie with a port and lemon.

'How much land?' asked Hattie, after Daniel had explained the situation to her.

'Fifteen acres. I had the letter from the estate agent this morning. With my mother's patch, that makes eighteen. It's not much, but it'll do for a start. It's good, rich land – we'd have enough to feed us and to sell a bit at the market. And it's cheap, Hattie – land prices have tumbled since the War.'

Hattie, no fool, said, '*Us?* Who's "us", Danny?'

The small room was crowded and overheated. Daniel tried to imagine himself in the Fens with Fay, arm in arm beneath the vast skies.

'There's a girl I've been seeing. She's called Fay.'

Hattie nodded slowly. 'I thought so. Haven't seen too much of you lately, Danny.' She looked at him more closely. 'We can go outside if you wish, love. It's always a bit of a crush in here on a Friday night.'

He shook his head. He had never told her about his claustrophobia, his dislike of crowds, but she had guessed.

'I must go soon. I just wondered if you'd think about it, Hat. It would take a while, but I reckon I'd be able to buy it back from you within two years.'

She drained her glass dry. Her plump, ringed fingers folded round Daniel's. 'I don't need to think about it. It'll be the best thing in the world for you, Danny. You don't belong here – you never did. I can't bear the countryside myself – too quiet, and there's nothing to do – but I'm sure it would be just the thing for you.'

He stood up, and bent his head, and kissed her on the mouth in front of all the staff and customers of The George and Dragon.

'Dear Hattie. I won't let you down.'

She did not let go of his hands. 'Is she a nice girl, Danny? Is she the right girl for you?'

He thought of Fay, with her clear skin and bright eyes and curling dark hair. He could have howled like a dog with hunger for her.

'I'm sure she is.'

Over the past month Fay had feared, sometimes, that she had

miscalculated. That she had said no once too often, that Daniel Gillory had wearied of the whole thing, that she had misjudged the delicate balance.

Over the previous week she had several times almost written to him, but had managed to stop herself. Men didn't respect a girl who ran after them. Especially men like Daniel Gillory. Daniel was a gentleman – he spoke like a gentleman, he had the manners of a gentleman, and the first time she had met him he had been wearing an officer's uniform. Best of all, he owned a little farm somewhere in the country. So he was *landed* gentry. Phyl had been ever so envious when Fay had told her that.

Because Daniel Gillory was the best chance Fay had had in years, she was very careful. Men like Daniel were scarce now – gentlemen, that is, with all four limbs intact, and the full capacities of their senses. Fay had known when she had dropped her handkerchief on the bank of the Serpentine that opportunities for girls such as herself were few and far between since the War. She knew herself to be pretty and smart, she knew that she deserved something better than a labourer or a clerk, or some old crock with only one leg or half a mind. She wanted money and a decent sort of life. She deserved it.

To Daniel, she always referred to her home as 'my lodgings'. She thought it sounded better, more grown up. She would have hated him to have seen the small terraced house in Kilburn, with its dirty scrap of a back garden, its cluttered, ugly rooms. Fay always kept her own room nice. She went round every day with a duster, and laundered her bed-linen and towels herself.

Because she was neat and smart, she had landed herself the job in Kensington. She had trained herself to speak well, never missing off aitches and putting them in the wrong place like her mother did. She made sure her stockings were unholed, her blouse always crisply ironed, her shoes always polished. She rose early in the morning to dress herself and take the long journey into the centre of London. She would go without food rather than appear slovenly. Because of this, she knew that she deserved Daniel.

In the ladies' cloakroom at Chantal's, Fay examined her appearance before leaving the shop. She was wearing the navy skirt and the white blouse, and the scarlet bow in her hair. Fay powdered her nose and checked her stockings for holes. As she walked out through the shop, she saw that Daniel was waiting for her in the street. For a moment she studied him through the glass door: Daniel Gillory was undeniably attractive. She had sometimes found herself getting carried away in the back of the cinema, or after one of their picnics in the park. Never too carried away, of course – she had made that mistake before, and had regretted it. Men didn't respect you if you were easy. Men didn't *marry* you if you were easy.

'Hello, Daniel.'

He bent his head to kiss her, and she threaded her gloved hand through his arm.

'Where shall we go?'

'Are you hungry?'

She shook her head. 'One of the girls had a birthday, so we all had a piece of cake. There's a picture I'd like to see, though.'

She sensed his edginess, yet felt too tired herself to want to talk much. Sometimes he tried to talk to her about his war experiences, but she always cleverly changed the subject. She didn't want to hear talk about gas, or dead bodies, or horrible injuries. All that was over and done with and, besides, a man shouldn't expect a girl to listen to that sort of thing. Though the evening was warm, it would be better to sit in the darkness of a picture house, and let him kiss and cuddle her a bit. That usually made him a little less fidgety.

They saw *Daddy Long Legs*, which Fay had seen three times already. They sat in the back row, with all the other lovers, and Fay reckoned that she watched only a fraction of the film. Daniel's caresses seemed more urgent, more desperate that evening, and Fay found herself responding to him. He was both clever and gentle, which made him very difficult to resist. She wanted him to touch her; she found herself wanting him more than she ever had before.

When the film ended, she tidied her clothes and they left the cinema. In almost complete silence, they walked to Hyde Park. He was still restless, he walked too fast for her. In the park, she did not suggest a boat or an ice, but went instead with him to the haze of trees and shrubs that they had used before. There, they lay in the grass together, sheltered by a lilac bush. Daniel put his jacket on the ground, Fay took off her shoes. She didn't want them scuffed, or grass stains on her blouse. She held out her arms to him, and let him kiss her again. When he undid the buttons of her blouse, she did not protest.

She pushed him away, though, when his hand crept beneath her skirt. It was quite an effort. She wanted him to go on, but knew that she must not let him. 'No, Daniel,' Fay said sharply, and sat up. She began to rebutton her blouse.

He had turned away from her, his head buried in his hands. Then he looked back, quite suddenly, and said, 'Fay. I can't go on like this. Will you marry me?'

She heard her own sharp intake of breath. Her heart was beating very fast. 'How could we, Daniel? Where would we live?'

He was kneeling beside her; he caught her hands in his. 'You remember that I told you about my mother's smallholding. Well, some land adjacent to it has just come up for sale. It's not much, Fay, but it'll be enough to live on if we're careful. I'll work hard for you, I promise.'

She hardly heard his last words. A breeze had begun to rustle through the bushes and grass, but she did not notice it. 'You're buying this land?' she said. 'So that it belongs to your farm?'

'Yes. More or less. It's lovely, Fay. Such good land. I want you to see it. I want you to live at Drakesden with me.'

Drakesden, she thought. Mrs Fay Gillory of Drakesden. It had such a distinguished ring to it.

'The cottage is rather dilapidated – it'll take me a while to make it good enough for you. But you don't mind waiting a month or two, do you, Fay?'

Slowly, she shook her head. She imagined herself sitting in the garden of a pretty little cottage, like the ones on the chocolate boxes. Pink-walled perhaps, with small, daintily-curtained windows and a neatly thatched roof. She would give afternoon tea-parties. Mrs Fay Gillory of Drakesden. The Captain's wife. She would wear a flowery dress and a wide picture hat.

'Will you marry me, Fay?'

She felt a warm wave of relief wash over her. She had got it right, after all. Not too little, not too much. She congratulated herself on her skill.

Fay smiled at Daniel. 'Yes, I will. Of course I will.'

Clive reminded Thomasine about the vine and the porch, and Thomasine became adept at climbing out of the first-floor window and running to Clive, waiting at the corner of the street. Sometimes, her hands full of vine leaves, her shoes slipping on the wrought-iron roof of the porch, Thomasine was horrified at herself. She knew that what she was doing was terribly wrong, she guessed how distressed her aunts would be if they found out. Well then, she comforted herself, they must never find out. As long as she was careful and quiet, as long as she did not lose her job, no one need ever know.

When she was with Clive she never felt guilty. Lying in his arms, sharing his bed, always felt so perfectly right. As he had told her, what they did together got better in time. She knew now what had been missing in her life. She had needed someone to love: someone like Clive, who was clever and handsome and sophisticated. She was grown-up now, no longer an innocent child, but a woman capable of creating her own destiny.

In the gaps between seeing Clive, concerned about the show's falling attendance, she began again to search for work. Her two auditions were hopeless: the first only wanted dark-haired girls, the second asked her to pose naked except for a frill of spangly tulle. She did not want to go back to London. It would seem like a defeat. Only to herself did Thomasine admit that her plans for the future now included Clive. She imagined them travelling round Europe together, moving from theatre to theatre, their love a constant in a transient and glittering world.

Each night Thomasine gazed out to the auditorium and saw the scattered empty seats, heard the unenthusiastic applause. Every day she scanned the music papers, looking at the job advertisements. Clive was still vague about his future plans. In company, he did not single her out for any special attention. Because of the chaperone, Clive said – liaisons between the English dancers and the male singers and actors were strictly forbidden. They were not a couple, as the female ingénue and the principal male dancer were a couple. She was just one of the chorus, to be acknowledged perhaps with a nod of the head in the corridor, possibly not even that. His inattention sometimes hurt her, and Thomasine felt herself humiliated by it. But when they were alone, Clive was charming, amusing and attentive.

She believed that, in time, things would change. She knew that an actor's life was a disrupted one, with little continuity. Although in her blackest moments she was uncertain of his affection for her, Thomasine knew that she had never loved anyone as she now loved Clive Curran. In time, Clive would be able to be more open in expressing his affection. In time, they would do the sort of things other couples did. They would window-shop in the Faubourg St-Honoré, or search for treasures in the Marché aux Puces. They would picnic in the Bois de Vincennes, or take a boat-trip down the Seine. They would be proud of being seen together in public; they would no longer hide guiltily away, as though their affection was something shameful.

Paris in the springtime seemed only an appropriate back-ground to their love affair. The sun shone more brightly every day, and the trees that lined the boulevards sprouted acid-green leaves. The banal words of the love songs in the revue expressed all that Thomasine felt. She could not eat, could not sleep. She lost weight, so that all her costumes had to be taken in. When she looked at herself in the mirror, she saw a new Thomasine: pale-faced, bright-eyed, the last childish plumpness of jaw and cheekbone whittled away. Men's eyes followed her in the street; admirers left roses in the dressing-room.

Nicholas and Lally arrived in Paris in early May. Nicholas was driving the new Delage; Lally was kneeling up on the passenger-seat, clutching the door, her hat held on with her free hand, looking around her.

'There's the Seine – and look, Nicky – the Eiffel Tower!'

Nicholas, concentrating on his driving, grinned at her. The motor-car handled beautifully. They had travelled since the early hours of the morning, motoring up through the lush green valleys of the Loire.

'Isn't it wonderful?' shouted Lally.

'Wonderful,' Nicholas agreed.

He had spent the last six months of the War in Paris. Looking around, he saw that it was all different. The streets were full, the pavement cafés packed. During the bombardment of 1918, the civilian population had hidden away in the cellars beneath the city. Now, like butterflies emerged from their chrysalids, their colours were bright and startling – silks of lavender, lemon, pink and lime gathered under the awnings of the cafés.

'Lots of clothes,' said Lally thoughtfully, staring at the girls in their summer dresses. 'I'm going to buy lots and lots of clothes. You'll give me some money, won't you, Nick?'

He nodded, slowing at an intersection. The Delage braked smoothly, and Lally collapsed back on the seat.

'I think this is going to be the best. Rome and Monaco were wonderful, but Paris will be the best. Besides, I'm nineteen soon.'

'Are we going to celebrate, Baby?'

'We're going to have the most marvellous dinner. And we're going to dance until three in the morning. In one of these darling little cafés, perhaps.'

The horse and cart blocking Nicholas's route moved off, and Nicholas put the motor-car into gear. He did not need Lally to read the map; he knew the way to their hotel. The streets, as he drove through them, were familiar, but not frighteningly familiar. The Avenue des Champs-Elysées seemed brighter and sunnier – even the plane trees appeared to Nicholas to be more thickly leaved than they had been two years ago. As they neared the Place de la Concorde, Nicholas thought that perhaps it was over, perhaps he had forgotten, perhaps things were all right. When he drove, when he was in company, he could believe that.

They checked into the Crillon Hotel, and were shown their rooms. After he had bathed and changed, Nicholas knocked on Lally's door. 'I'd better go to Cook's. We're running a bit short of cash. There's no need to come, Lal – I'll see you at dinner.'

A bundle of letters and a cheque were waiting for Nicholas at the travel agency. All were from his mother. He cashed the cheque, and then found an empty seat at a pavement café, ordered coffee and a pastry, and opened the first letter. Drakesden seemed very far away now, almost impossible to imagine. He and Lally had left East Anglia in the middle of winter, when the rain had been swelling the dykes and turning the floodlands to marsh. Their departure had been delayed by his mother's reluctance to be parted from him again, and by Nicholas's own uncertain health. Away from England, though, in the early shimmering sun of Italy and Monaco, the day visions had receded, until he could cope with them again. Lally's company – any company – helped him.

He scanned through all six of the letters, swallowed his coffee, and ate the pastry. Back at the hotel, he knocked on Lally's bedroom door again.

'You can read them if you like.' He tossed the letters on to her bed.

'Nothing for me?' Lally was combing out her hair. She glanced at the inscriptions on the letters. 'Oh, dear. What a disappointment.'

He could never tell whether she minded or not. 'Mama sends her love,' he said hastily. 'There's not much news, anyway. The usual stuff – Marjorie's children, Mama's efforts at economizing, that sort of thing. Oh, and Pa's sold that bit of land. To a Mrs Harriet Someone-or-other, of Bethnal Green.'

Lally giggled. 'A Cockney lady farmer. Can you imagine, Nicky? She'll call all the villagers "ducky", and expect trees to grow in rows.'

Nicholas lay full-length on Lally's bed and closed his eyes, suddenly tired. He often found it easier to sleep in the day than at night.

Lally sat down on the bed beside him. Her small hand enfolded his fingers.

'This is fun, isn't it, Nick? Everything's going to be all right now, isn't it?'

He recognized the anxiety in her voice. ''Course it is,' he said sleepily. 'Julian and Belle should be here tomorrow. Ettie may travel with them.'

'Ettie has bobbed her hair.' Lally's voice flickered in and out of Nicholas's consciousness as he drifted off to sleep. 'Do you think that I should bob my hair?'

CHAPTER FIVE

'THE end of the month, Poppy.' Thomasine stared gloomily into the bottom of her glass. 'We close at the end of the month.'

Poppy sucked the cherry off her cocktail stick. 'It's rotten, isn't it?'

They were in the café beside the theatre. It was the fourteenth of July, Bastille Day, so they had been allowed to stay out late. The café was decorated in the colours of the French tricolour: red, white and blue. They had pulled several tables together, and were seated round them, chairs jostled closely to each other, the tables already cluttered with bottles and glasses. Clive was seated at the far end of the table, between Clara Rose and the director.

'What will you do?' asked Thomasine.

'Oh,' Poppy shrugged. 'Go home, I think. I've had enough of this. I miss my mum . . . and London.' She looked sideways at Thomasine. 'What about you?'

Thomasine could not help but glance up to the other end of the table, to where Clive was sitting. As she watched, he put one arm around Clara Rose and kissed her on the cheek. Thomasine felt a rush of misery; her confidence in the future was slipping away from her.

'I don't know. Stay here for a while, perhaps.'

Yet without her weekly wage from the revue, she would not be able to support herself. She must find another job, quickly. She decided that on her next free morning she would go round all the theatres in Paris, asking if they had any vacancies. Even if she was losing Clive, she thought, at least she still had her career.

'I thought you and Alice would go home.'

The assistant stage manager, who was sweet on her, had

placed another cocktail in front of Thomasine. She smiled absently at him, and stirred the coloured liquid vigorously. 'Alice hasn't made up her mind yet.'

The truth was that she and Alice now hardly spoke to each other. They no longer ate their meals together, or borrowed each other's clothes, or provided mutual alibis to the chaperone for social engagements. Alice's distancing of herself from Thomasine had been a steady but inexorable process since Thomasine had begun to see Clive.

'Alice should ease off a bit,' whispered Poppy. 'She'll lose her looks if she goes on like that.'

Alice had already drained her glass. She was laughing, her cheeks as scarlet as her painted lips.

The musicians, slouched around the piano, had begun to play. Clive led Clara Rose to the centre of the floor.

Poppy lit herself a cigarette, and smiled. 'So that's started up again. Well, wouldn't you know it? Clara's rich boyfriend's going to finance a tour for her, I've heard. Dear old Clive must be making sure of a starring role for himself.'

Thomasine was aware of a great ache inside her. She wanted to run out of the café and back to the *pension* and howl for hours, but she would not let herself. She did not look at Clive and Clara Rose dancing together, but instead forced herself to gather her pride, and smile and talk and laugh.

They had spent the early evening in a nightclub, and now they were wandering from café to bar, bar to café, having a drink in each. There were eight of them: Nicholas and Lally Blythe, Ettie, Boy and Julian and Belle and the two Frenchmen. Belle was a cousin of the Blythes. They were celebrating Lally Blythe's nineteenth birthday.

Nicholas, arm in arm with Lally and Belle as they wove along the crowded pavements, told himself that he was having a terrific time. The show they saw at the nightclub was like nothing he had ever seen before. He had not taken the opportunity to visit such places when he had been in Paris in 1918. To-night, along with Boy and Julian, he cheered and whistled at the dancers. Some of the showgirls were naked except for a small patch of sequinned material attached to their groins. They stood quite still, posed carefully in some improbable scenario: a classical temple, or a crater on the moon. Julian focused his opera-glasses, but in the darkness of the theatre Nicholas looked away. It was as though he still heard his mother's voice scolding him for staring at the nude statues in the walled garden. *Don't look, Nicky. It isn't nice.*

After the nightclub, they walked through the streets, stopping at the cafés and bars. It was dark now. Nicholas had lost track of time, but he guessed it must be the early hours of the morning.

'I'm going to have nineteen cocktails,' said Lally, beside him. 'One for each year.'

'You'll be ill.' Nicholas's voice was mild. 'Very ill.'

'This one.' Lally had stopped outside another café. 'Julian . . . Boy . . .'

They went inside. The café was already crowded. Couples were dancing in the centre of the room. The light was very dim, so that at first Nicholas could see only vague shapes in the darkness.

'Music. *Lovely*,' said Belle.

Julian dragged some tables and chairs together. The girls sat down, and Julian and Boy waited, as they always did, for Nicholas to fumble in his pocket for some coins. When he had found a few francs, they went to the bar.

Nicholas found a seat and opened his cigarette-case. His fingers trembled slightly as he struck the match. His unease worried him; he could not see the cause of it tonight. He was in company, which usually helped, and he had all the drink and cigarettes he needed. It was very hot in the café, so he took off his jacket and hung it over the back of the chair, rolling up his shirt-sleeves. The low, reddish lighting delineated the scars on his arm very clearly, painting them a dark scarlet-brown. Nicholas hurriedly swallowed his daiquiri, and looked away.

Lally sat down beside him. 'Do I look nice?' she said.

He managed to smile. 'You look very nice. That frock's a lovely colour.'

'It's called Lanvin blue. It suits me better than brown, don't you think?'

'Much better.' Now, he could hardly picture Lally in a school uniform. The frock she wore was a pale purplish-blue embroidered silk, loosely draped but clinging to her figure. Her hair was coiled in thick black ropes round her ears. She was still a little plump, but the dress, one of half a dozen that Nicholas had bought her for her birthday, effectively disguised the childish roundness of her body.

Julian placed a cocktail in front of each of them. 'Ettie's being sick,' he said. 'She thinks it was the *boeuf bourguignon*.'

Belle giggled. Lally's eyes, dark and slanted, studied Nicholas carefully. 'We'll go back to the hotel if you like,' she whispered.

He shook his head and tried to look cheerful. 'Certainly not, Baby. This is your birthday treat.'

A roar of laughter issued from the far side of the café, where a large group of people were seated round several tables. When they spoke, Nicholas realized that they were English. He watched them for a while, his eyes now accustomed to the light. He thought, as he inhaled his cigarette and threw a few more francs on the table for drinks, that he understood his unhappiness. He had realized that the best of them had died, and now he was left with the dregs. That men like Julian and Boy could not compare with fellows like Richardson or Holtby. That he himself, because he had survived, and because of what he had done, must remain third-rate for the rest of his days. Even the girls, he thought, were different to how they had been before the War.

His eyes half-closed, he watched the girls at the table across the room. The two blondes, the red-head. When the red-head turned and smiled at the man beside her, Nicholas realized that she was Thomasine Thorne.

★

133

At last Clive asked her to dance. Thomasine almost refused him, but the seesaw dip of her emotions tilted the other way when he smiled at her. She tried to relax, to enjoy the sensation of his arms around her, the warmth of his body against hers. But it was no good. Anger simmered inside her, a deep rich vein that she could not quite quell.

'Relax, Toots,' Clive whispered in her ear. 'You're all stiff.'

'Poppy says that you're going on tour with Clara Rose. Is that true?'

Clive laughed. 'What would Poppy know about it? Poppy will be on a boat to England at the end of the month.'

She almost lost her temper, almost stalked from the dance-floor and left him empty-armed. '*Clive!*' she hissed furiously.

He looked down at her, and shrugged. 'Clara Rose is still desperately making up to her banker. She could be out of a job like the rest of us in a month's time.'

She was not sure whether she believed him. She said bluntly, 'After the show closes, Clive, what will happen to us?'

She could see the irritation in his eyes. 'Don't fuss, Toots,' he said. 'I can't bear a girl who fusses. We'll just have to see.'

He had made much the same reply to much the same question over and over again throughout the past few weeks. Thomasine tried once more to make him understand her predicament.

'I'm still looking for work here. I've been through the papers, but there's nothing.'

'It's a devil, isn't it?'

She could see that he wasn't really listening. His blue eyes gazed, distracted, around the café, and his brow was furrowed.

'Chin up, Toots,' said Clive vaguely. 'It's not the end of the world, you know, a lousy revue closing.'

The music had stopped. They stood in the centre of the dance-floor, still touching each other, but they might as well, thought Thomasine, have been a thousand miles apart.

'I won't go home,' she said. She could hear the desperation in her voice. 'I couldn't bear it.'

Clive stooped and dropped a kiss on the crown of her head. 'We'll talk about it later, darling. Something will turn up.'

Lally was trying to choose which of the men at her table she should sleep with that night. It was not an easy choice, because she had no experience of such things. After that first, experimental kiss with Daniel Gillory, there had been a long, fallow period. School and Drakesden had not greatly enlarged her sexual experience. She was still embarrassingly lumbered with her virginity, but was determined to rid herself of it tonight. A special nineteenth birthday present to herself.

She sat back in her chair and surveyed the group seated round the table. Nicholas was her brother, of course, so he was not a possibility. Boy – well, Boy wore his sparse brown hair parted in the centre and plastered down close to his scalp. He knew simply everyone, which was why he was useful. But his pale eyes bulged, and Lally had not been able to convince herself that Boy found her attractive. He had suggested a frock in the violet-blue colour for her, and the suggestion had proved a good one, but Lally suspected that his interest in her was more artistic than sexual.

Julian. Julian was Belle's husband, and it had been via Belle that Lally had been able to fill in certain gaps in her education. Mama had told her nothing, of course, so that the onset of her periods at school had been both embarrassing and distressing. Until she had spoken to Belle, Lally hadn't even been sure what periods were for. Otherwise, her rather idiosyncratic sex education had been picked up from the biology teacher at Lady Mary's (cowslips and bees), from some well-hidden postcards in Pa's study, and by simply using her eyes.

She had pretended a certain level of sophistication to Belle, and Belle had obligingly filled in the rest. Julian had not been Belle's first lover, nor had he been her last. Belle had enjoyed discussing her various lovers. Lally's eyes lingered on Julian for a moment, taking in the fair curling hair, the small bristly moustache, and then moved on to the two Frenchmen.

They were called Jean-Luc and Marcel. Jean-Luc was the younger of the two, and probably the better looking, but Lally's eyes always returned to Marcel. Marcel, Boy had told her, was a Count. He had a house in Paris and a château somewhere else. He was also old – at least forty, guessed Lally. It had occurred to Lally that it might be preferable to lose her virginity to a man of forty rather than to a man of twenty. At least then one of them might know what they were doing.

'*Lally.*' Nicholas touched her shoulder. She turned to him and smiled. It was a strange thing to her to be needed – something both unaccustomed and unexpected. She had never been needed before, but she had known since she had left Lady Mary's that Nicholas needed her.

'Lally – look.'

She followed the direction of his gaze. There were two groups in the café: the Blythes' set, and a larger group of people clustered in the opposite corner. Carefully, Lally studied the strangers.

'They're English.'

'Yes,' said Nicholas impatiently. 'Don't you see? Look again – the red-haired girl.'

Lally stared. She was rather short-sighted, so she had to screw her eyes up a little. She picked out a very glamorous dark-haired woman, about ten years older than herself, and a good-looking man. A couple more men, and two young fair-haired girls. Then she saw the red-head. Her hair was cut short and level round her face, and her straight fringe touched her eyebrows. At that moment Lally determined to bob her hair. Mama would hate it. She screwed up her eyes again.

Nicholas, leaning over her shoulder, said, 'That's Thomasine Thorne, Lally. Don't you remember?'

She did remember, of course. How could she ever forget? She didn't believe him at first, because Nicholas had once been in love with Thomasine Thorne and, since the War, he had often seen things that were not really there. Instead of the shadows of war, this time he was conjuring a different memory from the darkness.

Then she looked at him, and she saw that his face did not have that awful glazed, still look. Nicholas had risen from the chair and was crossing the room, weaving between the dancers, brushing aside the scarlet and blue streamers that trailed from the ceiling. The red-haired girl looked up to Nicholas as he reached her, and Lally's fingers folded tightly round her glass as she saw that it was indeed Thomasine Thorne.

'We arrived in Paris three weeks ago,' Nicholas was saying. 'I'm with my sister and my cousin. You remember Lally, don't you, Miss Thorne?'

Of course she remembered Lally. Lally should have been wearing a pinafore and plaits, but instead she was dressed in a frock that must have cost ten times the price of Thomasine's, and her long black hair was coiled in smooth shells around her ears.

'And this is my cousin, Isabel. And you must meet Julian and Ettie . . . and Boy . . .'

She would hardly, Thomasine thought, have recognized Nicholas Blythe. The years had aged him, removing the last traces of childhood from his features. He had always been tall, but the spare ranginess of adolescence had been replaced by a greater solidity of muscle and sinew. His clothes were well cut and his skin was deeply tanned, but his eyes were exactly as she remembered them: that dark, intense brown.

'You look terrific, Nicholas. How marvellous to see you.'

'*You* look stunning, Thomasine. But then, you always did.'

She believed that the compliment was sincere. She did not think Nicholas Blythe capable of insincerity. They had pushed the tables together, so that the Blythes' set sat down adjacent to the group from the theatre, a great long, straggling tail of celebrants, isolating the musicians and dancers to one side of the café.

'You're to let me buy you all a drink.' Nicholas began to scoop money out of his pockets, sitting down beside Thomasine as the waiter came to take their order.

'It's my sister's nineteenth birthday,' he added. 'What a marvellous present, to see you again, Miss Thorne.'

Thomasine introduced the rest of the company – Poppy, Alice, Clara Rose, Clive, and half a dozen others. 'It's not much of a celebration for us,' Thomasine explained. 'More of a wake. Our revue's closing in less than a month.'

'You're an actress?'

Thomasine shook her head. 'A dancer. I've been working in Paris since last August, and before that I was dancing and teaching in London. What about you, Nicholas? It's been so *long*.'

'Oh . . .' He grimaced. 'The War, of course. And then I was ill for a while, but I'm better now. I spent a year or so mouldering at Drakesden, but Lal and I have been on the Continent for the last few months. *Much* more fun.'

Lally, standing behind them, rested a hand on the back of Nicholas's chair. 'We've been to Rome, Florence, Monaco and Nice, Miss Thorne. Nicky has bought the most adorable motor-car.'

'A Delage.' The musicians had begun to play again, and Nicholas had to shout to make himself heard. 'She's a beauty. And we flew from Dover to Calais. It was terrific.'

'Cold.' Lally folded her arms round herself.

Nicholas stood up. 'Will you dance with me, Thomasine?'

The dance was a foxtrot. Nicholas danced well, steering Thomasine through the forest of red, blue and white streamers, guiding her past Alice, slumped at a table, her head cradled in her arms, past Lally, dancing with the bearded Frenchman, and past Clive, dancing again with Clara Rose. Looking quickly away from Clive, Thomasine saw that Nicholas was still gazing at her, his dark eyes opaque.

'I wanted to kill Daniel Gillory,' he said suddenly. 'I tried to, in fact.'

She stopped dancing. Another couple collided with them and then stumbled away.

'Daniel? What has Daniel to do with anything?'

'He took it, of course.'

She couldn't at first think what he was talking about. But Nicholas fumbled in his jacket and drew out his cigarette-case and added, 'We never found the Firedrake, you know. Gillory must have sold it. He went to London quite soon after you left Drakesden – it's quite easy to sell something like that in London.'

Thomasine recalled Armistice Day – Daniel driving her in the stolen Rolls-Royce, his knuckles white, his face unsmiling as he described what had happened to him since he had left Drakesden.

'You're wrong, Nicholas. Daniel wouldn't have done something like that.'

Nicholas didn't reply. He held out the cigarette-case to her, and Thomasine shook her head. She saw how his hand trembled when he lit his own cigarette. She spoke more gently.

'I was so sorry about Gerald.'

He grimaced. 'Poor blighter. Didn't last out the first six months.'

The foxtrot had ended. A hand touched Thomasine's shoulder. Clive said, 'Do you mind, old chap? This one's mine.'

Nicholas inclined his head briefly, and wandered back to the table.

'Clara Rose has gone,' whispered Clive into Thomasine's ear. 'Thank God. She can't dance, you know, darling – compared to you she's like an elephant. But I had to find out about this tour Poppy's been talking about.'

Looking up, she saw herself reflected in his blue eyes.

'All nonsense, I think,' said Clive. 'Just rumour. Couldn't have stood another six months with the silly cow, anyway.'

Lally borrowed a pair of scissors from the barman and sat on the table. Ettie, still a little pale, held up the mirror of her powder-compact. Lally uncoiled her thick black hair and began to cut.

As the scissors opened and closed, and locks of hair scattered all around her, she began to feel better. She imagined the scissors slicing Thomasine Thorne's wavy hair, or the tips of the blades digging into her smooth fair skin. When she had finished cutting the fringe and the sides of her hair, Lally found that she was gasping for breath.

'Let me,' said a voice.

Marcel was standing beside her. He took the scissors from Lally's hand, and began to cut the back of her hair, where she could not see. When she looked up, she saw that Miss Thorne was no longer dancing with Nicholas, but was encircling the floor with the good-looking singer. Lally felt a wave of relief as she watched the singer brush his lips against Thomasine's.

'That's it,' said Marcel, putting down the scissors. 'You look *épatante*, Mademoiselle Blythe.'

She smiled. 'Would you excuse me a moment, Monsieur de Seignelay?'

She crossed the dance-floor. Lally noticed that Thomasine's green dress was of a cheap material, her bright Indian beads ten a penny at all the market stalls. Glancing at the couple a second time, she thought that Miss Thorne was in love with the good-looking singer. Clive, she had heard someone call him.

Nicholas was dancing with Belle. Lally whispered in his ear, and he nodded and mumbled something. He was a little drunk.

And so was she. As she walked back to Marcel, Lally knew that she could not have gone through with this had she not been rather tipsy. She might seek out new experiences, but she feared them as well. It was as if she had to test herself continually, to peer always over the edge into the void.

'I'm a little tired. Would you take me home, Monsieur de Seignelay?'

Marcel wrapped her silk shawl around her shoulders. When they went out of the café Lally saw that, to the east, the rooftops and spires of Paris were dusted with rose-pink.

'The Hotel de Crillon, is it not, *mademoiselle*?'

She turned to look at him, conscious of the lightness of her bobbed hair. 'Actually, I think it would be better if I went home with you. And if you called me Lally.'

Nicholas hardly noticed Lally leave the café. He still did not quite believe it – that after so long a parting he had found Thomasine here, in Paris. He was half afraid that she might vanish again, that she was only a more pleasant figment of his damaged imagination. He watched her hungrily, waiting for that lounge-lizard actor to finish dancing with her. He did not intend to lose her again.

When the dance ended, Nicholas went to her side. 'It's late,' he said. 'Let me see you home.'

Thomasine looked up at him, startled. He saw how white her face was, how dark the blue shadows were beneath her eyes. She was every bit as beautiful as he remembered, though. The tawny hair, the sea-green eyes, the flawless skin. When so many had been fouled by the War, the past, it seemed to Nicholas that only she remained untouched.

'Your sister . . .?' Thomasine said.

'Lally has gone already. Have you had enough?'

She nodded. Crossing the room, Thomasine picked up a silk scarf from the chair and threw it over her shoulders. Nicholas followed her out into the street. The birds that gathered in the plane trees were singing, and the sky had lightened.

'I'm late,' she said. She was walking very fast.

Nicholas's earlier black mood had gone. He had not, in the little Montmartre café, seen again the mud-fields of Flanders. The thought crossed his mind that it was Thomasine who had banished his nightmares.

She had paused at the doorway of a house, fumbling in her bag for a key. Nicholas mentally noted the number of the house, the name of the street.

'You'll let me see you again, won't you, Thomasine?'

She glanced back at him. Her eyes were wide and dark. He thought she looked ill.

'Of course, Nicholas.'

He almost reached out and touched her, almost took her in his arms. But the habits of home, of school, were too deeply ingrained in him for physical spontaneity. Blythes did not kiss or hug, except when society dictated that they must. And besides, she had turned away.

'It was lovely to see you again, Nick. Bye.'

'Toodle-oo,' said Nicholas, and stood there quite still in the street for ten minutes after she had gone.

Inside the *pension*, Thomasine went immediately to the bathroom. There she was violently sick, trying to stifle the sounds as much as possible, so as not to call attention to her late arrival.

Afterwards, she washed her face with cold water and sat down on the floor, propped against the wall, her head resting on her knees. She must have caught a stomach bug, she thought crossly. She had been unwell the previous morning, and since then had eaten hardly anything. She had not enjoyed the cocktails that she had drunk that night, but she had hoped that they might make her feel better. They hadn't.

Eventually she rose, and went to her room. Alice's bed was still empty, the window ajar and unshuttered. The early morning sunlight washed over the clutter of clothes, the ribbons and powder and combs scattered on the single chest of drawers. In a few short hours she would have to be in the theatre again. She had never felt less like dancing. Yet again, she tried to remember exactly what Clive had said to her that night, pinning down his words, examining them minutely for indications of commitment or affection. She realized with a stab of pain that he had never once told her that he loved her.

Marcel took Lally back to his apartment in the Rue St-Honoré. The walls of his bedroom were decorated with *trompe l'œil* arches of sea-green and gold; painted peacock feathers and sunflowers drooped gracefully within the arches. The curtains were drawn. The room was dark and green, lit by a few small gold lamps.

Lally wandered round the room, her fingers trailing uninterestedly over a statuette, a bookcase, an art nouveau lamp. She picked up a photograph from the dressing-table.

'My wife,' said Marcel. 'She is staying at present in my château in Touraine. She is expecting our fifth child. Do you mind?'

Lally replaced the photograph. 'Should I?'

'You are very young. And you are English.' He was helping her out of her coat. She felt him kiss the back of her neck. 'Young girls can be very romantic, *ma chère* Lally.'

'I'm not romantic at all. And I thought you might help me become a little less young, and perhaps a little less English.'

He laughed. 'It would be a pleasure.'

He kissed the back of her neck again. He was a head taller than Lally, but then, at just over five foot, she seemed to have stopped growing. She could see their reflections in the looking-glass opposite: his hands resting on her shoulders, his bent head, his short dark-grey beard contrasting oddly with the whiteness of her skin. She raised a hand and touched the clipped ends of her hair.

'Do you think it suits me?'

Marcel, too, looked at the mirror. Lally was pleased that his answer was not quick and false, that he took time to think.

'You should cut it even shorter, perhaps. Like this.' His hands cupped her bobbed hair, so that it rested just below her cheekbones. 'The colour of the dress is good – the short sleeves suit you, but the neckline is too plain. On the whole, I would say that a woman as young as yourself should wear simple clothes – but with you, *Mademoiselle* Blythe . . .' He frowned. As he spoke, he began to undo the buttons at the back of Lally's dress. 'You will never be beautiful, but you have a look about you that is perhaps more interesting than beauty. You are a little wicked, perhaps. A little . . .'

'Decadent,' finished Lally. She smiled.

Her dress had dropped to the floor, a shimmer of lavender blue. She thought, looking at her white limbs, and at the curve of her stomach and bust beneath her slip, that her years of exile at boarding school still continued to make their mark.

'You are frowning,' said Marcel. 'Why are you frowning, Lally?'

She turned to face him. 'Because I had to go to school. It was a dreadful place. And the food . . .' She ran her hands down her body.

Marcel shook his head. 'You frown because you do not look like a boy, like all the other English girls. You are foolish, Lally Blythe. It is good not to look like a boy.'

He turned her to face him. His hands followed the path that Lally's own hands had traced. Slowly, from her shoulders to her breasts, to her waist, her stomach. When his palms were cupped round her buttocks, he paused. She raised her face to him, and he kissed her. She closed her eyes, and in an instant's pleasurable recollection saw herself kissing Daniel Gillory, the rain battering against the walls of the potting-shed. When she opened her eyes she glimpsed her reflection in the mirror: her body in its silk slip pressed against Marcel's. Marcel's hand slipped between her legs. Lally gasped.

He led her to the bed then. There, he divested her of her underclothes and stockings: there, he kissed her and stroked her until she could not wait for him, and cried out with pleasure at the touch of his hand. Only then did he relieve her of her unwanted virginity. Slowly, carefully, he aroused her again, and then gently eased himself inside her, so that it hardly hurt at all.

When it was over, he slept, his arms around her. Surreptitiously, she slid her thumb into her mouth and sucked, for comfort. Opening her eyes, she saw the photograph on the dressing-table. That was the best part of it, Lally thought, that she had made love to another woman's husband in another woman's bed.

★

During every available weekend, Daniel went to Drakesden, to work on the cottage and land. He repaired the window-frames and doors himself, sanding down and repainting what he could, replacing any rotten timber. He swept out the mess of years of dereliction from both rooms of the tiny house, and took great pleasure in knocking down the lean-to that had been the black-smith's workshop. When he lit the bonfire to burn the rotten timber and the debris from the workshop, he could have danced like a pagan around the flames. Except that by then, after a long day's work, his limp had returned, and he had hardly the strength to walk, let alone dance.

He began to clear the smallholding of weeds. In the patch where his mother had once grown cabbages and celery, purple opium poppies flourished and thistles heaved their grey-green spiky heads towards the sky. The pigsty, the well-head and the hen-house were tumbledown grey oases in the middle of the riotous weeds. Daniel sharpened the scythe that he had found in the clutter of the lean-to and set to work.

By the end of July he had cleared away the weeds and begun to dig the ground. Often, before beginning the walk back to Ely station, he would walk to the dyke and, standing on the bank, look back across to the land that had once belonged to the Blythes and, providing he worked hard and was lucky, would soon belong to him. Looking at the thin strip of field between the allotment and the dyke, and along to the area where the strip opened out into a wide, flat meadow, Daniel felt sure that he would continue to be lucky. This year, his fortunes had altered.

He had not yet taken Fay to Drakesden. She worked at the shop on Saturdays and, besides, he wanted to make everything perfect for her before she came. The seven day week that he was working was exhausting, but Daniel did not grudge a moment of it. They had fixed the wedding-day for September – so what did it matter if Daniel was too tired to eat most evenings? Each night, he dreamed of Drakesden, and Fay. He saw the corn growing tall, and he held the woman he loved in his arms. Out there, he could breathe. Out there, he did not feel confined by walls or roofs – the wide blue arc of the sky was his only limitation. Out there, he felt free.

If it had not been for her continuing poor health and uncertainty about the future, then the week after Bastille Day would have been an enjoyable one for Thomasine.

Nicholas called several times for her, between the afternoon and evening performances. Because he was English, and because his father was Sir William Blythe, there was little objection from the chaperone to Nicholas taking Thomasine for tea at Fouquet's or the Café Anglais. He was pleasant company. Compared to the exhausting emotional seesaw of her relationship with Clive, the afternoons with Nicholas were delightful. Nicholas was always encouraging, never critical. He was as happy just to sit on a bench with Thomasine and watch the children playing in the park as he was to escort her to the most exotic nightclub. She rediscovered the pleasures of their friendship at Drakesden, a friendship that had scarcely had time to blossom before it had been curtailed. Nicholas was never devious, never unreasonably demanding. If Thomasine sometimes sensed in him a fragility belied by his handsome and healthy appearance, then she put it down to his years in Flanders, and was especially gentle with him in consequence. The contrast between her friendship with Nicholas and her love affair with Clive was sometimes glaring, to Clive's detriment.

Throughout the week, though, she was still troubled with colic. It usually attacked her in the early morning or occasionally late at night, or when she was faced with some particularly lavish meal. Glancing down at the pastries she had ordered in Fouquet's, rich with cream and cherries and icing sugar, Thomasine had to make a rapid journey to the ladies' cloakroom. When she returned, Nicholas was concerned, anxious. Thomasine refused his offer to escort her to a doctor, telling him untruthfully that she had seen a doctor already. The truth was that she could not afford a doctor. And she was not, after all, used to rich food. The War years and lack of money had deprived her of that.

Later, she knew that the week with Nicholas had been the lull before the storm. The storm broke on Sunday morning, the one day of the week on which they were allowed to lie late in bed. Awakening from an uneasy dream, Thomasine had to dash for the bathroom. When she returned, cold and shivering, Alice was sitting up in bed.

'You were sick yesterday morning.' Alice's voice was accusing.

Thomasine climbed cautiously back between the sheets, curling up, pulling the quilt over her head. 'I've been sick almost every morning this week. I must have eaten something.'

Alice was silent for a while. Then, 'Are you well otherwise? I mean – have you had the curse?'

Thomasine had closed her eyes. 'It's not the curse,' she said sleepily. 'That's a bit late, actually.'

'How late?'

Thomasine just wanted to roll over and go back to sleep again. She and Alice had hardly spoken for weeks; Alice's sudden interest in her health was irritating.

'*How* late, Thomasine?'

Crossly, she began to count up. 'About three weeks, I think. Something like that.'

'*Christ,*' said Alice softly.

Something in Alice's tone of voice made Thomasine open her eyes. 'Why? I don't think it's anything to do with the stomach-ache.'

Bright sunlight filtered through the shutters. Alice had pulled on a dressing-gown and was scrabbling in her bag for a packet of cigarettes.

'What have you and Clive been up to?'

Thomasine felt her face go scarlet. She did not reply.

'You've let him mess around with you, haven't you? For God's sake, couldn't you have been more careful?'

Suddenly, anger overcame her weariness. That Alice should criticize her – Alice, who hardly ever occupied her own bed for a whole night.

'Leave me alone, Alice. It's nothing to do with you.'

Alice heaved open the shutters, and lit a cigarette. 'Like hell, it isn't! How am I ever going to look Mrs Russell in the face again? I was supposed to be keeping an eye on you.'

Thomasine sat up and stared at Alice. The nausea was stirring again, a vengeful black beast that lurked restlessly in the pit of her stomach.

'There's no need for Aunt Tony to know about me and Clive. You wouldn't tell her, would you, Alice?'

Alice said tartly, 'I won't need to tell her, will I?' And then, impatiently tapping her cigarette ash out of the window, 'You still don't know, do you? You're up the spout, Thomasine. You're going to have a baby.'

If she lay down again, the sickness might go away. 'Don't be silly, Alice, I'm not married,' Thomasine said, and pulled the covers over her head.

The quilt was dragged back. Alice looked exasperated. 'Didn't those aunts of yours tell you anything? No – I bet they bloody didn't.'

Thomasine's old annoyance at Alice's assumed worldliness returned. 'Oh, leave me alone, for heaven's sake, Alice.'

'I'd like to kill bloody Clive Curran.'

She couldn't understand why Alice was making so much fuss, but Thomasine found that she had begun to feel a little frightened.

Alice said sharply, 'If you've let that rotter take liberties with you, Thomasine, then you could be pregnant – expecting a baby, that is. It can happen if you're not married, you know, whatever Auntie So-and-so has told you. It happened to my sister Clemmie – sick as a dog every morning for a month. That was how she knew – that and the curse hadn't come, of course. She had to get hitched double-quick or else Mum would have killed her.'

It was the concern on Alice's face that alarmed Thomasine, rather than what she was actually saying. What she said still did not make sense.

Alice rubbed at her eyes. 'Christ – my poor old head.' She turned back to Thomasine. 'Have you been to a doctor yet?'

Thomasine shook her head. In the untidy, familiar room, with the sounds of the street and the market-place not far distant, the conversation seemed utterly unreal.

'Then you'd better. As soon as possible. And if I'm right, then you'd best go and see lover-boy straight away, before he does a bunk.'

Alice arranged the doctor's appointment and went with Thomasine to the surgery. Returning to the waiting-room after she had seen the doctor, Thomasine felt dirty, fouled. She had been touched by a stranger where previously only Clive, whom she loved, had touched her. The doctor had been cold, brusque, disapproving. What he had said was too awful to be believed.

They walked out into the street. Out in the open air, it began to seem real. The road still bustled with people. Paris was as bright, as lovely as before. It was only she who felt for the first time unclean and ashamed.

She cried out as they walked along the pavement, Alice's arm linked through hers, 'What am I going to *do*?'

'He'll have to marry you,' said Alice thoughtfully. 'You're going to have to get Clive Curran to marry you.'

For the first time, the following afternoon, Thomasine went to Clive Curran's apartment on her own accord. Previously, she had only called there at his invitation. The concierge stared at her as she made her way up the stairs, and Thomasine was convinced that the woman had guessed her awful secret.

She knocked at Clive's door. Eventually, from inside there was a shuffling of feet and a grating noise as he turned the key in the lock.

She said quickly, when the door opened, 'Clive – I have to speak to you. I'm sorry to turn up out of the blue like this, but it's important.'

'It's not awfully convenient, I'm afraid, Toots. I've got letters to write, bills to pay, that sort of thing.'

'Please, Clive. Just for a few minutes.'

She thought again, looking around his apartment, how empty it all appeared. It was not a home, but a temporary bolt-hole, a place to leave his few belongings. She could see no paper or pen on the table, but the door of the bedroom in which Clive kept his desk was closed.

'What is it, Toots? I'm sorry to hurry you, but you know how it is.'

She had worried all night about finding the right way to tell him, but in the end the words just fell out, hopeless and unimproved. 'I'm pregnant,' she said baldly. 'I'm going to have a baby, Clive.'

She thought, almost wanting to smile, that at the beginning of the week she hadn't even known what the word 'pregnant' meant. She had learned a great deal since the beginning of the week. She didn't stop looking at him, but she could not read his expression. He was, after all, an actor.

'Christ,' he said, at last. 'Poor poppet. I did tell you to get yourself fixed up, though, didn't I?'

Alice had explained that one. There were things you could use to prevent yourself having a baby, but they were difficult to get hold of, especially if you were unmarried.

'I didn't know what you meant.'

She thought, wearily, that now she was telling the truth to Clive for the first time. Before, she had always chosen her words carefully, to disguise her own lack of sophistication.

'Of course not,' Clive said automatically. He had sat down,

his elbow resting on the arm of the sofa, his knuckles pressed against his mouth. After a while he looked up. 'Are you sure, darling?'

She thought that there was hope in his eyes. She did not dare think about that. She killed the hope. 'I went to see a doctor.'

'Ah.'

She sat down, because she needed to summon up all her courage. 'You must help me, Clive. After all, it's our baby.'

Alice had explained that to her, as well. That it took two people to make a baby, that they didn't have to be married, they merely had to do what she and Clive had done together. In this room, on that sofa.

Clive gave a short, nervous laugh. 'Don't look so cross and gloomy, sugar. It gets me down. I'll think of something. It's not the end of the world.'

He still had not said the words she needed to hear. Despairingly, Thomasine cried, 'It will be the end of the world for me if I have a baby out of wedlock, Clive!'

'Then we'll have to make sure it isn't out of wedlock. That's it, we'll get married.'

As soon as he said it, the relief almost swamped her. She couldn't speak. Instead, she rose from the chair and sat down on the couch beside him, her face buried in his shoulder, her arms around his neck.

He patted her back. 'See, Toots – I told you I'd think of something. Now you must run along. I'll fix everything – don't you worry.'

When he had first said it, he had meant it. It was only afterwards, when the door had closed behind her, that Clive began to think it through. Marriage was a state that he neither looked forward to nor dreaded. And Thomasine was a sweetie: stunning to look at, and good fun. She could probably cook and sew – how nice, Clive thought, looking round his apartment, to have someone waiting for you when you came back from the theatre at night.

A decent meal, and no more buttons missing from his shirts. And if he found the prospect of monogamy uninteresting, then a married man did not necessarily have to be monogamous.

Then the bedroom door opened and Clara Rose called out, 'Has she gone?'

Clive found himself praying that Clara had not overheard his conversation with Thomasine. He had been very careful to close the door.

'Yes. Just the concierge's daughter. There's been some trouble with the roof, apparently.'

He did not know whether she believed him or not, but her expression was bland and uninterested. He watched her unroll her stockings on to her legs.

'It's all go, darling, by the way,' she said. 'The tour. Armand's come up trumps.'

Clive felt a flicker of excitement. His heart began to pound a little faster. 'Where?'

'Oh – the South of France, Monaco, Italy . . . Back to London eventually, if things go well.'

Standing up, Clara pulled her dress over her head. Clive went to her side and began to do up the buttons. 'And me?'

'Leading man, of course, darling. I'm leaving for Marseilles in a couple of days. I really don't see any point in sticking out this shambles until the bitter end, do you?'

Clive shook his head. He watched Clara pick up her bag and run a comb through her hair. At the door, she kissed him lightly on the cheek.

'Let me know tomorrow, Clive. If you aren't interested, I'll have to find someone else.'

He didn't remember Thomasine until Clara Rose had gone. Then she seemed an irrelevancy, an irritation, a temporary distraction from the most important thing: his future. The scales dropped from his eyes. He imagined himself touring Europe, a wife and a wailing baby in tow. It was quite impossible, of course. He could not marry – Clara would drop him like a stone.

He told himself that Thomasine had tricked him. He reminded himself that he had never made any false promises to her, that he had always emphasized that whatever she did was her choice, and hers alone. Besides, how could he be sure that the baby was his? Thomasine Thorne wouldn't be the first pretty chorus-girl who'd tried to trick him into marrying her.

Clive felt a twinge of guilt when he recalled that Thomasine had been a virgin. But guilt only exacerbated his ill-temper, and he found himself disliking her for the very first time.

The following morning she bought a new dress. It was white, with an embroidered border around the neck and hem. The sleeves were short, the waist low, almost around the hips. She could dye her tap shoes turquoise to match the trim, thought Thomasine, and one of the girls would surely lend her a hat. Something borrowed, something blue. She felt a little guilty, buying a white dress to be married in; she knew that she was not entitled to it.

In the afternoon, she and Alice walked to the theatre together. It was almost the end of July; the sky was an intense violet-blue, the pavements hazy with heat. The city seemed sleepy and deserted. Every Parisian was packing up and heading for the seaside, for Le Touquet or Cannes.

When they reached the theatre, there was a small group of people clustered outside. A notice was pasted over the doors, which were closed. Girls' voices chirped through the thick afternoon heat, angry or relieved or despairing. Poppy, coming towards them from out of the crowd, spread out her hands in a gesture of resignation and said, 'It's closed a week early. I'll have to change my boat ticket.'

'Bugger,' said Alice. She pushed forward towards the doors.

Thomasine watched her. She felt languid with the heat and tiredness. She did not mind in the least that the revue had closed early. She was too tired for dancing anyway. Besides, she was going to marry Clive and have his baby. Clive would easily find work in another theatre, and she would go with him. When the baby was born she would be able to start work again; this child need not mean the destruction of all her ambitions.

Alice was shaking her arm. She looked furious. 'Clara Rose has gone. That's why it's closed. Left a note with the management, and scarpered. She knows they won't sue her for breach of contract when there's only a week to go.'

Alice had hold of Thomasine's elbow. She was steering her away from the throng on the pavement. She seemed to be struggling for words suddenly, which was unusual for Alice.

'They couldn't keep the revue running without the leading lady, I suppose.'

'And the leading man,' said Alice bitterly. She turned to face Thomasine. 'Clive's gone, love. He left early this morning with Clara. He's cut and run, I'm afraid.'

Much later, Alice said tentatively, 'There is another way, of course.'

Thomasine hardly heard her. She could not recall having walked back from the theatre to the *pension*. She could not recall any of the conversation that had since taken place. Yet she knew that Alice had remained with her all the time, that Alice had talked and brought her cups of tea. The cups of tea were piled up on the chest of drawers. She had not been able to drink any of them. She felt quite numb, almost unable to see or hear or think. Most of all, unable to think.

Alice unwrapped Thomasine's clenched fingers and placed a glass in her hand. 'Drink up, love. Might even do some good, and if not, it'll help you forget about that bastard. Oh, sorry. I meant –'

It wasn't a baby, of course, it was a bastard. One of the maidservants at the Chalk Farm had had a bastard. Thomasine had heard them talking about her at the shop in Drakesden. They had stopped talking when Thomasine had come in to the shop, of course, but she had caught that ugly word. Bastard. She had not known then what it had meant. She knew now, though.

She raised the glass and drank. The gin scalded her throat, but jerked her mind into some sort of action. 'What do you mean, another way?'

'Well.' Alice poured some gin into her toothmug, and swallowed. 'Some girls try gin and a hot bath, but I've never heard that it worked. Or a shilling's worth of pennyroyal. Clemmie tried that, though, and it just made her ill. I heard of a woman who used carbolic, but . . .' she grimaced and looked up at Thomasine. 'To get rid of the baby, I mean, love.'

'Get rid of it?' Her voice was shaking.

Alice looked defensive. 'Well, what else are you going to do, now that lover-boy's gone? Go back to auntie?'

Thomasine, crouched on the bed, lowered her head to her bent knees, and closed her eyes very tightly. She saw herself going back to Antonia in Teddington with a swollen stomach and no ring on her finger. Or to Aunt Hilly, who had just written to her that she had found a suitable house for her school.

'No. Of course not. It would be quite impossible.'

'Then there's the workhouse,' said Alice. 'Homes for "wayward" girls. They treat 'em like prisoners there.'

Thomasine shuddered. She had once attended a service in Ely Cathedral, and the girls from the workhouse had been there, all clad in identical coarse dresses and aprons and caps, hair scraped severely back from their thin, defeated faces. She shook her head.

Alice poured more gin into her glass. 'Drink it up. I've almost half a bottle, and you never know, it might work. I'll run you a hot bath. If it doesn't do the trick – well, one of the girls at the bar has given me the name of a woman who might be able to help you out. You'll have to pay, mind.'

Thomasine nodded. She felt as though she was in a different country, with different rules. The rules of her childhood – the simple, straightforward rules taught to her by Rose and Hilda Harker – no longer applied. Those rules might work in Drakesden; they did not work here. She thought of her aunts seeing her now, in a dingy room, her hair and clothes a mess, drinking glass after glass of gin. Planning to kill the child that she had believed to be the product of love. Then she thought of Clive, and how casually he had deserted her. Thomasine rolled on to her side and covered her face with her hands.

The gin and the hot bath only made her violently sick and gave her an appalling headache. Alice came back from the café one lunch-time with an address scribbled on a scrap of paper. Borrowing from Alice, selling the white dress to a singer in the café, emptying out her purse and pockets, Thomasine managed to raise the necessary money. She was given a date, a time. She went alone through the streets of Montmartre late one evening. The moonlight picked out the roofs and chimney-pots of the houses, lining them with silver. The noise from the bars and cafés seemed shut off, eerie, nothing to do with reality.

She walked alongside the Cimetière de Montmartre. The moon and the street-lamps washed over the tombstones and statues and trees. It lingered, silvering the family tombs, those square, ornate houses of the dead. She thought, as she narrowed her eyes to read the street-signs in the dark, how futile all her dreams had been. How foolish, how naïve. She had gone out into the world incompletely armed, with the morals and ignorance of a dead generation.

Walking through the Pigalle, the bright lights of the nightclubs and theatres flickered in the darkness, harsh shades of orange and green and electric blue. She caught a glimpse of a woman standing in an alleyway, and in the flicker of a street-lamp she could see the tawdry clothes, the look of defeat in the kohl-rimmed eyes. A man called out to her and Thomasine walked on, the collar of her raincoat pulled up around her face, her eyes staring straight ahead so that she need not see the crude paintings and photographs that adorned the entrances to the bars.

She saw the street-sign, and glanced down at the scrap of

paper in her hand. Then she began to walk down the road, glancing from left to right at the numbers of the houses. She found the number she was looking for at the corner of a small alleyway. It was a tenement house, divided into apartments, the names of each inhabitant inscribed in faded ink on a collection of tattered cards outside the front door. Only a few of the windows of the house were lit, but Thomasine could see that the panes were smeared with dust and cobwebs. The paint on the sills and on the doors was cracked and peeling. The alleyway sloped uphill, the damp cobbles gleaming dimly with the reflected light of the windows. A skinny black and white cat prowled across the steps, rubbing its head against Thomasine's leg.

She glanced at her watch. Twenty minutes past ten. Ten minutes to wait. She sank back into the shadows of the alley, leaning against the wall. The sounds of the house began to distinguish themselves from the sounds of the night. A couple quarrelling in an upstairs room, a child moaning in its sleep. The cat, yowling in the privacy of the alleyway. Mud and dead leaves and empty wine bottles filled the gutters. She was alone and the minutes were ticking by, and soon she would walk up those steps and knock on the door of that house, and in some dingy room a stranger would relieve her of her bastard child. She did not know how. She could not bear to think how.

It was half-past ten. Thomasine crossed the alleyway, climbed the steps and stood at the door, her fist bunched. But she was overwhelmed suddenly by a terrible and nameless fear, an almost tangible blackness. She, who had rarely experienced fear, was nearly overcome by it. She could not do it; her knuckles would not strike the wood. A memory that she had shut away for years returned to her: herself as a young girl, riding alone through a parched and alien landscape, her baby sister cradled on her back. She had known fear then also: that she would lose her way, that she was alone, that the baby would die.

Turning aside, she began to run fast, back to the *pension*.

★

157

'You didn't do it? What do you mean, you didn't do it?'

'I couldn't go through with it, Alice. I'm sorry, but I just couldn't.' With Alice staring at her as though she was insane, Thomasine was unable to explain the revulsion that had seized her in that dirty alleyway.

'All the trouble I went to!' Alice was furious. 'You do know, I suppose, that what I was helping you do was illegal? That we could both have ended up in some filthy French prison? And the *money —*'

'I'll pay you back as soon as I can, Alice.' She was shivering, her coat still clutched around her.

Alice, dressed in her nightgown, was throwing things into a suitcase. 'With what? Where are you going to get money? How are you going to feed yourself and the brat? Had you thought about that?'

Thomasine shook her head. She had not planned, she had not been careful. She had nothing with which to support herself. Her belief that she would be able to continue to dance had been a self-delusion, she now knew — pregnant or with a tiny baby, she would not be able to dance.

'Well, you're on your own now,' Alice said sharply. She sat on her suitcase in order to clip the locks. 'I'm off first thing tomorrow morning — I've found a job. I've got to look after myself, haven't I? I've tried to help you, Thomasine, but if you won't be helped . . .'

Alice climbed into bed and switched out the light. Sitting on the edge of the bed, staring into the darkness, Thomasine's mind darted round like a rat in a trap searching for a way out. But she could see only blind alleyways and unclimbable obstacles.

Early in the morning, Alice, still angry, made a cold farewell. When she had gone, the room seemed empty, and the paucity of her own possessions alarmed Thomasine. An empty purse, a few clothes, writing paper and pens. Poppy had left Paris the previous day; most of the other English girls had found work or had already returned home. She was alone in a foreign country.

Thomasine threw on her clothes and went outside, unable to bear the silence of the room. She would have to quit the *pension* anyway: she had no money to pay the rent. She walked in no particular direction, but eventually found herself facing the wide glittering expanse of the Seine. The sunlight mocked her, failing to erase the dark terror of the previous night.

All Paris was on holiday, so there were no boatloads of laughing tourists travelling up and down the river, and few ferrymen. The Jardin des Tuileries lay behind her, the Pont Royal spanning the river to the Left Bank. Thomasine walked along the bridge, stopping about halfway, leaning her arms on the parapet. The river, deep and flat and calm, gleamed beneath her. She realized that for the first time in her life she simply had no idea where she was going. Always before – on that nightmarish ride to the mission hospital, on the long voyage from Africa, then travelling first to Drakesden, and, years later, to London – she had had a destination in mind. But now she was directionless. Now the future trapped her, and she could not see which way to travel.

At the beginning of August they began to drift away from Paris: first Jean-Luc, then Ettie, then Julian and Belle, and at last, Boy.

Nicholas witnessed their departures with a well-disguised alarm. He did not like to be alone. Although Lally was nominally still staying at the Crillon, Nicholas saw less of her. That morning Lally, too, had made her farewells. 'No one's in Paris now, Nick,' she told him. 'And Marcel has the most adorable little place in Le Touquet. Do come.'

Nicholas did not explain to Lally his reluctance to quit Paris during its dead season. He stayed for Thomasine, because Thomasine gave him something that he thought he had lost for ever. Her strength nourished him: her energy and vitality infected him, replacing what the War had taken from him. She gave him direction. With her, he could abandon some of the destructive rituals that had sustained him over the past years; with her, he did not hate himself quite so much. He believed that if he could stay with Thomasine, if he need not return to Drakesden for a very long time, he could pick up the pieces again and fix them together into something almost like a man.

That morning, he walked to Thomasine's *pension*. As he turned the corner into the narrow street, he caught sight of her just a few yards ahead of him, fitting her key to the door. He called out her name and she spun round.

'Nick.'

He noticed how pale she was, how dark-eyed. He felt a flutter of panic. Tuberculosis, he thought, caused by the sort of life she led – the late nights, the poor and infrequent meals . . .

He said anxiously, 'Are you all right? You look ill.'

She shook her head. 'I'm fine. Just a little tired, that's all. And worried.'

He took her arm and said, 'Tell me what you're worried about, Thomasine. I may be able to help.'

He noticed the bleakness in her eyes. In the interval of silence, the list of horrors that might have befallen her multiplied in his mind. Sickness . . . injury . . . trouble with the authorities . . .

'The show's closed, Nick. The thing is . . . it's awfully silly and awfully embarrassing, but I haven't enough money to get home. I haven't enough for the ferry and train fare.'

At first, he almost wanted to laugh with relief. Such a trivial thing, the lack of a few francs for a train fare. Then he thought, *home*. Thomasine was going back to England.

'I shouldn't ask you, Nicholas, I know it isn't right. But most of my friends have already gone, and I can't find any more work. I have tried, but . . .' Her voice trailed away.

Nicholas delved into the inside pocket of his jacket, fishing out the crumpled notes and odd coins. 'Look. Here you are. Have as much as you need.' The money fell into her hands, spilling on to the pavement. Several hundred-franc notes, a stream of francs and centimes.

'Oh – I don't need all that! It's too much – really, Nick –'

He said anxiously, 'Where will you go when you return to England? To London? To Drakesden?'

She shook her head. 'I don't know. I haven't decided.'

'Do you *want* to go back to England, Thomasine?'

She smiled at last, a watery, tentative smile. 'Not really. But I can't think what else to do.'

He said, 'Stay here with me.'

She stared at him. Nicholas knelt on the pavement, picking up some of the fallen money. A ten-franc piece rolled unheeded into the gutter, a gust of hot dry wind blew one of the notes on to the road. Kneeling there, he saw with a clarity he had not experienced for years what he must do. The idea almost paralysed him, almost made him unable to speak.

'Marry me,' he croaked, looking up at her.

He knew, as soon as he had asked her, that she must accept him. He could not bear to lose her again. Without her, his life would begin to fall apart once more.

'Please, Thomasine,' he said. He could not keep the desperation out of his voice. 'Please marry me.'

He could not believe his good fortune when, slowly, still staring at him, she inclined her head. He rose then, and put his arm round her. The gesture of affection seemed natural, merited. He knew that she would change him, that she would make something better of him. He bent and kissed the top of her head, and her hair felt soft and silky against his face. His hand curled around her shoulder, so small and thin-boned, and he marvelled at his new-found ability to touch, to express love.

'Marry me,' Nicholas Blythe had said, and then he had hailed a taxi and taken her to the luxurious hotel in which he was staying, and fed her sips of champagne and morsels of smoked salmon.

And she had accepted him. She had experienced such violent swings of emotion over the past week that now all that was left to her was a sort of uneasy disbelief, an inability to accept the fact that Nicholas Blythe had asked her to marry him, and that she had accepted.

'We'll go to Le Touquet,' Nicholas was saying. 'The others are all there. We'll find a good hotel. We'll go out to restaurants every day and dance into the small hours every night. I'll buy you all the frocks you want, Thomasine, all the jewellery. And in the autumn we'll tour Europe. The south of France . . . Spain . . . Italy . . .'

At last, some of Nicholas's pleasure and excitement began to infect her. She need not return to England; she could travel again. How glorious, to see those places, to breathe that different air . . .

'But – Drakesden,' she said suddenly. 'Don't you have to go back to Drakesden?'

Nicholas shook his head and poured out some more champagne. 'Oh, no, Pa'll look after the place for ages yet. He doesn't need me. Besides, I'm no earthly good at farming. It bores me stiff. We wouldn't need to go back for simply years.'

'But your *mother*,' she whispered.

'Mama? What's Mama got to do with it?'

She tried to explain. 'Lady Blythe would want someone better for you, Nick. A debutante – an heiress. Not someone like me.'

Not Thomasine Thorne. Not the Misses Harkers' niece, who had never fitted in at Drakesden, who had never given the Blythes the respect they believed their due. Who had never known her place.

'Thomasine.' Nicholas took her hands in his. 'I've never wanted to marry anyone but you. Not ever.'

She looked up at him and saw the naked love in his eyes. She knew suddenly that, compared to Nicholas's feelings for her, her love for Clive Curran had been a tawdry affair, composed only of duplicity and physical desire. She had mistaken desire for love; she would not make that mistake again.

And yet it was Clive's baby that she carried. Lady Blythe's cold blue eyes watched her, negating the excitement and happiness in Nicholas's voice. *Girls of your type can so easily go to the bad.* She could not go through with it. She could not do this to Nicholas, to herself. She could not carry out such a vast deception. Thomasine started to speak, but Nicholas silenced her.

'Do you want a big wedding? White dress, all the frills? Or something quieter?'

She heard herself whisper, 'Something quieter, please, Nick.'

If she did not marry Nicholas Blythe, then what would she do? Would she shame the women who had so generously and so lovingly brought her up? Would she attempt for a second time to kill the child growing in her womb? Would she go to the workhouse? Or worse – she recalled an unfortunate pregnant maid from Drakesden, who had ended up not at the workhouse, but immured indefinitely in the asylum, her immorality supposedly the product of hereditary feeble-mindedness. The recollection made her shiver.

'I'm so glad.' Nicholas squeezed her hand. 'That's what I think, too. I should loathe all that fuss, but if you really wanted it . . . And I don't think we should wait too long, do you, Thomasine?'

Mutely, she shook her head.

'I'll tell you what – I'll get a special licence. I know a chap at the consulate. It can all be done within a couple of weeks. I'm twenty-three now, so I don't need my parents' permission. What about you, Thomasine?'

'I was twenty-one in June.' Over the last few weeks she had become fond of Nicholas Blythe; and long ago in Drakesden, she had liked him for his generosity, his eagerness to please.

'Then we don't need to ask anyone's permission,' he said, smiling.

CHAPTER SIX

THEY married two weeks later. Thomasine wore a silk dress from Fortuny, a waterfall of sea-green swirling pleats. Nicholas had wanted to buy her a white dress, but she had refused. 'I'm too pale,' she said. 'I'll look like a ghost.'

The wedding took place at the British Consulate in the Rue Montolivet. Nicholas's schoolfriend acted as a witness at the brief ceremony. Thomasine carried the small posy of rosebuds that Nicholas had bought her from a market-stall that morning. The sun glared through the blinds covering the consulate's windows, and dust-motes danced in the bleached, dirty light.

Halfway through the ceremony she thought, I am marrying Nicholas Blythe and planning to cheat him in the worst possible way. She knew, with utter certainty, that what she was doing was wrong. It was as though her life had slid on to an incorrect course, and there was only a moment left to halt that sliding.

She did not grasp the moment. She heard herself repeating the words, felt Nicholas's ring as he slipped it on to her finger. When they had finished signing their names, they walked out of the building and into the sunshine. Nicholas's schoolfriend pelted them with rice and rose petals, and strangers smiled as they ran down the steps.

She was his wife.

'I'd better send a telegram,' Nicholas said uneasily, as they walked away from the consulate.

In the *bureau de poste*, he concocted messages to send to his parents, to Lally. 'We'll drive north this afternoon. I won't give a forwarding address.'

Nicholas's eyes were bright, conspiratorial. He reminded Thomasine of how he had looked when, years ago, he had uncovered the bottle of wine that he had hidden beneath the statue of the Firedrake. As though marriage, too, was a schoolboy prank, something he would not do while his mother was watching.

'You should telegraph your aunts.'

She could not think what to write. In the end she scribbled: 'Married Nicholas Blythe at 11 a.m. today. All love, Thomasine', and prayed wordlessly that somehow Hilda and Antonia would understand.

'Do you want to dine in Paris?' Nicholas asked, when the telegrams had been sent. 'Or shall we drive a little first?'

'We'll drive a little.'

She wanted to leave Paris as soon as possible. Threading her hand around Nicholas's arm, Thomasine tried to smile at him. She thought once again how different he was to Clive. There were no endearments with Nicholas, and he rarely touched her. Yet she did not doubt that he loved her: the joy in his eyes as he had slipped the ring on to her finger had been blatant.

At the hotel they packed their bags and Nicholas paid the bill. All Thomasine's possessions fitted into the small, battered suitcase she had taken with her from London. Nicholas's suitcases were of matching leather: valises and a briefcase and hat-boxes. The motor-car was driven out of the hotel's garage for him and into the Place de la Concorde. Nicholas bent over the Delage lovingly, touching the shining paintwork with care and pride.

'Isn't she beautiful? Isn't she absolutely topping, Thomasine?'

'Topping,' she said.

He held open the door for her, and she climbed in. She had travelled in a motor-car only once before, on Armistice Day. The Delage smelt of leather and petrol and polish. Nicholas started up the engine and they swung out of the hotel forecourt, weaving around horses and carts, pedestrians and cyclists. Nicholas drove faster than Daniel had. The breeze tossed Thomasine's short hair about and tugged at the pleated folds of her dress.

'Are you cold?' shouted Nicholas, as they passed through Paris's boundaries and headed in the direction of Amiens.

'Not at all.'

The air seemed cooler, more sweetly scented. There were thick banks of flowers at the sides of the roads, and the corn stood high and golden in the fields. Flocks of birds scattered from the trees as Nicholas steered the motor-car round the narrow, winding roads; a cat darted in front of the vehicle, missing the wheels by inches. Turning another corner, Thomasine saw the herd of cows that were straggled across the track in front of them and called out. Nicholas jammed his foot on the brake, and the Delage screeched to a halt. A cloud of dust billowed in the air behind them.

The cows ambled across the road, through the open gate into a meadow. Nicholas started up the car again. He had flung off his jacket and rolled up his shirt-sleeves.

Thomasine said, 'You look so happy, Nick.'

He looked at her. He didn't speak for a moment, and then he said, 'It's odd, isn't it, how things work out? To find you in Paris – maybe my luck's changed for the better at last. I'd almost forgotten what it's like to be happy.'

She watched him turn the steering-wheel, carefully now, and noticed for the first time the long thin scars that pitted his arms from the inside of his wrists to the crooks of his elbows.

'Your poor arms,' she said.

His eyelids flickered as he looked down. 'That was the worst time. I wanted to die.'

She could tell that he was speaking the truth. She thought of Daniel, limping out of the crowds of London. *Just a scratch at Passchendaele.*

'The War?' she said.

He nodded. 'The Somme.' He didn't say any more for a while, and then he added shakily, 'But that's all over now, isn't it? I've got you.'

She felt a rush of affection for him. She sensed that he had suffered, and thought that if she could in some way ameliorate that suffering then perhaps that would begin to compensate for the awful lie that she was living. She wondered, gathering up all her courage, whether she could bring herself to say, 'I am carrying a child, Nicholas.' Whether he would forgive her, whether he could bring up another man's child as his own.

Of course not. She dismissed the idea immediately. Impossible that Nicholas Blythe, who could count back the generations for three centuries or more, should accept a bastard child as his own. A bastard as his heir, perhaps. Yet she must tell him – she must tell him today, before it was too late. When they stopped, when their every word was not almost drowned by the noise of the engine, when she felt better, then she would tell him about Clive's baby and accept the consequences, whatever they might be. Just now she was too tired and her back ached dreadfully. When, at the next village, they stopped to dine, she had to drag herself out of the motor-car. The sun was searingly hot; Thomasine rummaged in her suitcase for a hat.

'You look all in,' Nicholas said anxiously, replacing her suitcase in the Delage.

'It's been a long day. I'll be better when I've had something to eat.'

She couldn't eat, though. She did not seem to be able to swallow the food. She moved the ham and artichokes around with a fork, trying to make them seem less. Shaded by the leaves of a large walnut tree, she and Nicholas drank a bottle of tart red wine. The wine dulled the backache, and dulled her guilt. When she climbed back into the motor-car and Nicholas began to drive, she felt lulled by the rhythm of the wheels on the rough surface of the road. Travelling, she had to face neither the past nor the future. The problems of the future were enormous, terrible, but she did not have to deal with them now. All the decisions that must be made could be postponed for a little while.

She was almost asleep when she felt it. The small flow of

blood between her legs, something she was accustomed to dealing with each month. Only it should not be happening now. Alice had told her that when a girl was expecting a baby, the curse stopped.

Nicholas drove on in silence. Houses, fields, rivers flashed by. The roads were empty of people and traffic, the sun still high in the sky. Thomasine felt the small wetness again, and this time she was sure. Her back and the lower part of her belly ached. She found herself thinking, My dress. I'll spoil my lovely Fortuny dress.

Nicholas said, 'Are you all right? Are you feeling ill?'

She managed to get hold of herself. 'I'm fine. It's just that –' she felt herself going red – 'I need to powder my nose.'

Nicholas too flushed. 'I'm so sorry – I didn't think –' He slowed the motor-car and stared wildly about. There were only fields and trees and streams.

'Can you wait until the next village?'

'I don't think so. Just stop here, Nicholas. There's a hedge over there I can hide behind. There's no one around.'

Thomasine found herself trampling through a field of sunflowers, clutching her handbag. She wanted to laugh at the ludicrousness of it all, but when she squatted and looked and saw the spots of blood on her underclothes, she didn't want to laugh any more. She wanted Alice, she wanted Aunt Hilly. She wanted someone to explain to her what was happening. She didn't have any towels in her handbag, so she rolled up a handkerchief and hoped for the best. Heading back through the sunflowers, she knew that she could not tell Nicholas. She herself did not understand what was happening to her and, besides, she did not have the vocabulary for such things. Women's bodies were shameful and secret; you did not talk about them, least of all to men.

Nicholas looked worried when she returned. Thomasine forced herself to smile at him.

'Perhaps we shouldn't drive much further, Nick. After all, it must be quite late.'

He glanced at his watch. 'It's almost seven. Thoughtless of me, to drag you so far.'

'Not at all – I've enjoyed it. It's lovely to get away from Paris.'

Her words sounded to her own ears so ordinary, so banal. As they drove on, the backache intensified. Is my baby dying? she thought. What if I should die?

Nicholas drove to the next small town. In the lobby of the town's only hotel, he signed the register. Mr and Mrs Nicholas Blythe, he wrote, and gave their address as Drakesden Abbey, Drakesden, Cambridgeshire, England. To Thomasine it all seemed increasingly unreal, as though she had accidentally strayed into someone else's dream. One room, she thought, as he pocketed the key. Stupid of her not to have thought of that before. They were man and wife – of course they would share a room.

She found a ladies' lavatory while Nicholas carried their suitcases into the bedroom. Inside the lavatory, she sat shaking with fear and panic. Something was going wrong; she did not know what to do. The ache was a pain now, and her handkerchief was soaked in blood. She dealt with the mess as best as she could. Back in the bedroom, Nicholas was dressing for dinner, knotting a black tie around the stiff collar of his shirt.

'Could you . . .?' he said, indicating the tie. 'I'm never much good with these things. Mama or Lally usually tie them for me.'

'I don't know how. I've no brothers, remember, Nick – no father.'

'Poor darling.'

It was the first time he had called her that. She went to him then, and leaned her head against his chest. He put his arms around her, and he stroked her hair. She needed comfort, and Nicholas was offering her comfort.

'I'll be your father, your brothers,' he whispered. 'I'll look after you, Thomasine. You'll never have to worry about money again – you'll never have to work again. I'll make everything all right for you.'

She could see the scars on his inner arm, deeply and cruelly incised. They were both damaged, she thought – Nicholas with his disfigured arms, she with the child that seemed to be oozing out of her body. She closed her eyes, and felt his arms around her, warm and strong.

Thomasine guessed by nightfall that she was losing her child. The spots of blood thickened, became clotted. In the blessed privacy of an hotel bathroom, she ran the bath taps as an alibi, but did not dare climb into the bath. When the cramps became unbearable, she crouched on the lavatory and could not afterwards bear to look down. She felt as though her insides had disgorged themselves, along with her unwanted child. She lost track of how long she remained in the unfamiliar room, curled up in a corner, her head on her knees.

Eventually she cut up one of the hotel towels with her nail scissors, wrapping it between her legs. Somehow she got through dinner, eating nothing, terrified that she might faint. She drank more wine, and it enabled her to walk back up the narrow, winding stairs to the bedroom. Inside the bedroom, with the door closed and the lamps on, Nicholas looked awkward, embarrassed. He was fumbling with his tie again. His stiff white shirt crackled as he wrestled with the studs to take it off. Thomasine glanced at the big double bed with its square French bolsters and patchwork quilt.

Of course, they had been married today. She did not feel like Nicholas's wife – more like his friend, or perhaps his sister. Marriages had to be consummated.

Yet this marriage could not yet be consummated. She felt her face grow hotter and redder, and sweat prickled on her scalp. When Nicholas was dressed in his pyjamas and he came to sit on the edge of the bed beside her, she knew that she could not put off the moment any longer.

'Nicholas. I'm sorry. I can't . . .'

'I won't hurt you,' he said. 'I'd never hurt you, Thomasine – you must believe that.'

She hated herself. 'It's not that. It's just that — I can't tonight. I've the curse, you see.'

A wave of relief mingled with the pain and exhaustion. She had found the right words, the right lie. When she looked up at Nicholas, Thomasine was surprised to see relief on his face too, mixed with embarrassment.

'Oh. I didn't know . . .'

She managed to smile. 'Why should you? It's just bad timing.'

He said hesitantly, 'Shall I get another room? Would you rather be alone?'

'No. There's no need for that. We can cuddle, can't we?'

They climbed into bed together and Nicholas put out the light. He did not touch her at first, but then his arms went round her, and they lay together, curled like spoons, her back against his front. Gradually the ache in her belly began to lessen.

At last, Nicholas slept. The tears moved then only very slowly and silently down Thomasine's face. She was glad then of the comfort of Nicholas Blythe's arms, glad that she was not alone.

Daniel and Fay married in September. The reception was held at Fay's parents' house in Kilburn. It was an awkward, stilted affair; Fay's younger sisters silent with the effort of behaving well, Daniel's sister Nell awed into similar silence by her first visit to London. Hattie and Fay's mother struggled to keep the conversation going. The cold ham and egg sandwiches curled in the mid-September heat. The icing on the wedding-cake crumbled as Daniel and Fay cut the first slice.

They took the train from Liverpool Street to Ely that afternoon, and Daniel hired a cab to take them from Ely to Drakesden. They had heavy luggage, and Fay was wearing light, high-heeled shoes.

'Just here,' said Daniel, as the cab approached the cottage.

He hauled out Fay's suitcase and his own haversack. It was

early evening and the weather was still fine and clear. Daniel slung the haversack over his shoulder and picked up the suitcase.

As always, when he came back to Drakesden after a long absence, he let his gaze travel slowly over the allotment, across the field that had once belonged to the Blythes, to the dyke. The dyke was a flat, high, green line against the sky. The sky was vast.

Then he glanced back at Fay. She looked so beautiful in her cream-coloured dress, the spray of pink rosebuds he had given her that morning still pinned to her breast. He could not quite make out the expression on her face, though. He waited for her to say something, to remark on the hours of work he had completed in the allotment, or the beauty of her new home. But she said nothing. She was tired, of course. It had been a long, confusing day. And she was a little homesick, perhaps.

Daniel squeezed her hand. 'We're going to have to go in through the back door, Fay, I'm afraid. The front's been nailed up for decades.'

She glanced from the cottage, to the field, and back to the cottage again. 'This is it? *This?*'

He realized then how different Drakesden was from all that she was used to. 'It's only a small cottage, darling, but it'll do us for a while. And when I've money to spare, we can easily build an extra room or two alongside. There's plenty of land.'

Fay said wildly, 'But I thought – I thought it would be *thatched . . .*'

Daniel explained, 'Some of the houses in the village are thatched with sedge, but my father had the cottage roofed with tiles the year he married my mother. He was a blacksmith, you see, and thatch would have been a terrible fire risk.'

She was staring at him. 'Your father was a blacksmith?'

He nodded. 'I used to help him. There was a lean-to built against that wall, but it fell derelict during the War. I'll build you something better, Fay. I promise you. And now –'

He lifted her up in his arms, then. Her eyes, as she looked up at him, were bright and dark and her face was slightly flushed. As he carried her over the threshold of the cottage, he thought how light she was, scarcely any weight at all. He was aware suddenly of the responsibility he had taken on, of the promises he had made that morning, of how it was now his duty, and his alone, to protect her.

He set her down on the floor very carefully. He noticed that she was trembling slightly. He said, very gently, 'I know it isn't much, Fay, but it's ours. I'll work hard for you, I promise, and things will soon get better. The land is good and fertile, and who knows? In time I may be able to buy more. I'll work night and day, I swear it.'

'But where do we eat?' said Fay, suddenly looking round. 'And where do we sleep?'

'We eat in here. We used to fit seven of us round this table. But I'll build a drawing-room or parlour for you soon, where the old lean-to used to be. I'll knock through a door, and then you can have tea-parties or whatever you want.'

She was beginning to look a little happier. Carefully, Daniel lifted off her lavender-coloured close-fitting hat, so that he could kiss the top of her head.

'And as for a bed – well, I can show you that.'

He led her to the foot of the ladder. There, he took her in his arms and kissed her on her forehead, her cheeks, her mouth, her neck. Then he followed up the ladder after her.

When Daniel described to her what he intended to do to the cottage and the farm, Fay saw it all for a while through his eyes, and was comforted. He would build a drawing-room downstairs to one side of the kitchen, and a scullery and bathroom to the other. Upstairs, he would add a second bedroom. He would replace that dreadful ladder with a proper staircase.

When Daniel was not there, however, the dreams faded. Fay needed Daniel to ignite her own rather limited imagination. When he was working on the farm, which seemed to Fay to be all of the time, then her discontent and disillusionment returned and she saw only the meanness of the tiny house, the dreariness of the flat, featureless lands.

She tried, though. The same ambition and self-interest that had enabled her to rise at dawn each day to travel from Kilburn to Kensington, that had enabled her, in her cramped home, to be always neatly turned out, helped her try to make something of her marriage. She recognized too that, although Daniel was not the gentleman she had believed him to be, he was nevertheless respected in the small village. The rector spoke to Daniel and Fay for a good ten minutes when they met him in the street one day, and various neighbours inspected the allotment and the cottage and complimented Daniel on the improvements he had made. Fay offered the neighbours tea and cakes, while secretly despising them. Their clothes were dreadful – twenty years out of date – and they spoke in a peculiar flat, drawling accent. She did not, as Daniel had hoped she might, consider any of the women as possible friends. They were not her sort and, besides, she had never really had friends. Phyllis had been useful, a necessary companion for trips to the cinema or the shops, but that was all.

She tried hard to cope with the inconveniences of the cottage and the village. The grocer's shop was hopeless – a few flyblown tin-cans in the window, a rusty advertisement for Reckitts Blue, and nothing interesting to look at inside. She went with Daniel to the market in Ely, and Ely, thank goodness, had a little more to offer. Once a week or so, a pedlar or carter would call round and Fay would buy herself a length of ribbon or a piece of material. She was determined to look after herself, not to let herself go like so many of the other women in the village.

It was all so different to London. Often she woke at night, startled by the silence. There was nowhere to walk, nothing to look at. No picture-house or theatre, no dress shops. Fay was proud that Daniel did not expect her to work in the fields. Many of the village women worked in the fields alongside their husbands, and Fay despised them for it. They looked like dirty peasants, she thought, with their straw hats and old headscarves, their shapeless black skirts and hessian aprons. A few of the women even helped with the turf cutting. By the time they reached middle age, their bodies were bowed and twisted, their faces permanently bent towards the soil.

Daniel taught Fay to feed the hens, to search for eggs. She thought the hens ugly, with their red-lidded eyes, their silly, nodding gait. There was some satisfaction in finding an egg, though, warm and freckled-brown, hidden in a corner of the garden. Fay always kept her eyes averted from the pigsty. The pig, with its small, stupid black eyes, frightened her.

The cottage itself was inconvenient and hard to look after. Dirt gathered in the gaps in the brick floor, and there always seemed to be a layer of black dust on the window-sills and mantelpiece. Water had to be collected each day from the butt or the well. The water-closet was a horror: the night-soil man emptied it daily, but Fay could not bring herself to clean it. The kitchen range, with its doors and pipes and hot-plates, was impossible. Her mother had always cooked for her; Fay did not like to cook.

Daniel was out one day, and Fay made a pie. The steak that she had bought from the butcher had cost almost all of the rest of the week's housekeeping money, and she had great difficulty making the pastry stick together. She was sure, though, that when it was cooked, it would be delicious. Daniel never complained about her cooking, but they seemed to have eaten an awful lot of tinned soup and sardines recently.

She had forgotten to feed the range and the fire had gone out hours ago, so Fay placed the turf in the range as Daniel had shown her, and dumped a handful of kindling on top. Then, kneeling on the brick floor, she struck a match. The kindling flared, fizzled, and went out. Fay lit another match. The same thing happened. She jabbed the turf with the poker, and struck a third match. Her knees were getting sore and she had the beginnings of a headache.

When she had used a dozen matches and the fire had failed to light, Fay seized a handful of the remaining matches, flung them on top of the kindling and dropped a lit match on top. Then, her face in the doorway of the range, she blew. Black smoke blew back at her and she coughed and choked.

'*Beastly* thing!' cried Fay, standing up and stamping her foot.

She heard Daniel say from the doorway, 'You look like something from *The Arabian Nights*. You're all black.'

Tears of frustration streamed down her face, making tracks through the soot. 'It doesn't work! There's something wrong with the beastly thing!'

Daniel peered into the doorway of the range. 'You've used the damp turf, that's all. The driest is in the pile next to the wall.' He straightened up. 'Oh, darling, don't cry. You'll get used to it.'

'Never!' cried Fay. 'Never!'

Daniel dipped his handkerchief into the water-bucket. 'It's just a bit cranky, that's all.' He squeezed Fay's shoulder. 'Most of the other cottages only have open fires. It's better than that, isn't it, Fay?'

Slightly mollified, she turned towards him. He began to wipe the smuts from her face with his handkerchief.

'I was making you a pie,' she said sulkily.

He looked at the dish in the oven. The pastry looked grey and hard, and some of the fluted edges had collapsed.

Daniel said doubtfully, 'It looks lovely. Dry your face, darling, and I'll light the range.'

While he was raking out the damp turf and replacing it with dry, Fay combed her hair and powdered her nose. She felt hot and cross and dispirited.

When the fire had caught and the oven was starting to warm up, Daniel said, 'I've bought you a present. Well – it's for both of us, really, but you must use it whenever you want.'

He looked very pleased with himself. Dragging her heels, shaking the soot from her dress, Fay followed him out into the courtyard.

'Look,' said Daniel.

176

She followed the direction of his gaze. A bicycle was propped against the wall-head.

'I know you're not too keen on poor old Nelson, so I thought that would be the very thing. It'll mean you can get about a bit more. I bought it in Ely. It needs a new coat of paint, that's all.'

Fay said, alarmed, 'But I can't ride a bicycle!'

'I know.' Daniel slid his arm around her shoulders and hugged her. 'I'm going to teach you.'

She allowed herself to be led over to the machine. The wheels looked enormous, the saddle was miles from the ground. There was a crossbar.

'I haven't the right clothes – my skirt will tear –'

'You can wear my old corduroys.' Daniel picked up the machine and gave the pedals an experimental twirl. 'Roll up the legs or something. Go on, Fay – it's time for your first lesson.'

'*Trousers,*' she said weakly. She had never in her life worn trousers.

He was grinning. 'Trousers. You'll ruin your good clothes otherwise.'

When she reappeared from the bedroom five minutes later, Fay was wearing her husband's old and much-patched corduroy trousers, belted in at the waist, rolled up and tied with string at the ankles.

'I look ridiculous.'

'You look adorable.' She saw by the expression on his face that he meant it. That, even though in her own eyes she appeared ugly and foolish, to Daniel she was always beautiful She felt a momentary thrill at the power she had over him.

He was holding the bicycle steady. 'Climb on, darling. That's it. Now – you hold the handlebars and put your feet on the pedals, and I'll push.'

When the bicycle began to move, she shrieked. The hens, shrieking too, scattered out of the way, but Daniel did not stop pushing.

'Try and pedal, Fay. Push with each foot in turn. You'll soon get the hang of it.'

Her feet slipped on the pedals, and when Daniel tried to let go of the saddle the bicycle began to rock alarmingly until he caught it again. It was as bad as the kitchen range, thought Fay crossly.

'I know,' said Daniel, when he had recovered his breath, 'I'll ride and you sit on the crossbar. You might get the feel of it, then.'

Fay felt very precarious, perched on the crossbar, both legs to one side, her hands on the handlebars between Daniel's. But when he started to pedal and the bicycle gathered speed and they were travelling out of the allotment and along the edge of the field, she began to see some sense in it. She still screamed whenever they turned a corner, and still closed her eyes when finally, amid a cloud of dust and a squeal of brakes, they cycled back into the courtyard. But the speed was exhilarating and enjoyable.

Daniel slid off the saddle and caught Fay in his arms. 'There. What do you think?'

His eyes were green and glittering. She knew that he wanted her, and she knew also that, rather to her surprise, she wanted him. Then she saw the cloud of black smoke issuing from out of the kitchen door.

'The pie!' Fay cried, and ran inside.

Away from London, working outdoors all day, Daniel's health improved rapidly. His leg still ached at the end of each day, but now that was the normal ache of tiredness. He slept soundly at night, waking early to feed the animals. Fay slept in for an hour or two more. Dressing each morning, Daniel loved to watch her as she slept.

He worked from sunrise to sunset, and as he worked he felt the shadows of the last years, of the War and its aftermath, slip steadily away from him. His fear of confined spaces did not taunt him, because out here nothing seemed confined. Less and less at night he heard the cries of his fellow-officers trapped beneath the mud. If he did dream, then there was Fay beside him, to hold until he was comforted.

He began to read again, borrowing books from the Public Library in Ely, occasionally buying them from the second-hand bookshops. Sometimes, when he was digging or ploughing, phrases, sentences, occasionally even paragraphs began to form in his mind. Fragments of stories, a recounting of some of the things that he had seen. He did not write anything down: he was afraid that as soon as he put pen to paper what few words he had would dissolve and disappear, and he would be left as mute and confused as he had been before.

He had bought an old army horse to help with the ploughing. Nelson was a battered and nervous casualty of the Somme. Like his namesake, he was one-eyed; like Daniel, he shunned loud noises and bustle. He was a good worker, though, and if treated with care and respect would consent to be ridden. Nelson patiently dragged the plough and the harrow through Daniel's eighteen acres of land, making the soil ready for the spring planting.

For Daniel, during the first autumn of his marriage, it was as though things had started to come right for him again after six years of veering off-course. He knew who was responsible for his happiness, and he did his best to see that Fay, too, was content. She found the adjustment to country life more difficult than he expected, however. The paucity of shops, the hours of physical labour involved in farming seemed a source of continuing surprise to her. Daniel made sure that he did as much of the hard labour as possible. He promised himself that he would never make a drudge of Fay: the memory of his mother, her body misshapen by years of continual childbearing, her hands red and worn with work, was always with him. Remembering his mother, he made sure that he and Fay would not immediately have children. Better to put off parenthood for a year or two, until the farm was running smoothly and a little money was put by. Daniel intended to give his children the sort of things he had been denied: an education, and freedom from having to work at too early an age.

He tried to teach Fay about the Fens, sure that if she understood the complicated workings of this fragile land, then she too would grow to love it. One rainy afternoon he tried to persuade her to put on galoshes and jacket and walk with him along the dyke.

'It'll ruin my hair,' she said. 'It's raining.'

She was clearing up the remains of their midday meal, a peculiar combination of rubbery scrambled egg and tinned pilchards.

'It's only a bit of drizzle,' said Daniel patiently. 'Look – it's clearing to the east.'

Eventually she pulled on her galoshes and tied a scarf round her hair. Daniel took her arm as they walked across the courtyard and allotment.

'The hens are doing well,' he said. 'That was almost three dozen eggs you collected last week, Fay.'

'The rector had a dozen and a half of them,' said Fay. 'I wish you'd come to church, Daniel. We might meet some people, then.'

They had had this conversation before, and he had tried, and failed, to explain to her that after the War all that sort of thing had seemed meaningless. What she said made him feel guilty, though. He was aware that he had taken Fay a long way from her family and friends, and that she had as yet made no friends in the village to replace them.

'Who can you meet at church that you cannot meet in the post office or at the shop?'

'The rector himself, and his wife,' said Fay. Her voice had begun to sound a little sulky. She picked her way carefully through the mud and grass. 'And the Blythes.'

They had reached the boundary of the allotment, the fence that had once marked the boundary of the Gillorys' land. Mine, soon, thought Daniel proudly, glancing at the fields that Hattie had bought.

He tried to explain. 'You don't know what it's like here, Fay.

The rector would never invite you or I into his house – we aren't his equals. I used to work for Mr Fanshawe, sometimes, when I was a boy, weeding his garden. Things haven't changed that much since. He'll buy our eggs and vegetables, but we'll never sit at the same table.'

'But the *War* –' said Fay. 'You were an *officer* –'

'That doesn't make any difference here. Here, I'm still Daniel Gillory, the blacksmith's son.'

He gave her his hand and helped her over the fence. 'As for the Blythes –' he began carefully – 'well – you don't "meet" people like them. You work for them, or you doff your cap or curtsy to them in the street. If you break their rules, then you'll find yourself out of a job and out of your home. Most of the cottages in Drakesden are tied to Drakesden Abbey, Fay. *Owned* by the Blythes, that is.'

He heard the bitterness in his voice, but could not disguise it. He took Fay's hand, following the narrow path that led round the edge of the ploughed field towards the dyke.

He heard her say, 'But not our cottage, Daniel.'

'No.' This time there was grim satisfaction and pride in his voice. 'My great-grandfather bought the cottage and the land. It's prone to flooding, but I'll make something of it.'

They had reached the foot of the dyke. Daniel climbed up a little way, and held out his hand to Fay.

'It's so slippery – I'm going to fall –'

'I won't let you fall.' He steadied her, and then she was there beside him, on top of the bank. To one side of them was the field that Hattie had bought for him, to the other, the dyke, swollen with the autumn rains. 'Be careful – don't go too near the edge of the dyke.'

Fay glanced down at the water. 'It's horrible. So dark and muddy.'

'And dangerous. If a horse or a cow falls in the water, Fay, then they're often lost, because no one has the strength to pull them out. And every winter you hear of a child drowned.'

'Horrible,' said Fay again.

'But necessary. Without the dyke to hold in the water, we wouldn't have the farm. It would all be inundated.'

He explained to her then how different the Fens were now from how they had been four hundred years before. How Vermuyden and his Dutchmen had changed the landscape for ever – or until the waters found their way back again, and the land returned to the swamps and lakes from which it had been stolen. He explained to her that neither Vermuyden nor anyone else had foreseen the problem that grew more critical each year: that as the peat dried out, it sank, forcing the Fens gradually further and further below sea-level.

He wasn't sure whether she was listening. The wind had picked up, whipping up her hair and blowing it against her face.

'I don't know why they bothered,' Fay said, unimpressed. 'It sounds a lot of trouble for a few fields.'

'The best farmland in England,' said Daniel softly. 'That's why they bothered.'

'We'll be rich, then?'

He laughed. 'I hope so. Especially if I can buy more land.'

From where they stood, high on the dyke-wall, the pattern of fields and rivers and ditches was spread out before them. The village of Drakesden to one side, their own cottage and allotment straggling away from the village, the island to the other. To the right of Daniel, all the fields were Abbey land.

'I'd like to buy more,' he explained. 'I'd like that field – and that.' He pointed to the ploughed black earth in front of them. 'I'd have more than twenty acres then, which would entitle me to become a Drainage Commissioner. The drainage in the South Level is a mess – and no one will do anything about it, no doubt, until there's a bad winter, and we all end up under water. Perhaps if I was a commissioner I could give someone a kick up the backside.'

'*Daniel,*' said Fay reprovingly. Then, 'When will you buy those fields?'

'I don't know.' He grimaced. 'When I've money enough. When they are for sale.'

182

He thought, when the Blythes have to rid themselves of a bit more of their land to pay for their peacocks and their fountains and their fancy jewellery. *Soon.*

She had wandered a short distance away from him, down the bank, towards the clump of stunted trees that stood at the corner of Hattie's fields. He wondered whether Nicholas Blythe had learned yet that he, Daniel Gillory, whom Nicholas believed to be a thief and a liar, farmed the land that his family had once owned. It was a small, but very enjoyable, vengeance. The land that he now farmed would earn him little until next summer, and there was still his debt to Hattie to repay. The money that he had saved from his year in the advertising agency was dwindling rapidly. The initial outlay on the farm had been unavoidably large, even though he had bought second-hand equipment where possible. Housekeeping seemed to cost Fay rather more than Daniel had originally estimated, and although prices for agricultural products were now high, Daniel was unconvinced that they would remain high. He knew that he must be careful, very careful, particularly in this first year.

'Daniel! *Daniel!*'

Fay's voice broke through his thoughts. He heard terror in her calling of his name, and a matching terror made sweat break out on his forehead as he ran down the bank towards her. She was standing in the clump of trees. Her face was white, her features rigid with fear.

'Darling – what is it?'

She pointed with a quivering finger to the hollowed, muddy roots of the hawthorn tree. A snake lay coiled in the roots, sheltered from the drizzle, old and brown and sleeping. Fay was sobbing.

'It's only an old grass snake,' said Daniel gently, drawing her to him, stroking her head. 'It won't hurt you, love.'

'I thought – I thought it would sting me –'

'Grass snakes don't bite, darling. Honestly.'

He began to kiss her, his lips brushing against her damp eyelids, her wet mouth. His fingers threaded through her dark hair, and he drew her towards him. The snake uncoiled itself and slid away into the longer grass of the bank, and Daniel pulled Fay down to the ground and made love to her there, the fragrance of her skin mingling with the scent of the warm, wet earth.

Lady Blythe saw him on the way to church one morning. William's rheumatism increasingly discouraged him from stirring out of the house, and the drizzle was constant, making it impossible for Gwendoline to walk. She rode stiff-backed in the rear seat of the Daimler, travelling along the uneven road at a steady ten miles an hour.

He was walking towards her from the far end of the village, in the direction of the church. She noticed him because his head was uncovered, even in the drizzle, even though it was Sunday. A scruffy young man, she thought contemptuously, not yet recognizing him. Standards had declined so much since the War. The young woman at his side wore a coat and hat, both lavender coloured. The small bunches of artificial silk flowers pinned to her hat and her coat were wilting in the rain. She looked a vulgar type, thought Gwendoline Blythe. Her mouth appeared to be reddened with lipstick. For *church*.

The Daimler drew up outside the lych-gate. The young couple had almost reached the church. The chauffeur opened the door, and Lady Blythe, in a great gathering of Edwardian skirts and coat, allowed herself to be helped out.

She found herself face to face with him, then. Daniel Gillory was taller, older, of course, but she recognized him instantly. The golden-brown hair, curled by the rain, the straight nose and mouth. The same green-hazel eyes stared at her with much the same shocked expression as they had more than six years ago. She almost expected to hear the thunder that should accompany the rain, to see lightning flare in the dull grey sky. His physical presence seemed almost overpowering as she recalled quite clearly, as though it were yesterday, this man embracing her daughter. The expression in his eyes changed now from shock to a sort of insolent amusement mixed with triumph.

She walked past Daniel Gillory, making, of course, no acknowledgement. She was aware, though, that he had taken his leave of the young woman, and was walking away from the church. Heads bowed and bobbed as she passed the villagers and entered the porch, but Daniel Gillory had not bowed. She felt, as she had felt when she had found him with Lally all those years ago, physically ill. If anything, it was worse now, because he was a man and not a boy.

Lady Blythe's thoughts as she prayed were not ones of Christian forgiveness and reconciliation. All the pent-up anger of the previous months consumed her. She was late with the responses, unable to remember the melodies of the hymns.

When the service was over, she was, as usual, the first to leave the church. She said, pausing briefly in the porch, 'You must call at the Abbey this afternoon, Rector. Around four o'clock will be convenient.' Then she walked to the waiting motor-car.

Sir William was in the conservatory when Lady Blythe returned from church. She peeled off her kid gloves, but did not sit down.

'Dull sermon, Gwennie?' enquired Sir William, refilling the spray.

'I don't remember.' Gwendoline picked a few dead leaves from the plumbago. 'I saw Daniel Gillory, William.' She had to force the name out: it felt like acid in her throat.

'Gillory?' said William vaguely. 'The blacksmith . . .?'

'His son. Jack Gillory is dead.'

She did not say, 'Jack Gillory was killed in the War.' To do so would have been to classify him with heroes, like Gerald.

'Oh.' William sounded uninterested. He filled a terracotta pot with compost. 'Well, Drakesden is the boy's home, Gwennie. Hardly surprising, really . . .' His voice trailed away, his sentence unfinished.

Such an economy with words was an increasingly common

thing with William, nowadays. Never talkative, his phrases frequently dangled in the air, unended, as though speech, as well as money, was now in short supply at Drakesden Abbey. Gwendoline found the habit unbearably irritating.

'Gillory – *Daniel* Gillory – left Drakesden just after the War broke out, if you recall, William. Just upped and went.'

Carefully, William placed the seedling orchid in the damp soil. 'Probably joined up, Gwennie.'

A sprig of plumbago broke off in Gwendoline's hand and sky-blue petals scattered over the tiled floor. She hissed, 'He was working for us, William!'

'Yes.' He put aside his plants and glanced at her. 'It was uncivil of him, Gwendoline, but hardly important.'

She wondered, as she had wondered so many times over the years, whether she had done right to hide from William the episode involving Lally and Daniel Gillory. But to have spoken about it would have meant talking about things that she did not even like to think about. She struggled to control her revulsion.

'It is just that the Gillory boy was here, too, that summer. And since then, everything has seemed wrong.'

She turned away from him and went to the window. The glass was steamed with the heat and damp of the conservatory. When she touched the pane with her fingertips, great drops of water trickled down the glass, mimicking the rain outside.

'Nicholas and the Thorne girl,' she whispered. 'How *could* he, William? I had such hopes . . .'

When the telegram announcing Nicholas's marriage to Thomasine Thorne had arrived three months earlier, Gwendoline's first thought had been to travel to France, to dissolve the appalling and foolish match. William had dissuaded her, however. He had pointed out that as Nicholas was now over twenty-one, there were no grounds for dissolving the marriage. More significantly, as Nicholas had married, surely, for love, to cast doubts on the suitability of his bride might only alienate him. Gwendoline was sufficiently aware of Nicholas's fragile mental state to believe this to be possible. She could not have borne to lose Nicholas for ever, as she had lost Gerald. Nothing more could be done until Nicholas returned to England.

She did not believe that Nicholas had married for love, however. He had married because the Thorne girl had ensnared him, reviving his adolescent infatuation, taking advantage of his temporary weakness to secure what she had always wanted: Drakesden Abbey. The hasty marriage justified everything she had ever believed of Miss Thorne. The thought of that ill-bred young woman sharing her beloved son's bed, or carrying out the duties of the mistress of Drakesden Abbey, outraged her.

The Reverend Fanshawe arrived promptly at four o'clock. Over tea in the drawing-room, Gwendoline made the necessary enquiries.

'I was surprised to see that Daniel Gillory has returned to Drakesden, Rector.'

Her visitor squirmed guiltily in his seat, from which Lady Blythe concluded that he had known of Daniel Gillory's residence in Drakesden for some time. She continued inexorably, 'When did he come back?'

The Reverend Fanshawe helped himself to a scone, and did not meet her eyes. 'Oh – I'm not certain – a month or two, perhaps . . .'

'And the young woman he is with?'

'Mrs Gillory? She is from London. They married in September.'

There was a brief silence. It had stopped raining at last, and through the drawing-room windows a pale sun could be seen, washing the fields with silver.

'The boy's a smithy, like his father, is he?' said William suddenly. 'Less call for it now . . .'

'Ah, I don't believe that the motor-car will ever oust the horse from Drakesden, Sir William.' The rector gave a polite laugh. 'But no – Daniel is not carrying on his father's trade. He is farming.'

The news pleased Lady Blythe. 'Then he'll be gone soon

enough, no doubt,' she said briskly. 'There's not a living to be had from that squalid little patch of land.'

'Oh, no, your ladyship –' said the rector, and then stopped, his face a dull red, his teacup clanking in its saucer.

'Yes, Rector?' said Lady Blythe. Her voice was hard, like steel. 'You were saying?'

'Daniel has bought another fifteen acres. The fields that lie adjacent to the Gillory allotment.'

She did not at first realize what Mr Fanshawe meant. Then suddenly she did understand, and she had to use all her immense self-possession not to show her fury.

'*Our* fields?'

Fanshawe nodded. He looked terrified.

William said, 'But those fields were sold to a London woman. I can't remember her name . . .'

Suddenly Gwendoline guessed what Daniel Gillory had done. 'As you said, Mr Fanshawe, Gillory has spent the last few years in London. This woman is an acquaintance of his, presumably. He knew that we would not sell Blythe land to *him*.'

Her voice was like ice. She had to concentrate very hard on the simple tasks of folding her napkin and putting aside her teacup and saucer. 'You will excuse me – William, Rector.'

Inside her bedroom, Gwendoline stood at the window and looked out at the gardens, the fields, the line where earth and horizon met. She understood now the nature of the triumph she had seen that morning in Daniel Gillory's green-gold eyes. She understood also the bitterness of the battle she fought. That he might own even the smallest part of Blythe land was intolerable to her. Yet a part of her welcomed the commencement of hostilities, recognizing how much the inaction of the previous months had cost her. Once again, as in 1914, the figures of Thomasine Thorne and Daniel Gillory melded together and became one enemy, one intruder.

PART THREE

1921–1923

Though there's nothing in the larder
Don't we have fun!
Times are hard and getting harder,
Still we have fun.

(Popular Song)

CHAPTER SEVEN

THE Blythes returned to England at the beginning of 1921. Dirty snow edged the pavements, and the sky, even at midday, was dull and steely. At the corners of the streets ex-soldiers, many of them lacking an arm or a leg, held out their hats for pennies.

They took rooms in Claridges. Peering through the window at the London she had left almost eighteen months previously, Thomasine reflected on the first six months of her marriage. They had spent August in Le Touquet and then darted with increasing speed around France: Deauville, Trouville, Biarritz, Nice and Montpellier. But then letters had arrived from Nicholas's accountant and they had slowly and unwillingly driven back to Calais. Peering out at the sunless afternoon, Thomasine realized that since her wedding-day the days and weeks had muddled themselves together, so that she could not recall in which month she had visited which town, or in whose company she had sunbathed on the beach, or danced, or engaged in bright, meaningless conversation.

In one of the endless succession of French seaside towns she had visited a doctor. She had told him something of her history, and had blurted out something of her fear. That the early and unattended miscarriage had damaged her permanently, that she would not be able to have the child that both she and Nicholas longed for. She had not, of course, mentioned her other problem. She had far too much pride to explain that though her husband loved her, he only occasionally desired her.

The sympathetic French doctor offered some reassurance and prescribed a tonic. She was very young, he said. She had plenty of time. Yesterday, standing on the deck of the Channel ferry, watching the jagged waves heave and slap themselves against the sides of the boat, Thomasine had thought him wrong. She did not have plenty of time: time, and Nicholas's temporary lack of funds, had funnelled them into this boat, which would spit them out at Dover. Neither she nor Nicholas had any desire to return to England.

Doubt intruded on Thomasine when she woke in the small hours of the night, or when Nicholas insisted on yet another party, yet another evening out. Or, worst of all, after they had tried and failed to make love. They did not always fail. She did not suffer, she reminded herself, the constant jarring humiliation of an unconsummated marriage. Neither did she truly believe that Nicholas's lack of passion indicated a lack of love. His devotion to her seemed to Thomasine to be undiminished. It was her own feelings that she doubted. Her belief in the validity of a marriage prompted by necessity, and undertaken in the conviction that friendship was of greater importance than passion, had faded over the months. The one thing that might have assuaged her doubts − the conception of a child − had not happened. Each month she suffered the misery of hoping, and then of seeing her hopes crushed. Every time Nicholas turned away from her at night after no more than a chaste embrace, her misgivings increased.

Nicholas was standing behind her. He laid one hand on her shoulder in a tentative gesture of affection.

'Foul, isn't it? Like someone's pulled a curtain.'

She smiled, looking out at the heavy yellow-grey sky. 'It might snow. I'd like that.'

'We won't have to stay in England for long, Thomasine, I promise. I'll go and see my accountant and sort things out. It's just a hiccup.' Nicholas scrabbled in his pocket for his cigarette-case.

She said, voicing the greatest of her doubts, 'Will we go to Drakesden?'

Nicholas shook his head. 'Not yet. I've written to Mama.' He extracted a crumpled envelope from his pocket and waved it at Thomasine. 'Told her we're in London, would be delighted to see her, that sort of thing. I thought that was the thing to do . . . I mean . . . rather tactless just to turn up at Drakesden, perhaps . . .' His voice trailed away.

She thought of driving to Drakesden Abbey with Nicholas and walking through that great front door into the hall, with the stuffed birds and animals glassy-eyed and staring in their cages. A cold, hard knot formed in her stomach, but she said, 'I'm sure that's the right thing to do. Let's go out, shall we, Nick? I'm hungry.'

Thomasine wore a delphinium blue dress, with white silk stockings. The dress was drop-waisted, its hem halfway between ankle and knee. Round her forehead she tied a diamanté band. Nicholas, gazing at her, thought how lovely she looked. Shoving his worries to the back of his mind, he told himself that it was all right now, that he had plenty of friends in London, that he would be a better husband to Thomasine, that they would have fun.

They went to a little restaurant in Hanover Square. It was quite early, seven o'clock, and only half the tables were occupied. The comparative quiet of the restaurant made Nicholas, who preferred noise and bustle, feel uneasy, and he was glad when the pianist started to play. The music, a slow, smooth blues, seemed to pull people inside from out of the cold and the darkness. Nicholas glanced at every customer, looking for faces that he knew.

A crowd arrived at around half past eight, as Nicholas was lighting up the last cigarette in his case and stirring sugar into his coffee. When the door opened to let the new arrivals into the restaurant, they seemed to give colour and light to the room, to drown the notes of the piano with their shrieks of laughter. The girls' dresses glittered with jewellery and the shoulders of the men's coats sparkled with snow, like diamonds.

Nicholas studied the new arrivals, recognizing some of their faces. He remembered Bobby Monkfield from Winchester – Bobby had been a year or two younger than Nicholas, but that didn't matter nowadays. If Nicholas had counted up his classmates, he would have found a third of them gone, killed in the Great War. Nicholas also remembered Bobby's sister, Lavender, from cricket matches and Speech Days. She had changed. The sturdy schoolgirl had metamorphosed into a tall young woman, her shoulders fashionably drooping, her gestures languid.

Some of the other faces he thought he remembered from Deauville or Le Touquet, but he could not pin names to them. He felt a brief flicker of recognition as his gaze alighted on the fair-haired man sitting next to Lavender Monkfield. Cigarette ash spilled on to the white tablecloth as Nicholas's fingers began to tremble. But he realized almost immediately that the recognition was false, an unkind illusion, because that was not his dead friend Richardson sitting there, calling for cocktails, but a stranger. The similarity was in the fair hair, the blue eyes, the muscular, graceful body.

He heard Thomasine say, 'It looks so pretty, doesn't it?' and could not for a moment think what she was talking about. Then he saw the snow, and the concerned look in her eyes as she glanced at him, and he said, 'Frightfully pretty. Like a Christmas card.' Stubbing out his cigarette, Nicholas added, 'There's a chap I know at that table over there. Come and meet him.'

Monkfield's crowd were drinking dry martinis and scanning the menu. Nicholas, crossing the restaurant, touched Bobby's shoulder to gain his attention.

'Monkfield? Good to see you.'

Bobby Monkfield had a florid face and reddish hair. He blinked. 'Blythe? Good Lord – it is, isn't it? Haven't seen you for decades, old chap.'

Nicholas recalled that he had disliked Bobby Monkfield at Winchester. 'I've been abroad for a while, and before that on the family estate. My wife and I came back to London just this morning.'

He still felt immense pride and some disbelief whenever he said 'my wife'. He had never been able to believe his luck in finding Thomasine in Paris, still less had he been able to believe that she had actually married him. Often now his other, older fears paled beside a new terror: that she would leave him when she discovered what a useless, cowardly husk of a man he really was. His incompetent efforts in bed must already be teaching her the truth.

He groped in his pocket for his cigarette-case as he took Thomasine's hand and led her forward. 'This is Thomasine – we were married six months ago.'

Lavender Monkfield stared at Thomasine. 'We know. We all heard that Nicky Blythe had had a whirlwind romance with a French ballet dancer. *Too* thrilling.'

Nicholas struggled to correct a few inaccuracies. 'Thomasine isn't French, she's English. We knew each other before the War.'

'*Too* romantic.'

Nicholas's cigarette-case was empty. He felt edgy, nervous. In France it had been easy to forget that in marrying Thomasine he had, to a great extent, broken the rules. He thought, unable this time to brush the thought aside, of his mother. He dreaded the inevitable fuss.

A voice said, 'Have one of mine, old chap.'

The golden-haired man who had reminded Nicholas momentarily of Richardson was holding out a cigarette-case. A flick of a lighter. Nicholas bent his head and inhaled.

'Simon Melville,' said the man, and held out his hand.

Nicholas's friend Bobby introduced them all to Thomasine.

'This is my big sis, Lavender, and this is Lavvie's fiancé, Maurice Douglas. And this is Tiny, for obvious reasons, and here are Lois and Rosemary and Bunty. And that clown is

Teddy Sefton, and the fellow with the loud tie is Teddy's little brother Colin. And this is my great chum, Simon.'

Thomasine, like Nicholas, was aware that a time of reckoning had come. Faces stared at her, voices called out greetings, someone pulled out a chair and she sat down.

'You'll dine with us,' said Lavender Monkfield.

'We've already dined.'

'A drink then.' Lavender signalled to the waiter. 'Everyone says that the Blythes are simply *furious*. About you and Nicky, I mean. Have they cut poor Nicky off without a penny?'

Thomasine laughed. 'Not that I know of.'

Their present financial problems were, Nicholas had explained to her, merely short-term. Their extended honeymoon in France had used up the remainder of his severance pay, plus his last quarter's allowance and much of the small legacy he had received from his uncle who had died in the War. They had returned temporarily to England, Nicholas had said, to sort out his tedious financial situation and to secure, hopefully, from the Drakesden Abbey estate an allowance more suited to a married man.

'Terribly naughty of Nicholas,' went on Lavender. 'Mummy told me that Lady Blythe had masses of debs simply lining up. A registry office, wasn't it? What fun – almost worth it, not telling anyone – to see the look on one's family's faces –'

'Perhaps,' drawled the man sitting beside Lavender, 'they were in love.'

'I didn't mean –' began Lavender. Her face, under its layer of powder, went the same dusky red as her brother's. 'I didn't mean to imply, Teddy –'

Thomasine said lightly, 'Actually, we were married at the British Consulate. And neither of us wanted a big wedding. And Nicholas has had plenty of letters from his mother. She seems to have accepted the situation.'

She did not quite believe her final sentence herself. The Lady Blythe who had written the short, affectionate letters that

Nicholas had sometimes shown her could not be reconciled with the Lady Blythe of Thomasine's memory. *You are not welcome at Drakesden Abbey, Miss Thorne. You will never speak to my son again.*

'You've chosen a poor time to return to London, Mrs Blythe,' someone said. 'It's simply dead in January, of course.'

'Quite deserted at weekends. Everyone's in the country.'

'At least one doesn't have to queue so long for the pictures.'

'Frightfully dull.'

Thomasine put aside her glass. 'Then why are you all here?'

A small, dark girl said, 'It'th Thimon'th idea. We do winter thingth in the thummer, and thummer thingth in the winter. Thuch fun.'

'Tiny means,' explained Lavender Monkfield, 'that we play tennis and bathe *now*, and in the summer we'll have house parties and hunt. Simon thought it would be amusing.'

Teddy Sefton blew a smoke ring. 'Simon's a communist, Mrs Blythe,' he explained lazily. 'Death to the idle rich, which is us, of course, and power to the working-classes. Only he can't quite manage a revolution here, like in Russia, so he's doing it more gradually, by freezing us to death. Yesterday we went for a dip at Brighton. You see? He's a very clever chap, is Simon.'

Lavender said, 'Oh, *Teddy!*'

After the restaurant, they went to the Frolics Club, at the back of Regent Street. As they walked the short distance, the snow glittered in the yellow light of the lamps, transforming London into something magical and entrancing. The music – piano, ukelele and percussion – assailed them as soon as they entered the nightclub. Thomasine was suddenly very aware, looking around at the dancers and drinkers and chatterers, of what class she had married into. Here the women wore long strands of real pearls, not glass beads; here there were no homemade frocks, and no one bothered to question the price of a drink.

A voice said, 'You should be in your element, Mrs Blythe. A

French ballet dancer like you should be showing us all how to shimmy.'

She grinned and accepted the glass that Teddy Sefton held out to her.

'I'm English, I'm afraid, Mr Sefton, not French. And I was never a real ballet dancer. I was a Little Snowdrop, to begin with. We used to put on concerts in the War, that sort of thing.'

'I remember a concert I saw when I was convalescing. There were a dozen fat little girls dressed as sparrows. They wore brown crêpe tunics and yellow caps that I eventually realized were supposed to be beaks. Eleven of them always went in the right direction, but the twelfth was always wrong. I had a fever, and I thought I was hallucinating. It was *wonderful!*'

Nicholas was dancing with Tiny; Lavender Monkfield, all flailing beads and floating chiffon, whirled around her fiancé. The nightclub was noisy and crowded. Women's voices brayed over the rackety music, and men in immaculate dinner suits sprayed bottles of champagne over the dance-floor.

'They're not so bad once you get to know them,' drawled Teddy. 'There's a few sharks, of course, but it passes the time, doesn't it, Mrs Blythe?'

'Thomasine,' she said firmly.

'Thomasine.' He smiled. 'I've never met a Thomasine before. Not outside the pages of Thomas Hardy, anyway. And you must call me Teddy. Or idiot, or ass, if you wish, just like everyone else does.'

The band had begun to play again. They were shouting out the words of the song:

> *Though there's nothing in the larder*
> *Don't we have fun!*
> *Times are hard and getting harder,*
> *Still we have fun.*

It didn't matter, Thomasine told herself, that she had never until her marriage owned a strand of real pearls. It didn't matter that in Paris she had painted her legs white with make-up because she couldn't afford silk stockings. She was Thomasine Blythe, who had been brought up by the best aunts in the world, who had worked and earned her own living, and whose name was as good as anybody's. She took Teddy Sefton's hand and smiled at him.

'Shall we dance?'

He followed her to the centre of the floor. The syncopated rhythms seized her and held her; she gave her body and soul to them. The music erased all doubt, just as it always did, and she felt as though she could have danced all night, never making a mistake. The floor cleared, so that she and Teddy Sefton danced alone, and when the music stopped, there was a ripple of applause.

When the nightclub closed at two o'clock, they took taxis to a party in Bayswater. The party was in an artist's studio at the top of an old house split into apartments. The artist was called Marcus Dorn, and his paintings were fixed to the walls of the studio, or propped against the furniture, or balanced on top of the piano. Red, purple and black tunnels and caves, crimson tubular structures narrowing into dark pinpoints stared out from every corner.

'Very Freudian,' said Colin Sefton.

'Marcuth hath a mother fixthation,' said Tiny.

They were handed drinks in pottery mugs. Thomasine, mistaking hers for lemon tea, took a large mouthful and choked.

'Marcus calls it Painter's Poison,' said Teddy. 'I believe he mixes brandy and gin together, and then chucks in anything liquid he can find. You know, lemonade, ginger ale, bath oil . . .'

Colin sat down and began to play the piano. Thomasine discovered that if she kept on drinking, she didn't notice the taste any more. The night became more disjointed, more unreal. She forgot people's names as soon as she was introduced to them.

'Too sick-making —' A tall woman with a black turban waved a gloved hand vaguely in the air.

'The cocktail?'

'The paintings. I had my tonsils removed a fortnight ago, and they make me think . . . well, you know . . .'

Sometimes the piano was louder than the conversation, sometimes the other way round. *'How you're gonna keep 'em, down on the Farm'* . . . A face swam in front of Thomasine, mouthing silently. She leaned forward, straining to hear.

'Pardon?'

'I said, you must sit for me.' A short man with a protruding stomach, a ragged white shirt and a bow-tie and no jacket grabbed her hand and kissed it. 'Marcus Dorn.'

Someone was ladling something into her mug. She smiled. 'Thomasine Blythe.'

'I'd dress you in red, of course. Blue is so insipid.'

Teddy whispered in her ear, 'Don't do it. You'll be a red tube with a bobble on the end.'

She started to laugh. The liquid in her mug lapped against the sides and then overflowed. She looked around the room, but could not see Nicholas. Through the haze of alcohol and exhilaration, she realized that she had not spoken to him since the taxi ride. She touched Teddy's arm.

'Nicholas —'

'Haven't seen him for ages. I shouldn't worry.' He glanced down at Thomasine. 'Ah. You *do* worry.' His expression changed.

'He is — moody.'

Teddy took her arm and steered her through the throng. 'Since the War? I thought so. You can pick 'em out. The ones who went through it, the ones who were too young for it, the ones who managed to worm their way out of it — the lucky bastards.'

They had reached the kitchen. Through the crowd that gathered round the cluttered table and sink, Thomasine distinguished Nicholas beside the window. He was talking to Simon Melville.

'Thank goodness. He looks fine. You'll think me silly, but I just wondered –'

Teddy's expression was thoughtful. 'Now, Simon was one of the ones who wriggled out of it. He was on the other side of the Atlantic in 1914. Or so he says. I'm not sure how it all fits in with being a communist and the illegitimate son of an Irish Countess and being sent down from Oxford. Personally, I don't believe a word of it.'

She didn't care. She only saw from Nicholas's expression that he looked happier than he had for weeks.

Teddy, leaning against the door–jamb, had taken a hip-flask from his pocket. 'I shouldn't drink any more of that foul muck, my dear Mrs Blythe. Help yourself to some of this, or you'll have the most frightful headache tomorrow.'

They went back to their hotel soon afterwards. The others disappeared for a game of tennis on someone's floodlit court, but Nicholas and Thomasine pleaded exhaustion. Thomasine staggered as they made their way along the corridor towards their rooms. Nicholas put his arm round her, steadying her.

'A jolly crowd, aren't they?'

She nodded. They had reached the bedroom; the ceiling was spinning. 'Very jolly.' She added accusingly, 'You're not tiddly, Nick. I'm tiddly. Why aren't you tiddly?' She collapsed on the bed, fully dressed.

Nicholas said, 'I don't like to drink. I have horrible dreams. Anyway, that stuff of Marcus's was foul. Simon says that his drink's as decadent as his paintings.'

'Painter's Poison,' murmured Thomasine, and giggled. She tried to sit up, failed, and fell back on the pillows. 'I can't reach my shoes, Nick.'

He sat on the end of the bed and carefully unbuttoned her shoes. 'Such lovely little feet. I do like feet.'

Thomasine had closed her eyes. 'Tiny would say you had an Oedipus complex. Or an Oediputh complexth.'

He was kissing her foot. She felt deliciously lazy, lying there as Nicholas unrolled her stockings. She could have drifted off to sleep.

She realized that she must not sleep when Nicholas pushed up the skirt of her dress and began to fumble with her camiknickers. She made herself help him then, unbuttoning his shirt and trousers, caressing him, whispering in his ear. She felt elation as he moved inside her, utter relief as he shuddered and gasped.

Afterwards, she saw the relief and pride in his eyes as well. She held him in her arms, pulling the bedspread over them both, gently brushing back the dark locks of hair from his eyes.

'It's going to be fine, isn't it, dearest?' he whispered. 'England's going to be fine.'

She believed then that he was right.

In February the water came up through the floor of the Gillorys' cottage. The white February gave way to a black one as the snow melted, laying bare the peat fields as water rose perilously close to the banks of the dykes and gathered in great puddles on the level ground.

Daniel swore when he climbed down the ladder into the kitchen one morning and water lapped around his ankles. Fay's face, huddled in a blanket, appeared at the top of the ladder.

'It's flooded, damn it. I should have moved the furniture last night.'

He sent her back to bed and worked alone, cursing himself. He had been tired the previous night, and had not paid heed to the swollen black clouds, the waterlogged ground underfoot. Now dark, dirty water oozed up through the brick floor, leaving rings of mud on the walls and on the legs of the table and chairs. The dustpan floated in the corner of the kitchen; the twigs of the broom dripped when he lifted it. Daniel began to sweep the water out through the front door, but he knew that it was hopeless. Outside, it was raining, and the farmyard and fields were glazed with a thin film of water. The peat was like a sponge, sucking and swelling with every drop of moisture.

He did what had to be done. Most springs of his childhood, his family had performed the same ritual: hauling the lighter furniture upstairs, using bricks to raise anything that could be raised off the ground. He thanked heaven he had stored their food, wood and turf on stacks, and he prayed that his crops of winter vegetables, not yet ready for harvest, might not be washed away.

As dawn began to glimmer on the horizon, and Daniel finished clearing up the worst of the mess, Fay appeared. She paused two rungs from the foot of the ladder.

'It's still all wet! I thought you'd swept it out!'

'I can't.' Daniel chucked several dirty cloths into a bucket. 'The water's in the peat, Fay, and this house is built on peat. It's directly under the floor. That's why there's no cement between the floor-bricks – it makes the water easier to drain away when the flood level goes down. No repair work to do, you see.'

'But how can I cook? I can't walk on *that*.'

She pointed to the kitchen floor, wet and shiny with an inch or two of water still lying on top of the bricks. She sounded angry rather than tearful.

For the first time, Daniel was aware of an answering anger in himself. He was tired, damp and cold, and worried about his crops. 'You put on my old trousers and the galoshes I bought you, for a start.'

She was wearing a thin woollen dress, cherry red, edged in white. At any other moment he would have thought how it suited her, but now, with the lower storey of his house flooded, he felt only irritation. He was aware that he was being unfair: how many other country dwellers expected to wade in water for part of the year?

He said, trying to comfort her, 'We're much better off than most, darling. Lots of people in Drakesden have to prop up their beds on bricks and paddle to them each night.'

Fay sniffed. 'It's ridiculous. It's uncivilized. Surely something could be done.'

'Well, the big landowners could spend a bit more on drainage, I daresay. And the Commissioners could wake up to the fact that sooner or later there's going to be a disaster, rather than just a few puddles on the floor. But, frankly, neither of those things seems very likely just now.'

He relieved his feeling by throwing more coal into the range. The water had not risen high enough, thank God, to put out the fire.

'There's no need to shout,' said Fay.

When he turned and glanced at her, she was still standing on the ladder. She looked small and cold and miserable. He reached out to her, intending to hug her, but she moved away from him.

'You're all coal-dust.'

His hands were black and his feet were soaking. He said, as kindly as he could, 'Go back to bed, darling. I'll bring you a cup of tea when the kettle's boiled.'

As she began to climb back up the ladder, he realized how much he had wanted her to say, 'Don't be silly, Daniel. I'll make the tea.' How much he had wanted her to put on her oldest clothes and grab a broom, and share with him the baling out of their house. How much he had wanted companionship, as well as desire.

After their first month in England, the Blythes moved out of Claridges, and took a little house in Chelsea. Their return to the Continent had been postponed indefinitely: Nicholas's interview with his accountant had not been a pleasant one. The rented house was not large; its rooms were low-ceilinged and pastel-washed, the furniture spindly and insubstantial. Nicholas engaged a cook and a maid, and rented a garage for the Delage. The severity of the weather eased, the snow melted and the streets were washed by rain.

Once they were settled in the little mews house, Nicholas went to bed later and later each night, and in consequence rose later and later each morning. It was almost as though, having lost the structure that hotel life had imposed upon him, he had forgotten how to arrange his own life. Thomasine, unable to lose the habit of early rising, spent the mornings alone. On some afternoons, she and Nicholas went to the pictures or for a drive. On others, when Nicholas tinkered with his motor-car, she sewed or shopped or played the piano that Nicholas had bought for her. Yet it was not enough. The hours stretched purposelessly in front of her. She could not grow used to the emptiness of her days, to the absence of work. Nicholas's set considered work neither necessary nor desirable; the pursuit of pleasure was their only occupation. All Thomasine's efforts at useful employment were ultimately futile. There was no need to sew when Nicholas insisted on buying her numerous gowns, and no need to shop or cook when she could just give orders to the servant, or pick up a telephone and order groceries from Harrods. To fill the empty days she read for hours, sometimes until her eyes were red and sore.

Aunt Hilly visited one weekend in April. The maid showed her in, her arms full of parcels and packages and bunches of flowers.

'I thought, if the mountain does not come to Mahomet . . .'

Thomasine gave a crow of delight, and embraced her visitor.

'A bit much, I know,' said Hilda, when she was released, 'to turn up out of the blue like this. But one of my older pupils unexpectedly needed escorting to London, and it just seemed too good an opportunity to miss. There was no time to write.'

The maid took Hilda's coat, and Thomasine ran to the kitchen for vases for the bunches of tulips and daffodils.

Hilda said, 'It has been so *long!* Far too long.'

'Almost two years.' Thomasine arranged the flowers in cut-glass vases. 'Before I went to Paris.'

Hilda had sat down on the couch. 'You must tell me all about

Paris. I do envy you – the museums and art galleries, such wonderful architecture –'

They discussed Paris until the maid arrived with tea and cakes. Thomasine sat down at the spindly occasional table. 'Tea, Aunt Hilly?'

'Please.'

'Nicholas is out at the moment, I'm afraid. He and his friend are replacing a tyre on his motor-car.'

Thomasine poured the tea and scrabbled in her pocket for her cigarette-case.

Hilda shook her head when Thomasine held the case out to her. 'I managed to give it up. It was a dreadful struggle.' She smiled, and Thomasine found herself smiling in reply.

'Oh, Aunt Hilly. You haven't changed a bit.'

It was true, she thought. Hilda's dress was a simple navy blue and white, the ankle-length hemline making little concession to fashion. Her hair was scraped back in an untidy bun, held together by an uncompromising collection of pins and clips, just as it always had been.

'*You* have changed, my dear.' Hilda pushed her spectacles back to the bridge of her nose to look at Thomasine. 'You are so grown up now, so elegant. And the short hair is so much more practical, isn't it? I wish I had the courage . . .'

Thomasine laughed. 'A headmistress with bobbed hair! What are you thinking of, Aunt Hilly?'

For a moment, then, they had slipped back into their old, easy relationship. The intervening years – London, Paris – had fallen away, leaving no scar.

Hilda accepted the teacup from Thomasine. 'I have the evening free . . . I need not return to Sheffield before tomorrow morning. I hoped that perhaps . . .'

Thomasine shook her head regretfully. 'Nicholas and I are engaged to dine this evening with the Monkfields, I'm afraid. Bobby was an old schoolfriend of Nicholas's. And then we're to go to a party – dressing up as Russians – Cossacks, that sort of thing . . .'

She recognized the expression on Hilda's face. She had seen that expression before: on the occasion that she had neglected her English grammar and instead ridden the rector's pony; on the occasion that she had stayed out too long boating with Daniel Gillory and had not returned home until it was dark; on any other occasion when she had failed to reach Hilda's own high standards of behaviour.

She said defensively, 'It's just a bit of fun, Aunt Hilly. Nicholas likes to see his friends.'

'I know that you are a grown woman now, Thomasine, a married woman, and that I have no right to interfere in your life, but . . .'

Angrily Thomasine pushed away the thought that Hilda's disapproval only echoed her own increasing dissatisfaction with her life.

She tried to explain. 'When I married Nicholas, I married his way of life. Parties and dinners and theatre trips are part of his way of life. Besides, nothing's the same now, Aunt Hilly – everything's changed since the War.'

But she knew, looking at Hilda, that what she said was untrue. Hilda had not changed: her standards, her ethics, were unaltered. She had never made the mistakes that Thomasine had made, had never had to make the choices that Thomasine had had to make. Those mistakes, those choices, she thought miserably, had put a vast gulf between them, a gulf that could never be bridged.

But Hilda only said, 'I understand that there are obligations connected with rank. It only seems to me that frivolity is not necessarily a part of that obligation. And dressing up as *Russians* . . . when you consider the deprivations that country has endured . . . when so many have died . . . when it seems likely that even the Tsar and his family have been put to death . . . There is *famine* in Russia now, Thomasine.'

She found herself angry that Hilda, who had taught her so little of some aspects of life, should criticize her. 'What would you have me do, Aunt Hilly? Take baskets of food to the deserving poor? Play Lady Bountiful, like Nicholas's mother?'

'Yes,' said Hilda simply. Her forehead was creased in a frown. She pushed back a few strands of hair that had escaped from their imprisonment of pins, and said more gently, 'Come and sit next to me, *please*, Thomasine. You look so *wild*.'

Half-unwillingly, she sat down on the couch next to her aunt.

'I don't mean to criticize you, my dear. Of course you should enjoy yourself – and of course you have social obligations to fulfil. It just seems to me that there is so much hardship now . . . both in London and in the countryside . . . that as you are married to Nicholas Blythe –'

'That as I am married to Nicholas Blythe I have both position and money, and therefore can change the world, just as you have always wanted to, Aunt Hilly.' Thomasine leaned back against the couch. 'Only we haven't money, you see, we spent it all in France. And everyone knows I'm just a jumped-up little chorus-girl, and though some people don't mind, others do.'

In the silence, Thomasine could hear the rain pounding against the window-pane, the howl of the wind around the chimney-pots.

She heard Hilda say hesitantly, 'Lady Blythe . . . does she mind?'

'I don't know. I really don't know.'

She stood up, and began to tidy cups and saucers back on to the tray. She would let no one, not even Hilda, know how she dreaded going to Drakesden.

'You must tell me everything, Aunt Hilly. Have you seen Antonia recently? I had tea with her in Gorringes a fortnight ago. And your school – I've been longing to hear about it. You have twenty pupils now . . . thirty?'

The water-level dropped and the dampness oozed between the loose brick floor of the cottage, back into the peat. Daniel carried the furniture back downstairs, and scrubbed black mud from the floor and walls. Spring flickered fitfully in the air. His crops and stock had survived the flooding, and Fay, since she no longer had to cook wearing galoshes, cheered up a little. Looking out at pale skies pasted with ragged white clouds, Daniel felt quite happy.

He took on one of the villagers to help with the farmwork. Harry Dockerill was a couple of years younger than Daniel, and had missed all but the last nine months of the War. Those nine months had been enough, though. A long time ago, in another world, Harry and his brothers had pelted Daniel, returning home from grammar school in his swanky school uniform, with pebbles. Now Harry, like Daniel, was quieter, more subdued, content with silence and empty spaces. Harry had been gassed during the War, but was capable of all but the heaviest tasks. Sometimes, working with him, he reminded Daniel of his own younger brother who had also been called Harry, and who had died in 1918.

To pay a labourer's wages was a struggle but, as Daniel saw it, a necessary struggle. Once a week he read the *Daily Herald* at Ely library, as well as the *Farmer and Stock-breeder*. He did not believe that the good times – the industrial and agricultural boom that had occurred just after the end of the War – would last. The occasional letter from Hattie told him about the mounting queues of unemployed in London; he wondered how long the Government would continue with its wartime policy of protecting the price of wheat. At the moment, the great landowners, crippled by death duties and raised taxes, were suffering. Looking up at the shallow swell of the island that protected Drakesden Abbey from the waters, Daniel did not care a jot about the landowners. But he wondered how long it would be until the farmers, the smallholders, the agricultural labourers would themselves be touched by the cold wind of change.

Not long, he thought, so he tried to protect himself and Fay. If the price of wheat collapsed, then he must not be totally dependent on wheat in order to be able to survive. He planted potatoes and root vegetables, and made plans for strawberry beds and raspberry canes. Anything that could not be more easily and more cheaply imported from abroad, anything that would grow in the soft black soil of the Fens; every square inch of his smallholding must grow something.

On market-days, Daniel and Fay went to Ely. If the weather was good, Fay enjoyed selling eggs in the market-place. She always dressed in her best: her hemlines were shorter than any other woman's, her lips reddened with a discreet dab of lipstick. After completing his own business, walking across the square back towards her, Daniel would still feel immensely proud.

Had he the time, though, he would have read endlessly. It was as though a vast well had opened up in him, just waiting to be filled. He read anything and everything: biography, history, novels, poetry. Reading, he recognized his own ignorance, the paucity of his truncated education. He read all the classics he had never got round to reading as a child: Dickens and Thackeray, and Meredith and Hardy. He tried, at first, to share his pleasure with Fay, showing her the books he had borrowed, summarizing the stories. Reading hurt her eyes, she told him; she was too tired for anything more than *Woman's Weekly* by the evening. So he read to her aloud one night, by the light of the oil-lamp, when the range had warmed the little cottage and insulated them from the raw weather outside. But when he had read a page or so, he glanced up and saw that her dark eyes were glazed, dull, so he put the book aside, and went to her, and took her in his arms and made love to her.

Thomasine, too, read. Dr Marie Stopes's *Married Love* was not an easy book to buy, but, reading it, Thomasine was surprised to find tears running down her face. Tears of anger. She resolved never to be the victim of her own ignorance again. Good works and a lifetime's virginity might have worked well for Hilda and Rose; they had not suited Thomasine.

She heard the sound of Nicholas's key in the door, his footsteps as he ran up the stairs. Quickly she hid *Married Love* under the pillow.

Nicholas opened the bedroom door. 'You're not ready, darling. Hurry – we'll have to leave soon.'

She had forgotten the time, and their plans for the evening. 'Where are we going?'

'On a picnic. You remember – Simon's been planning it for weeks.'

'A *picnic.*' Thomasine glanced out of the window. 'It's raining, Nick.'

'I know.' Nicholas was struggling into his shirt, throwing socks and handkerchiefs aside to find a collar. 'It'll be a hoot. Simon's made up some clues. If we follow them correctly, we'll pick up champagne and stuff for the picnic. Frightfully brainy clues, of course, being Simon's. Bobby's getting into a lather, apparently – thinks they'll be too difficult for him – no food, you see. He always was a bit of a duffer.'

Nicholas had found a collar and was struggling with a black tie. Thomasine, rising from the bed, went to help him.

'What should I wear?'

'Something warm,' said Nicholas vaguely. 'And I'll put umbrellas in the car. But do hurry. We have to be in Trafalgar Square by six, or we'll miss the first clue.'

The picnic turned out to be in the New Forest. Nicholas and Thomasine arrived there just after midnight, leaving the motorcar at the side of the road, tracking their way through the trees, following the arrows made of sticks, leaves and fungi that Simon had used to mark their path.

He was waiting in a clearing. 'The victors!' he cried. 'A prize for the victors!'

Thomasine felt a wet wreath of laurel leaves thrown over her head, a kiss planted on her cheek. The same for Nicholas, the wreath and the kiss.

'What do you think?' said Simon.

Thomasine looked around the clearing. Rain still dripped through the heavily branched trees. To one side of the clearing was a tent, open at the front. Inside, white cloths were spread on the ground, with cutlery and plates and glasses. Candelabra hung from the trees, sheltered from the rain by makeshift canvas awnings. A bonfire burned, struggling against the dark and the dampness. There was even a piano nestling in a thicket of bushes, its pedals and ornately carved feet scattered with dead leaves.

'It's splendid,' said Nicholas. 'Absolutely splendid. Simon – you're a genius.'

Simon smiled. The orange light of the fire underlit his face, darkening his blue eyes, blackening the shadows at eye-socket and cheekbone. 'Too kind. Now – did you collect anything *en route?*'

Nicholas fumbled in the basket he had carried from the car. 'Two bottles of champers, a salmon and some Bath Olivers.'

'Heavenly.' Simon began to ease the cork from one of the champagne bottles.

Thomasine said, 'But the others . . .?'

'Will be here soon enough.' Simon's words were for Thomasine, but he was looking at Nicholas. 'Unless none of the rest of them manage to sort out my little puzzles.' Champagne gushed over the forest floor, mingling with the rainwater.

Nicholas held out three glasses. 'The Seftons and Tiny and Lois should be here any moment. And Lavender and Maurice, I think. I don't know about poor old Bobby – last time I saw him he was driving around Newbury, trying to work out what "an arch that spans the water" meant.' He handed glasses of champagne to Simon and Thomasine.

'A glowing testament to the efficiency of the English public school system, old Bobby,' said Simon. 'A skull an inch thick and filled only with cotton-wool.'

Thomasine found herself disliking Simon intensely. 'But you

accept Bobby's hospitality,' she said, and Simon just looked at her, his eyes cold and considering.

There was the sound of breaking twigs and shrieks of laughter.

'Paradise lost. More picnickers, I think. Throw a bit more wood on the bonfire, Nick – it's getting rather low.'

Nicholas wandered around the clearing, gathering fallen branches. Thomasine, huddled in her coat under her umbrella, drank her champagne as Simon went to meet the new arrivals.

'Have we won, darling?'

'We motored ever so fast –'

Thomasine caught part of Simon's reply. 'I'm afraid Nicky Blythe and his little parvenu have pipped you at the post –' and just for a moment she shivered as she watched Nicholas throw branches on to the fire. But she held up her head as the clearing filled with people. Damn them all, she thought. She would not be judged. She was as good as any of them.

Teddy Sefton crowded under the shelter of Thomasine's umbrella. 'Runners-up as usual. Blasted Blythes.' Then he hugged her.

'Nicholas drove extremely fast,' said Thomasine. Smiling, she kissed Teddy on the cheek.

'One of Simon's less inspired ideas,' muttered Teddy, pouring more champagne into Thomasine's glass and finding a glass for himself. 'The flower of the English upper classes are about to perish from pneumonia. Where's Nick?'

'Building up the bonfire. Simon told him to.'

The flames of the fire leapt higher and higher into the air. The intense heat and the gaudiness of the flames suddenly cancelled out the dark and the cold.

'He'll set the whole bloody forest alight,' said Teddy casually. 'I'll go and say hello. See you in a moment, poppet.'

More footsteps through the undergrowth, more greetings yelled through the night. Lavender Monkfield and her fiancé Maurice appeared. Bunty Warburton was leaning on Maurice's other arm, and limping.

'*Too* frightful –'

'Quite sick-making –'

'Bunty has holed her stocking.'

'You are wicked, Simon, absolutely wicked.'

'Poor Bobby has a puncture.'

Impossibly, music had begun to play. Colin Sefton was seated at the piano, and in the darkness Thomasine could see the red tip of his cigarette and the outline of his overcoat and hat, scarlet in the reflected light of the bonfire. Lois and Lavender had thrown off their coats and hats, and were dancing together on the uneven ground.

Later, in the tent, huddled with the rest of the dozen, Thomasine began to feel warm again. There was hot soup, cold chicken and salmon, salad and fruit.

'Thtrawberrieth!' cried Tiny. 'Where did you find thtrawberrieth in April, Thimon?'

Simon smiled. He had a smile like a cat's, thought Thomasine, slow and feline and calculating.

'I know a rich old widow with a hothouse.'

Teddy Sefton helped himself to a strawberry. 'Will she leave you all her money, Simon?'

Simon was distributing strawberries, grapes, pears. 'A little *bourgeois*, don't you think, Sefton, to talk about money at dinner?'

Teddy said mildly, 'But we are *bourgeois*, my dear Simon. Irredeemably so. As you keep reminding us.'

There was a flicker of annoyance in Simon Melville's eyes. He turned to Nicholas. 'Wind up the gramophone, Nick. We need some music.'

Nicholas fitted a new needle to the arm of the gramophone and turned the handle. Thomasine had taken her coat off to dance and now, in her sleeveless velvet dress, she had begun to feel cold again. Music issued from the wooden loudspeaker of the gramophone.

Ev'ry morning, ev'ry evening,
Ain't we got fun,
Not much money, Oh, but honey,
Ain't we got fun.

The rain had lessened, but huge drops of water still tumbled from the treetops. Simon had turned, was taking something out of a hamper, and placing it on the tablecloth.

'A birthday cake!' cried Lavender Monkfield. 'Whose birthday, Simon?'

'Mine.' Simon took a knife out of the hamper. 'A dreadful custom, I suppose, but I thought it would be rather fun.'

'Just like the nursery . . .'

'Shall we have candles?'

'Nick?'

Nicholas had candles. He took them out of his pocket and pushed them into the icing. Thomasine watched him take a box of matches from his pocket and carefully light the candles, one by one. Twenty-five tiny lights fluttered in the immense darkness of the forest. The festivities seemed to Thomasine to be forced, mechanical. As though, somewhere in the endless search for diversion, they had mistaken what pleasure really was. She shuddered. She heard Teddy say, 'Have my jacket. You look freezing,' and was grateful for his dinner jacket slung over her shoulders.

More champagne bottles, slices of pink and white cake placed on pretty china plates, more kisses. This time, Thomasine sensed that Simon Melville's kiss was cold, grudging. When the cake was a broken mess of icing sugar and crumbs and every one of the candles had gone out, they went outside again. Colin began to play the piano. Nicholas took Thomasine in his arms.

'That jacket –'

'It's Teddy's. I couldn't find my coat and I was cold.'

Nicholas frowned. 'You could have had mine.'

'You were busy lighting the cake. I'm sorry – do I look frightful?'

215

He relaxed a little. 'Not at all. Just a bit – disconcerting. With your short hair . . . it's rather like dancing with one of the chaps.'

She laughed. She nestled into his shoulder, enjoying, just as she always did, the warmth of his body, the feel of his arms around her. If it could always be like this, she thought. If it could always be so easy, so uncomplicated. The champagne and the music seemed to take away their mutual clumsiness, their inability to please each other.

Then Nicholas said, 'Hasn't this been the best night ever? Isn't Simon simply marvellous?'

The spell was broken. She could feel herself drawing away from him.

He added, 'He reminds me of someone I once knew. A fellow who was killed in the War.'

When she looked up at him, she saw both the pain and the happiness in his face. She found herself wanting to protect him, to guard him against both what he feared and what he hoped for. Standing on tiptoes, she kissed him on the mouth and felt him respond to her.

A voice said, 'There's time enough for the continuation of your decadent line, Blythe. The bonfire's dying down again.'

Thomasine opened her eyes. Simon Melville was standing beside Nicholas, one hand resting possessively on Nicholas's shoulder, his expression saying – she did not know what. Something challenging, something amused.

She lost track of time. The rain had stopped, but the ground was still sodden underfoot. Water trailed along the curled fronds of the ferns and made the great grey trunks of the beech trees gleam silver. Thomasine leaned against the piano, chin on hand, an elbow on the lid, watching Colin.

'Half the notes aren't playing – the rain's got inside it.' Colin ran his hands over the keys. 'Bloody stupid idea . . . A good piano *ruined!*'

Suddenly he slammed the lid shut. When the strings had stopped reverberating, the silence was immense. Most of the candles in the trees had blown out. The dancers staggered to a halt. They seemed very small against the vast forest. Almost lost.

Teddy Sefton had come to stand beside his brother. 'We'll go, Col. I've had enough. Thomasine?'

She was about to nod, to go and find Nicholas, when she heard Simon Melville call out, 'Our revels now are ended. Or almost ended. One more thing, ladies and gentlemen . . . A final competition, to warm us all up. Nothing too intellectually demanding, you'll be glad to hear, Bobby. Just a simple race back to London. The first one back in Trafalgar Square can name the theme of the fancy dress party I'm going to give next month.'

'*Simon's* giving a *party*,' whispered Teddy. 'Wonders will never cease.'

'The rich widow will pay for it,' said Colin. He had risen from the ruined piano. He did not bother to lower his voice.

'Well – what are you waiting for?' said Simon. 'Off you go.'

Teddy touched Thomasine's arm. 'You can come with us, if you like, Thomasine. Colin can travel in the dickey seat.'

She smiled and shook her head. Nicholas had reappeared, waving to her to hurry.

'Your jacket, Teddy.'

'Keep it. If I find your coat, I'll bring it to you.'

Nicholas, excited, had grabbed Thomasine's arm and was already pulling her away from the clearing. When Thomasine looked back, she saw that only Teddy and Colin were left. Colin was wiping the rain from the piano with the tablecloth, and Teddy was throwing earth on to the bonfire, extinguishing the flames.

Nicholas, speeding along the narrow roads, was explaining to her about his motor-car. Something to do with horsepower and tyres and cylinders.

'I've a full can of petrol on the running-board, and she's going like a dream. The others haven't a chance. Bobby has a Hispano-Suiza, but I've always thought the Delage the better motor-car.'

They had already driven out of the green, secret wilderness of the New Forest. The rain held off, but in the first glimmerings of dawn Thomasine could see the glaze of dampness that covered the surface of the road, the deep puddles that gathered at the edges of the verge.

Nicholas, his hands on the steering-wheel, his foot on the accelerator, glanced across at her. 'All right, darling? Comfortable?'

The endearment was such a rarity that she smiled. 'I'm fine. Perfectly comfortable.'

Although the Delage, driven at speed, rattled and bumped along the uneven road, and cold air whistled through the unglazed side-windows, Thomasine hardly noticed the discomfort. The champagne she had drunk and the exhaustion that had begun to overtake her insulated her from all feeling. She had even ceased to feel cold. Curled up in the seat with Teddy Sefton's dinner-jacket pulled up around her ears, she felt as though they were cut off from the rest of the world.

'Tell me if you need me to stop. If you feel unwell or anything.'

She said again, 'I'm fine. I might go to sleep.'

She could not sleep properly, though. Disjointed dream images flickered through her brain, mixed with memories of the evening's entertainment. *Ev'ry morning, ev'ry evening, ain't we got fun.* Colin Sefton slamming down the lid of the piano. Bobby Monkfield trailing disconsolately round Newbury, crying, 'An arch? What does he mean, an arch?' Simon Melville saying, 'Nicky Blythe and his little parvenu . . .'

The motor-car swerved violently. She heard Nicholas cry out. When she opened her eyes, there was a sharp, fast succession of sky and field and hedgerow as the Delage hurtled out of control. A shape formed out of the dim dawn light, a face turned oh so slowly towards her, so close that she could see the features, the expression clearly. The old woman's mouth was open in a silent scream.

The Delage swerved, skidded and buried its nose in the hedge at the side of the road. Leaves and grass rose up into the air, steam hissed. The force of the impact rammed Thomasine's forehead against the dashboard and knocked the breath from her body.

She heard Nicholas cry, 'Are you all right, Thomasine? Are you all right?'

He was hauling her upright, shaking her. When she could speak, she said, 'Yes, fine,' and struggled around in the seat, looking desperately out at the road and the verge.

But there was no broken body, no bloody corpse. She heard footsteps and then, in the leaden dawn light, picked out the bowed figure scurrying away down the road. She called out, 'Are you hurt? Wait –' But there was no reply. She recognized fear in every line of that small, hunched departing figure.

Nicholas cried out, 'She was in the middle of the road! One of the tyres went. She was in the middle of the bloody road, Thomasine!'

She said flatly, 'She was old, Nick. And this is the countryside. People aren't used to motor-cars.' Then she climbed out and sat, shaking, crouched in the hedgerow, while he changed the tyre.

They did not arrive in London until mid-morning. The motor-car limped slowly back, its front mudguard buckled, the bonnet refusing to stay properly shut. Throughout the remainder of the journey, Thomasine could not sleep. Every time she closed her eyes she saw the old woman's terrified face. Only when they had reached the city streets again and mingled with the hundreds of other motors and lorries and buses, did she cease to feel an interloper, a trespasser, someone who had spoilt something simply by her presence.

When, finally, they arrived back at the Chelsea house, there was a letter waiting for them. The letter was from Lady Blythe, inviting them to stay at Drakesden.

CHAPTER EIGHT

THEY drove to Drakesden on the first Saturday in May. The Delage, its bodywork repaired, took the rutted roads smoothly and easily. The sky was clear and blue; across the Fens they could see the Isle of Ely and the silhouette of the cathedral, purplish-grey on the skyline. The heavy, sweet scent of may blossom perfumed the air, and the waterways were glittery lengths of silver lace.

The village grew out of the skyline: the church, the straggling yellow-bricked cottages, the outlying farms and smallholdings. And above all the other buildings, high and secure, Drakesden Abbey. As they drove through the village, Thomasine let out small squawks of pleasure and reminiscence.

'There's the Dockerills' cottage . . . and look at all the advertisements outside the grocer's, Nick. It looks so *modern*. And Quince Cottage – oh, it's just the same . . .'

They headed up the incline towards the gates of Drakesden Abbey. When they were halfway along the drive, Nicholas stopped the car. Thomasine, glancing at him, saw that he looked dazed and nervous.

'What is it, Nick?'

Nicholas shook his head. 'It's changed. Look . . .' He rubbed at his eyes. 'So *overgrown*. There's weeds in the gravel. There were never *weeds!* There was a boy whose only job was to pull the weeds out of the drive.'

Thomasine saw that the garden did not quite now match the clipped perfection of her memory; that some of the bushes needed pruning, that the flowers and shrubs had not been tamed with quite their former severity.

'Even the *house* –' he added disbelievingly. 'The window-frames could do with a coat of paint.'

His hands shook as they rested on the steering-wheel. His glance flickered towards Thomasine and he whispered, 'I was ill the last time I was here. I don't want to be ill again.'

She laid her hand over his, quelling the shivering. 'You were ill because of the War, Nick,' she said gently. 'That's all been over with for three years now.'

He said nothing, but sat, staring ahead at the great house, the vast gardens. Then he muttered, 'Can't you hear it, Thomasine? The silence. I don't like silence. I like noise –'

There was only the rustle of the breeze in the trees, the small sounds of birds and insects. Thomasine said comfortingly, 'You might be able to sleep better, Nick, if it's quiet. You've been looking so tired recently.'

Often over the past weeks they had not gone to bed until dawn. There were shadows like purple thumbprints beneath Nicholas's eyes, and his tanned skin had paled since their arrival in England. Frequently concerned about his health, Thomasine had tried to persuade him to rest, to slow down the frenetic round of nightclubs and theatre and parties. But he had refused or, if occasionally he had wavered, there had always been Simon, egging him on, mocking him for being unable to keep up with the others. She loathed Simon now, and Simon, she thought, felt the same about her.

'I need *people* –'

'You've got me, Nick. You've still got me.' Thomasine hugged him, acknowledging the irony that she had, in the end, been glad that Lady Blythe had invited them to Drakesden. Thomasine was convinced that an absence from London, and a separation from Simon Melville, could do Nicholas nothing but good. 'And you want to see your parents, don't you?'

He smiled at last. 'Yes, of course. Dear Mama –' He pressed his foot on the accelerator and drove to the front of the house. There, he pulled on the hand-brake and climbed out of the Delage.

'Here's Hawkins.'

The butler greeted them; a boy hovered nearby to take their luggage. Nicholas opened the car door and Thomasine climbed out.

And then another figure appeared at the great front doors of Drakesden Abbey. A woman wearing a soft mauve gown, caught in at the waist, a white lace collar threaded with pearls standing high around her neck. Lady Blythe's gown was still of the era before the War; her fair hair, immaculately arranged, was untouched by grey.

'Nicky!' Slowly, gracefully, Lady Blythe walked down the steps to her son's side. 'Darling – how wonderful! We have missed you so much.' She took Nicholas's hands in hers and reached up and kissed him on the cheek. Then she stepped back. 'But you look so pale – so tired.' Her brow creased, her tone of voice was concerned. 'Too much gadding about, I daresay. And I don't expect you have been eating properly.'

'Mama.' Nicholas murmured something in his mother's ear.

'Of course.' The smile returned to Lady Blythe's face. Thomasine's heart lurched. Nicholas took her hand, leading her forward.

'Mama, this is my wife, Thomasine. You remember Thomasine, don't you, Mama?'

The air was perfumed with carnations as Lady Blythe's lips brushed her cheek. A rustle of silk, a murmured greeting, and Thomasine would have felt immensely relieved had she not glimpsed that small narrowing of those ice-blue eyes, that almost imperceptible appraising twist to the corners of that pretty mouth.

The bed in Thomasine's room was a four-poster, high and hung with heavy drapes. Her suitcases were already unpacked, her evening-clothes freshly ironed and laid out on the bed. The bathroom was along the corridor, the housemaid had explained before leaving the room, but if Mrs Blythe needed hot water she had only to ring for it. Thomasine stared at the bell-pull, the wash-stand. She could not imagine ringing that bell, summoning some wretched girl who would scuttle away to the depths of the house to fetch her a jug of hot water.

Outside, the sky had begun to dim and the air to chill. Now that the sun had gone in, the May evening was cold. There was no fire lit in the room: the hearth gleamed, unsullied by coal or ash. No electric light, of course, only an oil-lamp unlit on the table. Thomasine, searching, could find no matches. She shivered and, turning, looked out of the window.

The room faced north, looking over the front gardens and driveway. Ornamental trees – a cedar, a monkey-puzzle, a copper-beech – somehow survived the chill winds of the Fens to grow on the lawn. Below the front garden was the paddock. She could glimpse the spire of the church, and the distant line of the dyke that contained the tributary of the Lark. She thought she could see the blacksmith's cottage, at the end of the spur that broke away from the protective shelter of the village, but the little house was lost in shadows, and the fields that backed it were blue-grey in the twilight.

She felt dusty with the journey; she must dress for dinner. Gathering her towels and sponge-bag, Thomasine left the room and walked down the corridor in search of a bathroom.

She could not remember which room the maid had indicated was a bathroom. She tried to recall the geography of the house from her previous, disastrous visit to Drakesden Abbey, but could visualize only the hot, humid conservatory, and the kitchen with the cook and the scullery-maids all staring at her.

A maid appeared from out of one of the rooms, and Thomasine could have hugged her with relief. She recognized Ellen Dockerill, one of the vast tribe of Dockerills who had grown up in the two-roomed cottage in Beck's Row.

'*Ellen!* How lovely to see you. I'm looking for the bathroom. I must have a bath before dinner ... the journey ...' She stopped.

'I'll fetch the water, ma'am. Joseph will bring the bath to your room.'

The maid scurried away down the corridor. Thomasine did not move. Ellen Dockerill, with whom she had played tag as a girl, had *curtsied*.

Sir William Blythe joined them just before dinner.

'Here's Thomasine, Pa,' said Nicholas. 'We drove up from London this afternoon.'

Sir William took Thomasine's hand. 'Welcome to Drakesden Abbey. A pleasure to see you both. A sherry, my dear? Dashed pretty dress.'

Thomasine had worn the sea-green Fortuny gown Nicholas had bought her in Paris. 'This was my wedding-dress, Sir William.'

Sir William looked approving. 'Marjorie had to have the whole shebang − white stuff and a veil down to her ankles. Never worn the thing since, I daresay. That was in nineteen-fifteen, of course.'

'The frock is very becoming,' said Lady Blythe. 'Not so *traditional*, though, William.'

Nicholas had lit a cigarette. 'Paris is different, Mama. You wouldn't believe the things that go on there.'

Lady Blythe was still smiling. 'I don't doubt it, Nicky.'

'When in Rome, and all that . . .' said Sir William vaguely.

Lady Blythe had turned back to Thomasine. 'Oh, just a little word.' She drew Thomasine aside, so that they were slightly separate from the two men. 'I believe you had a fire lit in your bedroom, and a hot bath?'

Thomasine nodded, bewildered.

Lady Blythe's voice was low, confidential. 'Well, if you wouldn't, in future. It gives so much work to the servants, and it just isn't done to trouble them so, especially at such an inconvenient time of day. And we never have fires lit in the bedrooms. Never.'

★

Afterwards, Thomasine remembered the entire evening as a succession of awkward or embarrassing moments. At dinner, Sir William asked after his younger daughter.

'Not too good with a pen, old Lally. Sent her to some ridiculously expensive school, but she still can't spell for toffee. Takes after her father, I'm afraid.'

'Belle is looking after her.' Nicholas, aware that Belle's chaperonage was at best intermittent, and at worst non-existent, avoided his father's eye. 'In Biarritz, I think.'

'Dashed convenient,' said Sir William approvingly, 'her cousin helping her out. Always felt the poor girl was done out of her coming-out parties and what-not.'

Lady Blythe said, 'Lally didn't want to be presented at court, William. You know that. Many girls don't, nowadays. And travel can be just as beneficial to a girl of her age. She is fortunate that Isabel is prepared to look after her.'

Appetizer, fish dish, entrée, main course, dessert, savoury. Conversations about London, Paris, Italy, the Riviera. About friends and relations of the Blythes, a few of whom Thomasine knew, most of whom she didn't. Recollections of Nicholas's childhood, his schooldays. Thomasine, choosing from the array of sparkling cutlery set out before her, chose wrong, and ended up with only a knife to eat her dessert. Lady Blythe, smiling graciously, sent the footman to the butler's pantry for an extra place setting. Nicholas and his father talked about horses, motor-cars and farming over their glasses of port. Alone in the drawing-room, Lady Blythe questioned Thomasine about the Chelsea house, their furnishings, their servants.

'Only two servants, dear? A cook and a maid?'

'We eat out a great deal,' explained Thomasine.

'But London restaurants are so expensive ... And one can never quite trust the quality of the food, don't you think? Before the War we had produce from Drakesden sent up by train each day when we were up in Town for the Season. Then one could be sure. We used never to eat in restaurants. Nicky had such a delicate stomach as a child . . .'

The manservant arrived with the tray of cups and saucers and the pot of coffee.

'Of course, we all suffered during the War.' Lady Blythe began to pour the coffee. 'But one has to try to maintain standards, don't you agree?'

Thomasine could only nod. Drakesden Abbey, which she remembered from her childhood as being full of light and treasures, seemed to have darkened, become heavy and oppressive. The coral-coloured walls of the drawing-room were blood-red in the candlelight, crowded with ornaments, portraits, photographs. Faces of dead Blythes stared back at her as she stirred her coffee. She had to ask Lady Blythe to repeat her last question.

'I said, you surely must have a manservant?'

Thomasine shook her head. She felt, at last, on reasonably steady ground. 'Manservants are very hard to come by since the War, Lady Blythe.'

'But the motor-car . . . Such troublesome machines . . .'

'Nicholas enjoys tinkering with the motor-car. He wouldn't want anyone else to do that.'

Lady Blythe frowned. Putting aside her coffee, she murmured confidingly, 'He may not have mentioned it, but poor Nicky was quite unwell after the War. Such a dreadful experience for us all. I think Nicholas felt Gerald's death almost as much as I did. Nicky still has to be careful not to overtire himself. He is looking rather under the weather, don't you think?'

Thomasine could not speak. She stirred her coffee so furiously that some of the liquid slopped over into the saucer. Lady Blythe gave a signal to the waiting footman and a clean saucer appeared, gleaming porcelain edged with gold.

When, at the end of the evening, they walked up the stairs together, Nicholas whispered, 'There. It wasn't so bad, was it?'

Thomasine waited until she was inside her bedroom and

Nicholas, following after her, had closed the door behind him.

'*It wasn't so bad?* Nick – she *hates* me!' They had been given candles to lighten the darkness; the flame of Thomasine's guttered as she placed it on the writing-table.

Nicholas blinked. 'Nonsense, darling. You were chatting away all through dinner. Getting on like a house on fire, I thought.'

She stared at him. 'Can't you *see?*'

He looked bewildered. 'See what?'

'That your mother has forgotten nothing. Oh, Nick – don't be so obtuse! I'm still just a girl from the village to her. And there was the Firedrake, of course.'

He had sat down in a chair. The fire had died long ago; the room was cold and unwelcoming.

'Now that really is nonsense,' Nicholas said. 'Mama hasn't mentioned the Firedrake for years. I expect she's forgotten it.'

Thomasine sat on the bed, her cold feet curled under her. She thought that Lady Blythe forgot nothing, that ancient hatreds simmered behind those cornflower-blue eyes. She repeated simply, 'She hates me.'

The candles made amber circles of light in the darkness. Nicholas rubbed at his eyes. 'It's just her manner. Mama is very formal – old-fashioned, I suppose. Some people find it off-putting. But really, Thomasine, she was trying to put you at your ease. I was afraid it would be much worse. She talked to you all evening.'

'Nagging me,' she hissed. 'Hinting that I don't look after you properly. Making me look a fool in front of the servants. Telling me off for having a bath before dinner and a fire lit.'

Nicholas laughed. 'You didn't, did you? In the *bedroom?* I'd have loved to have seen the servants' faces. I don't think fires have been lit in the bedrooms for *decades*. I'm surprised the chimney didn't catch alight.'

He rose from the chair. He took the candlestick from Thomasine's hands and placed it on the bedside table. Then he sat down beside her.

'You can't expect it to be easy, Thomasine. Mama would have loved me to have a big wedding, all the trimmings. We didn't really think of her feelings, did we? She probably feels cheated.'

Throughout the evening, all her doubts concerning her marriage had crowded back. She had to force herself to ask her next question. 'And you, Nick. Do you feel cheated? Do you regret what we did?'

'No. Of course not.' Once more, she could read the truth in his eyes. 'How can you ask? It was perfect. It's still perfect – or it would be if I wasn't such a duffer.'

She shook her head, squeezing his fingers. 'It's just taking a bit of time, that's all. That's not uncommon.' Dr Stopes had taught her that plenty of newly-married couples had trouble starting a family. Because of ignorance, or anxiety, or simply the time it took for two people to get used to each other.

In the silence she could hear the wind and see the flicker of the curtains as cold air crept into the room. When she looked back, she saw that Nicholas had turned away from her, his head bowed.

'Stay the night, Nick. Please.'

Reaching out, she touched him on the shoulder. When he turned to her, she kissed his furrowed forehead until, eventually, he smiled.

Thomasine woke early the next morning. A jug of hot water had already been left on the wash-stand by some silent-footed servant. Without waking Nicholas, she rose and washed and dressed.

As she walked through the house, sunlight spread in dust-dappled squares from the high windows, and the colours of paintwork and furnishings seemed brighter, less oppressive. She realized that the previous night she had been foolish. Nicholas had been right; Lady Blythe did not hate her. She only resented, understandably, the hastiness of her son's marriage, the difference in station between Nicholas and her new daughter-in-law. It was up to Thomasine to prove to Lady Blythe that her son had not made a mistake in marrying Patricia Thorne's daughter.

After breakfast, she and Sir William walked in the garden. The sky was a cloudless forget-me-not blue. Sunlight glimmered on the lawn, turning the dew into a thousand coloured jewels. Sir William pointed with his walking-stick towards the paddock.

'They say you can still make out the outline of the old abbey there. Can't see it m'self. Whole caboodle was knocked down by Henry the Eighth when he got rid of the monasteries, and some lucky Blythe was there to pick up the pieces. I used to grub around in the earth as a boy, looking for buried treasure. Never found a thing, of course.' He chuckled, and held out his arm to Thomasine.

They walked beneath the circular shadows of the copper-beech, the monkey-puzzle, the cedar. Drakesden Abbey lay to one side of them, many of its windows still closed and curtained. To the other side, the lawn sloped away, merging eventually with the paddock, then with farmland. They passed the gardeners' sheds, the greenhouses, the shrubbery.

Sir William nodded in the direction of the sheds. 'We'd have had a dozen fellows working there once. Before the War, that is. Cutting and pruning, planting out seedlings, potting them up. Now there's just Dilley and the boy. Dilley's almost seventy now.'

The laurel hedge ended and the path that was the entrance to the Labyrinth opened out before them. Branches, their new bright green leaves uncurling, hung over the path, making a roof. The grass was long and wet underfoot. Only every now and then did the sunlight break through, scattering speckled light on the old brick wall, catching on cobwebs and brambles.

When she saw the gate, Thomasine let out a gasp of pleasure, of recollection. 'Oh! The secret garden. Could we . . .?'

'Try the door, my dear. I don't think it's locked.'

She turned the handle. Slowly, creaking a little, the door opened. The walled garden lay before her, its rose-beds and lawns and statues just as before.

'It's perfect,' she said. 'I always thought this garden was perfect.'

'M'father planned it.' Beginning to walk again, Sir William struck at some of the long grass with his stick. 'That was his hobby, gardening. Or obsession, you might say. I remember, when I was a boy, the Abbey gardens were magnificent. But it's sadly overgrown now. Dilley and the boy manage to keep the front of the house tidy enough, and the kitchen gardens, but this . . . hasn't seen a scythe for years. I tried to cut back the roses myself last winter, but this damned rheumatism . . . begging your pardon, Thomasine.'

She smiled at him. 'It's still beautiful. And the roses are budding already.'

He snapped off one of the partly-opened blooms and handed it to her. It was pale pink, gloriously perfumed. 'Albertine. My favourite. Much nicer than those dreadful modern things with no scent. One of the few things Gwennie and I agree on, when it comes to gardening.' His dark brown eyes, Nicholas's eyes, looked around the walled garden. 'I'm glad that you saw it before the War. I'm glad that you saw it at its best. Something to tell your children about.'

She slid the rose through her lapel buttonhole.

Sir William added, 'The house is much too big for us now, of course. We should sell, like everyone else. Only I'm fond of the place, and besides, it will be Nicholas's soon enough. It wouldn't seem right to barter his inheritance.'

They had reached the statue of the Firedrake. The ferns that had once hidden a stolen bottle of wine were tall now, green and many-tongued in the water that dripped from the dragon's mouth.

'It was the War, y'know,' said Sir William. 'The poor boy was very ill after the War.'

She could smell the Albertine rose in her buttonhole, hear only the whispering of the gentle wind in the trees. She waited mutely for him to continue.

'Nicholas was wounded at the Somme. His arms were torn to ribbons – a terrible mess. He was recommended for an MC, y'know. We were so proud of him, Gwennie and I. But somehow . . . never quite the same after that . . . never able to settle . . . sometimes didn't seem quite *here* . . .' Sir William broke off the dead head of a rose, and crumbled the powdery petals between his fingers.

She had been looking forward to this for so long. It had been over a year since Gwendoline Blythe had spoken to her younger son – since Gerald's death, her only son – over a year since she had had his company to herself. Yesterday she had had to share him with the Thorne girl (she could not yet bring herself even to think, 'Thomasine' or 'Nicholas's wife').

As usual, Lady Blythe passed the hours after breakfast writing letters and discussing the ordering of the day's meals with Cook. At ten o'clock, Nicholas knocked at her door. She embraced him, smoothing the untidy dark hair out of his eyes with one hand.

'Did you sleep well, Nicky?'

He nodded. 'Like a log.'

'So good that you could come to Drakesden, Nicky. We need you so much.'

He blinked, and lit a cigarette. 'Has Pa been very unwell? You said in your letters, just a touch of rheumatism –'

She poured two cups of coffee, stirring cream into them. 'William suffers in the cold damp weather. He was quite unable to walk in the spring, which was why we did not ask you to Drakesden earlier. It would have been miserable for you.'

He looked uneasy. 'But it isn't . . . it isn't – *dangerous?*'

She gave a short trill of laughter and gave Nicholas his cup. 'Oh, no, not at all. Just inconvenient and depressing. You mustn't worry.'

'It's just that . . . well, I had a bit of a shock coming up the drive yesterday. Drakesden has gone to seed, hasn't it? I suppose . . . not having seen the place for a while . . .'

'We can't get the men, Nicky. Nor the girls, if it comes to that. They all seem to prefer to work in *offices*, these days.' Lady Blythe's mouth curled. 'Things have changed so much since the War. And I believe there are financial problems. Taxes, that sort of thing. William will want to talk to you, of course. We have made economies, naturally, but one feels so beleaguered nowadays.'

'Quite a lot of chaps' parents are having to sell. The Mortlakes – two lots of death duties, you know, Mama – the father, then Johnnie Mortlake died in 1916.' His voice was careless, uninterested.

Lady Blythe told herself that it was just Nicholas's manner. She believed that beneath his superficial disinterest, Drakesden Abbey was as important to him as it was to her. It had to be: he was a Blythe.

'I thought we should have a little chat,' she said. 'Letters are so *unsatisfactory*, don't you agree?'

Nicholas had sat down in one of the small chintz armchairs. 'You should have telephones installed, Mama.'

'Telephones! I don't think so.'

Nicholas frowned. 'Impractical, I suppose. Drakesden is just too far from civilization. But you really should have electricity. It's ridiculous, still to rely on oil-lamps and candles. Too medieval.'

'We are too remote. None of the villages have electricity.'

Nicholas said impatiently, 'The Abbey is hardly the same as a squalid little village like Drakesden. Drakesden will remain in the Dark Ages, no doubt, for the next half-century. There's no reason for the Abbey to do likewise.' He stubbed his cigarette out in the ashtray.

'The expense . . .' murmured Gwendoline. 'And is it safe?'

'Of course it is, Mama. Perfectly safe. If Drakesden was mine, the first thing I would do would be to install a generator. Then . . . radiators, electric lights, hot running water. It's absolutely ludicrous that poor Thomasine couldn't have a bath without half the servants having to run up and downstairs for hours with jugs of hot water. And the bedrooms are like ice-boxes for nine months of the year.'

'I was brought up to believe that an over-heated bedroom was bad for the health.'

Nicholas snorted. 'I'm not suggesting anything tropical. Simply that you don't suffer from frostbite every time you put a foot out from under the blankets.'

Gwendoline recognized in her son an enthusiasm which she had rarely seen before. If she found electricity, telephones and suchlike both incomprehensible and unnecessary, she realized that Nicholas did not.

She said carefully, 'You know that the Gillory boy is back in Drakesden, don't you, Nicholas?'

He stared at her. 'Gillory? Which Gillory?'

'Daniel.' She disliked saying his name, but she managed to hide her distaste. She still remembered the way Daniel Gillory had looked at her outside the church . . . insolence, and triumph.

He was frowning, shaking his head. 'I thought he'd gone for good. I thought we'd seen the back of him years ago.'

Her heart was beating rather fast. 'I'm afraid not. He is working in Drakesden now.'

'Smithying?' Nicholas's laugh was short and unamused. 'He used to think himself a cut above that.'

'Daniel Gillory isn't a blacksmith. He is a farmer.'

She hadn't told him before, because she had wanted to tell him face to face, like this. She had wanted to see how he would react. Whether the old antipathies of childhood still remained. Whether he felt as she did about Drakesden Abbey.

'He has bought more land. He farms the Abbey acres that William sold a year ago. The woman who bought it must have been a friend of his.'

Nicholas stared at her. She saw the colour ebb slowly from his face.

'He is married, Nicholas. His wife is a Londoner. A common little thing. She wears lipstick to *church*.'

Nicholas rose from his chair and went to stand at the window. She could see how white his knuckles were as he gripped the sill.

'Daniel Gillory is farming Blythe land?' he whispered. 'Daniel Gillory tricked us into selling him Blythe land?'

'Yes.'

When he turned, she saw the depth of the hatred in his eyes. It almost took her by surprise, and then she was aware of a deep river of happiness, of relief, welling up inside her. She knew that this was something they would always share, she and Nicholas, this need to keep Drakesden Abbey inviolate.

'It is intolerable,' he said.

'Yes,' she answered simply. 'Quite intolerable.'

That year the summer broke all records. The July of 1921 was the driest ever recorded. The dykes and ditches dried up, and there was no rain for the water-butts to catch. The leaves of the most delicate plants scorched in the hot sunshine, and the foliage of others shrank and yellowed through lack of water.

Cycling back from Ely one afternoon, Daniel thought it ironic that his labours that day had been to do with an abundance of water instead of a shortage of it. He had spoken that midday to an informal gathering of Drainage Commissioners, land-owners and farmers in one of the Ely public houses. He had tried to make them see that for Drakesden, with its inadequate and ill-repaired dykes and ditches, there was a disaster waiting to happen.

But they hadn't listened. They had been, unsurprisingly, too absorbed with the present problems of water-shortage and drought. Too easily distracted by all landowners' and farmers' worries about falling grain prices, high mortgages and rising costs. Those problems concerned Daniel too, although in some respects he was slightly better off than most. Having foreseen what had happened – that the Government would stop subsidizing wheat prices – he had already diversified, planting potatoes and other root crops as well as soft fruit. And Hattie, dear Hattie, charged him no interest on the money that he had borrowed.

Daniel climbed off his bicycle, wheeling it over the rickety plank that spanned the dyke. There was no water now in the dyke, only, in some places, a layer of thick, fetid mud. Stranded eels floundered in the mud. The sight of the writhing, flyblown bodies sickened him, so he looked grimly ahead, pushing the cycle quickly across the wobbling plank. Then he began to ride again down the dry, rutted drove.

He would survive, he thought. He must find other ways of bringing attention to the threat of flooding, and other ways of earning money. He had explained to Fay only that morning just how careful they must be. That, whenever possible, they should eat the produce of the farm instead of buying tinned food from the grocer's or meat from the butchers. That they could not, for a while at least, afford much in the way of new clothes or new things for the house. Daniel had already stopped buying second-hand books. He had done all he could to protect himself and Fay from the man-made disasters caused by the economic policies of the Government. He had tried, that day, to protect them in future years from the potentially much greater disasters of nature, but so far he had failed.

The Gillorys' cottage, built on the lowest-lying land and close to the dyke, was particularly vulnerable to flooding. That was why, during every spring of their childhood, Daniel and all his brothers and sisters had paddled bare-foot inside their kitchen for a week or two. There was nothing he could do at the moment to prevent that. The cottage would flood this spring, next spring, the spring after that. The peat soaked up water like a sponge, and spewed it out through the loose bricks of the Gillorys' floor. When he had money, when he had time, when

Sir William Blythe decided to sell the fields that Daniel coveted – those fields that were just that little bit higher – then Daniel would build a better cottage with a downstairs parlour and a bathroom, just like Fay wanted. Every week Daniel struggled to put aside a small amount of money, waiting for the time when the Blythes would have to sell.

The next drain was bridged with a log of bog oak. Daniel dismounted and hauled the bicycle across. He could see the blacksmith's cottage now and Fay in the garden, unpegging the washing. Standing on top of the dyke, Daniel waved and called her name, and cycled the last few hundred yards along the narrow rim of the bank.

She was waiting in the yard for him. She looked happy, excited, her eyes bright, her lips rosy-red. She was a changeable person, he had realized during the ten months of their marriage. He could never guess in what frame of mind she was going to be from one day to the next.

She folded up a pillowcase and put it in the wicker basket. 'How did you get on?'

He shook his head. 'Not too well, I'm afraid. I think they thought I was insane for haranguing them about water at a time like this.'

He propped the bicycle against the wall of the barn and rubbed his sleeve against his forehead. He felt hot, dusty and sweaty.

'Have we any beer?'

'A little. I haven't had time to go to The Otter. Come inside, Daniel – there's something I must show you.'

He followed her to the house. As he crossed the dusty yard, he said, 'None of them can see further than the ends of their noses, that's the trouble. The Commissioners, I mean. And when they do decide to do something, it's at a snail's pace.'

He stepped inside the cottage. Fay handed him a glass of beer. It was lukewarm, the dregs of the barrel. 'Look,' she said.

He looked to where she was pointing. A strange contraption

stood across the kitchen from him, in pride of place on the floor in front of the dresser. An odd collection of cylinder, switches, hose, wires. His mind still on agricultural equipment and steam-pumps, he couldn't at first think what it was. Then he said, 'It's a vacuum cleaner.'

Fay said proudly, 'Yes. Isn't it smart, Daniel? Isn't it modern? The salesman said that I'd be able to clean this room in a fraction of the time. You can even use it to dust curtains.'

He rubbed his eyes. His head ached with the heat, with tension and thirst. 'You *bought* it?' he said disbelievingly.

She nodded. 'A gentleman came round just half an hour ago. He's going round all the cottages in Drakesden.'

He stared at her, but she still smiled, still looked pleased with herself. 'Fay,' he said very softly. 'How did you pay for it?'

Even then, she did not falter. 'Oh, that's all right. You don't need to fuss. We don't have to pay all of it at once. The gentleman said that we could pay over a year. He was ever so nice, Daniel, ever so polite. You just have to sign the papers. He'll be back in a little while to collect them.'

He saw the papers lying on the table. Rifling through them, rapidly scanning the print, he said, 'You bought it on hire purchase, Fay. You bought this – this monstrosity – on hire purchase.'

Swinging round to look at her, he saw her expression change at last. Her small mouth pursed up, her brow became sulky. 'There's no need to shout, Daniel. I thought you'd be pleased.'

'We haven't any bloody electricity!' he yelled.

'I know *that*. I'm not stupid. But we will have soon – the gentleman said so. Every house in England will have electricity in six months' time. He showed me a newspaper article about it.'

He opened his mouth to try and explain that it would be years – decades, perhaps – before somewhere like Drakesden had electricity. To point out to her the difference between the cost price of that useless contraption and the hire purchase price. To point out that, had the thing cost ten shillings or ten pounds or ten thousand pounds, they still could not have afforded it.

But he understood suddenly, looking at her, that all such protests would be futile. She was winding a strand of hair around one of her small, slim fingers. The realization that she was not listening to him, that she had not the perception to understand if she had been listening, shocked him.

He grabbed the papers off the table, stuffed them in his pocket and bundled up the vacuum cleaner in his arms. It was easy to find the salesman: the motor-car marked his presence in the Dockerills' house. Flo Dockerill, mother of ten, a cannier woman altogether than Daniel's Fay, was arguing with the unfortunate salesman.

Daniel opened the boot of the salesman's car and dropped the vacuum cleaner inside. Then he rapped on the door of the Dockerills' cottage. When he had torn up the hire purchase agreement and scattered the pieces over the spotless brick floor of Flo Dockerill's kitchen, he told the salesman, in uncompromising terms, what he could do with his vacuum cleaner. Then, apologizing to Flo for the mess he had made, he tramped off back to the cottage.

It was a week before Fay forgave him. When he tried to touch her at night, she moved away from him silently, offering no quarter, curled up and closed on the clammy sheets.

The summer passed, febrile and overheated. London was unbearable, but they were able to escape to the Continent only for a couple of weekends. Lack of funds, Nicholas explained. They spent a week in Bournemouth, baking with a thousand others on the hot yellow sand. Bournemouth's night-life did not compare with London's; Simon and Tiny drove back to Town one day, Nicholas and Thomasine the next.

One morning in early September, Teddy arrived at the Chelsea house. Greeting him, Thomasine kissed him on the cheek.

'Busy?' he asked. There were lengths of material, reels of

thread, packets of pins scattered all over the drawing-room floor.

'I've almost finished cutting it out.' She folded the cut pieces of material and began to put them away. 'It's too hot for sewing, though.'

'We could go to the Savoy. Have a dance. Or is Nick . . .?' Teddy pushed some pins into the pin-cushion.

'Nick has gone out.'

Teddy said nothing, just looked at her.

She said, exasperated, 'Yes, he's with Simon. And, yes, we quarrelled. Again. About his bloody mother, actually.'

He was offended by neither her language nor her tone. Teddy was never offended. 'Steady on, old thing,' he said gently.

They went to Kew Gardens. It was cool in the shelter of the trees; Thomasine could almost imagine herself in the countryside. After they had walked for an hour or so, they had tea among the palms and wrought-iron and wicker furniture of the restaurant.

'Tell me about Nicholas's mother,' said Teddy, after Thomasine had poured the tea.

She thought of Lady Blythe, whom she had last seen at Drakesden over four months ago. 'She's like Queen Mary, only not so tall. Perfect deportment. Beautiful. And is utterly, utterly devoted to Nick.'

'Ah.' Teddy stirred his tea. 'She sounds detestable.'

Thomasine, scowling, put down her teacup. 'Sometimes I think she is, and sometimes I think that it's me. That I imagine that she is detestable. That I imagine she hates me.'

'Explain.' Teddy offered a cigarette to Thomasine, who shook her head.

'When we visited Drakesden Abbey – that's the Blythes' house – it was awful. I knew it was going to be difficult – because of who I am, and because of the way we married in Paris – but I didn't think it would be quite so bad. But it was. Except for Sir William – Nick's father. He was perfectly sweet.'

She paused for a moment, and then she added, shaking her head, 'But it's so hard to pinpoint exactly why it was awful. I keep going through it, over and over again and, really, Lady Blythe didn't say a single cross or unkind word to me. It just all felt so *uncomfortable*, Teddy. Nicholas can't see it, of course.'

'Which is why you quarrel.' Teddy pushed a plate of scones in Thomasine's direction. 'Eat up, poppet. No point in being miserable on an empty stomach.'

She took a scone and split it and buttered it, mentally reliving once more that weekend at Drakesden.

'What did you mean when you said you knew it was going to be difficult because of who you were?'

Thomasine looked up at him. 'Well, Teddy, would your mother want you to marry the girl who lived in the cottage two doors down from the post office? Assuming your parents *owned* most of the village, that is.'

He laughed. 'My mother would be delighted to see me hitched to the scullery-maid, if she was a respectable girl. She's a bit worried that I've reached the grand old age of thirty without bringing home any girl who isn't, as she sees it, a painted vamp or an empty-headed flapper.'

She smiled, but continued doggedly, 'You know what I mean, though, Teddy. Nicholas was supposed to marry some deb with a dowry. Instead, his mama finds that he's suddenly hitched to a chorus-girl he's met in Paris. Worse, a chorus-girl from the village he grew up in.'

Her hand, resting on the tablecloth, was clenched. Teddy laid his fingers over hers, so that her muscles relaxed a little.

'It'll get better. It'll just take time. I'm sure that once she gets to know you, Lady Blythe will realize how lucky Nick is.'

She smiled at him again. 'You really should marry, Teddy. You'd make a perfectly sweet husband.'

He said nothing, but leaned back in his chair and lit another cigarette. Even if she found some of Nicholas's friends vapid and ignorant and others self-seeking and affected, Thomasine had known for some time that she had found a friend in Teddy Sefton. Teddy had a shambling sort of elegance: his suits always seemed to be missing a button, his shirt-cuffs were often frayed. Yet his lazy diffidence was appealingly refreshing. With Teddy she never felt judged, never felt looked down on.

'We only stayed for a weekend, though. Nick wanted to get back to London. You know what he's like, Teddy – you know how he always wants to be on the go.'

'I know what he's like. I was the same.' Teddy blew a smoke ring. 'It just didn't last so long with me, that's all.'

Thomasine glanced at him sharply. 'You had neurasthenia, Teddy?'

'Mmm. Shellshock, the newspapers call it.'

Thomasine recalled the letter she had recently received from Hilda.

'I wrote to one of my aunts about Nick. She nursed in France, and afterwards worked in a convalescent home. She wrote to me that the symptoms of neurasthenia are nightmares, obsessions, restlessness and an inability to settle to anything. Well, that's Nick, isn't it? He never sleeps well, and everything always has to be just so. The maid hung his shirts in the wrong order a couple of days ago and he nearly threw a blue fit. And he's out every afternoon and every night. He just can't bear to do nothing. I'm worried about him.'

'Does he see a doctor?'

Thomasine shook her head. 'He saw doctors during and after the War, but apparently they couldn't do much. They told him to take lots of exercise and cold showers, not to dwell on the past, that sort of thing. To be a *man*.' Her voice was scathing.

Teddy's mouth twisted in the smallest of smiles. Then he said, 'Does he talk about it to you?'

'Not really. Hardly at all. I have tried, Teddy, lots of times, but it makes him so edgy that I'm afraid of making things worse.'

The waitress arrived with the bill. Teddy handed her a florin. Outside, they began to walk again.

'I was wounded in nineteen-sixteen,' explained Teddy. He was walking rather fast, with Thomasine's hand looped over his arm. 'Afterwards, when I was back in England, supposedly recuperating, I kept seeing it – the mud, the rats, the whole damned mess. Bits of people. Men with their faces or their legs shot away. Men literally coughing up their lungs because they'd been gassed. I remember going to Buckingham Palace to collect my medal. It felt so odd – half the time I wasn't really there, I was still at the Front. They called me a hero. And I was a hero. Every man that went through it was a damned hero. Only it wasn't heroic. Not one bit. Do you see?'

Thomasine thought back to the War years that she had spent with Antonia in London. 'I didn't know anyone at the Front,' she said slowly. 'Well, there were men I knew, like Nick, and Daniel, but I'd lost touch with them. No one wrote to me, and no one told me what it was like. I read the newspapers, of course, but they didn't say –'

'I know.' Teddy's voice was savage. 'It's called censorship, Thomasine. Besides, no one told their people back home what it was really like. I had to censor my men's letters. "Dear Mum, hoping this finds you as it leaves me. I am in good health, and cheery spirits." *God!*' Teddy threw his cigarette-butt into a flower-bed.

Thomasine, too, felt a sudden wave of anger. 'But you should have told us. Just because we're women, that's no reason to treat us as though we were idiots – or *children* –'

'Can you imagine experiencing something so awful that you couldn't talk about it to anyone else? Can you, Thomasine?'

Her anger died. She looked away from him. She thought of Paris, her pregnancy, the attempted abortion, the miscarriage. Only Alice knew part of it; she had never spoken of it to anyone else.

'Yes. I see.'

She saw, too, how late it had become. How the sun had begun to lower itself towards the horizon. How the heat of the day, the summer, had begun to diminish at last.

CHAPTER NINE

THE weeks passed, a muddle of fancy dress parties, swimming parties and treasure hunts. Nicholas's exhaustion was visible in the dark shadows that marked his face and in the unnatural brightness of his eyes. His moods were brittle and uncertain, lurching too easily from elation to despair. Thomasine, sensing the influence that Simon had over him, made sure that she was with Nicholas as much as possible. But she too began to feel tired and drained, so that when at first her period was overdue she put it down to the late nights and frantic days. But gradually, a new suspicion took hold of her, and eventually she allowed herself to hope. Excited, she made an appointment to see a doctor.

Leaving the doctor's, riding back in a taxi to the Chelsea house, Thomasine thought that they had been allowed a new start. The child that had begun inside her body might compensate for the child who had died last summer, might compensate too for the lives Nicholas had seen destroyed in the War. This child might restore Nicholas's shattered belief in himself, and might give her a real purpose in life.

Nicholas was out when Thomasine returned home. A note was stuffed behind the clock on the mantelpiece. 'Simon called. At the garage for an hour or two. All love.' She sat down on the couch, slightly deflated. All the way back from Harley Street she had pictured Nicholas's face as she told him her news.

The telephone rang and Thomasine answered it. Teddy was persuasive, amusing. She found herself putting her coat and hat back on, and walking to the Underground station.

They went to an exhibition of prints and textiles in a Grafton

Street gallery. Angular black and white birds soared into the air on advertising posters; women, their necks elongated and their eyes almond-shaped, gazed down at her from prints and lithographs.

'Do you like them?' asked Teddy. 'Or do you prefer Marcus Dorn's red tubes?'

She laughed. 'I like them. So elegant. So serene.'

'Like you,' said Teddy.

She wanted to laugh again, but only shook her head.

'I mean it, Thomasine. You're one of those people who, when you're with them, everything seems to sort itself out. What terrible grammar – I do apologize.'

They were alone in the room, apart from the doe-eyed girls and the stylized birds. It crossed her mind, just for a moment, that she might confide in him. That she might share with Teddy the burden of guilt that still accompanied her memories of Paris and her marriage, allowing him to judge her with the intelligence, humour and tolerance that she had come to expect from him. But she did not, because she did not wish to witness the disappointment and disillusion in his eyes, and because to confide in another man would be a betrayal of Nicholas. Instead she walked on a little further.

And then Teddy said, 'I mean it, though. I only stay with the rest of them because of you. Bobby's an ass, and Simon's a gold-digger. Colin's taking off to Spain soon. The girls are good fun, but I'd be away with old Col tomorrow if it wasn't for you.'

She began to understand what he was telling her. Her face burned. 'That's kind of you, Teddy, but . . .'

'But you're a happily married woman, and I'm a drivelling idiot. Enough said.' He smiled his slightly twisted smile and walked with her into the next room. 'The worst of it is that Nicky Blythe doesn't even seem to realize what a lucky devil he is. I'll shut up now. Just remember that you have a friend. For life, I'm afraid.'

Later, when she was tired, he bought them both ices and they

244

sat at an open-air tea-shop in Hyde Park, eating them. The warm summer had lingered on into autumn, but now the air had chilled and leaves had begun to tumble from the trees, so that the grass was speckled gold, bronze, crimson.

She said when she had finished her ice, 'What did you mean, Teddy, when you said that Simon Melville was a gold-digger?'

He lit two cigarettes and passed one to Thomasine. 'Only that Simon latched on to Bobby because Bobby is rather well-heeled. Not because of Bobby's sparkling wit or challenging conversation. Simon was courting another rich young idiot before that. And there's the wealthy widow, of course.'

'You don't like him either?'

'He's a fraud. I don't give a damn who his parents were, what his politics are, it's not that. God knows, we all have to scrabble around a bit nowadays for something to believe in. But Simon sells his pretences for money and then expects the object of his greed to adore him. He sees people's weaknesses and exploits them. He had a go at me once, you see. Soon found out I hadn't a bean. Well, not like this poor chap –' Teddy nodded at the beggar walking from table to table, his cap outstretched – 'but you know what I mean.'

Teddy threw a handful of coins into the cap, and Thomasine fumbled in her purse for money. The note pinned to the beggar's greatcoat said 'Ex-serviceman – wife and five kids to support.' Dead leaves floated on the water and ducks squabbled over a piece of bread thrown by a child.

When she arrived back at the Chelsea house, Nicholas was in the bedroom, struggling with the stiff fastenings of his dress-shirt.

'Where have you *been?* It's seven o'clock.'

Guiltily, Thomasine glanced at her watch. 'I was with Teddy. We got talking. I forgot the time.'

He was trying to thread his cuff-links through his sleeve. He mumbled something.

Thomasine said, 'Let me do that.' She took the gold link and began to push it through his cuff. She started to speak, to tell him her wonderful news, but he interrupted her.

'I said, you seem to be spending a hell of a lot of time with Teddy Sefton.'

Looking up at him, she realized how angry he was. 'What do you mean, Nick?'

He jerked away from her. The cuff-link, unfastened, fell to the floor. 'What I said. That you seem to be spending a lot of time with bloody Teddy Sefton.'

Some of her happiness drained away and was replaced by anger. 'I don't like spending every afternoon stuck in here on my own while you're out with Simon, that's all.'

He was scrabbling about on the floor for the fallen cuff-link. 'It's hardly the same.'

'You fiddle with your motor-car, I go to look at paintings. What's the difference?'

'*Christ.*' Nicholas abandoned the search. Standing up, he pulled a drawer out of the dressing-table and threw its contents on the bed. 'There's every difference, isn't there?' He stared at the tangle of ties, handkerchiefs and jewellery on the eiderdown. 'None of them bloody match –'

She noticed then how his hands were shaking. Sitting on the bed, forcing herself to remain calm, she started to help him pair the cuff-links.

'Teddy can give you a better time than I can, is that it, Thomasine?'

She looked up at him then. When she understood what he was saying, she wanted to hit him. To strike those familiar handsome, mistrusting features until he understood, until he listened to her.

'How *dare* you –'

'Simon pointed out to me how keen Teddy was on you. You've spent every afternoon this week with him, haven't you?'

'Colin was with us yesterday. And the day before –'

'And today?'

She did not answer him quickly enough. She struggled for the right words.

Nicholas added bitterly, 'I was such a fool not to have noticed it before. He's in love with you, isn't he?'

She remembered the expression on Teddy's face when he had spoken to her in the art gallery. Thomasine stared wordlessly at Nicholas's busy hands, at his long, elegant fingers. He was rolling up the ties, tidying them with hurried, meticulous, obsessive thoroughness, replacing them in the drawer. He said, 'I thought so. You can't deny it, can you?'

It was true, she could not. She said stiffly, 'Whatever Teddy's feelings are for me, I feel only friendship for him. You must believe me, Nick.'

He was folding the handkerchiefs now, creasing the white linen so that the corners matched perfectly and the refolded squares were exact. Then he placed them in the drawer beside the watches, which he had laid out in parallel lines, and the cuff-links, all now exactly paired. He said nothing, but she could see the disbelief in his eyes.

Thomasine grabbed a towel and her dressing-gown. 'I'm going to have a bath,' she said furiously and slammed the door behind her.

Lally had returned to England in mid-October, but had not yet contacted her parents, brother or sister. Rather short of money, she took a room in one of the less expensive hotels and slept, on and off, for a week. The summer cold that had lingered into the autumn disappeared at last and, eventually, she got out of bed. At first she continued to take her meals in her room, but then once or twice she wandered down to the dining-room or the bar. She received a few stares at first, sitting alone at a table, smoking and drinking without an escort. Sometimes they refused to serve her, often she brazened it out. At the end of a fortnight, when she felt able to face the outside world again, she began to make discreet enquiries.

She discovered that Nicholas was living in a dreadful little house in Chelsea, from which she concluded that he, too, was short of funds. Acquaintances of acquaintances described to her Nicholas's friends, his social life, his new red-headed wife. Lally managed to wangle herself an invitation to a party in Mayfair.

Nicholas was not yet there when she arrived, so she had to put up with the attentions of her escort. He was handsome, rich and dull. In France, after Marcel, she had lost count of the men. She remembered faces, names, at random. She was aware that, though each one had courted her assiduously, none had wept at her departure.

The Mayfair house, although large, was crowded. People were crammed into all the downstairs rooms and jostled each other in the hall and on the stairs. Many of the women were dressed as men: dinner jackets and trousers, hair slicked back against their heads, white faces and scarlet lips.

Lally's escort, staring, turned back to her. 'You haven't dressed up. You'd have looked terrific as a chap.'

Lally took a cocktail from the tray offered to her. She disliked fancy dress parties; she preferred always to wear the same sort of clothes. Black, or other dark colours, subtle, shimmery, satiny materials. Marcel had taught her, and besides, though she had lost weight in France, she still saw herself as a dumpy schoolgirl.

'I don't like to dress up. Have you a cigarette, Pip?'

Her escort opened his cigarette-case. Virginia on one side, Turkish on the other. Lally chose Turkish. They wandered through the house. A jazz band was playing in the large back room: five musicians, each with skin as black as ebony. The room opened out into a conservatory where geraniums, ten-foot high, grew against the walls. There was a sweet, heavy scent in the air that Lally could not identify as belonging to any of Mama's conservatory plants at Drakesden.

'Dance?' said her escort.

The room was full of dancers. Limbs flailed, beads were swung, sweat glimmered on straining faces.

'I don't think so.'

'Another drink, then?'

Lally watched him disappear into the crowd. Once more, she glanced at all the other guests, and then she turned and walked into the conservatory.

The conservatory was cool and dark. Someone had opened the wide double doors, letting in the cold autumn air. 'The orchids will die,' muttered Lally out loud, and broke one of the blooms from its stem. It was chartreuse-coloured, with a flush of crimson staining its open throat. She pinned it to her hair with a diamond clip that Marcel had bought her. When she glanced at her reflection in the window, she found that it was pleasing. The dark hair, the dark, slanted eyes, the white skin, the acid-green flower the only bright colour. Lally smiled. Then she saw the couple in the garden.

They were standing beside the fountain and they were kissing. She saw the two dinner suits, the two high white collars, the two smooth, dark heads. They looked like reflections of each other. She realized that they were both women, and watched for a while, fascinated. Scarlet lip against scarlet lip; a long, slender white hand caressing an equally slender white neck.

When at last Lally looked away, she saw, through the blur of dancers, Nicholas and Thomasine.

There had been no opportunity to make up the quarrel because Simon and Tiny had arrived while Thomasine was having her bath, and then they had all travelled together in the Delage to Mayfair. Besides, she was still almost too angry to speak to Nicholas.

The first person she saw at the party was Lally Blythe. Thomasine hardly recognized her. The plump schoolgirl was utterly gone, and in her place was a small, elfin creature in dark crimson, a lime-green flower in her hair. Lally waved at them, then fought through the dancers and gave both Thomasine and Nicholas a restrained, Blythe-like peck on the cheek. Thomasine noticed the pleasure in Lally's eyes, though, when she looked at Nicholas.

'This is Tiny, and this is Simon,' said Nicholas. 'Meet my younger sister, Lally.'

Thomasine said, 'How lovely to see you, Lally. How long have you been back from France?'

'Oh – a week or two. Isn't this divine? There are two women in the garden, *kissing*. Too decadent.'

Thomasine glanced down at her chiffon dress. 'I didn't know . . .'

Tiny was wearing trousers, a waistcoat, a white shirt. Simon Melville said carelessly, 'Didn't Nick tell you? Peggy's little get-together is a homage to the altar of Sappho.'

Nicholas said, 'Have you been home, Lally? Have you been to Drakesden?'

Lally shook her head. 'Not yet. I'll write, I suppose.'

'We're going down in a week or two. You could come with us.'

Lally looked unenthusiastic. 'Perhaps. Are they well? Is everything just the same?'

'Mama is very well. Pa's a bit creaky. So's Drakesden, come to that. Weeds in the drive and the floors no longer polished daily.'

'*Not* the thing,' said Lally mockingly.

Simon Melville yawned. 'So dull, all this family chit-chat. You should do as I did, Nick, old thing, and cut yourself off from the lot of them.'

The band had begun to play again. Simon said, 'Shall we dance?'

They danced together, exchanging partners at the end of each tune. Lally found herself in Simon Melville's arms.

He glanced down at her. 'What are you looking at?'

'You.' She was studying his well-cut fair hair, his straight, sculpted features, his blue-grey eyes. 'You are the most handsome man I've met in months.'

Her voice was matter-of-fact, not flirtatious. Lally never flirted. Simon just laughed.

She said curiously, 'Are you really a communist?'

'Why? Does it shock you?'

She shrugged. 'No. I'm not in the least bit interested in politics. I just wondered whether it was true, or whether you said it for effect.'

His glance this time was a little sharper, a little longer lasting.

'It doesn't matter,' she said reassuringly. 'It's just that political people can be so dull. And I thought we might talk.'

She led him upstairs, climbing over the embracing couples, the inebriated couples. On the landing, the sweet, musky smell that she had noticed in the conservatory was stronger.

'Are you planning to seduce me?' said Simon.

She glanced at him consideringly. He really was a most attractive man. 'Perhaps. Not just now. I want to talk to you about Nick.'

'Ah.'

'He's my only brother. My elder brother was killed in the War.'

They were leaning against the balustrade, looking down to the hall. Simon said, 'The inestimable Gerald.'

'The unbearable Gerald,' said Lally. 'He was dull, Simon, utterly dull. He hardly ever spoke to me. Mama thought he was wonderful, of course.'

A girl pushed past them, running across the landing to the stairs, her painted face streaked with tears. Simon yawned.

'I'm sorry,' said Lally. 'Family chit-chat again. Only I wanted to know, have they quarrelled? Nicky and Thomasine, I mean.'

She had noticed, watching her brother and his wife, that they had neither spoken to each other, nor looked at each other. When they had danced, it had been stiffly, awkwardly, as though they were strangers.

'Little marital tiff?' drawled Simon. 'Probably. I hadn't noticed.'

Liar, thought Lally. You notice everything. 'Are they happy, do you think?' The urgency in her voice took her by surprise.

'Happy . . .?' He was resting his elbows on the banister, watching the crowd below. 'I haven't a clue. Ghastly institution, marriage, don't you agree?'

She nodded. Though she would probably have to marry sometime in order to secure an income, she would put off that day as long as possible.

'Like being smothered in a soft, fluffy blanket,' added Simon. 'Or wading through syrup.'

She laughed, resting her arms on the balustrade next to his, so that their elbows touched. He neither pressed against her, nor moved away. She said, 'What do you think of her? What do you think of Thomasine?'

Simon pursed his beautiful mouth. His eyes were hard and cold. 'Hardly out of the top-drawer. She was a chorus-girl, I believe. Rather lacking in class.'

'People don't bother about things like that nowadays, do they? Not since the War.'

'Do you think so?' He swung back round to look at Lally. 'I don't agree. I think that they care just as much – perhaps more. They can see it all crumbling away. They are struggling to keep hold of what they have, before it slips from beneath them . . .'

His voice was low, amused. When Lally saw the expression in his eyes, she shivered. He was voicing what she most feared, the loss of the familiar order of things. Though her upbringing had bored her, the thought of an unpredictable, chaotic future was frightening.

She pushed those thoughts out of her mind. Wrinkling her nose, she said, 'What is that peculiar smell?'

Simon took a deep breath. 'Oh – marijuana. Peggy adores it. Haven't you tried it? You must. Come on.'

They were getting ready to leave the Mayfair house when it happened. There was an almighty crash and the glass in the large front window of the drawing-room shattered. Nicholas covered his head with his hands and ducked, and Thomasine felt herself dragged back towards the wall by Teddy's hand.

'Are you all right?'

She looked down at herself. Her chiffon dress sparkled, but that was the crystal beads sewn to the fabric, not shards of glass. The floor was littered with glass, like diamonds.

'I'm fine. Nick . . .?'

He lowered his hands and stood up straight again. He looked white, dazed. 'Sorry. Behaving like an ass. Thought it was a mortar . . .' He tried to laugh. Then he left the room.

Teddy said, 'A stone, I think. Someone's chucked a bloody stone through the window.' He crossed the room, treading carefully through the fragments of glass to the broken window.

Thomasine shivered. Cold air wafted in through the large jagged hole in the pane. The window faced out on to the street; she could hear voices calling outside and running footsteps. In the back room, the jazz band still played, the syncopated music muffled by distance. Servants arrived to sweep up the mess. People stood back from the shattered glass, staring and silent. The stone, the size of a man's fist, lay in the centre of the floor.

Thomasine whispered, 'Do you think it was an accident?'

Teddy's brother Colin, rather out of breath, muttered, 'Not likely. There were a couple of men in the road. Some of the chaps tried to chase them, but they took off.'

'Same thing happened a week ago, at the Montgomeries'.' Bobby Monkfield peered around the door, his sister on his arm. 'They were having a party and the window was smashed. Some damned beggar.'

'It's just envy,' cried Lavender. 'Too sick-making.'

'People are starting only to use the rooms at the back of their houses when they have parties. Frightful, isn't it, when you can't do what you want in your own home?'

Filled with a sudden revulsion, Thomasine moved away. She recalled clearly the beggar that she and Teddy had seen in Hyde

Park that afternoon. *Ex-serviceman – wife and five kids to support.* Suddenly the lavish food and endless bottles of champagne, the opulent furnishings and overheated house seemed contemptible; distaste overwhelmed her and she longed to leave.

She found Nicholas by the front door, wrapping his scarf around his neck, his fingers fumbling. She touched his arm. 'Shall we go home?'

He shook his head. His eyes were bright and feverish. 'It's only two. Can't go home yet. Plenty of time for a drive.'

'Please, Nick. I'm tired. It's late.'

She was about to explain, to tell him there and then in this noisy hallway about the baby, their baby, when Simon appeared, Lally at his side.

'If you don't want to come,' drawled Simon, 'then I'm sure one of the Seftons would be only too happy to take you home.'

She went with them, of course. Squashed in the dickey seat of the Delage with Lally Blythe, Thomasine was aware that she had not gone home because she feared for Nicholas, and because she feared for their future.

On the drive, she slept a little. When the motor-car drew to a halt and they went into the house, Thomasine felt dazed and disorientated. They walked through huge rooms, one of them octagonal, with jasper pillars and *trompe l'œil* murals.

'It'th Thimon'th rich widow'th houthe,' whispered Tiny. 'Lady Lilian Thomething-or-other.'

They were led into the garden. A huge rectangular swimming-pool was set into a marble terrace. Archways of intricate tracery surrounded the courtyard in which the pool was set.

'Frightfully Arabian Nights,' said Lavender Monkfield.

'There's bathing-dresses in the changing-rooms,' called Simon. 'That side for girls, this side for boys.'

'Aren't you . . .?' said Nicholas to Thomasine.

She shook her head and tried to smile. 'Too cold. I'll watch.'

She sat there alone on a marble bench, while the rest of them disappeared into the changing-rooms. There was no sign of the Seftons. Moonlight gleamed on the still surface of the pool and she could smell the scent of the box trees in their terracotta pots. As she watched, Thomasine saw someone dive into the pool, a clean, straight line, breaking the smooth water like a knife-cut. The swimmer disappeared and then re-emerged, and she recognized Simon Melville's fair head.

Nicholas swam for a while, hoping that the cold and the exercise would calm him. The events of the evening seemed to have jumbled together, so that he felt disturbed and unsettled. Around him, people were shrieking and laughing and playing with inflatable rubber rafts. He tried to shut himself off from them, forcing himself to think, to work things out. It was the quarrel with Thomasine that had upset him, of course. He realized now that he had been stupid, jealous. He could see her sitting there at the end of the pool, all hunched up on the marble seat. He felt a terrible wave of guilt: it was, after all, his duty as her husband to make her happy. And yet here he was, fooling around in a swimming-pool while she shivered alone in the darkness.

He swam to the edge of the pool and clambered out. Inside the changing-room, which looked, Nicholas thought, like something out of a harem, he pulled on his trousers and began to towel his hair.

A voice said, 'Had enough, Nick?'

Nicholas glanced back and grinned at Simon. Simon's body gleamed with droplets of water; his blond hair was darkened and stuck to his scalp. 'Too noisy for me,' he said, 'after that bloody stone. My ears are still ringing.'

'You've been looking a bit jumpy tonight.'

Simon's hand rested on his shoulder. Nicholas lowered the towel. 'Tired, I suppose,' he said awkwardly. 'Too many late nights.'

There was a silence. Though from school and the army he

was used to male nakedness, he found now that he felt tense, ill at ease.

'You don't have to stay with her, you know,' said Simon softly.

Nicholas turned round. He was still clutching the damp towel. 'What do you mean?' he whispered.

'Oh, come on, Nick. You understand me perfectly well. Lilian's made me her sole heir, you know, so there'd be no shortage of cash. Besides, I'd be very discreet. No need for Mummy and Daddy to know about us.'

Confused thoughts rushed through Nicholas's head. He couldn't concentrate, he couldn't think clearly. It took him a while to form one coherent sentence. At last he said, his voice choked and thick, 'You are suggesting that I leave Thomasine?'

'Well, it isn't working out, is it? The bitch isn't your type, Nick, is she? All that soft white flesh – that vulgar hair –'

Nicholas saw then the disgust in Simon Melville's eyes. Simon's hand still rested on his shoulder, but then slowly, deliberately, it ran down Nicholas's bare chest, to his stomach, towards his thigh.

With a cry of horror, he pulled himself away. His hands flailed out, wildly at first, and then with violent purpose. He heard himself cry, 'How could you – how could you think that of me?'

As he backed towards the door, grabbing his shoes and shirt, he saw that his fist had caught Simon on the chin and that blood trickled from the corner of his friend's mouth.

Simon touched the wound disbelievingly. 'You've hurt me.' He wiped his mouth with the back of his hand; scarlet smeared his fingers. Then he said, 'You're the same as the rest of them, aren't you, Blythe? I thought you were different, but I was wrong. A wife and a couple of howling brats and a long slow death trying to hold on to the remains of the family fortune.' He looked up at Nicholas, his eyes dark and glittering. 'Well, you won't, you know. None of you will. For your lot, it's over.'

★

She went to look for him. Thomasine had seen Nicholas run out of the changing-room; Simon had stayed inside.

He had disappeared into the darkness. She searched the house first, peering into glittering and unfamiliar rooms. The vast chambers were echoing and empty, the house seemed deserted. Then she searched the garden. The swimming-pool was empty now, littered with inflatable rafts, discarded bathing-caps and a smear of dead leaves blown on to the surface of the water. The wind had become chill. The grass, as Thomasine walked through it, was already crisp with frost.

The Delage was still there, parked in front of the house. She began to run then, sensing disaster, through rose-beds, past statues and ornamental ponds. Moonlight painted the garden; the flood-lights from around the pool allowed her to make out her path.

She found him in the summer-house at the end of the pergola. Nicholas was hunched in the corner-seat, his knees under his chin, rocking slightly. She said his name, but he did not respond. When she crossed the floor to him, she realized that he neither saw her nor heard her. His eyes were wide, frightened, the pupils flicking this way and that. She knew that he saw something completely other than the distant shape of the house, the broad sweep of the garden.

She cried out, 'What are you seeing, Nick? *What are you seeing?*'

He did not answer her. She heard his low moan of despair, and she put her arms around him so that his head lay against her breast, while she gently smoothed the damp black hair away from his face. She said, over and over again, 'Nick – it's me, Thomasine. You're with me, and you're safe. There's nothing out there to hurt you.'

And eventually his fingers that gripped her flimsy dress relaxed, and she saw his staring eyes close, and she heard the moan become a groan of relief, of remembered pain. Stroking his face, she repeated, 'There's nothing out there, Nick. Just the trees and the garden. I'm here with you. Nothing's going to hurt you.'

Slowly, he sat up. His hands were balled against his eyes. 'Oh God. I'm so sorry . . .'

She said firmly, 'There's no reason to be sorry. You've done nothing to be ashamed of. You just had – a sort of nightmare, that's all.'

His face was pale and crumpled. He lay back against the wooden wall of the summer-house.

'Just sit there a while. Then we'll go home. I'll drive, if you like. I've watched you often enough.'

He wasn't listening. He said, 'If you want to go – to call it a day – then I'll understand. I've been a rotten husband, I know.'

She could not bear to see the pain in his eyes. Still, clearly visible, was that awful naked love. Although she had doubted many, many times over the past year that they should ever have married, she understood now that the battered and bruised remnants of affection still remained.

Thomasine took a deep breath. 'Do you want me to go, Nick?'

There were black shadows under his eyes, but she thought that he was seeing her clearly for the first time. He said slowly, 'I love you so much, Thomasine. In the War, I used to think about you. I'd imagine going to the meadow at Drakesden . . . and you would be there, and it would be just like it was before . . . Please don't leave me. Please.'

'I won't leave you, Nick.' Her voice wobbled. 'What would people think? I'm going to have a baby, Nick. I'm going to have your baby.'

She saw his look of disbelief, then heard his small gasp of uncertain delight. He took her in his arms then, and her eyes closed as she nestled her head against his shoulder, and he kissed the crown of her head.

Neither of them saw Lally glance through the open door of the summer-house, and then turn away, walking quickly through the garden.

★

They drove back through the dawn. They took it in turns to drive, brushing away the remaining shadows of the night in laughter as the motor-car kangarooed round corners when Thomasine brought up the clutch too quickly, or stalled when she forgot to change gear. If the laughter was a little forced, then it was better than tears.

When they reached the Chelsea house a telegram was waiting for them. Nicholas's face, pale to begin with, grew white as he tore it open and read what was written inside.

The wait, as he struggled to find words, was intolerable. At last he said, 'It's Pa, Thomasine. He died yesterday afternoon. A stroke.'

He handed her the telegram. The white paper shook in her hands like a leaf about to fall. Nicholas walked to the window. The shafts of early morning sunlight seemed weak, dissipated. Thomasine went to him and took him in her arms. There were no tears in his eyes, only a shocked blankness.

'You realize what this means, Thomasine,' he whispered. 'We'll have to go to Drakesden. We'll have to live at Drakesden. It's mine, now.'

Almost the entire village of Drakesden attended the funeral of Sir William Blythe. The wind was cold and fidgety, directionless, working its way through the crooked doors and window-frames of the Drakesden cottages.

They had quarrelled most of the morning, Daniel and Fay. Or, not quarrelled, exactly – more a series of short silences, punctuated on Fay's part by bewildered resentment, on Daniel's by stubbornness and sarcasm.

She was putting on her hat, checking her lipstick in her powder-compact. There was a new black ribbon around the mauve hat. Daniel noticed the ribbon but just managed to say nothing. Fay closed her compact with a snap and looked at Daniel. He was dressed in old corduroys, a shirt and a muddy jacket. His working clothes.

'So you're really not going.'

'I'm really not going.' He tried not to let his impatience show in his voice.

She began to button up her coat. 'If you don't go to church, things like that, how can you better yourself?'

Daniel took a deep breath and pointed to the pile of library books on the table. '*That* is how I better myself.'

She glanced at the books disparagingly. 'Those old things. You'd do well, Daniel Gillory, to talk to the right sort of people, to try and be a bit more civil to your betters.'

This time he could not keep the sarcasm from his voice. 'You mean, doff my cap to the Blythes? Bow and scrape? No, thanks – I finished with all that years ago.'

Fay picked up her handbag. Her eyes were dark and angry. 'And where's your pride got you? Look at this place . . . Even my mother had a bit of linoleum on her floor.'

Anger welled up in him. He said curtly, 'I've got work to do,' and walked out into the farmyard. He went to the stable and began to bridle Nelson. His hands were too quick, too clumsy, and the old horse turned and looked at him reproach-fully. He stopped and laid his head against Nelson's neck for a moment, his eyes closed. The smell of horse and stable was comforting, soothing. Daniel told himself that all newly-married couples had differences, that no one went through life without a cross word. He hardly knew whether to believe himself, though. He had begun to suspect, recently, that his and Fay's differences were a little more fundamental than many people's.

He pushed the unwelcome thoughts out of his head and led Nelson out of the stable. The restless wind tugged at his hair and clothes. Daniel walked away from the cottage and farmyard, not looking back, towards his furthermost field, which had once belonged to the Blythes. He waved to Harry Dockerill standing in the field, another horse beside him.

'Jack didn't mind?' asked Daniel, glancing at the second horse.

Harry shook his head. 'Needs her back later on, though, after they've laid the old squire to rest.'

260

The church bells were tolling. A single chime for each year of Sir William Blythe's life.

'You're not going?' asked Daniel.

Harry was yoking the two horses together. 'No. Can't abide churches. I might go for a moment or two later on, though, just to pay my respects.'

'Whatever you like.' Daniel led the two horses round. 'I won't, myself.'

'You're getting a reputation, Gillory,' said Harry. 'A bit of a Red.'

Daniel smiled, but said nothing. In a small, tight-knit community like Drakesden every deviation from the norm was noted, commented on, stored away for future reference. Daniel had married an outsider; he read books and newspapers. He did not attend Sunday morning service – worse, he would not stand outside the churchyard, cap meekly in hand, as they carried the Squire's body into the church.

Harry was still teasing him. 'Dad was asking me the other night whether you'd take the lads out on strike if they cut the farmhands' wages any more. Ma said she'd tan your hide if you did, for what would we bloody eat?'

Daniel wasn't really listening. 'Bog oak,' he said absently, staring at the black branches that protruded from the unploughed earth in the centre of the field.

'She's a bugger,' said Harry, and whistled.

Ploughing the previous day, Daniel had unearthed the tree. Bog oaks littered the Fens: ancient trees, buried in the peat, a remnant from pre-history. As the level of the peat sunk each year, the trees were revealed, often as the earth was turned by ploughing. If the tree was buried deep enough, there was little anyone could do to shift it. Daniel knew that he might have to wait until the peat gradually sank, until wind and water leeched the top-soil away and nature herself revealed her prize. Until then, he was stuck with a field that could not be fully ploughed, that could not be fully planted. And, just now, every square inch of earth mattered.

'Do you know how big she is?'

Daniel shook his head. 'No idea. Damned thing bent the plough, though.'

He had spent the previous evening repairing the damage that the buried oak had inflicted on his plough. His father's work: hammering the distorted prongs back into place, using intense heat to make the iron malleable.

'I've dug around, but it goes deep. I thought I'd try with the horses.'

Harry helped Daniel tie chains to the protruding branches of the prehistoric tree. When the chains were fixed, they coaxed the two horses forward. The tolling of the church bell rang through Daniel's head, counting out the rhythm of his labours. The chains went taut, the horses strained, sweat gleaming on their coats, their manes and tails flicking in the wind, but the bog oak did not shift at all.

'Hell,' Daniel muttered.

Harry rubbed his forehead and nodded in the direction of the church. 'Must clean myself up.'

'Of course.' Daniel managed to smile. 'I'll see you later, Harry.'

He watched Harry Dockerill run across the field in the direction of his mother's cottage. The chiming of the bell still pounded across the flat fields. Fay would be there by now, as the bearers carried the body into the church, ranks of Blythes following it. The widowed Lady Blythe, the two daughters, Lally and Marjorie, and Nicholas, the heir. And Nicholas's wife.

My God, he thought. Thomasine. Lady Blythe. *Lady Thomasine Blythe*.

He had known for some time, of course, that Thomasine Thorne the Harkers' niece had married Nicholas Blythe. The unequal match had been discussed endlessly in the pub, at the Harvest Supper, in the village shops. Daniel, uninterested in village gossip, had not joined in the discussions. He had found it hard to reconcile himself, though, to the news that the girl who had once been his friend had married the man who had helped deprive him of his education, his home, his family. When he recalled the Thomasine of his childhood, or the Thomasine whom he had found sick and alone on Armistice Day in London, he felt a surge of anger and a sense of betrayal. He thought bitterly, had she married Nicholas Blythe for love or for land? Had she forgotten the past, or did she discount it as unimportant?

Daniel rapidly checked the chains where they hooked on to the black fingers of bog oak. Then he began to coax the horses forward again, so that the chains went taut.

He wondered what Sir William Blythe's death would mean to him. Sir William might have been careless enough to sell him land; would his son make the same mistake? He still remembered the expression in Nicholas's eyes when they had fought each other. *So you're foul-mouthed as well as a thief, are you, Gillory?*

In desperation, Daniel added his own strength to that of the horses, dragging them forward, leaning back against the wind so that his weight was pivoted against that of the great tree. But the buried monster moved not an inch and he fell to his knees in the ploughed black soil, every muscle in his body juddering with exhaustion, knowing that he was beaten.

Fay found a space at the back of the church, crushed in with the rest of the villagers behind the ranks of Blythe relatives and servants. Afterwards, sheltering under the branches of a yew tree, she watched the burial. She soon stopped listening to the words of the service and instead studied the family around the grave. The women's features she could see little of, as they were all veiled, but she envied them their fur coats and their stylish, modern hats and shoes. Fay was wearing the coat and hat in which she had married. She had retrimmed the hat and had cleaned and pressed the coat before coming out, but she knew enough about clothes to recognize the difference in quality between hers and the Blythe women's. She hadn't had a new thing to wear this autumn. She sighed. Daniel was such a misery nowadays, forever harping on about lack of money, and expecting her to scrimp and save. He had changed since they had married.

She let her gaze drift over the men. They wore black coats and top hats. Fay nudged her neighbour.

'Who's that?' she whispered.

Letty Gotobed said, 'The dark-haired one is Mr Nicholas. *Sir* Nicholas now. And the poor gentleman in the wheelchair is Miss Marjorie's husband.'

'And the gentleman behind?'

Letty squinted. 'Oh, he's not one of them. That's Dr Lawrence. He lives in Ely.'

Fay studied him. He was tall, sandy-haired, hawk-nosed.

Letty whispered, 'He was Sir William's doctor, after Doctor Cooper died. My sister says he's Scottish, from Edinburgh. A handsome man, ain't he?'

The words of the burial service rebounded against the high walls of the church. 'We therefore commit his body to the ground; earth to earth, ashes to ashes, dust to dust.'

Fay shivered. 'I wouldn't know,' she said proudly, and moved away.

Two days after the funeral, Gwendoline Blythe took to her bed, claiming illness. Nicholas, coming downstairs from visiting his mother, was worried.

'She's never ill, Thomasine. The occasional headache, that's all.'

'Will you send for a doctor?' Thomasine poured Nicholas a cup of coffee.

He shook his head. 'Mama won't hear of it. I've offered to drive to Ely to fetch Doctor Lawrence, but she utterly refuses.'

Thomasine looked at him carefully. Nicholas had found the week since his father's death gruelling and exhausting. His weariness was written in the dark shadows beneath his eyes, the way his fingers drummed on the edge of the table. She went to stand behind him, kissing the dark crown of his head.

'I expect she's just tired and grieving. Should I go and see her?'

His fingers stopped drumming as she gently covered his hand with hers. 'I don't think so. She said she'd go back to sleep. I'll look in on her later.'

'I'll go for a walk, then.' Through the window the sky beckoned, a clear, cold forget-me-not blue. The wind had dropped and the last few rust-coloured leaves on the trees danced in the gentler breeze. 'Will you come, Nick?'

He grimaced. 'Max Feltham is calling this morning. Pa's accountant. I really should go through his desk . . . the safe . . . all his things . . . I've put it off too long already.'

Walking through the newly fallen copper-beech leaves, Thomasine told herself that the worst was over, that she had survived the funeral and the breakfast that had followed it, as well as the lunches and dinners and long, long evenings spent in the company of inquisitive and tearful Blythes. She had managed to avoid being sick at embarrassing moments; she had tried to ensure that the demands of his family did not return Nicholas to the near-breakdown of a week ago.

Yesterday, Lally had returned to London by train, and Marjorie and Edward and their two young sons had motored back to Hampshire. Now Drakesden Abbey seemed empty, echoing, curiously hollow, as though the house itself noted the loss of its former squire. If she no longer felt an interloper there, still Thomasine found it hard to think of herself as anything more than a visitor, a temporary guest.

Outside, the island on which Drakesden Abbey was built reaffirmed once more the house and gardens as a part of the surrounding countryside. Rising above it, yet belonging to it. The air tasted sharp and clear and cold, and Thomasine could see where the lawn ended and the paddock began, where the paddock ended and the fields and river and banks drifted endlessly to the horizon. She began to walk down the hill, away from the house. Unconsciously, she let one of her palms rest on her stomach as she walked. There was not even the smallest swelling yet beneath the layers of black material, but she felt calm and hopeful nevertheless. Because of the baby, because of the precious scrap of life that would grow inside her until, next summer, she held her own child in her arms. She could picture her child, warm and smiling and content. She would belong to Drakesden Abbey when she had given the Blythes an heir.

Methodically, Nicholas began to sort through the contents of his father's study. The job distressed him: because of the nature of it, the finality of it, and because his father had never shared his own attachment to tidiness and order.

Max Feltham arrived punctually at half past ten. Nicholas liked Max: Max was a gentleman, not some jumped-up little clerk. He shook Max's hand. Max offered condolences and enquired after Nicholas's mother and wife. Nicholas found Max a chair, and sent the maidservant for tea.

'Journey all right?' he enquired. 'I know it's a bit of a haul.'

Max smiled. 'Spot on time. I thought of motoring up, but the train seemed a better bet at this time of year.'

Nicholas, sitting back down at the desk, untied a ribbon from a bundle of papers. 'The roads aren't up to much. Mud in the winter and rutted in the summer.' Staring at the papers, he sighed. 'Decent of you to come up, old chap.'

'It was the least I could do.' Max glanced at Nicholas, and the piles of papers and files and account books on the desk. 'Dreadful job, isn't it? I remember when my father died, this was the worst of it. Having to pick through all his things. It felt — barbaric.'

'I'd like just to leave it all. Let it lie.' Nicholas's voice was savage.

Max said gently, 'We have to talk, Nick. That's why I came down. It can't be left.'

Nicholas looked up at him. 'Are things that bad?'

'Well, they're not good. There'll be heavy death duties to pay, I'm afraid, and to be frank the Abbey's affairs weren't in a healthy state before Sir William died.'

Nicholas pulled open more of the desk drawers. 'Such a *mess* . . .' he said despairingly. 'There are tailors' bills tucked inside rent books from the cottages, receipts for saddles and things in with the decorating bills. My God, I've just found a bill for the flowers for Marjorie's wedding . . .'

Max was tactfully silent.

Nicholas added, 'I'd no idea things were so bad. Why the hell didn't he get another secretary after Cresswell went off to the army?'

'Cost, I suppose,' said Max. 'Damned difficult to get staff, too.'

'Damned difficult to get staff at a place like Drakesden, you mean,' said Nicholas grimly. 'The peasants can't read or write properly, and no one with a decent education is going to want to bury himself in the sticks.' Restless, he rose from the desk and went to the window. Looking outside, he could see Dilley and the boy sweeping up leaves. The leaves were still falling as they swept. The futility of it all depressed him.

Max said carefully, 'The thing is, Nicholas, that it's all got somewhat out of hand. Stern measures are going to be necessary, I'm afraid, to sort things out. You're going to have to think seriously about selling some land.'

The door opened, and the maid came in with the tea and biscuits. As she arranged them on a small table, the men were silent. Nicholas felt shocked, as though someone had hit him. He pulled aside the small velvet curtain that covered the safe and turned the combination lock.

When the maid had gone, Nicholas said hopelessly, 'Sell what? Look at it, Max, scattered in bits and bobs halfway to Ely. Some of it is good arable land, but some of it is swamp. What should I sell?'

He began to fumble through the contents of the safe: jewellery caskets, papers, the locked tin boxes that contained the labourers' wages. He found a map and unrolled it on the desk, pointing out the salient features of the area to the accountant: the river, the village, the dykes and ditches and droves.

'Drakesden is about two-thirds ours. The rest was parcelled off in the last century – a smallholding in exchange for a sack of potatoes, that sort of thing. This is ours – and this, and this, and this.' Nicholas's finger stabbed at the paper.

'The cottages are tied?'

Nicholas nodded. 'The rent is pitiful, though. I was looking at father's books before you arrived. He paid more for repairs than he earned in rent.' Nicholas put aside his tea and opened a cigarette-box.

Max was frowning. 'It's a buyer's market, of course, that's the hell of it. People aren't buying agricultural land now. We have to try, though.' Accepting a cigarette, he lit it and inhaled, staring at the map. 'Your father sold a few acres near the village. There's already been some interest expressed as to whether the adjacent field might be put up for sale. That would be the best place to start. I'll have a word with the estate agent.'

Nicholas could not at first think what Max Feltham meant, but then, following the line of the River Lark and its ditches and tributaries, he reached the hamlet of Drakesden. And pictured the spur of untidy shacks that led from the village, and the blacksmith's cottage at the end of it.

Nicholas shook his head. 'No. Not that land. I won't sell that.'

'There's a ready-made buyer, Nick. Take it, for God's sake.' Max had glanced sharply at him.

Nicholas said softly, 'I know who wants to buy it. And I shall never sell to him.'

Max stood up. 'This is senseless . . . Sell, Nick – you may never find another buyer. As your accountant, I have to recommend you in the strongest possible terms to sell. Take a good offer while it's on the table.'

'Never,' said Nicholas. 'No, Max. Never.' He was arranging the scraps of paper into neat piles. He noticed the dust on the desk-top, on the sill, on the bookshelves. He must have the room thoroughly cleaned, he thought, dusted, washed, scrubbed. He could not bear dirt and disorder.

When she returned to the house after her walk, Thomasine felt warm, pink-cheeked, healthy. She unbuttoned her old black coat and, sitting at the bottom of the stairs, began to prise off her muddy shoes. She heard the sound of stout boots on the marble floor, bombazine skirts scratching and rustling. She looked up.

'Mrs Blatch – good morning.' Thomasine smiled. 'Can I help you?'

The cook's short, vast frame was covered in voluminous black skirts and bodice, enveloped with a frilled white apron. She did not smile back.

'It's eleven o'clock, your ladyship, and the menus haven't been settled. If the menus aren't settled, then the boy can't send up to the greenhouses nor the shops, and the scullery-maids are just twiddling their thumbs.'

Thomasine frowned. 'I thought Lady Blythe . . . I mean, the Dowager Lady Blythe . . .'

'Lady Blythe always came down to the kitchens at ten, regular as clockwork.' Great channels of disapproval etched themselves down Mrs Blatch's thickly-padded brow and cheeks. 'I didn't like to disturb the poor lady when she was unwell . . . *If you could spare a moment, your ladyship . . .*'

She wasn't sure whether she detected sarcasm in the conventional phrase, or whether it was only her imagination. Thomasine began to walk towards the kitchens.

Half an hour later she found Nicholas in his father's study. Her words tumbled out over themselves, hot with embarrassment and fury.

'And I was in my stocking-soles, Nicholas! In the kitchen! How they all *stared* –'

He laughed. 'They'll talk about it for weeks. It'll be in every public house in Ely by midday. How the new Lady Blythe doesn't dress properly before she goes to the kitchen to give Cook her orders.'

'It didn't occur to me that I had to! Go to the kitchens, that is. I thought they just made it up themselves.' Thomasine perched on the window-sill, running her fingers through her windblown hair. 'And goodness only knows what we'll be eating for dinner today. That awful woman was no help at all. I kept asking her for suggestions, and she just said that her ladyship always worked out lovely menus. So I just said the first things that came into my head.'

'So what will it be – eel pie followed by lobster thermidor with a jam roly-poly to follow?'

She glared at him. 'It's all very well for you to laugh, Nicholas, but you should have seen the way she looked at me. Like I was a *worm*.'

'Lally and I used to call Mrs Blatch the Basilisk. When Lally was little, she was convinced that the old harridan could turn her to stone.' Nicholas took two cigarettes out of the box, lit them both, and handed one to Thomasine. 'You'll get used to her, Thomasine,' he said comfortingly.

'Will I?' She inhaled the cigarette and then, disliking the taste, returned it to the ashtray. Pregnancy made everything taste peculiar. 'I'm not sure. I wasn't brought up for all this, Nick.'

'You could ask Mama to help you.'

'Yes. Perhaps.' She did not voice to him her resentment that Gwendoline Blythe had not warned her of the duties that would be expected of her as chatelaine of Drakesden Abbey; that Gwendoline Blythe had simply taken to her bed and left her inexperienced, ignorant daughter-in-law to muddle through.

She glanced round the study. She disliked the room. It held too many bad memories.

'Has your accountant gone?'

'Max? No – he'll be staying the weekend. He's hoping to get in some shooting. He's with Mama at present. Max was always one of her favourites.'

Paper covered the entire surface of Sir William's desk. A great many of the pieces of paper looked, thought Thomasine, like bills.

'Can I help, Nick? I used to do Antonia's accounts. I'm quite good at that sort of thing.'

'Oh, no need.' Nicholas looked up from the desk, and smiled briefly. 'It's not as bad as it looks, old thing. You stick to sorting out the staff. Most of this just needs filing. If you could arrange for this room to be cleaned – it really is too ghastly.' He glanced at his watch. 'Must go and see Mama. I said I'd look in.'

CHAPTER TEN

THE capacity for making a fool of herself in a house the size of Drakesden Abbey seemed unlimited to Thomasine. She gave Max the wrong bedroom – *Max always has the crimson room, my dear. He is an old friend of the family, not an employee –*, and the meals, that first day, were awful. In her rooms, Lady Blythe ate delicate consommés and lightly cooked omelettes; downstairs, Nicholas and Max Feltham nobly fought their way through an appalling mixture of nursery food and ill-cooked French dishes.

After struggling blindly for a week, Thomasine eventually discovered a set of menus in the morning-room desk. Studying them carefully, she worked out Mrs Blatch's strengths and weaknesses, and concluded something about the art of putting a menu together. Not to be too ambitious, and to use the fresh ingredients that the kitchen garden produced. Good old-fashioned English food, simply cooked. Nicholas stopped having indigestion; Thomasine herself began to be able to look at her dinner without feeling ill.

Once a week she had to give out the stores to the servants. She gave the best candles to the kitchen staff, and the family ended up with household candles in the drawing-rooms and bedrooms. The smell of the cheap candles gave Lady Blythe a migraine. Nicholas sat at his mother's bedside, bathing her forehead with lavender water whilst making the finishing touches to his plans to install electricity at Drakesden Abbey. Thomasine managed to sort out the candles, but then there was a disaster with the soap. Somehow, Nicholas's stuffy old godparents, their guests one weekend, ended up with brown salt soap on their wash-stands, while all the maids were suspiciously delicately perfumed. When she managed to get the soap under control, there was the linen-room, a minefield of social embarrassment and error. The most important guests always seemed to end up sleeping on scratchy cotton sheets, and the finest linen lay unused at the back of the vast cupboards.

The trouble was, Thomasine admitted mutely to herself, that her heart simply wasn't in it. She didn't see why they couldn't all have the same sort of soap or candles or sheets, but when she suggested this to the housekeeper, she was met with outrage. Neither did she see why the three of them had to have four long and complicated meals each day. Thomasine herself could not eat breakfast during her pregnancy, Lady Blythe always had a small appetite and Nicholas loathed the tedious institution of afternoon tea. Yet if all the rituals were not religiously adhered to, then Thomasine met with resistance not only from the housekeeper, but also from both Lady Blythe and Nicholas. Thomasine acknowledged that she was the newcomer, that others knew far better than she how to run a great house. So she managed to quell her boredom and irritation, most of the time.

She was careful not to overtire herself in the first three precarious months of pregnancy. She did not ride and she rested each afternoon. The sickness passed by the time the tenth week was out, and she did not experience again the awful draining exhaustion that had characterized her disastrous first pregnancy. She wrote long letters to both Hilda and Antonia, making fun of her own social gaffes and asking their advice. She admitted to neither aunt her increasing boredom and frustration: boredom, Hilda had frequently said to her, was only a sign of a lack of inner resources.

Fay's remark about Daniel needing to better himself had stung. He signed up for Workers' Educational Association classes in Ely, cycling there twice a week. He attended lectures on the League of Nations, and on the Treaty of Versailles and its possible consequences, and on the causes and cures of the current economic depression. Often he looked out at the fields adjacent to his, longing for the day when the Blythes, forced to pay substantial death duties, would scrabble for money, just as he did. The land Daniel wanted was the logical piece of land to sell, cut off as it was from the rest of the Blythes' acres. Carefully, he put every spare penny aside.

But no For Sale board appeared. Daniel worked out some of his frustration by marking out the area where he would build Fay her parlour next summer. When he described it to her – the cosy room with a table and rocking-chair and standard lamp – she smiled. She had not smiled much, recently. It worried him that Fay still did not seem to adapt to village life. She carried out the duties of a country housewife with little efficiency and no enthusiasm. Daniel knew that the life he had brought her to was harsh, and he tried to take the worst of the burden from her. When they spent an afternoon at Ely's Electric Cinema, or when Fay was able to buy new clothes, then she cheered up and he saw again the bright, sensual Fay who had originally enchanted him. But afternoons out were rare, and there was little money for treats. She could not seem to find compensation in the things that Daniel loved: the books, the sense of freedom from other people's mastery, the silence and peace of the landscape. He thought that she might be longing for a child, but when he spoke of it to her she looked at him scornfully and shook her head.

He began, at last, to write. It started as a farming diary, something in which to record dates of planting and ploughing, something that might enable him to see where he had succeeded and where he had failed. He found himself adding pieces of description, and then, occasionally, his memories and dreams. The writing did not flow easily at first, but he began to see that it could be a release for him, a necessary piece in the jigsaw. Eventually he managed, with many starts and stops and a great deal of wasted paper, to compose an article for the local newspaper. Late one night, he read through the final version and it seemed to him vivid and clear, but when he delivered it by hand to the newspaper's offices in Ely, that sense of clarity had gone, and he flinched at his presumption.

Pieces of the electric generator that Nicholas had ordered began to arrive by train at Ely, or towed in barges along the river, travelling the last few difficult miles on the back of a horse-drawn cart. Workmen – an army of electricians, plasterers and carpenters – invaded Drakesden Abbey. The house resounded to the noise of holes being hacked in the ancient plaster, as old, hand-painted wallpaper was stripped away to thread an intricate web of wires throughout the fabric of the house.

Lady Blythe, fully recovered, rose from her bed. Nicholas ensured that the workmen disturbed her favourite room, the morning-room, as little as possible. Thomasine collected flowers from the greenhouses to place in the morning-room to celebrate her mother-in-law's return to health. Scarlet poinsettias, fragrant lilies. The gardener, Mr Dilley, was furious. 'Dilley regards the greenhouses as his private terrain,' explained Lady Blythe, kindly. The scent of the lilies gave Lady Blythe a headache, so they all had to be taken back to the greenhouses.

Thomasine's sense of her own superfluousness did not lessen: she had a strong suspicion that she would never run Drakesden Abbey as efficiently as Lady Blythe. There was little in the way of distraction: no art galleries, no theatres, and only a single picture-house in Ely. There was, thank goodness, the Abbey's wonderful library, which Thomasine plundered more and more frequently as the days grew shorter and colder. Often she recalled her earlier years in Drakesden, her awareness of the narrowness and isolation of the village, her impatience with its attachment to a way of life that seemed to her to be outworn. If she, now that she was Lady Blythe, was now part of that anachronistic way of life, then it irked her none the less, because the customs and rituals that bound her life seemed futile and stifling.

The weather grew colder and Thomasine slept with socks, mittens, a jumper over her nightdress and a stone hot water-bottle. She asked Nicholas to share her bed, partially for the warmth, but partially because they had not made love since Sir William's death. But the experiment was not a success. His nightmares interrupted her sleep, his guilt at interrupting her sleep made the nightmares worse. If she managed to coax him into making love to her, then still he would often rise at midnight or later, retreating to his father's study, now cleaned, scrubbed and re-papered, and to his detailed plans for the electrification of the house. Columns of figures, complex calculations, strange and esoteric diagrams gathered on his desk.

Lally, Belle, Julian, Ettie and Boy stayed for Christmas. Thomasine organized the cleaning and airing of the bedrooms and attempted to plan menus for the festivities. Geese and hams and turkeys and puddings; fruit cakes, trifles, pies, blancmanges. The visitors arrived on Christmas morning, a whirl of bright colour against the grey Fen landscape, their motor-cars packed with useless and expensive presents. At night, when the house was dark and cold, and Lady Blythe had already gone to her bed, they played sardines. Stumbling across Ettie and Julian in a giggling embrace in the conservatory, Thomasine retreated silently. She found Nicholas sitting on the stairs, smoking. 'Such fun,' he said. But he looked tired and red-eyed as he lit a new cigarette from the butt of the last. Thomasine sat beside him for a long time, watching through the high windows the yellow crescent moon lying on its back in an inky sky.

In February, Nicholas dismissed his farm manager. The cottage beside the paddock was vacated. He would run the Home Farm himself, he explained to Thomasine – economies must be made, and reducing the wages bill was an obvious first step. Thomasine welcomed the change: Nicholas was always happier if he was busy. That he was taking on new duties made her hopeful that he had accepted the alteration in his life which had accompanied his father's death.

When the wind died down, the countryside was covered with a flat icing of white. The skies were yellow and swollen with snow, and drifts curled over the gardens and countryside. They tramped round the garden, their boots making the first scars on the bleached landscape. The Labyrinth was more subterranean than ever, the overhanging boughs heavy with snow, shutting out the dull gleam of sunlight. In the walled garden they built a snowman, short and stout with black stones for eyes. 'It looks like Mrs Blatch,' said Thomasine, and they pelted it with snowballs until they collapsed together in the drifts, laughing.

Until the snow cleared, Daniel could do little work outdoors. In the evenings he wrote, and by day he tended the animals in the yard and made sure the cottage was weatherproof. When the blizzard eased, he rummaged in the outhouse and, eventually discovering what he had been looking for, carried his trophy carefully wrapped in layers of sacking into the kitchen.

The kitchen was snug and warm. Fay was mashing potatoes; something was cooking in the stove. Daniel placed the bundle on the table and began to unpeel the layers of sacking.

'Ugh,' said Fay, turning. 'That's all spidery. Couldn't you do that outside?'

He said nothing, but triumphantly held up his prize. 'Look.'

'Bits of old metal,' said Fay, looking bewildered.

'Skates.' Daniel was smiling. 'These belonged to my father and mother. My father was a champion speed-skater once. They're good skates, Fay. Metal, not bone. My father made them.'

He began to rub at the leather straps with a cloth dabbed into a tin of dubbin. The leather was cracked and greenish, but as he worked it softened. 'As soon as we've eaten, we're going skating,' he said.

'Skating?' squawked Fay. 'I can't skate. You know I can't, Daniel.'

He grinned. 'You couldn't cycle, could you? Now you're riding all over the place on that bike.'

After dinner, he persuaded her to put on a pleated skirt and jumper, coat, scarf, woollen hat and mittens. Then they walked the half-mile to the River Lark, the skates slung over Daniel's shoulder.

The ice that covered the frozen river was hard and gleaming, the sun a rim of pink around the clouds. Disused windmills stood flat and black against the sky, stilled by time and by the snow that choked their sails. Men and women swirled and sped on the ice, children laughed and tumbled. Daniel helped Fay with her skates and led her on to the ice.

She was frightened at first, clutching at his jacket, her feet sliding away in unpredictable directions. But he took both her hands, not letting her fall, and led her away from the crowds to a quieter corner. There she began to relax and find a rhythm. They skated alongside each other for a while, slowly at first, but then gradually gathering speed. Fay looked beautiful, the dark strands of hair peeping out from beneath the scarlet brim of her woollen hat, her eyes bright. As he skated, Daniel noticed the Delage belonging to the Blythes arrive at the Fen, driving cautiously on the compacted snow. This land belonged to Nicholas Blythe.

Fay slid to a halt, out of breath. Daniel took her in his arms and kissed her. 'Not now, Daniel − it's ever so public.' She pushed him away, but she did not sound cross.

Someone had set up a brazier at the edge of the ice and was roasting chestnuts. Daniel bought a handful, so hot he could hardly hold them. He shelled some for Fay as they stood on the bank watching the skaters. The Fens were magically transformed, the waterways ribbons of gleaming silver that cut through the whiteness. Another motor-car arrived, skidding its way along the icy drove. *Two* motor-cars in Drakesden, thought Daniel. My God, times must be changing.

Harry Dockerill called out, 'A race, Gillory! Come on!'

Daniel turned to Fay. 'Do you mind?'

She shook her head. The young men were lining up to one

side of the crowds of skaters: representatives of the tribes of Dockerill, Gotobed, Hayhoe and Dilley. Daniel crossed the ice to join them.

'You haven't a bloody hope, Gillory,' said Harry, with a grin. 'My dad beat your dad in nineteen-o-five. And my grandad twenty-five years afore that.'

Daniel cursed him in a friendly fashion. Someone lined the five of them up and started the race. The landscape of windmill, hedgerow and bank sped up, joined together, became seamless. Daniel, head bowed, arms swinging, saw only the ice between his feet, the mark that his skates made, and heard the cheers from the crowds as he pushed past all the others.

Afterwards, he was clapped on the back and given hot ale to drink. He felt elated, light-headed. The elation was tinged with sadness, though. Ten years ago, there would have been twice that many young men racing. Harry's brother, his own, so many others . . .

Fay was skating again, by herself this time. The sadness slowly ebbed away as Daniel watched the swirl of her bright pleated skirt, the flush in her normally pale face. He saw that Nicholas Blythe was skating. Daniel knew now what all the rest of the village had known months ago: that Thomasine Blythe was expecting a child. Thomasine was standing by the car, wrapped in her furs. Just for a moment she turned and her eyes met his, and a smile touched the corners of her mouth. But he looked instantly away, refusing to acknowledge her. The distance between them was far, far greater than the yards of snowy turf that separated them. She was Thomasine Blythe now, and so a stranger – perhaps an enemy. The affection they had once felt for each other had been obliterated by the passing years.

There was a cry from the ice and Daniel spun round. Fay was sprawled by the bank. Harry Dockerill was helping her up, but she could not keep to her feet. Daniel's blood ran cold when he saw how her foot buckled beneath her. He ran back on to the ice, pushing his way to her side.

Her small face was contorted with pain. 'Darling –' he whispered, putting his arm around her. Together, he and Harry helped her off the ice. Someone threw down a piece of sacking and they placed Fay on it. Kneeling beside her, Daniel unbuckled the straps of her skate. Her ankle was already beginning to swell as he unknotted the laces of her boot. She let out a sob of pain and, dry-mouthed, he thought of broken bones, of all he had suffered five years ago, when his leg had been crushed.

'It's all right, Fay, it's all right,' he said, but inside he was panicking.

A voice said, 'Let me,' and a man knelt down beside him. He looked a few years older than Daniel, ginger-haired, Roman-nosed.

'That's Doctor Lawrence,' whispered Harry Dockerill respectfully.

The boot was unlaced efficiently, the swollen ankle poked and prodded and manipulated. 'Well, I don't think it's broken, Mrs . . .' said the doctor eventually.

'Gillory,' said Fay. 'Mrs Fay Gillory.' Her eyes sparkled with unshed tears.

'A nasty sprain, though. You'll have to rest it.'

Daniel felt weak with relief. 'I'll carry you home.'

'No – no.' Doctor Lawrence, standing up, shook his head. 'I'll take you both in my motor. You live in the village, don't you?'

In the end, they had to walk half the distance anyway, because the doctor's Morris Oxford couldn't manage the last, snow-filled trek along the drove to the blacksmith's cottage.

Daniel carried Fay in his arms. She felt so light, so fragile. She was no weight at all. All the colour had gone from her face and she looked shocked and white. Inside the house, which was still cluttered with the midday meal's dirty dishes, he sat her carefully on the settle.

'Snug wee place,' said Doctor Lawrence, opening his medical bag. 'Have you lived here long?'

280

Daniel, filling the kettle to make tea, mumbled something. Fay said weakly, 'Only a year and a half, since we married. I come from London.'

The doctor, bandaging her foot, smiled. 'Another city dweller, like myself, then. I'm from Edinburgh. Quite a change, isn't it?'

'Quite a change,' echoed Fay. Her voice had altered; her vowels had become pinched and careful. 'The best teacups, remember, Daniel.'

Fay had found the best cups in a junk shop in Ely: bone china with gold paint round the rim. Daniel filled the tiny cups with tea, but could not drink. Fay's foot was bandaged and a little colour had begun to return to her cheeks, but he felt sickened and exhausted. He had a sense of having narrowly avoided disaster, of having been careless and almost paid the price for it. He saw the doctor back to his motor-car, thanking him and discreetly paying him, and then returned to the cottage and Fay, hardly able to believe that she was still there, still safe.

The snow thawed, and the tax-demands arrived: the figures on them horrified Nicholas. He stuffed the copies of the demands, together with Max's letter, into his father's desk. He could not yet think about all that.

Drakesden Abbey was filled with guests to celebrate the switching on of the new generator. Nicholas had planned an elaborate ceremony: a seven-course dinner followed by dancing, complete with balloons and games and cases and cases of champagne.

After dinner, Nicholas left for the boiler room and Hawkins extinguished the candles. Only the firelight relieved the darkness. There was a distant rumble as the generator's diesel motor surged into life. Then the lamps flickered and glowed, and everyone gasped. Briefly, the light dipped and died, and there was a momentary return to darkness before it flooded the room again, strong and bright and clear.

Nicholas ran back into the hallway.

'Darling –'

'Congratulations, Sir Nicholas.'

'Well *done.*'

'Awfully clever –'

Thomasine could hear the servants clapping and cheering in the kitchen. Nicholas looked immensely proud of himself. He went to his mother.

'Well, Mama – doesn't the old place look bright?'

The more intense light revealed the shabbiness of the old furniture, the worn threads of the carpet, the fading and discolouration of the papered walls. The stuffed birds and animals in their glass cases seemed tawdry and ridiculous, a remnant from another age.

Everyone had crowded round the window. The curtains were not drawn. Looking outside, they could see squares of reflected light marked on the lawn, silvering the blades of grass, turning the drizzle to strands of gold.

'We should go outside.'

'Frightfully pretty –'

'The garden's floodlit, Nicky.'

'Yes.' Nicholas's voice was excited. 'Mama – come and see the Abbey as you've never seen it before.'

Lady Blythe gave a short trill of laughter. 'It would be rather thrilling. It is raining a little, but if you would find an umbrella, Nicky . . .'

The front doors were opened; they spilled down the steps, the women's jewelled headbands and beaded dresses shimmering in the wash of light.

'We must fetch the gramophone.'

'Hawkins shall take the champagne, won't you, Hawkins?'

'The lawn will be a topping place to dance.'

Thomasine had taken her raincoat from the lobby. She was about to follow the others outside, when a hand caught her arm and a voice whispered in her ear.

'You are not intending to go outside, Thomasine, surely?

Your condition, my dear. The smallest slip . . . it would be so unwise.'

Then Lady Blythe released her grip on Thomasine's arm, and walked out of the house at her son's side. Obstinately, Thomasine continued to button up her raincoat. She was alone now; all the others had run out into the illuminated garden. She caught sight of her reflection in the window: the distended stomach, and the narrow arms and legs that were out of proportion to her thickened figure, and she felt, just for a moment, ugly. She could hear, more and more distantly, their guests' exclamations of wonder and pleasure. Then she looked away from the window, and straightened up and walked outside to join them.

Daniel, walking along the river-bank late that evening, saw the lights of Drakesden Abbey. The house seemed to float in the darkness, a great beacon that blazed halfway across the Fens. He stood still, watching for a long while, half-willing the lights to extinguish themselves, to die, so that Drakesden Abbey would be returned to the night.

But they did not die. The many squares of light remained unwavering, unnaturally bright, altering for ever the skyline he had known since boyhood. Very distantly he could hear music and laughter, and glimpse in the great panels of light the glittering figures on the lawn. When he glanced back at his cottage and saw the gleam of candlelight through the kitchen window, he felt for a moment utterly defeated, without purpose.

He began to walk along the muddy rim of the dyke. The snow had thawed weeks ago, and since then the rains had been heavy. Just now the drizzle was no more than a fog of moisture, wetting his hair and face. The lantern he carried showed him how high the water had risen in the dyke. When he reached the boundary of his land, he swung the lantern forward, seeing again the poor state of the earthworks, the perilous closeness of the water to the summit of the bank. Nicholas Blythe had money enough to install electricity at Drakesden Abbey, but insufficient, it seemed, to maintain his lands, or to pay more than a pittance to the men who worked for him.

Returning to the cottage, the soft peat in the back yard squelched beneath Daniel's feet. Inside, he lifted the chairs on top of the table, rolled up rugs and placed them beside the chairs. He could already see the water glimmering blackly between the bricks. We live like beasts, he thought angrily. Like beasts.

Their guests left, and Nicholas became absorbed in his new scheme of plumbing in hot water at the Abbey. Thomasine gave out household supplies, consulted with Mrs Blatch about endless meals, and entertained various local dignitaries and their wives to lunch and tea. Irritated almost beyond endurance by the trivia of her daily life, she took to going for long walks each afternoon, her swollen figure enveloped in an old velvet evening cloak that had once belonged to Marjorie Blythe.

It was on one of these walks that she met Daniel. She had wandered down the Abbey lawns, across the paddock to the dyke. She did not climb the wall of the dyke, because she was afraid of losing her footing on the slippery grass. The day was grey, the landscape monochrome. Thomasine walked briskly along the foot of the dyke, beside the Abbey fields. Mud clung in great clods to her galoshes, but the air was sharp and cold, invigorating after the stifling airlessness of Drakesden Abbey.

When she looked up and saw him, she recognized him immediately. The fair hair, ruffled by the breeze, the strong, well-made body. Those fields had once belonged to the Abbey. Nicholas had told her, his fury undisguised, how Daniel Gillory had tricked his father into selling him Abbey land. It did not seem like trickery to Thomasine: only the sort of transaction that had gone on in the village for decades. But she had known that where Daniel Gillory was concerned, Nicholas was irrational.

Daniel was pulling weeds out from the furrows of earth. There was a haze of green over Daniel's land, whereas the Abbey fields, adjacent to it, were still black. Thomasine stood still for a moment on the boundary between the two fields, and then she called out his name.

'Daniel? Daniel – hello!'

She expected him to smile and walk towards her. Instead, he turned slowly round and straightened up. She was near enough to see that not the smallest smile touched his mouth, that he made not the slightest movement in her direction.

He nodded his head in a mockery of a bow. If he'd worn a cloth cap, Thomasine thought savagely, then he'd have raised it, overlaying the gesture of deference with a thick vein of contempt.

'Your ladyship,' he said. Then he turned his back to her and returned to his work.

She stood quite still for a moment, staring at him. Then she wrapped her cloak tighter around herself and began to walk fast down the boundary of the two fields towards the drove. Her face was hot and she was out of breath by the time she reached the drove, but she kept on walking. She did not slow her pace until she encountered Nicholas's foreman, talking to some of his labourers by the side of the drove.

She struggled to recover her dignity, to slow her footsteps and greet the men.

'Mr Carter.'

'Your ladyship.'

She thought she could hear much the same expression in Joe Carter's voice as she had heard in Daniel Gillory's. Better disguised, perhaps, but there, all the same.

'The wheat seems rather behindhand this year, Mr Carter.' Her own voice was sharp.

There was a flicker of resentment in the foreman's eyes, quickly hidden. 'It's been a poor spring, your ladyship.'

Every farmer's excuse, thought Thomasine. 'Other Drakesden

fields are further on,' she said bluntly. 'Mr Gillory's, for instance.' She glanced around her, still trying to keep her temper. The labourers were staring at her open-mouthed. 'And the ditches need dredging,' she added, pointing to where reeds clogged the bands of black water that divided the fields. 'This field's always prone to flooding.'

She thought she detected then just a glimmer of respect in Joe Carter's eyes. She knew which fields flooded first because for five years as a child she had ridden round this village until she had been intimate with every waterway, every island, every flat expanse of black earth.

Carter nodded. 'I'll get the men on to it, your ladyship.'

Thomasine turned to go. It must be almost four o'clock, time for tea. Back to the drawing-room, and to the ridiculous business of making Indian and Chinese tea and handing out cakes and sandwiches to three people, none of whom were in the least bit hungry.

As she started up the slope of the island, she heard one of the labourers mutter, 'Her should keep to the nursery, her should,' and then, shortly afterwards, the sound of scythes cutting the reeds in the ditch.

A few weeks later, Lady Blythe and Thomasine were alone in the drawing-room after dinner. Nicholas was drinking his port and smoking a cigarette in the dining-room.

Lady Blythe poured out the coffee. 'Excellent news, my dear. I have managed to find you a suitable nanny.'

'A *nanny*?' Thomasine's hand paused in the action of accepting the coffee-cup from Lady Blythe.

'For the little one, Thomasine.' Lady Blythe's expression was bland and composed. 'A friend of mine, Lady Faversham, knows of a suitable woman. Athene Faversham assures me that Nanny Harper is a most superior person.'

The baby was due in ten weeks' time, at the beginning of June. Thomasine began, 'I hadn't thought of engaging a nanny – '

'I realized that, dear.' Lady Blythe's smile was sympathetic. 'It is so easy to overlook such matters, especially when one is not used to running an establishment of this size, don't you agree? But I am always delighted to help you.'

'I mean,' said Thomasine more firmly, 'I didn't think we needed a nanny. Plenty of people bring up their children themselves nowadays.'

'*Some* people,' said Lady Blythe, still smiling. 'And I think you'll find, Thomasine, that those people are not *our* sort of people.'

Thomasine couldn't drink the coffee. Every night Lady Blythe poured it for her, and every night it stood untouched. Both coffee and cigarettes had been unpleasant to her throughout her pregnancy.

'I thought, when they were babies . . .' She struggled to explain herself. 'It seems so awful to give them to a stranger when they are babies.'

The familiar trill of laughter. 'A stranger? What nonsense, my dear. A newborn child cannot tell the difference between one person and another.'

Thomasine was unconvinced. 'But I want to look after my child, Lady Blythe. I'm looking forward to it so much. I don't want to give it to someone else.'

Yesterday she had visited a cottage in the village where a new baby had been born. She had loved to hold the tiny scrap in her arms, to feel the warmth of that fragile body.

'No one is suggesting that you neglect your child, Thomasine. But I must point out to you that now you are the mistress of Drakesden, you have certain duties. Those duties must take precedence over changing napkins, washing out baby clothes — that sort of menial work. A competent nanny will relieve you of the more tedious aspects of motherhood. She will allow you time to carry out your other duties.'

Tea-parties and luncheons, thought Thomasine savagely. Tedious house parties and far too much time spent twiddling her thumbs, wondering what on earth she should do next.

287

She said nothing, but she was aware of a small hard core of rebellion growing inside her. When Lady Blythe reached across and patted her hand, Thomasine thought that her fingertips were cold, fleeting.

'You'll see that I'm right, dear.'

Spring came fitfully, a succession of sun and showers and cold, blustery winds. One evening, when they were walking back over the fields, Harry Dockerill drew a crumpled piece of newsprint from his pocket and showed it to Daniel.

It was a cutting of his article on the South Level, published the previous week. 'Annie Hayhoe's dad showed it to me. We didn't know you were famous.'

Daniel snorted. 'I'm not giving up farming yet, Harry. It's the *Ely Standard*, not *The Times*.'

He had felt, though, a tremendous pride when he had received the letter telling him of the acceptance of his article, and the cheque that had gone with it. The cheque, though small, was useful, and the letter asking for more articles on a similar subject had given him a real sense of achievement.

He realized that Harry, never the most talkative of people, was trying to say something else.

'What is it, Harry?'

Harry stopped at the edge of the field, rubbing his moustache. 'Well, the thing is . . . Some of the lads thought . . .'

'Come on, Harry, out with it. There's only Nelson and me.'

The sun was setting in a great purple band across the horizon, painting the furrowed black earth with stripes of mauve and pink.

Harry said, 'You know that Annie's sister lost her little 'un?'

Daniel nodded. Annie was Harry's sweetheart, her sister Rose a scrawny little thing with a handful of undernourished infants. The youngest girl had died of a fever the previous week.

'Couldn't afford the doctor, see. They're always sickening for summat. Ma says it's the air from the marsh.'

288

Daniel thought privately that the family's illnesses had more to do with a lack of good food and the squalid conditions in which they lived. But he said, 'I was sorry to hear about the little girl. Let's hope it was an isolated case. But if any of the other children are sick, I can lend Rose the ten shillings for the doctor.'

Harry's tanned face went brick-red. 'It ain't that, Daniel. You know Rose wouldn't . . . It's just that they used to be able to manage, and now they can't.'

The line between survival and penury was very thin, very precarious. Daniel said, 'Because of the new baby?'

Harry shook his head. 'Because Squire's cut wages. Rose could allus manage afore that.'

Daniel scowled. The great flaming rays of the sun died away, returning the land to a pattern of dull greens and greys. 'I didn't know,' he said slowly. 'Have the Blythes cut all the labourers' wages?'

Harry nodded. 'And put up rents. And some of the lads thought . . .'

'Spit it out, Harry.'

Harry was still clutching the cutting. 'Some of the lads thought you might have a word with Squire. Seeings as you wrote this. And seeings as you've had an education, and can speak proper . . .'

Daniel began to walk again, leading Nelson by the bridle. Futile to explain to Harry that his education had been useless, or worse than useless, because it had shown him possibilities, yet refused him access to any of those possibilities. Futile also to try and explain to Harry that he was probably the last person Nicholas Blythe would listen to. The effort it had cost Harry to ask him this favour had been obvious. He could not refuse.

'Yes, of course,' he said. 'I'll do what I can.'

Nicholas received another letter from Max. The contents of the letter made his heart pound and his forehead break out in a sweat. Running a shaking finger down the enclosed column of figures, he could not at first believe the numbers that he saw. Too many noughts, surely.

This letter could not, like the others, be put away at the back of the drawer. From the safe he took out the old map of Drakesden, staring at the snaking black lines of the river, the criss-cross of dyke and ditch. He could make no decision, though; his thoughts were not coherent.

There was a knock at the door. Nicholas looked up, relieved by the interruption. 'Yes, Hawkins?' His voice was dry and scratchy.

'There's a – a gentleman to see you, Sir Nicholas.'

'Who is it, Hawkins?'

'Mr Gillory, sir.'

Nicholas stared at the butler. He said sharply, '*Daniel* Gillory?'

'Yes, sir. He was most insistent, sir.'

He wanted to say, 'Throw him out. I will not allow him on my land.' But if he stayed here, trapped in this room, his father's room, then there was the letter, and the map, and the decision that he was somehow expected to take. He thought then, did Daniel Gillory *know* somehow? Servants' gossip, perhaps . . . Disguising the chaos in his heart, Nicholas followed the butler downstairs.

It had cost Daniel Gillory a great deal to walk to Drakesden Abbey that morning, to knock at the side door of the house. He wore his best clothes, the suit in which he had been married, but no hat, because he could not have borne to raise his hat to Nicholas Blythe. It was as much as he could do to make himself call at the tradesman's entrance rather than the front door. Waiting in one of the dingier downstairs rooms, Daniel forced himself to concentrate on the present, rather than the past.

Then the butler escorted Nicholas Blythe into the room. Daniel realized immediately that he had got it all wrong:

Nicholas was dressed in well-cut tweed jacket and trousers, the gentle colours set off by a knitted sleeveless pullover. Daniel, who rarely bothered much about clothes, suddenly saw his outfit for what it was: an ill-fitting city clerk's suit, either baggy or tight in all the wrong places. The butler hovered in a corner of the room. As though he was dangerous, thought Daniel. As though he needed to be watched.

'Yes, Gillory? Your business, if you please. I don't have much time to spare.' Nicholas's voice, as Daniel had expected, was cold.

'I'm not here on my own behalf, Sir Nicholas. I'm here on behalf of some of the villagers – your tenants and labourers. They asked me to speak to you.'

'Concerning what, Gillory?'

'Concerning rents and wages. You've put their rents up and reduced their wages. These people live from hand to mouth. Their margin of survival is very slim indeed – any loss of income is disastrous.'

Nicholas had sat down in one of the armchairs. 'So?'

'So I'm asking if you would reconsider. If you'd consider restoring wages to the levels of last year.'

Nicholas was silent for a moment. His fingers fiddled constantly with the tasselled trim of the chair. 'I'm sure you know, Gillory, that wages had risen unprecedently high. I have merely returned them to pre-War levels. The correct level.'

Daniel's voice was soft. 'But you have not returned *prices* to pre-War levels.'

'Prices are not particularly relevant to these people. They buy little of their food from shops. Surely you are aware of that, Gillory?'

He meant, Daniel knew, 'You yourself come from a rural slum.'

Daniel said; 'They eat their own produce because they cannot afford to do otherwise. That's why their diet is hopelessly inadequate, that's why they are poorly clothed. That's why they can't pay doctors' fees, and that's why their children die each spring from fevers and infections.'

Nicholas said coldly, 'I hope you are not blaming me, Gillory, for the infant mortality rate.'

'You have a responsibility.'

Nicholas sighed. 'The children die because their parents are unintelligent and ignorant. Because they produce a brat each year regardless of their income, and because they spend their money on ale instead of medicines.'

This time, the challenge in Nicholas Blythe's eyes was unmistakable. A thousand replies, all of them insulting, flickered through Daniel's brain. He said slowly, 'Do you ever go and look at your tied cottages? Do you ever see how your tenants live? Are you aware that most of the cottages – the cottages that you own – flood each spring, and that they are infested with insects and vermin because of the damp? Have you ever thought how *you* would manage in such conditions?'

Just for a moment, then, he saw Nicholas flinch. A twitch of the eyes and for an instant his fingers paused in their plaiting and unplaiting of the tassels. Ruthlessly, Daniel followed up his advantage.

'And are you aware of the condition of the land that you own? That the poor state of your ditches and dykes contributes to the flooding in the village?'

He heard the butler say, 'Shall I show him out, Sir Nicholas?' But Nicholas had risen from the chair and was walking towards him.

'Ah.' Nicholas's eyes glittered, hard and black. 'I thought so. Now we come to the real motive of this interview. I didn't think you had called for reasons of altruism, Gillory.'

Daniel's eyes narrowed. 'Meaning . . .?'

'Meaning that I had a visit from one of the Commissioners a while ago . . . Have you been speaking to them, Gillory?'

He said levelly, 'I've spoken to the Drainage Commissioners several times over the past year. I've pointed out to them the poor state of the banks and ditches in Drakesden, and the consequent danger of flooding.'

Nicholas had gone to stand by the window. He twitched the curtain aside to stare out at the garden and then swung back round to Daniel. 'You have fourteen acres . . . fifteen . . .?'

'Eighteen,' said Daniel. Which you know damn well, he thought angrily.

'Ah. It requires twenty, does it not, for a landholder to become a Drainage Commissioner?'

Daniel's fists, by his sides, were clenched. 'Yes.'

'You have no voice then.'

It was a statement of fact, but Daniel could see the triumph in Nicholas Blythe's dark eyes.

'I cannot yet become a Commissioner, no. But I can speak to people – write to them.'

'Of course. The Grammar School boy.' Nicholas's lip curled.

There was a brief, taut silence. Then Daniel, making a last heroic effort, said, 'I have had no success with the Commissioners. They are short of money – Government gives little priority to the needs of parts of the country as isolated as the Fens. If the banks collapse, then your land, Sir Nicholas, will be inundated along with mine. Our interest is mutual.'

Nicholas was smiling. '*Part* of my land, Gillory. Part of my land will be inundated. A small fraction of it. This is the difference between us – or one of the differences. I have three hundred acres. You have eighteen.'

For a moment he could not speak. Sunlight streamed through the window, illuminating the carpets, the furniture, the electric lamps. Through the slightly open window a breeze tugged at the curtains. At last Daniel said, 'Flooding can be prevented – a little work now, and we need have no fear –'

'*I* have no fear. It does not trouble me in the least.'

Daniel's temper, precariously held, began to slip away from him. 'Have you been there? Do you ever look at your vast acres of land? Do you see the rabbit-holes that undermine the banks on your property, the pitiful condition of the paths? My God, you have money enough for electric lights – for whatever foolishness you are constructing out there –' He gestured wildly to the window. A channel of brown earth seared the green expanse of front lawn. Twenty workmen in hob-nailed boots and muddy corduroys laboured for Nicholas Blythe. Daniel took a deep breath. 'I came here this morning because I hoped that we could be civilized – that we could discuss these matters as gentlemen.'

'*Gentlemen?*' The sneer was unmistakable now.

The loathing that Daniel had felt for so many years returned in full flood. A loathing, not only for Nicholas Blythe himself, but for what Nicholas and his family represented.

'Whatever your feelings towards me, would you sacrifice the rest of the village? Do you even understand the situation? Do you understand that the peat is sinking each year – sinking faster since diesel pumps were installed – and that a serious flood is ultimately inevitable? Do you understand that if – *when* – that happens, it will not only be my house and lands that are inundated, but the two beside me in the drove, and perhaps half the village as well?'

Nicholas said coldly, 'That is your opinion, Gillory – no one else's. It is not the opinion of the Drainage Commissioners.'

'The Drainage Commissioners,' hissed Daniel furiously, 'are in your pocket.'

Nicholas's face blanched. 'Hawkins. Would you fetch Robert, please?'

Daniel felt as though he was choking for breath. This room, this house, suffocated him.

Nicholas said, 'You are not to put a foot on my land, Gillory. Not to touch my ditches, my banks, my paths. It is *my* land, remember, and it will always be my land. I shall have you prosecuted as a common trespasser should you touch as much as a blade of grass.'

The butler had returned, accompanied by a footman. Nicholas

said, 'Throw him out, Hawkins,' and two men grabbed Daniel, dragging him out of the room.

At first he did not fight, and then he did. Utterly futile, of course. There was some satisfaction in wiping the smug smile from that bastard Hawkins's face, some satisfaction in seeing the footman, whom Daniel remembered from elementary school, collapse to the floor, gasping for breath. But then there were half a dozen more men, dragging him through the garden to the boundary, throwing him out of the gate.

There was blood in his mouth and his clothes were torn and muddy. He was sickened with the Blythes, sickened with himself. Daniel dragged himself to his feet and began to walk back down the slope. He had achieved nothing.

Nicholas went upstairs to the study. There, he sat down at the desk, his head in his hands, and thought. He found himself glad that Thomasine was out, that she had not witnessed that ugly little scene. But he knew now that Daniel Gillory had no inkling of the Abbey's precarious financial state. Nicholas realized that his previous fears had been foolish. Only Nicholas himself – not even Thomasine, not even Mama – knew the implications of that piece of paper on the desk.

The implications had now to be faced. Sitting down at the desk, Nicholas closed his eyes and stabbed at the open map with his forefinger. Then he looked down. The eastern side of the village and half of Burnt Fen. Three tied cottages and a tenant farm. Nicholas noted it down in neat, careful handwriting. Eyes closed, finger searching again. A collection of boggy fields halfway to Ely. One last time, and his questing forefinger found good arable land behind the island.

That should be enough, he thought. That should satisfy Max. Conscious of a job well done, Nicholas leaned back in the chair and wiped the sweat from his forehead with his handkerchief.

The epidemic started slowly, and then gathered an inexorable momentum. Thomasine first heard about it from the foreman, Joe Carter. She had spent an increasing number of afternoons with the foreman since the beginning of spring. Hostile at first, he seemed to have gradually accepted that her interest in the land was genuine; that from her past – her years as a child on her father's farm in Africa, and the five years she had earlier spent in Drakesden – she had come to understand a little of the cycle of the seasons and crops.

The weather was still raw and wet. Thomasine gripped her cloak tightly around her as she walked at the foreman's side along the boundary of the largest Abbey field.

'Wheat's coming up nicely in the higher ground, your ladyship. Water don't seem to drain off here, though.'

The fields that clung to the slope of the far side of the island were now a cloudy emerald green. But flat silver swathes of water still glazed the lowest ground, turning the earth into swamp.

'Hasn't Sir Nicholas asked the men to work on the dykes and ditches yet, Joe?'

The foreman shook his head. 'There aren't the men, your ladyship. Some of 'em are digging the new well up at the Abbey, and there's a handful off sick, of course. There's a lot of fever about this year.'

A little girl had died in the village only a fortnight ago. Thomasine remembered earlier winters, tramping with Aunt Hilly from cottage to cottage, trying to alleviate some of the misery and deprivation enclosed in the shabby clunch walls.

She did not return to Drakesden Abbey her usual way, through the paddock and lawn, but instead continued along the drove towards the village. It seemed to her that there were fewer children than usual playing in the streets, and she could see no crowds of gossiping women clustered around the village pump. The unsurfaced roads were striped with furrows from cartwheels, the hollows of the furrows awash with water. She knocked at the door of the Gotobeds' cottage.

Mrs Gotobed opened the door. She was a gaunt woman of forty or so, her shoulders badly stooped from summers spent cutting peat to earn the family a little extra money. Since her marriage at the age of twenty she had, Thomasine knew, produced a baby each year, some of whom lived and some of whom did not. All the Gotobed babies were pretty, blue-eyed and golden-haired, a prettiness that faded quickly as they grew older.

Thomasine smiled as she was shown into the tiny two-roomed cottage. 'I came to ask after the new baby, Mrs Gotobed.'

Some Drakesden babies slept in beautiful carved cradles, remnants of days when there had been a craftsman carpenter in every Fen village. Others slept in drawers or in withy baskets. The Gotobed baby grizzled in a cardboard box begged from the grocer's shop.

'Evelina ain't too well, your ladyship. She's sickening for summat.'

The infant looked hot and restless. Very gently, Thomasine picked her up and cradled her against her shoulder. She could hear the child's breathing, a soft, stertorous groan with every rise and fall of the tiny chest.

'Poor little mite. Has she seen a doctor, Mrs Gotobed?'

Mrs Gotobed's eyes evaded Thomasine's. 'I don't hold with doctors, your ladyship. I've boiled an onion and wrapped it in her shawl.'

There was a strong smell of onion emanating from the tattered grey shawl. Thomasine was aware that she had visited empty-handed, that she had failed in her duties. The villagers of Drakesden tolerated the interferences of the Blythes, tolerated the ladies poking around their cottages and making tactless recommendations as to the upbringing of their children, because the Blythes, in their turn, dispensed charity. The Blythes passed on to the villagers their old sheets and blankets when they could no longer be sides-to-middled; the Blythes, in particularly harsh winters, gave out rations of soup and bread.

The cottage was cold and damp, the floor still blackened by recent flooding. The open fire seemed to give off no heat. Carefully, Thomasine placed the baby back in her cardboard box.

'I'll come back tomorrow, Mrs Gotobed. I've some shawls and nightgowns that might be useful for Evelina.'

The nursery cupboards at Drakesden Abbey were crammed with cot sheets, blankets, quilts, shawls, napkins and tiny little garments. All had once belonged to Gerald, Nicholas, Marjorie and Lally. Thomasine crammed a shopping-bag full of the warmest things, stole two bottles of blackcurrant cordial from the housekeeper's room and returned to the Gotobeds' cottage the following afternoon.

This time, three other little Gotobed children, all huddled together on one straw mattress, coughed along with Evelina in her cardboard box. There was a smell of damp and peat smoke, but the fire seemed neither to heat nor to light the small cottage. Thomasine helped change and dress the baby. The infant's cheeks were scarlet, her breathing still noisy. If she isn't well, thought Thomasine desperately, as least now she is warm.

When she left the cottage, she did not return to the Abbey. It was not yet tea-time and, besides, there were a dozen other cottages to visit. She went from door to door, trailing through the mud, resolution hardening in her as she visited each dingy dwelling.

CHAPTER ELEVEN

THOMASINE spoke to Nicholas that evening, between tea and dinner. He was bent over the desk in his study, drawing intricate plans, his brow furrowed, but he looked up and smiled at her when she came in to the room.

'Come and see. I've been talking to the plumber all afternoon and I think everything's finalized now.'

He showed her his plans for installing hot running water in the house, telling her about the new well, the soakaways and piping.

'Just think, Thomasine, you'll be able to have a hot bath whenever you like. No more asking the servants to run up and downstairs with jugs of hot water. Won't it be terrific?'

'Terrific,' she agreed. She could not at the moment echo his enthusiasm. She was too preoccupied by the scenes she had witnessed that afternoon. 'Nicholas – I have to ask you a favour. Could you let me have some money?'

She hated this, she found it humiliating. She earned no money now, and she had no control over the money that was spent at Drakesden Abbey. Nicholas paid the bills and dealt with his accountant.

'Have as much as you want, darling,' he said carelessly. 'What's it for? Clothes? I thought I'd take you to Paris after the baby was born. We both deserve a treat, don't you think?'

Thomasine shook her head. 'I don't need any more clothes, Nick. It's not for me. There's a lot of sickness in the village, and no one can afford to pay a doctor. People need medicine – fuel – decent food. I've taken some blankets and things, but it's not enough.'

Nicholas unscrewed the cap from his fountain pen. Then he

said, 'Money's a bit tight at the moment, actually, Thomasine.'

She stared at him. It had not crossed her mind that he might refuse her. He had always been unfailingly generous.

'But you just said – we may go to Paris – that I could buy clothes –'

'I'll always give you the best, Thomasine,' he said anxiously, looking up at her. 'I promised you that. I won't renege on that promise.'

She hadn't explained things properly, Thomasine thought. She pushed her hair out of her eyes and started again.

'The Gotobeds' new baby is very sick, Nicholas. She has a fever and I don't like the sound of her breathing. Three of Mrs Gotobed's other children are ill as well –'

'The *Gotobeds*,' interrupted Nicholas, and shook his head. His expression was scornful. 'They always were a feckless lot, weren't they? You can't help people like the Gotobeds.'

'You can help them pay for a doctor – you can give them turf for their fire –'

'And where do you stop, Thomasine?' Nicholas flung out his hands in a gesture of despair. 'Where do you stop? Do you feed and clothe every one of their umpteen children? Do you send Abbey housemaids to clean out that disgusting flea-ridden shack that they live in?'

She said furiously, 'It's *your* shack, Nicholas. The Gotobeds live in a tied cottage.'

'So do the Dockerills. Yet they manage to keep theirs clean and warm and tidy.'

She was silenced for a moment. What Nicholas said was true: there was a world of difference between the Gotobeds' squalid cottage and the Dockerills'. The Dockerills' home, though equally small and equally spartan, was *clean*.

'Mrs Dockerill is one in a thousand,' continued Thomasine obstinately. 'She is healthier than Mrs Gotobed – more intelligent – a better manager –'

'Exactly.' Nicholas placed a ruler on the paper and began to draw again. 'What you have to learn, Thomasine, is that there is a world of difference between the deserving and the undeserving poor. The Dockerills fall into one category and the Gotobeds into the other.'

For a moment, she disliked him. 'That sounds – harsh.'

He shrugged. 'Maybe. But you can't change people like the Gotobeds. They don't help themselves, you see.'

She watched him draw for a while: the neat black lines, the tiny annotations in the margins. Then she said slowly, 'What do you mean?'

'Well.' His snort of laughter was contemptuous. 'A baby every year. That doesn't exactly help, does it?'

Her temper, often short these days, was slipping out of her control.

'Should I send Mrs Gotobed to London to Dr Stopes's clinic, Nicholas? Should I?'

He reddened. 'I meant – restraint. They could practise a little more restraint, couldn't they?'

They were glaring at each other across the wide oak desk. 'Besides,' Nicholas added, 'they have so many children they probably scarcely notice the loss of one. They're not like their betters, Thomasine – they don't have the same capacity for feeling. They live such a hand-to-mouth existence, they're more like animals, really.'

She had to look away from him; she was afraid of saying something unforgivable. Her gaze flicked rapidly round the room, taking in the old, well-polished furniture, the paintings, the books, all the trappings of centuries of wealth.

She said coldly, 'You sound like your mother, Nicholas. Prepared to give patronage, but not to try and change things.'

The colour drained from his face. Thomasine could almost feel Nicholas's tension in the ensuing silence.

'And you sound like Daniel Gillory,' he said eventually. 'He's writing nonsense for the local newspaper now. Did you know, Thomasine? Stirring them all up, trying to convert them to

Socialism.' The sneer in Nicholas's voice was blatant. 'Have you been reading his rubbish?'

For a moment they just stared at each other. They were in the same room, thought Thomasine bleakly, but they might as well have been a thousand miles apart.

'Don't be ridiculous, Nick,' she whispered. 'You have a responsibility, that's all.'

She saw him flinch. Nicholas looked back at his plans, and began to draw again. His hand was shaking though, and a small black blot formed in the centre of the white paper. Immediately he reached for the blotting paper, and then began to scratch away at the tiny mark until the blemish was eradicated. It occurred to Thomasine that Nicholas's latest obsessions were just another way of evading the responsibilities that his brother's and his father's deaths had forced upon him.

'You have a responsibility,' she repeated. 'Whether you wanted it or not, the people of Drakesden are your responsibility, Nick.' Then she left the room.

Daniel's cuts were superficial, and the bruises Nicholas's men had made faded in a few days. The wounding of his pride, his soul, was far deeper, far more dangerous. Daniel knew now that Nicholas Blythe would never sell to him. He had seen the depths of the hatred in Nicholas's eyes, a hatred that was mutual, exaggerated rather than diminished by time. He would never build a better house for Fay on the higher land. He would never own the fields that he coveted. Fay would have to grow accustomed to the water that seeped up through the kitchen floor each spring; Daniel would have to build her parlour on peat that would take foundations of hardly any depth at all. Drakesden infants would continue to die of diseases that a decent diet and a dry home would have prevented, and Daniel's own house and land would be under a greater and greater threat of flooding as each year passed.

★

Thomasine continued to raid Drakesden Abbey's airing cupboards and clothes'-presses for warm blankets and garments. Carrying bags down the slope of the island tired her. One day, when the late spring sky went black and became peppered with stars, she had to sit and rest in the copse for fully ten minutes before she could begin to walk again. Afterwards, she drove the Delage to the village, steering it carefully through the muddy rutted roads.

The argument with Nicholas had not been resolved. It had merely, thought Thomasine bitterly, been swept away, disregarded. Nicholas evaded conflict and anger just as he evaded responsibility. It was as though, she often thought, he had built a wall around himself, a wall that not even she could scale.

She decided to go and see Mrs Dockerill. As Nicholas had pointed out, the Dockerills seemed to survive the worst that poverty and the harsh landscape could throw at them. When Mrs Dockerill showed Thomasine into the two-roomed cottage, she was taken back for a moment to the years before the War. Nothing had changed, she thought. There was still the stove, still the scrubbed and scarred table, still the delicious scent of the pudding boiling away in a saucepan.

And yet, she was wrong. Something had changed. Mrs Dockerill had not turned back to her pastry-making, telling Thomasine to help herself to raisins from the tin. Instead she stood, drying her hands on her apron, watching her warily.

Thomasine said crossly, 'I'm not going to start poking round in your saucepans, Mrs Dockerill, telling you what to cook!' and she saw a slight relaxation of the expression on the older woman's face. A chair was pulled out and dusted with a floury apron.

'Sit you down, then, and tell me what you are here for, then, your ladyship.'

The formality made Thomasine wince. But she sat down, aware that her legs and back ached, as they so often did nowadays.

'I came to ask your advice, Mrs Dockerill.'

Mrs Dockerill had returned to the pastry. Her large red hands pounded the dough and sprinkled flour on a board.

'About this epidemic, I mean. Three children have died so far –'

'Four,' interrupted Mrs Dockerill, and Thomasine stared at her.

'Mary Gotobed's little 'un died this morning.'

For a moment, she closed her eyes. She had visited the infant almost every day since it had fallen ill, and had grown attached to the tiny struggling creature.

She said weakly, 'But I thought she was *better*. I thought yesterday she was coughing less –'

A cup of tea was placed on the table in front of her. Mrs Dockerill said more kindly, 'Here, drink that, love.' The endearment made her eyes blur even more, but she picked up the mug and swallowed a mouthful of hot, sweet, stewed tea.

'It turned to pneumonia,' explained Mrs Dockerill. 'No one could have done nothing. Not even a doctor.'

Thomasine blew her nose. All her efforts over the last week seemed futile and feeble. 'If I'd got her a doctor earlier . . .' she whispered. 'I hadn't the *money* –'

She did not finish her sentence. She sat for a moment, gazing at the bleached surface of the table. Then she gulped another mouthful of tea and blew her nose again. She knew that Mrs Dockerill was staring at her, that Mrs Dockerill could not conceive of the possibility that she, Lady Thomasine Blythe, had not endless supplies of money to spend how she wished. She took a deep breath, and sat up straighter.

'I came to ask if you could suggest anything more that I could do. I've brought blankets and food and things, and I asked Joe Carter to share out some turves, but –' Again she could not finish her sentence. It was not enough – it could never be enough. She was haunted by a recollection of that tiny baby in its cardboard box cot.

But Mrs Dockerill said acidly, 'Well – you could ask your husband to stop cutting labourers' wages. And putting up rents.' And Thomasine turned and looked at the other woman, her eyes wide.

Reddening slightly, Mrs Dockerill picked up her rolling-pin. 'I beg your pardon, your ladyship. I spoke out of turn.'

'I didn't know.' Thomasine shook her head as if to clear it. 'Nicholas has cut the men's wages . . .?'

Mrs Dockerill looked at her for a long moment, and then she nodded. 'A couple of months back. Once they've paid their rent, bought a few things from the grocer's, and the man's had his pint or two at The Otter . . .' She shrugged. 'Well, there's not an awful lot left.'

Thomasine put down the half-finished cup of tea and stood up. She was aware of a gathering anger in her, an anger that could hardly be contained.

'I'll have a word with Nicholas,' she said, and turned to go.

Mrs Dockerill opened the door for her. One floury hand touched Thomasine's arm as she stepped through the doorway: a remnant of a time when they had been friends, thought Thomasine sadly.

'Don't fret yourself too much, love. Summer's almost here, so the fever will have burnt itself out in a week or two. And you ought to be looking after yourself – it isn't long until the baby's due, is it?'

Thomasine managed a watery smile. 'Four weeks,' she said, looking down at herself. 'I feel like an elephant.'

Once, she would have hugged Mrs Dockerill before taking her leave. But not now. Instead she walked to the motor-car, and started to drive back through the village and up the incline of the island.

She tramped all over the garden and house, looking for Nicholas, and then she found him in one of the bathrooms, washing his hands.

When she repeated what Mrs Dockerill had said, he just looked away from her, and muttered, 'I told you we were short of cash. Max said I had to make economies.'

'With people's livelihoods?' The drive back to the Abbey had not lessened her fury. 'For pity's sake, Nick – when I think of the food we threw away at Christmas –'

He said nothing, just refilled the basin, picked up the nail-brush and started scrubbing his hands again.

'You could have told me! I've been such a fool – going down there, thinking I could help them, and all the time we've just been making things worse!'

He poured more water into the basin. 'I told you there was nothing you could do, Thomasine. I said you couldn't change things.'

She whispered, 'The Gotobeds' baby died, Nick. Little Evelina. *God!*' She rubbed at her eyes with her fists. 'Such a bloody ridiculous name –' Her voice broke, and she squeezed her eyes shut.

When she opened them again, Thomasine saw that Nicholas was pouring out the used water from the basin, and refilling it once more. The water was quite clean, yet he continued to rub soap into his hands, to scrub at his skin with the nail-brush, to pick imaginary fragments of dirt from his fingers. She realized that he was hardly listening to what she said, that he was totally absorbed in this futile, obsessive washing. She watched him for a long while, seeing the intent expression in his eyes as he examined his hands for any trace of dirt. The skin of his hands was always reddened and rough, and she guessed that this was a ritual he had gone through many, many times before. Watching him, Thomasine was aware of a sickened feeling in her belly, an unnameable fear for the future, and she turned away from him and walked blindly along the corridor.

In Ely one afternoon, Fay left the cycle by some railings and began to walk around the shops. She had always enjoyed window-shopping, looking at pretty things. There was quite a good dress shop in the High Street (although it did not, of course, compare with Chantal's), and she gazed for some time at the outfits displayed in the window. There was a very pretty dress, pale pink, layered over a white underskirt. Examining it with a professional eye, Fay concluded that the pink material was chiffon, the white artificial silk. The effect was light, summery, modern.

Some of Fay's pleasure in the afternoon began to wear off. The dress she wore now she had made herself two years ago. Since then, she had altered the trim and taken up the hemline so that it now rested only a couple of inches below her knees, but it was still a two-year-old cotton dress. 'Twenty-seven and six,' whispered Fay crossly, staring at the price card beside the pink chiffon. She knew precisely how much was in her purse: two pounds and ten shillings, her housekeeping money for the week, given to her by Daniel that morning.

She wandered away from the dress shop and, to cheer herself up, went into the little café next door. Drinking her tea, she appreciated the nice china cups, the silver tea-service, the damask tablecloth. Momentarily, she imagined herself with a similar tea-service, entertaining the envious ladies of Drakesden. But the dream collapsed when she saw herself back in her awful poky kitchen with the brick floor and the smelly old stove. Besides, there were no ladies in Drakesden. Or none that would take tea with the wife of a smallholder.

In her mind's eye, she pictured the little house she longed for. In a town, not the countryside, with two living-rooms as well as a kitchen. Neat and pretty, and with a maid to do the heavy work. The dream dissolved again and, disconsolately, Fay paid the waitress her sixpence and left the café.

She was wandering aimlessly through the streets when someone called out her name. Turning, she saw Doctor Lawrence walking down the steps of one of the adjacent houses. Fay glimpsed the brass plate beside the door of the square, brick-built house.

'Doctor Lawrence! How delightful.'

'You look well, Mrs Gillory. And quite charming. How are you?'

She saw the admiration in his light blue, heavy-lidded, sandy-lashed eyes. He had remembered her name.

'I'm very well, Doctor Lawrence. My foot is quite recovered.'

'I'm pleased to hear it.' He smiled.

Fitful sunlight glittered on the flower-beds and shrubs outside his house. Fay said, 'Your wife must be feeling the benefit of the better weather, doctor.'

He laughed. 'Och, I'm not married, Mrs Gillory. I'm just a poor lonely bachelor. I haven't found any lassie willing to take pity on me yet.'

She murmured, 'Oh, I find that hard to believe,' and noticed again the flicker of interest in his eyes. Her heart beat a little faster: she realized how much she had missed this sort of excitement. None of the men in Drakesden were worth a second glance. Country hayseeds, the lot of them.

She said, 'Well, I must be on my way,' and she held out her hand. She felt the pressure of his fingers through her thin gloves. When he had walked away out of sight round the corner of the street, she turned quickly back to his house. Cautiously, she tiptoed up the path and read the brass plate.

'Dr A. Lawrence MD' it said. As she headed back to the High Street, Fay speculated happily on that enticing letter 'A'. Adam, Alan, Albert . . . none seemed quite right for him.

When she reached the dress shop, she opened the door and went in. 'I'd like to try the pink chiffon in the window,' she said haughtily to the assistant.

Inside the changing-room, Fay looked at herself in the mirror. The dress fitted perfectly.

It became all too easy to live quite separate lives: Nicholas supervising the workmen's noisy and invasive attempts to install hot running water, Thomasine spending much of the day outdoors.

May was dry and warm. The fever, as Mrs Dockerill had predicted, fizzled out as the damp cottages dried in the sunnier weather. The warm weather brought out the insects, though. Once, after calling at a particularly flea-ridden cottage, Thomasine scratched her way through afternoon tea. Dressing for dinner later, she found a rash of scarlet flea-bites over her body. Revolted, she scrubbed herself clean in one of Nicholas's half-built bathrooms, and washed out her clothes herself until she was sure that the infestation had gone.

In a stupor of discomfort and weariness she heaved herself from the Abbey to the village, from the village around the farm. She could no longer drive the Delage; she simply couldn't fit in it. Dr Lawrence scolded her and told her to rest, but she could not. She could find nowhere comfortable. The conservatory was too hot and the rest of the house full of pipes and workmen, hammering and sawing. The rift between herself and Nicholas had not been mended, and she was far too aware of Lady Blythe's censorious eyes to feel at ease in her mother-in-law's company. Sometimes she admitted to herself that she was, at Drakesden Abbey, lonely. Outside, at least there was Joe Carter to talk to, or Mrs Dockerill with whom to share the occasional cup of tea. She still felt almost overwhelmed by a sense of her own uselessness. But, if she could not pay the men properly, at least she could take to the poorest households some of the left-over food from the Abbey table. If she despised herself for doling out the charity that she had once regarded with such contempt, then it was, for now, all she could do.

She knew that Dr Lawrence had been right to scold her when, halfway through the meadow with a basket of groceries slung over one arm, she felt faint. She sat down on the grass, her eyes closed. A wave of pain washed over her entire torso, her back, her belly, her thighs. When she opened her eyes, Thomasine knew that the alleviation of pain was only temporary, that she must return to Drakesden Abbey. She was alone, the adjacent fields were bare of labourers and none of the cottages was within shouting distance. Leaving the basket in the middle of the meadow, she began the slow crawl back to the house. Every now and again she had to pause, leaning against a tree-trunk or just standing, desperately trying to keep her balance while the dreadful pain gripped her again.

When at last she stumbled through the gate to the orchard, she glimpsed one of the kitchen-maids ahead, pulling rhubarb for pies. She managed to call out the girl's name, and it almost made her laugh to wonder which of them was the more frightened, herself or the scrawny thirteen-year-old on whose shoulder she leant as she hobbled back to the house.

Dr Lawrence offered her chloroform, but she pushed him away. She had not endured twelve hours of agony to be robbed of the moment of her child's birth. When, with a dreadful tearing push she gave birth to the baby's head, she felt simultaneously both the worst pain and her greatest triumph. With a final slither and twist, the infant separated from her, and the pain, thank God, was over.

'It's a boy,' said Dr Lawrence, and Thomasine was aware of an all-enveloping, exhausted happiness. The baby was bathed and dressed and given to her to hold. His dark eyes darted, momentarily focusing on her. His tiny puckered mouth opened and closed when she stroked his soft, crumpled cheek with her fingertip. 'Sweetheart,' she whispered, and kissed her son's small head.

Nicholas was shown into the room. He looked pale and anxious, and when he bent to look at his son Thomasine saw that there were tears in his eyes. Suddenly, their differences of the past year seemed trivial.

They called the baby William Gerald, after Nicholas's father and brother. He had come into the world three weeks early, but in spite of that he was strong and lusty. Compared with William, nothing else was important. The love she felt for her child diminished everything else, so that she forgot all her previous difficulties. The days and nights adopted a different rhythm, the rhythm of a newborn baby's feeding and sleeping. She did not read, she forgot the village and neglected the house. If William was not near her she felt strangely bereft.

Daniel, leading Nelson by the bridle, was walking back with Harry Dockerill to the blacksmith's cottage. The sun gleamed high overhead, a bright, hard disc. Their boots and clothes were black with dust.

'Mark Hayhoe's been given notice to leave his cottage,' said Harry. 'Three kids and his wife expecting the fourth. Criminal, I call it.'

Daniel, startled, glanced at him. 'Mark? Why?'

'Squire's put land up for sale, ain't he?' Harry spat on the ground. 'Tied, ain't it? As soon as Master sells land, the Hayhoes will have to go. And the Bentons, and the Carters.'

They had reached the back yard. Daniel said slowly, 'I hadn't heard the Blythes were selling.'

'That's 'acos you don't go to The Otter. Nor to church. My Ma heard from Lizzie Hayhoe.'

Settling Nelson in his stable, Daniel had a few seconds to think. His conclusions were not pleasant. 'Come in for a beer, Harry,' he said.

Harry accepted thankfully. He pulled off his cloth cap as he stepped inside the kitchen, tucking it inside his shirt. 'Awful close weather, missus,' he said, nodding politely to Fay.

Fay sniffed and poured out two tankards of beer. Thunder rumbled distantly as she poured, making her hand jump, so that beer spilled on the table-top. Silently, she handed the two men the tankards.

Daniel said, 'You are not powerless, Harry. Your family – the Hayhoes and Carters – may depend on the Blythes, but the Blythes also depend on you.'

Harry drained his tankard in one gulp. 'I doubt if Squire's worrying how he'll feed the new baby.'

'Of course not. But Nicholas Blythe can't work his land alone. He doesn't plough the furrows, or cut the corn. He needs you to do that for him.'

Harry was staring at him. He put down his tankard. 'Strike, do you mean?' He laughed. 'Never. Not here. They'd think you were a bloody Red, if you suggested that. And how would they feed their families?'

'Can they feed them now? Where will they go, Harry, the Hayhoes and the Carters and the Bentons? Besides, I wasn't thinking of an all-out strike. More – more a tactical withdrawal of labour.'

'You're barmy, Gillory.'

Harry wiped his mouth with the back of his hand, muttered thanks to Fay and ducked out through the doorway, a big, muscular man, too large for the confined spaces of Fenland cottages. 'Storm's brewing,' he added, squinting up at the sky.

When he had gone, Fay said, 'You shouldn't let him speak to you like that. It isn't right.'

'Harry's a good worker – a good friend. I don't give a damn how he speaks to me.'

'A *friend*?' Fay turned her back to Daniel as she fried eggs on the range. 'Harry Dockerill isn't your friend, Daniel. He's your employee.'

The weather, his increasingly familiar exhaustion, the news that Harry had just told him, all made Daniel's temper short. 'For God's sake, Fay – what do you want? Do you want Harry to treat me like one of the bloody Blythes?'

As always, when he lost his temper, she did not reply to him, but reprimanded him. 'There's no need to swear, Daniel.' Only this time her voice shook.

He went to her. Eggs fried unappetizingly in the pan, swathed in grease, their yolks burst and their whites blackened. A tear plopped into the hot fat, making it sizzle.

Daniel touched her shoulder. 'Fay,' he said, more gently, 'what is it?'

'The *thunder*.' Her voice was only a whisper. She began to cry.

He almost laughed with relief. But, always practical, he helped her lift the eggs on to the plates and put aside the pan. Then he began to explain about thunder. That it was far away at present, that she had only to count the gap between lightning flash and thunderbolt to know that the storm was at least twenty miles away. That, even had it been overhead, they would be safe because thunder always went for the highest spot, not the lowest. Like the church, or Drakesden Abbey.

As he spoke, he experienced a brief, sharp flicker of memory, recalling himself, only fifteen years old, explaining the same phenomena to a frightened Lally Blythe. At least, he thought she had been frightened, though sometimes since then he had wondered whether he had mistaken excitement for fear. Whether the kiss that she had so fatally bestowed upon him had been planned from the moment she had met him in the Labyrinth, or whether it had been the consequence of her terror, of the intensity of the moment. He would never know.

Neither he nor Fay wanted to eat. Fay was too upset, and Daniel found the sight of the burnt egg and flabby luncheon meat unenticing. So he sat Fay on his knee and, as her trembling eased, he began to kiss her.

After a while she responded to him just as warmly as she had during the first happy months of their marriage. He could never quite equate this passionate side of her character with the other side, the side that increasingly jarred him, pernickity, small-minded, obsessed with appearance. When he led her up the ladder to their bed, she did not protest. Her eyes were dark and bright, her skin almost white. As the lightning flashed and the rain beat against the roof of the cottage, he made love to her with a passion that she seemed to welcome, so that he felt he was righting some of the wrongs, the small hairline cracks that had begun to appear in their marriage. Afterwards, he held her in his arms, stroking back the tangled hair from her face. He tried to put into words the fears that had haunted him for several months.

'If you weren't happy, you would tell me, wouldn't you, Fay? If you weren't content . . .'

He thought for a moment that she was asleep, that she had not heard him. Then the thunder crashed again, and she opened her eyes wide.

He persevered. 'I know it's been hard, darling, but it will get better, I promise you.'

But even to his own ears his promises sounded increasingly hollow. He had now no hope that Nicholas Blythe would sell him the land that he wanted. Nicholas Blythe had put up for sale different acres of land, land with tied cottages, land that the same families had lived on for years.

He was alarmed by her silence. 'Speak to me, Fay, please,' he whispered. 'Tell me.' He forced himself to ask the question. 'Is it me? Is it, Fay?'

She shook her head, and his relief was intense. Her fingers clutched at him, bruising him. He whispered, 'Then is it the house? Is it because I can't give you pretty clothes, that sort of thing?'

Again, she said nothing, but he could see the truth in her eyes. He saw that what was enough for him was deficient for her.

He said gently, 'And – are you lonely?'

She spoke at last. 'It gets ever so lonely, sometimes, Daniel. It's so quiet here. I wouldn't have believed anywhere could be so quiet. I can't bear it.'

He needed this land, though. He needed it because he feared that to return to the city would return him to ill-health and poverty. And because there was so much that was incomplete, unavenged. Fleetingly, Daniel wondered whether his suggestion to Harry Dockerill had been prompted by a concern for the villagers' welfare, or by his own need to ruin Nicholas Blythe, to even up the debt between them – to force the Blythes into selling the land that Daniel coveted. He pushed the thought aside.

'Poor old Fay – I haven't been much company lately, have I?' Daniel stroked her long, soft dark hair, loving the feel of it as it ran through his fingers. He had a sudden inspiration. 'Listen. How would you like this? We'll go to London for the day. Get up early, catch the first train from Ely, and spend the whole day there. You could go and see your family, if you like.'

He saw her smile at last. He ignored the nagging voice in his head that pointed out how little he could afford a day out. A whole day's work lost, and his financial reserves were low. Agricultural prices were still falling.

'Oh, Daniel – oh, Daniel – that would be ever so nice.'

He heard Harry Dockerill call at the door downstairs and ignored him. He began to kiss Fay again. Let Harry draw his own conclusions.

Antonia visited Drakesden at the beginning of June. Thomasine took her first to the nursery, where Antonia agreed that William was, of course, the most adorable baby ever born, and then they had luncheon with Lady Blythe and Nicholas. Lady Blythe was condescending; Antonia, as always, was elegant and charming. Afterwards, Thomasine pushed the huge old perambulator around the Abbey gardens, Antonia at her side.

Antonia talked about her dancing-school. 'I have engaged a new teacher, Thomasine. She is a very competent dancer, but not as patient with the little ones as you were.'

Thomasine looked down at herself and grimaced. 'Look at me – I'm such a lump. I can't imagine ever being able to dance again. Thank goodness dresses don't have waists these days.'

Antonia said firmly, 'It is only three weeks since William was born, dearest. You must be patient. You are looking well, I think.'

Thomasine adjusted the canopy on the perambulator, so that William was shaded from the sun.

'I'll be glad when I can ride again, Aunt Tony. Dr Lawrence says I should wait until six weeks after the birth, though.'

They walked on a little further. 'And Nicholas –' Antonia's voice was hesitant – 'is he well?'

Thomasine glanced at her sharply. Recently, her former unease about Nicholas's state of mind had begun to creep back.

'He doesn't sleep well, Aunt Tony. To be honest, he's never really settled back at Drakesden. But then he never settled anywhere. He was happiest when we were on the move.'

She had thought once that she could make Nicholas happy. But lately it had seemed to Thomasine that they were, perhaps, too different, too pulled apart by background and by history. She would admit to the precarious state of her marriage to no one, though, not even to Antonia. She said, more cheerfully, 'But his electric lights and hot running water are marvellous, aren't they, Aunt Tony?'

'Marvellous,' agreed Antonia. 'I've always thought – these big old houses – they are so wonderful, of course, so much *history*, yet so tiresome to run, I should imagine. You must need so many servants, and yet everyone says that good people are so difficult to get hold of nowadays.'

They were walking down the edge of the lawn, beside the Wilderness. Ahead of her, Thomasine could see the paddock, the dyke, the fields. Clouds were gathering on the horizon, casting black shadows on the sunlit wheat.

'William's nanny arrives on Monday,' she said suddenly. 'I do wish –' She stopped herself just in time. She could not imagine sharing William with a stranger. She could not imagine allowing a stranger to feed her baby, to bathe him, to play with him. She realized that Antonia was looking at her, her eyes troubled.

'It is the usual thing,' said Antonia gently. 'All the titled ladies who send their daughters to my school – well, they all employ nannies.'

The rain clouds were creeping closer. Thomasine turned the

perambulator round, and began to walk fast up the island, back to the house.

'I had a letter from Aunt Hilly yesterday,' she said brightly. 'Apparently she has met a kind and intelligent gentleman. Do you think that there is any chance . . .?'

Much later, Daniel remembered the trip to London as the last time that things between himself and Fay seemed right. She wore a dress that he had not seen before: pale, floaty pink stuff that emphasized both the ethereal paleness of her skin and the dark sheen of her hair.

London had changed during the twenty months of their absence. Huge traffic jams clogged the centre of the city; the fumes made them both choke. In the West End, window-shopping, they heard an ex-servicemen's band playing in the street. Fay exclaimed over the pretty things in the shop windows, while Daniel kicked his heels on the pavement, hating London, hating the lousy, rotten country that reduced even its War heroes to beggars.

They had lunch in Selfridges, and Fay bought a hat and a dress. The articles that Daniel had written for the *Ely Standard* paid for the clothes. Later, travelling by bus to see Hattie in Bethnal Green while Fay met her mother in Gorringes, he composed more articles in his head. For national newspapers, for magazines and periodicals. He must earn more money, so that he could give Fay the things she wanted. A better house, pretty clothes – children, perhaps. He had realized that he could never earn sufficient from eighteen acres of swampy land.

Bethnal Green had not changed at all: barefoot children still ran in the gutters and the women still looked old at twenty-five. Hattie hugged and kissed him, but could not disguise the cough that racked her body. Widowed six months previously, she brushed away Daniel's concern about her health, plying him with food and drink, listening avidly to his news.

Then they returned to Drakesden, and life reverted to its

usual pattern: Daniel working all hours of the day, Fay uninterested in house or farm. Soon her disinterest hardened to neglect. Meals failed to appear, the range choked when the ash-can was not emptied. They seemed to lead increasingly separate lives – Daniel always either farming or writing, Fay increasingly restless, moping round the house, wandering round the village or cycling in the afternoons to Ely. Daniel found himself unable to halt the slow, steady progress of their estrangement. Tired and worried himself, he could not pinpoint what was wrong. Only sometimes, when he went out to lock the hen-house at night, and the stars in the sky were reduced by the gleaming unnatural bulk of Drakesden Abbey, did Daniel blame the quirks of history that had placed him in the swampy ground by the river, and Nicholas Blythe up there, safe, untouched.

William was four weeks old when Nicholas collected Nanny Harper from Ely station. That morning Thomasine had, to her delight, managed to get into one of the skirts she had worn before the birth. Her hair, she thought as she looked in the mirror, desperately needed cutting, but it was nice to have her figure back again, and to be able to run upstairs without getting out of breath.

Thomasine escorted the new arrival to the nursery, showing her the large, airy day-nursery and adjoining bathroom and night-nursery, and introducing her to the nursemaid, Martha. Nanny Harper was about forty-five years old, bony, strong-featured, her cape and bonnet immaculate. She bent over William's cradle.

'What was the child's weight at birth, your ladyship?'

'Almost seven and a half pounds,' Thomasine answered proudly.

'A good weight. Six feeds a day, then, Martha,' Miss Harper said, addressing the nursemaid, 'at regular four-hourly intervals. A bath morning and night, of course. I'm sure the little mite will be no trouble at all.'

318

Fondly, Thomasine looked down at the baby in the cradle. He was beginning to stir.

'He seems to be a bit grizzly in the evenings, Nanny. I have to give him an extra bottle sometimes.'

Nanny Harper had taken off her cape, and was hanging it on the back of the door. She smoothed the creases out of her dress.

'Regularity is most important for an infant of that age, Lady Blythe. Bad habits must be nipped in the bud, before they can get out of hand. Extra feeds – unnecessary fussing – those are the type of practices that lead to a sickly, discontented child.'

Nanny Harper smiled. She seemed, thought Thomasine, dazed, to have rather a lot of teeth: large, perfectly white and gleaming. Her eyes were a cold blue-grey. She was opening drawers and baskets, checking the nursery equipment.

'It all seems quite satisfactory, your ladyship. Another dozen napkins, perhaps, and the bathroom sink could be a little shinier, but otherwise it seems most satisfactory.'

The baby's grumbles were gathering in momentum, ready to turn into full-throated cries. Thomasine lifted William out of his cradle, holding him against her shoulder and gently patting his back.

'When was the infant last fed, your ladyship?'

Thomasine frowned, thinking. 'Just after lunch, I think. At about two o'clock. I didn't look at the time –'

Nanny Harper permitted herself the smallest sigh. 'We really must keep better account of things, mustn't we? The child's feeds should be timed to the minute. It is most important. Two o'clock? Then his next feed should be at six.'

William's face was a red crumpled ball. His cries filled the room.

'But he's hungry now, Miss Harper –'

'It is good for the infant to cry. It will exercise his lungs. Now, Lady Blythe, I won't keep you any longer. Everything seems quite satisfactory.'

Thomasine said obstinately, 'William's hungry, Nanny.' And

she sat down in the nursing chair by the window and unbuttoned her blouse. But either William had been kept waiting too long, or the nanny's disapproving stare curdled her milk, for he fed badly, letting go of the nipple frequently to voice his displeasure and regurgitating mouthfuls of wind and stale milk when he was finally taken away from the breast.

Planning William's christening was like planning a battle campaign. Lady Blythe graciously stepped aside, promising that she would not interfere, so all the arrangements were left to Thomasine. Nicholas was still wholly absorbed in plumbing. Problems had developed with the construction of the septic tank, the site he had originally chosen proving to be little more than swamp a few feet below ground. Pipes had had to be relaid, new trenches dug.

Thomasine made lists, drew up plans. At dinner, husbands and wives must not be seated next to each other, each guest must sit beside a guest of the opposite sex, and each guest must sit next to a different guest at each different meal. It was, Thomasine thought, like algebra. She sat one day at the drawing-room table, surrounded by pieces of paper, pens and timetables, cutting out small squares of cardboard, writing the name of a guest on each one. It took almost the entire afternoon, shuffling the cards in different patterns, to plan the seating arrangements for every evening. And then, when, triumphant and tired at six o'clock in the evening, she thought she had finished, Lady Blythe appeared, casually inspecting the seating plans on her way to her rooms to dress for dinner. 'Oh, dear, you have not taken account of precedent – these really will not do, Thomasine.' Max Feltham was the nephew of an earl, Marjorie's husband Edward, an Honourable. These things, apparently, mattered. Thomasine gritted her teeth and began once again to rearrange the cards.

She had intended to plan the formal breakfast that would follow the christening by checking back through the old menus in the morning-room desk. But they were not to be found. Lady Blythe disclaimed all knowledge of them, and Thomasine was left to wonder uneasily whether she had mislaid them during the last few forgetful weeks of pregnancy. Often, these days, things were not where she thought she had left them, and she sometimes had no knowledge of messages that her mother-in-law claimed to have given her. Asking Lady Blythe's advice about the breakfast, she was told not to worry, that Mrs Blatch had cooked for the christenings of Marjorie, Gerald, Nicholas and Lally, and would know what to do. Thomasine put aside that problem, and concentrated on the next: the preparation and allocation of the bedrooms.

The difficulties began as soon as the first guests started to arrive, the day before the christening. The problems with the septic tank had delayed the completion of the plumbing, and Nicholas had a harassed, apprehensive appearance as he welcomed his guests. One of the maids tripped over a heap of piping and sprained her ankle, and the new flush lavatories refused to flush. And, somehow, the bedrooms were wrong. Close relatives were at opposite sides of the house, incontinent great-aunts were housed at vast distances from the nearest bathroom. Max's uncle the Earl had a poky bedroom with cotton sheets instead of linen and – horrors – a tablet of that wretched brown salt soap.

Lady Blythe stepped into the breach, smoothing away all the difficulties, rearranging all the bedrooms with calm efficiency. When Thomasine glimpsed herself in the looking-glass before rushing out to greet yet another carload of guests, she saw a white-faced young woman, her hair uncombed, her pistachio green dress streaked with builder's dust.

The first evening passed without further mishap, and the christening itself went well. Nanny Harper handed William to Thomasine when they were inside the church. He was the perfect baby, sleeping throughout the service. Standing inside the church, her son in her arms, Thomasine felt immensely proud. When she glanced from Nicholas to Hilda and to Antonia, she saw her own pride reflected in their eyes, and felt perfectly happy.

But when she had given William back to Nanny, and they had motored the short distance back to the Abbey, everything started to go wrong again. The placements for the christening breakfast were a muddle. Gentlemen were beside gentlemen, ladies beside the guest they had sat next to the previous night, and the wretched Earl had been completely forgotten. Yet she had checked the place cards only that morning . . . Nicholas was looking at her, expecting her to sort it all out. Lady Blythe was nowhere to be seen. The butler and maids were waiting for their orders.

Thomasine longed just to tell them all to sit down and be quiet, as she had years ago with the unruly infants at Antonia's dancing school. Instead, Marjorie, Nick's elder sister, stepped in and made order out of chaos. After all, she knew one guest from the other, and could actually recall who was married to whom, and who was related to some minor member of the aristocracy.

The food, Thomasine realized as the first course was served, was awful. Too rich, too dry, burnt, tasteless. Nothing quite fitted together; Mrs Blatch had been over-ambitious. Thomasine muttered apologies for the stuffed and blackened pike, the sugary, soggy trifle. The bishop, to one side of her, choked on a fishbone; Lady Blythe, at the far end of the table, shook her head to the cream-laden, over-decorated pudding. Afterwards, Thomasine grabbed Hilda's hand and escaped with her to the nursery.

'You must come and talk to me while I feed William. Else we shall never have a proper conversation.'

In the nursery, while Nanny Harper bullied Martha unmercifully in one of the adjoining rooms, Thomasine put the baby to her breast, and Hilda talked about her pupils.

'My youngest girl is only six years old. Her parents are in India, poor little thing.'

William was feeding well. Away from guests and formality, Thomasine had begun to feel calmer. She said softly, 'How can her parents bear to send her so far away?'

'The climate in India is not suitable for small children. And it is the expected thing.' Fondly, Hilda glanced across at the feeding infant. 'Nicholas and Gerald Blythe were sent away from home at much the same age, I recall.'

William was growing sleepy, his eyes beginning to close.

'Not William,' Thomasine whispered. 'I shall never send William away from me. Never.'

The following day, many of the guests went out to shoot wild duck. Thomasine was left with the older or less energetic members of the party to entertain.

The day started badly. After the excitement of the christening, everyone seemed bored and aimless. The intermittent drizzle made the thought of walks or tennis unattractive. That afternoon, taking Lally to visit her nephew, Thomasine discovered that William had started a chill. He squirmed in his cradle, hot and red and cross.

'He looks feverish.' Anxiously, Thomasine placed her hand against the baby's forehead. 'I think I should send for the doctor.'

'I have already done that, your ladyship.' Nanny Harper, counting napkins and vests, smiled smugly. 'I'm sure it's just a little cold, picked up in that draughty church, but it's always wise to make sure.'

Thomasine cradled her son against her. His cries seemed to ease a little as she gently rocked him.

Lally studied her nephew curiously. 'They're never like babies in picture-books, are they? So much uglier. I won't hold him, if you don't mind, Thomasine – he looks rather damp. Besides, I never know what to do with babies.'

Lally's day-dress was of purple satin, and she was smoking. Ostentatiously, Nanny Harper opened the nursery window. She glanced at her watch. 'His feed isn't due for another hour, your ladyship. Martha will change him, and then he really must go back to his cot.'

The crying had lessened, but the small, reddened eyes still gazed up at Thomasine piteously.

'Perhaps he's thirsty, Nanny – a cold can make you feel thirsty.'

Nanny Harper smiled patiently. 'I think, if I may say so, that I know best, your ladyship. After all, William is your first child, but he is my sixth.'

Thomasine had to bite her tongue for a moment in order to force herself to pause and choose the right words. She said softly, 'You may have looked after other people's children, Nanny, but William is mine, and I know him best. And I think that it would be cruel to force him to wait another hour for anything to eat or drink, and cruel to put him back in his cot when he's obviously happier being held.'

There was a silence. Thomasine was aware of Martha, her hand clasped over her mouth as her gaze flicked from Nanny Harper to Thomasine, and back to Nanny again; aware also of Lally watching her curiously, with neither sympathy nor criticism in her dark, slanted eyes.

Miss Harper seemed to draw herself up to her full height, so that her bosom protruded like a pouter pigeon's chest.

'I have *never*, in all my years as a children's nurse, had my professional expertise questioned, Lady Blythe –'

Lally interrupted, 'It's tea-time, Thomasine. They'll be pawing the drawing-room floor, desperate for their scones.' She glanced out of the open window. '*Awful* place. Look at it – so grey. It's supposed to be summer. How can you and Nick bear it? I would go quite mad if I had to live here again.'

When she looked at the nursery clock, Thomasine saw that it was almost ten past four. She made herself look Miss Harper in the eye.

'You're to give William a drink of water, Nanny. And if he

starts to cry again, you're to fetch me. And I wish to be told when Dr Lawrence arrives.'

Very gently then, she tucked William back into his cot. She realized, as she left the nursery and began to walk downstairs, that she was shaking. She heard Lally say as they went down the stairs, 'She probably does know best, you know. Babies are frightfully complicated things.'

Outside the drawing-room door Thomasine paused. Lally added, 'I should go in and get it over and done with. Or Marjie'll do the honours again, and that would be unbearable. I can't bear Marjorie when she's being magnanimous.'

Thomasine took a deep breath, and walked into the drawing-room. The tray, with the teapots and divided tea-caddy and kettles and spirit-lamp, was already on the table. Maids were bringing in plates of scones and sandwiches and cakes. Thomasine sat down in the only vacant seat, next to the tea-kettles. She had always hated the contraption. Its usefulness did not match its elegance: the silver handles of the crested jugs and kettles were narrow and elaborately curved, so that the user risked burning her knuckles. The flame of the spirit-lamp used to heat the water was apt to flare too high or go out altogether.

She made herself concentrate hard. Forget about the embarrassments of the previous day, forget about the look of betrayal in William's eyes when she had put him back in his cot. Remember instead in which teapot she had put the Indian tea, which the Chinese. Wait until the water was really boiling, so that the leaves infused properly. Stop imagining that everyone was staring at her, waiting for her to make a mistake.

She made the tea without accident, spilling not a drop of water. She even remembered to ask the bishop's wife whether she took milk or lemon. But when she stood up to hand her guest the cup of tea, Lady Blythe said loudly, 'Did you remember to see William, Thomasine? I thought he was looking rather unwell.' She just stared at her mother-in-law for a moment and then, dropping the tiny teacup so that it shattered on the stone hearth, she ran out of the drawing-room and out of the house.

Her lungs ached as she tumbled across the lawn, down the shallow slope of the island towards the paddock. Clambering through the fence, her dress tore and the rough wood snagged her stockings.

She slid to a halt when she had climbed the bank that bordered the tributary of the Lark. Her heart pounded and her shoes were clogged with mud. Drakesden Abbey, which had swallowed her, consumed her, had now spat her out, unwanted and displaced. For a long while she just looked down at the grey water in the dyke, and then eventually up to the sullen sky that curved over her. Her nails had dug into her palms, making small, red, swollen half-moons. She stood up, clasping her arms around herself. The clouds overhead formed and reformed, their blustery shapes making a mountain, a castle, a dragon's fiery mouth. Cold and shivering, she was forced to face the truth. That even though she had presented Drakesden Abbey with an heir, she still did not belong there. You had to be taught from birth how to live that sort of life. The Blythes knew, but she did not.

Thomasine began to walk, her head bowed against the restless wind, along the rim of the bank. As she walked, she noticed the crumbling surface of the banks, the places where the water lapped dangerously near to the downtrodden earthworks. The flat, flat land, that would return to the waters if the dyke was breeched. The rotting planks of the crude bridges that spanned the water, and the tares and thistles in the fields that bordered the dyke.

She stood for a long time, just staring at it all. Then she began to walk back to the house. If it felt like returning to a sort of prison, then she pushed that thought out of her head. She had no choice. Her husband and her son needed her.

Before she went back to London, Lally had a half-hour alone

with her mother in the small sitting-room that adjoined Lady Blythe's bedroom. Lally was restless and bored, surrounded by chintz and frills and china ornaments. She stood at the window, looking out to the front lawn, as her mother poured the coffee. Nanny Harper was walking along the drive, pushing a large perambulator. William's morning constitutional, thought Lally, and yawned.

She said, turning back to her mother, 'Where did you find that awful woman?'

Lady Blythe looked up calmly. 'I don't know what you mean, Lally.'

'The harpy. Poor old William's nanny.'

'Miss Harper came to me with the highest recommendations. Do sit down, Lally – your coffee will get cold.'

There was a silence for a while. Lally drank her coffee. Eventually, she said, 'You can't bear her, can you?'

'Who?'

'Thomasine, of course.'

Lady Blythe gave the short trill of laughter that Lally always associated with her mother at her most deceitful, her most manipulative. 'Don't be ridiculous, Lally.'

Lally was not to be deflected. She watched her mother, fascinated. 'Nicholas loves her, you know.'

Lady Blythe's expression of bland composure altered to one of rage. 'Nicholas is infatuated. Any clever, passably attractive woman can infatuate a man if she sets her mind to it.'

Lally said, putting together what she had observed, 'So you undermine Thomasine constantly. You make her doubt herself.'

'I show her what she truly is.' Lady Blythe's voice was clipped and cold. 'I merely point out to her that she is not good enough for Nicholas, and never will be. She has not the breeding. She does not belong here.'

It was almost, Lally thought then, worth staying at Drakesden just to see how things developed. Just to watch her mother, splendid in her unyielding, amoral authority, destroy Thomasine

Thorne. But Drakesden would drive her to distraction within a week. Lally rose from her chair.

'Don't worry, I won't say a word to Nicholas. You're probably right. They should never have married.'

A slight chill, said Dr Lawrence, after he had examined William. Plenty of fluids, keep the bairn warm but not overheated and he'll be as right as rain in a day or two. Thomasine, buttoning up William's matinée jacket, was aware of an overwhelming feeling of relief.

The guests left the following day, an intermittent stream of motor-cars and cabs trailing down the drive and out through the village. As soon as she had said her farewells to the last of their guests, Thomasine went up to the nursery.

She could hear William's hiccuping sobs before she even opened the nursery door. They were the hopeless sobs of a child who has cried long and hard and been disregarded. Inside the nursery, she stood for a moment, looking around her at the gleaming floor and basin and bath, at the dustless furniture and shining crockery. At the piles of napkins, blankets and cot sheets, all precisely folded and put away in their proper place. At the rows of sterilized bottles, the washed and ironed bibs. Even William's rattles were placed in a neat, orderly row on a named shelf in the cupboard.

Nanny Harper was fitting rubber teats to glass bottles; Martha was scrubbing the baby bath. Thomasine lifted William out of his cot.

He did not even smile at her. His look of exhausted defeat, and the sound of his convulsive, choking sobs almost broke her heart. His face was blotched red from crying and his small body trembled as Thomasine cradled him against her.

If it had not been for William then she would, Thomasine thought, have been capable of physical violence. A terrible primitive rage had taken hold of her. She would have liked to pull Nanny Harper's neatly pinned hair from her scalp, or to batter her fists against that smooth, large, uncaring face. But, with her baby in her arms, she could use only words.

She found it hard to speak, though. At last she managed to say, 'How long has William been crying?' She could not bear to address the woman by name.

The last rubber teat was efficiently stretched over the mouth of the bottle.

'Half an hour or so, your ladyship. William has been very fractious this morning.'

'*Half an hour* –' Again, she was reduced to wordlessness.

'Rather a naughty little boy, I'm afraid, your ladyship.'

Thomasine knew suddenly that it was futile to argue. That if she tried to explain that William was unwell, that he was only two months old, that he simply was not yet capable of naughtiness, then she would be met only by a smug incomprehension. She saw, quite suddenly and clearly, what she must do.

'Would you pack your bags, please, Miss Harper? I have no further use for your services. I will pay you two months' wages in lieu of notice, of course.'

She had the woman's attention at last. She had succeeded in breaking through that self-satisfied veneer. Briefly the cold grey fish-eyes widened, and the mouth, with its rows of white tombstone teeth, opened and shut. 'You are dismissing me, Lady Blythe?'

'I am dismissing you, Miss Harper.' She had begun to feel calmer. Thomasine turned to Martha, gawping in the bathroom.

'Martha – will you take William and give him a bottle of water while I go and collect Miss Harper's wages.'

This was the difficult part. In her room, Thomasine searched through bags and purses and managed to find three shillings and sixpence. Another sixpence was in the pocket of a dress, and a threepenny bit in her handkerchief drawer.

She found Nicholas talking to his mother in the conservatory. She knew that there was no point in drawing him aside and speaking to him quietly, no point in not facing up now to the consequences of her action.

'I'm afraid I have to ask you for some money, Nick. I've just dismissed Miss Harper, and I have to pay her two months' wages in lieu of notice.'

Her voice sounded strong and clear, like a challenge. She couldn't make herself sound apologetic, or propitiatory: she could recall too clearly the despair in William's eyes, the awful spasms of his sobs.

'You've *sacked* Nanny –' said Nicholas, disbelieving.

'Yes. I don't want her looking after my child, Nick.'

Nicholas, bewildered, had turned to his mother. Lady Blythe said coolly, 'May one ask why you have taken this step, Thomasine?'

'Because she is cruel. Because she seems to believe that it does William good to be unhappy.'

'Because she does not immediately gratify the child's every wish?' Lady Blythe put aside her embroidery frame. 'Come, Thomasine – you do not want William to become spoilt, surely?'

'Of course I don't.' Yet again she was aware of the gulf that yawned between herself and the Blythes; how almost everything that she believed in must be questioned by them. She struggled to explain, for Nicholas's sake, not for Lady Blythe's.

'William is far too young for there to be any risk of spoiling. I don't want him to be left crying and alone just because he's woken an hour early for his feed. How can that be good for him?' She touched Nicholas's hand. 'Please, Nick – I need Miss Harper's wages – I want her gone today. If you can't let me have it, then I shall have to take it from the housekeeping money.'

She thought for a moment that he was going to refuse. His gaze moved from her face to his mother's, and back to her again. Then he walked out of the conservatory and up the stairs to his study.

CHAPTER TWELVE

MARTHA the nursemaid took over William's day-to-day care. Within a week, he had recovered from his cold and started to smile and to put on weight again.

Thomasine took one of the horses from the stable, and rode out through the paddock and around the island. The August sun struggled to peer out from behind a battery of fluffy white clouds as she trotted the mare along the track. The wheat in both Daniel's and Nicholas's fields was growing high – Thomasine looked at the swathes of undulating gold with satisfaction, glad that her conversations with Joe Carter seemed to have borne some fruit in these, the most fertile and most fragile of Nicholas's lands.

Putting her heels to the horse's sides, she continued along the drove, around to the far side of the island. The track was very uneven now, and the chestnut mare trod delicately beside fields that spread over the flat sweep of the earth like a patchwork quilt. Many fields were sown with wheat, but a few were still untouched, and on the black earth a mass of weeds had sprung up: sow-thistle and poppy and flax.

Uneasily, she reined in and climbed out of the saddle. In the later stages of pregnancy she had been unable to travel out to these furthermost fields: it had been too far to walk, and the motor-car could not have taken the muddy track. The land was fallow, wasted. Thomasine, stooping, let a handful of fine black, peaty earth trickle through her fingers. She would speak to Nicholas, she thought, and find out why these fields had not been farmed.

Looping the reins around the dipping branch of a tree, Thomasine began to walk, taking the path that led beside the threadwork of ditches and dykes. The ditches were filled with six inches or so of shallow water. Holes pocked the foundations of the dyke, and the thick mud and reeds halted the progress of the fetid, cloudy water. On the horizon the sails of the disused windmills, half eaten away by the elements, were motionless and the land had an unkempt, neglected appearance. The patches of swamp seemed to have merged with the fields, and the feathery reeds that grew in the boggy ground encroached on what had once been arable land. Poppy petals drifted in the air, and the remaining seed-heads were a pale, swollen bluish-green. It was as though the Fens were slowly regaining their own, inch by inch, stealthily, secretly. She could see the three tied cottages a hundred yards or so away, little more than tumbledown shacks, isolated from the rest of the village. Stacked outside them were boxes, sacks, a few pathetic sticks of furniture. A cart was being dragged along the lane towards the cottages. One of the cottagers glanced at her and Thomasine raised her hand to wave. But the woman turned her back, making no reply. Puzzled and apprehensive, Thomasine headed home.

August was, for Daniel, the busiest time of year. The strawberries were all sold, but there were still raspberries on the canes and the blackcurrants and redcurrants were ripening fast. The soft fruit was fiddly and time-consuming to pick. Reluctantly, Daniel asked Fay to help. At midday, the Gillorys and Harry Dockerill went back together to the cottage to eat.

Harry said, as he kicked the mud off his boots outside the back door, 'Some of the men are with you, Daniel, over this business with Squire. Specially the young 'uns. You should come to The Otter tonight – have a word with 'em.'

Daniel nodded. Inside the kitchen he opened the cupboards and peered inside the oven. He could find nothing but a tin of sardines and a packet of water-biscuits.

Fay was cleaning her nails. 'The hens haven't been laying,' she said peevishly to Daniel's enquiry. 'And I haven't had time to go to the shop.'

'Then find your purse, and we'll go now.'

She looked evasive. 'I haven't a lot of money, Daniel.'

Harry Dockerill was standing in the doorway, tactfully pretending to be absorbed in the view.

'It's only Tuesday,' whispered Daniel. 'You must have enough for a loaf of bread.'

Fay's purse was on the sideboard. Opening it, she peered inside. 'Twopence.'

'*Twopence!*' Daniel forgot to whisper. 'But I gave you two pounds ten shillings on Friday afternoon. Where's it all gone?'

'I haven't had time to cook,' she said defensively. 'Not with having to work outside. So I had to buy things from the shop. Tins and things. And I had to get a new hat, otherwise my face would burn. And gloves.'

He stared at her. He tried to quell the panic that was rising in him. 'Fay. We can't go on like this. We really can't. I've only just about broken even these last few weeks. Could you try a little harder, *please*, to economize?'

'*Economize?*' she repeated scornfully. 'That's all I ever do – always scrimping and saving. There's no fun any more, and I never have anything new.'

'I have to save, Fay – how else can I make things better for you? How else can I buy more land or improve the house? It's only for a while.'

'It's only for a while,' she mimicked. 'You've been saying that ever since we married, Daniel Gillory. And we're still here, aren't we, in this hovel? I've still no parlour, and no bath, and there's still that awful water-closet –'

Daniel said furiously, 'You've a roof over your head, and enough money to feed and clothe yourself properly, Fay. I'll give you the other things as soon as I can – *if* we can save. My God, Harry's mother brought up ten children on less than half the money that you have –'

'*Harry's mother?*' Fay screwed her face up in a grimace of distaste. 'They live like animals, don't they? Three to a bed, and there's so many of them they can't all sit down together at dinner. They wash their hair twice a year, and bathe in an old bucket outside the kitchen door. I'd rather die!'

Just for a moment, then, she looked quite ugly. Her face was white, with two spots of scarlet on her cheeks, and her mouth was twisted in a sneer. When he looked quickly round, Daniel saw that Harry was already halfway out of the back yard, walking in the direction of his mother's cottage. Daniel's fist struck the table hard. He struggled not to speak; he knew that he teetered on the brink of saying something that would make the rift between them permanent.

Fay pushed past him, running across the yard. For a moment, he thought she had gone to make her apologies to Harry. But then he saw her duck inside the shed and emerge with the bicycle. Daniel did not call after her. He sat down at the table, exhausted, his head in his hands.

Fay cycled to Ely, throwing the bicycle down on a verge near the cathedral, walking furiously around the shops until her temper cooled.

Eventually she found herself on the pavement outside the doctor's house. The street was lined with trees; sheltering under one of them, she tidied her hair and clothes with quick, careful hands, and was rewarded at last for her patience by seeing Doctor Lawrence step out of his front door.

She registered surprise on her face when she called out to him. 'Why – Doctor Lawrence.'

'Mrs Gillory. Shopping again?'

'Window shopping,' she said. 'It's ever so hot, though.'

For a moment he said nothing, but just stood, looking at her. She knew that she could not have borne the disappointment had he just raised his hat and walked away.

But he did not walk away. Instead, he said, 'I was just out for a wee bite to eat. I wonder if you'd be kind enough to keep me company, Mrs Gillory?'

★

Doctor Lawrence ordered tea and cakes, and settled back in his seat, watching Fay. She found the directness of his gaze unnerving. In another man she might have considered it insolent, but in him she found it oddly disturbing, slightly frightening and – exciting. Yes, exciting. She felt herself flush, and she began to talk.

'What does the "A" stand for, doctor? On the name-plate outside your door. I thought Albert, perhaps, or Andrew . . .'

'Alexander,' he said, and smiled.

'Alexander. How charming. Such an unusual name.'

'In England, perhaps. Not so in Scotland.'

The waitress arrived with the tea, and Fay, thankful for the distraction, busied herself pouring and stirring in milk and sugar.

'Do you miss Scotland, Doctor Lawrence?'

He put his head to one side, considering. His eyes were a light, washed-out blue, heavy lidded, the fairness of his colouring giving them a curiously lashless appearance. Like some sort of animal, thought Fay, who was not usually given to imaginative comparisons. A lizard, or a snake . . .

'Not at all, just now, Mrs Gillory.'

She felt herself blush again, and was mortified by her lack of control.

He seemed to take pity on her. 'I came down to East Anglia for my work, Mrs Gillory,' he explained. 'I'm very interested in rheumatic diseases, you see – I'm writing a paper on their causes and treatment. There's a very high incidence of rheumatism in the Fens.'

'Oh.' She could think of nothing to say; neither could she eat. She stirred her tea over and over again.

'It's the dampness, Mrs Gillory. The low-lying land. People cannae keep warm.'

'Our cottage is very damp in the spring. Water comes up through the floor.' Her words were jerky and uneven, as though she did not have full control of her voice. She was aware, suddenly and transiently, of the danger of her situation. She resolved never to cycle alone to Ely again, never again to compromise her reputation in such a way, never again to be at the mercy of this man's eyes, this man's clever, seductive voice.

'And do you have rheumatism, Mrs Gillory? Aches and pains in the joints?'

'No – no. Just thorns.' She giggled. 'I've a thorn in my finger from picking raspberries. It's rather painful.'

She knew that she was gabbling like a fool, but she could not stop herself. She had not eaten a morsel of her macaroon, but instead had ground it between her fingers until it was a pale, sandy heap of crumbs in the centre of her plate.

'Let me see.'

She gave him her hand. She could not have done otherwise. 'Just there. On my index finger.'

'Ah. I see it.' He looked up at her. 'You shouldn't neglect something like that, Mrs Gillory. It could become infected.'

She was quite, quite dumb. When he raised her hand to his mouth and placed his lips around the sore tip of her finger, sucking the tiny thorn from her flesh, she let out a small squeal of pleasure, of fear, of shame.

'You taste of almonds,' he said.

Dinner was always the most elaborate meal of the day: six courses punctuated by meaningless conversation, served by a silent butler and footman.

They had reached dessert. Soon, Thomasine and Lady Blythe would retire from the table for the drawing-room, leaving Nicholas to smoke his cigar and drink his port alone. Nicholas's dessert was untouched, his fingers drummed the table. Thomasine gently placed her hand over his, stifling the small repetitive sounds.

'Nick – I rode around the island today. Many of the fields are doing well and are nearly ready to be harvested. But the ones near Burnt Fen are fallow.'

Nicholas said vaguely, 'Carter is supposed to keep an eye on all that, Thomasine.'

'I know. I'll talk to Joe tomorrow. But, Nick, the families are leaving those three cottages. All their furniture is piled up in the drove. Do you know why?'

Nicholas slid away his hand from beneath hers. He reached in his pocket for his cigarette-case.

'I'm selling the land,' he said eventually.

She stared at him. The footman stooped and whisked away her plate. Thomasine hardly noticed him.

'*Selling* it . . .'

He nodded. 'A chap's going to build a garage there. Says there's a fortune to be made in garaging – there'll be garages all over the country soon.' He was fumbling with his lighter, trying to ignite his cigarette.

Lady Blythe said, 'I think Nicholas wishes to smoke, Thomasine.'

The footman was already hovering behind Thomasine's chair, ready to move it out so that she could retire to the drawing-room with her mother-in-law.

Nicholas added defensively, 'The cottages went with the land. It can't be helped.'

She felt winded, as though she had been struck. 'You could sell other land!' she whispered. 'Where will those people go?'

'They'll find somewhere else. The Fens are littered with labourers' cottages.'

'No one is taking on extra labourers. You know that, Nick.'

He shrugged. 'I had no choice. I needed the money.'

She did not believe him. When she looked around her, she saw the sparkling silverware, the Venetian glass, the crested and monogrammed crockery. All the trappings of wealth and security.

'You have money enough for electric lights . . . to give us hot water . . .'

Nicholas, his shoulders hunched, did not immediately reply.

The desolation in his eyes alarmed Thomasine, and she was aware once again of a feeling of powerlessness, an inability to alter the centuries of patronage and custom. It harmed Nicholas too, she thought, crushing him between the opposing forces of tradition and modernity. Forcing him to choose between his mother's standards and her own.

'I have to pay death duties, Thomasine.' His voice was a sullen mumble. 'I put other land up for sale, but it hasn't sold. Some of the fields were too marshy, and no one's interested in arable land just now. It was damned lucky about the garage.'

Rising, she went to his side, not caring that Lady Blythe and the servants were watching. She crouched down beside his chair.

'Nick,' she said very gently. 'Would you reconsider? Sell half the land, perhaps – or make it a condition of sale that the garage owner allows those people to remain in their cottages? Would you think about it? Please? For me?'

She had taken hold of his hand, and his dark, troubled eyes met hers. Slowly, Nicholas inclined his head.

'Yes,' he said. 'I'll think about it.'

His mother spoke to him when Thomasine was upstairs in the nursery, feeding the baby. Nicholas's head ached, and he was aware of the muscle that jerked constantly at the corner of his eye, but he knew that, though he was tired, he would not sleep.

His mother sensed that he was tired, though, and came to sit on the footstool beside him. The gesture touched him. She looked younger, the slight hollows and fading of middle-age subtracted from her face by the gentle evening light.

'Nicky, darling,' she said, and then she paused. When she looked up at him her eyes were round and blue, and he could smell her faint scent of carnations. As always, that scent took him back to childhood. He was leaving Drakesden for his prep school, and she was kissing him, and he could smell carnations . . .

'Nicky. I'm sure that Thomasine is trying to do her best, but, my dear, she really is out of her milieu, don't you agree?'

He looked at her blankly. His headache was growing worse. 'What do you mean, Mama?'

'Well —' Her voice was hesitant, her words tentative. 'This business about the land. And the nanny. And the christening.'

'Oh.' He rubbed at the furrow between his brows with his forefinger. He had not expected such a litany of wrongs. 'The *christening?*'

A small flutter of laughter. 'Well, it really was a bit of a shambles, wasn't it? The breakfast — if Marjorie and I had not been there to reorganize things ... And the menu that Thomasine had planned was so unsuitable. I don't want to criticize, Nicholas, but ...' Lady Blythe allowed the sentence to trail off into silence.

Nicholas, looking at her, tried to recall William's christening. It seemed terribly long ago, though. Odd, how events of five or six years past could still seem to him so crystal clear, and yet recent time had melded together into a formless, confusing lump.

'The food was rather ghastly,' he said, vaguely recalling some unpleasantly burnt fish.

'And to dismiss Nanny!' Lady Blythe shook her head regretfully.

Nicholas sensed that his mother was finding it hard to discuss these matters with him.

'After I had tried so hard to find the right woman ... Miss Harper was sent to me on Athene Faversham's specific recommendation, you know, Nicky ... so hurtful ... and to leave the poor child in Martha's sole care! It will not do, it really will not do. Thomasine is taking too much on herself.'

He was uncomfortably aware that she was speaking the truth. There had always been nannies and nursemaids: one was cared for by nanny until one went to prep school.

He tried to explain. 'It was different for Thomasine, Mama. She was brought up on some ramshackle farm in Africa. And then —' He stopped suddenly, aware of the hole he was digging

339

for himself. Yet he thought uneasily that Mama was right, that Thomasine and he quarrelled at Drakesden because Thomasine hadn't learned to fit in.

Lady Blythe remained tactfully silent. Nicholas's headache had begun to interfere with his vision. It did that sometimes nowadays, so that he feared in the flickering lights of migraine a return to the day visions that had tormented him in the years after the War. He wanted to hide away somewhere warm and dark and alone, until he could see properly again, until he didn't have to think any more.

Mama had sensed his pain; she was dabbing her own cologne-scented handkerchief against his throbbing forehead.

'There's no need to worry, Nicky. I will make sure that William's upbringing is not affected, and I will keep an eye on the running of the house. And of course you must sell that land. If it is necessary in order to keep the Drakesden estate together, then you must sell. After all, Thomasine's business is the house and the child. The farm is your responsibility.'

The word 'responsibility' made him flinch. He knew that he had not fulfilled his responsibilities; he knew that it should have been he who had died, not Gerald. Gerald had been strong, fair, competent, *manly*. Nicholas knew that his own survival had been dishonourable, the act of a coward. He loathed himself for living.

His mother rested her head against his shoulder. He breathed in her scent and felt, just for a moment, safer.

'There, there,' said Lady Blythe softly, stroking his hair. 'Poor Nicky. Poor, dear Nicky.'

When Nicholas's foreman came to him, explaining that he could not recruit men to gather the harvest, Nicholas was sitting at his father's desk, writing letters.

'What do you mean, Carter – you can't get the men?'

The foreman was twisting the cloth cap that he clutched in his hands. 'I've been round all the cottages, sir,' he repeated doggedly. 'They say they can't do the work.'

Nicholas was bewildered. 'But the Gotobeds, the Dockerills, the Bentons . . . They've always worked for us.'

'Bentons aren't in Drakesden no more, sir,' said the foreman. He was looking up at the ceiling, refusing to meet Nicholas's eyes.

Nicholas glared at him, and then he remembered. The Bentons had lived in one of the tied cottages at Burnt Fen. He had sold Burnt Fen. He began to understand.

'*Can't* do the work,' he said slowly, 'or *won't* do it?'

Carter said nothing. Nicholas recalled that one of the other tied cottages had belonged to a family by the name of Carter. This man's sister's family . . . his mother's . . .? Fear uncurled in Nicholas's stomach. He tried to think.

'If the men in Drakesden are foolish enough to refuse work, then you must ask in the neighbouring villages, Carter. In Prickwillow – or Soham.'

'Won't do no good, Sir Nicholas. They've work of their own.'

Nicholas's fist slammed the table. 'Then offer them extra money, man! I cannot leave my harvest to rot in the fields. There's three or four weeks' work out there, for Christ's sake! Do they all live in such luxury that they can afford to turn down *that*?'

The foreman's eyes met Nicholas's. Just for a moment, Nicholas saw such scorn, such resentment, that the fear inside him grew cold and hard and solidified into something permanent. Dismissing the man, he had a sudden leap of intuition.

'Carter. One moment. Tell me – is Daniel Gillory behind this?'

The foreman did not reply.

Nicholas said softly, 'I want to know, Carter. The truth, mind. If you wish to keep your job, that is.'

Carter shuffled uneasily. 'Mr Gillory spoke to some of the men, sir, I believe. There was a meeting in The Otter a week ago.'

As the foreman left the room, Nicholas thought, *Mr* Gillory. The drunken blacksmith's uneducated and uncouth son, who was a liar and a thief, who had marked both Thomasine's life and Nicholas's own, was *Mr* Gillory. Then he just sat, staring at the worn surface of his father's desk until the light darkened and the dinner bell rang out its summons.

Daniel and Harry and a handful of the other villagers harvested the wheat when Daniel saw that the weather was about to change. Rubbing the swollen amber grains between finger and thumb, he would have liked to have given the crop a day or two longer, but when he looked out across the Fens he could see the thick white clouds that rolled restlessly on the horizon. As the day lengthened, the clouds darkened to grey, crawling closer.

It was past midnight when they finished. They worked by lantern-light towards the end, gathering in the last few stooks. As he worked, Daniel often glanced at the adjacent fields. The corn there, too, had grown high and ripe, but no reapers walked among them, wielding their scythes. Excitement grew in him as he worked, keeping him going throughout the endless hours, hatred and triumph providing a salve to bitterness and exhaustion.

The rain started as they tied the final tarpaulin over the harvested wheat, struggling to make the knots secure against the violence of the wind. When he returned alone to the cottage it was dark and cold, and the wind snarled at the doors and windows, rattling the panes. They had run out of beer, so Daniel drank water, dipping his head into the bucket, drinking as though his thirst would never be quenched. His hands and arms were covered with a thousand tiny scratches from the sharp stalks, and his fingers were blistered from gripping the scythe. He was too tired to climb the ladder upstairs, so he lay on the settle, fully clothed, listening to the rain and the wind.

At dawn he woke and went outside. The season had changed

overnight from summer to autumn, and the sky was a sullen, leaden grey, the rain pounding in thick straight rods to the ground. Black puddles shone throughout the yard, but the tarpaulin that covered Daniel's grain was secure, unmoved by the gale.

He walked along the top of the bank towards his fields. He had to bend his head against the wind and he was soon soaked to the skin. The dyke, that only yesterday had been almost empty, was filling fast, the black water seething and bubbling. Several times Daniel almost lost his footing as he walked along the narrow, slippery path.

When he reached the boundary of his land, he stopped. Not one step further. He would not, as Nicholas Blythe had insisted, crush one blade of his grass.

He did not need to. The god that ruled over this harsh, forsaken country had done that task for him. The wheat which the previous day had grown tall and yellow was battered to a discoloured pulp, crushed this way and that, so that hardly a single stalk was left standing.

Thomasine woke at six for William's early morning feed. The wind still howled, almost drowning William's small noises of contentment, and she could see through the window the leaves and branches that littered the lawn.

As soon as William was asleep, Thomasine ran to her room and dressed in jodhpurs, a jumper and a mackintosh. The house was quiet, except for the silent-footed maids sweeping out the grates. Outside, the wind thwacked at her hair and clothes and the rain lashed against her face. She saddled her chestnut mare and rode out of the stables. The paths were clogged with mud and debris: she could not have driven even as far as the village in the motor-car.

As she rode out of the paddock and towards the drove, Thomasine saw that her worst fears had been realized. The Abbey fields had not been harvested. Instead, the storm had reaped the ripened wheat, strewing it carelessly this way and that, and flattening it into great, flat, sodden circles. As far as the eye could see, Drakesden Abbey's harvest was lost, consumed by the gale. She told herself that the other fields would be safe, that Nicholas must have ordered the men to begin harvesting the fields, but as she circled the island hope died and was replaced by a cold mixture of fear and anger. Every field was reduced to chaos. Not a single bale of wheat seemed to have been gathered in. Rain slithered down the collar of Thomasine's mackintosh, rain seeped inside her riding-boots and glued her hair to her scalp, but she did not notice. When she slid off her horse to pick out of the wreckage an ear of wheat, the grains were damp, glued together by mud and water.

At last she encountered Joe Carter, standing alone at the edge of a field. She did not speak to him; she did not need to. She knew that the expression in his eyes echoed the expression in her own: a shocked despair, a sickening realization of the waste of it all.

Back at Drakesden, Thomasine paused only long enough to fling off her riding-boots and mackintosh, and to towel-dry her hair. Then she went in search of Nicholas.

She found him in his study, silhouetted by the window. He did not answer her knock, but she pushed open the door nevertheless. He was standing up, looking out, his back to her. She knew immediately that he, too, knew what had happened.

'The harvest –' she said. Her voice sounded strange, jerky. 'Nick – we've lost it all –'

'*All?*' It was hardly a question, more a confirmation of a terrible fear.

'Everything. Nick – what happened?'

He was silent for a moment, and then he said, 'I couldn't hire the men.'

Blankly, she stared at his back. 'You couldn't hire the men? Nick – I don't understand –'

'They wouldn't work for me, Thomasine.'

Every now and then his head bowed, and his arms bent in a small movement. She did not know what he was doing. She did not care.

'The men refused to work for me. Joe Carter asked in the other villages, but . . . Too many aunts and cousins and things in Drakesden . . .' Nicholas's voice trailed away. Then he added, 'Daniel Gillory's to blame.'

'*Daniel?* What has Daniel to do with it?'

Nicholas's head bent, his arm made that small rhythmic movement. His voice was toneless. 'Gillory told the men not to work for me because I sold the tied cottages.'

She heard her own rapid exhalation of breath. Her hands clenched. 'You sold them, Nick? After I asked you not to . . .' For a moment she could not go on.

Nicholas whispered, 'It's our land, Thomasine. Besides – I had to. Max's orders.'

Shock was turning rapidly to anger. 'If the villagers would not work for you, Nick, then that's because you treat them with contempt. What do you expect, when you throw them out of the houses they have lived in all their lives?'

'Three families.' His head bent again. 'That's all – three lousy families.'

'Those three families are related to every other family in the village. Matthew Carter is married to Letty Gotobed, Rose Hayhoe's sister is walking out with one of the Dockerill boys, the Bentons and the Dilleys have intermarried for generations –'

'Yes – yes – I know all that –'

'Do you, Nick?' She stared at him, thinking again how poorly he had adapted to the role that his father's and elder brother's deaths had enforced upon him. 'Do you?'

He did not reply. Instead he bent his head again, and made the same small movement. For the first time she looked at the desk, the window-sill, the bookshelves. All were covered with neat piles of paper, arranged so that their corners exactly touched, and were parallel to the edges of the furniture. Nicholas did not speak again, and did not move. As she watched him, Thomasine forgot the harvest, the tied cottages. She realized that he had not turned to look at her once. His voice had throughout been toneless, uninterested. It was as though he was absorbed in something more important, more fascinating even than the loss of Drakesden Abbey's livelihood. Disturbed, she went towards him.

When she saw what he was doing, she was almost physically sick. He held a razor-blade in his right hand: the small rhythmic movement that she had observed had been the drawing of the blade along the inside of his forearm. His left arm was already scored with countless cuts, all echoing the scars that were his legacy from the War. He did not look at her when she gasped in horror, but instead continued to draw the blade along his skin. His eyes were intent, his expression calm. Blood oozed from the narrow wounds, staining his shirt-sleeve, falling in dark red drops to the carpet.

When he moved the blade away, Thomasine folded her hand over his. His fist was strong, resistant.

She whispered, 'Drop it, Nick. Drop it.'

Dumbly, he shook his head.

'Please, my darling – you mustn't do this to yourself. Let it go, please. For me – for William –'

At last he looked away from his wounded arm. When his eyes met Thomasine's, his face creased and crumpled. The razor-blade fell to the floor and she stooped and picked it up and, wrapping it in her handkerchief, shoved it in the pocket of her jacket.

'I'll send someone for Dr Lawrence,' she said, but he grabbed at her.

'No, Thomasine. No doctors.'

'But Nick – your poor arm –'

'It'll heal.' His grin was short-lived, ghastly. 'It always does.'

She had to sit down then. She still felt nauseous. She knew suddenly that he had done this before, countless times, secretly and alone. Nicholas, who always wore a shirt, jacket and tie, even on the hottest days. Nicholas, who always insisted that they made love in the dark. So that she could not see –

Her stomach heaved, and she closed her eyes very tightly. Then, mustering all her self-control, she opened them again, and said, '*Why*, Nick?'

'Because it makes me feel better.' His voice was light, matter-of-fact. The haunted look had gone from his eyes. He frightened her. She looked away from him, and saw again the sheaves of paper on the desk, the sill. Only now she was near enough to see that they were accounts, letters, bills. When she glanced at the figures written on them, her heart pounded even faster.

'I'll get some bandages,' she said quickly. She had to get out of this small, dark, terrible room. Her impulse was to grab William from his nursery and to run out of the house, away from Drakesden. To go to Hilda, or to Antonia – anywhere. To leave the sickness and darkness that seemed to her now to be an integral part of Drakesden Abbey. But she fought the impulse and went instead to the bathroom, and fetched lint and band-ages and disinfectant. Back in the study she cleaned Nicholas's arm and bandaged it carefully. Then she brought him a clean shirt and helped him into it. He looked pale and exhausted.

When she had finished, she touched one of the piles of bills on the desk.

'Did these frighten you, Nick? Did they?'

He nodded. Just for a moment the haunted look returned to his face.

He mumbled, 'Got in such a mess. No earthly use at this sort of thing. No bloody good. Gerald should have done it –'

'Gerald's dead, Nick.' Thomasine smoothed back the dark hair from his face. 'But that doesn't mean you have to do it all on your own. I can help you.'

He looked up at her. Eventually he shook his head. 'That wouldn't be right. You've got the house – you have to entertain people – and there's the baby –'

She said firmly, 'Martha's good with William – and he still sleeps a lot of the time. As for the entertaining – well, I'd be happy never to have another tea-party in my entire life. And I think if you asked your mother, she'd run the house again, don't you?'

Very slowly, he nodded. He was looking up at her, and his eyes were trusting and obedient.

'I'm going to help you, Nick,' she said gently. 'You won't have to hurt yourself again. It's going to be all right.' And cursed herself for doubting her own words even as she spoke.

Another reconciliation, another new start. Thomasine knew that each falling apart drove a greater distance between herself and Nicholas, that each coming together was more precarious. She feared that one day she would not have the strength to try again, and they would drift apart for ever, two tiny boats set on different currents.

She spent the day looking at account-books, bills and bank statements. Running a finger down the column of numbers, she was disturbed and shocked. She sent a note to the kitchens giving orders that a cold collation only be served for lunch and dinner, and wrote another note in response to Mrs Blatch's outraged reply. By the end of the day she had a fair idea of Drakesden Abbey's debts and assets. She saw that the estate had been lurching for several years towards disaster, that there was, even now, hardly enough time to draw them back from the brink. At night, when the wind and rain had at last died down, and the grey sky had turned to indigo, she and Nicholas shared a bed for the first time since William's birth. They did not make love; instead she held him in her arms, and tried not to think of what the future might bring.

She went to see Daniel. Thomasine waited until Nicholas had left the house one day, and then walked down through the wood and the meadow and into the village. She saw the hostility of the villagers in the cursory bows of the men, the coldness of the women's eyes. She was relieved to take the track that led towards the blacksmith's cottage, to escape from the curious and critical faces.

She did not attempt to knock at the Gillorys' front door, standing as it did several crooked feet above the sunken peat. Instead she walked into the back yard, and called out to the woman pegging washing on the line.

'Mrs Gillory? Is Daniel in, please?'

She had seen Fay Gillory at church, and admired the neatness of her figure, the clothes that had been chosen with obvious care. To put out the washing Fay Gillory wore a well-pressed pale blue cotton dress, white stockings and lipstick. Thomasine was suddenly very conscious of her galoshes, her plain skirt and jumper.

'He's ploughing, your ladyship. Shall I fetch him for you?'

Thomasine shook her head. 'I'll go and find him, if I may. I won't disturb you.'

She set off in search of Daniel, politely refusing Fay Gillory's offer of a cup of tea and a seat indoors. She had a strong suspicion that it might be better to speak to Daniel outside, where Daniel's prickly notions of class and pride might be less easily offended. As she walked she noticed the alterations that Daniel had made to the smallholding: the clumps of small fruit bushes (redcurrants and blackcurrants, she discovered, on closer inspection), the raspberry canes and strawberry beds. The rows of winter vegetables, their dull blue-green leaves small blossoms against the black earth.

She glimpsed Daniel in the furthermost field, guiding the two horses that pulled the plough. She waited until he had completed another long straight row, and then she called his name. He looked up.

'Lady Blythe.'

She felt a surge of irritation with him. They had scarcely spoken to each other since she had returned to Drakesden, and

349

she could already sense the hostility in him, the inclination to be difficult.

'Daniel,' she called. 'I'm sorry to interrupt your work, but I need to talk.'

'Talk away, then.'

'Here, please, Daniel. I don't want to get in the way of your ploughing, and I've no wish for a sore throat.'

She saw him pause, and then shrug and come towards her.

'The horses could do with a few minutes' rest.'

He had unbuckled the two animals from the yoke. There was a long silence as Thomasine searched for the right words. They would not come.

'I've come to ask you,' she said baldly, 'to tell the men to go back to work.'

He looked up at her. For a moment there was malicious laughter in the familiar hazel eyes. 'Ask *me*? *Tell* them? My dear Lady Blythe, you attribute to me an influence I do not possess.'

'*Thomasine!*' she said angrily. 'Heavens, Daniel – do you have to make this so impossible?'

He said nothing, but clapped both horses on the neck, so that they trotted off to a far corner of the field. Thomasine tried again.

'You have some influence, Daniel – I know you have. I've seen your articles in the paper. Things like that give you a reputation here.'

'Which articles? The one on the League of Nations in the *East Anglian Daily Times*? Or perhaps it was the bit of cod psychology I did for the *Spalding Guardian*? "Amazing Stories from the Casebook of Doctor Freud". I was thinking of *Red Star Weekly* next, but my knitting's a bit rusty –'

'The articles you've written for the *Ely Standard*,' interrupted Thomasine furiously. 'About the South Level. And farm labourers' wages. And tied cottages.'

His eyes met hers at last. 'Ah. Farming's not a profitable business at present, you see, Thomasine. That's why I've diversified.'

She said very softly, 'And that's why I'm here. Farming hasn't been too profitable for Nicholas or myself just lately, either.'

He shrugged. 'The wind's blowing on rich and poor alike, then? What a shame.'

'And I hear you've been – helping to work the bellows, Daniel.'

'Who do you hear that from?' He had come to stand beside her. The breeze had picked up, so that she felt cold in her thin jumper and skirt. She was aware, looking at Daniel Gillory, of how much he had altered over the past years, so that the boy she remembered was utterly gone, so that there was hardly any trace of the wounded soldier.

'Nicholas told me. And I believe him. He has also told me why the men refused to work for him.'

Daniel's eyes were cold. 'Then you know that they had reasons of their own for doing what they did. And that those reasons were nothing to do with me.'

She understood the threat that someone like Daniel represented to someone like Nicholas. 'I don't think that's true,' she said calmly. 'You're clever, Daniel. You always were. You're good with words. It's just a question of choosing the right words, isn't it? And then unrest becomes a little more than a few mutterings in the pub on a Friday night.'

His smile was arrogant and unconcerned. She wanted to seize him and shake him, or to turn on her heel and walk away from him, but she made herself plough on doggedly.

'We've made some wrong decisions, I admit that, Daniel. Decisions that have harmed people. Incompetence, though – thoughtlessness. Never a wish to harm.'

She looked him in the eye. The long eyelashes flickered and he turned away, his expression altered.

'I told you – you are suggesting I have power that I simply don't possess. People make their own decisions. I can't bend things to my will.' His hands gripped her shoulders then, turning her round so that she faced the field. 'Look, Thomasine.'

He was pointing at the centre of the field where bare black branches protruded from the earth.

'Four hundred years the Blythes' ploughs must have turned that soil. And that monster lay buried all the time. I unearthed it the second winter I ploughed. I can't move it. It'll sit there for the next decade, breaking my plough, cutting down my profits. It wouldn't matter to someone like Nicholas, who owns acre upon acre, but it does matter to me.' He released his hold on her and dug his hands back into the pockets of his jacket. His eyes were bleak. 'You're asking me to forget the past, Thomasine. That's too much to ask. *You* may be able to forget, but *I* can't.'

She cried out, 'Things happened in our childhood which changed our lives. But that was years ago! This – this enmity – cannot go on and on. It will destroy us all, I'm sure of that. Speak to the men – please, Daniel.'

He shook his head. His tone was cold and final. 'No. It's your problem, not mine. You work it out. And now, I've got work to do, if you will excuse me, Lady Blythe.'

All Fay's good resolutions crumbled to nothingness. She cycled to Ely a week after she had taken tea with Alexander Lawrence. She told herself that there was nothing wrong in it, that there was no harm in a married woman drinking a cup of tea with a respectable man. She was entitled to a life of her own.

This time, it was as though he was waiting for her. When she reached his house the door opened, and he walked down the steps towards her.

'Doctor Lawrence. How unexpected.'

He smiled, and for a moment Fay thought she saw mockery in those heavy-lidded eyes. His teeth were small, sharp, white. He was standing by the gate-post, watching her with that disconcerting gaze.

Fay floundered, out of her depth. 'I've finished my shopping now – I was just going for a cup of tea. That dear little tea-shop that you took me to . . . it's just around the corner, isn't it?'

He spoke at last. 'Your shopping-basket's empty, Mrs Gillory.'

She glanced at it, and blushed. She said haughtily, 'I couldn't find what I wanted.'

'Couldn't you? I would have thought you were very good at getting what you wanted, Mrs Gillory. You strike me as a very competent person.'

She was not quite convinced that he was complimenting her. She struggled, wrong-footed. 'I'm going to the tea-shop. It's getting late.'

For a long, awful moment, Fay thought he was going to let her walk away. But he said suddenly, 'I was going to go out for a drive, Mrs Gillory. Would you like to come with me?'

As they drove through Ely, Fay knew that she had crossed a sort of boundary. That there was a difference between this journey and the previous week's cup of tea. She told herself that she was just having a bit of fun, that there was no harm in it. That what Daniel did not know about, he could not possibly mind. That she had no intention of going any further.

They drove out of Ely, travelling north. They spoke little; the Morris Oxford was noisy and bumpy. Eventually Doctor Lawrence braked and pulled in beside the road. The countryside was bleak and open. There was a high bank ahead of them that seemed to run for ever to either side, cutting the land in two. Windmills dotted the skyline.

He said, 'I'm going back to Edinburgh soon. On Saturday, to be precise.'

Fay stared at him. She was aware of a crushing disappointment, a feeling of life returning, far too soon, to its dull, bleak course. 'For ever?' she whispered.

He laughed. 'No, no. For six weeks or so. I've my parents to see, and my paper to give.' Briefly, his fingers touched hers. 'Will you miss me?'

She knew that she should rebuff him. *Miss you, why should I miss you?* But the touch of his hand was frightening and wonderful, and she muttered, 'Yes.'

'Good.'

He did not, as she had hoped, tell her that he would miss her too. Instead, he climbed out of the motor-car and opened the door for her.

'Where are we going?'

He had taken her arm. He said, nodding at the skyline, 'That barn. There's a grand view of the countryside.'

It was muddy, as it always seemed to be in the Fens, and Fay's shoes were soon black and clogged. The wind whipped her hair against her face, and though it was only early autumn the air felt cold and wintry. Doctor Lawrence helped her climb the wooden ladder inside the barn.

'Look,' he said softly.

She gazed out of the small window. Now she could see the thick strip of water that filled the immense dyke, travelling on and on, endless, towards the sea.

'That's the Hundred Foot Drain. If you look carefully you can see the Old Bedford River beyond it. In the winter, they flood the washland between the two, to protect the surrounding lands. It looks . . . magnificent.'

Momentarily she felt irritated with him. He sounded like Daniel, going on endlessly about this beastly countryside with its bogs and ditches and horrible weather. Besides, there was something about the vast stretch of water that frightened her.

'I hate it. It makes me feel – unimportant.'

The amusement had returned to his eyes. She was very aware of the confined space in which they stood, the closeness of his body to hers.

'Unimportant? You're very important, Fay. Very important to me.'

He had spoken the words she had wanted to hear, but somehow she wasn't sure whether he meant them. She did not yet know him well enough, perhaps, to interpret his tone of voice. Again, she shivered.

'Are you cold?' He caught her hand in his, slipping off her glove. He laid her fingers against his cheek, and then kissed the back of her hand. Slowly, carefully, his lips pressed against her knuckles, against her palm. Her heart was pounding, her breath tight in her throat.

Then he drew her towards him, kissing her face. Her brow, her eyes, her cheeks. And her mouth. His tongue parted her lips, and she felt herself pressing against him, as if to draw the warmth and the energy from his body. She knew that she should pull away from him, that she should stop this now, before she had done anything really wrong. Strangers kissed – at parties, greeting and parting. There was no harm in kissing. She had done nothing wrong.

But his hands were unbuttoning the front of her dress and he was caressing and kissing her breasts. A very small part of her remained separate, watching herself. Expecting herself to push him away, to stop him before he went too far, as she had, before her marriage, always stopped Daniel. Unable to believe that she would allow this man to make love to her in this squalid little barn, standing up, pressed against the wall.

But she did not cry out, did not stop him. Soon she no longer watched herself. Soon she was utterly lost, drowning, begging for him.

In the little box-room next to the library, Thomasine set up a small desk for herself and shelves for her files and account books. The box-room was unheated and damp, but it was hers. Increasingly, she gave up her position as hostess, as mistress of Drakesden Abbey, to Lady Blythe. It happened easily, almost as though the house itself was content to slide back into old habits, recognizing that Lady Blythe was, simply, better at that sort of thing. The great house returned with a sigh of relief to its proper mistress, and Thomasine sometimes thought that was what Lady Blythe had intended all along. She no longer even tried to win her mother-in-law's approval, but fought instead to hold on to the place she was carving out for herself.

She worked to preserve her son's inheritance. William had Nicholas's dark hair and fine features, and his blue eyes had just begun to echo Thomasine's sea-green ones. Thomasine pinned Nicholas's old map of Drakesden to the wall, so that whenever she looked up from her desk, there it was, William's future. Often, struggling to make sense of Nicholas's incomplete account books, she would glance up, and remember what she was working for.

And yet, as the weeks and months passed, she knew that she worked not only for William, but for herself as well. She began by paying the bills that Nicholas could not even face looking at, but then, very gradually, her sphere began to widen a little. What began as tentative reminders to Nicholas (Potters' Field should be ploughed, the ditches to the north of the island must be dredged) became, at Nicholas's request, orders from Thomasine directly to Nicholas's foreman. She asked Joe Carter's advice, and then, with increasing confidence, made decisions. As Thomasine's involvement with the land increased, so Nicholas's declined. Though sometimes, when things went wrong – when she sowed some of the fields too early, so that the February floods washed the valuable seedlings away – she almost abandoned the attempt, almost placed the advertisement in the newspaper for the farm manager they could not afford, somehow she managed to grit her teeth and carry on. One day, riding along the boundary of a field, with Joe Carter on a pony beside her, Thomasine made an extraordinary discovery: that she was learning to love the land. That although she still found the Abbey stifling, and although her marriage had decayed into passionless acquaintance, she no longer loathed Drakesden. She had become a part of it: she, like others, fought to preserve it.

She looked back through every record of the estate that she could find. Account-books, wages books, bills and invoices, letters and maps and planting schedules. What should be sown, and when to sow it. Which crop grew best in which field. Records of ditch-dredging, land-clearance, dyke-construction. The vital, endless process of draining the constantly threatened land: first by windmills, then by steam-pump, now by diesel pump. As she worked, she saw how the slow process of neglect had almost drowned Drakesden. She could not tell precisely when the neglect had begun, but she recognized that it had intensified during the War, growing more severe during the first few years of the twenties. Fragile land like Drakesden's could not survive inattention. Time and time again Thomasine rode over the estate, examining every ditch, every path. The condition of the countryside concerned her, and often at night she lay awake, calculations running through her head, knowing that the outgoings necessary to make the estate secure were grossly in excess of Drakesden's income.

She struggled constantly to gain acceptance from the men she gave orders to: men who had known her as a child, men who had never before worked for a woman. She learned to dress carefully, so that she was attractive but not vampish, practical but not mannish. She knew what a fine line she had to tread, how easily she would merit nothing but insolence or derision. She made time to talk to the villagers of Drakesden, to listen to their needs and grumbles. She was aware that the farmland was still trapped in the past, burdened by old-fashioned working practices and crops that no one wanted to buy.

Nicholas retreated from the tasks that had always bored him, returning to those which he enjoyed. His beloved machinery: his motor-car, his electrical generator, his plumbing. He began to construct a wireless set, an elaborate assembly of valves and batteries, tinkering endlessly with it, triumphant when ghost voices flickered from the huge loudspeakers. At weekends his London friends visited: the Monkfields, Julian and Belle and Ettie and Boy. They seized his mind from its old, troubled paths and distracted him, for a while.

And yet Nicholas too knew that he and Thomasine had grown apart again, existing within the same house, but in different worlds. He could not fail to see Thomasine's satisfaction and pride in her work. He could not fail to notice the small improvements, the slow but steady retreat from ruin. His resentment was born of his own sense of failure. *He* was a Blythe, not Thomasine, and yet he had failed. A woman now successfully carried out what should have been a man's job. All Nicholas's old fears, that he was somehow less than a man, reasserted themselves. Thomasine had so little time for him. She seemed constantly busy, constantly preoccupied. Nicholas, who needed company, found himself spending more and more time with his mother. Lady Blythe, though she had regained control of the house, resented Thomasine's control of the land. 'It's what she always wanted,' she said, caressing her handsome son's dark head. His mother's fear of change echoed his own. Talking to her, Nicholas began to wonder whether Thomasine had not intentionally usurped him.

CHAPTER THIRTEEN

To celebrate Howard Carter's discovery of the tomb of King Tutankhamun at the beginning of 1923, the Mayfair nightclub was decorated in Egyptian style: hieroglyphs on the walls, papier-mâché grave-goods beside the dance-floor, and a huge sarcophagus, its painted eyes black-rimmed and staring, balanced precariously beside the entrance to the ladies' room.

Lally had dressed appropriately in sand-coloured silk, embroidered with scarabs. Her escort, greeting her with a peck on the cheek, wore flowing white robes over his dinner suit.

'*Too* Tutankhamun, darling.'

'Rudolph Valentino would be madly jealous, Hugo.'

She perched at the table while he went to find her a drink. She was quite proud of Hugo: he had lasted longer than most. The room was very crowded and hot. Lally, coughing, searched in her bag for a cigarette and a handkerchief.

By the time Hugo returned with her drink, the band had started to play, and they had to shout to make themselves heard.

'Still got the sniffles, darling?'

Lally blew her nose and fitted a cigarette into the holder. 'Almost gone. It's been quite a wretched one, though.'

She had caught a cold just after Christmas, and it had refused to go. Sniffing and coughing her way through late winter and early spring, she had begun to feel quite tired and down.

'Perhaps you should let up a bit,' said Hugo. 'A few early nights, don't you know.'

'*Darling,*' mocked Lally, more out of force of habit than anything else, and for the sheer pleasure of seeing him blush. He was not, she thought, her usual sort of man. Quite handsome, but terribly English. She usually preferred something a little more exotic. He was rich, though, and she had begun lately to think that to marry Hugo Grafton-Page might not be such a bad idea. Lally was permanently short of money, and there was always, because of the War, a depressing shortage of men.

She lit her cigarette, and touched his arm. 'Had you thought about America?'

He shook his head. 'Not on, I'm afraid, sweetheart. Can't leave the old family estates for that long, I'm afraid. A week or two in France, perhaps.'

She frowned. 'But you *said* . . . I want to go to Mexico . . . and to Hollywood.'

'No go, I'm afraid, old thing. Sorry.'

Inhaling her cigarette, she began to cough again. She had not realized, until he had refused, just how desperate she was to leave England. When she had finally managed to stop coughing, Lally said, 'You do look quite ridiculous in that get-up, you know, Hugo. Like you'd forgotten to get dressed after visiting a Turkish Baths.'

The band had stopped playing. Lally saw the flicker of anger in Hugo's eyes. He stood up. 'And you look like you always look. Like a cat. Bastet, the cat goddess.'

He strode away, and she was left on her own with the drink and the cigarette and a hundred dull people making fools of themselves to pass the time. She knew that she would not be alone for long, because girls like her never were alone for long. Girls who went all the way. She tried to work out what had gone wrong between her and Hugo, but it was at the same time too complicated and too simple. The way to make a man want you was to offer (mutely, of course) to sleep with them, yet if you slept with them, they despised you. Hugo would marry some fat blonde deb that his mama approved of. Normally Lally rarely thought of the future; now it crept up on her, full of insidious glimpses of old age and ugliness and loneliness, frightening her.

She began to feel rather ill. She put it down to her anger, which boiled and bubbled inside her. She did not go home. Instead she remained where she was, drinking steadily, dancing occasionally. When she coughed, her heart seemed to rattle against her rib-cage. Once, she looked down at herself, at the arms that protruded like sticks from the pale gold material of her dress, and thought, surprised, *That's not me, that's not Lally Blythe*. Lally Blythe was dumpy, rather overweight, because of all those school puddings.

People that she knew came and went: Julian and Boy and Simon and Pip. Sometimes she danced with them, sometimes she talked to them. They bought her drinks, lit her cigarettes, kissed her fleetingly on the cheek. Their faces muddled together; she could not remember their names. The anger and the fear burned in her all the time, an accompaniment to the rhythm of the ragtime. She felt closed off from the rest of the company, quite alone. She thought that the people who spoke to her – her friends, surely – must notice how she felt, but they did not. They came and went, spoke or were silent, laughed and danced. Eventually she began to wonder whether they were real. Whether she was here at all, or whether she was dreaming. Her fear intensified to something approaching panic, and she rose from her chair, pushing her way through the pulsating crowd of sheikhs and Nefertitis and Egyptian slave-girls to the ladies' room.

She thought that if she looked into the mirror and saw her reflection she would be reassured. She would see that she was here, that she was real, that there was no need to be frightened. Then she would call a cab and go back to Belle's house. Lally elbowed her way past the sarcophagus, down the corridor that was decorated to look like the entrance to a pyramid, and into the ladies' cloakroom.

Only a couple of girls and the attendant were in the room. The attendant was tacking up one girl's fallen hem; the other girl was touching up the kohl around her eyes. Drawings of Egyptian gods were pinned to the cubicle doors, and the ceiling and walls were draped with a shimmering gold material. The room was close, overheated. Lally washed her hands, wiped the condensation from the looking-glass and stared at her reflection.

She saw a small, hollowed face, dead white, framed by severely-cut black hair. The eyes were two pits of black. It was not her face, but someone else's face, a dead person's face. To one side of that corpse-face was a falcon, to the other a jackal.

Lally opened her mouth to scream, but no sound came out. She was utterly relieved when the images in front of her blurred and dissolved, so that there was nothing left but darkness.

By spring, Thomasine was aware of a flicker of satisfaction as she rode with Joe Carter around the Drakesden Abbey estate. At the edge of Potters' Field she dismounted, looking out to where tiny shoots of green broke through the black earth.

'It's all coming on nicely, Joe. You've all done so well.'

Joe Carter's response was a grunt. He pulled at the tips of his moustache, though, a sure sign that he was pleased.

This harvest was vital to replace the lost harvest of the previous summer. Thomasine was all too well aware that Drakesden Abbey could not survive another bad year.

'I thought –' Always conscious of her comparative ignorance and inexperience, Thomasine's voice was tentative. 'I thought we should diversify. There's not much of a profit to be had from wheat, is there, Joe?'

The foreman spat on the ground. 'Abbey fields have always grown wheat, your ladyship. That's what the land's good for.'

The spring breeze was biting. Thomasine did up the top button of her coat.

'Then it'll be good for growing other crops as well.'

Again, Carter was silent, but he did not look at her, as once he might have, with that mixture of resentment and scorn. She knew that he was waiting for her to continue.

'I thought – blackcurrants and redcurrants, that sort of thing.'

She had two pictures in her mind's eye. One was of the

garden of Quince Cottage, which green-fingered Rose had always crammed with plump blackcurrants, redcurrants, raspberries and gooseberries. The other was of Daniel Gillory's land, the land that was adjacent to Drakesden Abbey's. The netted rows of soft fruits that she had glimpsed when she had visited Daniel the previous year.

'Troublesome crops, your ladyship,' Carter was saying dubiously. 'If the birds don't get 'em, the greenfly do –'

'Then we shall net them, and spray them with derris powder,' Thomasine said firmly. She mounted her horse. 'Think about it, Joe. I'm going to drive over to the nursery in Soham some time to look at some plants. You can come with me, if you like.'

She began to ride back to the house. It must be almost time for William's bath, an hour she cherished above all others out of the day. She was aware of a feeling of contentment as she opened the gate to the paddock and rode up the incline of the island. She found immense satisfaction in her work. She had an adorable baby son. She had food, clothes, a home. She had everything.

And yet, she knew that she was deceiving herself. She knew that at the centre of her life was a great hollow, a vacuum. If she looked too closely at it, doubt and failure stared her in the eye. She had thought she could live without passion, but she had learned recently that she could not. At night her dreams reminded her of what she had lost, of what had perhaps never truly been hers. The night cast up past lovers, so that she woke, her body hot and aching, her arms empty. She dreamed of Clive – vivid, passionate dreams that recalled to her Clive's lovemaking, yet passed over his faithlessness. She dreamed, once, of Daniel Gillory: of standing in the shadows of the copse, her hand touching his face, his lips caressing hers. And yet in the dream they had been naked, their bodies white like the marble statues of the walled garden. When she woke she was ashamed, and yet the physical hunger lingered, undiminished by guilt.

★

When her fever subsided, Lally returned to Drakesden to convalesce. At first, it was a relief to be in familiar surroundings, to be brought bowls of blancmange or soup at frequent intervals, to be able just to lie still and quiet. She forced herself to swallow all the horrible medicines the doctor prescribed for her, and take the rest that he insisted on. Doctor Lawrence scolded her for dieting, and recommended X-rays, which Lally refused.

She got up and dressed for the first time at the end of May, on William's birthday. The table was set on the terrace, outside the conservatory. Lally was fussed over briefly, given a wicker chair to sit in, and a shawl tucked round her shoulders. Then all the attention returned to William in his high-chair, clapping his hands at the sight of his birthday cake.

Lally's gaze wandered from her mother, to her brother, to Thomasine. Thomasine sat between William and Nicholas, feeding William little morsels of icing, picking up his spoon when he threw it to the paving-stones. How happy she looks, thought Lally. Thomasine had everything – a husband, a baby, a home. Once, Nicholas had needed her, Lally, but that had been a long time ago, before Paris. I have nothing, Lally thought bitterly. Nothing.

Forbidden by the doctor to return to London, unable to afford to go abroad, she had no option but to remain at Drakesden. But Drakesden bored her, as it always had, and she began to slip back into her old habits, to get up later and later each morning, to go to bed later and later each night, to wander aimlessly round the house and gardens. Lally took to borrowing Nicholas's Delage and motoring out into the countryside. Sometimes Nicholas went with her, which was nice, almost like old times. On other occasions Lally drove alone, stopping perhaps at a pub for a drink, enjoying the outraged stares of the locals.

Motoring round the village one day, she found herself at the end of a cul-de-sac. Three small houses lined the track: she could see no room to turn. Lally drove on a little further, looking for a field entrance or cart-track. The motor-car lurched and bumped and then staggered abruptly to a halt as the engine stalled. Crossly, Lally restarted the ignition, jamming her foot down hard on the accelerator when the car refused to move. The engine made a terrible whining noise, and clods of mud flew up into the air. Lally climbed out. The Delage's offside wheel was jammed in a deep rut, and when Lally shoved at the bonnet, it moved not an inch. Lally looked around her, trying to decide at which squalid little cottage she should ask for help. Then she saw the men working in the field.

Two men. One brown-haired, thickset, ruddy-complexioned; the other of medium height, lithe, his golden-brown hair bleached by the sun. Lally stared at him for a moment. Daniel Gillory, she thought with a delicious shiver of recollection. Suddenly she was back in the gardener's shed at Drakesden and the rain was beating on the roof and the thunder was rumbling. She was kissing Daniel Gillory. They said you never forgot your first kiss.

The two men were doing something with hoes and rakes. Lally, hidden beneath a silk headscarf and tinted glasses, left the motor-car, and walked across the field towards them.

'Hello, Daniel.'

Both men looked up. She realized that Daniel did not know her.

'Lally Blythe,' she said, reminding him. 'Don't you remember?'

A flicker of shock passed over his face. The day was hot and close, and his ragged shirt was half-unbuttoned, the sleeves rolled up. From behind her dark glasses, Lally studied his taut golden skin, the firm musculature of his torso.

'Oh, I remember, Miss Blythe.'

'Good. The thing is, one of my motor's wheels is stuck in a rut. I wondered whether you and your friend would move it for me.'

The other man was grinning openly now, staring at her. Lally smiled back. Her dress was very short, just touching the knee, the material semi-transparent.

For a moment Daniel said nothing. Then he threw down his hoe, and began to walk across the field towards the Delage. Lally and the other man followed him.

They had the Delage out of the rut in no time. Lally would have liked them to take longer. She enjoyed watching Daniel: she realized how attracted she always was to strength, to the naked sort of power that some men possessed. Daniel Gillory was so utterly different to Hugo, to Pip, to Marcel . . .

When they had pushed the vehicle on to more level ground, Daniel made as if to walk away. Lally touched his arm, halting him.

'I'm afraid I'll get it stuck again. Would you . . .?' She held out the car keys.

Again, he said nothing. She watched him climb in and start the engine. She had guessed that he would be able to drive, and drive well. He turned the Delage in three neat movements, so that it was facing back to Drakesden.

'Too sweet of you,' said Lally. 'You always were so frightfully clever, Daniel.'

Lally looked for Daniel in church that Sunday, but could not see him. Strolling outside into the sunlight after the service had ended, she checked that her mother was out of earshot and whispered to Nicholas, 'Don't the Gillorys come to church?'

Nicholas blinked. 'Daniel Gillory doesn't . . . his wife does, I believe.'

'His *wife*. He's *married*?'

'He married some tart from London. That's her.' Nicholas nodded in the direction of a young woman just leaving the church.

Lally studied Daniel's wife carefully. She wore a pink chiffon dress, a close-fitting white hat and gloves. The dress was ready-made, cheap-looking. Mrs Gillory was small, dark-haired, fair-skinned.

'She's pretty,' said Lally.

'Do you think so? Rather common, I'd have said. Sluttish.'

Lally watched Daniel's wife walk out through the lych-gate and down the road in the direction of the blacksmith's cottage. The small feet, clad in unsuitably high-heeled shoes, slipped and slid on the rutted road.

'Rumour is,' said Nicholas, offering his cigarette-case to Lally, 'that the marriage is on the rocks.'

'Oh, *Nick*.' Lally accepted a cigarette. 'You've been listening to gossip! How delicious.'

A flush stained his skin. She noticed how his hand shook as he tried and failed to ignite his lighter. She thought, he hates him. Nicholas *hates* Daniel. Then she thought of Daniel Gillory making love to that flashy, dark-haired woman, and her mouth went dry and her heart began to pound a little faster.

'Let me,' said Lally and, taking the lighter out of Nicholas's hand, ignited it immediately.

Bored, smoking in the conservatory after lunch, they discussed how to pass the afternoon.

'We could take out the boat,' said Nicholas.

'*Dull*,' said Boy, with a yawn.

Nicholas managed to persuade his friends to come up to Drakesden Abbey once a month or so during the summer. He was always uncomfortably aware though that Drakesden had little to offer in the way of entertainment.

'You should come with us to the Riviera, Nicky,' said Ettie, voicing his thoughts. 'So much more to do.'

'Thomasine doesn't like to leave William,' said Nicholas, lighting a cigarette.

'The sweetie,' said Ettie. She was halfway through her third gin and it, and slightly squiffy. 'But his nanny, surely . . .?'

Nicholas shook his head. Thomasine said, 'And there's the estate. We are so busy at this time of year.'

'Frightfully emancipated,' breathed Belle.

Boy sniggered, and Nicholas felt his face go hot. Though he

had been glad to cast off some of the burdens of Drakesden Abbey, he felt the anomaly of his position increasingly. Thomasine was taking over a man's job. Only occasionally did Nicholas admit to himself that Thomasine's lack of conformity, which had originally so enchanted him, had begun sometimes to irk him.

There was a silence. Then Belle said, 'We'll go out for a walk, shall we? Take a few picnic things. And a tennis tournament, perhaps.'

They wandered out into the garden. The afternoon passed slowly, but Nicholas told himself that he was having fun. They played doubles, and Nicholas and Lavender Monkfield beat Belle and Maurice Douglas. Lally didn't play, because she still tired easily, and Boy didn't play because he loathed hearty tennis-playing types. And Thomasine had gone back to the house at some point, muttering about a letter she had to write. Her departure annoyed Nicholas, though he could not have explained exactly why.

After tennis, they picnicked and drank more gin and its, and wandered down through the paddock towards the dyke. Staggering rather tipsily along the bank of the dyke became, somehow, a game of follow-my-leader. They had played follow-my-leader only a week ago, in Harrods, explained Ettie. Such fun. The dyke led them up the drove and into the village. In the grocer's shop, Boy, who was the leader, emptied a bag of broken biscuits over the floor, so they all had to copy him and the floor was soon awash with crumbs and currants and fragments of icing. Mrs Carter, who owned the shop, didn't say anything of course, but just stood there, watching. None of the others noticed, but Nicholas saw the expression in her eyes. And there, in the middle of the shabby little shop, the awful emptiness washed over him again, reducing him from elation to despair in the passing of seconds. If he had had a knife, he would have put it to his wrists and done the job properly for once, as he had intended to, over and over again. But instead, loathing himself for his cowardice, he followed them out of the shop and up through the meadow and the copse. Not one of them noticed how he felt. Back at the house, he wanted Thomasine: he wanted to lay his head on her breast and her arms to encircle him and make him feel safe. But she was nowhere to be seen, and instead his mother took control, thank God, entertaining his guests, arranging dinner and filling in gaps in the conversation.

A few days later Thomasine was driving back from Soham with Joe Carter, her mind full of fruit bushes and raspberry canes, when she saw from a distance the small figure silhouetted against the skyline.

'Look, Joe – there's a child playing on the dyke.'

The foreman squinted. 'Looks a little 'un.'

Thomasine pressed her foot down on the Daimler's accelerator. The drowning of a child in a dyke was not an infrequent event in the Fens. And that child looked very young, far too young to be playing by itself, without a mother or an elder sister nearby. Much the same age as William, in fact.

The Daimler's wheels churned up dust. Thomasine's gaze darted frequently from the road to the small, bobbing figure, perilously close to the water. She narrowed her eyes, trying to cut out the glaring sunlight. The toddler seemed to be wearing a white sailor suit. Like William's. Yet Drakesden children commonly wore old pinafores, or sturdy leggings and their fathers' cut-down shirts ... She slammed her foot down so hard on the accelerator that the old motor-car skidded momentarily on the unsurfaced road.

'William,' she whispered, and Joe Carter swore as he almost fell out of his seat. The Daimler slewed round the bend in the path, and Thomasine leapt over the door, leaving the engine running.

She couldn't seem to run fast enough. William was tottering along the bank of the dyke, his small plump legs unsteady on the tussocky ground. She was afraid to call out his name in case, caught by surprise, he lost his footing and tumbled into the water. Her chest hurt as she pulled herself up the steep bank, scrabbling on all-fours. Then William turned and looked at her, his mouth a round red 'O' of pleasure, and just as he wobbled precariously she lurched forward and caught him in her arms.

For a moment she knelt on the sparse grass at the summit of the dyke, her eyes closed, clutching his small warm body against her own.

'Mama,' said William eventually, wriggling and pulling her hair.

'Oh, William!' She hugged and kissed him again. There were tears in her eyes as she looked down at him. 'What were you doing? Where's Martha?'

Looking wildly around her, Thomasine saw, further down the dyke, Ettie, carrying a picnic basket. And more distantly, the Delage parked beneath the shadow of a tree, Nicholas standing beside it.

Ettie was trying to load the picnic basket into the rowing-boat. The tiny craft bobbed on the water, threatening to float out of her reach. At any other time, Thomasine thought grimly, she might have found it funny: Ettie Taylor-Graves, in a hopelessly unsuitable frock and beaded headband, trying to launch the Blythes' rowing-boat. But just now, the sound of Ettie's alternate curses and giggles and the sight of the half-empty champagne bottle on the grass beside her almost paralysed Thomasine with rage.

She managed to get up, though, and to walk, William still held tightly in her arms, towards the Delage. She was still shaking. She realized what Nicholas was doing. He was cleaning the car, buffing the dust from the gleaming paintwork, scraping minute specks from the windscreen. He didn't see her at first, and for a moment she was unable to speak.

Then she said, 'William was playing beside the dyke, Nicholas. He could have fallen in.'

Nicholas spun round, dropping his cloth. 'Thomasine!' He looked utterly confused. 'William was with Ettie –'

A sudden flicker of fear crossed his face, but this time she felt not an ounce of sympathy for him. 'He could have *drowned*,' she said, and her voice trembled.

'Is he all right?' And then, when she did not answer, 'For God's sake, Thomasine –'

'He's fine. But if I hadn't come along –' Fury washed over her again. 'What were you *doing*, Nicholas? Why was no one watching him? Where's Martha?'

His face whitened. 'Ettie wanted to take William for a picnic. In the boat. She's very fond of William.'

'Ettie couldn't look after a *dog*, Nicholas, let alone a small child!'

He winced, and turned away. Picking up his cloth, he began to rub at the glass. 'Flies,' he muttered. 'All over the windscreen.'

She stood there, watching him. She knew suddenly, with cold and terrifying certainty, that her position was untenable, that her marriage had no future. That she could not, as she had hoped, just muddle on, disregarding the great desert of her marriage to Nicholas. That her belief that she could help Nicholas had always been self-delusory. He was beyond her help. That for the first time, Nicholas's illness had threatened not only Nicholas himself, but William also.

'You must see a doctor, Nick,' she said. 'Will you let me call Dr Lawrence?'

He stopped polishing and shook his head violently. 'No. I told you. No.'

Behind her, Thomasine could hear Ettie calling William's name. She said clearly, 'If you ever put William at risk again, Nicholas, then I shall leave you, and take him with me. Remember that.' Then she walked back to the Daimler, her baby clutched in her arms.

Throughout the summer, the misery which the winter had seeded inside Daniel festered, so that it blighted his every waking hour. Fay's extravagance and lack of consideration he could have coped with, just; the belated realization that the two of them had hardly anything in common reduced him to loneliness and despair.

Ironically, his writing prospered. The fame that Harry Dockerill had once jokingly referred to was now, in a very small way, his. He earned more from freelance journalism than from farming. He was asked to speak at meetings of the local Labour Party and the Farmers' Union. When a number of South Level smallholders, concerned, like him, about the state of drainage in the Fens, voted to attempt to put pressure on the Ministry of Agriculture, it was Daniel who wrote the ensuing letter.

Yet he understood now the trap he had made for himself. Fay resented the fact that he worked all hours, and Fay could not, or would not, economize. The only way that Daniel could pay for what she spent was to work harder. Yet if he worked longer hours, then Fay, in her boredom and dissatisfaction, spent more. If he did not work, then she taunted him with their lack of material comfort and position.

When he tried to explain their situation to her, she became petulant. Explanations became remonstrations, petulance became sullenness. Remonstrations turned into recriminations and sullenness hardened to spite. Fay would storm out of the house to Ely, and Daniel would do what he had always promised himself never to do, and reach for the bottle he had bought at The Otter, and pour a long measure. If he drank, he could sleep. If he drank, he could quell some of his pent-up rage and misery.

Thomasine wrote to Hilda and arranged to meet her one Saturday afternoon in Cambridge. In a small tea-shop in King's Parade, she stirred her tea and tried to find the right words.

They would not come. She had, she thought miserably, treasured her independence for so long that she was now unable to admit to anyone, even Hilda, that she had an insoluble and awful problem.

But Hilda placed her hand over Thomasine's and said, 'You look tired, dear. Such hard work, running a place as big as Drakesden Abbey.'

She shook her head and tried to smile. 'It's not that. I enjoy my work.'

'Then ... William?' said Hilda, frowning. 'Or is Lady Blythe ...?'

'William is quite well. And Lady Blythe and I have established a truce, I think. We each keep to our own territory.' Thomasine stared out of the tea-shop window at the glorious traceried silhouette of King's College Chapel. 'It's Nicholas,' she said eventually.

Hilda sat very straight in her chair, looking at Thomasine. 'I believe that a great many marriages go through difficulties in their earlier years ... and the arrival of a baby can bring extra problems.'

Thomasine thought grimly that if it had not been for William, she would have left Drakesden long ago. She said baldly, 'Nicholas is ill. He hasn't really been well since the War. I didn't realize just how ill he was at first, because he's become rather good at hiding it. But I do know now and, Aunt Hilly, I am *frightened*.'

She shut her eyes very tightly. The waitress, hovering nearby, dumped a plate of sandwiches and cakes on the table. She heard Hilda say, 'Oh, my *dear*.'

Thomasine opened her eyes. She didn't want sympathy, she thought, she wanted practical help, something that Hilda had always been so good at. She said, 'I thought, if you still wrote to your nursing friends ... I just wondered if there was any new sort of treatment. Nicholas saw doctors immediately after the War, but they were useless. He refuses to see anyone – he won't even admit that he's ill. But we can't go on like this, Aunt Hilly – we just can't.'

Her voice was bleak. She didn't want the sandwiches or the cake, but she made herself drink the tea.

Hilda was silent for a while. Thomasine could see that she was choosing her words carefully. She felt a sudden rush of love for Hilda, who had abandoned her beloved school for an afternoon and rushed all the way to Cambridge on the strength of a rather enigmatic letter from her niece.

'The treatment of severe neurasthenia is always a long drawn-out affair, Thomasine.' Hilda's voice was gentle. 'But I have heard of doctors who have achieved quite a large measure of success. The cure involves talking – which may sound ridiculously easy – but, of course, it isn't. Nicholas would have to remember things he does not want to remember, to talk about things he finds extremely painful even to think about. The technique is called psychoanalysis – it was developed by Dr Freud in Vienna, just before the War. But I believe that there are practitioners of psychoanalysis in England. I could find out some names for you, if you wish, Thomasine.'

She began, for the first time since that awful incident with William, to feel a little hope. Thomasine nodded.

'Yes, if you would, Aunt Hilly. That would be marvellous.'

July was rainless and hot. In the village, the women had to walk long distances to fetch water. At Drakesden Abbey, Nicholas closed off the supply to the ornamental pond and fountain, fearful that even the new deep well he had sunk would run dry.

The house seemed to be even hotter at night, the air close and clammy. Often Lally heard the baby cry, often there were footsteps treading along the corridors. Once, getting up and opening the windows wide, she saw Nicholas on the lawn below, walking in the moonlight in his pyjamas and dressing-gown. She could not tell whether he was sleepwalking or not.

Curled up naked in her bed, Lally fantasized, rearranging things in her head, making them different, making them how she wanted them. She saw Drakesden without the interloper, Thomasine; she saw Nicholas needing her once more. She saw herself in Daniel Gillory's arms. She saw herself rediscovering the Firedrake. *Turn back the clock, make it different.* Sometimes, drifting at last into sleep, she believed herself capable of that.

She continued by day to wander around the hard, dusty roads of the Fens. The countryside was, on the whole, appallingly dull. She hardly ever saw anyone she knew, rarely encountered another vehicle. And then, one day, driving back to Drakesden, she glimpsed the motor-car that was parked off the road, half-hidden behind a small clump of trees. Lally slowed, screwing up her eyes. The car was smaller, less sporty than the Delage, and Lally recognized it as the Morris Oxford belonging to Doctor Lawrence, who had treated her during her illness.

The Morris Oxford's door opened, and Lally was about to press the Delage's horn and call and wave when she saw the driver climb out. And his passenger. The motorist was Doctor Lawrence, the passenger . . .

The passenger was Mrs Gillory, Daniel's wife. Lally screwed her eyes up again and her hands gripped the steering-wheel very tightly. She watched the couple walk from the motor to the disused windmill that stood at the corner of the field. At the entrance to the mill, as though to remove any last doubt she could possibly have concerning their relationship, they embraced. They seemed to melt into each other. When they finally let go and walked through the doorway, Lally released her breath in one great gasp.

Reluctantly, she started up the Delage. She would have liked more than anything to go to the windmill to watch the lovers, but she knew that the countryside was too open, too silent. As she drove home, Lally hugged her secret to herself, treasuring it. She had always liked secrets.

Daniel and Fay ate their evening meal, as they so often did nowadays, in silence, and then Fay, complaining of a headache, went upstairs to bed. Daniel found a book and the whisky bottle and struggled to keep at bay the angry, repetitive thoughts that rattled through his head.

It was after midnight when he looked up from the book and noticed the faint haze that blurred the clarity of the sky. Rising, going to the doorway, he stared out into the darkness. Clouds, he thought, rain at last. But then, looking again, he knew that it was not rain and those were not clouds, and he ran outside, across the yard, towards his fields.

A weird orange light had settled on his most distant field. The acrid scent of the smoke grew stronger, filling his nostrils. The centre of the field glowed with the flames that flickered beneath the surface of the earth. The peat was on fire.

For a moment he watched, unable to move as the devils that lurked in the soil devoured the wheat, consuming it, reducing it to black fragments of ash. He heard in the crackling of the flames the destruction of all that he had worked for. Then he began to run. When he reached Flo Dockerill's cottage he pounded on the door, over and over again. Candles flared in the windows of adjacent cottages and there was the sound of shuffling footsteps.

'Harry!' he called. 'My field's on fire – the peat's burning!'

Faces loomed at him from out of the darkness of the tiny cottage. Someone called out, 'We'll bring spades and shovels.' Daniel ran back to his own cottage, grabbing the tools from the shed.

They dug around the fire which was blistering a great circle in the centre of the field, swallowing up the bog oak that protruded like a black-fingered hand. The flames were burning underground through the dry peaty soil, and water, even if it had been available, would have been of little use. Daniel's only hope was to dig a trench around the smouldering peat, a trench deep enough to reach the clay that lay beneath, so that the flames could be cut off. The half-dozen men worked desperately, aware that a peat fire, unchecked, could burn for days. Fragments of Daniel's wheat, that should have been harvested in only a few weeks, whirled into the air, spinning upwards in a golden vortex. The flames licked outwards. To Daniel, hacking away at the hard earth, they were like a living thing, greedy and voracious. They wanted what he had worked for. They wanted to take his livelihood from him. They wanted to complete the ruin of his crumbling marriage. Sweat streamed from his body, his fingers blistered and his muscles ached. The air was hot, tainted by the smoke, and so humid that it seemed to Daniel he could have seized it in his hands.

Returning to her bedroom in the early hours of the morning, Thomasine threw wide the curtains and windows. She saw immediately the smudge of light on the horizon, and thought at first that it was a thunderstorm. But the sky was quiet, the air still. Frowning, she struggled to make sense of what she saw. The light was muted and coppery.

Nicholas opened the bedroom door. 'I couldn't sleep,' he said. 'I saw it from the garden. A bonfire, d'you think?'

'No. Who'd have a bonfire at this time of night, in this weather?' Once more, Thomasine stared anxiously out of the window. 'It's a peat fire, Nick, I'm sure of it. *Where . . .?*'

She was pulling her sandals back on as she spoke. Whose fields, whose lands and crops were being ruined by the slow, creeping, flames?

Nicholas followed her as she ran downstairs to the motor-car. The orange light came from one side of Drakesden village. As they drove out of the house and down the incline of the island, Thomasine's hands were clenched into fists, her gaze always fixed on that baleful gleam. A peat fire in a wheat-field, begun perhaps by a piece of broken glass or a carelessly thrown cigarette-end, could turn profit to loss in the course of a single night. Nicholas swung the Delage through the village, out along the drove that led towards the tributary of the Lark.

The air thickened, became acrid. Fragments of straw, black and grey and blood-red, floated in the heavy air. And yet, as they reached the end of the drove, Thomasine could see that the Blythes' fields were untouched by the flames. Charred strands of straw lay like wisps of black lace on the pale gold wheat, but the stalks still stood high and proud, the plump grains unburnt. The flames had blighted the adjacent field, the smoke had veiled the crop with a grey haze of ash.

'Daniel Gillory's land,' said Nicholas suddenly, softly.

Thomasine knelt up on the car-seat. She glimpsed the long line of the dyke that enclosed the water and, before it, the dark silhouettes of the men, beating at the smouldering stubble with flails.

Nicholas said, 'Then let it burn,' and she stared at him, horrified.

'*Nick* –' she whispered, but he repeated calmly, 'Let it burn.' There was a sort of exultancy in his eyes.

'That's callous. Uncivilized.' Thomasine's voice was brittle.

He was smiling now. His eyes were dark and opaque, and just then she despised him. That he could allow jealousy and suspicion to breed in such a way, so that it took away from him the most basic decencies – that he could permit the petty tragedies of childhood to fester for so long was intolerable.

She could not bear to look at him any longer. Turning quickly away, she glimpsed Daniel, standing alone to one side of the circle of labourers. In the sallow moonlight and the flickering, unnatural light of the dying flames, his face looked white and unearthly. There was defeat and exhaustion in every line of his body. Thomasine could see no sign of Mrs Gillory. Beyond Daniel lay the field with the great black crater, tiny devils of smoke still leaking from its scarred surface.

Before Nicholas could stop her, she jumped over the motor-car door, and ran through the burnt corn towards that solitary, beaten figure. The charred straw was hot beneath the thin soles of her shoes. Running towards Daniel, she called out his name.

'Daniel! I'm so sorry. What rotten luck.'

Slowly, he turned to face her. His mouth curled ill-humouredly and his eyes, chill and green, focused on her with derision.

He said, 'You're trespassing. You're trespassing on my land.'

She heard her own sudden indrawn breath. She cried out and took a step towards him, clutching at his sleeve. But hard, unforgiving hostility was etched into his every feature, and the enmity in his eyes struck her with almost physical force. Her hand slipped, and Thomasine found herself stumbling back to the motor-car, treading with superstitious despair along the Blythes' side of the path.

Back at Drakesden Abbey Nicholas followed her into her own bedroom. He had not spoken to her since they had left Daniel Gillory's blighted land. His hands fumbled with the buttons of her jacket and dress and tore at the fragile ribbons of her camiknickers. She had to fight an impulse to struggle, to push him away. Nicholas was tugging his tie from his neck and pulling his braces over his shoulders.

'You shouldn't speak to him,' was all he said as he pushed her on to the bed.

'I'll speak to whom I choose,' she screamed, but the scream was a silent one. He was pressing up against her, his body hard and demanding, but she could see the desperation in his eyes. When he forced himself into her it hurt, but she pushed her mouth against his shoulder and refused to let the tears fall from her eyes.

All his anger and jealousy left him as he climaxed. Nicholas lay still for a moment, his body heavy on Thomasine's, his head against hers. Then he whispered, 'I'm sorry', and slowly stood up. Standing at the hand-basin he began to wash every inch of his body thoroughly and carefully. Then he dressed again.

When he looked back at her, she saw disgust in his eyes. She did not know whether the disgust was with himself, or with her, sprawled naked and defiled on the bed.

Lally, rising late, was rather sorry to have missed the excitement of the fire. After lunch, when everyone else was either working or dozing, she put on the purple satin dress and left the house.

Indolent by nature, she disliked walking. She knew that it would be unwise to take the motor-car, so she took the footpath through the copse and meadow, passing below the thickly-leaved darkness of the trees, crossing her fingers against the devils that still, for her, lurked in the undergrowth. Skirting the village, she followed the path at the foot of the dyke. The mud in the dyke smelt fetid. When she was level with the back of Daniel's house, she stood for a while, looking.

She could see Daniel in the back yard, unbuckling the horse's bridle. There was no sign of his wife. Lally walked from the bank, through the field, towards the Gillory allotment.

'Daniel,' called Lally. 'How nice to see you again.'

He had unbridled the horse and one of his hands rested on the creature's glossy neck. His hands were not gentleman's hands – they were strong, calloused, sun-tanned.

'Let me see,' said Daniel, glancing at her. 'You've had a puncture. Your motor-car's fallen in the dyke –'

'Don't be silly,' said Lally. 'I was out for a walk.'

'Ah.' Daniel's smile was a small curling of the corners of his mouth. 'You've come to survey the wreckage.'

For a moment she could not think what he meant. Then she saw the charred wisps of straw that littered the yard, the black smudges on his clothes and skin. 'Oh! That. No – I'm not in the least bit interested in farming. I leave all that to Thomasine.'

He had turned away from her. He picked up the bridle, hanging it on a hook in the stables. Lally kept her distance from the horse, a huge, clumsy-looking thing that she distrusted instinctively.

'Is Mrs Gillory in?' she said suddenly.

Daniel said, 'I'm not sure. Why?'

'Because I'd like a drink of water. I'm terribly thirsty.'

He led the horse into the stable, giving it a final pat on the back, and then walked across the yard to the cottage. Lally followed him. Opening the door, he called out, 'Fay!' but there was no reply.

Lally felt a thrill of excitement. 'She's out,' she said. 'Does she go out a lot?'

He did not reply. Dirty dishes were piled up in the sink and flies crawled over an uncovered pat of butter. The tiny kitchen was squalid, awful. Daniel found, eventually, a clean cup. He was about to dip it in the water bucket, when Lally said, 'Not that. It's lukewarm, I expect. Haven't you anything else?'

Daniel's mouth set in a thin, hard line. He leant against the range, watching her warily. 'What had you in mind, Miss Blythe? Champagne, perhaps?'

'I never drink champagne. I don't like it. Beer will be fine, Daniel, if you have it.'

He said nothing, but poured her a cupful from the stone jar that stood on the dresser. Lally drank. She had begun, for the first time that year, to feel well again, to feel alive. Some of the fear and lethargy that had seized her for so many months drifted away. She could change things. Things had gone wrong for her years ago, when her mother had found her kissing Daniel Gillory. That kiss was still unfinished, but its memory was powerful and beguiling. It needed to be finished.

She put aside the cup. He was standing at the sink. She touched his arm and felt the warmth of his skin.

'What do you want?' His voice was dry, throaty.

'What do you think? I want you, Daniel.' She spoke the truth. She had, she thought, never wanted a man so much. It was as though she had caught up the thread that she had begun in childhood and, an adult now, that thread was so much brighter, so much stronger.

He whispered, 'Go home, Lally, go home.'

She did not believe that he meant what he said. Standing on tiptoes, her lips brushed his cheek, his mouth. Her eyes closed, and she buried her face in the crook of his neck and his skin tasted warm and salty.

He pulled away from her, and she was left cold, her hands empty.

'Get out.'

Her surprise was complete. She had never considered that he might refuse her. No one had ever refused her before.

'You don't need to worry,' she said. 'I won't tell anyone.'

'What do you *really* want, Lally? Or is this your version of helping out the poor . . . Mummy doles out baskets of groceries, and you're generous with your favours –'

'Don't be ridiculous, Daniel. I'm bored, that's all, stuck in this god-forsaken place. Don't you get bored?'

He almost smiled. 'Not really. No, I wouldn't say boredom was one of my big problems.'

She went to him, then. She laid her two palms against his chest, and looked up at him. He made her feel safe, protected. She knew that he wanted her: she could hear the fast beating of his heart and feel the hardness of his body. She began to caress him.

His voice, though, was cold. 'I'm married, Lally.'

For the first time, she began to feel angry. 'Oh, don't be so lower-middle-class, Daniel.'

He took her wrists in his hands, pushing her away from him. 'Go away, Lally – you don't belong here. Don't humble yourself.'

She cried out, 'But you *can't* not want me! We're friends, aren't we, Daniel? We were always friends, weren't we?'

She could not believe what she saw in his eyes. Impatience, anger and disinterest. The disinterest was worst.

'Friends? No. Never.'

'But we were – when we were children! Don't you remember?'

He shook his head. His hands slipped from her. He was standing at the door, waiting for her to go. Her thumb slid into her mouth, and for a moment she sucked desperately, overcome by a wave of desolation and anger. Then she said, 'I saw your wife last week. She was with Doctor Lawrence.'

He looked at her sharply. 'Fay's not ill.'

Lally laughed. 'She looked very well. Very happy. They were going into the windmill at the corner of Potters' Field.'

Her whole body tautened, and she waited, angry and exultant. The colour bleached from his face. When she saw the expression in his eyes she began for the first time to feel frightened.

'I don't believe you.'

She gathered up the remains of her bravado. 'It's true. They were embracing. Perhaps she's with him now –'

His eyes were wild. He hissed, 'You're lying. Nicholas has told you to say this –'

And she cried out, 'I wouldn't lie to you, Daniel – you're my friend!'

He pushed her out of the door, so that she fell to her knees in the dust. The door slammed shut. Scrambling to her feet, Lally began to run, her small body making a sharp zigzag line through the cornfield.

When she had gone, Daniel stood still for a moment, watching his hands shake. He was gasping for breath. She had been lying, she must have been lying. Nicholas had told his sister to tell him such a terrible lie, because Nicholas hated him. Daniel picked up a plate, then a cup and a saucer, hurling them against the wall so that they smashed to smithereens. Then he took the whisky bottle from the cupboard.

As he drank, he thought. Somehow he could not quite convince himself that Nicholas Blythe would concoct that sort of lie. He thought of Fay. The alteration in her that he had noticed over the previous months, her feverishness, her restlessness. Often now at night she turned to him, and yet her embraces felt to Daniel increasingly desperate and unloving.

Doctor Lawrence. The more he thought about it, the more possible it seemed. She had met him, of course, skating on the Lark. He thought of Fay's frequent trips to Ely, and the new dresses and hats and lipsticks that she had bought. He recalled too his own first meeting with her. The dropped handkerchief – accidental, he had thought at the time. An old trick, he now guessed. It was as though a mirror had reversed, so that he saw the last few years through a darker glass. Daniel began to doubt every hour they had spent together, from their meeting on the banks of the Serpentine, to their present silences by day, their frantic lovemaking by night. His thoughts were a torment to him and he drank steadily, longing for unconsciousness, until he heard the footsteps outside.

Fay pushed open the door. She stared at the broken china.

'What have you done? That's one of my best cups –'

She made as if to cross the room, but he grabbed at her, halting her. 'Where have you been, Fay?' he whispered. 'Where have you been?'

'To the shop, of course –'

'Don't lie to me! You've been with *him*, haven't you?'

Her face, until then startled, offended, altered, becoming closed and secretive. 'I don't know what you're talking about, Daniel.'

'I bet you bloody don't!' He was yelling now. 'I'm talking about Doctor Lawrence, Fay.'

She said stiffly, 'Let me go. I've been to the shop. Look.' She showed him her basket.

Daniel's hands slipped from her and he stared inside the wicker basket, seeing the tin of soup, the loaf of bread. He longed to believe her and yet he could not.

'Fay, tell me the truth. You've been seen together. Someone saw you.'

A deep flush stained her pale skin. 'Who told you this?'

'It doesn't matter who told me. Tell me the truth, Fay.'

She moved away from him. Crouching on the floor so that her back was to him, she began to pick up the broken pieces of china. 'Someone's telling you lies, Daniel. One of the old gossips in this village, I expect. They all hate me.'

'I'll kill him, Fay. If it's true, I'll kill him.'

He watched her carefully place the pieces of blue china on the dresser. Her hands were small and fragile. It sickened him to think of those white hands touching another man's body. Then she rose to her feet and began to put away the contents of her shopping basket. Her face was calm, her movements neat and assured.

He shouted, 'Don't do that now! I want to know the truth!'

Fay closed the cupboard door. 'Don't talk to me like that, Daniel Gillory. You've no right to talk to me like that.'

'I have every right – I am your husband –'

'Yes.' Her eyes were filled with scorn. 'And a fool I was ever to allow you to become *that.*'

He dragged her towards him. 'So it's true, then –'

She tried to pull away from him. 'No. No. *No* –'

He hated her then. He loathed her every feature, her every mannerism. He seized her shoulders, forcing her against the wall. He wanted to hurt her, he wanted to force the truth from her. He wanted to break through the veneer of selfishness and vanity, to make her understand just how much she hurt him. Daniel raised his hand, and Fay screamed. He saw the fear on her face and, horrified at himself, his hand dropped to his side. Fay ran out across the yard. Daniel stared at the door, banging backwards and forwards in the restless breeze, and then at the footprints her high-heeled shoes had left in the dust. By the time he had begun to drink again, the wind had filled in the small hollows her shoes had made, so that there was nothing left to show her path.

Fay did what she had never done before, and sent a message via one of the Hayhoe children to Ely. She did not dare go back to the house for the bicycle, and she could not walk all the way to Ely. She repeated her message to Jackie Hayhoe.

'Tell him he's to come to the usual place. Tell him it's important.' She took a sixpence out of her pocket.

She watched the child set off across the fields, his hobnailed boots beating up the black dust. Then she began to walk away from the village, towards Potters' Field. The mile seemed longer than usual. The mud on the bank was hard and rutted; the water in the ditch smelt disgusting. Fay followed the dyke because she was afraid of getting lost, but the sight of the eels writhing in the shallow greasy black water sickened her.

When she reached the old windmill, she sat down in the doorway, waiting. She began to plan, picking the words to explain her predicament to Alexander. 'I can't stay with Daniel any longer,' she would say. 'He hurt me.' She would show him her bruised shoulders, and he would be horrified, outraged. Then he would ask her to marry him. Fay had only a vague idea of the laws of divorce, but she was sure that any judge would be sympathetic to her. No one could expect her to remain tied to someone like Daniel Gillory, in a place like Drakesden.

As the afternoon wore on, though, and Alexander Lawrence did not come, some of the happy confidence of her fantasies began to fade. She was unable clearly to imagine Alexander proposing to her. She tried, but the words were not convincing, and there was always that touch of cynicism behind the washed-out blue of his eyes. She kept looking up the drove, expecting to hear the sound of his motor-car, but there was only silence. Eventually the silence was filled by the rustling of the wind in the trees and the corn, and the sky, that had been a pure flawless blue for days and days, darkened. Fay, sitting on the steps, could see the fast, upwards whirling motion of the clouds. The weather had become suddenly cooler. She shivered in her thin dress.

She had lost track of time, but guessed it was by now late afternoon. She had waited for hours and hours. He must come, she thought, he must. Slowly her confidence drained away, and she felt lonely and abandoned. The emptiness of the countryside frightened her. She jumped at all the creakings and whirrings that the wind and the old mill produced. The great black clouds crowding the sky cast dark shadows on the cornfields. When she heard the first rumble of thunder, she sprang to her feet and ran inside the windmill.

The rain began, pounding on the holed wooden slats in drops

the size of a penny. The drops were sparse at first, a dark pitting of the dust in the drove, but then they gathered in frequency, echoing in the emptiness, a thousand drummers beating out a relentless rhythm. Great jagged spikes of lightning split the horizon. Fay huddled inside the windmill, watching through the doorway as the sky changed from grey to black to lilac-pink. Then the thunder clashed again, an appalling clamour of sound, and Fay shrieked, covering her ears with her hands. Daniel's voice said over and over again, *Lightning always goes for the highest point, Fay.* When she stared, terrified, outside, she saw only the flat, flat fields, the few stubby trees, the line of the dyke. The windmill in which she sheltered was the highest point.

The lightning forked violently, illuminating the interior of the mill so brightly that for one appalling moment Fay thought it had already been struck. The crash of the thunder was deafening, and when it finally faded she heard another sound, a terrible creaking whine, as the old sails, forced into life by the gale, began to rotate. The noise seemed to fill her head and Fay found herself running outside, towards the dyke.

He would not come. She knew now that he would not come. Just for a moment, she faced the truth. She was nothing to Alexander Lawrence and he would never ask her to marry him. Yet she could not bear to be left here alone in this terrible storm, in this awful place. She began to run back towards the village. The rain battered down, filling the dyke, churning the dust to mud. Her feet, in their flimsy high-heeled shoes, slipped and slid. In a few minutes she was soaked to the skin. The lightning flashes increased in frequency and the thunder rolls were deafening. Count the seconds, Fay thought, panicking, count the seconds between lightning and thunder. Out loud she sobbed: *one, two, three, four, five . . .* each time she counted the gap was smaller. Tears were streaming down her face, mingling with the rain.

She could not see clearly, she could only struggle to follow the line of the dyke. The only illumination was the flare of lightning – the evening sky had darkened almost to blackness, and the countryside had always all looked the same to her. She did not know how far she was from Drakesden. She had lost track of distance and time. Sometimes the sky was as light as day, an eldritch, violet gleam, broken by a craquelure of white. Fay clambered up the bank of the dyke, sliding back a couple of times, clutching at the sodden tufts of grass.

When she reached the top, there was a lull in the thunderstorm, a strange silence, so that Fay could just make out the plank that bridged the dyke. As she began to cross it, she glimpsed the outline of the village not far away. Her breath came in great sobbing gulps. She had never felt so frightened.

Halfway across the plank her foot slipped on the wet wood and she struggled for balance, her hands flailing out for something to grip. Fay struck the black mud and water in the dyke with a force that knocked the breath from her body. For a moment she could not move and muddy water filled her eyes, her nostrils, her mouth. Then she began to thresh wildly about, struggling to drag herself out of the mire.

But the mud was thick and grasping, and Fay was exhausted. The more she struggled, the more the mud gripped her, sucking her down. At last she no longer fought, and she closed her eyes as the thunderstorm raged overhead.

Thomasine received the letter from Hilda by the afternoon post, the only glimmer of hope in an oppressive day. The events of the previous night fell like a shadow over her. She did not see Nicholas at all until the afternoon, when at four o'clock they assembled in the drawing-room for tea. It seemed to Thomasine that the entire house shook with the force of the thunderbolts, that the air inside the house had become heavy, almost unbreathable.

After tea, she followed Nicholas out on to the terrace. For a moment they just stood side by side, staring at the lightning. A parody of a happily married couple, thought Thomasine bitterly. Fingering the letter folded in her pocket, she made herself touch his sleeve and speak to him.

'Nick – there's something I must talk to you about.'

He had moved away from her, as though he too was recalling the joyless embrace of the previous night. At last his gaze moved from the purple lightning flashes on the horizon to Thomasine.

'Talk ahead, old thing.'

'Not here, Nick. It's too noisy.'

The thunder almost drowned their words. Nicholas looked at her blankly. Rain streamed down his face, plastering his hair to his scalp. Thomasine glanced desperately around her. Lady Blythe was still in the drawing-room. Thomasine had no idea where Lally was. Servants were scattered all over the house, drawing curtains and closing windows.

'Come into the conservatory, Nick.'

He followed her. Like a dog, she thought, that expects to be punished.

In the conservatory, rain streamed in great rivers down the glass panes of the roof. Nicholas waited until she had sat down on one of the wicker chairs, and then he said, 'I'm so sorry, Thomasine. About last night. I behaved like a cad –'

'It doesn't matter, Nick. Sit down, please. It really doesn't matter.' She knew that she lied, that the gulf between them was now almost too wide to be breached. That was why she clutched so desperately at the scrap of paper in her pocket. She took a deep breath and tried to catch his uncertain, flickering gaze.

'I saw my Aunt Hilda a fortnight ago, Nick. Do you remember that she was a nurse in the War?'

He nodded dumbly. A flare of lightning robbed all colour from the plants that crowded the conservatory.

'She told me that she nursed men in the War who had suffered from shellshock. Men like you, Nick. She told me that there are new ways of treating shellshock nowadays – good ways. Effective ways.'

He blinked, and reached inside his jacket for his cigarette-case. She took the lighter from his unsteady hand and lit the cigarette for him.

'She gave me the name of a doctor, Nick, who should be able to help you. He's called David Franks, and he's very well-known and kind, and he practises in –'

'No.' Nicholas stood up, shaking his head. 'No, Thomasine. I told you. No doctors.'

She persisted stubbornly. 'He wouldn't be like the other doctors, Nick. No cold baths or exercise routines – none of that sort of nonsense. He'd just want to talk to you.'

'No.' The word was almost masked by the thunder, but Thomasine could see the violent shake of his head, the stubborn refusal in his eyes. 'Don't you see? That's what I can't do. It would be quite impossible.'

Nicholas stubbed out his unfinished cigarette in a plant-pot and then, turning on his heel, left her alone in the conservatory, with the rain beating like pebbles on the glass roof.

Daniel, exhausted by the events of the day and the previous night, drank himself into insensibility.

He was woken by the thunder. Struggling to emerge out of a nightmare, he heaved his head off the table. The empty bottle rolled to the floor, smashing on the bricks, and he opened his eyes.

For a moment he just watched the thunderstorm. The rain pounding the yard, the livid sky. His head ached, his mouth was dry and his eyes were gritty. Huge puddles had formed outside and rain streamed from the roofs of the outbuildings.

Then he thought, *Fay*, and all the appalling events of the day came back to him. Lally. The quarrel with Fay. Himself, almost hitting her. He had seen his father in himself then, and it had horrified him. Daniel struggled to his feet, knocking over his chair, calling out her name, but the thunder mocked him, drowning the sound of his voice. He began to climb unsteadily up the ladder, his movements still blurred by alcohol. The upper storey of the cottage was empty.

He ran out into the yard, searching each one of the outbuildings. The bicycle still stood in the shed. Without the bicycle she could not have gone far. The drove was empty, the village appeared deserted, all the inhabitants driven indoors by the force of the storm. He could not think of anyone in the village that she would have gone to. And then he remembered the windmill. Potters' Field.

Grabbing a lantern, Daniel cut through the fields, taking the quickest route. Great forks of lightning branched intermittently through the sky. He realized, when he slipped in the mud and fell on his face, what it all reminded him of. For one long, dreadful moment he was back in Flanders and the thunder was the crash of mortars, the lightning their impact as they found their target. His face and hands were covered with mud and he could not breathe.

Scrambling to his feet, he headed on through the storm, trampling down the thistles, the poppies, the flax. When he reached the windmill, he half-fell through the door.

But the mill was empty, silent except for the churning of the ruined sails. She has gone to Ely, he thought. She was already with her lover . . .

He could see, lit up by the violence of the sky, the black line of the dyke. He began to run again, his head full of crazy thoughts of cycling to Ely, of forcing her back to her home. Clambering up the sticky surface of the bank, he stared to left and right. A single great flash of lightning lit up the sky so that for a moment he saw with perfect clarity the village, the fields, the path to Ely. But the drove itself was empty and desolate. Holding out the lantern, Daniel looked wildly around him. And then he saw, not far from where he stood, something wedged in the plank that spanned the dyke.

A high-heeled shoe. He could hardly bear to look down.

The pink chiffon dress was so blackened and torn it appeared to be no more than a collection of dirty rags. Daniel jumped into the water, pulling at her, trying to release Fay's body from the grip of the mud. The mud would not at first let her go, but he strained and heaved and finally it released its prize. He held her cold body to his own, trying to warm her. Mud filled the cavities of her face and tarnished the white marble of her skin. Her dark hair, that he had loved to touch and to kiss, was a thick, matted rag. He knew that there was no life in her, had not been, perhaps, for hours, and yet he felt desperately for a pulse, a heartbeat. Then he raised his head and called out her name, his despairing lament drowned by the crash of the thunder.

CHAPTER FOURTEEN

ALTHOUGH a witness had heard raised voices coming from the Gillorys' cottage on the day of Mrs Gillory's death, the child Jackie Hayhoe, almost bursting with self-importance, told the coroner about the message Fay Gillory had given him that afternoon, and the labourer Harry Dockerill described how, peering through the window of the blacksmith's cottage, he had seen Daniel Gillory asleep at the kitchen table. The police were satisfied, and the verdict of the inquest was one of accidental death.

Thomasine attended the funeral. That the small church was almost full was, she knew now, a tribute to Daniel and not to Fay. The inquest, brutal in its cold succession of facts and dates, had shown how little Fay Gillory had been liked in Drakesden. Though anyone must pity the horror of Daniel's wife's death, whispered voices murmured about the events that had led up to it, passing harsh judgement. One face, all too visible at the inquest, was conspicuously absent from the funeral: that of Alexander Lawrence.

Seated at the front of the church, Thomasine was only a few feet away from Daniel. When she greeted him he made no acknowledgement. He stood up or knelt when the service demanded it, but his lips did not move to sing the hymn or to mutter the prayers. He walked like an automaton to follow his wife's coffin out of the church to the graveyard, his face pale beneath its summer tan, his eyes shocked and blank. To one side of Daniel was his sister, to the other was Harry Dockerill. The summer's day was bright and clear, the violence of the thunderstorm long past. None of the comforting clichés, the platitudes that usually help mourners through funerals were appropriate. Fay's death had not been a merciful release; it had not marked the end of painful illness or vexatious old age. When it was over, taking Daniel's unresponding hand in farewell, Thomasine said only, very gently, 'I'm so sorry, Daniel. I'll come and see you. Soon.'

Two days later Thomasine walked to the Gillorys' cottage. The yard was deserted except for the hens pecking at the earth and the pig snuffling in its trough.

She knocked at the back door and, after waiting a few moments, called out Daniel's name. She tried the handle and found that the door was locked. Hearing footsteps, Thomasine turned and saw Harry Dockerill.

'Is Mr Gillory out working?'

Harry, who had raised his cap, shook his head. 'Haven't seen him since the funeral. Not for want of trying, mind. Daft bugger won't open the door to no one – begging your pardon, your ladyship.'

Thomasine peered through the kitchen window. Through the grimy pane she could see a mass of dirty cups and plates piled high in the sink, and a trail of ash from the stove.

'Isn't Daniel's sister staying with him?'

Harry shook his head. 'Sent her away the day afore yesterday, didn't he? Ma tried last night – shouted at him to come and open the door for a half hour, but it didn't do no good.'

Thomasine glanced uneasily at Harry. 'Perhaps he's gone back to London.' Yet she was not convinced. The Daniel she had seen at Fay's funeral had not seemed capable of taking such a step. It occurred to her that Daniel could be ill; the state of the kitchen told her that he was not taking care of himself.

Harry said doubtfully, 'I could break the door down, your ladyship.'

'Could you?' She realized that Harry Dockerill was waiting for her to make the decision. 'Yes. Go ahead, Harry. I think you must.'

Harry fetched a pickaxe from the tool-shed and swung it against the kitchen door. Fragments of wood spun into the air, and there was a clang as the head bit the metal lock. He stood aside as Thomasine walked into the house.

The kitchen was hot, fetid, rank. Flies fed on a jug of sour milk, wasps buzzed around the sticky neck of a jamjar. Thomasine's stomach churned. She seized the milk jug and emptied the reeking contents out into the yard.

'Could you light the range, Harry? I'm going to look upstairs.'

She climbed up the ladder. It took a while for her eyes to accustom themselves to the gloom of the loft, and then she glimpsed him, sprawled on the mattress, quite still. For a second she thought that the fear she had not allowed herself to give voice to had been proved true: that Daniel, maddened by grief, had made sure that he would not have to live without Fay. But then, with a great sigh of relief, she noticed the small rise and fall of his chest and the empty bottles scattered over the floor.

She called downstairs. 'Harry? Daniel's up here. He's all right – drunk, I think.'

She could hear Harry fiddling with the doors of the kitchen-range. Thomasine knelt on the edge of the mattress, seized one of Daniel's shoulders and shook him.

'Daniel. Wake up. You must wake up.'

There was no response, so she shook harder. Daniel's eyes opened briefly and failed to focus. 'Go away,' he mumbled, and rolled on to his side, pulling the blankets over his head.

She knelt there, exasperated, looking at him for a moment, and then she scrambled back down the ladder to the kitchen. Searching through the debris of dirty crockery, Thomasine found what she wanted: a large pitcher. Filling it with water from the bucket, she hauled it back up the ladder while Harry watched curiously.

'Daniel,' said Thomasine again loudly. There was no reply, so she upended the cold water over his head.

There was a roar of protest, and Daniel tumbled in a tangle of blankets to the floor.

'What the *hell* –'

'I'm sorry, Daniel, but I had to wake you up. You've had a lot to drink, and you might be sick.'

'*Jesus!*' He struggled back on to the mattress, rubbing the drops of water from his eyes with the palm of his hand. Then he stared up at Thomasine. 'Go away. For God's sake, go away.' He looked furious.

She crouched down beside him. 'No. I won't,' she said firmly. 'Have you eaten since the funeral, Daniel? Have you drunk anything except this?' She indicated the empty bottle of whisky.

'None of your damned business,' muttered Daniel. His eyes were red-rimmed, and there was a two-day growth of beard around his chin. His hair clung in wet, darkened locks to his scalp. 'Go away, Thomasine. Push off. I don't need you.'

For a moment they just glared at each other. The silence was filled by the sound of Harry tactfully tiptoeing out of the kitchen below.

'I'll go,' said Thomasine carefully, 'if you'll drink a cup of tea. Yes, Daniel?'

She knew that her own temper was short these days. Only her intuition of the misery that lay beneath his rudeness and anger enabled her to keep her patience. His eyes focused finally on her, then he looked away and gave the smallest nod of his head.

'Good.' Thomasine scrambled back down the ladder.

Harry Dockerill had lit the range and filled the buckets with clean water. Through the window, Thomasine could see him crossing the farmyard, heading out towards the fields, scythe in hand. For a moment she could not think where in the filthy kitchen to start. It was awful, worse than the Gotobeds' cottage. The brick floor was clogged with mud and straw from the fields, the range was ringed with dark, burnt encrustations.

Every surface – the table, the dresser, the settle – was littered with dirty crockery, empty tins, old newspapers, unopened letters. Thomasine rolled up her sleeves and set to work.

There was the sound of footsteps on the ladder as she heaped cups and dishes into the sink. She did not look round, but began to scrub at the plates with a piece of wire wool. She had already filled the kettle and placed it on the range; a little warmth was beginning to seep up through the hot-plate.

She said, 'I'll just tidy things up a bit. Then I'll make you a cup of tea, and then I'll go.'

She heard the hiss of Daniel's exhaled breath. She could hear him pacing about behind her, flicking at the unopened letters, kicking at the debris on the floor.

'Ah. The lady of the manor, come to do her bit for the ignorant peasants.' His voice was bitter.

'Don't be silly, Daniel.' Thomasine poured more water into the sink. 'You wouldn't open the door to Harry, and Harry was nervous about battering his employer's door down without permission. So you ended up with me.'

'I don't want anyone.' Daniel's voice was taut, dangerously soft. 'I'm asking you – *telling* you – to leave me alone, Thomasine. I don't need a goddamned nanny.'

She paused for a moment, her hands still immersed in water. She knew that he had come very close to her, that very briefly his body had brushed against hers as he continued his restless pacing round the room. She was aware of a barely suppressed violence in him, and aware too of a response in herself that she simply had not predicted. She scrubbed harder at the dirty dishes and heard him move away to the door, then to the table, then back to the door. When the kettle was almost boiled, she looked round for a tea-caddy.

Daniel was leaning against the door-jamb, looking out to the yard. Yet she knew that he was not looking, that he saw nothing. There was so much that needed to be said, but she could not find the words, and she cursed herself for her inadequacy. She knew how, looking at her, he must be reminded of the woman who had once worked in this kitchen, the woman he had loved, the woman who had betrayed him. The name 'Fay' resounded in the squalid room, but could not yet be voiced.

She made the tea. 'There's no milk, but I've put lots of sugar in it.' She placed the cup on the table. 'Drink it, Daniel, please -- it'll make you feel better.'

Thomasine watched him shuffle from the door to the table. For a long moment he stared at the cup as though he didn't know what to do with it, and then his fist swung out, sending the scalding liquid streaming across the scarred table-top, smashing the earthenware cup against the wall. She took a step backwards. But she heard him whisper, 'I killed her, Thomasine. I killed her,' and she stood, frozen, gazing at him, her heart pounding, unable to believe what she heard.

He must have understood the expression on her face. His fists uncurled and he laughed humourlessly and said, 'Oh, I didn't push her into the dyke – I didn't hold her head under the water. But I killed her just the same.' She could hear the anguish in his voice.

'Fay died because of the thunderstorm, Daniel. She died because it was dark, and she couldn't see properly, and the bridge was slippery. It happens every year – you know that. You didn't kill her.'

'Oh, I did.' Just for a moment then, his eyes were quite sane, quite sober. 'I did. I wish to God I'd never brought her here.'

Nicholas always took morning coffee with his mother. 'Our little treat', Mama called it. The custom suited Nicholas: he liked every part of the day parcelled out, assigned a purpose and an occupation.

Mama was stirring sugar into his coffee when Thomasine came into the room. Usually Thomasine took her coffee upstairs, in her office. She had a sheaf of papers in her hand, which she dropped into Nicholas's lap. He tried to catch them and failed, and they skated over the polished floor of the morning-room.

'I found these in your desk, Nick,' she said. Her voice was taut.

He knelt on the floor and began to pick up the fragments of paper. He heard his mother say, 'It isn't the thing, Thomasine, to look through someone's private possessions.'

'And it isn't the thing, is it, Nick, to hide letters from the bank manager?'

Nicholas glanced quickly from his mother to his wife and back to his mother again. His mother was looking furiously at Thomasine; Thomasine was looking furiously at him. He could not bear anger, conflict. He concentrated on picking up the bills, the letters, the invoices, filing them neatly into categories. If he could keep control of the small things, then the bigger things – family, home, what the hell he was supposed to do with the rest of his life – might also fall into order.

Thomasine added, 'I had a letter from the bank this morning. It said that unless they hear from us within a fortnight, they're calling in the overdraft.'

He had all the invoices together now, and all the IOUs. He did not have the letters from the bank, because he had burnt them. They had been addressed to him, of course, because Drakesden Abbey was his and the money (what was left of it) was also his, not Thomasine's. But somehow he had never been good with money, and those increasingly awful letters had only succeeded in reducing him to a sort of blind panic, a confirmation of failure and inadequacy.

'I found bills for wireless components and for spare parts for the motor-car. And there's a huge bill for champagne, and another for picnic stuff from Fortnum's. And two withdrawals for five hundred pounds that I can't account for at all.'

Nicholas rifled through the IOUs, withdrawing two of them. He'd explain everything to Thomasine, and then Thomasine – clever, level-headed Thomasine – would sort it all out.

'Boy asked me to lend him a few bob.' He handed her the IOUs.

Thomasine glanced at the scraps of paper. '*A few bob?* A thousand pounds, Nick – a thousand pounds!'

The anxiety in her eyes worried Nicholas. He had expected reassurance, understanding. Once, she would have given him understanding. But she had changed since they had come to Drakesden Abbey: she had become harder, less forgiving. Often now, when she looked at him he saw a mixture of criticism and pity on her face. He could not bear either.

'Boy will pay me back,' Nicholas muttered defensively. 'He said he would. He was short of funds for a while, that's all. He'll pay me back.'

He heard her snort of derision. He had realized a long time ago that Thomasine despised his friends. He had tried to explain to her that he needed them, that they filled in the gaps, the silences. He repeated, 'Boy's a friend, Thomasine.'

Mama said, 'Of course Nicky must help his friends if they are in trouble. It would be inconceivable for him not to do so.' And he looked at her gratefully, glad that she, as always, understood.

He had the beginnings of a headache, so early in the day. He had planned a long drive that morning – he would persuade Lally to get out of bed so that he had some company, and they would head off for Cambridge. There were shops and restaurants and things in Cambridge, and a pal or two who had returned to the University to finish an education that had been disrupted by the War.

'Boy won't pay you back, Nick,' said Thomasine. 'Boy's not really a friend. He'll stay with you as long as you pay for his drinks and his cigarettes, but that's all.'

He couldn't bear it when she spoke to him like that. Such judgement in her eyes. He whispered, 'I need *company*.'

'I know you do, Nick.' She went to him then, and laid her hand on his arm. Her eyes, such a lovely bluish-green, had softened. 'I know you do.'

When she looked at him like that, when she spoke to him like that, he was aware once again of the love he felt for her, the love that nothing could quite kill. He felt a new resolve spring up inside himself. He would sort things out, he would be better with money, he would be a *man* –

Then Mama said, 'What you have never quite understood, Thomasine, is that people like us – the Blythes of Drakesden Abbey – have a duty towards the rest of our class. We are not farmers or bookkeepers, and we do not behave like farmers or bookkeepers. We are something more than that.'

Nicholas knew that Mama was furious. She only showed her disapproval in small ways; she was far too much the lady ever to stamp her foot or shout. Her voice just became cold, and her eyes like steel. Her anger always made Nicholas feel sick inside. It reduced him to a seven-year-old boy, sobbing in her lap because he didn't want to go back to boarding-school. *Control yourself, Nicholas. Be a man.* It didn't matter that Mama's anger was directed at Thomasine, rather than at Nicholas himself; he still feared and dreaded the inevitable confrontation.

Thomasine's voice was equally cold. 'And what you must understand, Lady Blythe, is that there simply won't be a Drakesden Abbey unless you change. We have to make economies – you no longer have the money for a houseful of servants, a stable full of horses, two motor-cars –'

'You are not suggesting that Nicky sells his motor-car, are you, Thomasine?'

Nicholas glanced at Thomasine in horror. He needed the motor-car; it allowed him to escape from this god-forsaken hole. It was inconceivable that he sell the motor-car.

'No – of course not,' said Thomasine, and Nicholas breathed a huge sigh of relief. 'I'm suggesting that we manage with a couple less servants – that we sell a horse or two – they are not all ridden regularly.'

Thomasine took one of his hands in hers and brushed his hair from his aching forehead. Her touch was cool and soothing.

'We just have to economize a little, Nick, that's all. It won't be so bad.'

There was a ripple of laughter from Lady Blythe. 'Thomasine wants us to wait on ourselves, Nicky. To scrub our own floors and wash our own linen. Well, you may be accustomed to that sort of life, Thomasine, but Nicholas and I could never be!'

He knew that Mama spoke the truth. It was all right for Thomasine who had, one must admit, been used to a hand-to-mouth sort of existence, but the thought of living in squalor appalled him. He needed a clean house, clean clothes, the sort of ordered existence that only a multiplicity of servants could ensure. He couldn't live like the people in the village. His months in the trenches had shown him how much he needed the routine and cleanliness that went with his sort of upbringing.

Mama would sort everything out, just as she always did. Mama understood what he needed; Thomasine did not, because she was different. Once, he had adored her for that difference; now it threatened him. Thomasine asked him to do impossible things: to talk about what had happened in the War, to abandon the self-created rules and customs that allowed him to keep going. Nicholas kissed his mother on the cheek, placed the bundle of papers in Thomasine's hands, and went out of the room in search of Lally.

As she walked down the drove, Thomasine made calculations in her head. There must be sufficient profit from the harvest to pay off enough of the overdraft to satisfy the bank manager. Would there then still be cash to buy the fruit bushes that she believed necessary to guarantee their future survival? She would write to Max and ask him to use all his charm and influence in staving off their creditors.

The door of the Gillorys' cottage, its lock unrepaired, was ajar. Thomasine, looking inside, could see Daniel making ineffectual attempts to clear the table. She could also see the whisky bottle standing on the dirty oilcloth.

Daniel looked up. 'My God. I've just got rid of the bloody vicar. Now its Lady Bountiful again.'

She almost turned on her heel and walked back to Drakesden Abbey. Yet she had needed, more than anything, to escape. The discovery of the unpaid bills and the conversation in the morning-room still troubled her profoundly. She jutted out her chin and stepped inside. 'I came to see how you are.'

'I'm terrific.' Daniel gestured wildly around the kitchen. 'Well-wishers every five minutes or so, and Harry's ma keeps sending her brats round with offerings. So I'm terrific. Nothing for you to do, Lady Blythe.'

A collection of plates, all piled high with various sorts of food, balanced precariously on top of the range.

'You haven't *eaten* the food Mrs Dockerill has sent you, Daniel.'

He sloshed some whisky into a tumbler and sat down, rather suddenly, on the settle. 'Wasn't hungry.'

She went to the range. 'I'll heat something up for you. You can't let all this go to waste.'

'Oh, for pity's sake, give it to the bloody pig. I told you – I'm not hungry.'

She turned and looked at him carefully. In the years they had known each other their relationship had lurched between friendship and dislike, affection and resentment. Yet he had always seemed competent, strong. Now he reminded her too much of Nicholas: that awful edginess, the blank look in his eyes. A slovenliness that Nicholas would have found unendurable. Yet Daniel, like Nicholas, was trying to shut out the past. Nicholas just didn't use alcohol.

'You're not hungry because you're drinking too much, Daniel. You'll make yourself ill.'

His gaze wandered, failing to focus on Thomasine. The anger suddenly died. 'Does it matter?'

She knew that Nicholas was slowly destroying himself; she could not bear to watch Daniel do likewise.

'Yes, it does. It's a waste.'

'I don't think so.' Daniel took another mouthful of scotch.

Thomasine left the stove and went to sit beside him. She had never, she thought, chosen her words so carefully.

'What happened to Fay was so utterly, utterly awful – so wrong. But it won't make things right for you to destroy yourself as well, Daniel. It won't bring her back.'

Clichés, she thought. Clichés. Yet he glanced at her briefly, and blinked.

'I know that.' The glass shook in his hand. 'But it stops me thinking, you see.'

She knew that there were no words that could alleviate this sort of grief. Eventually, if you were strong enough, you learned to live with it. Eventually you bundled up the people you had lost into a little box of memory. And only sometimes did you turn the key and peer inside. Most of the time you couldn't even bear to look.

'Such a dreadful way to die,' he whispered. 'I keep thinking about it. The mud . . . in your mouth . . . your eyes. Blinding you. Choking you. I can't sleep . . . that she should die like *that* . . . the mud . . . and the water . . . and the thunderstorm. She was frightened of thunder, Thomasine!'

She glimpsed the tears in his eyes. The glass slipped out of his fingers, shattering on the brick floor. He covered his face with his hands and his shoulders shook, and she put her arms round him, pressing her head against his, stroking his hair.

After a long time, she heard him groan, 'What they said about her at the inquest – it wasn't like that. At least, not at first. I loved her. She was so beautiful.'

As she held him, she was aware of the warmth of his body against hers, the roughness of his chin. Aware of the obvious, unavoidable fact that he was a man and she a woman. She stood up and went to the stove, and opened the coal-door. Her hands were not steady, though, as she threw pieces of turf on top of the smouldering ashes.

'You know what it's like in Drakesden,' she said eventually. 'It's different for you, Daniel – you were born here. It takes so long for anyone from outside to be accepted. It must have been hard for Fay.'

Staring bleakly at the uneaten plates of food on top of the range, Thomasine remembered her own early years at Drakesden, the struggle to adjust to the cold, the wind, the flat, featureless landscape. The people who had stared at her in the street, the mutterings behind her back. She remembered Fay Gillory – pretty, smart Fay Gillory with her lipstick and her high-heeled shoes and her London ways. How the gossips must have muttered about her. With what shocked delight they must have learned of her faithlessness.

Daniel had risen from the seat, rubbing his eyes with the back of his sleeve. Shuffling to the sink, he too stared at the plates of food.

'I'll heat something up for you,' said Thomasine. 'You'll eat it, won't you, Daniel?'

He nodded.

'Some of these look rather old. Scrape them into the bucket, please, Daniel.'

Make him do something, anything. Work allows you to endure pain. Make him begin to care for something again.

'Harry's been feeding the animals,' she said, 'but you can give most of this to the pig. Mrs Dockerill needn't know. This pie looks all right – it'll heat up in a few minutes.'

She placed the dish in the oven. Daniel's movements were slow and clumsy, as though the simple tasks were a huge effort. It hurt her to witness the concentration he had to summon to sort out the cutlery, to stack the plates and bowls.

She heard him whisper, 'I meant what I said the other day, Thomasine. It wasn't just the whisky talking. I was responsible for Fay's death, because I brought her here, to a place where she couldn't possibly be happy. She needed – oh! – pretty clothes and visits to the pictures and some sort of pretence of gentility. I couldn't give her that. I don't care about things like that. I should never have married her.'

'Daniel –'

He shook his head, silencing her. 'It's true. We were happy at first, I think, but gradually . . . it all wore away, Thomasine. There was nothing left.'

After she heard of Fay Gillory's death, Lally waited, frightened, for some sort of retribution.

Retribution did not come, however. Although the inquest had pieced together the chain of events that had led to the tragedy, one link of the chain had not been disclosed. Daniel had not told the police about Lally's visit to the blacksmith's cottage. She did not question his motives for silence but, reading the report of the inquest in the local paper, had felt a deep sense of relief.

Soon she found herself as bored and lonely as ever, though. Lally longed to return to London, but London, at that time of year, was deserted. She received letters from Simon, from Belle and Pip. Irritably, she counted the days. Casting round for occupation, she retreated to her old pastimes of watching and fantasizing.

Thomasine often absented herself from the house. Interest flickered and ignited when Lally noticed that Thomasine's absences usually took place when Nicky, too, was away. Occasionally Thomasine drove; mostly she walked. One afternoon Lally followed her. Trailing some distance behind, she tracked her sister-in-law's path through the orchard, the wood, the meadow.

When Thomasine started down the spur that led from the village towards the Gillorys' cottage, Lally held back, hiding in the curve of the road. She waited, her heart battering against her rib-cage, watching as Thomasine disappeared down the path towards Daniel's house. Lally heard, very faintly, Thomasine call out Daniel's name. There was an easy familiarity in her tone of voice, as though she had made this same journey, called that same name many times before. Lally's nails dug deep into her palms, searing the skin, and there was a red haze of anger and jealousy in front of her eyes.

In September, Belle, Julian, Boy and Ettie arrived at Drakesden to collect Lally. After lunch they lounged in the drawing-room.

'So good to see you,' said Nicholas. 'We've been buried here all summer.'

Belle shrieked. 'Nicky, how frightful! Everyone goes away for August. Simply everyone.'

'Thomasine's been awfully busy. It ties us rather.' Nicholas's voice was sulky. He was sitting on a sofa, his head cushioned by his palms.

'Aunt Gwendoline's gone now.' Belle squeezed his arm. 'We can be naughty. Tell us the gossip.'

'Oh . . . nothing much. Drakesden's such a frightful hole.'

'There's Doctor Lawrence,' said Lally slyly. 'Awfully scandalous.'

'One for the popsies, was he, old thing?' Julian lit himself a cigarette.

'He was . . . um –' Nicholas's eyes were half-closed – '*consorting* with one of the local farmers' wives.'

'*Delicious.*'

Lally said, 'Doctor Lawrence had simply oodles of sex-appeal, you see, Belle. And Mrs Gillory was terribly pretty. They were fornicating like mad all over the place. Barns . . . fields . . . the back of his motor-car. It's centuries since anything so shocking has happened in Drakesden.'

Nicholas grinned. 'Apparently the cuckolded husband paid a social call a few days ago. Poor old Lawrence will be going back to bonnie Scotland minus a tooth or two.'

Belle giggled. Thomasine glanced down at Nicholas sharply. 'It isn't true! Who told you that?'

'One of the farmhands. Gillory always was an aggressive little beast.'

Boy said, 'And the errant wife? Has she fled to Gretna Green with the seductive doctor, or has the farmer tied her to his bedpost?'

There was a short silence. 'Neither,' said Thomasine harshly. 'She's dead. She was found drowned just over a month ago.' Thomasine rose from her seat. Her gaze passed coldly from Belle to Ettie, from Ettie to Boy. 'Amusing, don't you think? *Such fun.*'

She could hear their voices as she slammed the door behind her.

'*Such* a spoilsport –'

'What shall we do?'

'A séance. My Ouija-board is in the motor-car.'

'Too light – in the evening, perhaps –'

'Mah-jong?'

'Hide-and-seek! We used to have the most wonderful games of hide-and-seek at Drakesden.'

'Masses of places to hide.'

'I've my own special place. You'll never guess.'

'Such fun!'

Thomasine ran upstairs to the nursery. William was asleep in his cot. She bent over him, touching his soft cheek with her forefinger. His dark hair clung in curls to his forehead and his closed eyelids were pale and translucent, marbled with blue. She smiled at Martha, knitting in the corner of the nursery, and closed the door very quietly behind her. She found herself longing for the safe untenanted silence of her study.

And yet the room that she regarded as her sanctuary was not untenanted, was not silent. Thomasine heard the rustle of papers as she walked down the corridor and smelt – just a faint signature lingering in the air – the scent of carnations.

The door to the study was a few inches ajar. Inside the study, Lady Blythe was leafing through the papers on the desk, picking up and reading first one, and then another. And then, as Thomasine watched, Lady Blythe upended the inkwell with elegant precision, so that a thin stream of black drowned all the carefully written words and figures.

★

The following day Lally left Drakesden with their visitors, calling out her farewells from the dickey seat of Ettie's motor-car. In her office, Thomasine rewrote columns of figures and scrubbed at the black trails of ink on her desk. But the stains would not come out, and she made mistakes with the figures, so that when she tried to add them the numbers were nonsensical. She put aside her pen and sat, her eyes closed, her fists pressing against her forehead. Such hatred, she thought, and despised herself for running away yesterday, for failing to confront Lady Blythe. Yet the knowledge that such a confrontation would have been futile was worse even than her self-hatred.

She did not sleep that night, nor the next. She went through the motions of working: ordering blackcurrant and redcurrant bushes from the nursery at Soham, asking the men to begin the clearance of the summer's growth of sedge from the ditches. But the fascination she had once felt with her tasks was absent. Whenever she shut her eyes she saw that thin stream of black ink, like a bayonet cut. How often in the past two years had she blamed herself for accidents, omissions, blunders? She questioned the years she had lived at Drakesden Abbey, seeing behind her own apparent early incompetence and doubt a malice that was truly chilling. A malice that she could not fight against. To damage Nicholas's image of his mother would be to damage the powerful bond that tied mother and son. To break that bond would, Thomasine believed, destroy Nicholas.

When she went again to see Daniel, he was out in the yard, grooming the horse. She crossed the yard to join him.

'He's beautiful.' Thomasine patted Nelson's glossy mane.

'He's a disaster. Jumps at the sight of a mouse, and his good eye's giving out.' Affectionately, Daniel fed the horse chunks of carrot and apple. Thomasine studied him carefully. He looked better, she thought, than when she had last seen him, three weeks before. Apart, that was, from the faded remains of a black eye. Alexander Lawrence, Thomasine thought grimly, must have fought back.

'I came to ask your advice, Daniel.'

He was emptying a bucket of water into the horse trough. 'Advice? Not sure I'm the right person. I've fouled up fairly spectacularly recently, haven't I?' His voice was bitter.

She winced. 'I don't mean about . . . people.'

He lugged a bale of straw into the stable and cut the twine that bound it with his knife. 'You've done rather better than I have in that respect, haven't you, Thomasine?'

She could not answer him. When eventually he looked up at her, he stuck the knife back into his belt, and said, 'Hell. What have I said?' He kicked the remainder of the straw into the stable and moved towards her. 'I'd always assumed —'

'That I was happily married?' She glared at him. 'I'd assumed much the same about you, Daniel.'

She wanted to call the words back as soon as she had spoken them, but he only blinked and rubbed his forehead, and said, 'I deserved that.' Then he put his arms round her and hugged her. 'Sorry.'

Such a rare thing, an apology from touchy, arrogant Daniel Gillory. Thomasine shut her eyes for a moment, resting her head against his shoulder. The embrace was not awkward, as all Nicholas's embraces were awkward: it was natural, easy, the gesture of a man used to showing physical affection. So easy, too, just to raise her head, just to ask for a little more comfort . . .

She pulled out of his arms and walked towards the house. 'Can I make a cup of tea, Daniel? I'm terribly thirsty.' Yet it was an effort to keep her voice steady.

Daniel made the tea, Thomasine sat at the table. The silence was lengthy, weighted with tension.

Eventually she said, 'I wanted to ask your advice about the farm, Daniel. I've ordered two dozen each of redcurrant and blackcurrant bushes, and I was thinking about strawberry plants. They grow so well in the Abbey's kitchen gardens. But I don't know how many I'd have to buy to make a reasonable profit – or where to sell them –'

Farming, she thought. Such a nice, safe subject. If you talked about yields and profits and transport problems, you couldn't possibly think about how much you'd like to go to bed with the man you were talking to. How much you'd like to climb that ladder and fall on to that grubby straw mattress and feel this man's body against yours . . .

Daniel had taken a pen and was noting figures on a scrap of paper. 'You could sell some of the strawberries in Cambridge, Thomasine, but you'd get the best price if you sent them to Covent Garden. That would mean loading them on to the early train – quite feasible, though – just a question of taking the stuff by horse and cart to Ely station.'

Daniel, of course, would be sickened if he knew what she was thinking. Daniel's embrace had been prompted by friendship and affection. Drinking her tea, watching him write, she thanked God that she had been sensible, that she had pulled away from him and resisted the compulsion to make a fool of herself. She knew that it was not even really Daniel Gillory that she desired. She was throwing herself at the first attractive man she had met in months simply because her marriage was a sham, a façade, and had been so for years.

When she said her farewells to Daniel, Thomasine knew that she must not see him again. Harry Dockerill must make sure that Daniel ate and looked after his stock and did not drink himself to sleep each night. She could not. It was too dangerous.

They were taking tea on the lawn, catching the last sun of a fading summer. William was toddling on the grass when Nicholas arrived back from the county fair he had been visiting.

'Deadly dull. All those marrows and bottled plums and cakes. Just a cup of tea, if you please, Mama.'

'You must have something to eat, Nicky. You look tired.' Lady Blythe heaped sandwiches and fruit cake on to Nicholas's plate.

Nicholas sat down at the wrought-iron table. 'You should

have seen the tractors and combine harvesters, though, Thomasine. All the latest models. Perfectly ripping machines. Twincylinders, most of them.'

To relieve the boredom and tension of afternoon tea, Thomasine had recently insisted that William join the family at this time. Just now, William was pulling marigolds out of the border.

'Some of the more modern farms hardly keep any horses any more. Everything's done by tractor. Terrific idea, don't you think?' Nicholas's restless fingers crumbled his cake to dust.

Thomasine, struggling to extract orange petals from an uncooperative William's mouth, glanced uneasily at Nicholas.

'You are making crumbs, Nicky,' whispered Lady Blythe tactfully.

Nicholas glanced at his tea-plate, and hurriedly withdrew his hand. 'I beg your pardon, Mama.'

Thomasine, having cleaned up William, returned to the table and her unfinished sandwich. 'Tractors were tried out in East Anglia during the War, Nick. They're fine when there's a lot of heavy work to be done, but they can't do everything. And they're awfully expensive.'

'There's a lot of heavy work on the farm,' said Nicholas obstinately. 'Max says our labour costs are crippling.'

'Max is right. But we really can't afford to spend a large amount of money just now.'

William had climbed on to his father's lap and was licking the cake crumbs off his plate. Nicholas wiped the child's sticky hands with his handkerchief. 'Mechanizing Drakesden would be an investment, Thomasine. The farm's still in the nineteenth century.'

Lady Blythe murmured, 'You should listen to Nicholas, dear. He knows Drakesden better than you do, after all. He was born here. These things do make a difference.' She removed Nicholas's plate from William's grasp. Furious, William banged his small fists on the table.

'Anyway, I've ordered a tractor. It'll be utterly topping. They offered me a special price. I'd have been a fool not to take it.' There was defiance on Nicholas's face as his eyes met Thomasine's.

She felt suddenly an almost overwhelming sense of panic. All her work and plans of the previous year would come to nothing, because she could not withstand the combination of Lady Blythe's innate conservatism and Nicholas's inability to face reality.

'But I told you – we're planting strawberries and raspberries next year – I *told* you, Nick! They'll sell so much easier than the wheat –'

Lady Blythe's laugh was high and brittle. 'What an extraordinary idea. When I called at little Rose Carter's cottage the other day, they were eating dumplings and bread and margarine. Not even the smallest piece of meat, let alone fruit. *Strawberries!*'

William started to yell. Lady Blythe shook her head. 'I did warn you, Thomasine. He really isn't old enough to be allowed to join the family at meal-times. He is over-excited.'

'Frightful mess . . .' Meticulously, Nicholas brushed cake-crumbs from his trousers.

Thomasine struggled for patience. 'The villagers eat dull food because they can't afford to buy anything better. I mean people in the towns, the suburbs. People who have a little money to spare. It's happening all over the Fens, Nick. Farmers aren't bothering with wheat, they're planting celery and chicory and raspberries and redcurrants. For heaven's sake,' she heard herself finish desperately, 'how could you just go ahead and buy a tractor? Don't you see – we simply haven't the cash. I showed you the bank statements –'

'Nicky is quite right not to trouble himself with clerical work. Neither his father nor his grandfather concerned themselves with the day-to-day running of the farm. That is what you fail to understand, Thomasine. Shopkeepers and the merchant classes may spend their time scribbling rows of figures, but we do not.' Lady Blythe smiled patronizingly.

Which is why, thought Thomasine, you risk losing everything. Why the land crumbles away and the house falls into disrepair. It was as though she was standing on the dyke, watching the water rise higher and higher until it touched the edge of the bank and first trickled, and then flooded, on to the land.

Thwarted, William banged the table-top with the flat of his hands. One of the tiny teacups jumped and overturned, spilling its contents all over the tablecloth.

'*Christ!*' said Nicholas. Tea dripped from the cloth on to his clothes. Standing up, he passed William to Thomasine.

'The child is out of hand,' said Lady Blythe repressively. 'You really must engage another nanny. Martha is not a suitable person to have sole care of him.'

Nicholas dabbed splashes of tea from his trousers. 'Mama's right, Thomasine. He'll be a little horror by the time he's seven.'

'Seven?' repeated Thomasine, bewildered.

'When he goes away to prep school. He'll be ragged fearfully by the other boys if he still behaves like a spoilt brat.'

She stared at Nicholas. 'William isn't going to boarding-school when he's *seven!*'

'Of course he is.' Nicholas added irritably, 'You can't keep the poor little chap tied to your apron strings for ever, Thomasine.'

Lady Blythe signalled to the maidservant to take away the tea-things. 'Perhaps Thomasine intends William to attend the elementary school, Nicholas.'

Nicholas lit himself a cigarette. One of the muscles beside his eye was twitching. 'Nonsense, Mama. Can't have a Blythe in with that rabble. William will go to Winchester – Blythes always do, don't they?'

The maidservant began to clear away the tea-things. They sat in rigid silence – one could not, after all, quarrel in front of the servants. William was almost eighteen months old, thought Thomasine desperately. In just five and a half years' time they intended to send him away to boarding-school. She would see him then for only three or four months of the year. The school would make of him what it had made of Nicholas: someone who had learned as a small child that you must not show the distress you felt at being sent away from the person you most loved; someone who would try, at whatever cost, to conform to his peers' idea of manhood. No. She could not permit it. It was intolerable.

The Grafton Galleries always closed at 2 a.m. Lally, who was wearing a backless silver dress and silver stockings and the gloves that the Galleries deemed necessary for dancing, shivered as she stepped out into the street.

'Tired?' asked Simon Melville, draping her cape around her shoulders.

'Not at all.' Lally looked back. 'Where's Tiny?'

'Tiny's gone home with the pianist.'

The Grafton Galleries employed a negro jazz band. Lally glanced at Simon. 'Frightfully decadent.'

'Tiny always had a penchant for the gutter.' A flicker of distaste crossed Simon's handsome face. 'Where now?'

The London streets were chill and autumnal. Mist swirled in the dips of the road, a harbinger of the thick fogs the winter would bring. Lally's restlessness had increased since she had left Drakesden.

'Oh – I don't know, Simon. Somewhere different.'

'Rectors? The Forty-three?'

Lally shook her head. 'Pip took me to the Forty-three last week. And everyone goes to Rectors now.'

Simon was silent for a moment. Looking up at him, she could see only the scarlet tip of his cigarette and the sheen of his golden hair in the mist-dimmed street-lamp. They had been, at various times during the two years of their acquaintance, lovers. Yet there was still something about Simon that frightened as well as fascinated Lally – something cold, reptilian, detached.

Sometimes she sought his company, sometimes she avoided him for weeks.

'I know just the place,' said Simon, hailing a cab.

He took her to a club in Soho. The doorway was narrow, flanked by a huge doorman and several lurid posters. In the street beyond, painted women smiled emptily in dark alleyways and drunks staggered on the dank cobbles.

Inside the club the other customers all stared at them. Lally could see a few seats and tables, a tiny dance-floor and bar, and a small stage. There were no other women except, of course, for the women on the stage. Blinking to accustom her eyes to the dim light, Lally sipped cocktails and watched the show. Half a dozen girls danced, not quite in time with each other, on the wooden platform. The gramophone blared out, 'Yes, we have no bananas' as the girls danced. They were bare-chested, wearing only raffia skirts and high-heels. Various fruits were attached to the raffia: apples, oranges, pears and, of course, bananas. Lally giggled.

A tattered curtain came down, and there was a little half-hearted applause.

'Do you want to dance?' asked Simon.

They danced the tango on the six-foot square of threadbare carpet in front of the stage. Lally knew that every man in the room was staring at her. She enjoyed the sensation. She needed men to want her, to desire her. It helped to make up for the terrible rejection she had suffered earlier in the year.

The curtain was raised again, and the music altered to 'The Sheikh of Araby'. This time only one woman reclined on the stage amid a pile of tasselled cushions and lengths of cloth. She wore shimmering harem pants and a silk shawl, and a yashmak covered the lower half of her face. When she began to dance, swaying sinuously to the music, Lally saw that though her eyes were dark, her hair was blonde.

Lally frowned and squinted. The dancer let fall her silk shawl, revealing a chiffon bodice beneath. Slowly, dreamily, the girl began to undo the buttons of the bodice. Her eyes, with their encircling of kohl, were blank and black. The bodice dropped to the floor and the dancer unhooked one side of her yashmak. Some of the men in the audience were staring at her, their eyes intense and hungry, others were carrying on their conversations, uninterested.

Lally said, 'Lend me your opera glasses, Simon.'

Simon, amused, handed her the glasses. Lally focused on the Eastern dancer, trying to compensate for her short sight.

Simon said lazily, 'Well, you do surprise me, darling. Still — there's no accounting for taste.'

She was sure now. 'I've seen her before. In Paris.'

'At the Folies? She's come down in the world a bit, then.'

Lally shook her head. 'Not at the Folies. In a café in Montmartre. It was July — my nineteenth birthday. Thomasine was dancing in a revue in Paris. That girl —' Lally nodded to the stage — 'was one of the other dancers.'

Lally's hand was clenched around the stem of her glass. Simon murmured, 'Careful, darling, you'll break it,' and eased the glass out of her grasp.

She hissed, 'We were having such a fine time until then. We'd been to Rome and Monaco. Just Nicky and me and a few friends. Then we met *her* again. Thomasine.'

Thomasine had first taken Nicky, and now she had taken Daniel. At Drakesden the impulse to make public Thomasine's illicit liaison with Daniel Gillory had been almost irresistible. Only the fear that had accompanied the news of Fay Gillory's death had kept Lally silent, understanding something of the havoc that sort of revelation could wreak.

There were tears in Lally's eyes, though whether of anger or of grief she was not sure. Simon said, 'Take it easy, darling,' but a flicker of interest crossed his face. He added, 'When did they marry?'

'A month later. Six weeks. I can't remember.'

The curtain came down amid a flutter of applause. Simon drawled, 'Frightfully quick, don't you agree?'

'I suppose so.'

'I mean, didn't you think . . .?'

She glanced at him. 'What do you mean, Simon?' she said sharply, frowning. '*Oh*. You think they *had* to get married?'

He shrugged. 'Could be. Otherwise – why the hurry? Your brother's such a conventional chap, after all.'

There was the hint of a sneer in his voice. Lally, ignoring it, stared at the empty dance-floor and thought. 'No,' she said at last. 'William wasn't born for simply ages after they married.'

She had always assumed that Nicky had been a virgin when he had married. He had never seemed at ease among attractive women, inclined either to idolize or to fear them. Vaguely, she had concluded that Nicky was a bit funny about women because of Mama. And yet, it had been odd, uncharacteristic, that hasty marriage.

Thomasine walked down to the village, pushing William in his perambulator. Nicholas had driven to Cambridge that morning, and she needed to discuss her plans for improving the labourers' cottages with Mrs Dockerill.

William pounded a piece of bread dough into a grey sausage while Thomasine and Flo Dockerill talked about drainage, dampness and infestations. There was, Thomasine acknowledged, only a limited amount that could be done until Drakesden Abbey's finances were on a more even keel. Most of the problems in the cottages were a consequence of the waterlogged land, and only a vast amount of work would stop Drakesden flooding each spring. There simply wasn't the money to carry out the work at present. And even if there had been, Thomasine suspected that neither Nicholas nor Lady Blythe would agree to her spending it on something not of direct profit to Drakesden Abbey.

After she left Flo, she walked out to the great dyke that confined the tributary of the Lark. Taking William out of his pram, she held his hand while they climbed the bank.

'Water,' said William, pointing, making bubbling sounds.

'Water,' agreed Thomasine absently, assessing the sedge that gathered thickly on the banks, the weed and lilies that impeded the smooth flow of the river. Following along the straight line of the dyke, she could see where the banks crumbled, holed by burrowing animals and eroded by the wind. Troubled, she let her gaze drift north, out towards the fields, to the distant proud silhouette of Ely cathedral. The land was so flat on this side of the village. She knew what would happen if this dyke should break: the water would flood the fields for miles around, laying waste crops, houses and livestock.

When, at last, she turned away from the dyke, she saw the cyclist freewheeling along the rutted path back to the village. She recognized Daniel Gillory immediately. Picking up William, she climbed back down the bank. She had not seen Daniel for six weeks. She was confident that she had successfully quenched any fleeting attraction she had felt for him. She waved as he approached.

He skidded to a halt, small fragments of mud flying up from the bicycle's clogged wheels.

'How are you, Daniel?'

'I'm well.' He ruffled William's dark head and threw the bicycle on to the grass. 'I'm glad we've met. I wanted to speak to you.' He paused for a moment, frowning. Then he said, 'I'm leaving Drakesden, Thomasine. I wanted to say goodbye.'

She held William to her, hugging him just a little bit harder. The day, that had seemed bright and sharp, chilled.

'Where are you going, Daniel?'

'To London, first. I can't stay here. Everything reminds me of her.'

Silently, she nodded. 'Of course.'

'I've been left some money. A friend of mine that I lived with for a while in London has died. She was a widow – and she had no children, so you see . . .' His voice trailed away. She could glimpse the bleakness still behind his eyes, and sense the effort it cost him to think about the future.

'I lived with Hattie in Bethnal Green for a couple of years at the beginning of the War. She lent me money to buy the Drakesden land. It was because of Hattie that I was able to marry Fay and get the farm going again. She was a good sort.' Daniel smiled, and then the smile died abruptly. He kicked at the muddy ground. 'Though when I got the letter from her solicitor, I found myself thinking, why not a month or two earlier?'

His voice was harsh. William wriggled out of Thomasine's grasp and squatted at the roadside, playing with some pebbles.

She said gently, 'I don't understand, Daniel.'

'No. Why should you? Nicholas protects you from all that. *Money*, Thomasine – or the lack of it. I found myself thinking, why couldn't Hattie, who'd been through hell from TB for years and years, have died just a few weeks earlier. It wouldn't have made much difference to her, would it? And it might have made all the difference to me. God forgive me for thinking that, but I did.' He looked up at Thomasine and shrugged. 'I couldn't give Fay enough, you see.'

She watched William for a few moments, piling the stones on top of each other, shoving pieces of grass and daisy between the pebbles.

'What will you do, Daniel?'

'I'm going to London. I had a letter this morning – the *Daily Herald*'s accepted an article of mine. And I've Hattie's estate to sort out and then I want to travel. I need to get away.'

'And the farm?'

'Harry Dockerill will manage the farm. He knows the work as well as I do. I wish him joy of it – in another decade most of it will be under water again, I daresay.' His eyes darkened. 'I'd be happy never to see the place again. But I realize that's impossible.'

It occurred to her then that she might never see him again. She flung her arms around him in a spontaneous gesture of affection.

'You look after yourself, Daniel. Make something of yourself. I want to see your name in all the best newspapers. I want to see your name on the jacket of a book.' Hugging him, she heard from behind her the sound of a motor-car coming round the bend in the road.

'*Daddy,*' said William.

'Hell,' said Daniel, and let her go.

She allowed herself just for a moment to hope that Nicholas had not witnessed their embrace. Hope died almost immediately. The Delage had skidded to a halt and Nicholas was jumping over the driver's door, and running towards them, his fists clenched.

'You little swine –' was all he said before he lunged at Daniel.

Thomasine ran to William's side. Daniel had ducked Nicholas's first blow, and was trying to fend off his flailing fists.

'For Christ's sake, Blythe –'

She heard herself shout, 'Stop it, Nicholas! I was saying goodbye to Daniel, that's all –' and Nicholas swung round towards her, his face white with rage.

'I told you not to speak to him, Thomasine. I told you not to!' Then he threw all his weight on Daniel, so that the two of them tumbled to the ground.

She stood watching them for a moment, aware then of a fury that matched Nicholas's own. They were scrabbling on the ground like schoolboys. Nicholas thumped his fist into Daniel's face, Daniel twisted round, desperately trying to free himself. She knew that Daniel would lose, because Daniel, over the past couple of months, had lost the will to fight back. She pressed her face into William's black curls, trying to shut out the sounds.

Eventually they stopped. There was the sound of footsteps, and a hand seized her elbow, dragging her across the road towards the motor-car. Nicholas opened the door. She was pushed into the passenger seat. When she glanced back, Thomasine saw Daniel uncurl himself from the ground and rise, very shakily, to his feet. Then the engine roared into life, and Nicholas shoved his foot down on the accelerator.

He drove towards the village, the motor-car gathering speed with each furious twist of the steering-wheel. Houses and people whirled by, a blur of colour. Thomasine held William tightly against her. Nicholas's knuckles were white, and he did not glance at her once. She shouted out, 'Nicholas – slow down – for pity's sake –' but he did not seem to hear her. She pulled at his sleeve, trying to catch his attention, but he flung off her hand. His right foot was touching the floor.

He was driving too fast to turn through the gates of Drakesden Abbey. The wheels lost their grip as the motor-car skidded, and there was a whirling kaleidoscope of colour. Just before the Delage struck the tree, the passenger door was thrown open and Thomasine and William were hurled out on to the grass.

CHAPTER FIFTEEN

SOMEHOW she had managed to keep hold of him. She was lying on the grass and William was in the crook of her arm. He was lying still, like a rag-doll. She heard herself scream his name, a dreadful high-pitched sound that soared over the roaring of the engine. And then his eyes opened, and he moved, and she began to shake.

She managed to haul herself on to her knees, to hold him against her. She was struggling for breath, and William had begun to cry. She whispered, 'Let me look at you, sweetheart,' and then she ran her hands over his limbs, his fingers and toes, his reddened, tear-stained face.

He had a large graze on his elbow and a bruise on his head, but that was all. She heard a sound from the motor-car. She had forgotten Nicholas. At that moment she did not care whether he lived or died.

But the Delage's engine died at last, and Nicholas murmured, 'Thomasine?'

She staggered to her feet with William in her arms and went to him. Nicholas had climbed out of the motor-car and was standing, his hands resting on the buckled driver's door, staring at her.

He said, 'You're all right. Thank God. Thomasine – I'm so sorry –'

She could not speak to him. She knew, when he flinched and turned away, that her anger was emblazoned in her eyes. With William cradled carefully against her shoulder, she began to walk up the drive to Drakesden Abbey.

Servants stared at her as she entered the house, their shocked eyes taking in her ripped and dirty dress, her tousled hair. She said curtly to the butler, 'Sir Nicholas has crashed the motor-car at the bottom of the drive. You're to send someone to help him.' Then she climbed the stairs to the nursery.

In the nursery she and Martha undressed William, bathed him, dabbed arnica on his bruises, bandaged his elbow. When Martha hesitantly offered the lint and arnica to Thomasine, she shook her head.

'Please feed William and let him rest for ten minutes,' she said to Martha. 'And then dress him in his outdoor things.'

In her own room, Thomasine packed. One small suitcase, she thought. With a baby to carry, she wouldn't be able to take more. A dress, jumper, nightdress, underthings. She could send for the rest later. She wouldn't need the silks and satins, velvets and chiffons.

She threw her toilet-bag into the suitcase, and examined the contents of her handbag. Seven shillings and threepence. Inside Nicholas's study she took a ten-pound note from the safe. She didn't even feel guilty.

Back in her room she pulled on her coat and hat. When she glanced in her mirror to adjust her hat, she saw the bruise on her cheekbone, the scratches around her jaw. She pulled the brim of the cloche hat lower over her face, picked up her suitcase and walked to the nursery.

Martha stared at her when she came into the room. 'I'm going to stay with my aunt,' Thomasine said. Her voice sounded peculiar. 'I'd take you with me, Martha, but I couldn't pay your wages, I'm afraid.'

William was already dressed in his coat, boots and bonnet. She took his hand and led him down the stairs and out of the house. Odd how easy it was, in the end, to escape. She did not walk down the drive, but through the old path: the Labyrinth, the kitchen garden, the orchard. And then through the copse, where the falling leaves mingled with mud on the path.

She heard Nicholas call her name as she reached the stile. She waited patiently for him. When he reached her, she could see the tears in his eyes. She told him where she was going, and why. That she would stay with Antonia, that he had endangered their child's life and she could not allow that. Then she pressed Hilda's letter into his hand, the letter with the name and address of the London psychiatrist. 'When you've consulted him, come and see me,' she said, and helped William over the stile. She knew that she had done the right thing. For Nicholas, as well as for herself and William.

The meadow, the village, the drove. How they all stared. Yet she felt, as she walked out of Drakesden and took the road to Ely, free. Though William, tired, was balanced on her hip, though the suitcase pulled at her aching shoulder, she felt as though she had rid herself of an enormous burden.

A week after the accident, Nicholas was ill. He had two cracked ribs from the impact of the steering-wheel, but it wasn't that. It was the shame, the guilt, the sense of loss, the realization of what he had done.

On the desk in his study he placed the letter that Thomasine had given him. Several times he picked up pen and paper and tried to write. Once, he managed to scribble the address on an envelope. But the knowledge of what he would have to tell this stranger always halted him, and he put the pen aside, his head clutched in his hands.

He was sitting like that when his mother came into the room. He looked up at her, and said, 'I could have *killed* her!' His voice was hoarse and frightened.

Lady Blythe said firmly, 'Nonsense, Nicky. People don't die from a few cuts and bruises.'

'But the *baby* –' Nicholas could not finish his sentence. He recalled, his eyes squeezed shut, a succession of horrors. The thud as the motor-car had struck the tree, the terrible squeal as, too late, he had braked, the jangle of breaking glass. His own sobbing breath as he had leant against the steering-wheel, winded. His realization that the passenger door had burst open. He had believed them both dead.

He heard his mother say, 'The accident was very distressing, Nicky. But one day you may believe, as I do, that it was for the best.'

'*Mama* –'

She silenced him. 'Thomasine has demonstrated to you the extent of her loyalty. She has shown you just how much her marriage vows mean to her. She has shown –' she looked down at him – 'how much she cares for you, Nicky.'

The visions cleared, and Nicholas stared at his mother. The room was dark and silent, the only sounds the ticking of the grandfather clock, the crackle of the flames in the fire. He tried to understand what his mother was saying to him, but his mind, shocked and exhausted, refused to work.

'You have no further obligation to her. I will arrange for Mr Linton to call to discuss the arrangements for a legal separation. And in due course, a divorce. It is distasteful – there has never been a divorce in the family before – but it is unavoidable.'

'Lawyers?' whispered Nicholas. '*Divorce?* You think that I should *divorce* Thomasine?' He tried to rise from the chair, but his mother's palm pressed his shoulder, keeping him in place.

'I think you must, mustn't you? Nicky, Thomasine has left you. She does not want the marriage to continue.'

He understood then, gradually, that his mother was right. He did not blame Thomasine for wanting to be free of him, he did not blame her for hating him. His load of guilt was enormous, crushing him. He had hurt the person he most loved.

He whispered, 'And the child?'

He heard his mother say, 'William will return here, of course, Nicholas. The lawyers will deal with the question of custody. William is a Blythe – there is no question that he will not be brought up at Drakesden Abbey.'

She sat down in the chair opposite him. She was still speaking. He tried to follow what she said, but the effort of concentration was almost beyond him.

'You were very young, Nicky. Not much more than a boy. You made a mistake. Thomasine has acknowledged that, and so must you. You have to let her go. She wants you to let her go.'

Slowly, he nodded. He could not continue to trap Thomasine in a relationship that must only disgust her. To let her go was the decent thing to do.

'We shall make a new start. It will be just like old times, Nicky. Just like it was before the War.'

And yet there Mama was wrong. Before the War, he had been a whole person, a man. Now he was in fragments, the shards flying off all over the place like the shattered windscreen of a car. Nicholas began to shudder, his eyes wide and staring, no longer seeing the grandfather clock, the fire.

Antonia, as charming and as generous as ever, had welcomed both Thomasine and William into her home, exclaiming at their cuts and bruises, providing tea and a warm fire as an antidote to their exhaustion.

She did not ask questions, but Thomasine, when William was tucked up asleep in the room that had once been hers, attempted some sort of an explanation. If Antonia, who had been a conventional and obedient wife during the brief period of her marriage, and who had only permitted herself to rediscover her ambitions on her widowhood, disapproved, then she did not say so.

Thomasine had meant, that first day, to return to her old tasks of helping Antonia with the accounts and the teaching, but instead she woke late, stiff with bruises. William too still slept, curled up beside her. The mark on his forehead reminded her why she was here. She had woken in the middle of the night, panicking and unable to breathe. She had seen clearly the danger of her situation: she was pitting herself against the Blythes, with their money and influence and connections. She recalled a stream of black ink defiling a sheet of white paper, and she thought, staring into the darkness, that Lady Blythe would want vengeance.

Disturbed, she had hugged her son to her, breathing in the sweet smell of his skin, tears pouring down her face.

Fear dissolved with the morning. Thomasine, rising, told herself that Lady Blythe had what she had always wanted: her son. That cold, possessive love had been satisfied at last. And if Nicholas still wanted a wife – if he still wanted his son – then he knew what he must do. Thomasine understood how painful Nicholas would find it to trust a doctor again, but she also knew how vital it was. She hoped that her departure might shock Nicholas into taking that step.

Her flight from Drakesden to London reminded Thomasine of that other flight, almost ten years before. She had acted on impulse then, too, but she had never regretted her decision. As the days passed she was aware of a calmness, a peace of mind that she had thought long ago lost. If, sometimes, she regretted the land, the work she had begun to ensure the survival of the Drakesden estate, then she knew that there was other work to be done. And besides, her achievements had been illusory. There had always been the great immovable obstacle of Nicholas and his mother, a wall of custom and short-sightedness and an inability to change. Now she had control of her own life again. She began to look through the Situations Vacant columns in the newspaper, searching for work that she could do while looking after William.

Lally asked Simon to take her for a second time to the Soho club. Something Simon had said had remained with her, sparking her curiosity. *Why the hurry? Your brother's such a conventional chap, after all*. It occurred to her that Simon was right: Nicholas's hasty marriage to Thomasine Thorne had been utterly out of character.

After the show ended, Lally had the club manager take her to the Eastern dancer's dressing-room. The manager told Lally that the dancer's name was Alice Johnson. Lally knocked on the door and was shown in.

It was a dreadful little room, no larger than a broom cupboard, poorly illuminated by a single naked lightbulb. Two other girls were sharing the room with Miss Johnson. They were pulling combs through their hair, arranging tawdry costumes on coathangers.

Lally smiled. 'How lovely to see you, Alice. I thought I'd just call in.'

Alice Johnson turned round on her stool and looked up. She was still wearing the harem pants, bodice and curly-toed slippers. She had removed her head-dress, and her blonde hair tumbled round her face. Lally realized that Miss Johnson's eyes were not dark, as she had supposed, but blue. The blue had shrunk to a narrow ring around her distended pupils.

'We met in Paris,' added Lally cheerfully.

The other girls gathered up their belongings. 'We'll toddle off now,' said one, 'and leave you in peace. Bye-ee.' The door closed behind them.

'Paris?' Alice said uncertainly.

Lally took out her cigarette-case, and offered it to Alice. 'Yes. We have a mutual friend – don't you remember? Thomasine Thorne.'

'*Thomasine.*' Alice frowned. 'I always wondered. Lost touch. How's the kid? What'd she have?'

The dark, blue-ringed eyes focused hazily on Lally, and Lally felt for a moment utterly confused. *How's the kid? What'd she have?* She thought at first that Alice was referring to Thomasine herself as 'the kid', but no, that was wrong. Then she thought that Alice was talking about William. But that didn't quite fit either. Lally's heart started to pound. Secrets, she thought. Secrets. She watched Alice take a bottle of gin from beneath her tiny dressing-table and slop a measure into two tumblers. Alice was, Lally guessed, very drunk. And not only drunk, perhaps.

A memory flickered into Lally's mind as Alice passed her the tumbler of gin. Thomasine dancing with an actor in the café in Paris.

'Thomasine was awfully friendly with that actor, wasn't she? What was his name?' She dug back into the past. 'Clive, wasn't it?'

'Clive Curran.' Alice scowled into her gin. 'Lots of us were awfully friendly with Clive Curran. The bastard.'

Lally thought rapidly. 'She was having an affair with him, wasn't she?'

For the first time Alice looked wary. 'I wouldn't know.' Turning away from Lally, she began to rub cold-cream into her face.

'Oh, come on,' said Lally. 'You were her friend. I'm just curious, that's all. I'd love to know the details.' She sipped at her gin, which was neat and lukewarm, trying to keep calm. 'He was rather divine. Wouldn't have minded him myself.'

'A bloody disaster in bed, though, darling. Took me ages to realize that. Followed him all the way to Italy, like a fool. Selfish bastard. Only thought of himself.'

Alice was scrubbing away at the cold-cream, wiping it off with a rag. Her voice had become incoherent, mumbling. Any moment now, thought Lally, and she'll pass out and then I'll never know. *How's the kid? What'd she have?* Lally lit herself another cigarette to calm her nerves.

'He left Thomasine in the lurch, didn't he? Got her into trouble, and then upped and went?'

Alice said, 'She told you, then?' Lally's hand, clutching the cigarette-holder, began to shake. In the mirror, Alice's eyes met Lally's, and Alice whispered, 'You didn't know!'

Lally shook her head. 'Not until now.' Her voice was quite calm, but her mind raced, trying to work out the implications of what she had discovered. 'Thomasine married my brother, you see, a few weeks after he met her in Paris. I wonder if he knew about the baby? I wonder what happened to the baby?'

Alice rose from the stool. Bottles, cigarettes and handkerchiefs fell to the floor as she stumbled against the dressing-table.

'I made a mistake. Had too much to drink, love. Got Thomasine mixed up with one of the other girls.'

Lally opened her bag. Inside her purse was a five-pound note and a handful of coins.

'Sit down. I want to know everything, Alice.'

Alice did as she was told. She looked frightened, desperation clearly visible through the alcoholic haze. Lally went to Simon, who was waiting for her in the corridor.

'Give me your money, Simon. All of it. The most amazing thing – don't ask, I'll tell you everything in a while.'

Simon gave her almost thirty pounds. Back in the dressing-room, Lally laid the money in front of Alice.

'There you are. Thirty-five pounds, twelve shillings and ninepence. That would get you out of this dump, wouldn't it, Alice? All you have to do is to tell me all about Thomasine Thorne and Clive Curran.'

There was no reply. Alice was trembling.

Lally added, 'You have to tell me, Alice. If you don't, I'll tell your employer about the drink and stuff. What do you take – is it marijuana or cocaine? I can tell by your eyes, you see. The pupils. Where do you keep it? In your handbag . . . in this drawer . . .?'

Tears were oozing from Alice's blank black eyes.

Lally whispered, 'You wouldn't get a job anywhere. Not even in a hole like this. And then what, Alice? You know what – you've seen the girls in the streets outside. You don't want to end up like those girls, do you, Alice?'

Slowly, Alice shook her head. Then she said tremulously, 'I tried to help her. I really did. But the silly cow wouldn't go through with it.'

She was at the table in the bay window, checking through Antonia's debit ledger, when the motor-car drew up in the road outside. She noticed it because it was an old Daimler, just like the one they had at Drakesden Abbey. When a gloved hand drew the curtain that covered the side windows at the back of the motor-car, Thomasine saw that there were two women inside. One of the women was Lady Blythe.

431

Her heart began to pound. William was squatting in a corner of the room, scribbling with crayons on a piece of scrap paper. Thomasine had to fight an overwhelming, childish urge to grab him and run from the house. Then the front doorbell rang. She heard the maid answer it, and she stood up, smoothing her hair back from her face. The door was opened.

'Lady Gwendoline Blythe,' said the maid nervously.

'Lady Blythe.' Warily, Thomasine nodded her head in greeting to her mother-in-law.

'Gan,' said William, looking up.

'Won't you sit down, Lady Blythe? And Mary shall fetch some tea –'

Both the chair and the tea were refused. Thomasine dismissed the maid.

Lady Blythe had put back her veil. She wore pale mauve, the fashionable colour of the eighteen-nineties. Someone, thought Thomasine, dazed, must have told her years ago how much it suited her.

'Are you here to talk about Nicholas?' she said suddenly. 'Has he been to see the doctor yet?'

Her voice was abrupt, rude, yet she could not stop herself. There was something in that cold, measuring gaze that disturbed her, recalling the unpleasant dreams of her first night in London. She recognized suddenly what that something was. It was *triumph*.

'Nicholas doesn't need a doctor,' said Lady Blythe calmly. 'He just needs rest – peace of mind.'

She said nothing. Futile to try to explain that Nicholas had lost peace of mind long ago, on the battlefield of the Somme, and could not regain it on his own.

Lady Blythe added, 'I have asked Nicholas's solicitor to draw up a Deed of Separation. You should hear from him in a day or two.' The cold eyes focused on Thomasine. There was hatred there, as well as triumph. The mask had slipped permanently now. 'The Deed of Separation will be a precursor to a divorce.

So much better for these things to be on a legal footing, don't you agree?'

'Divorce? Nicholas is asking me for a divorce?'

'I am telling you, Thomasine, that a divorce will be arranged. It is a troublesome and distasteful matter, but it is essential. You are not a suitable person to be married to my son.'

William had left his crayons and was standing at Thomasine's side, tugging at her skirts. For once she did not stoop and pick him up.

The cold blue eyes focused on him. 'And neither are you a suitable person to have custody of a child.'

She said clearly, 'I'll not relinquish William, Lady Blythe. I am his mother.' She would work night and day, if necessary, to pay lawyers to guarantee her claim to her son. Antonia would help her – Hilda would help her. 'I'll not have him brought up at Drakesden. I'll not have him sent away to school when he's still only an infant. I'll not have him consigned to nannies and servants. I'll not have him treated as Nicholas was treated –'

Her voice was low and level, and she knew that the loathing in her eyes reflected the loathing in Lady Blythe's. She bent and put her hand on William's shoulder, holding him protectively to her. His gaze darted nervously from his mother to his grandmother.

'William will be brought up at Drakesden Abbey. He is a Blythe. What have you to offer him, Thomasine?' Lady Blythe glanced scornfully round the small room with its old, clean but commonplace furniture, its clutter of photographs and mementoes, of no value to anyone except their owner. 'You have nothing. You are nothing. If a scullery-maid had behaved like you she would be dismissed without a character.'

She said proudly, 'I left Nicholas because I feared for the safety of my child –' but Lady Blythe interrupted her.

'I say again, you are not a fit person to have custody of a child. Any court in the land would agree with me. I have already consulted lawyers, Thomasine.'

Something cold seemed to be forming inside her, like a lump of ice, beneath her ribs. Lady Blythe had moved towards the vase of lilies on the piano and was adjusting the pale, delicate petals.

'I have been in contact with a young woman called Alice Johnson. I believe that you and she were friends?'

Thomasine stared at her. Appalling possibilities suggested themselves to her; possibilities she could hardly bear to consider. Somehow she managed to say, 'Alice and I attended the same dancing-school.'

'Quite. And she went with yóu to Paris in nineteen-nineteen.'

The fear solidified. The ice pressed against her ribs. Lady Blythe twitched a lily-stem into position.

'Miss Johnson told me that you had a . . . a liaison with an actor in Paris. Also that you conceived this person's child. I do not know, however, what became of the child.'

The older woman's pale face was stained with pink. Flushed with victory, thought Thomasine. Her knees were shaking. She had to lean back against the edge of the table to keep her balance.

'You are silent. Yet you usually have so much to say for yourself. You do not deny it, then?'

She recalled, with horrible vividness, those last few terrible weeks in Paris. Clive's desertion, Nicholas's proposal. Her silence, she knew, was an admission of guilt.

'And the child? Your lover's by-blow? Miss Johnson said that you refused to have the creature aborted. Did you change your mind?'

She managed to speak at last. 'No. I did not change my mind.'

'So you were pregnant when you married my son?'

'Yes.' She stared out of the window at the dull, grey sky, remembering the peculiar brightness of the day when she and Nicholas had driven through the French countryside. The unreality of it all. The sunflowers growing high by the roads, and the dusty heat.

'I had a miscarriage. It just happened. Nicholas never knew. I told him it was the wrong time of the month.'

And Nicholas, who had known almost nothing about women, had believed her, and had turned away with a small sigh of relief, excused the duties of a husband for a few more nights.

'So you intended to pass off another man's child as Nicholas's?'

Momentarily, Lady Blythe reminded Thomasine of Lally. She had never before perceived a similarity between mother and daughter, but now it was there, in the cat-like narrowing of Gwendoline Blythe's cold and curious eyes.

'Yes,' said Thomasine simply. 'But I thought that I loved Nicholas.' Words she was uncertain if Lady Blythe even heard. It would have made no difference, anyway.

'You do see,' continued Lady Blythe, 'that this alters everything?'

The Lally-look had gone, and Lady Blythe was her old self again – magnificent, victorious, intimidating.

Thomasine whispered, 'What do you mean?'

'You do realize, don't you, that no court in the land would give someone like you custody of a child?'

She began, then, to understand why Lady Blythe was here.

'No –'

'I could not leave my grandson in your care.'

Thomasine's gaze darted from the child at her side to the motor-car still parked in the street.

'None of this surprises me,' Lady Blythe continued. 'You were never worthy of my son. You have only confirmed my opinion of you. William shall return to Drakesden.'

Condemnation and punishment were issued in short, staccato phrases.

Thomasine cried out, 'I made a mistake! I was stupid – innocent! I know that it was wrong to deceive Nicholas, but I was desperate. And I knew that he loved me – I thought that I could make him happy –'

435

Lady Blythe's smile was a baring of small, perfect white teeth. '*You* – make Nicholas happy? Never! There was never the smallest chance that you might make Nicholas happy.' Hatred was there, festering beneath that glacial English exterior, those perfect manners and impeccable appearance.

Lady Blythe crossed the room and rapped on the window. The chauffeur climbed out of the Daimler and opened the back door of the car. Now Thomasine recognized the other passenger: the tall, bony figure, the large, raw features, the crisp black dress and white cuffs . . .

'Miss Harper . . . you've brought Miss Harper . . .?'

'So fortunate that Nanny was available, don't you agree, Thomasine? So essential that William is cared for by a professional.'

Antonia's maid had opened the front door to the nanny. Thomasine swung William into her arms, clutching him to her.

'You'll not take him . . . I'll never let you take him . . .'

The door opened. 'A moment,' said Lady Blythe calmly. 'You are to wait in the hall, Miss Harper.'

They were alone in the room again. Lady Blythe said softly, 'I want you to consider what is best for William, Thomasine. I think you understand that you will not, in the end, have custody of him. You would be judged to be morally deficient and capable of both conspiracy and deception. The world would know that you had considered the criminal act of aborting your child.' Lady Blythe paused for a moment, letting her words sink in.

I cannot argue, thought Thomasine desperately. Her instinct was to claw at this woman's face, to drive her physically from the room, to use any means to keep her from her child. And yet she knew that Lady Blythe spoke the truth. Everyone must condemn what she had done.

'You do not dispute that fact. So. You have a choice. You may, if you choose, drag both Nicholas and William through a protracted and sensational court case. Your conduct will be written about in the newspapers for all the world to read. Nicholas is not a farmhand or a labourer, remember, Thomasine, he is a Blythe. Everyone – including William's future schoolfriends – will know that his mother was a fornicator and a liar. They will taunt him – boys can be quite unkind, you know. His schoolmasters will know, his peers will know. His name and, by association, his reputation, will be tarnished long before he reaches adulthood.' She paused. 'Or, there is another way. You may voluntarily give custody of the child to Nicholas. Nicholas will admit to an adulterous relationship with some woman of doubtful reputation – these things are after all so much more forgivable in a man – and William will be spared a great deal of pain. Whichever you choose, the outcome will be the same. William will be brought up at Drakesden Abbey, where he belongs.'

It was a long time before she could speak. Words, images jangled randomly in her head, making no sense.

'Would you leave me for five minutes, Lady Blythe?'

A small nod of the head. 'I know you will be sensible, Thomasine.'

When the door had closed behind Lady Blythe, she sat down in an armchair, William on her knee. At first she could not speak, but just gazed at him. She did not need to learn his features, though: she knew them by heart. Then at last she whispered, 'Would you like to go for a ride in the motor-car, William, with Gan? Would you like to see Daddy?'

William clapped his hands together and bounced on her lap, straining to pull away from her. He loved the motor-car. She only knew that there were tears streaming down her face when William pulled her handkerchief from her pocket, and dabbed with careful clumsy concentration at her eyes. Then she pulled him to her, and whispered, 'Be a good boy, William. Don't forget me,' and she rose to her feet.

She packed his bag herself. She made sure that Nanny Harper understood that Rabbit was necessary for William to sleep, that

William didn't like milk pudding or kidneys, that his book of Grimm's fairy tales frightened him too much.

When they had gone, she sat on the bottom stair, her head buried in her hands. The hallway was filled with an awful low moaning noise, and it was a while before she understood that it was herself, weeping for the loss of her son.

Returning to his Bayswater lodgings after attending a stormy political meeting, Daniel was waylaid by his landlady on entering the house.

'You've a visitor, Mr Gillory. I've put her in the parlour.'

Daniel went into the ground-floor parlour. Although it was only mid-afternoon, the day was already darkening, necessitating the use of electric lights. A woman was standing in the bay window, staring out through the net curtains at the dusky street. At first Daniel did not recognize her. Then, when she turned towards him, he said incredulously, 'Miss Harker!'

'Daniel. How lovely to see you.' Hilda Harker came out of the shadows and offered Daniel her hand.

He found that he was smiling. It was years since he had seen Hilda Harker but she had not, he thought, changed at all. Perhaps the mid-calf-length skirts were some concession to modernity, and under the shapeless felt hat he could see that her brown hair was cropped to chin-length and peppered with grey, but otherwise she looked just the same.

'I don't know what to say.' He stared at her, a ghost from his past. 'I feel I should be wearing my school uniform, and you should be explaining sonnet form to me. Will you have tea, Miss Harker? Mrs Black is very proud of her baking.'

He noticed then, the worried look in her eyes, and the mud and damp on her shoes. He said gently, 'You should sit down, Miss Harker, and warm yourself by the fire.'

'Yes. Of course. So impolite of me.' She sat down, and Daniel, throwing his notebook, pen and scarf on to a settee, ran to the kitchen to ask his landlady for refreshments.

When he returned, Hilda Harker was spreading out her fingers to the fire. She looked up as Daniel came back.

'I obtained your address from Harry Dockerill, Daniel. I went to Drakesden, you see.' She paused for a moment, and then she added, 'I was so sorry to hear about your wife. Such a dreadful thing to happen. How you must miss her.'

He bowed his head. Since leaving Drakesden, he had made sure always to keep very, very busy. If he was busy, then he was all right, he kept going. There were, of course, certain parts of London he had to avoid, like Hyde Park and Kensington, just as there were photographs he could not look at, and snatches of verse he dare not recall. But he was teaching himself the art of getting through each day, each night.

Just now Fay's face was replaced momentarily by a different face: red hair, green eyes sparkling with laughter.

'You went to Drakesden,' he said encouragingly to Hilda, 'to see Thomasine?'

Hilda had poured out the tea. Her hand paused in the act of stirring in the sugar. 'Not really – it was a rather forlorn hope . . .'

Daniel was confused. 'Have the Blythes left Drakesden?'

'I do apologize, Daniel. I'm not explaining this at all well.' Hilda put aside the sugar basin and sat up straight, her hands folded in her lap. 'Thomasine is *missing*. I simply don't know where she is. I thought perhaps you could help me find her.'

Anger was replaced by bewilderment. *'Missing?'* he repeated.

Hilda managed a small, watery smile. 'If one of my pupils were explaining matters as poorly as I, then I would tell her to take a deep breath, marshal her thoughts and start again. Well, then.' She paused, her lips folded together, eyes closed.

'That's better.' She tried to smile. 'I don't know if you are aware, Daniel, that I am the headmistress of a small school in Yorkshire. I share the responsibility of running the school with a gentleman. Robert and I are soon to marry.'

Daniel blinked. 'Congratulations, Miss Harker.'

439

'Thank you, Daniel.' Hilda passed Daniel his teacup, and then sighed. 'Thomasine left Nicholas several weeks ago. The marriage had been in difficulties for some time, I'm afraid. She took William with her, and went to stay with my sister Antonia in London. She seemed quite happy there. And then, a fortnight ago, she left. Quite suddenly, and without the child. Antonia's maid said that an older lady had called and had driven away with William. From the girl's description, Antonia and I concluded that the woman was Lady Blythe. Thomasine had not left a note – anything – to indicate where she has gone. Just packed her bags and left. Antonia telephoned me in Yorkshire. We waited a while, but there was no letter, no telephone call. So last weekend, I decided to go to Drakesden.' Hilda shook her head. 'I spoke to Lady Blythe. She would not let me see Nicholas. She was not helpful, Daniel – in fact, she was quite rude. She told me that Thomasine had agreed to let Nicholas divorce her. And that Nicholas is to have custody of the little boy.'

Something in Hilda seemed to crumble and almost collapse. The fighting light present in her eye ever since Daniel had known her, which he recognized also in her niece, seemed to dim and die.

Daniel said gently, 'Drink your tea, Miss Harker. I'm sure things can't be as bad as they seem.'

He went to the window and, moving the net curtain aside, stared out. The drizzle had thickened to fog, yellow and opaque. He could not immediately absorb the impact of Hilda's news. His mind, always efficient and analytical, flicked it over, but failed to take it in.

He heard Hilda say, 'Thomasine and I have had our differences over the past years. And I never approved of her marriage to Nicholas. But to think that she would *divorce* him . . . to think that she would abandon her child . . . I cannot believe it. I cannot.'

And neither could Daniel. It did not fit with the Thomasine

he knew. He tried to be practical. 'You said that you thought I might be able to help you, Miss Harker.'

'Yes. It is presumptuous of me, I know. Harry Dockerill explained that you were working for a newspaper, Daniel.'

'No specific newspaper,' said Daniel. 'I'd have to put in a bit more legwork before I can do that. But I've done a couple of pieces for the *Daily Herald*. Part of a series on the election.' The election was in just over a week's time. 'It should be an interesting contest,' he added. 'They're calling it the "Tariff Election". At the meeting I just attended, Mr Lloyd George was telling the crowd that if the Tories win again, we'll only be able to afford to eat tinned salmon – everything else will be taxed. Except wheat, of course. We'll still be importing foreign wheat.'

As he had intended, some of the anxiety died from Hilda's eyes and was replaced by interest. She had drunk her tea, eaten a slice of cake.

'And you, Daniel,' she said. 'Would it be impudent of me to enquire your opinion?'

'Oh, I shall vote for Ramsay MacDonald,' said Daniel. 'We've had every combination of Liberal and Tory since the War, and there's still over a million men out of work. I think it's time for a change.'

'I agree, Daniel,' said Hilda Harker firmly. 'I, too, shall vote for Mr MacDonald. My father would turn in his grave, but . . .'

Daniel grinned. 'I always thought you were a Red. Underneath that respectable exterior beats the heart of a Socialist.' He had come to sit down opposite her. He said curiously, 'What makes you think that Thomasine is in London?'

'Without William she must have been so unhappy. Isn't London a good place in which to hide when you are unhappy, when you wish to be alone?'

Daniel himself had more than once used London as a hiding-place, retreating to its darker corners, sheltered by its anonymity. He said carefully, 'If Thomasine wishes to be left alone, Miss Harker, then perhaps you should respect that wish.'

She was silent for a long time. Then she said, 'Daniel – I am *frightened* for her,' and he looked at her and nodded.

'I'll do what I can, but it may take a while. Give me your telephone number, Miss Harker, and I'll contact you as soon as I have any news.'

When she left Antonia's house, Thomasine had no idea where she was going. She had six pounds in her purse, the remainder of the ten pounds she had taken from Drakesden Abbey's safe. She found a jeweller and sold all the jewellery she possessed. A necklace, an art deco brooch, her engagement and wedding rings. Then she began to look for somewhere to stay. Taking the Tube, she travelled into the centre of London. She avoided the sort of places she and Nicholas had frequented: Mayfair, Chelsea, Knightsbridge. Those were for other people now. Getting off the train at Camden Town, she walked until she saw a grimy card pasted in the window of a house: 'Rooms to Let'. She knocked, and went in.

Inside, the temporary surge of energy left her and she was overcome by misery and despair. She didn't spend much, because she didn't eat much. She lost count of the days, because they all melded into each other, grey and indistinguishable. Great events in the world passed her by. She read the result of the General Election on the newspaper hoarding, but it seemed unimportant, of no interest to her. She bought a newspaper and scanned the Situations Vacant columns, but neither wrote nor telephoned to enquire after work.

She bought herself an iced bun one day, out shopping for thread to darn her stockings. She knew that things were sliding out of control: that her hair needed washing, that her stockings were holed, her sweater grubby. Forcing herself to eat, she recalled William, screaming with laughter as she fed him fragments of icing from his birthday cake. She abandoned the bun; tears trailed from her eyes. There was a knock at the door.

When she opened it, she thought at first she was dreaming.

She had expected her landlord, come to collect the week's rent; instead, Daniel Gillory stood there.

'Can I come in?' asked Daniel.

Thomasine stood aside, and watched him step inside the small room. He was real, then. Her tired mind had not muddled up past and present and conjured him to Camden, out of place, out of time.

'Why are you here, Daniel?'

'I was looking for you. Your Aunt Hilda was worried about you.'

'Oh.' She frowned, and sat down on the bed by the window. There was one chair, and a bed, and a rather rickety table.

'I've been looking for you for the last fortnight,' Daniel added. 'A girl with red hair. I asked in all the pubs.'

'You shouldn't have. You should have left me alone.'

'Are you ill?'

She shook her head. 'No. Just tired.'

There was a silence. She resented Daniel's sudden intrusion into her solitude. She wanted him to leave.

'Miss Harker told me that you are divorcing Nicholas.'

She looked up at him. His expression was neutral: neither critical nor victorious. 'Yes. Or Nicholas is divorcing me. I'm not sure of the details.'

'And the child?'

'Nicholas will have custody of William. He will remain at Drakesden.'

So easy to say, yet so hard to believe ... that she would not see her son again, or would see him only on occasional visits, too brief for any true involvement.

'That is your *choice?*'

Suddenly she felt angry. The first real emotion, apart from misery and regret, that she had experienced for weeks.

'No. Of course it's not my choice. I had no choice.'

He was still scowling. 'Is it money?' he said suddenly. 'I have money, Thomasine – Hattie's money. I can give you some, if you need lawyers –'

443

'I don't need money. It wouldn't make any difference.'

She saw suddenly that she was going to have to explain to him. That he would not leave, that he would nag her, worrying at her as a cat worries a fallen bird until she told him the truth.

'Lady Blythe found out that I was pregnant when I married Nicholas,' she said baldly. 'Pregnant with someone else's child.'

She saw his eyes, that familiar mixture of green and gold, open wide. *'Christ,'* he whispered.

Her anger increased. 'I was very young, and very stupid. When I went to Paris after the War, I knew *nothing*. I thought babies were found under gooseberry bushes, and I thought marriage meant putting a ring on your finger. None of my aunts had explained anything to me. Hilda and Rose probably didn't know much more than I did, and Antonia believed that innocence itself was a protection. And the other girls in the chorus thought of me as a baby . . . Antonia's naïve little niece.' She looked up at him. 'Innocence didn't help me at all, Daniel. Not one bit.'

He was frowning, running his hands through his untidy hair. He had, as always, a slightly unkempt look. 'So you met someone?'

'An actor. He was in the same show. I fell madly in love with him, worshipped the ground he walked on.' She could hear the bitterness in her voice. 'I would have done anything for him. Do you understand?'

For a moment he looked away, and she recalled that he, too, grieved.

'Yes. I understand.'

'Do you? It's different for men, isn't it, Daniel? Different rules. Anyway, my lover promised to marry me, and then ran away overnight to Marseilles. One of the girls offered to arrange an abortion. But I couldn't go through with it.'

She could see that her words shocked him. That his picture of good, capable Thomasine Thorne was crumbling. She did not let up: she wanted to hurt someone – Daniel Gillory – anyone.

444

'So when Nicholas asked me to marry him, I accepted. A lousy thing to do, wasn't it, Daniel? Anyway, I lost the baby – miscarried on my wedding night. Nicholas never knew.'

She half expected him to walk out of the room, there and then. But he did not. Instead, he came and sat down on the bed next to her. He said nothing, only laid his fingers over her clenched fist so that eventually her muscles relaxed and her fingers uncurled.

She whispered, 'Don't you hate me?'

'No. How could I?'

She saw that he was speaking the truth. She felt Daniel pull her towards him. As she cried, he stroked her head.

'Poor old thing. You've had a rotten time.'

Eventually she said, 'Your shirt's all wet. And I haven't washed my hair for weeks,' and she sat up, blowing her nose on the handkerchief he held out to her.

'So Lady Blythe found out about the actor?'

'Yes. God knows how – it doesn't matter, does it? She told me that there wasn't a court in the land that would give me custody of William, if they knew what I had done. And she was right, wasn't she?'

He nodded. She could see the pity in his eyes. 'I suppose so. But will Nicholas allow Lady Blythe . . .?'

'Nicholas will do whatever his mother tells him to do, Daniel. He always has done. Or maybe he was different before the War. I don't know.'

Daniel was frowning. Thomasine said flatly, 'Nicholas suffers from neurasthenia. He can't settle to anything – he needs to keep busy. Then he's all right. Drakesden was hopeless for him. Too much time to think and brood. And I thought I could help him, but I couldn't.'

She blew her nose loudly. She had been through it all, over and over again, lying awake at night through these last awful weeks, and had come every time to the same conclusion. That for now, she was beaten.

'I'll have to write to Hilda and Antonia, I suppose. Tell them the truth.'

She stood up, her arms folded round her. Outside, the clouds had parted a little to show patches of blue.

'Put on your coat. I'm taking you out for lunch. You don't look as though you've had a decent meal for weeks.'

'I'm such a sight. My eyes . . . my hair . . .'

'You've a hat,' he said unsympathetically. 'And we'll go to some nice, poky pub, where no one will notice that you've been crying.' He held out her coat for her, and she stood, hesitating.

'You bullied me into living again once, Thomasine,' he reminded her. 'Now I'm doing the same to you.'

They went to a pub by Camden Lock, and Daniel ordered steak pie and potatoes and glasses of stout. Daniel talked, distracting her.

'I've been writing articles about the election. Now that Ramsay MacDonald's in Number Ten, I'll do a few more – first socialist Prime Minister, the agenda for change, that sort of thing. Not that I think there will be much of a change – Asquith's pulling the strings, after all. I wouldn't be surprised if there was another election within the year. And in the spring, I'm going to travel.'

The food and the beer warmed her. The pub was cramped and busy. Daniel had chosen a seat near the window.

Thomasine put down her glass. 'Where, Daniel?'

'Anywhere. I've got to get away, and I've only been abroad to fight. I can't bear England just now. It feels so small, so dingy. Besides, I need to read . . . and to write. To see things. Sometimes I feel so bloody ignorant. It would be good to see a bit more of France than mud and trenches. And then there's Spain, Italy . . . Germany, perhaps.'

'Paris was lovely,' she said, remembering.

He said nothing for a while. She knew that he still grieved, that sorrow and regret were visible every now and then behind the energy and hopes for the future. We are both bruised and battered, she thought. She pulled her coat round her, as cold as if she was outside in the icy December wind.

'It beat me in the end,' said Daniel slowly. 'The land. It destroyed Fay, and it almost destroyed me. I don't think I'll ever want to go home again.'

She drew her finger along the condensation on the inside of the window-pane and drops of water trailed down the glass, like tears.

'And you, Thomasine? What will you do?'

She took a deep breath. 'Oh, I shall find work,' she said. 'And I shall earn money. And I shall get my son back.' She repeated, almost to herself, 'I'm going to get him back, Daniel. I don't know how, but I'm going to get him back.'

PART FOUR

1926−1927

Fear no more the lightning-flash
Nor the all-dreaded thunder-stone:
Fear not slander, censure rash;
Thou hast finish'd joy and moan.
All lovers young, all lovers must
Consign to thee, and come to dust.

(William Shakespeare, *Cymbeline*)

CHAPTER SIXTEEN

THE cage hurtled downwards into the mine – thirty, forty, fifty miles an hour. The only light was the glow of the Davy-lamps. When the cage slowed and then shuddered to a halt, the men climbed out.

Daniel followed them. His ears were bursting and he had left his stomach behind at the pit-head. He managed to ask, 'How far are we below ground?'

'About four hundred yards.'

Daniel scribbled the figure down in his notebook, and tried not to think about it. He looked around him, his eyes slowly accustoming themselves to the poor light. He was standing in what appeared to be a small room cut from the rock. Most of the men with whom he had shared the cage had already disappeared down the passages that led from the room: only Jem Harris remained beside him.

'Is this where you work?'

Jem's grin was a flicker of white teeth in the darkness. 'Not yet. We've a little way to go, lad. Follow me.' He began to walk down one of the passages.

Daniel realized, after he had walked only a hundred yards or so, that not only did his claustrophobia make him unsuitable for mines, so did his height. He guessed, with a sense of humiliation, that Jem, ten years his senior, was slowing his pace to suit his own. Yet he could walk no faster, because the roof of the passage down which he travelled sunk steadily lower. Several times he struck his head on one of the beams that supported the ceiling. In a sense, the physical pain was welcome, because it distracted his thoughts. *Four hundred yards underground.* Above him was an incalculable weight of stone and earth. The air was hot and dusty, but he made himself breathe slowly. He would be underground for the length of Jem's shift – seven hours plus travelling time. He simply could not afford to panic.

The roof of the tunnel dipped even more, and Daniel was forced to crouch, his back and knees bent in an agonizing position. His eyes fixed on the dim gleam of Jem's Davy-lamp, his only thought was to keep going, for his muscles not to lock in their unnatural position so that he collapsed, shamed, to the ground. When, for a short distance, the height of the tunnel was raised by the rubble of an old roof-fall, it was a pleasure simply to be able to stand upright. He forgot that he was four hundred yards underground, and savoured the release from cramp.

But the relief was only temporary. Soon he was crouching again and then, for fifty yards or so, crawling through the passageway on hands and knees. The fragments of coal and shale on the ground tore his skin to shreds, but it seemed preferable to move this way than in that awful Neanderthal position. When, finally, they drew to a halt, Daniel discarded pride and collapsed to the floor, shaking. His shudders were not due to fear, though, but to exhaustion.

'How far . . .?' he managed to say.

'Oh, that were only about half a mile. Not a bad distance. Some of t'men have to travel three mile or more.'

Jem had already seized his pick and set to work. Because of the stifling heat he wore only breeches, clogs, gloves and knee-pads. The noise of the pick in the cramped corridor was appalling. Even more appalling to Daniel was the fact that the miner worked kneeling, so that all the work of wielding the pick was done by his arms and torso. Daniel tried to imagine digging trenches without the assistance of his legs to force the shovel into the earth, or pulling a bog oak from the soil with only his arms and back. He had never before, in all his twenty-seven years, felt physically feeble, but now, looking at the troll-like figure before him hewing coal from the rock, the muscles in his shoulders like gleaming knots of ebony, he felt effete, pampered. Carefully, and with hands that still trembled from exhaustion, Daniel took his notebook and pen out from inside his shirt.

When, more than seven hours later, he was released into the open air again, Daniel was aware of an intoxicating rush of freedom. Relieved, too, that he had survived eight hours underground without making too much of a fool of himself. Even the bleak Leeds landscape with its slag heaps and smoke and chimneys looked, for a moment, beautiful.

Jem's house, one in a row of back-to-backs, was a short omnibus ride from the pit. The April sky, viewed through the muddy windows of the bus, was a smooth flat blue, marred only by the smoke that belched from the chimneys. They had gone down the mine at half past five in the morning, when the sky was still misty and purple-grey. The alteration from chill dawn to spring sunlight seemed to Daniel miraculous.

They spoke little until they had eaten. Jem's wife, small and tired-looking, but neatly dressed, served them bacon and cabbage and potatoes. Daniel discovered that he was ravenous.

'Tha' looks a bit less green, lad,' said Jem, when they had finished.

Daniel grinned apologetically. 'I'd hoped it was hidden by the coal-dust.'

The tea was poured out. Jem said, 'There's nowt to be ashamed of. Some of us are used to hard work, and some of us aren't.'

It was as though he had been set a test, which he had failed. Daniel felt an illogical urge to justify himself.

'I was a farmer until two and a half years ago. And before that I was in the Army.'

Jem remained unimpressed. 'But you write stories now.'

Daniel, stirring sugar into his tea, smiled and resigned himself to being thought of as soft. 'I don't write stories. I write about what I see. I've written about agricultural labouring – it's what I know about. I've been tramping round Europe for the last couple of years, seeing whether they do things better there. But I'm going to write a piece about mining now.'

Jem's wife had set a bowl of hot water on the table. More water was heating on the copper. Jem scowled and plunged his hands into the bowl.

'What do you think?' asked Daniel curiously. 'Will it come to a strike?'

'Wait till Friday, lad, and find out. Only it won't be a strike, it'll be a lockout. If t'Miners' Federation don't accept wages t'owners' offer, then they'll lock us out of t'pits.'

'The mine-owners haven't made an offer yet, have they?'

Jem shook his head. Mrs Harris began to clean his coal-blackened back with a flannel. Daniel thought through the events of the past year. In the summer of 1925, the second summer Daniel had spent abroad, the Mining Association, representing the owners of over a thousand mining companies throughout the country, had given notice that they intended to terminate the existing agreements on miners' hours and wages. A Court of Enquiry had met and had made recommendations, largely favourable to the miners, concerning wages and the reorganization of the mines. The pit-owners had refused the Court of Enquiry's recommendations. The situation that the Conservative Government had always feared had emerged from the squabbling and bitterness: that the transport and rail unions would back any measures the miners might choose to take, should they be asked by their employers to accept lower wages. The Conservative Prime Minister, Stanley Baldwin, had taken the step of staving off trouble by paying a subsidy to the miners for nine months, while the Enquiry continued.

Jem was drying himself with a towel. Daniel said, 'The subsidy runs out at the end of this week, doesn't it, Jem?'

'Aye. Last day of April.'

'So the Mining Association will have to make its offer by then?'

454

Jem nodded and pulled his shirt over his head. The water in the bowl in front of him was black with coal-dust. 'Let me show you something, lad.' He rose, and went to a chest of drawers.

'Let the lad have a wash first, Jem,' said Mrs Harris.

'In a while, woman, in a while.' Jem thrust several pieces of paper on the table in front of Daniel. 'Tell 'em about these in your writing.'

The pieces of paper were wage-slips. Daniel studied the figures carefully. The sum paid to the miner per week, the deductions for the sharpening of his tools, the hire of the Davy-lamp, the Union fees.

Daniel said slowly, 'You're lucky if you clear two pounds a week.'

Jem pulled a comb through his short greying hair. 'I don't work every week, mind. In the summer there's often lay-offs.'

Jem had a wife and four children, the youngest of whom was at that moment in the back yard, admiring Daniel's Royal Enfield motor-cycle. Daniel tried to imagine feeding a family of six on less than two pounds a week. He had seen the effects of that sort of poverty in the Fens: the poorest agricultural labourers might be able, unlike the miners, to give their children fresh air, but bare feet, empty bellies and susceptibility to disease were common to both.

'And the Mining Association's talking of wage-cuts of . . .?'

'Up to twenty-seven per cent in some places. T'men would be better off on t'dole!' Jem's voice was bitter.

Mrs Harris placed a bowl of clean water in front of Daniel. He began to sluice off some of the coal-dust.

'Royalties have to be paid to the landowners, don't they? And all the pits are in competition with each other.'

'Aye. So Yorkshire Main undercuts Ashington, and the Manchester Collieries undercut Butterley, and so on. And Lord So-and-so who owns t'land above mine must have his piece of profit.'

'I went down a mine in Germany, Jem. It was so different. There was machinery to do a lot of the heavy work – automatic picks and coal-cutters – underground trains to take the miners to the places where they worked. No crawling along tunnels, which –' Daniel glanced at the pay-slips again – 'you don't get paid for.'

The water in front of Daniel was now black. Yet he still felt dirty, as though the coal-dust had ingrained itself into his skin. The small kitchen, which must be grimy with coal-dust five days of the week, was spotless, though. He could only guess at the amount of scrubbing and polishing that entailed.

Daniel stood up, buttoning his shirt. 'So what do you think, then, Jem? Do you think it'll come to a General Strike?'

'We'll see, lad, we'll see.' Jem shrugged, but his eyes were grim.

Daniel glanced out of the window. 'I'll give young Jimmy a spin on the bike, Mrs Harris. That'll keep him out of your hair for a while. And then I'll buy you a drink, if I may, Jem.'

In her lunch hour Thomasine went to see Mr Gibson, of Gibson, Paul and Gibson. Gibson, Paul and Gibson were lawyers who had made a reputation for themselves in the field of divorce law. After waiting in a glossy anteroom, watched over by a superior secretary, she was shown into Mr Gibson's office.

'Ah, Lady Blythe.' Mr Gibson, who was tall and thin and grey, and who wore a morning suit over a wing-collared shirt, held out his hand.

'Miss Thorne, if you please, Mr Gibson. I have reverted to my maiden name since my divorce.'

'Ah.' Mr Gibson sat down behind his desk and pressed the tips of his outstretched fingers together. Here is the church, here is the steeple, thought Thomasine. How many times had she recited that rhyme to William?

'As I said to you on the telephone, Miss Thorne, I have read your letter.' Mr Gibson indicated the piece of paper that lay on the desk in front of him. 'Your situation does not look – ah – hopeless. But there are a few points I am not quite – ah – clear about.'

His smile was a crinkling of the muscles around his mouth, but his eyes remained grey, cold, uninterested. Thomasine took a deep breath.

'I couldn't explain everything in my letter. There were things that weren't mentioned at the Divorce Courts. I must have your assurance that what I am about to tell you is strictly confidential.'

'Naturally, Miss Thorne.'

She explained, clearly and emotionlessly, about Clive and her first pregnancy and her marriage to Nicholas and the miscarriage. She could not detect disgust in Mr Gibson's eyes, as she had detected disgust in the eyes of some of the other lawyers, merely a glassy disinterest.

When she had finished, he was silent. Then he said, 'There is really nothing I can do for you, Miss Thorne. Nothing at all.'

Her heart began to pound. She never intended to invest hope in these interviews, but somehow she always did.

'Surely there is *something*, Mr Gibson. If not now, then perhaps in the future –'

'Miss Thorne.' The steepled hands folded and spread out in a gesture of resignation. 'You considered – ah – aborting a child, which is illegal, of course. A skilled lawyer might imply that you *had* in fact aborted that child. He would also point out that you had led an – ah – immoral life. In addition, any judge must be swayed by the fact that you intended to – ah – profess your lover's child to be, in fact, your husband's. You married, after all, into an old and respected family. I am sorry, Miss Thorne, but there really is nothing I can do for you. I am afraid you must reconcile yourself to the loss of your son.'

He had risen from his seat. Thomasine, too, rose. In spite of the spring warmth of the day, she felt cold. The lawyer opened the door for her.

As she stepped back into the anteroom, she said suddenly, 'Mr Gibson. If you cannot help me, then perhaps you could recommend someone who might be able to. I really can't reconcile myself to losing William. I just can't.'

The lawyer looked down his long, thin nose at her. If there was not disgust in those eyes then there was, thought Thomasine, distaste.

But he said, 'You could try Sir Alfred Duke. He has had some surprising successes with the – ah – *stickier* type of case. You could approach him, I suppose. If, that is' – again, that grimacing smile – 'the revolution does not take place next week.'

She could not at first think, and nor did she care, what he meant. But as she walked back to the store in which she worked in the accounts department, Thomasine noticed the headlines on the newspaper hoardings: 'Miners' lockout looms', 'Fear of General Strike'. She hurried past the newsboys; she was late.

After the department store had closed, she walked home. Mostly she caught an underground train or omnibus, but tonight she wanted to think. Besides, the air was soft and warm: spring seemed to have found its way even to London. As she walked, she tried to remember how much she had in her savings account. She refused to believe that she would be, yet again, wasting her hard-earned money. 'Sir Alfred Duke.' She said the name out loud, ignoring the stares of passers-by. It sounded honest, reliable, imposing. Surely Sir Alfred Duke would be able to help her.

It was almost eight o'clock when she reached her lodgings. She had moved to better lodgings within a couple of months of coming to live in Camden Town. The first, awful place had not been big enough to store her clothes and possessions. She had the wardrobe of a duchess, she had thought, staring at the boxes that had been sent from Drakesden, and the dwelling-place of a factory-girl. She had sold most of the furs, but kept the evening-dresses, hanging them in the wardrobe, wrapped in brown paper and mothballs. They hung there still, remnants of a different life. Sometimes, when she needed to remember that other life, she opened the wardrobe and breathed in the scents of the silks, the satins and velvets.

The street outside her lodging-house was busy. Housewives stood in the doorways and talked to each other, children played hopscotch in the street and men in cloth caps and shirt-sleeves lounged outside the pub. A young man with a motor-cycle was waiting outside her lodgings. The evening sunlight gleamed on his tow-coloured hair.

Thomasine felt, as she always did at Daniel's infrequent re-appearances, a mixture of irritation and pleasure. Pleasure because he was always good company, irritation because he invariably expected her to drop everything and rearrange her life to fit in with some scheme of his. She smiled, though, as she approached him.

'Daniel. What a surprise. How was Italy?'

'Too many uniforms for my taste. Mussolini's boys enjoy flexing their muscles.' He bent his head and kissed Thomasine on the cheek.

'When did you get back?'

'A fortnight ago. I've been in Yorkshire, scaring myself witless down coal-mines.' He looked tanned, healthy and confident.

'Coal-mines? Why coal-mines?'

'Because, my dear Thomasine, the miners are about to precipi-tate the most widespread strike this country's ever seen. The offer the mine-owners came up with this morning involves cutting wages by thirteen per cent and adding an hour to the working day. Some of the more rabid Tory gentlemen – Mr Churchill, for instance – are predicting a revolution.'

She laughed. 'That's ridiculous. Look around you.'

Daniel glanced down the street and grinned. 'I know what you mean. The dispossessed proletariat don't exactly look ready for battle. But something's going to happen. If the lockout begins tonight, and the TUC and the Government don't manage to sort something out, there'll be no buses or trains on Tuesday.'

'Then I'll walk to work.' Thomasine had put aside her basket and sat down on the front doorstep.

'Still at the sweatshop?'

'The select department store, if you don't mind, Daniel. Yes.' Proudly, she glanced at him. 'I'm chief clerk now. Not bad for a woman who's committed the double sin of being first married and then divorced.'

'They recognized gold when they saw it. Congratulations, Thomasine.' He gave her a quick hug. 'The money's rotten, I suppose?'

She shrugged, her eyes turned towards the children playing hopscotch. 'With the extra I get from teaching, I can make it up to the same as a male clerk's wages. So it's not too bad.'

'Teaching?'

'Dancing. I've started to take a few pupils in the evenings and at weekends – little ones, mostly. Mrs Price lets me use her front parlour. For a small fee, of course. She thinks it gives the place a touch of class.'

'And William?' Daniel's voice was gentle.

'I've seen him once a month since the divorce was finalized. Nicholas comes down to London and brings Nanny and William with him, and William and I have an afternoon together. We go to the park, or I take him to tea. I took him to a picture house last month, Daniel. He thought it was wonderful.'

There was a silence. Thomasine's eyes focused on the smallest boy playing hopscotch, the slender dark-haired one, who looked a bit like William. Only he wasn't like William at all, really. No one was like William.

She looked up at Daniel. 'Anyway,' she said brightly, 'how long are you here for? Five minutes – two days? Have we time for a sandwich or a cup of tea?'

He looked only slightly abashed. 'I have to dash now. But I'm taking you out tomorrow night. You're to wear a party dress . . . something glittery . . .' He added irritably, 'My book came out a few days ago. The publisher's putting on some sort of a bash.'

'Oh, Daniel. You'll be dining with Lady Ottoline Morrell next. Weekends at Garsington.'

He scowled. 'Rot. I suppose I ought to go, though. What do you think?'

She cried, exasperated, 'Daniel! Of course you must go! It would be terribly rude of you not to.'

'I suppose so.' He had crossed the pavement to the Enfield, and was kicking the starter. 'It just seems such a waste of time at the moment. Still. Eight o'clock, then. I'll pick you up.' The motor-cycle's engine roared into sound and the children scattered back to the pavement, their eyes wide.

She called, 'Not on that thing!' but he was already gone, round the corner, out of sight. Thomasine picked up her basket and fitted her key to the lock and let herself into the lodging-house.

It was strange, choosing a dress for the party. Like leafing back through an old diary. The chiffon dress with the crystals that she had worn to the Mayfair party where someone had thrown a stone through the window, the sleeveless velvet she had worn at the New Forest picnic. The pistachio green silk in which she had received the guests for William's christening, and the delphinium blue in which she had forayed into Bohemia. The Fortuny gown in which she had been married, a shimmer of sea-green pleats. At the Probate, Divorce and Admiralty Division of the High Court she had worn a high-collared coat and a hat pulled low over her brow. As though she was trying to make herself invisible.

She returned the Fortuny dress to its brown paper and took out a chiffon frock. It was pale apricot, ornamented with a soft multicoloured flower design and trimmed with a long and floating handkerchief hemline. It had always been one of her favourites. It was, she thought, one of the few dresses that suited a red-head best. When she slipped it on, she felt for a moment young and free and adventurous, as though anything might happen. She had not felt like that for years. The silver beading sewn on to the chiffon clung to her hips, emphasizing her slenderness.

She had only time to check her face quickly in the mirror before Mrs Price called up the stairs, 'Miss Thorne! There's a gentleman to see you!' Then she grabbed a shawl and her bag and left the room. Daniel was waiting outside. His eyes lightened as she emerged out of the hallway.

'Stunning. What amazing stuff – like cobwebs. You'll need a jumper, though.'

Thomasine groaned. She had forgotten the wretched motor-cycle. 'I'll wrap my shawl round me. I really can't go to a smart party wearing a woolly jumper over a chiffon frock.'

In the end, she wore Daniel's dinner jacket and stuffed the silk scarf into her bag. The ride to the Bloomsbury house was fast, exhilarating and inelegant. The handkerchief hemline of the chiffon dress hung dangerously close to the wheels of the motor-cycle and had to be tied out of the way. My stockings, thought Thomasine, as they swung round corners, zoomed through alleyways. Yet she felt safe, secure. Daniel never drove faster than conditions safely allowed.

'That was the easy bit,' said Daniel, as they drew to a halt outside a tall, white-painted house. 'Sit still. I'll untangle you.'

The handkerchief hemline was sorted out, the dinner jacket returned to its rightful owner. Doubtfully Thomasine tweaked his lapels into place. 'You look . . . I'm not sure . . . was this *made* for you, Daniel?'

He shook his head. 'I borrowed it. Do I look passable?' She realized that he was nervous.

Thomasine smiled and kissed him on the cheek. 'Of course you do. Eminently passable.'

The drawing-room was crowded. Pausing at the doorway, Daniel muttered, *'Christ',* and then ducked his head and plunged into the throng. Like diving into a millpond, he thought. Or going over the top, except that instead of a bayonet in his hand, there was Thomasine, her arm looped through his.

'Daniel. My dear boy.'

Daniel turned and saw Harold Markham, his publisher. Markham Books was a small, select imprint, each publication carefully chosen and beautifully produced. He'd be lucky, Daniel knew, if *The Black Earth* sold five hundred copies. Markham Books continued to survive only because of Harold Markham's vast personal fortune.

'Harold.' Daniel held out his hand.

'We were afraid we'd mislaid you, dear boy. Thought you'd been picking quarrels with Signor Mussolini.'

Daniel grinned. 'I'm only half an hour late. Oh – Harold. This is Miss Thorne, a friend of mine.'

Harold beamed at Thomasine and kissed her hand. Harold Markham was forty, overweight and one of the few people who made Daniel feel impeccably dressed.

'I didn't think there'd be so many people.'

Harold surveyed the crowd. 'Most of them are Paul's friends. Paul Penhaligon, you know, the poet. I published his second collection earlier in the week. A slim volume.'

A servant arrived with glasses of champagne and trays of canapés. Daniel and Thomasine helped themselves.

Harold said, 'Let me introduce you to our poet, my dear boy. Such a contrast. I couldn't resist publishing both of you in the same week.'

She found it hard, at first, to recall when she had last been to a party. William's christening, thought Thomasine painfully, and swallowed another glass of champagne. Or some awful Christmas festivity at Drakesden Abbey.

She wandered around the room, threading through the guests. She could not put a name to any of the vaguely familiar faces: she must have met them, she thought, long ago, at some seaside resort or fancy dress party. Odd how that part of her life had folded and compressed, so that memories of an era that had lasted for years seemed scarcely enough to fill a week.

She found herself at the fringes of a literary conversation. Two well turned out young men of thirty-five or so, a shingled blonde and an older lady wearing a feathered turban.

'Paul is hoping to start up a quarterly. The best poetry, a few woodcuts, that sort of thing.'

'I shall invite him to one of my evenings.' The turbanned lady fitted a cigarette into her holder. 'I can introduce him to all sorts of useful people.'

'Do you write, Miss . . .?'

Thomasine shook her head. 'Miss Thorne. Only letters and shopping lists, I'm afraid. And account books.'

'How extraordinary.' The blonde stared at her. 'I never could make head or tail of figures. Can you, Leo?'

'Only royalty cheques, Anthea.' One of the smooth-haired men reached over and lit the turbanned lady's cigarette.

A tinkle of laughter from the blonde. 'Now look, Leo. I've been meaning to ask you for ages. Who is that simply *farouche* young man?'

Thomasine followed the direction of Anthea's gaze. Past the beautiful young women and elegant young men, to the far corner of the room. To Daniel, whose hair still bore the imprint of the wind from the motor-cycle, whose dinner jacket already looked rumpled.

'*Divine*,' breathed Anthea. There was a greedy look in her eyes.

'His name's Daniel Gillory.' Thomasine accepted another glass of wine from the servant. 'He wrote *The Black Earth*.'

'You *know* him?' The small sharp eyes were looking curiously at Thomasine.

'He's an old friend of mine. We've known each other since we were children.'

'*Divine.*'

'I had a peep at the book.' Leo yawned. 'Frightfully odd. Not at all Harold's usual stuff.'

'*The Black Earth*,' mused the other gentleman. 'Lawrentian, I assume?'

Leo shook his head. 'Not at all. Rural poverty, set in some ghastly East Anglian bog.'

'*A la* Mary Webb? Impenetrable accents and unspeakable passions?'

There was a ripple of laughter. Thomasine interrupted, 'It's not a novel. It's just a factual account of life in a rather forgotten part of England. And Daniel writes very clearly and concisely.' She made no attempt to hide her irritation. All three were staring at her, but she did not care.

'It sounds divine. You must introduce me.' Anthea looked at Thomasine again. 'I'm sure I've seen you somewhere before. I really can't think . . .'

The room had become hot and stuffy. Daniel flung wide one of the windows and glanced surreptitiously at his watch.

'I shall drive a tram,' someone was saying. 'I signed up for the OMS simply ages ago. I'm sure I'd be frightfully good at driving a tram.'

The Organization for the Maintenance of Supplies had been set up the previous year by Lord Hardinge of Penshurst to arrange volunteer services in the event of a General Strike. Daniel glanced at the prospective tram-driver, a pale youth with soft hands and a yellow waistcoat, and managed to keep his mouth shut.

'A train might be more fun, though. It would remind one of being in the nursery, don't you think?'

A dark-haired girl said, 'Real trains are a teeny bit bigger, Bunny.'

'But what would one *wear*?'

'Oh – overalls and a cloth cap,' said Daniel maliciously, giving up the battle to remain silent. 'And just think of having to shovel the coal into the furnace. Hell of an effort.'

'Damned Bolsheviks.' An older man was speaking. 'Damned Baldwin, too. Never thought he was up to much. Useless lot in charge since the War. Shilly-shallying about while a handful of workers hold the country to ransom. Shoot a few of 'em, that's what I say – *pour encourager les autres*, don't you know.'

Daniel put aside his glass. 'Shooting a few of the women would work better, don't you think, sir? Take a pot-shot at the odd miner's wife, and they'd soon be back to work.'

'That's the spirit –'

'Or infants. Even better. Prop half a dozen babes in arms up against the wall, and the Revolution would be nipped in the bud.'

'Daniel.' When he looked down, Thomasine was standing beside him. Daniel understood the expression in her eyes and subsided.

'You've offended him.' The older man had disappeared into the crowd. Thomasine introduced the woman at her side. 'Daniel – this is Miss Millford. Miss Millford, this is Daniel Gillory, who wrote *The Black Earth*.'

Miss Millford was tall, slender, with hair so short and fair it looked silvery. Her dress, a tube of silver and white, barely reached her knees. She had, Daniel noticed, nice legs.

'Mr Gillory, I'm *longing* to read your book. It looks simply *wonderful*.' The small blue eyes studied him, registering interest and approval.

Thomasine powdered her nose and tidied her hair, and was pausing in the chill darkness of the corridor when she overheard the conversation. The two ladies were coming out of the bedroom set aside as a ladies' powder room.

One of them whispered, 'That was Thomasine Thorne. *You* remember, Dorothy, Thomasine Blythe that was. Divorced Nicky Blythe more than a year ago. He did the honourable thing and admitted adultery, but there's the most delicious rumours about *her*.'

'I haven't seen Nicky Blythe for years.'

'Hasn't a bean to rub together, darling. Gussie Fenchurch thought of snapping him up, but when she saw how things were . . .'

'Do tell me. I love gossip.'

'Well, I was dining with Simon Melville – you know, he was frightfully chummy with Lally Blythe. It seems that sweet little Thomasine wasn't quite as sweet as we all thought she was . . .'

The women disappeared down the corridor, their voices fading into inaudibility. Thomasine, hidden by the shadows, watched as the shimmer of their dresses merged with the silks and satins in the drawing-room. For a moment, she leaned her forehead against the cold window-pane, closing her eyes. And then she walked back into the cloakroom and asked the maid for her shawl.

Out in the street, she looked round for a cab. There were omnibuses, lorries and vans still pounding through the roads even though it was almost midnight, but no cabs. As Thomasine began to walk in the direction of the Underground, she heard footsteps, and a voice called out her name.

'Thomasine. I saw you from the window. Where on earth are you going?'

She tried to smile. 'I'm going home, Daniel. I was tired.'

'I'll take you home.' He turned towards the side-street where he had parked the Enfield. She laid her hand on his arm, halting him.

'No, Daniel. I'll go home myself.' She added rapidly, 'I'm tired, that's all. And it's your party – you should stay.'

'I've had enough, Thomasine. What a collection of innocents and ignoramuses.'

She said mockingly, 'Miss Millford thought you were rather *farouche.*'

'Dear God.' The street-lamp shadowed his face, drawing out the colour of his eyes and hair. He had undone the dinner jacket, and his bow tie was askew. You don't fit in with those people, thought Thomasine, and neither do I, any more. I don't think I ever did.

'You could come back to my flat for a drink,' said Daniel. 'It's not far from here.'

His words were casual, but the expression in his eyes was not. She had seen him that evening through another woman's eyes, and that sudden vision lingered. Fleetingly, she pictured herself loving Daniel as she had once loved Clive, had once loved Nicholas. She did not think she would ever trust a man sufficiently again to love him like that. And besides, she hadn't time for love: her undertaking to reclaim her son absorbed all her energy and exertion. She enjoyed her work and treasured her success and her independence. No man was worth jeopardizing all that she had achieved.

'I don't think I'd better,' she said lightly. 'It's awfully late. If you'd just hail me a cab.'

When she woke for work on Tuesday morning, she thought for a moment that she was back in Drakesden. She could hear the birds singing. Thomasine lay in bed, rubbing her eyes. Her clock told her that it was half past six – yet there was something wrong, something odd.

She realized that she could hear the birds because there was no traffic. Pulling a jumper over her nightdress, she went to the window and moved aside the curtain.

There were no buses, no lorries. Only a few people walking on the pavements and the occasional bicycle freewheeling, clear and unimpeded, along the road. She thought, it's happened then, with a slight feeling of shock, but remained at the window a little while, soaking in the peaceful sunshine.

By breakfast time on Tuesday, 4 May, around two million workers were on strike throughout Great Britain. Transport workers, dockers, iron and steel workers, printers and builders had all been called out by their unions. The million or so members of the Miners' Federation of Great Britain had been locked out of the pits since Friday night.

The Government opened recruiting stations for volunteers. Special constables were employed to assist the police. Although some members of the Cabinet called for troops to be brought in, the more level-headed knew that the sight of armed soldiers marching through city streets might only ignite a highly flammable situation. The response to the strike-call was overwhelming. London's presses were silent as the printers downed tools, and London itself slithered to a halt, its Underground trains, trams and buses unmanned. Private cars jammed the streets, travelling at a snail's pace. Transport regressed to an earlier century as people walked, or rode bicycles or horses.

Dr David Franks's office overlooked Hyde Park. From the second floor window of the building, Sir Nicholas Blythe watched the apparently endless snake of lorries and mounted police and armoured cars wind slowly along the road towards the Park.

'They left for the docks at half past four this morning. One hundred and seventy lorries,' said Dr Franks. 'My next-door neighbour counted them.'

Nicholas glanced at his copy of the *British Gazette*. Winston Churchill says here that it's going to get much worse: "Orders have been sent by the leaders of the Railway and Transport Unions to do their utmost to paralyse and break down the supply of food and the necessaries of life",' he read.

'Does that trouble you?'

Nicholas had turned away from the window. 'Not really. For a while the armoured cars . . . the guns . . . made me feel . . . uneasy. But I'll motor back to Drakesden this evening. And nothing changes there.' His crack of laughter was short, humourless. 'Nothing at all.'

David Franks looked down at his notes. 'How are things at home, Nicholas?'

'Oh, tickety-boo. Perfectly fine.'

There was a silence. From the street outside wafted the sound of cheering as the convoy of lorries headed into Hyde Park.

'Do you *want* things to change?'

Nicholas folded up the newspaper and moved away from the window. There was a couch and a chair; he chose the chair. 'Oh – I don't think so. I thought I did, once. But now I don't much care. And anyway, it's unalterable.'

Another silence. Then David said gently, 'Nothing is unalterable, Nicholas.'

'I was taught that God is. And the past is. And Drakesden is.'

'We will leave religion for another day, I think. And we can alter how we perceive the past, perhaps. But tell me, Nicholas – why do you think Drakesden is unalterable?'

Nicholas lit himself a cigarette. 'Well – you should see it, David. You plant some wretched vegetables and if the dykes don't overflow and drown the lot of them, then the wind blows in from bloody Siberia and rips them out. As fast as you try and make the place civilized, it turns back to primeval swamp.'

'Yet you stay there. You have chosen to stay there, Nicholas.'

Nicholas blinked. 'I *chose* . . . I suppose it's a choice.'

He sat for a while, thinking. Until this moment, he had viewed his decision to remain at Drakesden in the same light as he had viewed most of his life since 1914. A mixture of duty and apathy, not choice.

David said, 'You could sell up. Move to the city.'

Nicholas grinned. 'Mama would be outraged to hear such heretical talk, David. Blythes have immured themselves in the Fens for the last four hundred years.' Yet he knew, even as he spoke, that the psychiatrist was right, that he had chosen to stay at Drakesden. He had, to some extent, accepted what he was and the duties that went with that position. He did not remain at Drakesden solely out of a sense of duty to – or fear of – his mother.

He said wonderingly, 'I *protect* her. I protect Mama,' and he looked up at David, doubtful that his sudden and startling perception could be correct.

David's smile was rare and hard-earned. 'You are discovering how you feel about your mother, Nicholas. This is very good. Would you like to explore these feelings a little more?'

Nicholas frowned. He no longer heard the roaring of the crowd outside or the great grinding of the wheels of the lorries and armoured cars. He said slowly, 'I'm not sure that I *love* her. I used to love her. When I was a kid, I didn't see her often of course, so she always seemed perfect. When I left each term for school, she'd kiss me. It was the only time. She smelt of carnations. She was beautiful.'

The room was silent, waiting. Nicholas added, 'But after the divorce . . .' His hand shook. Ash sprinkled from his cigarette on to the carpet. He stooped to try and clear it up with his handkerchief.

'It doesn't matter about that, Nicholas.' David's voice was calm. 'Take your time.'

Eventually Nicholas said, 'You know I was ill after the car crash. It was like a great, dark pit. When you helped me begin to climb out, I saw how pleased Mama was about the divorce. She'd never liked Thomasine, thought she wasn't good enough for me – blamed her for things that had gone wrong. I hadn't realized she still felt like that. But after I was ill, I could see clearly – and, well, I can't feel the same about Mama. I just can't.'

There was another silence. Then Nicholas said, 'I always wondered why Thomasine married me. It always seemed so utterly amazing. Like a miracle. When Thomasine left me . . . and when Mama told me she wanted a divorce . . . it didn't surprise me.'

There were a couple of paper-bags propped up by Nicholas's chair. He fumbled in one and brought out a book. 'Rather an amazing thing. Daniel Gillory's written this. You remember I told you about him, David. Thought I'd have a dekko at it. Always detested the fellow, but now . . .' He shrugged, and then looked up at David. 'I don't seem to feel anything very much. All that –' he gestured to the window, to the strikers and soldiers outside – 'I'm just an observer. Can't get worked up about it. It's nothing to do with me.'

David said gently, 'That is a symptom of your depression, Nicholas. It does not mean that you will not feel emotions – or experience happiness – in the future.'

Nicholas rose from the chair and went back to the window. He could clearly see the dark, stubby shapes of the armoured cars and the mounted special constables with their white helmets and batons.

'I don't look for happiness. The War took that possibility away.'

Hyde Park did not, though, blur and transform itself into the mud-fields of the Somme, and nor did the cheers of the crowd transmute into the dying screams of his fellow soldiers. It had been a year and a half since he had suffered from day visions. David was responsible for that.

'We should talk about the War, Nicholas. You should come to visit me more often – fortnightly, at least, or weekly would be best. Will you do that?'

Nicholas smiled. 'Can't afford it, old chap. I'm selling the family silver as it is.'

'Then we shall continue to make excellent progress in our monthly sessions. Till June, then, Nicholas.' David Franks held out his hand.

Unable to bear the solitude of her room, Thomasine walked through the streets on Sunday morning. Although the strike had altered the whole landscape of London, crowding the streets with pickets and police, the events of the week seemed at that moment so much less important than the events of the previous day. That she had taken William to the Natural History Museum, and shown him the dinosaur fossils for the very first time, and had then parted from him, was all that mattered.

The water that flowed beneath Camden Lock Bridge glittered in the sunlight, reflecting the brightly painted boats and barges. Thomasine walked fast, away from Camden but in no particular direction, trying to exorcize the feelings of anger and desolation that always followed her afternoons with her son.

She had no idea of her whereabouts when she turned a corner and saw the crowds that straggled across the road beside a factory gate. The strike pickets carried banners and posters and chanted the slogan that had echoed throughout London for the past week, 'Not a penny off the pay, not a minute on the day.' The chanting altered to a sudden howl of anger as a bus swept round the bend in the road in the direction of the crowd. Its driver was, Thomasine realized, accompanied by two special constables. 'Scab!' someone yelled. 'Blackleg!' The rest of the throng took up the cry. As the people struggled to get out of its way, the bus swerved suddenly, mounting the pavement, and the howl of the crowd sharpened to a full-throated scream. The bus squealed to a halt, its front bumper only half a yard from the shop-fronts that lined the street. Knocked to the ground by the panicking crowd, people struggled to pick themselves up. Thomasine helped a woman to her feet. She was old and thin and fragile and there was a rip in her cardigan where her elbow had struck the paving stones.

There was a dull *clunk* as the first of the bricks struck the metal bonnet of the omnibus. Thomasine focused briefly on the driver, a young man wearing a Fair Isle jumper and a golfing cap. Then, hearing horses' hooves behind her, she turned and looked up the road.

A column of special constables was riding towards them. Their batons swung through the crowd, striking at random. Thomasine saw a young woman collapse on the road, a red weal across her face, and an old man trampled on by horses' hooves. And she herself, she knew suddenly, was trapped. The specials were to one side of her and the bus to the other. Missiles hurled through the air – bricks, stones, bottles from the bin outside the nearby pub. When one of the bottles shattered to the ground only a few feet away from her, Thomasine began to push through towards the stricken bus, away from the police.

The crowd had become a single entity, pulling her this way and that. It would have been easy to have become caught up in their anger, their desire for revenge. Elbows bruised her, the soaring stones rained around her. She was afraid that she might fall to the ground and be crushed underfoot. She was afraid of arrest, of imprisonment. She could see, glancing back at the special constables, that the arrests were as indiscriminate as the blows.

Squeezing herself between the bonnet of the bus and the wall, Thomasine glimpsed for a moment the stricken face of the driver. She had seen a hare, once, cornered by Sir William Blythe's hunting dogs. The expression on the young man's face reminded her of the hare: fixed, terrified, overwhelmed by a much stronger force. Then she pushed past, forcing herself through the tide of people. An elbow struck her in the stomach and she choked, her knees buckling. When she heard a familiar voice call out her name, she thought for a moment she had dreamt it.

But then, searching frantically through the crowds, she saw the motor-cycle and Daniel. Struggling through to the outskirts of the mob, Thomasine kept her eyes on the Royal Enfield and its rider as Daniel circled and drove slowly towards her. The crowd parted miraculously, allowing him through.

He did not waste time with words. 'Get on the pillion,' he said, and Thomasine climbed on to the back seat, and they headed away from the riot.

She looped her arms around Daniel's waist, and leaned her head against his back, her eyes closed. The roar of the crowd was lost in the roar of the wind in her ears. The power of the mob receded into the distance, and there was only her and Daniel. It was a long time before she looked up and took in her surroundings. Then, raising her head, she saw that they were heading away from London, through the northern suburbs.

'Where are we?' She had to shout her question before he heard her.

The Enfield slowed to a halt, and Daniel looked back at her and said, 'Walthamstow.'

'Walthamstow? Why?'

Daniel gestured to the panniers at the side of the motor-cycle. 'I've some letters to deliver. I've spent the week working as a courier for TUC Headquarters in Eccleston Square.'

Only then did she notice the letters TUC pasted to the side of the Enfield. Which was why, of course, the crowd had let him through.

'What the hell,' he said suddenly, 'were you doing there?'

She realized that he was angry, and climbed off the motor-cycle. 'Walking,' Thomasine said stiffly. 'I always go for a walk on Sunday.' She glared back at him.

'For Christ's sake. You could have been killed.'

A thousand replies sprung to her lips, but she bit them all back. Back there, she had experienced the violence and irrationality bred by riot and anger. She had felt herself sucked into a terrifying vortex, no longer an individual, but a single cell in one great mindless monster.

'It was awful.' Her voice was subdued. 'The police were hitting *anybody*. Women – children. And the driver of the omnibus – he looked terrified.' She closed her eyes again at the memory, shaking her head.

She felt Daniel's arm around her, hugging her. 'Come on, hop back on the bike and we'll head off. We've to go to Woodford and Buckhurst Hill. And then Epping Forest, I thought. I'm told the bluebells are very lovely at this time of year.'

They drove to the beech-woods at Epping. They had bought bread and cheese and a bottle of wine in a shop on the edge of the forest, and now they sat between the gnarled roots of a beech tree, the half-empty wine bottle beside them. The sunlight filtered through the trees, great columns of gold growing from the sky to the forest floor. The bluebells were a haze of azure among the uncurling ferns. The air was pleasantly warm.

Daniel told Thomasine about his week. 'I've been biking all over the country. The TUC needs all the couriers it can get. The post isn't getting through because the mail-trains have been cancelled, and hardly any of the TUC secretaries have telephones. I've been to Wales – Scotland – Cornwall. Once I was on the road for thirty-six hours.'

'You must be exhausted.'

Daniel shook his head. 'You're buoyed up by a kind of elation, I suppose. A belief that this chaos might have a good result. That it might change things.'

'Do you think it will?'

Daniel shrugged. 'I don't know. I hope so. All this confrontation seems so . . . so *wasteful*. If only the Government had stood up to the coal-owners. If only Lloyd George had accepted the Royal Commission's mandate for nationalization in nineteen-nineteen. It's not like it says in the *British Gazette*, Thomasine. No one wants a revolution, least of all the TUC.'

Thomasine threw some crumbs of bread to a nearby robin. 'I don't read the *British Gazette*.'

'Aha.' He stood up. In the warmth of the afternoon he had taken off his tie and rolled up his shirt-sleeves. Thomasine sat on his discarded jacket. Daniel stepped on to the lowest branch of the tree and looked down at her and grinned. 'A convert from the middle-classes. The *British Worker*, then?'

She shook her head. 'Neither, I'm afraid. I go to work in the day, I teach my girls in the evening and then I go to sleep. There doesn't seem to be much time for anything else.'

He was searching for hand and footholds in the trunk, shinning up the beech tree. 'It sounds dull, Thomasine.'

'Work isn't dull,' she said defensively. 'I enjoy it. And I need to earn money for the lawyers.'

She had not intended to explain to him about the lawyers. She had told no one about them – neither Antonia, nor Hilda, nor any of the people with whom she worked. Too often in the past she had created her own difficulties by her openness, her impulsiveness. It was better to be cautious and careful. The wine must have loosened her tongue.

Daniel was now twenty feet above her. 'What lawyers?' A shower of lichen and fragments of bark accompanied his words, making her jump to her feet.

'*Honestly*, Daniel!' Thomasine brushed herself clean. 'The lawyers I see about William. They're terribly expensive.' She glanced up at him. 'I can't talk to you up there. Do come down.'

'No. You come up. There's the most amazing view.'

He was hardly visible now, lost in a haze of acid green leaves. Thomasine muttered, 'My *shoes* —' and then, weary suddenly of caution, she kicked off her shoes and stockings and began to scramble up the tree after him.

There were plenty of footholds in the smooth, grey trunk of the beech. Branches spread out at frequent intervals, wide and easy to grip with her bare feet. Small puddles of brackish water, sprinkled with beechnuts, nestled in the crevices where the branches met the trunk. When she looked down Thomasine saw that the ground had receded, making the scattered jackets and shoes and Daniel's motor-cycle a fraction of their true size. It was like looking through a telescope the wrong way.

In a few minutes she was level with him. 'This is ridiculous,' she said. 'Utterly ridiculous.' But she was smiling.

Daniel shifted up the branch so that she could sit down. He said, 'You lost William because Nicholas had the money to pay for any number of lawyers. And because you knew that any jury would be impressed by his name and title. That's what this strike is about — giving everybody the same rights, the same possibility of a decent life.'

'No. You're wrong, Daniel.' Thomasine shook her head violently. She had had years to think about this. 'I lost William because I'm a woman. It's all right for a man to get a girl pregnant out of wedlock, isn't it? A man can have any number of lovers and still be thought respectable — rather admired, in fact. A bit of a lad. And I was stupid — and careless.'

Yet she knew that Daniel was partially right. The unwanted babies of well-off girls were born in discreet German spa towns, fostered out and conveniently forgotten. Or disposed of in a luxurious and tactful clinic, mentioned only in the clinic's records as a small gynaecological problem. She struggled to shake off her dark mood, to enjoy the sunlit warmth of the day, the glorious carpets of flowers. These were things that had once given her joy. Joy now was confined to one afternoon a month, and that happiness was tainted by its brevity. Sometimes she thought that it was as though her heart had withered over the years, sharpening her tongue, making her see everything in a colder and less favourable light. The years had altered her and she was not sure that she liked the alteration.

'Look,' he said gently.

They were high enough to see the tops of the smaller trees. The swathes of bluebells were violet and misty, like water. There was neither a house nor another human being to be seen, only the forest which rolled away to either side of them, a sea of green and brown and blue.

'I used to climb the trees in the coppice by the meadow at Drakesden,' said Thomasine suddenly. 'You could see everything from there. It was better than standing on the dyke. I made such a mess of my clothes – Aunt Rose used to be quite cross.'

The breeze rocked the tree tops. Daniel's arm was around her. He said, 'I remember you riding the Blythes' stallion. You weren't in the least bit afraid. You never seemed to be afraid of anything.'

She turned to look at him. The beech leaves scattered a pattern of light and dark across his face. 'Oh, I'm afraid of lots of things. Simply masses of things.'

He shook his head. 'I can't think of a single other lady of my acquaintance who would have climbed this tree. Can you imagine Miss Millford, who thinks me so *farouche*, climbing a tree?'

Her smile answered his. 'That's because Miss Millford is a lady, and I, no matter how hard I try, am not.'

She remained still, her back propped against the trunk, her legs dangling into the air, letting the sunlight and peace of the forest seep into her bones and warm her soul. The only sensations were the gentle rocking of the tree, and the warmth of Daniel's arm around her shoulders. The tallest trees rose high above them, higher than the biggest dinosaurs in the Natural History Museum. In the museum yesterday, one of William's boots had become unbuttoned and she had sat on the bottom stair, the child on her lap, to button it. She could recall so vividly the warmth of his small body, the clean scent of his hair and skin. She had hugged her son, and he had said in a small, clear, detached voice, 'Mummy, you are squeezing me too tight.' She had released him immediately, and he had run back to the dinosaurs. Her heart had ached. She had known that he was growing away from her.

Her heart still ached. She was glad of the presence of the man beside her. There was reassurance in the warmth of his skin, the sinewy feel of his muscles. She had touched no one – kissed no one – except William and her aunts for two and a half years. She had not realized how much she had missed the comfort that human contact gave. Up here, in the different world of the sky and the tree-tops, human contact did not seem so dangerous.

Her arms were full of bluebells as they walked back through the forest to the verge. At the roadside, Daniel kicked the motorcycle's starter. Nothing happened. He kicked again and again. The road was deserted. Thomasine stood on the verge as Daniel, cursing under his breath, began to examine the workings of the Enfield closely.

'What's wrong with it?'

'I haven't a clue. Damn thing's a bit temperamental. I should be able to fix it, though.'

Thomasine sat on top of a five-bar gate while Daniel tinkered with the engine. She knew something about the workings of tractors and motor-cars, nothing at all about motor-cycles.

Glancing up and down the long, straight road, she could see no houses, no garage. She pulled her jumper back on: it was still spring, and the days chilled early.

After twenty minutes or so, Daniel said, 'I think it's the carburettor. Blast!'

'Can you repair it?' Thomasine jumped down off the fence.

'I don't think so. This little bit's gone – see?'

She looked at where he was pointing. The component parts of the engine were covered in black oil; so were Daniel's hands.

'We'll have to find a garage, I'm afraid. Do you mind a walk?'

She shook her head, and silently offered Daniel her handkerchief. Wiping off some of the oil, he began to push the Enfield along the road, Thomasine at his side.

After they had walked for almost an hour, they came across a pub. Daniel went inside to enquire about a garage, and Thomasine sat on a rickety bench by the front door. She felt footsore and weary after the long walk. The sky had darkened to violet grey, and long shadows were pasted across the forecourt of the inn.

Daniel reappeared. 'The nearest garage is fifteen miles away. The only form of transport they have here is an old nag that looks as though it's about to peg out any moment.'

Thomasine said, 'A train?' and then, remembering, 'Oh. No trains. No buses. We'll have to stay here.'

Daniel's expression was unreadable. 'I asked about that, too. The landlady can do us some dinner and put us up for the night. But there's only one bedroom.'

She looked away from him. She heard him say, 'I can sleep out here with the motor-bike . . .' and she shook her head.

'It's cold, and you're tired. There's no need for that. You'll just have to –' She stopped, and felt herself going pink.

'Behave myself? Of course. I'll be the perfect gentleman.'

Daniel signed the register in the name of Mr and Mrs Daniel

Gillory. Thomasine kept her ringless left hand hidden in the sleeve of her jumper.

They ate roast chicken and treacle sponge in a tiny parlour adjoining the bar. The inn was ancient, all its floors and ceilings sloping, great draughts howling in around the window-frames. The fire roared in the grate, sparks flying up the chimney. The table wobbled and they huddled next to each other on a bench by the fire, trying to disregard the curious stares of the locals. They talked, once they had satisfied their initial hunger, endlessly – about the strike, its causes and possible outcome, about Daniel's journeys around Europe, about Thomasine's job. And eventually they spoke, as she had known they must, about the past.

Stirring sugar into her tea, Thomasine said hesitantly, 'Do you ever go back, Daniel?'

He understood, of course, what she meant. 'I went to Drakesden on the way up to the coal-fields. I'd had a letter from Harry Dockerill about the spring floods. And besides . . . I go to the churchyard when I can. I have to keep things tidy. She's got no one else.'

'Fay?' said Thomasine gently.

He nodded. 'Her family live too far away, you see. And she never had a friend in the village. I planted some bulbs. She always liked pretty things.'

Once more, she wished she could think of the right words to say. But there were, perhaps, no right words. Instead, she laid her hand over his, and he looked up and said, 'Terrible weather there this spring. Poor old Harry's had his work cut out. The land by the dyke is unusable.'

'Did the dyke burst?'

Daniel shook his head. 'No, thank God, or half the village would have been inundated. But the water comes up through the peat in that part of the village, and some of the ditches that feed into the dyke overflowed. It's going to happen, though, Thomasine. Next year – maybe the year after. I doubt if we'll reach the end of the decade without a serious flood. Harry was worried enough to send Annie and the baby to Annie's mother's in Soham for a couple of weeks.'

The noise of the pub seemed for a moment to recede, and she was back in Drakesden, watching the water in the dyke rising higher and higher, about to engulf them all. She realized that she was still clutching Daniel's hand. His fingers had folded round hers, his thumb touched her palm.

'I wish I knew how things were at Drakesden. I never see Nicholas. Nanny gives William to me, and takes him from me.'

Daniel was silent for a moment. Then he said, 'It's still a devil of a job to earn a decent living from farming. Harry told me that a lot of the servants have left Drakesden Abbey. They can earn so much more in the towns.'

'William said that old Mrs Blatch and Dilley the gardener have both died.' Thomasine recalled the ordeal of discussing menus with Mrs Blatch, and old Dilley's fury when she had picked the hothouse flowers. 'Has Nicholas put more land up for sale?'

Daniel shook his head. 'Not a square inch.'

'Lady Blythe hated him to sell anything.'

'It doesn't matter now, anyway. Look, Thomasine – the bar's almost empty. It's late.'

She saw that he was right. Only the landlady remained, polishing glasses behind the bar.

'Do you want to go up first? I can hang around here for a while, if you like.'

Yet his hand still touched hers, and the message in his eyes was clear. The world had changed in the past week, had become a strange and different place. The wine and beer she had drunk and her physical exhaustion made her feel relaxed and slightly euphoric. Some of Daniel's excitement and optimism had touched her, temporarily wiping away the cobwebs of the past. She was only twenty-seven and she did not want to sleep alone.

'No, Daniel,' she said. 'You should come up now.'

★

In the bedroom she took off her dress and stockings and underwear. It was almost as though she had to hurry, in case she changed her mind.

'You're beautiful. Quite perfect,' said Daniel. He was standing at the door. His eyes were dark and hungry.

'The light from the oil-lamps is very flattering. I have stretch marks and freckles.' *I'm not perfect, Daniel. Nicholas thought I was perfect. I want you to know the truth.*

'I love stretch marks and freckles. Come here.'

She went to sit on the bed beside him. '"Oh my America, my Newfoundland" . . .' he whispered. Pulling her towards him, he buried his face in her breasts, kissing them over and over again.

'Will I do?' Her hands stroked the head that caressed her breasts, her fingers threaded through his curls.

'*Do?*' He began to tear off his own clothes, flinging them haphazardly around the room. They scattered like random ghosts. A shirt caught on a chair-back, a sock marooned on the curtain-rail. 'Thomasine, I've been wanting to do this since I was fifteen –'

His mouth covered hers, silencing her. They fell backwards on to the pillows and she gasped for breath, but would not let him go. His tongue was inside her mouth, and she uncurled her body beneath his, so that they fitted exactly together, breast against breast, hip-bone to hip-bone. His fingers explored every part of her body, inciting her to want him. The hunger of years consumed her; the emptiness of her life fell away and became unimportant, and she pulled him into her. When they moved in rhythm she closed her eyes, lost in each increasingly powerful wave of pleasure. The climax, when it came, was almost painful.

When at last she opened her eyes, Daniel was looking down at her from the entanglement of sheet and pillow and blanket.

'There,' he said. His eyes were bright, filled with laughter. 'I told you I'd be the perfect gentleman.'

CHAPTER SEVENTEEN

His absence woke her. No warm body against hers, no arms around her. Opening her eyes, Thomasine saw the pale diffused light of the early morning sun streaming through the curtains. The bed and the room were empty. There was a note propped against the lamp. It said: 'Trying to fix the bike. Back soon, all love, Daniel.'

For a moment she pondered like a schoolgirl the significance of those two words, 'all love'. Then, as reality crowded back (she was going to be late for work), Thomasine rolled out of bed and began to dress.

She waited for him in the garden of the inn. A pink clematis trailed over the lilac hedge, and in the shade blades of grass glinted with the prismed light of dew. Someone was feeding hens: Thomasine could hear the sound of clucking and a woman's voice calling the creatures by name. 'Here, Nanny, Eliza, Chatterbox – have you laid for me today?' Far away, a dog barked.

She realized that she felt, just at that moment, happy. She had become unaccustomed to happiness: it had been forgotten in the struggle for independence and achievement. The sensation was intoxicating, but also slightly threatening. She suspected that her feeling of elation was as fragile as the dew-pearled spider webs that were slung across the bushes. A puff of wind, an overbright sun, and it would disappear.

There was the sound of an engine, and a motor-cycle coasted into the forecourt of the inn. Thomasine called out Daniel's name. Looking up, he crossed the forecourt to join her.

'I found a blacksmith. He made up a spare.' Daniel looked

down at Thomasine, sitting on the bench. 'I thought you'd still be asleep. I was going to bring you breakfast in bed.'

'It's too lovely a day to waste. Look at it, Daniel. It reminds me of –' She broke off. She had been going to say, 'It reminds me of home.' But Drakesden was no longer her home. Drakesden, now that her relationship with Nicholas had been severed, now that Rose and Hilda were gone, was just another little English village. She was aware of a wave of sadness.

Daniel's hand touched her shoulder. 'What is it?'

'Oh . . . I suppose we should go. I must get to work.'

Daniel grinned. 'I'll telephone, tell them you've been kidnapped by white slavers and won't be in until tomorrow. Ze beautiful Mees Thorne is in my power –'

'They'd only dock my pay.' She stood up. 'We should go.'

'Hey.' He had taken her in his arms; his lips brushed against her face. 'Don't look like that, love. This isn't the end – it's a beginning. Isn't it?'

She nodded, trying to believe him. She could smell the salty scent of his skin along with the lilac blossom and the indefinable fragrance of a sunny May morning.

They set off within half an hour. As they neared London the trees thinned out and were replaced by houses and factories, and the silence was filled by the rumble of traffic. The air was no longer sweet. It seemed to Thomasine as though the landscape was closing in, trapping her, returning her to all the problems of the present. The city drew them both in and swallowed them up, discounting passion, driving a wedge of reality between them.

The strike drifted into its second week. The disruption caused by the absence of transport workers was offset by the efforts of volunteers: university students, debutantes and flappers. Well-fed young men in plus-fours or cricket whites drove trams and buses, manned telephone exchanges and loaded goods on to lorries. More people died as a result of railway accidents caused by amateur drivers than in the sporadic rioting that flared up like pockets of naphtha gas in the cities.

On Thursday, 6 May, Sir Herbert Samuel had returned to England from Italy. In Dover he had been met by Major Segrave, a famous racing motorist, who whisked him to London in his fast Sunbeam car. There, he approached the TUC with an offer to mediate in the dispute. As the negotiations between Government and workers and owners reached a stalemate, the TUC leaders, desperate for a settlement, gratefully accepted Sir Herbert's offer.

When Thomasine left work on Wednesday evening, Daniel was waiting for her.

'The strike's over, isn't it?' She gave him a kiss. 'One of the girls in the office told me it was over.'

'We've been sending out messages to all the Strike Committees, telling everyone to go back to work.' Daniel looked distracted and uneasy, though.

Thomasine squeezed his hand. 'I thought you'd be ecstatic, Daniel.'

'I'm not sure that we've won.' He scowled, kicking an old tin-can from the pavement. 'When the news came at midday, everyone thought it was a terrific victory. We were all celebrating. But now there are rumours ...' He shook his head and shoved his hands in his pockets.

The news hoardings were still blank, Thomasine noticed, and the talk in the streets was confused and bewildered. People jostled them on the pavement, hurrying to and fro. Every now and then an armoured car or troop of special constables would hurl themselves down the road. The special constables, unlike the regular police, were careless of pedestrians and arrogant in their assumption of a right-of-way. In the distance, Thomasine heard the sound of shouting and breaking glass.

'Do you mind if we go back to my flat?' said Daniel suddenly. 'There might be messages.'

They began to walk in the direction of King's Cross. As they rounded the corner of Euston Road, the sounds of turmoil grew louder. Ahead of them, the windows of a pub had been broken. Half a dozen specials were smashing the remaining panes with their batons.

'They're drunk.' Daniel gripped Thomasine's arm protectively, hurrying her along. 'There's been carloads of specials roaming the streets ever since the news of the end of the strike was broadcast.'

'Perhaps we should –' Thomasine began, and then stopped.

Perhaps we should what? Run for a policeman? But these thugs were policemen – or at least they had assumed the duties and the privileges of the police throughout these unreal days. Besides, the local people appeared to have taken the situation into their own hands. Gangs of youths and men dressed in cloth caps and shirt-sleeves had surrounded the drunken specials, and a fist-fight was underway. Outnumbered and made incapable by drink, the specials were no match for their opponents. Some attempted to run away, others tried to fight back. The pavement was soon littered with broken glass and spars of wood.

'I think we'll push off.' Daniel began to steer Thomasine away from the tussle. 'This is getting unpleasant.'

But as she watched, sickened by the violence, one of the special constables broke away from the fight and began to run in her direction. His gait was uneven, loping. Tripping in the litter of broken glass and detritus from the wrecked inn, he sprawled in the gutter at Thomasine's feet. His white helmet rolled from his head and he looked up at her. When two of the local men ran forward, and were about to hit him again, Thomasine spoke.

'No. Don't. I know him.'

'He's a friend of yours, love?' The endearment was a sneer.

She shook her head. 'No. An acquaintance.'

In the gutter, blood pouring from the wound in his forehead, lay Simon Melville.

As they helped Simon to Daniel's flat, Thomasine could feel the stares of the men, hear the muttered comments. Their eyes, following her, burned holes in her back. She was glad of Daniel, supporting Simon Melville's other arm. When he closed the door of his flat behind them she felt a cold wash of relief.

The room was high-ceilinged, untidy, littered with books. Daniel sat Simon in a chair. 'I'll get some water and bandages.' He disappeared into the bathroom, returning a couple of minutes later with a basin of cold water and a handful of lint and gauze.

Simon's blond hair was stained with blood and his skin was waxy. Thomasine worked quickly and efficiently, but she was aware of a distaste for her task. She had always disliked and distrusted Simon. She distrusted him still more since that whispered conversation at the Bloomsbury party. She kept her mouth closed in a thin, straight line as she used the lint to mop the deep, messy cut that seared Simon Melville's forehead.

Simon muttered, 'The *swines*. England doesn't need scum like that.'

Daniel was sorting through his letters and messages. He looked up and said contemptuously, 'Nor do we need uniformed louts like you.'

The bleeding had almost stopped. Thomasine placed a clean piece of lint over the cut. 'You should get it stitched, perhaps, but I'll patch it up for now. What on earth were you doing, Simon? It's all over now, anyway.'

'A little victory celebration. That's all. Just doing my patriotic duty.' He was, she realized, very drunk.

'*Victory* . . .' Thomasine glanced quickly at Daniel, who was rapidly scanning the heap of papers.

'They're all Reds,' mumbled Simon, as Thomasine wound gauze round his head. 'Whole bloody lot of them.'

'Nonsense.' Suddenly she could not remain silent. 'They're just ordinary people like you and me. They just want to be able to feed their families – to have somewhere decent to live –'

His lip curled. 'They're animals. Brutes – they're scarcely

human. Just look at them — at their twisted bodies, their coarse features —'

Now, suddenly, he frightened her. There was a fanatical gleam in his eye, and she knew that he believed every word he was saying.

Daniel glanced sharply at Simon. 'You're a Fascist, I suppose? One of bloody Arthur Hardinge's lot, no doubt.' He crumpled a pile of empty envelopes into a ball as he explained to Thomasine, 'Arthur Hardinge was on the executive of the British Fascists. His cousin's the president of the OMS.'

Simon smiled, a horrible distorting of his bruised and grazed face. 'I was a member of the British Fascists. I became a Loyalist in order to join the OMS. Someone's got to do something — England's becoming overrun by Bolshevik swine. Even the upper classes are affected.'

A flare of anger crossed Daniel's face. Thomasine said quickly, 'Shall I try and telephone Lally to fetch you, Simon?'

He was brushing the dust and dirt from his jacket. 'Who?'

'Lally Blythe. She could take you home. You are friendly with Lally, aren't you?' Her voice, recalling the conversation she had overheard at the literary party, was sarcastic.

'Friendly?' A small crow of laughter, but the blue eyes were cold. 'Being friendly with Lally Blythe would be like being friendly with a wildcat. Lovely to look at, but God help you if she unsheathes her talons.' Looking at Thomasine, he began to laugh. His shoulders quivered, his whole body shook. 'I don't believe it. You've never realized, have you? You were her sister-in-law. You must be as stupid as your ex-husband.'

In one movement, Daniel gripped the torn lapels of Simon's jacket, forcing him backwards.

'You little —'

'No, Daniel. Don't. Mr Melville is going now. I'll see him out.'

Slowly Daniel's hands relaxed. He gave Simon a final shake before releasing him. 'I have to make a few phone calls. I expect you to be gone by the time I come back.'

Simon straightened his clothes as Daniel left the room. The fear faded from his eyes, giving way to amusement.

'Besides, Lally's besotted with brother Nicholas. You should know.'

Thomasine's distaste hardened to revulsion. Simon was watching her, enjoying her discomfiture.

'I've sometimes wondered if the relationship isn't quite . . . healthy.' His tone was thoughtful. 'But then, I can't imagine dear Nicky involving himself in something so naughty. He'd probably have a nervous breakdown if anyone suggested his sister fancied him. Sorry. *Another* nervous breakdown.'

Thomasine hissed, 'Get out. You disgust me. Get out,' and she turned her back, unable to look at him any longer. She heard the front door slam behind him and she walked to the window, flinging it wide, breathing in the fresh air as though Simon Melville had tainted the atmosphere inside the room. Her fists still clenched, she watched Simon's limping progress up the road, and then, a few minutes later, Daniel's return from the telephone kiosk at the corner of the road.

She could tell from the expression on his face as he entered the flat that his news was bad. He flung out his arms in a gesture of despair.

'They've just crumbled. All that work, Thomasine. I had such hopes.' His voice was brittle with anger.

She stared at him. 'What do you mean?'

'The Government haven't given in. It's the TUC that have given in. They've abandoned the miners.'

'But everyone was cheering at work. They all thought . . .' Her voice trailed away.

'Not a penny off the pay, not a minute on the day,' Daniel muttered savagely. 'Actually, it hasn't quite worked out like that. The TUC's accepted some memorandum drawn up by Sir Herbert Samuel. The miners haven't accepted it, though. So when the rest of the country goes back to work, they'll still be locked out of the pits. Only now the owners can just starve them back to work.'

He sat down suddenly on the sofa and buried his head in his hands. She saw then how exhausted and demoralized he was, and felt an answering weariness inside her. Nothing changed. You thought it might, for a while, but it didn't.

'The worst of it is that there's no guarantee that the Government will accept the Samuel Memorandum. The TUC believes that they will, but there's no certainty. And no promise from Baldwin that the strikers won't be victimized when they go back to work. Some employers are already insisting on lower wages for their night-shift men.'

'Then it's all been for nothing?'

'It looks like that.' Daniel's eyes were bleak. He shook his head. 'The TUC should never have called the printers out. That was a capital error. The Government's got the British Broadcasting Company under its thumb – Baldwin's made excellent use of the wireless. If the Liberal papers had been allowed to publish, then perhaps the middle-classes would have had some idea . . .' He broke off. His fist thumped the arm of the sofa, and then he was silent.

Automatically Thomasine began to clear up the gauze and lint. Simon Melville's words still echoed in her ears, disquieting her. *Being friendly with Lally Blythe is like being friendly with a wildcat. Lovely to look at, but God help you if she unsheathes her talons.* She stood quite still, the bandages and scissors clutched in her hand.

Daniel glanced at her. 'What is it?'

'Simon. What he said about Lally.' Thomasine dropped the soiled dressings into the bin in the kitchen.

'She can be a bitch, you know.' Daniel had followed her into the kitchen. Thomasine suspected that he was not really thinking about Lally Blythe, but was preoccupied with the disastrous outcome of the strike.

But he added, 'It was Lally who told me about Fay,' and she stared at him, horrified.

'You mean – Fay and the doctor?' There was disbelief in her voice.

'Mmm. Fay and Alexander Lawrence.' He grimaced as he took a bottle of scotch and two tumblers from the cupboard. 'I should have guessed that something was going on, of course. God knows how I managed to deceive myself for so long.'

She was trying to think clearly. When Daniel handed her the tumbler she drank a mouthful rapidly, hoping the whisky would deaden her confusion and misery. 'Tell me what happened, Daniel.'

'Does it matter? It's all a hell of a long time ago.'

'*I* think it matters. *Please*, Daniel.'

He shrugged. 'Lally came to my house on the morning of the day Fay died. I didn't tell the inquest – there seemed no point. It wasn't relevant. I'd have found out about Fay sooner or later anyway – there was a limit to how long even I could delude myself.'

'But *why*, Daniel?' The words burst out of her. 'It was nothing to do with Lally. She hardly knows you. Why would she *bother?*'

He turned away, frowning. She thought, Tell me the truth, Daniel, you have to tell me the truth. And eventually he looked back at her and said warily, 'She . . . had a crush on me. She was angry when I didn't respond to her. She wanted to upset me, so she told me about Fay.'

'A *crush?* Lally wasn't a child, Daniel! She was – oh – twenty-one, I suppose. A grown woman.' And not an innocent, she thought. Lally Blythe had had a lover in Paris at the age of nineteen.

Thomasine went back into the living-room and sat down heavily on the sofa. Both Simon Melville, with his golden hair and loathing of his fellow human beings, and the sudden and anti-climactic end of the strike had shaken her. Daniel sat beside her.

She said thoughtfully, 'We all treated Lally like a child, though. She was always running along behind us, trying to catch up. Looking at what was going on, rather than being a part of it. I wonder what's happened to her? I haven't seen her for years.'

He did not reply. When she looked across, she saw that Daniel had put aside his glass, and that his head lolled against the back of the couch. His eyes were closed. She watched him as he slept: the long dark eyelashes, the untidy golden-brown curls, the straight lines of his profile. She thought how the past had entangled them, catching them in its snares, refusing to allow them any freedom of movement. She did not know what had tarnished her happiness: the events of the day, or Simon Melville's distorted philosophy, or the sudden unfolding of some of the past's secrets. But now she saw again what she had fleetingly evaded during the past week: that she dared not love Daniel Gillory. She had learned her lesson too well, and could commit herself to no one. She had lost so many that she had loved: her parents, her sister, her child. Every one of those losses had seared her, changed her, had made loving increasingly impossible.

Thomasine rose very quietly, and tiptoed out of the flat, closing the door behind her.

After old Dilley died, and after his grandson left Drakesden for work in the town, Drakesden Abbey was without a gardener. Sometimes Nicholas himself hacked away at the weeds and brambles; sometimes he pulled the mower over the long, gently sloping lawn. He enjoyed the physical work: he had always enjoyed working with his hands. But he was aware that it was a battle he could not win. Bindweed choked the roses in the walled garden, plantains and mosses mottled the green of the grass. Nicholas thought that the sense of approaching decay, of tumbling into chaos, had only really overtaken Drakesden since Thomasine had left. Whilst she had lived at the house – whilst she had overseen the running of the farm – things had slowly improved, had become ordered and rational. That Drakesden Abbey, just as much as he, needed Thomasine, Nicholas did not doubt. Now the wisteria that covered the walls of the house had become rampant after its lack of pruning in the spring. Looking up, Nicholas thought that one day it would cover the windows and seal up the doors so that nothing and no one could escape from the house. So that they were all trapped inside in their decaying Edwardian grandeur.

Just now he was staring at the left side of the house, peering upwards between the hazy purple flowers, the leaves and thick, twisting stems. He had thought, walking from the tangle of old sheds and compost heaps that led from the Labyrinth to the house, that he had glimpsed a flaw in the brickwork of the Abbey. The bright sunlight painted Drakesden Abbey with dappled blacks and whites. Nicholas, squinting, saw that the stems of the wisteria cast dark snaking lines on to the wall. He concluded that what he had believed he had seen had been only a trick of the light. The house had stood for almost two centuries. Drakesden Abbey's foundations had been constructed on the only solid earth for miles around.

'If you please, Sir Nicholas, her ladyship is asking for you.'

Nicholas left off his contemplation of the wall, and acknowledged the maid. 'Thank you, Ellen. This moment?'

'Yes, sir.'

Nicholas followed the maid back to the front door. It was four o'clock: tea-time. Often, Nicholas had the foresight to be away at four o'clock.

His mother was in the drawing-room, surrounded by the usual paraphernalia of kettles and tea-service, but she was not, as Nicholas had expected, alone. Nanny Harper was with her.

'Nanny.' Nicholas tried to smile jovially, but the woman always made him feel uneasy. 'I hope that your presence does not indicate that my son has misbehaved.'

'No, Sir Nicholas. I have given Lady Blythe my notice.'

Nicholas groaned inwardly. Staff at Drakesden Abbey now consisted of a cook, a parlourmaid, a nursemaid, and an idiot fourteen-year-old boy.

'Come now, Nanny.' He tried to be reassuring. He was aware of his mother watching him. 'I'm sure that isn't necessary. If William is disobedient . . . if you are not happy with your quarters . . .'

'It isn't that, sir.'

When the wretched woman looked at him in that way, Nicholas, too, felt like a naughty four-year-old. 'What is it, then? Is it Martha?'

'No, sir. Although the girl is vulgar and ill-educated.'

Nicholas fidgeted, momentarily at a loss. 'Then what, Nanny?'

'I have found a better position, sir. Lady Torrington in Surrey has offered me a post.'

'Oh,' said Nicholas weakly. He could think of nothing to say. The door closed after the departing nanny.

Lady Blythe spoke at last. 'Insolent woman! How dare she?'

'Leave us?' Nicholas wanted to laugh. 'One can't blame her, really. She must have watched the servants disappearing one by one, and the silver positively marching its way out of the cupboards and wondered what on earth was happening. She's just leaving a sinking ship, Mama. Quite sensible, really.'

'Don't be ridiculous, Nicky.' Lady Blythe, stiff-backed, began to pour the tea. 'You are exaggerating.'

When he glanced at her, he saw that she believed what she said. Her capacity for self-delusion was unlimited. 'No tea for me, Mama,' said Nicholas. 'I should go back to the garden while the light's still good.'

'You must eat, Nicky. You must take care of yourself.'

He shook his head. 'No, Mama.' His voice was gentle but firm.

She continued to pour the tea. 'I shall advertise for another Nanny.'

'No, Mama.' He saw that he was going to have to try and make her understand. 'There's no point. What competent woman would come here? What would we have to offer her?

Poor wages and a life of purdah. Martha can look after William. He likes Martha.'

'What William likes and what is good for him,' said Lady Blythe stiffly, 'are two different things.'

'Are they?' said Nicholas, looking down at her. 'I'm not so sure.'

She did not reply. She continued to carry out the outmoded ritual she had overseen almost every day since she had first come to Drakesden Abbey as a bride of twenty. Heating the kettle over the spirit-lamp, spooning Indian tea into one pot, Chinese into the other. Her dress was ankle-length, pinched impossibly tight at the waist, frilled round the neck. For some reason, the sight of her depressed Nicholas utterly. The frills of the Edwardian tea-dress framed a face that had at last begun to display the effects of time, and her hair, swept up on top of her head in a huge, puffy bun, was white now, not blonde. He could not recall when it had changed colour.

Sir Alfred Duke's fees were huge – twenty-five guineas for a half-hour's preliminary consultation. From her work in the accounts department, Thomasine earned only three pounds and ten shillings a week. She took dancing pupils at two shillings for a half-hour's lesson. When she arrived home from work, she had only a quarter of an hour in which to wash her face, tidy her hair and change into her ballet slippers. Often she did not eat until half past nine in the evening.

She had an ulterior motive, she knew, for keeping herself so busy. It helped her to avoid Daniel. She was simply not ready to commit herself to another man. Her relationship with Clive Curran, her marriage to Nicholas Blythe had shown her the folly of allowing her happiness to depend in any way upon a man. Now, when she found herself constantly longing to be with Daniel, she was reminded of the intoxicating love she had felt for Clive. She did not trust that sort of love.

Both Clive and Nicholas had, in their different ways, betrayed her. She might be attracted to Daniel, but how well did she know him? A childhood friendship, a fleeting reacquaintance after the War followed by something approaching enmity on his part during the period of their unhappy marriages. Since her separation from Nicholas, Daniel had largely been out of the country. She knew him to be complicated, driven perhaps by an unresolved and unjust past. She sensed that Daniel still fought the battle for recognition that had begun in his childhood. She knew that her own battles were now more confined, more personal. She did not want, and was not ready, to involve herself in Daniel Gillory's life. She knew that she must avoid the sort of hunger and desire for affection that had brought her to his bed. She could not afford to lose herself again.

She had discovered with Daniel a fleeting glimpse of happiness. But she was afraid of becoming dependent on that happiness. *You are not afraid of anything*, Daniel had said, but she had known that was not true. She was afraid of giving herself again to someone who might misuse her trust, her love. Since her return to London she had made no close friends, had confided in no one. The lack of intimacy had been entirely deliberate, a necessary protection against a hostile world. At work she was elegant, efficient, reliable. But never friendly, never intimate. She had learned to distrust intimacy.

She had heard rumours, too, of Drakesden Abbey's decline. That brief conversation at the literary party had only confirmed hints and innuendoes that she had heard from other sources: from Daniel, from William too. In the Blythes' decline she saw hope for herself. If they were to fall and she were to rise, then how much more hopeful might her claim to her son become? Thomasine worked hard, demonstrating always the flair and competence that had already promoted her beyond what was usual for a woman. If, years ago, she had almost lost her reputation, then she believed that eventually her achievements and trustworthiness might in the eyes of the world compensate for that earlier fall. And for that reason most of all, she could not involve herself with Daniel Gillory. She would allow nothing to jeopardize her independence. She would allow nothing to jeopardize the possibility that she might reclaim her son.

The success of his book took Daniel by surprise. The modest print-run of *The Black Earth* sold out within three months of publication. Harold Markham and Daniel celebrated in style at Harold's club. 'People are sick to death of hedonism,' said Harold, by way of an explanation. 'They buried their heads in the sand after the War – didn't want to read anything that might make them think. Now they're bored with improbable adventure stories and dreary romances about so-called Modern Girls. They want something with a bit of meat in it.'

Daniel thought privately that the small success of *The Black Earth* had more to do with the difference between life in the Fens and modern city life than with his ability somehow to tap into the spirit of the age. It amused him that people might consider his birthplace exotic. The cheque that eventually arrived from Markham Books was, nevertheless, extremely useful. It allowed Daniel to continue the life that Hattie's legacy had begun: to educate himself, to travel, to write. The itch to travel again had already returned – he had a longing to visit post-Revolutionary Russia – but something held him back. He needed to see for himself the aftermath of the General Strike – the miners were still, in September, locked out of the pits.

His feelings for Thomasine also held him back from leaving England. Those feelings were a confusing mixture of desire and affection and frustration. They seemed to spend so little time together. Thomasine herself worked five and a half days a week and, it seemed to Daniel, every evening as well. And the claims on Daniel's own time were, just now, huge. He knew that if he was to capitalize on the success of *The Black Earth* he must complete his series of articles before the book was forgotten. The drift back to the pits was anti-climactic, a slow and un-dramatic agony. Daniel wanted to write something that would jolt the middle-classes out of their complacency.

He returned to Leeds. He was writing about the work of the Relief Committees among the families of the locked-out miners. He had latched on to a worker from the Women's Committee – Miss Cecilia Morris, thirty or so, dark-haired, strong-featured, intelligent. Her day was an endless round of soup-kitchens, the distribution of second-hand clothes and checking that miner's wives and children were receiving their due from the Poor Law Guardians. Today, she was marching purposefully through the rows of back-to-back houses that Daniel had first encountered on his visit to the mine six months earlier. Things had changed since then: the air since the closure of the pits was cleaner, and the place had a quiet, sullen aspect. In the eyes of the men who hung around the street corners there was bitterness and defeat.

It was mid-afternoon when Miss Morris knocked on the last door in the row. This time Daniel waited outside, weary of the endless parade of hollow-eyed children and wives who struggled to put a brave face on poverty.

Within a few moments, though, she was outside again. 'I think you should see this, Mr Gillory.' When Daniel, surprised, looked at her, he saw anger in Cecilia Morris's dark eyes.

Inside the terraced house it took a while to accustom himself to the gloom. He thought at first that the room was empty – there was no furniture, only a tangle of rags on the floor. Only they weren't rags, he realized suddenly, they were a woman and a child.

The woman was ageless. Daniel could not tell whether she was sixteen or forty. Her hair was a tangle of black, and her skin was transparent. She wore a haphazard collection of women's skirts and shawls, men's jackets and mufflers. The house was so cold because it was always, Daniel guessed, deprived of sunlight. The room faced directly into the yard of the house behind it. Through the single grimy window Daniel could see the privy that this house must share with the rest of the row. Although there was a range it was not lit, and the coal-scuttle was empty.

Eventually, he forced himself to look at the baby. The infant's skin was grey, taut against the bones of its fragile skull. It too was wrapped in a bundle of rags. The woman – or girl – was clutching it to her skinny chest.

'Haven't got no milk,' she said. Her voice was husky, apologetic.

Daniel watched as Cecilia Morris knelt on the floor beside the mother. 'The baby's gone, dear,' she said very gently. 'Let me wrap him in my shawl.'

She sent Daniel for a doctor, though the time when a doctor could have made a difference was long past. When all the formalities, that Daniel found obscene in their uselessness, had been taken care of, and Daniel himself had in a surge of fury and impotence emptied the contents of his pockets into a chipped bowl from the cupboard, he walked back with Miss Morris to her lodgings, where they drank tea that neither of them wanted.

He made her talk about herself. Her fiancé had died at Ypres, and since then, being neither pretty nor wealthy, she had known that she was one of the many women whom the War had deprived of both marriage and motherhood.

'"Surplus" women, they call us,' she said, looking up at Daniel. 'It sounds so dreary, doesn't it? Like some unfashionable garment left over in a shop. My family seemed to think that with Albert's death my life had been completely wasted. So I thought I'd prove them wrong. I'd show them that I was still useful.'

He realized that she was crying. 'I thought I could make a difference, you see, Mr Gillory. But I was wrong, wasn't I?'

Between the six-year-old twins and the overweight thirteen-year-old, Thomasine had a break of twenty minutes. Usually, she spent those precious minutes collapsed in a corner of Mrs Price's parlour, a cup of tea cradled in her hands. This evening, however, Mrs Price stuck her head around the parlour door as the twins left.

'There's a gentleman to see you, Miss Thorne.'

Through the lace curtains of the parlour Thomasine could see the grey shape of the Royal Enfield motor-cycle. Pulling on her cardigan, she went outside.

'Daniel.' She kissed him on the cheek. The street was quiet, twilit, and the sharp November wind pulled at her clothes. Daniel wore a greatcoat and boots, and the goggles he used when he rode his motor-cycle were slung round his neck.

'Can we go inside?'

'I need some fresh air. I've another pupil in a quarter of an hour.' She evaded his eyes. She did not want him to come indoors because it was safer out here. Easier to keep him at arm's length.

He scowled. 'The pub, then?'

'There really isn't time. And I've my ballet slippers on. Everyone would stare.' She felt tired and irritated. She had carved out a life for herself over the past three years. An exhausting and challenging life, perhaps, but it was hers, and not to be trampled on by anyone else, even Daniel Gillory.

He was silent. The breeze whipped at the dead leaves in the gutter and whirled small vortices of dust along the pavements. Thomasine pulled her cardigan more tightly around her, and tried to recover her temper.

Daniel's smile was fleeting. 'It looks like ten minutes on the doorstep then, doesn't it? Come here.'

He put his arms around her. The thick material of his coat sheltered them both from the breeze. When they kissed, she forgot her troubles for a while. She found herself wanting him, as she had once wanted Clive, as she had never, perhaps, wanted Nicholas. But she pulled herself away from him and said lightly, 'How was Yorkshire?'

He frowned. 'Cold. Poverty-stricken. I'm glad to see the back of it.'

'Have you finished your piece?'

'Almost. If I lock myself in the flat and take a vow of silence, it should be done within the month.' She saw that there wasn't an ounce of humour in his eyes. In the twilight, their colour was a chill grey-green.

'I've had such a busy week. Two of the junior clerks have been ill, so I've had their work to do as well as my own. And a whole family of little girls have decided to take dancing lessons. Five of them at once in that small parlour for an hour –'

'Don't! For Christ's sake, don't!' Daniel's voice was sharp, cutting through the stream of trivia. His hand slipped from her shoulder. 'If you want me to push off, Thomasine, then tell me to push off. I'd rather you were honest with me. If you're sick of me, then say so.'

There was pain in his eyes. She struggled for words, and failed to find them. She had not opened her heart to anyone for years now – how could she peel through the protective layers and expose herself, raw and bleeding, to him?

So she made do with half-truths. 'It's not that, Daniel. It's just that I'm working so hard at the moment, I don't seem to have the time or energy for anything else. I get up at half-past six each morning, and I'm busy until nine o'clock at night. And then I have my hair to wash and mending to do and letters to write. I fell asleep darning a stocking the other day. I only woke up when I stuck the needle in my finger.'

He was standing in the shelter of the doorway, leaning back against the jamb. Some, but not all, of the pride and anger had faded from his eyes. He said, 'You're saving up so that you can pay a lawyer to help you get William back?'

'Yes.' The wind seemed to blow through the weave of her cardigan, and the pavement was icy beneath the thin soles of her ballet slippers.

'How many have you seen already?'

'Three. Sir Alfred Duke will be the fourth.'

Daniel's tone was clipped, practical. 'If you've seen three, and they can't help you, then is there any point in seeing a fourth?'

Again, she avoided his eyes. He voiced her greatest fear: the fear that woke her often in the middle of the night. That she had lost, and could not fight back. She said, feigning a confidence she did not possess, 'Sir Alfred Duke was recommended to me. He's supposed to be awfully good with difficult cases.'

A silence. She was afraid of what he would say next. Afraid that he might destroy her fragile hopes and leave her instead standing at the edge of a void.

'There'll come a point, surely, when you may have to accept the inevitable.'

She could not answer. Though she might know in her heart that Daniel was right, she could not yet bring herself to admit it.

'How much does this lawyer charge?'

'Twenty-five guineas for a preliminary consultation. That's why I have to work in the evenings. I've made an appointment for the end of the month.'

'I can let you have twenty-five guineas, Thomasine. I had a royalty cheque this morning.'

She looked upwards, away from him. The moon was a pale silver curl in the sky and the gaps between the inky black clouds were peppered with stars. She said softly, 'No.'

'Why not? I'm not being altruistic, Thomasine – it's just that I don't really appreciate only seeing you for ten minutes in a freezing doorway, like some furtive fifteen-year-old.'

She said angrily, 'And would you have accepted charity from me, Daniel, when I had plenty and you had nothing? When we were living in Drakesden and I was Lady Blythe and you were only a smallholder?'

'Jesus – it's not the same –'

'Of course it's the same! It's exactly the same! Or are you allowed to have pride, while I am not?'

'Hell!' He had pulled away from the doorway, his hands dug deep into his pockets. Lace curtains twitched and curious faces peered out at the raised voices. Walking towards them from the far end of the street, Thomasine could see the plump, gawky shape of her next pupil, accompanied by her mother.

'It's not the same,' said Daniel doggedly, 'because I thought there was something between us now. Which makes it different.'

She turned to him. 'Don't you see,' she hissed, 'that makes it quite impossible for me to accept money from you, Daniel? Quite impossible.'

She almost kicked open the door. As she struggled to twist her face into an expression of welcome for her pupil, she heard the roar of the Enfield as Daniel sped away down the street.

At the end of November, Daniel went back to Drakesden. The quarrel with Thomasine – patchily and inadequately made up – and the completion of his work, made him feel empty, restless, unable to settle to anything.

He had not visited Drakesden since April. Then the spring sunlight had softened the harshness of the landscape, and the vast blueness of the sky had compensated for the uniform level of field and water. Now the sky was steel-grey, swollen and menacing, yet refusing to rain. A vengeful wind blew dust round the edges of Daniel's goggles and into his eyes as he swung the Enfield through the village and along the spur towards the blacksmith's cottage.

He was given, as always, a warm welcome by Harry and Annie. He admired the baby, now eighteen months old and toddling purposefully around the kitchen, and ate the dinner that Annie put in front of him. It was still odd to be a guest in what had once been his home, yet there seemed to Daniel to be little trace of his previous life here. He did not now mistake the woman cooking at the range for that other woman, dark-haired and beguiling. The Dockerills had purchased new furniture and redecorated the cottage during the period of their tenancy: echoes of the past – the hammer of the blacksmith in the rebuilt lean-to next door, the sound of a bicycle freewheeling along the muddy track – had faded.

After dinner, while the baby had her nap, Daniel tramped round the fields with Harry. The narrow strip of land between

504

the yard and the dyke lay fallow, now permanently waterlogged. In the centre of his largest field the black branches of bog oak still broke from the earth like grasping fingers. Harry grew no wheat: the land was devoted during the summer months to flowers and soft fruits and potatoes, and in the winter to celery and root crops. Harry enthused about his carnations and sweet-peas. Just now a trial crop of chrysanthemums nodded their tawny heads above the black soil.

With Harry's permission, Daniel cut a bunch of chrysanthe-mums. Tactfully, Harry headed back to the cottage, leaving Daniel standing alone at the edge of the field, the flowers clutched in one hand. When he looked back towards the dyke, he could not help but notice the devastation of the adjacent fields, the reeds that clogged the ditches and the uneven rim of the dyke. Thistles and poppies broke through the stubbly remains of the wheat. The sight did not please him, as once it might have; instead he turned away, his edginess increased by the sight of the chill wind tugging spitefully at the blighted crops.

He walked to the churchyard, the flowers cradled in the crook of his arm. The collar of his army greatcoat was pulled up around his face. When he pushed open the lych-gate and walked beneath the yew-trees he knew that he was not alone.

Nicholas Blythe stood, silhouetted by the dull cloud, motion-less beside one of the gravestones. The Blythes had a patch of ground to themselves: their tombs were ornate, miniature echoes of their status within the village. Daniel could not tell whether Nicholas had noticed his arrival.

He knelt at Fay's grave and laid the bunch of chrysanthemums beneath the headstone. As he pulled the weeds from the grass, he did not pray, but muttered to himself the poem he always now associated with Fay: '"Fear no more the lightning-flash, nor the all-dreaded thunder-stone; Fear not slander, censure rash; Thou hast finished joy and moan."' The terrible bitterness and guilt that had almost swamped him during the weeks after her death did not return. He saw her death for what it had been: the appalling waste of a young, bright human life. It seemed to him for the first time that Fay's death had been an echo of a greater crime, the one that had blighted his life and so many other lives in the years between 1914 and 1918. His marriage to Fay had been in part a desperate attempt to claw back what he had lost in the War years: his youth, his optimism. And Fay, perhaps, had feared Cecilia Morris's fate, and had married him rather than add to the ranks of 'surplus' women. Their marriage, born of an inability to face the past and a fear of the future, had perhaps never had much of a chance.

Standing up, Daniel looked back to the other side of the churchyard, to Nicholas Blythe. Nicholas had not moved. He seemed carved in black marble, like the stone angels that surrounded him. Daniel took a deep breath and walked towards him.

'Sir Nicholas.'

When Daniel spoke his name, Nicholas Blythe jerked, his entire body suddenly snapping back to the present. His dark eyes fixed on Daniel.

'Gillory.' A brief nod of the head.

Daniel dug his hands into the pockets of his greatcoat, and scowled, struggling for words. 'Foul weather,' he said eventually. Feeble, but the best he could find.

Nicholas blinked. 'I keep expecting rain. It's been so dry. And rain always seems appropriate for a graveyard, doesn't it?'

So far, this halting dialogue was, Daniel thought, the most civilized conversation he and Nicholas Blythe had had in years. Daniel glanced at the headstone of the grave by which Nicholas Blythe was standing. It was of polished black marble, like all the other newer Blythe graves, wreaths of laurel incised round its border. The inscription said: 'Gerald William Blythe, 1896–1914.'

'Your brother?' said Daniel. 'Mons, wasn't it? Poor sod.'

Nicholas stared at the headstone. 'Oh, I don't know. I sometimes think it was easier for old Gerry. He's finished with it, isn't he?'

Daniel could not reply. Thomasine's voice echoed in his head: *Nicholas has neurasthenia.* He saw, looking at Nicholas, how much he had aged in the last three years. The lines drawn around his mouth and eyes gave him the appearance of a man in his late thirties, rather than his late twenties. There were a few grey hairs scattered among the dark locks around his temples.

Nicholas added, 'I don't think I'll ever be finished with it. Not until I'm nice and quiet and tucked up in Drakesden churchyard, anyway.' His voice was quite calm and matter-of-fact. 'You were in the army, weren't you, Gillory?'

Daniel nodded. 'The London Regiment of the Royal Fusiliers. I was a captain in the third battalion.'

'Did you see much action?'

'The Somme,' said Daniel, 'and Passchendaele.'

It was strange to be having this conversation with Nicholas Blythe at the end of 1926, in the churchyard in Drakesden. It was as though they had somehow missed out almost a decade, as though these words should have been spoken years and years ago, and their failure to be spoken had damaged them both.

And he knew that he had to push himself a little bit further. 'I know what you mean about never being finished with it.' Daniel's voice was rough, almost harsh with the effort of speech. 'Passchendaele was a bad show.'

Nicholas's eyes focused on him again. There was an intermittent blankness about them that disturbed Daniel. It was almost as though he himself bore the responsibility for dragging Nicholas Blythe back to reality.

'I was buried alive,' explained Daniel. 'Damned mortar fell on our dugout. I don't know how long I was there. Never knew. Everything was confused. I felt I'd lost days – weeks, even. And afterwards I couldn't bear enclosed spaces. To be shut in – in the dark – it brought it back every time. And I had such terrible dreams.'

Nicholas was staring at him now. His hands, in their black leather gloves, shook.

Daniel said, 'And you?'

Nicholas named his regiment. Then he said, 'They recommended me for the Military Cross. They shouldn't have, you know.'

Looking at Nicholas Blythe, Daniel's stomach squeezed, turned over. Nicholas was pulling off his coat and jacket, rolling up the sleeves of his shirt. 'Look,' he said. He held his arms out straight in front of him, the palms up.

Thin white lines were incised like pathways along the tanned inner forearms from hand to elbow. The scars were jagged, uncountable.

Nicholas said, 'I did it, you see.'

Just for a moment, Daniel did not understand him. Then he did, and his breath caught in his throat. He wanted to retreat, to leave the churchyard, Drakesden. He did not want his enemy's secrets. He did not want to know that his enemy was fallible, damaged.

But he knew that he could not leave. For whatever reason Nicholas Blythe's broken mind had offered up its secrets, those secrets were a precious gift, to be accepted with respect.

Daniel said, 'You wounded yourself. So that you could go home.'

Nicholas nodded. 'Like this.' His arms grappled with something unseen. 'On the barbed wire. Seventy stitches, the doctor told me. Almost shredded myself to bits. I was the only one of my battalion to survive. Do you think I should give my MC back?'

Daniel struggled to absorb what Nicholas had told him. He managed to shake his head. 'Of course not.' He made himself sound confident, unjudgemental, and some of the old, familiar anger reasserted itself. Only this time the anger was not with Nicholas Blythe, but with those who had made the War – the politicians, the generals, the profiteers. The Old Men. He said roughly, 'Everyone who was there was a hero. Everyone who slept in a trench with rats running over them, everyone who breathed in poison gas, everyone who saw his pal shot going over the top was a hero. We should all have had medals.'

He delved in his pocket, and drew out a flask of whisky. Unstoppering it, he offered it to Nicholas. 'Have some. And put your coat back on, old chap. It's damned cold.'

He watched Nicholas as he drank. A thousand thoughts flickered through his mind: a mingling of regret, of pity, of understanding. A little colour returned to Nicholas's cheeks as he swallowed. Daniel picked the discarded jacket and coat up from the grass and held them out.

'It gets easier,' he said as he helped Nicholas on with his jacket. 'Honestly. I was hopeless when I first came back from France. Couldn't go on the Tube. I remember forcing myself to travel one stop – Knightsbridge to Kensington – and getting into a blind funk. I had to run off the train. People thought I was drunk. That was why I came back here. You can't have claustrophobia in East Anglia, can you? I'm a lot better now, though. I went down a mine a few months ago, for my work. It was bloody awful, but I did it.'

Nicholas said suddenly, 'I'm reading your book.'

'Oh!' Daniel was startled. 'What do you think?'

'Topping. You always were a clever sod, weren't you?'

Daniel grinned. For a moment they were both silent.

Nicholas said, 'So you don't think it matters?'

'About what you did?' Daniel looked Nicholas in the eye, beginning to understand how his guilt must have festered over the past decade. How it must have diseased his life, poisoned his mind, refused to let him put aside the horrors of the War. 'Not a bit,' he said firmly and truthfully. 'A hell of a lot of us might have done the same if we'd had the chance.'

The wind howled over the distant network of marsh and water. A flock of starlings, black pinpoints in a leaden sky, swooped over the fields.

'We were very young,' Daniel added hesitantly. 'Perhaps we'd do things differently if we had the chance again, but . . .

it's too late, isn't it? I know that what happened to me in nineteen-fourteen – with Lally, and your mother – it altered everything for me. It made me so bitter. And then the War . . .' His voice trailed away, lost in the moan of the wind.

'*Lally?*'

Daniel scowled and shrugged. 'It seems so trivial now, doesn't it? Just a kiss. We were only kids, after all. But I can see what Lady Blythe must have thought.'

He thought for a moment, glancing up, that Nicholas was angry. But then he realized that it was not anger, but bewilderment which clouded Nicholas Blythe's dark eyes.

'You kissed *Lally?*'

Daniel shook his head. 'No. Lally kissed me.'

Twice Lally Blythe had kissed him, he recalled. And knew suddenly that neither of those kisses had been trivial. 'You didn't know?' he asked curiously.

Nicholas looked dazed. 'No. I knew you were at the Abbey that day, though . . . that was why I thought you'd taken the Firedrake.'

'Well, I didn't. Never saw the damn thing.'

'Tell me what happened.' Nicholas's tone was urgent. 'Tell me everything.'

Daniel told him. About his father hitting him and telling him he couldn't go to school any more. About running to Quince Cottage to look for Thomasine, and finding her gone. About guessing that Thomasine was with Nicholas, and feeling sick with desolation and jealousy. About trailing up to Drakesden Abbey and meeting Lally in the orchard. About the thunderstorm. *Fear no more the lightning-flash, nor the all-dreaded thunderstone.* About Lally taking him into the potting-shed and touching his wounded forehead and pressing her lips to his . . .

Her tongue darting into his mouth. *I've got a secret, Daniel . . . shall I tell it you?* Those things he did not tell to Nicholas Blythe, Lally's brother.

'And Mama came?' said Nicholas, when Daniel had finished.

He nodded. 'At the worst possible moment. And because I was nearly three years older than Lally . . . and one of the village boys . . . she must have thought . . . Can't blame her, really. So, anyway, she told Mr Fanshawe not to help with my school uniform any more, and that was that. It doesn't matter now.'

He realized that he spoke the truth. It didn't matter now. It was finished with. He had a future.

And part of that future, he hoped, was Thomasine. Daniel remembered suddenly why he had crossed the churchyard to talk to Nicholas.

'I wanted to speak to you about Thomasine. I see her occasionally in London.'

Nicholas's head, which had been bent towards the ground, jerked up. 'Do you? Is she . . . well?'

'She's well enough. Tired, though.' He took a deep breath and plunged in, aware that he might make matters worse rather than better, yet fearful of the consequences of not trying.

'The thing is, I just wanted to say . . . I know that it's none of my business, and you're entitled to tell me to push off, but, well – she misses the kid like hell, you know. I realize you won't let her have him back, but maybe you could let her see him more often . . . that might help . . . anything . . .'

'William? Are we talking about William?' Nicholas rubbed his eyes. 'I don't understand you, Gillory. Give him back? Thomasine willingly gave me custody of my son. She knew that I could provide a better life for him.'

It was Daniel's turn to frown. 'It wasn't quite like that, surely . . . She's spending a fortune on lawyers looking for a way to get him back, you know. Working day and night.'

The confusion on Nicholas Blythe's face matched, Daniel guessed, the confusion on his own. He thought suddenly, *secrets*. Talking to the Blythes was like running through the Labyrinth at Drakesden Abbey. A dark tunnel here, a locked door there. Branches overhead, shutting out the sun. Weeds at your feet, tripping you up.

'Forget it,' said Daniel suddenly. 'I shouldn't have spoken.' A sense of unease was growing inside him.

But Nicholas said, 'I'll speak to Mama about it. Try and sort something out. Tell Thomasine not to worry, Gillory.'

Daniel was not sure whether Nicholas's smile was genuine. But he nodded and turned on his heel and began to walk away from the lichen-covered tombs of the Blythes.

When he reached the yew-trees he heard Nicholas call out, 'I love her, you know, Gillory! Couldn't live with her, and can't live without her.'

But when he looked back, Nicholas was already gone, clambering over the wall at the edge of the churchyard and starting up the shallow slope of the island.

Walking home, Nicholas felt as though a heavy load had slipped from his shoulders. He could not at first understand why he had been able to tell Daniel Gillory what he had been unable to tell anyone else, including David Franks. His amazement accompanied him up the incline, through the Wilderness. Where the tennis-court had once been – where he and Daniel Gillory had once fought – he paused.

It was, he realized suddenly, because only Daniel Gillory could possibly have understood. Neither Mama nor his sisters nor Thomasine could have understood because they were women. David could not have understood because, unfit for service because of asthma, he had spent the years of the War studying in Vienna. And none of his surviving schoolfriends would have understood, because Old Wykehamists didn't do the sort of thing Nicholas had done.

Sitting on the bole of a beech tree at the edge of the Wilderness, rubbing his forehead, he tried to work it all out. He understood eventually that he had been able to tell Daniel Gillory that he had deliberately wounded himself so that he would be sent home from the Front precisely because Daniel Gillory's standards were different. The very things that Nicholas had always despised Daniel for – his lack of education and breeding and tradition – had allowed Daniel to say, 'It doesn't matter.' Those words had felt to Nicholas like forgiveness.

He had been able to talk to Daniel both because of their differences and their similarities. Daniel had shared the experience of war; he, like Nicholas, had lived with the unseen wounds inflicted by war. He too had suffered the recurrent nightmares, the fear of being returned to an unbearable past. He too had failed to function in normal society. He had told Nicholas that mere survival of those years was heroic. If Nicholas did not quite believe that, then he could, at last, manage to forgive himself a little. The medal lying in his bedroom drawer would not taunt him quite as much now, would not be quite such a constant reminder of failure.

So Daniel Gillory had pointed out to him a truth. It was all very odd.

Nicholas's head was beginning to ache. The sky had darkened, and the clouds that seemed to sink lower and lower to the earth were a dull purplish-grey. He had missed tea-time, Nicholas thought with relief. But he did not yet rise and go into the house.

If Daniel Gillory had voiced a truth, then must he, Nicholas Blythe, accept everything else he had said as the truth? Nicholas rather thought that he must. In which case . . .

In which case, Daniel Gillory had not taken the Firedrake. Nicholas found that he believed him. He, Nicholas, had confided his most terrible secret to Daniel, and it would have been easy for Daniel to have done likewise to him. Easy for Daniel to have said, 'I took the Firedrake and sold it in London. I was short of cash.' Nicholas knew that he would not even have been angry. Reading Daniel's book he had begun to understand what poverty meant to people like the Gillorys. It wasn't what Nicholas thought of as poverty – being down to your last four servants, and paying their wages by selling paintings and silver. It meant not having enough to eat. Or eating the same dull food day in and day out. It meant being unable to afford to pay a doctor if you were ill. It meant drinking away your last shilling in the ale-house because only alcohol gave you a brief respite from reality. Nicholas understood for the first time that the poor were not a different species from their betters – they were the same, but different things had happened to them. Previously, he had always lumped the rural poor together as one unattractive and uninspiring mass. He had recognized their sufferings but believed them to be largely self-inflicted.

Nicholas rose to his feet. He was left with a problem. If Daniel Gillory had not taken the Firedrake, then who had? His mind was crowded with thought; he could not immediately sort through his recollections.

Indoors, he found a whisky bottle and a tumbler and went to his room, pleading a sick headache. When, later, his mother tapped at the door he remained silent, pretending to be asleep. But he stayed awake all night, the curtains undrawn, looking out through the window to where the lawns, the paddock and the dyke lay bathed in darkness.

CHAPTER EIGHTEEN

THOMASINE took a day off work and went to see Sir Alfred Duke on the last Friday of November. The Lincoln's Inn Field office was piled high with books and legal documents. Curls of white paper bound with scarlet ribbon littered the desk and drawers. The single red eye of an electric heater gleamed in the fireplace. Sir Alfred was middle-aged, moustached and monocled, and wore a wing-collared shirt, a frock-coat and embroidered waistcoat.

'Miss Thorne.' He shook Thomasine's hand, and lifted a pile of books from a chair. 'Do sit down. I know your ex-husband slightly, Miss Thorne. Sir Nicholas's accountant, Max Feltham, is an acquaintance of mine.'

She caught a glimpse then of the intelligence behind the genial, slightly chaotic, appearance. Taking a deep breath, Thomasine said, 'You know from my letter that I'm here to ask your advice about reclaiming custody of my son. I should tell you that I've visited several other lawyers already, and have been advised that my efforts are futile. You are, I think, my last hope.' As she spoke, she knew that she told the truth. There was, as Daniel had said, a point where you had to accept the inevitable.

'Then I shall endeavour to do my utmost for you, Miss Thorne. I shall turn up the heater, and find myself a seat. And then, perhaps, you can explain matters to me a little more fully.'

So she explained to another stranger about Paris and Clive and the baby and Alice. It felt, as always, like a violation. When she had finished, she looked up at him defiantly, expecting as before, judgement and condemnation.

Sir Alfred was cleaning his monocle on a crumpled silk handkerchief. He said, 'I have four daughters, Miss Thorne, all younger than yourself. My wife and I have always been honest with them. I have never seen the point of deliberately fostering ignorance – not in any sphere. It would be like sending a soldier into battle without telling him what his bayonet is for.'

Her smile answered his.

'Tea, Miss Thorne?' asked Sir Alfred Duke. 'And then I must ask you a few questions, I'm afraid.'

He asked more than half an hour's worth of questions. Thomasine watched the hands of the clock move and thought, twenty-five guineas . . . thirty-seven and a half . . . Eventually he stood up and went to the window. The seconds stretched out, the minutes ticked expensively by.

At last Thomasine, unable to bear the suspense, said, 'It's hopeless, isn't it? I'm wasting your time.'

He turned back to her, shaking his head. 'Not at all, young lady, not at all.'

Her heart skipped a beat. She was, then, allowed to hope. She threaded her fingers together in her lap, squeezing the knuckles. 'Do you think that you can help me, Sir Alfred?'

'I believe so. There are . . . possibilities.'

She felt a ridiculous smile flower, then spread over her face. In the rebirth of hope she no longer noticed the chill damp of the winter weather, the bleak greyness of the sky.

Sir Alfred said, 'You mentioned that your husband has been unwell since the War?'

'Nicholas had a bad time in the War. He still suffers from neurasthenia – shellshock.'

Another silence. Then, 'And is he receiving treatment for this condition?'

'He visits a doctor in London every month. I have William for the afternoon while Nicholas sees the doctor. Nicholas had . . . a sort of breakdown after I left him. I suppose that forced him into doing something. He always refused to see anyone before that.'

The lawyer's avuncular manner encouraged her to say more, perhaps, than she had intended. She had been aware for many years of Nicholas's own shame of his illness, aware that he saw it as an unmanly weakness.

'A doctor ...' the lawyer said thoughtfully. 'You mean a psychiatrist, don't you, Miss Thorne?'

He had sat down at his desk again. Thomasine nodded. 'I don't see ...' Her voice tapered away uncertainly.

'Merely that your ex-husband, who has custody of William, is undergoing treatment for a mental illness. It could be suggested, perhaps, that a man with a diseased mind was not the ideal guardian for a young child.'

A little light rain pattered against the window; in the adjoining office a telephone rang. Sir Alfred frowned, and returned to polishing his monocle.

'An interesting dilemma, certainly. Should the custody of an infant be awarded to a parent suffering from an ailment of the mind, or to a parent who has, in the past, led an immoral life?' He looked across the cluttered desk at Thomasine. 'You are aware that you would, Miss Thorne, be branded by any reputable defence lawyer as a woman who has led an immoral life.' Sir Alfred's gaze moved slowly to the ceiling. 'Yes – an interesting dilemma. I cannot recall a comparable case. Woods versus Woods, perhaps ... No – the mother was crippled ... But, Miss Thorne, should you choose to engage my services, I am confident that I could put up a good fight for you. After all, your ex-husband's illness sadly continues, whilst *you* have, I feel confident, led a blameless existence since your divorce. Sir Nicholas Blythe must be considered to be still unpredictable – dangerous, even. Whereas in your case the foibles of the past could be attributed to the follies of youth. If I were a betting man – which I am not – I would wager two to one that the courts would award custody of the child in your favour.'

517

He was smiling, but at the same time he was watching her closely. 'Miss Thorne?' The lawyer's voice was gently enquiring.

She could not at that moment think clearly. The prospect of regaining William was so wonderful, so breathtaking. And yet . . .

'Think about it,' he said.

Nicholas stayed awake until dawn, and then dozed for a few hours. At mid-morning he rose, light-headed with lack of sleep. Lady Blythe was still in her room, writing letters, so Nicholas waited in the conservatory, smoking and drinking coffee. He saw through the tall glass windows that the thick cloud which had covered the sky for days had at last begun to break. Where small patches of pale blue showed through the cloud, thin rays of sunlight stabbed the earth. With the unnatural clarity of thought that insomnia sometimes brings, it occurred to Nicholas that the fracturing sky reflected his own state of mind. He was at last beginning to see things clearly.

His mother came downstairs and joined him. Nicholas sent for fresh coffee. As the windows magnified the heat of the sun, the room had become over-warm. The scent of the earth and the plants was strong and sour. Nicholas felt as though he had sat there for ever. The pattern of the tiles, the colour of the flowers and the arrangement of the terracotta pots was burnt into his mind. He lit another cigarette as Lady Blythe poured out the coffee. Watching his mother, Nicholas tried not to hate her.

He said, 'Thomasine has been visiting lawyers, Mama, to discover whether there is any chance of her regaining custody of William.'

A tinkle of laughter; her hand did not pause in the tilting of the jug. 'Really? Then she must have money to waste.'

'That's not the point.' Nicholas shook his head to the coffee-cup his mother held out. 'The point is, you told me that Thomasine *voluntarily* gave me custody of William.'

Throughout the night, he had struggled to recall the events of the months after the car crash. That time had been chaotic, blurred by illness. When, with David Franks's help, he had begun to emerge out of the darkness, it had been to find things organized along unfamiliar lines: Thomasine gone, arrangements made for the child to visit her in London once a month, divorce proceedings set in progress.

The flicker of a frown crossed Lady Blythe's brow, quickly hidden, but to Nicholas's unnaturally alert state of mind, unmistakable.

'It doesn't make sense, does it? I've been thinking about it all night. If Thomasine wished to have custody of William, then why didn't she fight for him at the time of the divorce? Why see lawyer after lawyer now – something that she can surely ill-afford.'

'Oh, she'll have money enough! Girls like her always have money.'

Nicholas paused in the lighting of another cigarette. 'What do you mean?'

'She will have admirers, Nicky. Girls of her sort always do.'

His mother's eyes were narrowed, small patches of blue in a pale, ruined face. He could see vividly how the years had altered her, dragging down the corners of her eyelids, marking deep lines from nose to mouth so that a smile was no longer a smile, but a grimace. Her prettiness had faded utterly, taking with it her ability to mask her feelings.

'I think you persuaded Thomasine not to ask for custody of William. I don't know how, but I think that's what you did.'

When she turned to him her gown rustled, a whisper of pale mauve silk and cream-coloured lace. 'And what if I did, Nicholas? William belongs at Drakesden. This is his inheritance.'

'*Inheritance!*' Nicholas found that he was laughing. 'William will be lucky if he inherits anything more than an empty house and an overgrown garden.' He managed to light his cigarette at last. 'Thomasine would have kept the place together. I can't do it.' He inhaled the cigarette, and blew blue smoke out through his nostrils. 'What did you say to Thomasine to make her give up William?'

'Don't be ridiculous, Nicky. And do open a window. The smoke –' She coughed into a lace handkerchief.

He disregarded her. '*Tell* me, mother.'

His voice was no longer steady. If he had risen from his seat, if he had crossed the room and touched her, then he would have squeezed and squeezed her tiny bones until she cried out in pain, until she told him the truth. So he remained where he was, watching her, and watching the scarlet tip of his cigarette tremble in his hand. His headache had returned, the cigarettes and coffee failing to stave it off.

His mother had spooned six sugars into the tiny china cup. The meniscus curve of the liquid bobbed against the gold-leaf rim. She looked up at Nicholas defiantly.

'Thomasine was pregnant when you married her. Pregnant with another man's child.'

Though it was December, some of the plants in the conservatory were in flower. The Christmas cactus, the amaryllis and the slipper flower, a few orchids. Harsh shades of pink and orange and yellow that hurt his head, clogged his thoughts.

Nicholas whispered, 'I don't believe you . . . Thomasine wasn't like that . . . You always hated her . . . You're lying, aren't you?'

'I didn't tell you because I thought it might upset you. Thomasine miscarried the child very early on in the pregnancy. It is distasteful to talk about such things, but perhaps it is better that you know. The child was fathered by an actor.'

Slowly, very slowly, the realization that she was telling the truth sank into his mind. It explained something that he had never understood – it explained, at last, why Thomasine had married him. His thoughts ran on, making connections, linking facts together with a sudden almost visible facility, like small fiery explosions, like mortar bombs, like the bright trumpeting snouts of the flowers. He felt sick.

'Pregnant . . . she had a *lover* . . .' Nicholas closed his eyes and pressed his fingertips against his throbbing temples, trying to stop them hurting. 'How could you know this? Who told you?'

Again, she did not answer him. She looked calm again, though, and Nicholas understood that her fleeting discomfort had been a consequence not of her own guilt, but of her aversion to talking of sexual matters.

'Thomasine understood, when we discussed the matter, that William should be brought up at Drakesden Abbey.'

Nicholas blinked. 'I said, who told you?'

A small shrug of the thin, silk-clad shoulders. 'Lally met a girl who had been a friend of Thomasine Thorne's in Paris. This girl – her name was Alice – told Lally everything. Lally thought it best to tell me.'

When Nicholas thought back, he could remember the three girls sitting together in the corner of the Montmartre café. Two blondes, one red-head. Alice and Poppy and Thomasine.

And he also remembered Lally. Lally in the lavender-blue dress he had bought for her; Lally sitting on a table and cutting her hair. The click of the scissors, the coal-black locks falling to the floor.

'So you see, Nicky, that Thomasine isn't a suitable person to have custody of a child.'

He looked away from her. He could hardly bear to be in the same room as her. It occurred to him that they had both had secrets, he and Thomasine. Just as he had hid from her his terrible experiences of war, so she had hid from him her own private wounds and defeats. He did not hate Thomasine: he understood impulse, guilt, regret too well.

He whispered, 'Thomasine shall have William, Mama. It is what I want. What you did was cruel – judgemental. Who are you to judge another human being?'

She had agreed to meet Daniel that afternoon. If there had been any way of cancelling the arrangement, then Thomasine would have done so. She wanted only to go back to her lodgings, to curl up in bed and try and work out what to do. But Daniel had no telephone, and there was no time to write to him. Waiting at a table in the Strand Corner House near Charing Cross station, Thomasine bit her nails and tried to think.

She could have William back. She could have the person she most loved with her every day. She could walk with him to school, give him his bath, cook him his food. Every one of those mundane tasks would be unmitigated delight. She could watch him grow up, take him to his first show at the theatre, go by train with him on seaside holidays. Her longing was terrible, all-consuming. And yet something held her back.

'Thomasine?'

She looked up. Daniel was sliding into the seat opposite her.

'I'm sorry I'm late. It was a long journey, and the wretched bike was playing up again.'

She struggled to be civil. 'Where have you been?'

The waitress appeared. Daniel ordered bread and butter and cakes.

'I went back to Drakesden.'

For a moment her mind was distracted from its desperate, haunted path. 'How was it?'

'Oh – much the same. Harry's little girl is walking now. Harry and Annie are growing chrysanthemums. And . . . and I saw Nicholas.'

She looked at him properly for the first time. Daniel's old army greatcoat was covered with a layer of dust and his hair was ruffled by the wind. And there was, unusually, a look of anxiety in his eyes.

'I mean,' he said, 'I *talked* to Nicholas.'

The tea arrived, and was ignored by them both.

'You *quarrelled* with Nicholas?'

Daniel shook his head. 'No. I mean talked. He was in the churchyard when I went to leave some flowers for Fay. So I spoke to him.'

His eyelids dropped, hiding his eyes from her. She looked at him for a long moment, and then she said softly, 'Come on, Daniel. I don't think you and Nicholas talked about the weather . . . or politics . . .'

'I asked him about William. I asked him whether there was any real prospect that you would ever get the child back.'

'You did *what?*' She stared at him, horrified. 'How dare you, Daniel? It's none of your business –'

'I'd hoped it was becoming my business. Your welfare, I mean.' He reached across the table and touched her hand. 'Look – I know I was interfering, but I can't bear to watch you flogging yourself to death like this. I really can't. And if the Blythes mean to hold on to the kid like glue, then perhaps it's better that you know.'

She snatched away her hand. She could not bear anyone to touch her just now, and nor could she work out the ramifications of this particular piece of interference. She only knew that today her interview with the lawyer had scratched away at the thin scab that covered her heart, leaving it raw and bleeding. Once more she thought, if I went back to court . . . She pictured herself in the witness-box, describing Nicholas's moodiness, his obsessions, his self-mutilation . . . For William, she reminded herself. For William.

She said coldly to Daniel, 'You had no right. None at all.'

An answering anger flickered in his eyes. 'No? Do you intend things to remain that way for ever, Thomasine?'

'What do you mean?'

'Well – you've kept me carefully at arm's length since May. I thought it was because of the child. That guff you told me about having to work all hours to pay for lawyers. But maybe I was wrong. Maybe it's involvement with me you don't want. Christ – I've been trying to pluck up courage to ask you to marry me for weeks. Maybe I've been fooling myself. Maybe you don't think I'm good enough for you.'

She was hardly listening to what he said. Again she saw herself in court, watching Nicholas's face as impassive voices detailed the symptoms of his illness and suggested possible prognoses. As his friends, relations, the Press listened in the Public Gallery. It would be like flaying him alive. She could not do it. She could not.

Her clenched fist struck the table, and tea splashed over the immaculate linen tablecloth.

'I don't want to marry you, Daniel! I don't want to marry you or anyone else just now!'

There was a sudden awful silence. A few feet away the waitress paused with her loaded tray, staring at them. The colour drained from Daniel's face.

He said slowly, 'My God, how you've changed. You dole out affection in teaspoon quantities these days, don't you, Thomasine?'

She did not reply. Tears stung behind her eyes. She blinked, trying to keep them at bay. She thought furiously that he was right, that she had altered beyond recognition, that the carefree girl who had ridden the dusty droves of the Fens could not be reclaimed.

He said suddenly, 'Or is it Nicholas? Are you still in love with Nicholas?'

'I have no capacity to love,' she almost screamed at him. But other customers were staring now, and the Nippie still hovered, tray in hand.

'Just leave me alone, Daniel.' Thomasine's voice was brittle. 'I just want to be left alone.'

Daniel rose to his feet and threw a ten-shilling note on to the table. 'Of course. As you wish.'

He strode out of the café. As soon as he had gone, she wanted to call him back. To explain to him that she had abandoned her child, to explain that she was only half a person, that she had lost perhaps the best part of herself over the preceding decade. To explain that if she could have loved any man, then that man would have been Daniel Gillory.

When he got back to his flat and sifted rapidly through the pile

524

of post by the front door, Daniel found the note from Anthea Millford. 'Darling,' it said, 'I am obliged to attend a terrifically ghastly party, and I haven't an escort. I'd be for ever in your debt if you'd help me out.'

The flat seemed very empty, very quiet. Daniel checked his calendar. Then he shoved the note into his pocket and, slamming the door of the flat shut behind him, walked to the telephone box at the corner of the street.

Throughout the afternoon the clouds dispersed, so that the house and gardens were bathed in pale winter sunlight. Nicholas walked down to the meadow, then back through the copse, the orchard and the Labyrinth. In the walled garden he stared at the three statues in their niches: Leda and Daphne and the Firedrake. *It's in Papa's study*, Lally's voice whispered. *In the safe.*

The walled garden was, like the rest of the grounds, hopelessly overgrown. Runners from the rose-bushes tangled into each other, yet still put forth a few late blooms. The grass was high and thickened with clumps of weed. Ivy trailed over the walls, pulling at the old bricks, its suckers eating away the dusty mortar. Dead leaves gathered at the edges of the flower-beds and in the corners of the walls. The autumn had been dry, so the leaves were brittle, brown and curled.

Leaving the walled garden, Nicholas circled the house. Sunlight struck the old yellow walls, delineating every brick. The leaves and flowers of the wisteria had died away, leaving only bare grey stalks. Nicholas glanced once at the east wall of the house, and then looked again.

Unable to believe what he saw, he walked closer. Reaching out, he touched the fine jagged line that had grown between the bricks. He could almost fit his smallest finger into the aperture. A stream of powdered mortar trickled to the grass as he scratched at the hollow. Looking upwards, he followed the progress of the narrow fissure, brick by brick. The wall that had stood for two centuries was tearing apart.

Cold with shock, Nicholas stumbled to the corner of the house. There he stood, looking along the line of the side wall to where it met the front lawn. The wall bulged, slightly but unmistakably, an obscene protrusion. Looked at straight on, the swelling would not have been visible. Only from here, only from this angle, could the cancerous growth that diseased Drakesden Abbey be seen.

He realized then that he'd got it all wrong. For years he had been looking at things from the wrong angle. Everything – the house, the past – depended on which way you looked at it.

He began to run towards the Daimler, parked at the front of the house. The uncut lawn tripped him, the disintegrating house mocked him. But something gave him the strength to turn the starting-handle, to fall into the front seat, to begin to drive.

Lally had said, *It's best just to take what you want. That's what I do.* He had to drive to London, to see Lally. He had to know what she had done. He saw things clearly at last.

Daniel had had several drinks by the time he and Anthea Millford reached the Mayfair party. The large, brightly lit house, busy with party-goers, was temporarily distracting. That and the alcohol and his companion stopped him from thinking of Thomasine for a while.

The music was loud, the chatter incessant. Everything seemed to glitter. Such a change, he thought, from a Fenland churchyard, or a row of back-to-backs in Leeds. He could have this sort of life if he chose, and all the things that went with it: a decent house, a motor-car, restaurants and the theatre. He had only to go on being clever and *farouche* and manage to shut up for a while about the gloomier aspects of life. It would be the sensible thing to do.

Anthea passed him a glass of champagne. 'Drink that, darling, and don't look so cross.'

Her short dress was of some shiny pink stuff trimmed with feathers. The band round her forehead held another feather. She looked, Daniel thought, like a rather pallid Red Indian.

'There's simply oodles of people I want to introduce you to, darling. Frightfully important people.'

He allowed himself to be led across the room and introduced to various men and women. He managed to be civil, to avoid discussing politics or social justice or any of the things that had been important to him over the past few years. He drank steadily, while the strains of the Charleston filtered from the adjoining room.

After a while he felt a hand at his elbow, and was steered away to the comparative silence of the hallway. He saw, to his surprise, that Anthea was furious.

'What is it? I behaved myself.'

'Too – bloody – well.' Her high-heeled shoe beat out the rhythm of her words. 'Listen, darling – if you want to get on, you'll have to try a bit harder than that. There's thousands out there like you, Daniel. Birth, money and looks – that's what it takes to succeed. They say you can manage with two of them. Well, sweetie – you've just one, so you're going to have to make an extra effort.'

She had fitted a cigarette into her holder. Daniel rummaged in his pocket for a box of matches and lit it for her.

'I thought I was doing rather well. I kept my mouth shut when that old buffer suggested that giving the vote to women under thirty would make Britain communist at the next General Election – I ummed and ahed when his wife said that the flappers would vote the way their husbands and fathers told them to –'

A white tapered fingertip touched his lips, silencing him. 'Don't be stupid, darling,' said Anthea Millford sweetly. 'I wanted you to argue with them. Why do you think I introduced you?'

He stared at her. He had drunk too much to think with his customary facility.

She said, 'People find it so amusing. It makes this sort of bash a little less boring.'

Her small, sapphire-hard eyes gazed at him coolly. Understanding, when it dawned, was like a wash of cold water.

'Ah,' he said softly. 'You wanted me to provoke? To break the rules a little?'

'Of course, darling. As I said, you've got the looks, but nothing else. Brains don't count with these people. But sometimes someone who's just a teeny bit . . . *different* can get a foothold in society.'

He was leaning against the chimney-breast, watching her. 'So you see me as . . . a sort of pet monkey. I'm here to perform tricks, show myself up in company, that sort of thing?'

He saw that it was precisely what she meant.

She said, 'Don't glower, sweetie. After all, you'll get your reward at the end of the evening.'

She was, he thought, perfectly confident that when she clicked her fingers he would run, turn somersaults, take her to bed. He leaned forward confidentially and whispered in her ear, 'The thing is, us louts from the sticks don't really know how to behave. And we're not much better in bed. You're lucky if we take our socks off beforehand. Are you really sure you want to go through with it?'

There were two spots of pink on her cheeks, and her lips were pressed together in a straight line.

'We could do it here if you like,' Daniel added. 'A quick one up against the wall, and you could make up your mind –'

The palm of her hand struck his face. As Anthea Millford stalked away Daniel watched her, rubbing his chin where her rings had caught it. And then, in the crowded ballroom ahead, he caught a glimpse of a familiar face. Lally Blythe.

Somehow, Thomasine got through the evening's dancing lessons. After her last pupil had gone, she closed the piano, collected the tray Mrs Price had left for her and went to her room.

She could not eat the Lancashire hot-pot and rice pudding. She was cold, and though she turned on the gas fire and wrapped herself in her eiderdown, she could not get warm. She thought of the son she had lost, and Daniel, whom she had hurt. She could do nothing now for William: he would grow away from her. In a few short years he would leave Drakesden for boarding-school. He would grow up as Nicholas had grown up, knowing only male company, cut off from his home and family, learning to hide his fears and desires. Thomasine thought of her own future, of the career she had carved out for herself. Yet tonight even that failed to offer her comfort. Tonight, success and money seemed a poor compensation for loneliness.

Sitting on her bed, her knees bunched up to her chin, Thomasine began to understand how much his proposal must have cost Daniel. How hard it must have been for him to risk commitment again, with the wreckage of his previous marriage strewn behind him. If he had interfered in her affairs, and if she had resented his interference, then she knew in her heart he had meddled only out of concern for her.

Thomasine pulled the blankets around her, trying to keep warm. She was so very tired. It was only nine o'clock, but the temptation to curl up and sleep was overwhelming. She wondered, as her head touched the pillow, whether she could marry Daniel Gillory. If she had no hope of regaining William, then did that alter things between her and Daniel? Did it leave her free to marry again?

She rather thought that it did. The idea of marriage still made her uneasy, but maybe one day she might feel differently. As her thoughts became random and disjointed and sleep blurred the edges of her consciousness, Thomasine thought that perhaps in time she would accept that she had at last met a man whom she could trust.

Eventually he spoke to Lally. He had known that he must; there was too much unfinished business between them.

Daniel had gone to fetch himself another drink. Scotch, this time, not that awful sickly champagne. When he turned away from the bar she was standing behind him. She wore a very plain, very short black dress of some flimsy material. Lally's hair was cut short in an Eton crop, parted on one side. Her mouth was a crimson Cupid's bow, and her eyes were very dark and brilliant.

'Daniel,' she said. 'How lovely to see you again.'

'Lally.' He glanced back towards the bar. 'Champagne? No – you don't, do you . . .?'

Not a hint of shame crossed her small elfin face, though he was convinced that she, like him, remembered every word of that fateful conversation three years ago.

'I'll have a scotch,' she said. 'Like you.'

Daniel signalled to the barman. He wondered whether Lally, like Anthea Millford, simply thought him unimportant. A fleeting amusement, something to relieve boredom. The whisky he drank did not quell his anger; rather, it fuelled it.

He passed a glass to Lally. She was coughing. 'A bit of a sniffle,' she explained. When she had finished coughing, Daniel said, 'I saw a friend of yours a few months ago. Simon Melville.'

The mask did not slip. 'Oh – Simon,' she said. 'I haven't seen much of him recently. He's gone abroad now.'

'And I saw your brother yesterday.'

There was then a slight narrowing of her tilted eyes. 'Nicky?' Her voice was guarded. 'How was he?'

'Fine. Well – shot to pieces, of course. I hadn't realized what a mess the War had made of the poor sod.'

'We're a very *tactful* family, Daniel. Cloistered. You can hide anything in a god-forsaken hole like Drakesden, can't you?'

She was, he realized, as drunk as he. Around them, people had begun to leave, some for their homes, others for nightclubs.

Daniel said, 'Yes, I suppose you can.'

Just for a moment the dark eyes flickered, evading him. Lally stifled another cough. He thought then that she was not quite like Anthea Millford. Lally Blythe was a little more dangerous. Destructive, even. There was something destructive about her touch, her kiss.

'Everyone's going,' she said. 'Shall we go, Daniel?'

'*We?* Where?'

'Well – back to your place, I thought. You do have some-where, don't you? I live with my cousin, so it wouldn't be suitable.'

He was, he thought, not quite that drunk. He shook his head. 'Not a good idea, Lally. Think of the consequences.'

She glanced up at him calmly. 'I never think of con-sequences.'

'No,' he said slowly. 'You don't, do you? But I do, and I think I'll pass, if you don't mind.'

He was making rather a habit of it, he thought. He had rejected two women that night – a personal record, surely. It wasn't that he didn't feel like it, it was just that the woman he wanted – the woman he ached for – didn't want him. Thomasine had said, 'I don't want to marry you, Daniel.' The message in her eyes had been clear. She wasn't interested; he had made a fool of himself.

He pushed his way out of the room, out of the house. In the street, where a thin drizzle laced the pavement, Lally Blythe's small white hand caught at him, curling round his elbow.

'I want to go home with you, Daniel.'

He shook his head, and her dark eyes blazed with anger. 'Why? Aren't you capable?'

'I just haven't the inclination.' He lied, he knew. He loathed the prospect of his empty bed.

'I don't believe you.' She was standing in front of him, clutching at the sleeves of his dinner jacket. 'Perhaps you can't make love to me. Yes – that would make sense, wouldn't it? Perhaps that's why Fay was fooling about with the doctor.'

She was smiling. In the dull light of the street-lamp, her eyes were shining. 'Is that it, Daniel? Couldn't you be a proper husband to Fay? Was that why she cheated on you?'

For a moment he could not move. And then he seized her thin wrist and dragged her over to the taxi waiting at the far side of the street.

When they reached his flat, Daniel bundled Lally out of the taxi, scrabbled in his pocket for money for the cabbie and pushed her through the front door. Kicking the door closed behind him, he pulled the thin straps of her dress from her shoulders. There was a ripping sound and the flimsy material slithered to the floor. He dragged off his jacket as she pulled him down to the rug in front of the fire. He didn't bother to turn on the fire, and the only light was the single bare electric bulb in the centre of the ceiling. She was wearing just white silk stockings and garters beneath her dress.

He did not bother with preliminaries. Her fingers efficiently unbuttoned his trousers, her open mouth searched for his. This time he responded to her kiss. She opened her legs and he forced himself into her, and heard her gasp. One of his hands threaded through her cropped hair, the other gripped her thin body against his. Her small teeth bit his shoulders, his chest. Her breasts pressed against him as she moved in rhythm with him. He had not fully undressed. *You're lucky if we take our socks off beforehand.*

Nicholas was driving to London to see Lally. Now, about halfway there, he had pieced most of the bits together. He drove as fast as the old Daimler would allow. His mind worked with a similar speed, racing down alleyways, making connections. Trees and hedges whirled by, lit only by the headlamps of the motor-car.

He was growing very tired. He had hardly slept the previous night, and the events of today and yesterday had been emotionally exhausting. He knew that even if he pulled in and tried to sleep, he would not be able to. His mind raced, refusing to allow him any rest. Besides, he had always enjoyed speed. It blanked things out. He remembered racing Titus along the drove, the dust kicked up by the horse's hooves in the heat, the sun on his back. Daniel Gillory had won that race, but Nicholas had not cared.

He rubbed at his eyes with one hand, struggling to fight back his fatigue. It occurred to him that it was futile, this drive. You could not alter the past. Whatever he said to Lally, or Lally said to him, could not change what had happened. It was like the crack in the wall of Drakesden Abbey: a single weakness in the foundations and the past began to fragment, a thousand hairline spidery faults shaking the entire edifice.

Nicholas saw suddenly that he did not have to go to London. He was tired, and he needed to rest. It was like riding Titus. All he had to do was push himself a little harder, and then he could lie again on the grass in the sunlight.

He pressed his foot down hard on the accelerator, and the old motor-car shook as it gathered speed. The speed was exhilarating, cleansing. It washed away everything, allowed him to start again. He was smiling and he no longer felt tired. The road stretched out long and dark in front of him, but he could see the end of it at last. When he felt the twist of the steering-wheel, the lurch as the tyres lost their grip on the surface of the road, he let out a cry of pleasure. He was free. He had escaped the chains of time.

Afterwards, Daniel closed his eyes for while and lay still. His anger had utterly gone, dissipated in the release of sexual tension. He felt rather tired and hazy, and was aware of the beginnings of a feeling of revulsion, largely directed against himself.

He opened his eyes when Lally started coughing. She was sitting up now, still naked, next to the unlit gas-fire. He could not at first believe that such a sound could come from so small a body. It was a dry, wracking cough and it shook her entire frame. Sitting up, pulling some of his clothes back on, Daniel stared at her. Her back was to him and he could see every one of her ribs. He could have counted the vertebrae of her spine; they seemed to pierce her skin.

She managed to stop coughing for a moment. 'Just a cold,' she said quickly, smiling at him. Her eyes were luminous.

Horrified, he managed to say, 'You've seen a doctor, haven't you?'

'Oh – a little while back. He wanted me to go to some beastly hospital. I couldn't, Daniel. I'm frightened of hospitals. Anyway, it's just a cold.'

She began to cough again. He could hardly bear the sound. Rising to his feet he lit the gas-fire and draped a blanket round her shoulders. When she looked up at him and said, 'You won't send me away, will you, Daniel? I don't want to be on my own. I hate being on my own,' he could not for a moment reply.

He looked down at her small shadowed face and knew that whatever harm she had done, she was going to pay for it, over and over again. No one should have to pay that price. So he said, 'You can stay till the morning, Lally. Just till the morning.'

She held out her arms to him like a child. He could see the need in her great hungry dark eyes. Helping her to her feet, he led her into the bedroom. There he found her one of his shirts to wear. She clung to him throughout the night, her dark cropped head nestled in the crook of his arm.

'Miss Thorne! Miss Thorne! There's a lady to see you.'

The knocking at her door interrupted muddled and exhausting dreams of William, of Daniel, of Drakesden. When Thomasine opened her eyes, she saw that it was still dark. Fumbling in the gloom to light the gas-mantle, she squinted at the clock. A quarter past six.

Pulling on her dressing-gown, she opened the door. 'Who is it, Mrs Price?'

'Her name's Lady Debden,' whispered Mrs Price. 'I've put her in the parlour.'

Still blurred with sleep, Thomasine did not for a moment recognize the name. Then she remembered: Lady Debden was Isabel Debden, formerly Isabel Blythe. Nicholas's Cousin Belle. She hadn't seen Belle for years.

Running down the stairs, she knew instinctively that something terrible had happened. *William* . . . William had pneumonia . . . or whooping cough . . . he had fallen downstairs . . .

All her worst forebodings were confirmed when she saw Belle. Belle was sitting at the table, a handkerchief scrunched up in her hands. Her eyes were red and swollen with weeping and her face was blotched pink and white.

She could hardly get the words out. 'Belle – what is it? *William* . . .?'

Belle shook her head. 'William's fine, Thomasine.' Her voice trembled. 'It's Nicky. A motor accident –' She broke off, mopped her eyes, and then took a deep breath. 'Nicky is dead, Thomasine.'

Thomasine sat down heavily on Mrs Price's horsehair sofa. She could not speak, she could only stare at Belle and note ridiculous details: the small hole at the ankle of Belle's gunmetal grey silk stocking, the jet bead on the tip of her hat-pin.

'It was last night. They think it must have been quite soon after midnight.' Belle rummaged in her bag for another handkerchief. 'A farmer found the motor-car in a ditch. The police told Aunt Gwendoline, and she telephoned me from the hospital. She had to . . . you know.'

Lady Blythe had had to identify the body of her son. Thomasine could not understand why her own eyes were dry when tears made constant furrows down Belle's powdered cheeks.

'Only,' Belle added tremulously, 'I can't find Lally, you see. Aunt Gwendoline asked me to break the news to her and Marjorie. But Lally didn't come home last night. She often doesn't, but I couldn't tell Aunt Gwendoline *that*, of course. So I said she was at a friend's house, and they hadn't a telephone. And I thought perhaps you might . . . I had to tell you anyway, since you and Nicky . . .' Her voice lurched wildly as she spoke her cousin's name, and she twisted her handkerchief into a sodden rope.

It all seemed quite unreal. It was almost as though she was still asleep and dreaming a particularly vivid nightmare. Soon she would wake up and know that Nicholas was still at Drakesden, and had not died in a motor accident at the age of twenty-nine. Thomasine dug her fingernails into her palms, trying to feel something, anything. She was aware of the lumpy springs of the sofa and the icy cold of the small, unheated parlour.

And yet there was an awful ring of truth about Belle's words. Even now, Thomasine could picture Nicholas's hands, white-knuckled as they clenched the steering-wheel, and see his eyes, fixed and staring on the road ahead.

She managed to speak at last. 'You want me to find Lally and tell her what's happened?'

Belle nodded. 'I'll have to travel down to Marjorie's by train – it's too ridiculous that they have no telephone. It doesn't seem right just to send a telegram. And there'll be arrangements to make . . . the funeral . . .' She looked up, her eyes screwing up again. 'It's all too frightful, isn't it, Thomasine? Just too frightful.'

Slowly, Thomasine nodded. It was beginning to seem real now. There was, at the edges of her consciousness, the beginnings of a raw pain.

'I know it's a beastly cheek, after all that's happened.' Belle blew her nose. 'But you knew some of Lally's set. And Julian is in India just now, and Boy says this sort of thing upsets him too much, and I really can't think what else to do. She could have left a note . . . or telephoned. I've asked everyone I can think of. So inconsiderate.' Her voice had become peevish and querulous. She flicked the veil of her hat over her swollen face and stood up.

Thomasine said, 'I'll do what I can, Belle. Someone must know where Lally is.'

After Belle had gone, Thomasine went to her room and rapidly dressed. A strange collection of clothes – an old tweed skirt, a blue jumper with a patch on the elbow, a pair of rather baggy black stockings. Even the normal everyday things of life, like getting dressed, had become difficult and disjointed. She shoved her purse into the deep pockets of her coat and pulled a cloche hat tightly over her hair. Then she ran out into the street to look for a taxi.

The lavender light in the east told her that dawn was approaching. The milkman's horse and cart clattered up the cobbles, and the newsboy had already set up his stand at the corner of the street. Thomasine found that she did not have the least idea where she was going. She tried to recall Lally Blythe's friends. There was Simon Melville, of course, though Simon had disclaimed friendship. Thomasine shivered. Who else? That boy at the Mayfair party – Thomasine could not remember his name – and Lally's lover in France. And Belle and Julian and Boy and Ettie. And yet somehow, standing there on the pavement in the icy dawn, Thomasine was not convinced that any of those people had truly been Lally's friend.

A taxi swung round the corner and Thomasine automatically put out her hand. The cab slowed to a halt.

'Where to, love?'

She hadn't a clue. Then, suddenly, she knew that there was someone who would help her. She gave the driver Daniel's address and settled back in the seat, the fur collar of her coat pulled up round her face. She had forgotten her gloves, and her hands were blue-tinged. Frost whitened the occasional small patches of grass beside the houses, and the sky was clear and cloudless. She thought, Nicholas is dead. Nicholas, who was my husband and who was the father of my child, is dead. The waste of it, the pointlessness of it, seared her. She thought bitterly that Nicholas had never had much of a life. What little happiness he had found had been illusory and transient. She pressed her knuckles against her eyes.

Daniel would help her. Daniel was good at finding things. He had helped her on Armistice Day, and he had found her in Camden Town after she had fled Antonia's house. He had trailed round Europe for three years and had driven the length and breadth of England. Daniel never got lost. He was the only person on whom she could, on this singularly awful day, rely. He would know how to find Lally.

The taxi slowed to a halt outside Daniel's flat. Thomasine handed a florin to the driver, and was left standing alone in the silent street. She rang the front doorbell.

Daniel, wearing only a pair of trousers, opened the door. Thomasine almost fell into the hallway of the flat. Her hands clutched at him.

'Oh – Daniel. The most terrible thing –'

There was a sound from behind him, as the bedroom door opened. A lazy, familiar voice said, 'It's a bit early for callers, isn't it, darling?'

Thomasine's hands slid from Daniel's arms. For a moment she stared at Lally Blythe, utterly confused. Lally was wearing a man's shirt, her short dark hair was tousled and her legs were bare. She was smiling. Thomasine took a step backwards. Her gaze flicked rapidly to Daniel and then back to Lally. Then she ran out into the street and back along the pavement.

He grabbed a jacket from the peg in the hall and ran after her. Lally called after him, but Daniel ignored her. He caught up with Thomasine just as she turned the corner.

'Thomasine. For God's sake –'

She did not stop walking, so he took hold of her elbow, halting her. When she turned to him, he saw the tears that glittered at the corners of her eyes.

'What do you want, Daniel?'

'To explain. It's not what you think.' Hopelessly, he gabbled clichés.

'Oh, I think it is. As she said, "It's a bit early in the morning for social calls." And she was wearing your shirt, Daniel!'

'Listen, please. Lally was at a party I went to last night. I'd drunk too much and I was in a foul mood after we quarrelled. For pity's sake, Thomasine – it wasn't important!'

She whispered, 'It is to me.'

There was a dreadful bleakness in her eyes, and her face, always pale, was quite white. He remembered then that she had said, 'The most terrible thing . . .' He asked urgently, 'What is it, Thomasine? What's happened?'

She laughed. It was a horrible sound, cracked and short and verging on the edge of hysteria. 'I was looking for Lally, actually, Daniel. It's quite convenient that she was with you. I've something to tell her.'

She began to walk again, pulling away from him. The great bulk of King's Cross station loomed behind her, blotting out the rising sun.

'But *you* can tell her now, can't you, Daniel? *You* can tell Lally Blythe that her brother is dead.'

He wanted to go to her, to hold her, to comfort her, but something in her expression halted him, keeping him at arm's length. 'Nicholas is dead? *How?*'

'A motor accident. Last night.' She had turned away from him.

As she walked away he watched the hunched lines of her narrow shoulders, the strands of red-gold hair that the wind lifted from beneath the brim of her hat. He could not accept that this was final, that through foolishness and anger and a desire for vengeance he had lost her.

He called out, 'Thomasine. Don't go! I love you!'

Just for a moment she paused. Fleetingly, she turned back to him.

'Do you, Daniel? I wonder if you do. No matter. It's over, isn't it? I don't ever want to see you again.'

He watched her leave him. He did not attempt to follow her. Instead, he walked back to his flat, and Lally.

'She's gone,' he said stupidly.

He caught sight then of the look of naked pleasure – of glee and triumph – on Lally's face, and he forgot her physical frailty and said suddenly and brutally, 'Nicholas is dead. He was killed in a motor accident last night.'

Her eyes rounded into two black circles, focused on him.

Then she began to cough. Daniel watched in horror as the blood gouted from Lally's mouth down the front of her borrowed shirt.

The funeral took place ten days later. It seemed to Thomasine that she had stood too often in the small church in Drakesden, had heard repeated too many times the words of the service for the Burial of the Dead. For Aunt Rose, for Sir William Blythe, for Fay Gillory, and now for Nicholas.

The day was cold and grey. Low clouds clung to the fields and marshes. She could not watch as the coffin was lowered into the grave. Instead, standing a little way away from the rest of the mourners, Thomasine looked out beyond the scattering of houses that made up the village and towards the dyke, that long, low barrier which divided earth from sky. When she remembered Nicholas now she no longer thought of the damaged man whom she had married, nor the jealous and obsessive husband from whom she had separated. She remembered instead the Nicholas of 1914, a boy of seventeen, darkly handsome, generous, eager to please. The Nicholas who had ridden with her and Daniel along the droves, who had led them through the twisting pathways of the Labyrinth. Who had shown her the wonderful treasures of Drakesden Abbey, who had laughed with her and Daniel, lying on the grass amongst the roses of the walled garden. Momentarily, Thomasine raised her head and looked back at the group of mourners around the grave. She could not, among the black-coated, veiled women, see Lally.

She realized that it was over. The circle of mourners was fragmenting into twos and threes. One of the veiled women was walking towards her, and Thomasine recognized Marjorie Blythe.

'We're having a little supper at the house,' said Marjorie. 'Nothing elaborate. I wondered if you would join us.'

Marjorie 'had inherited her father's heavier features, her mother's fair colouring. Lady Blythe's fragility had been passed only to her two younger children.

'That's very kind of you, Marjorie, but I don't think I'd better. If you would just give my condolences to your family.' She asked suddenly, 'Marjorie . . . where is Lally?'

Marjorie frowned. 'Lally is in hospital.'

'*Hospital?*'

'Well, a sanatorium, actually. She has tuberculosis.'

A sudden vivid picture of Lally Blythe as she had last seen her flashed through Thomasine's mind. Wearing Daniel's shirt, her hair untidy, her eyes still blurred with sleep. Her skin flushed, and her arms and legs like sticks.

'I didn't know.'

'None of us did.' The brisk upper-class confidence slipped for an instant. 'I sometimes think that none of us knew each other very well.' Marjorie's voice and expression were sad. 'She must have been unwell for years – she may even have contracted the disease at school. Anyway, she was taken very ill on the day after poor Nicky's accident. The shock, the doctor said.'

Marjorie took her leave and walked away. The mourners had dispersed now, walking home to their cottages, or following the path round to where the motor-cars waited by the lych-gate. Thomasine exchanged a few words with the rector and some of the villagers. She was aware that her position was now more ambiguous than ever: that she was neither widow nor wife nor divorcee. Curious eyes watched her furtively, voices whispered behind sheltering hands. Marjorie's gesture – initiated, Thomasine was certain, by Marjorie herself – had been a generous one, but at Drakesden Abbey, particularly, she would feel outcast, unwanted. She would not expose herself to that sort of scrutiny again. She would not let others judge her again.

She looked out on to the street. It was three years since she had lived in Drakesden and she had realized, travelling to the church from the guest-house in Ely in which she was staying, just how much everything had changed during that time. She had undertaken the journey from Ely by bus. The omnibus's route encircled half a dozen villages including Drakesden, before returning to the bus station in Ely. No more tramping through the fields, your boots embalmed by the muddy tracks, risking your life crossing the slippery bridges that spanned the dykes. On the bus, looking out of the window, she had seen the garage built on the outskirts of the village, near where they had once skated. It was a rickety affair of yellow brick and corrugated iron, but several motor-cars had stood in the forecourt and there had been two gleaming petrol pumps.

Change had touched the village as well. A tea-shop, of all things, had opened in the cottage next to the grocer's. Checked curtains hung in the windows and an advertisement pinned on the door offered ices and cakes. Mr Fanshawe had explained that during the summer charabanc outings visited the countryside from the cities, pausing frequently in Drakesden. Now, thirsty city-dwellers could drink tea or lemonade in Mrs Hayhoe's tea-shop. And by the roadside several stalls had been set up, offering winter vegetables and home-made jams and chutneys to the passing motorist. The machine that had engineered Nicholas's death was beginning to touch all their lives. Thomasine did not know whether the changes were for better or worse.

Gathering up her prayer-book and handbag, Thomasine walked over to the lych-gate. Peering out through the old lichened archway, she saw that the road was not, as she had thought, deserted. There was a Bentley parked on the curve of the road.

She had to walk past the Bentley in order to reach the bus-stop. As she drew level with the motor-car Thomasine saw that, though the driver was unfamiliar to her, in the back of the vehicle sat Lady Blythe. She hardly recognized the face beneath the raised veil. It was ruined, desolate, all trace of youth and beauty gone. There was a slight movement from the inside of the motor-car, a turning of the head, and just for a moment their eyes met. Thomasine saw utter defeat, a complete extinguishing of spirit in those faded blue eyes. To have outlived both your sons ... what more bitter fate, she thought, for any mother. Thomasine inclined her head, and walked on.

She would call Sir Alfred Duke tomorrow so that the process to win back her son might be set in motion. She knew that this time she would win. She would not stop fighting until she had custody of William again. Fleetingly, she wondered whether the broken woman she had glimpsed in the back of the Bentley was capable of any more struggle. She wondered if the impulse for possession had died even in that implacable heart.

Sunlight extruded in bands of gold from between the clouds. It bathed the village and the fields and fens in bright hues: coral and amber and orange and pink. The sky was a great palette of colour, painting the land with glory, marking the passing of dynasties, the beginnings of a different age.

That evening she began to go through Nicholas's things. Marjorie had offered, the maid had offered, but she had refused both of them. This last service only she could perform for her most beloved son.

Everything haunted her, though. She had approached the task believing that even in these nightmare days her old authority and ability to organize would not desert her, but now, faced with wardrobes, drawers, desk, bed, cupboards, all the inanimate objects that held such vivid traces of him, she was defeated, paralysed. When she closed her eyes, he was here in the room with her. The faint scent of him lingered in the shirts and the jackets. She believed that she could see the dent his head had made on the pillow. A single dark hair was threaded through the bristles of his hairbrush. 'Nicholas,' Lady Blythe whispered. She had given him the ivory-backed brush and its fellows: the comb, clothes-brush and looking-glass. Now she clutched the hairbrush to her, glimpsing perhaps for the first time since his accident the terrible endless void of his death, the desert that was the remainder of her life. He still spoke to her: she knew that she would hear his parting words to her for the rest of her days. *'Thomasine shall have the child, Mama . . . Who are you to judge another human being?'*

She shivered and looked out of the window. Now she saw clearly what the years had done to Drakesden Abbey: the overgrown gardens, the weed-filled paths, the silent fountain. She had never been a truly religious woman, attending church more as an affirmation of status than to fulfil spiritual need, but just now a phrase from the Book of Isaiah recalled itself to her, in all its unpitying beauty and sorrow: 'And thorns shall come up in her palaces, nettles and brambles in the fortresses thereof: and it shall be an habitation of dragons, and a court for owls.'

PART FIVE

1927–1928

Love, all alike, no season knowes, nor clime,
Nor houres, dayes, months, which are the rags of time.

(John Donne, 'The Sunne Rising')

CHAPTER NINETEEN

In the spring, Thomasine armed herself with secateurs, a wheel-barrow and heavy gardening gloves. William trailed behind her, a plump bundle of coat and mittens and scarf and buttoned boots. Inside the walled garden he played some distance away from her, rolling his ball through the long grass, but Thomasine knew that he watched her furtively.

Her secateurs clipped the roses; she swept up the tangled branches into the wheelbarrow. The roses had not, she realized, been pruned for years. She cut away all the diseased growth and the shoots that were too spindly to flower. The day was cold, but sunny. She worked methodically, pruning and tidying, raking away dead leaves and fallen rosehips, pulling out the weeds that pushed their heads through the soil.

'William. Come and see this.'

He came, obedient as always, and glanced at where she pointed.

'A caterpillar. Isn't he lovely?'

'I don't like insects,' said William. 'Nanny said insects are dirty.' He walked back to where he had been playing with the ball.

Thomasine removed the caterpillar to the sanctuary of the ferns beneath the Firedrake. Then she piled the pruned branches into the wheelbarrow, and put the secateurs in her pocket.

'Come on, William – that's enough work for one afternoon. Shall we make a bonfire to warm ourselves up?'

The child did not reply. He followed after Thomasine, a small, sullen, disinterested four-year-old, as she pushed the wheelbarrow out of the walled garden and back through the Labyrinth.

On the lawn, where once they had eaten cucumber sandwiches and drank tea from porcelain cups, she made the bonfire. Stuffing crumpled newspaper beneath the leaves and branches to ensure that it caught, she opened the box of matches.

'Do you want to help me light it, William?'

His eyes, a light blue-green that echoed her own, gleamed, but he said nothing.

'We'll hold the match together,' she said coaxingly.

'Nanny said matches are dangerous.'

Thomasine managed to hide her irritation. 'Well – so they are. But if we are very careful and very sensible, we won't get hurt.'

He remained standing on the far side of the bonfire, his lower lip stuck out. She showed him the matchbox one more time, but he shook his head obstinately, so she knelt on the grass and lit the fire herself.

She went to stand beside her small proud son as the newspaper caught and the leaves began to crackle and flare. As the branches burned, sparks danced up into the dusky sky, and Thomasine placed a hand on William's shoulder, making a fragile bridge between the two of them. But he twisted from her grasp, and ran up the steps and back into the empty house as the smoke billowed from the fire, misting the grass and trees.

Sometimes at night she dreamed about it – two yellow gleaming eyes and an open maw that hungered for her. Then she would wake up suddenly, staring wildly at the child in the cot as she fumbled to light her candle.

But William was always safe, and the only sound was the whine of the wind as it twisted through the chimneys. At night, apart from William and herself, the house was deserted. Sitting up alone in the huge four-poster, wrapped in cardigans and shawls and blankets to keep out the bitter cold, Thomasine would stare out at the darkness and think.

It had, in the end, been easy to reclaim her son. A clutch of lawyers' letters had hurtled to and fro, and out of them had come, eventually, the confirmation that Lady Blythe would not attempt to fight for custody of her grandson. Sir Alfred Duke had broken that news to Thomasine in person, and the other, even less expected, news. That Lady Blythe had left Drakesden Abbey to live with her daughter Marjorie.

Drakesden Abbey was entailed, therefore it belonged now to William. Gently, Sir Alfred Duke had put it to Thomasine that she could, if she chose, live at Drakesden Abbey with her son. She had been able to make no immediate decision. She had left the lawyer's office with her mind in turmoil, and had lain awake for three nights in succession trying to sort it all out. She had recalled the raw misery of many of her days at Drakesden Abbey, as well as the sense of pride she had felt when she had learned how to manage that hostile land. She had recalled the isolation, the backwardness of the Fens, as well as the soaring skyscapes, the sense of freedom. She had reminded herself of the career she had carved out, the promotion that she had fought long and hard to secure, the independence and security that her wages had given her.

She had, in the end, gone back for William. Because Drakesden Abbey had been William's home for all the years of his short life; because to uproot him, after all the partings he had suffered, would be cruel. Because he was, in the end, a Blythe, and Blythes had always lived at Drakesden Abbey. So she had packed her things, and given in her notice, and begun again, once more. Another journey, another unfathomable destination. Only this time, perhaps, alighting at Ely station, she had had a sense of homecoming.

Often, lying awake at night, she thought of the manner of Nicholas's death. The straight empty road, his years of driving, the fact that no other person had been involved in the accident. His sudden and unexplained decision to leave Drakesden that evening, his destination unknown to everyone. She would wonder over and over again whether Nicholas's death had been accidental, as the inquest had decided, or whether it had been something altogether blacker. She did not doubt that Nicholas had been capable of taking his own life, but she was unable to follow precisely the sequence of events that had preceded his death. It was like trying to put together a jigsaw puzzle when half the pieces were missing.

So she remained awake in the darkness, watching the stub of candle burn down. There were other things she must not think of: images of betrayal and love and death. All she had to do now was to survive, to feed, clothe and keep warm both her child and herself. Existence had been scraped down to the bare bone, and she was glad of that. It made everything simpler. She must ensure that the remaining lands flowered and fruited, so that she could feed her son both this year and the next. The dragon's name now was hunger, and she alone was responsible for keeping it at bay.

She had begun to sell land within a week of returning to Drakesden. Soon, Thomasine knew, there would be nothing left but the gardens of Drakesden Abbey itself and a few fields scattered around the village. The more valuable fields – the wide swathes of black earth between Drakesden and Ely – she had already sold. She signed the bills of sale without a qualm, knowing that only by so diminishing the estate could she retain a fraction of it for its owner, her son.

She had gone through Drakesden Abbey's accounts with Max Feltham, who had explained everything to her. That the estate, even before Nicholas's death, had been heavily indebted, kept afloat only by the sale of valuable items such as furniture or paintings. That the farm had not been profitable since Thomasine herself had quit it in 1923. That Nicholas's and Lady Blythe's expenditure had always been heavy. Max's advice was to sell up, to abandon Drakesden Abbey so that Thomasine was left perhaps with enough cash to buy a little suburban villa. Stubbornly, she refused. Max, sighing, began to calculate with her the death duties that would soon be payable, and the expected valuation of land and property. Eventually he conceded that survival was just about feasible. 'It'll be damned hard work,' he had said, as he had left for Ely station. 'Are you sure it's worth it?' Thomasine had only nodded and smiled.

Since then, she had worked through all the hours of daylight. The money that she had saved from her job as an accounts clerk had been eaten up already. The estate had a vast maw and an empty belly. But if there were no longer fields in which to grow wheat and barley, then there were still orchards, kitchen gardens and conservatories. Thomasine began with the conservatory. The plumbago, hoya and oleander she cut back or gave away, but she kept the passion flower, fig and apricot, looking forward to the summer when the fruit would grow fat against the warm walls of the conservatory. Exotic fruits would fetch a high price. Outside, the years of neglect had tangled the gardens into a wilderness. Thistles choked the kitchen garden. The trees in the orchard, unpruned for years, were blighted and straggly. Thomasine worked systematically, tearing away the weeds, giving the plants room to breathe. Often she thought that the garden had beaten her: clearing one patch of earth, she would discover the bright green heads of new weeds sprouting in the patch she had dug only the previous week. Stubbornly she persevered, aware that she could not afford to fail. She sowed seeds according to the type of soil and the aspect of the land, knowing the futility of attempting to force a plant to survive in unsuitable soil.

In the flower gardens she kept only the plants that could be sold as cut flowers – the roses, the bulbs and some of the perennials. They would grow no more neat rows of begonia and alyssum. Drakesden Abbey was turning into a market garden.

The seeds and cuttings she begged and wheedled from neighbours and acquaintances. She was shameless in her methods: a bat of her eyelashes and she had a set of lettuce seedlings from a farmer, a dull afternoon at the rectory discussing the perils of spiritualism and she went home with twists of paper containing carrot, onion and radish seeds harvested from Mr Fanshawe's kitchen garden.

She had only the boy from the village to help her with the heavy work. Eddie was fourteen years old, slow and silent, the product of a marriage between cousins. In return for his digging and fetching and carrying, Thomasine fed him and gave him a few shillings a week pocket money. Eddie could not have joined the exodus to the towns that had gathered momentum in the village of Drakesden, leaving some of the cottages untenanted and filling the bus each morning. He could neither read nor write. At Thomasine's suggestion, he watched, open-mouthed, as she taught William his letters, but when he attempted to scrawl his own name on the paper, his efforts were clumsy and illegible.

Sometimes, crawling up to bed at the end of an exhausting day, she caught sight of herself in the mirror. A battered tweed skirt or, increasingly often, an old pair of Nicholas's trousers, belted in at the waist. Several thick jumpers and a muffler round her neck. Her hair had grown to shoulder-length and was scraped back with a piece of ribbon.

A few of the fields she kept, not yet ready to sell them. They were the fields that abutted the Gillory land, now farmed by the Dockerills, edged by the dyke.

The generator failed at the end of February. Thomasine gazed at the complicated collection of pipes and motors and then firmly shut the boiler-room door. Searching through the house, she rediscovered candles and oil-lamps. It did not matter now that she used the best candles in the servants' rooms; they no longer had servants.

She soon realized that it was both impossible and unnecessary to heat and light the entire house. Downstairs, they began to live almost exclusively in the kitchen. Following the installation of electricity in Drakesden Abbey, the range had not been lit for years, but Thomasine cleaned and polished it and, after a great many attempts, discovered how to light it. She kept it burning constantly, fed by the logs that Eddie cut, so that there was always one warm room in the house. They ate their meals in the kitchen, she and William, perched at one end of the huge table round which the servants had dined. William loathed the arrangement. 'Kitchens are for servants,' he said, staring scornfully at Thomasine.

Initially, her happiness at being reunited with her son had been overwhelming. It was as though a part of her body had been amputated and then somehow reattached. At Drakesden with William, she had felt complete again. Soon, however, she had begun to understand that it wasn't quite that easy. William's memories of her were those of repeated desertion. If affection had blossomed during those three years of monthly meetings then it had always, on parting, been blighted. She knew that William's coldness with her was born of anger and pride and a fear that she would desert him again. She had not yet found a way to break through the barrier.

She knew also that he was confused and frightened by the series of sudden changes that had overtaken his life. The loss of his father, the absence of his grandmother. The earlier departure of his nanny and the more recent leaving of Martha the nurse-maid for a more lucrative job in a hairdresser's in Ely. William was obliged to eat his meals in the kitchen, to share a bedroom with his mother rather than sleep in the nursery, and to grub around in the garden. He had no nursemaid to help him dress and wash – worse, his mother was beginning to teach him to do those things for himself. Drakesden Abbey had become cold, empty, strange. Bewildered, he retreated into himself, hoping that the life he was accustomed to would soon return.

Thomasine recognized in William both her own pride and Nicholas's fear of disorder. He was polite and distant and controlled, already ashamed, as Nicholas had been, of his uncertainties. Thomasine's heart almost broke, understanding the battles fought in her small son's head. He did not, she discovered, know how to play. He knew how to read and how to write his name and recognize his numbers, but he did not know how to make a mud-pie or blow soap bubbles. If she told him to play, then he made neat rows of tin soldiers, or piled wooden bricks one on top of the other with careful and anxious concentration. When Thomasine opened the kitchen cupboards for him and showed him all the shelves of jelly moulds and saucepans and whisks and wooden spoons, he did not, as other small children would have done, crawl inside and examine every object. He just stared blankly at her, his eyes sea-green and uncomprehending.

April approached, and spring was more than a whisper of warmer air and bluer skies. Daffodils nodded on the lawn and the borders were crammed with tulips of every shade. Thomasine dressed William in his coat and boots and led him out of the gardens through the orchard. At the end of the orchard she opened the gate, and took his mittened hand in hers as they walked through the wood.

'Why are we going this way? I never go this way.'

Thomasine smiled. 'You can see the bluebells if you walk through the wood. And look, William – there's a butterfly.'

William glanced at the primrose yellow butterfly, resolutely unimpressed. He looked down at the path. 'It's muddy.'

'So it is. We'll be able to see our footprints.'

Studying the imprint of his own small foot, he said nothing.

'We're going to the Dockerills',' explained Thomasine, as they reached the stile. 'It's far quicker to walk through the wood than to go round by the drive.'

'I like the drive. I liked the motor-car.' William stared at the stile, as if he was not quite sure what to do with it. Thomasine climbed over first, and held out her hand.

'I can do it myself.' Proudly, he scrambled over the wooden bar. Thomasine waited for him while he brushed his coat clean.

'Nanny says God doesn't like dirty boys.'

She stared at him, appalled. Just then, he reminded her so vividly of Nicholas: the mop of dark hair, the meticulous picking of every speck of dirt from his clothes.

She said gently, 'God loves every sort of boy, William. He doesn't care in the least bit whether their clothes are clean or dirty, whether they've had a bath today or not, whether they've remembered to brush their hair or clean their teeth.'

Impulsively, she reached down and hugged him. He still resisted her, but not quite as resolutely, she thought, as he had three months earlier. 'I love you,' she whispered in his ear. 'I always have done and I always will.'

When they reached the end of the track, Thomasine took the familiar path round the side of the blacksmith's cottage.

'I'm hoping that Mr Dockerill will sell us some hens,' she explained. 'Then we could keep them in the garden. That would be nice, wouldn't it, William? We'd have lots of lovely eggs.'

He said nothing, but she thought she detected a flicker of interest in his eyes. Walking into the yard, Thomasine saw Harry Dockerill leading the horse out of the stable. She called his name and he turned, doffing his cap.

'Your ladyship . . . I mean . . .'

'Miss Thorne will be fine, Harry. Or Thomasine, if you prefer.'

Harry crossed the courtyard to join her. 'Annie!' he called. 'Missus is here.'

Annie Dockerill appeared, drying her hands on her apron. A small girl toddled after her, pulling at her mother's skirts.

'Missus.' A bob of the head. 'And young Master William.'

William eyed her. 'You used to clean the steps.'

Annie Dockerill laughed. 'So I did. The Abbey's steps was a never-ending job, too. I'd no sooner get to the top, and the bottom one would be dirty again.'

'Put the kettle on, Annie,' said Harry. 'You'll have a cup of tea, won't you, Miss Thorne?'

She agreed happily. Tea was poured out and drunk, a ginger-bread man found for William, and the weather, the farm and the children discussed.

Eventually Thomasine said, 'I came to ask you, Harry, whether we could perhaps make an exchange. I know that you sell cut daffodils in Ely market – well, I've hundreds and hundreds of tulips. Beautiful ones – all colours.'

Harry nodded. 'Abbey tulips are famous, Miss Thorne. I could sell 'em for you easy as anything.' He frowned. 'An exchange?'

'For hens, if you would, Harry. A few pullets, if you can spare them. I've plenty of wood and chicken wire and I'm sure, if I showed him how, Eddie could make me a hen-house. There's a good place for it near the potting-sheds. And I don't think we've too many foxes at the moment.'

Harry stood up. 'Come and choose half a dozen pullets now. They're good layers – did me proud last year. And I'll give Eddie Readman a hand with the hen-house, else it'll fall over at the first breeze.'

Out in the yard, Thomasine chose half a dozen plump pullets and made arrangements for the picking of the tulips and the building of the hen-house. When she looked back, Thomasine saw that William was not, as she had expected, glaring scornfully at the muddy farmyard. Instead he was standing beside the stables, looking up at the horse. She went over to him and crouched beside him.

'He's called Nelson, William. He's Mr Dockerill's horse – he does lots of work on the farm. Would you like to give him a sugar-lump?'

Her breath caught in her throat when William nodded, rather than push her away. Thomasine delved in her coat pocket for the sugar-lumps that she always carried with her in the countryside.

'You have to hold your hand out flat.' She placed the sugar in the centre of the child's palm. 'That's it. Now I'll lift you up, because Nelson is so big.'

She lifted him up and watched as the horse's velvety lips nuzzled at his small palm. William's eyes were huge and round and admiring.

'He likes to have his mane patted.'

William reached out a hand. From behind her, Harry Dockerill said, 'Isn't a bit afraid, is he, Miss Thorne? Blythes were allus good horsemen.'

At last William wriggled out of her grasp. Thomasine stared at Nelson thoughtfully.

'The stables are empty now – Nicholas had to sell all the horses. Harry – does the rector still keep a pony?'

Harry nodded. 'Old Bluebell died a few years back, but he bought another to pull the cart. Not that Mrs Fanshawe goes out in it more'n once a year, but he still likes to keep a pony.'

She found that she was smiling. 'Thank you, Harry. I'll go now, then. I think I've time to call on the rector before lunch.'

The following day, Thomasine borrowed the rector's pony and began to teach William to ride in the paddock. The pony was called Fancy, a plump, dappled version of Thomasine's old friend Bluebell. Watching William seated on Fancy's back, his short legs stuck out to either side of the fat belly, she was irresistibly taken back to the past. She, mounted on the rector's pony, Daniel riding along the drove beside her. She did not allow herself to think of Daniel Gillory; she had refused to think of Daniel Gillory since December. She had worked so hard over the last few months she had barely had time to think. That kind of love was a luxury now, abandoned with all the other luxuries that had once clung to Drakesden Abbey, like servants and scented soap and hot running water.

A few days later she had dozed off, exhausted, beside the kitchen range when she was woken by William's screams.

It was dark. Still drugged by sleep, Thomasine grabbed an oil-lamp from the table and ran for the kitchen door. A house the size of Drakesden Abbey held many dangers for a small child. He had tumbled downstairs, or caught his clothes on a candle . . .

'William! Where are you, William?'

He did not reply, he only continued to sob, but the sobbing was, she thought, a little closer. With the oil-lamp clutched in her hand, Thomasine ran past the butler's pantry, the storerooms, the buttery. In the hallway she glanced wildly into the morning-room and drawing-room. They were both empty. Then, raising the lamp and calling his name again, she spied him at the top of the stairs, curled up in the pool of moonlight that streamed from the window. She gathered him in her arms.

'William – sweetheart – what is it? Have you hurt yourself?'

He managed to shake his head. He could hardly speak for crying. 'I saw – I saw – a monster!'

Thomasine looked to where he pointed. There was only the moonlight and the curtains, moving slightly in the draught from the windows.

'There's nothing there, sweetheart. Only the silly old curtains. Look.'

William raised his head. His face was stained with tears and his body still shook. He whispered tremulously, 'It had great big teeth.'

'It's all gone now.' Thomasine pressed her face against his, rocking him. 'It won't come back.'

And yet she could almost imagine, looking round her, what William had seen. The vast empty house creaked and groaned in the wind; draughts blew currents of cold air around every window and door. If she opened the front door, old dry leaves would blow in, swirling in eddies in the hallway. Mould blossomed on the old wallpaper in some of the unheated rooms, and in the attics water seeped through the roof where damaged tiles had not been replaced. She felt very alone, and very aware of the responsibilities she had taken on.

William whispered, 'When's Daddy coming back?'

Thomasine's heart lurched. The small face stared up at her trustingly, the eyes solemn, waiting for an answer.

'Martha said Daddy had gone away for a while. Will he come back soon?'

'Oh, William.' Her voice was bleak, like a sigh. She rose to her feet, the child still clasped in her arms. 'We'll go to the kitchen and make some cocoa. It's warmer there. And we'll talk about Daddy.'

Parcels arrived from Marjorie Blythe and Aunt Hilly. Marjorie's parcel contained clothes passed down from her two sons: jumpers, shirts, shorts, coats, pyjamas and boots. Cutting the string and examining the contents of the brown paper parcel, Thomasine felt almost weak with relief. William seemed to grow visibly each month. She had been dreading the cost of buying his next pair of boots. In Hilda's parcel was a warm jumper for Thomasine herself, several packets of seeds from the school's kitchen-garden and a postal-order for ten guineas. 'A late birthday present,' the enclosed letter explained.

The hen-house was built, the pullets fetched from the Dockerills and installed in their new home. When they began to lay, Thomasine assigned to William the task of collecting the eggs. He enjoyed searching in the straw for the warm brown eggs, and placing them carefully in his basket.

Annie Dockerill called one day with a bundle of hay for the hen-house. 'Harry can often spare a sack or two, Missus. If you're ever short, just let us know.'

'*Thomasine,*' said Thomasine firmly. 'Look at me, Annie. My hair's a mess and I'm wearing *trousers*. I'm not Lady Blythe any more.'

'You do look a bit of a sight, Missus – I mean, Thomasine.' Annie grinned apologetically. 'It do take some getting used to, though. I mean – all this.'

Thomasine glanced at the neat rows of salad vegetables that grew to one side of the front lawn. 'It's a bit of a change, isn't it? You just wait, Annie – you won't recognize the place soon. I thought we could keep a few ducks on the pond. The fountain hasn't worked for years. I'll have to ask your Harry's advice about ducks, though.'

Annie said suddenly, 'Oh – the little rascal!'

Thomasine followed the direction of Annie's gaze. William, halfway back from the hen-house, had paused on the path. Carefully, one by one, he was dropping the eggs from his basket on to the stone path and watching them shatter on the flags.

'You'll lose the lot of 'em –' Annie began to walk towards the boy, but Thomasine grabbed her arm, halting her.

'No. Look, Annie.'

William had crouched on the flagstones and was dipping his finger in the mess. Thomasine found that she was smiling with pleasure as she watched him draw circles on the stones with the yellow yolks and scoop up and squeeze through his fingers the sticky transparent albumen, all with an expression of concentrated delight on his face.

'He's being *naughty!*' She turned back to Annie. 'Isn't it wonderful?'

Thomasine celebrated William's fifth birthday at the end of May with a picnic on the lawn at the side of the house. They drank home-made lemonade and ate sandwiches and buns. William's birthday cake, which Thomasine had baked the previous evening, was slightly sunk in the middle, but William didn't seem to mind. He blew out the candles with gusto and made a wish, his eyes screwed up tightly. They paddled in the pond and played hide-and-seek in the Labyrinth. She had played hide-and-seek in the Labyrinth before, but that was a long time ago, in another country. Afterwards, they cleared up the picnic things, bundling them together in an old tablecloth. William was pushing the cork back into the lemonade bottle when he paused, staring at the house.

'What is it, William?'

His brow was creased in a frown. 'That window looks funny.'

Thomasine looked at where he was pointing, at the side wall of the house. It was true, one of the windows did look odd. Though the sunlight glinted from the panes of five windows at a similar angle, from the sixth the light appeared peculiarly distorted. She began to run towards the house. The sill was swathed in wisteria. The greyish-purple pendant flowers hung like misty bunches of grapes all over the side and front of the house. The corners of the window were asymmetrical. Desperately, Thomasine began to scrabble through the forest of leaf and winding, wiry stem.

'Has someone broken it?' William sounded frightened.

Thomasine managed to shake her head. 'No, darling. See — the glass is still there.'

The wisteria clung to the old bricks. She could not break its hold, but she could tear aside the flowers and leaves and smaller shoots. And then she stopped, suddenly cold in the bright summer sunshine, staring at what she had uncovered.

'What's that, Mummy?'

Her heart was in her throat. She said slowly, 'It's a crack, William. The wall is cracked.'

She touched the treacherous space between brick and mortar. She knew what she would find if she continued to tear away at the wisteria — the fault snaked towards the roof of the house, pulling brick from brick, rending apart what had stood for centuries.

Thomasine used Hilda's ten guineas to pay for a surveyor from Ely. An Austin Seven clattered up the drive one bright June morning, laden with tools and instruments. For what seemed an unbearably long time, the surveyor crawled about the attics, dug away at the base of the walls and took sightings and measurements. As he worked, Thomasine and William pinched out tomatoes and removed caterpillars from lettuces. Thomasine's hands, normally careful, were clumsy with nervousness.

Eventually the surveyor strode across the lawn to join her.

'Oh dear, oh dear, Mrs Thorne. You've got yourself a tricky little problem here.' Smiling, he rubbed his hands together.

Thomasine, greeting him, managed to quell her impatience.

'How old is the house, Mrs Thorne?'

She calculated rapidly. 'It was built in the early eighteenth century, Mr Purbeck. There was a Tudor house on the site before that, and before that, an abbey.'

'No foundations, you see, Mrs Thorne, no foundations, that's your trouble. Or, at least, they skimped on the foundations. Used some of the old foundations to support the new walls, and only dug a foot or so into the ground. Builders in those days had no idea of the importance of firm foundations, especially on a site like this.' Mr Purbeck shook his head, smiling at past follies.

'But the house has stood for almost two hundred years,' she said, bewildered. 'Surely any settlement should have finished years ago?'

'The house isn't *settling*, Mrs Thorne – it's *subsiding*.'

Thomasine stared at him, horrified.

'You had a new well put in recently, didn't you, Mrs Thorne?'

For a moment, her mind would not work. Then she remembered the dark scars that had seared Drakesden Abbey's gardens at the time of William's birth.

'My husband had the new well sunk five years ago.' She was still confused, unable to see the connection between Nicholas's sinking of a new well to supply hot water and the crack in the wall.

The surveyor finally put aside his amusement, and took pity on her. Taking a pencil and notepad from his briefcase he began to draw. Thomasine sat down on a nearby bench, William on her lap. She felt slightly sick.

'You see, Mrs Thorne, you're on clay and surrounded by peat. That's the root of your trouble. If I may –' Thomasine nodded, and Mr Purbeck sat on the bench beside her, showing her the sketch. 'Drakesden island is clay, and around it there's the peat of the Fens. The peat is like a sponge, full of water. The well your husband sunk takes water from the peat, like so.' The pencil pointed to the diagram in the notepad. 'The peat dries up, and thus dries out the clay. We've had a series of wet springs and dry summers, which makes things worse, of course. The peat expands in the winter and contracts in the summer. And your trees won't help.'

'Trees?'

'Those.' The surveyor nodded in the direction of the copper-beech, the monkey-puzzle and the cedar. 'They'll suck up water in a dry summer. In August, this ground must be like powder.'

Every August, dust had filmed the windows, had been trodden into carpets and rugs. Servants had laboured endlessly, scrubbing and polishing to keep the forces of nature at bay.

'So the house has shifted on its foundations . . . the ground has sunk, and that's making the house subside.'

'That's right, Mrs Thorne. The wall is already bulging several inches out of true. Quite remarkable in so large a house – I've never seen anything like it.'

She thought then of the many Fen cottages with walls that listed at a crazy angle, windows that leaned drunkenly to the earth and doors several feet above the sinking peat. She had believed Drakesden Abbey to be different, safer.

'Of course,' continued Mr Purbeck gleefully, 'that's why there's so few great houses in these parts. Everyone knows the land won't take them.'

She said slowly, 'Is there nothing that can be done?'

Mr Purbeck pursed his mouth. 'You could try underpinning – digging beneath the house and laying new foundations.'

'And that would cost . . .?'

He named a sum so vast that she knew that it was pointless even to give it consideration. 'And if I can't do that?'

'You must stop using the new well. Re-open the old one –

it's further away from the house and won't dry the land out as quickly. And have those trees cut down. That might stave off the worst of it for a while, though it won't cure your problem.'

She stared at the cedar, the monkey-puzzle and the copper-beech. She hardly dared voice her worst fear.

'Will the house collapse, Mr Purbeck?'

He returned his notepad and pencil to his briefcase. 'In time, Mrs Thorne, in time. That wall will lean more and more out of true – and the roof will become unstable. The wallpaper's already tearing in some of the attic rooms. And the winter frosts will make things worse.'

When he had gone, Thomasine looked for a long while at the great house built on the summit of the island. It appeared so solid, so unassailable. And yet the ground was shifting beneath it, a slow invisible force that would in time destroy the entire edifice.

At the end of the month Thomasine and William moved to the farm manager's cottage. The cottage lay at the foot of the island, next to the paddock, not far from the dyke. It had a kitchen, scullery and parlour downstairs, and two bedrooms upstairs. Unused for years, the cottage was festooned with spider-webs, thick with black dust.

Thomasine enveloped herself in an apron and swept and scrubbed and whitewashed walls. William set himself the task of collecting the many spiders from their webs and transporting them to safety. He had forgotten his previous distaste for small creatures, and handled them with careful concentration. The boy Eddie hacked at the brambles and nettles in the garden and made huge bonfires, staring at them slack-mouthed as the flames soared high into the sky.

Eventually the cottage was habitable. Harry Dockerill and Eddie carried the heavy furniture down from the big house; Thomasine herself collected cooking utensils and bedding. She had to make several trips from the house to the cottage, William trailing along beside her, his arms full of spoons and soap and pillowcases. Inside Drakesden Abbey she felt like a thief, an invader. Disapproving ghosts lingered, watching her as she took plates from the kitchen, sheets and towels from the housekeeper's room, but she was ruthless and methodical in her spoliation.

William began to grow tired and querulous. Thomasine picked up her final load and walked out of the front door for the last time. Then she heard a voice call out her name.

Her heart began to pound. Turning, she saw Daniel Gillory. Her arms stiffened round the basket of blankets, and she waited silently as Daniel walked towards her.

'Harry said that you were moving house.'

'Harry didn't say he had visitors.'

His eyes met hers. 'I asked him not to.'

There was a silence. Then Daniel said, 'Shall I carry those for you?' And because it would have been churlish to refuse, and because she was tired, Thomasine nodded her head and passed him the basket.

The silence continued as they walked down the hill. When she thought how easy it had once been to talk to Daniel Gillory, her heart ached. The awkwardness confirmed what she had known since December, that whatever had once been between them was now over. But Daniel had not changed, she thought. She wished he would change, that he would grow unpleasing, unfamiliar. It would be so much easier then.

Inside the cottage she made a sandwich for William and poured him a cup of milk. William wandered out into the garden, bread clutched in one hand, cup in the other. When he was out of earshot, Daniel said, 'I know you didn't want to see me again, but there are a couple of things –'

'There's nothing, Daniel. Nothing at all.' Her tone was final.

'I've come to tell you that I'm going away.'

She was washing up – anything to keep busy. Anything to avoid looking at the man who had hurt her almost beyond endurance. She paused, though, her hands immersed in soapy water.

'The new book won't come, and I thought that if I travelled again I might find some sort of inspiration. Or at least accept that I haven't got it in me any more.'

She started to pile plates into the water, to scrub them viciously. Silence lengthened between them, a yawning desert. Eventually she said, 'When?'

'I'm sailing in a week's time. I came up here to leave the bike with Harry.'

A week. She should be feeling glad, and yet she was not. She felt as though another layer of stone was forming around her heart, a slow, petrifying drip. She glanced outside to check that William was playing safely and noted with dreary irritation that her vision was slightly blurred.

'So you've come to say goodbye?' Her tone was sarcastic. She saw him wince.

'Not quite. Worse than that. I've come to ask you a favour.'

Misery was for a moment swamped by bewilderment. Thomasine dried her hands on her apron and turned to face him. 'A favour?'

'I've come to ask if you would visit Lally while I'm away.'

For a moment she struggled for words. Then, 'I don't believe it, Daniel. How *could* you —'

'Please, Thomasine. Let me explain. You can tell me afterwards that I'm an arrogant and insensitive bastard.'

He was holding out a chair for her. She sat down heavily, unable to look at him.

'Lally is very ill. She has TB.'

'I know that. Her sister told me.' Thomasine's voice was stiff and furious.

'She's in a sanatorium in Hertfordshire — it's supposed to be a good place. Well — I've been visiting her every fortnight or so. A lot of the time they won't let me see her, so I just leave flowers or something.'

She said nothing, just stared at him mutely. Daniel sat down beside her.

'What I said last December was true. I'd got drunk at a party, Lally was there and insisted on coming home with me. And – yes – we made love. If you could call it that. I'm not trying to make excuses – I know that's not possible. I was stupid and angry, and because I was stupid and angry I lost you. I regret that bitterly.'

She looked outside to where William played. He was taking branches from the pile that Eddie had swept up and threading them together to make a den. She whispered, 'Lally must mean something to you, Daniel, or you wouldn't be visiting her.'

'Lally may *die*, Thomasine. And she has no one else. Both her brothers are dead. Her mother pays the fees for the sanatorium, but never visits. Her sister comes occasionally, but as she has an invalid husband she can't make the journey very often.'

'Belle and Julian,' said Thomasine wildly. 'Lally's London friends –' Yet she remembered, as she spoke, her suspicion that none of those bright, glittering people had really been Lally Blythe's friend.

Daniel shook his head. 'Plenty of people don't care for hospitals. Especially TB sanatoria. They're cold, draughty, miles from anywhere. I asked the doctors, Thomasine. Hardly anyone comes.'

'So you think that because I was her sister-in-law . . .?'

He shook his head. She saw that he was, unusually, searching for words. 'I'm not asking you because of that. It's just that –' and Daniel screwed up his eyes, scowling – 'we seem to have been interlinked. You and me and Nicholas and Lally.'

Like a dance, she thought. Nicholas and Lally and Daniel and she were trapped in one of those old country dances. Constantly weaving in and out, holding hands first with one partner, then with another.

She avoided Daniel's eyes. She knew that a thousand words lay unspoken between them and that she was still too brittle to voice them.

She heard him say, 'I feel responsible, you see, Thomasine. I felt responsible for Nicholas too.'

Now she looked at him, her eyes wide and troubled.

'Too much of a coincidence, wasn't it? I speak to Nicholas for the first time in years, we exchange a few of our guiltier secrets, and the next day Nicholas manages to break his neck on a straight stretch of road without another vehicle in sight.'

Thomasine shuddered. 'Secrets? What secrets?'

'Nicholas told me about what had happened to him in the War. And I told him about Lally. When we were kids, I mean. I must have said *something*. I don't know. Perhaps he regretted telling me so much . . . perhaps he still hated to think that his sister would kiss me –'

'Or perhaps he knew that he'd lost Drakesden.' Thomasine's voice was flat, attempting to disguise her pain. 'I've thought about it over and over again, Daniel. Perhaps Nicholas knew that he'd lost the house and the land.'

He looked up at her, frowning.

She explained, 'I've had to sell most of the land – even if Nicholas had lived he probably wouldn't have been able to hold on to it. The estate was heavily indebted. He shouldn't have been a farmer, you see. Gerald should have inherited, not Nicholas.'

'But the house . . .?'

'Why do you think we're living here now? The house is collapsing.'

'*Collapsing?*' Thomasine could hear the shock in Daniel's voice.

'The peat in the fen has sunk and the clay's dried out. The house has hardly any foundations, so the walls have begun to move. A cottage like yours will shift with the land it's built on, but a great house like Drakesden Abbey will simply fall to pieces. The roof may cave in, the surveyor says.'

'My God. I've always thought of Drakesden Abbey as indestructible.'

'Me too. I was wrong. And if Nicholas had realized . . .' Thomasine took a deep breath and fleetingly touched Daniel's hand. 'Daniel – we don't know whether Nicholas took his own life. We'll never know. And if he did – well, he could have done it at any time. The War changed him so much. I couldn't sleep for weeks, thinking about it, but now –' She shook her head. 'We just have to get on with things, don't we? I have to look after his son and try and keep the remains of the estate together. You have to write your books. You have to tell the truth.'

She looked around her at the small, comfortable kitchen, still littered with boxes of crockery and baskets of linen. 'Anyway, I like it here. It's the right size for William and me. We felt lost in that huge place.'

'Harry said you've been doing a grand job. Hens . . . salad vegetables . . . cut flowers.'

Thomasine rose to her feet and began to unpack one of the boxes of crockery. 'I've all the orchard fruits and the old kitchen garden, and you should see what I'm growing in the conservatory. I was lucky – it's been easy. It just needed tidying up a bit.'

She was unwrapping newspaper from around a cup. Daniel caught her hand, spreading out the fingers and palm. The callouses that marked the skin between the knuckles and the traces of old blisters on her palm were easily visible.

'*Easy?*' he said softly. 'It's never easy, Thomasine – I know that. It's unremitting hard work from dawn to dusk. I know. I've done it.'

She whispered, 'But it's worth it, isn't it?'

He did not reply, but she read his answer in his eyes. 'Where are you going, Daniel?' she said. 'Italy . . . France . . .?'

'Russia, eventually, I thought.' His eyes gleamed. 'Harold says I won't be socially acceptable after spending six months there. All Bolsheviks are atheists and murderers, according to the Tory Press. I thought I'd see for myself.'

She understood that Daniel was still restless and haunted, as Nicholas had been. He was trying to exorcise the demons of the past, and would settle nowhere until he had achieved some sort of equilibrium. She heard him say, 'Will you go and see Lally, Thomasine? Keep an eye on her? She has no one else.'

She did not look at him, but stared outside to where William scrabbled in his nest of leaves and mud and twigs. She understood that what Daniel felt for Lally was not the same as what he had once, she thought, felt for her. It was compounded of a mixture of regret and pity and duty – a sort of love, perhaps, but not the best sort.

'Yes. Yes – if you like.'

He found a piece of paper and a pencil and scribbled a few words. 'That's the address of the sanatorium, and my publisher's address as well. If you should need to get in touch with me, then just drop a note to Harold.' He rose from the chair. 'And here's some money for the train fares.' Daniel stuffed a bundle of notes into a jug on the dresser. 'You're not to refuse it.'

As they walked out of the door and down the path, she said suddenly, 'I'm teaching William to ride, Daniel. We borrow the rector's pony. William isn't the least bit afraid.'

Daniel's smile lit his eyes. 'Like his mother.'

She knew then that, even if neither of them had found quite the right words, then some sort of communication had passed silently between them. There was a possibility, she thought, that time and patience might repair the worst wounds. The soft evening sunlight, the froth of flowers along the rim of the dyke seemed to Thomasine just then to be especially beautiful.

She said, 'You'll look after yourself, won't you, Daniel?'

'You too.' He was staring at the dyke, the high bank of which was only fifty yards from the cottage. When he turned to her, his eyes were troubled. 'You're very low-lying here, Thomasine. And that dyke's always been in a poor state of repair. You must keep an eye on the water-level in the spring, if the rains are heavy. It's not like the Abbey – you haven't the height of the island to protect you from the water. You'll remember that, won't you?'

She assented. Then she watched him walk out of the garden and across the paddock and towards the dyke. When he had climbed the dyke and was a black figure silhouetted against the skyscape he turned, and waved his farewell.

In September, Thomasine went to visit Lally for the third time. The journey was complicated: a bus trip from Drakesden to Ely, then a train journey, changing at several stations. Finally the long walk from the station to the sanatorium, built miles from anywhere on the summit of a rolling hill.

The nurse showed her to a bed on the verandah, overlooking the great sweep of the valley. 'No physical contact, and she mustn't talk too much. You can have half an hour, Miss Thorne.'

When the nurse had gone Thomasine touched Lally's hand where it lay on the coverlet. She thought that if she looked hard enough she could have seen the pattern of the fabric through the skin and bone.

'You're looking better, Lally.'

Lally's eyes, brilliantly dark and mocking, stared vaguely at her. 'You mustn't make me laugh. I'm not allowed to laugh. I know how I look.'

Thomasine began to arrange the flowers she had taken with her in a vase. 'Abbey roses. Do you like them?'

Slowly, Lally turned her head. 'You brought me some before. You've been here before, haven't you?'

Thomasine nodded. 'They wouldn't let me speak to you, so I just left the flowers. I peeped through the window once, but you were asleep.'

'I recognized them. Mama's roses . . .'

'I sell lots of those in Ely market.'

Lally's sudden crack of laughter was followed by a bout of coughing. The nurse, seated at the end of the verandah, glared disapprovingly.

'Poor Mama. All those frightful people buying her precious

roses.' Lally's eyes focused for the first time on Thomasine. 'Why do you come here?'

Thomasine sat down on the chair at the side of the bed. 'Because Daniel asked me to. He's gone abroad, you know, Lally.'

Lally smiled. 'He wrote me such a nice letter.'

There was a silence. The light breeze stirred the leaves on the trees in the garden and ruffled Lally's bedclothes. Her eyes had closed, and Thomasine thought for a moment that she had fallen asleep. But eventually she murmured, 'Do you remember, Thomasine, when he used to come to the Abbey? We used to play hide-and-seek. I was good at hiding.'

'You shouldn't talk, Lally. Let me do the talking.'

'I want to talk.' Lally's tone was querulous. 'It's so dull here, just lying in bed all day, on my own, with nothing to look at.' Her face had screwed up in anger: *it isn't fair*.

'Very well,' said Thomasine soothingly. 'But you must just whisper, or the nurse will come.'

Lally said, 'Sometimes you wouldn't let me play with you. I hated that.'

And for a moment Thomasine too forgot the present, and was fifteen again, running through the Labyrinth. Or standing at the top of Drakesden Abbey's staircase on a hot, sultry August morning. *Push off, Lally. Do go away.*

Thomasine said softly, 'You took it, didn't you?'

Lally's slanted dark eyes focused on her. 'Took what?'

'The Firedrake.'

When Lally nodded, Thomasine realized that she had been holding her breath. Her exhalation sounded like a sigh.

'I wanted to show it to Daniel. It was my favourite thing. I was going to give it to him. Then he'd have always been my friend.'

Thomasine thought of the misery that had stemmed from that single action: her own leaving of Drakesden, Daniel's abandonment of school and home, Lally's dismissal to boarding-school. And the consequent chain of jealousy and love and hatred that had threaded their lives for more than a decade.

'Nicky left the safe open. I was watching, you see. There was no one about – Mama was away and all the servants were busy, so I just took it. It was easy.'

'But what *happened?*' Thomasine almost forgot to keep her voice low. 'You didn't give it to Daniel, did you, Lally? Did you lose it?'

Lally closed her eyes. She looked terribly tired. 'I looked everywhere for you. I asked Cook, and she said you were having a picnic. I thought Daniel would be with you and Nicky. It was always the three of you.'

Thomasine and Nicholas and Daniel. Riding together down the long, dusty droves, or lying among the roses of the walled garden, drinking wine from a bottle hidden among the ferns . . .

'I saw you and Nicky riding in the paddock. So I went down and watched you. But then I saw Mama . . .'

'Lady Blythe came back early,' said Thomasine, remembering, 'because of the War.'

'I was afraid Mama had seen me, so I hid the Firedrake in the grass. I didn't have a pocket in my dress, you see, and Mama would have been angry if she knew I'd taken it. And then I met Daniel.'

'I know. He told me. Lady Blythe found you kissing him. She must have been furious –'

'She was,' said Lally smugly. Her eyes had opened. They gleamed, narrowed and black, a fleeting reminder of the old Lally. 'And then I had hysterics and Mama put me to bed. And when I looked for the Firedrake the next day, I couldn't find it. I'd hidden it under a clump of grass in the paddock and I just couldn't remember exactly where. I looked for *hours*, Thomasine, but it all looked the same. Mama thought you'd taken it. I told her I hadn't seen it, and she knew it wasn't Daniel, because I said I was with him all the time.'

Lally's voice had faded so that it was almost inaudible. The scent of Lady Blythe's roses was powerful in the late afternoon sunshine.

Thomasine whispered, 'But couldn't you have told your mother the truth?'

'Why should I? I hated you.'

And Thomasine shivered, chilled to the bone by the simplicity of Lally's words. It was disturbing to come face to face with hatred: civilized society tamed it, dissembled about it, disguised it or ritualized it into war. But with Lally the veneer of civilization had always been thin, a fragile covering of a particular sort of ruthlessness. Simon Melville had said, 'God help you if she unsheathes her talons.' Lally had unsheathed them years ago, in the gardens of Drakesden Abbey.

'Why?'

'You had everything. You were allowed to go out on your own and you were pretty, you weren't fat, and you weren't scared of anything. Both Nicky and Daniel liked you. If it hadn't been for you they'd have been my friends. It wasn't fair.'

Thomasine stood up, suddenly unable to bear the stillness of the verandah, the unmoving patients in their beds, the muted sounds of the click of the nurse's knitting needles and the occasional cough. Standing at the edge of the decking, she stared out at the green and blue skyline. The three of them, she and Daniel and Nicholas, like a triangle, pulling apart, pressing together. And Lally always on the outside, never quite belonging.

'I suppose it wasn't,' she said slowly. 'It must have been . . . lonely.'

She looked down at the small figure on the bed. Lally was so fragile, in appearance as well as reality, and yet she had wreaked such havoc. Lally's hatred of Thomasine and hero-worship of Nicholas and Daniel had not ended with childhood. It had continued to distort Thomasine's own life, Fay's life, Daniel and Nicholas's lives. Lally's destructiveness had been vented not only at others, but also inwardly: the wild parties, the many lovers, the restless search for newer and greater pleasures had always had its blacker side. Lally had looked for the love that had been denied to her in childhood, but that search had long ago become fatally entangled with the impulse to destroy.

'I wanted Nicky to hate you. I thought he would if he believed you were a thief. But he blamed Daniel. And Mama sent me to school, which was awful. I wouldn't have had to go there if it hadn't been for you. And it was just too difficult to sort things out. Gerald died and Nicky joined up, and after the War he was different. I thought I'd tell him the truth one day, when it didn't matter any more, but it never seemed to be the right time. And then when you married Nicky ... and he didn't want me any more ... Well, it made me so angry. I thought that was what you'd wanted all along. That was what you'd planned, back in that summer.'

'But we were *children!*' Thomasine's voice was a low cry, a last lament for a time that was now done with.

'It still counted, though,' said Lally dreamily. 'Just because you're a child it doesn't mean it doesn't count. You still feel things.'

Thomasine understood then that what Lally had felt for Daniel could not easily be dismissed. In her own way, Lally had loved Daniel. If that love had always been hopeless, then that was Lally's tragedy.

'Do you still hate me?'

Lally was staring out at the distant vista of fields and trees. 'I don't think so,' she said eventually. 'I don't seem to feel anything much now. Except for this beastly illness, of course. When I was very bad I felt frightened because I thought I would die. But now I just feel bored.' She looked up at Thomasine. 'They say I might have to stay here another year. I don't know how I shall bear it.'

Her eyes flickered shut. The nurse had put aside her knitting and was tapping her watch. 'Time to go, Miss Thorne.' She smiled at Lally. 'Don't want to get too tired, do we, dear?'

'Old bag,' muttered Lally. But her cheeks were scarlet and feverish and her short black hair clung in damp tendrils to her forehead.

Thomasine picked up her purse and gloves. Lally grabbed her sleeve as she turned away. 'It doesn't matter now, does it, Thomasine?'

She knew that she spoke the truth when she said, 'No, it doesn't matter at all now, Lally.'

Because she arrived back late from the sanatorium, Thomasine did not collect William from the Dockerills until the following morning. He ran to meet her as she emerged from the path at the side of the house. She swept him up in her arms.

'Mummy! Mummy! I've ridden Nelson and Mr Dockerill has some ducklings for us and Rosie is such a *baby* –'

William was hugged and kissed. Annie Dockerill called from the kitchen, 'He's been such a good boy. You'll have a cup of tea, won't you, Thomasine?'

She accepted gratefully. Inside the kitchen she sat at the table, William on her knee, watching little Rosie Dockerill play with a bowlful of empty peapods. A cup of tea was placed in front of her.

Annie whispered, 'How is Miss Blythe?'

Thomasine was aware suddenly of how fortunate she was. She had friends, she had a child. At Drakesden she had created a home and work for herself. She had survived the slings and arrows of the past; she could look to the future with hope. Self-sufficient, at last. She could, eventually perhaps, allow herself to love.

'Lally's allowed visitors now. She stays outside all the time, Annie – day and night. The doctors are more hopeful than they were a few months ago.'

'Poor little thing.' Annie shook her head. 'Don't seem right, do it? That family was never so unlucky before the War. Still –' she tickled William under the chin – 'this little one seems fit as a fiddle, don't he?'

'He certainly does.' William's cheeks were ruddy with health, his hands and knees muddy from playing in the farmyard. Thomasine hugged him again.

'Annie – where is Harry? I've some business I need to discuss with him.'

'He's in the top field. I'll send the lad for him, if you like.'

She shook her head. 'I'd like the walk. William can come with me.'

They went together out of the yard and along the path that lay parallel to the dyke. William's hand was in hers, and he sang to himself as they walked along. It was early morning, and the sunlight caught the remaining pools of dew so that they sparkled, multicoloured. The feathery tips of the rushes shook in the gentle breeze. Harry Dockerill was cutting down the old pea-stalks. Thomasine waved, and the scythe stilled.

She had one more piece of business, she thought, as he approached. Something outstanding, something that should have been completed long ago. Nicholas, had he lived, would have agreed with her.

They exchanged greetings. Then Thomasine said, 'I've decided to put those fields up for sale, Harry. The ones that adjoin the Gillory land. I thought you might like to buy them.'

The land Daniel always wanted, she thought, but did not say. The land on which he could build a better house, away from the marshy ground by the dyke.

Harry, startled, rubbed at his forehead with the back of his hand. 'That's very good of you, Miss, and I'm sure Daniel will be pleased, but with him away just now ... I haven't the money, see, for something like that. He's left me something for emergencies, like, but ...'

'It's all right, Harry.' She smiled at him. 'I looked in Drakesden Abbey's records to see how much Ruth Gillory's grandfather paid for the field. A bushel of potatoes, the account book said. I estimate that three bushels would pay for these fields. Seedling potatoes, if you have them, Harry. I'm just about to start digging up the tennis court.'

CHAPTER TWENTY

THE day started badly. William grizzled as Thomasine helped
him dress for school, and complained that there wasn't enough
treacle on his porridge. Outside, it was raining again, a fine cold
rain made needle-sharp by the spiteful bursts of wind.

Thomasine scraped the uneaten porridge into the bin. The pig
could eat it. There was a limit to what work could be done on a
smallholding in February, but the animals had to be fed and the
housework had to be done. Today she had to go and see the
bank manager in Ely, so she had dressed in a tweed skirt that
had once been smart, and a Fair Isle jumper without any
obvious darns. After leaving William at the village school she
would have five minutes to walk to the bus-stop.

William said sullenly, 'My head hurts.'

'Go and wash your face, darling. That'll make you feel
better.'

Thomasine heard him stomp upstairs. She hadn't time to
wash the dishes, so she piled them in the sink and poured a
bucket of water over them. She would empty the contents of
the slop bucket into the pig's trough as they walked up the
island, and she had given the hens extra rations the previous
night. She was almost ready.

Then there was a sound, all too unmistakable, from the
landing. Thomasine threw down the tea-towel and dashed
upstairs.

'I was sick, Mummy,' said William tearfully. 'I couldn't reach
the bathroom.' He began to sob.

When she took off his soiled clothes she saw the scattering of
tiny red spots around his upper chest. His forehead was burning.

'You've got the measles, you poor old thing. You must have caught them from Rosie Dockerill.'

'Mr Dockerill said Rosie had spots all over.' Standing in the bathroom, William gazed down at himself, momentarily distracted from his misery. 'He said she looked like a currant pudding.'

Thomasine began to dress William in his pyjamas. She tried to quell the waves of anxiety that surged up inside her. William was five and a half now, well-fed and healthy, dosed with Virol each day, camphorated oil rubbed into his chest if he so much as sneezed. She must not think about the two Drakesden babies who had already died of measles during the current epidemic. They had been ill-nourished, poorly clothed, their homes lacking proper drainage or heating. She must not think of ear infections, blindness, pneumonia . . .

She tucked William up in bed, partially drawing the curtains to keep out the dull grey light. The nearest doctor was in Ely, but a doctor could do little for measles. Thomasine kissed his hot forehead.

'I'll clear up a bit and then I'll come and read you a story, darling.'

Thomasine changed out of her smart clothes and put on trousers and a thick jumper. Then she mopped the landing and flung all the soiled garments into the copper. The bank manager would have to wait.

Isolated in the little cottage, a quarter of a mile from the rest of the village, Thomasine saw no one but Eddie Readman. In her loneliness she found herself, once, talking to the pig. I shall become a mad old woman, she thought. I shall adopt stray cats and mumble to myself in the street.

She sponged William's hot little body, and fed him cups of weak sugary tea. He vomited frequently and was restless and miserable for much of the night. She dabbed his spots with calamine lotion, and told him stories in an attempt to distract him from scratching. Once he rolled on the floor, screaming with fury at the relentless itching, so she carried him to the bathroom and bathed him in cool water, and afterwards he fell asleep, curled in a towel in her arms in front of the range. Thomasine just sat quietly and watched him. The damp black hair, the closed, long-lashed eyes, the delicate skin pitted with a thousand crimson spots. The endless rain that battered at the roof and windows seemed a suitable accompaniment to illness and isolation.

Waking one morning, William asked, for the first time in five days, for food. Thomasine boiled an egg and cut fingers of toast. Her own head ached and she felt exhausted and dirty. All the hot water had been used for washing sheets and handkerchiefs and pyjamas. She could not remember when she had last had a bath. Every bone in her body throbbed. Closing her eyes momentarily, she recalled the hot baths she had once had at Drakesden Abbey. The running water, the perfumed bath salts, the thick, luxurious towels . . .

William slept for most of the day. Thomasine washed and ironed and scrubbed bowls and floors and tables. Reaching the last corner of the kitchen floor, she stood up and the room seemed to spin. She felt unbearably hot and her head pounded as though someone was striking it with a hammer. When, having lost all track of time, she climbed up the stairs to bed and began to peel off her grubby clothes, she was not really surprised to find a flecking of scarlet spots all over the top half of her body.

Daniel, arriving back in London, dumped his belongings at his flat and then went to see Harold Markham.

Markham Books was unchanged: piles of manuscripts and proofs and early editions were piled in the offices and corridors. Harold gave a cry of delight, shook Daniel's hand and dusted a seat with his handkerchief.

'Well, well, the prodigal returns. We thought you'd fallen among thieves. I was just starting to compose your obituary.'

Daniel was dishevelled and hollow-eyed. He grinned. 'How are you, Harold?'

'Blooming, dear boy, blooming. Though business is dreadful, of course.' Harold fumbled in a drawer and took out a bottle and two glasses. 'I'm hoping that you have something for me that will restore the shattered fortunes of Markham Books. Something exotic . . . passionate . . . Russian . . .'

Daniel shook his head. 'Sorry, Harold. Nothing exotic and passionate and Russian.'

Harold poured out two measures of whisky. He glanced at Daniel quizzically. 'Writer's block? Don't worry, dear boy – it happens to the best of 'em.'

'Oh, I've written something, Harold.' Daniel opened his haversack and took out a large envelope. 'It just wasn't what I'd intended to write.'

He placed the manuscript, handwritten and tied with a piece of string, on the desk in front of Harold. Harold's eyes gleamed.

'Ah. It's almost like going to bed with a woman for the first time. The expectation. The possibility that this might be the one . . .' Harold scrabbled about in the mess of paper-clips and pens and sealing-wax, and drew out a penknife. 'May I?'

'Go ahead.' Daniel sipped his whisky as Harold cut the string that bound the manuscript. As he drank, he found himself thinking of the last few weeks. The glorious exhilaration of finishing the book. The sense of release, the overwhelming compulsion to return home. The realization that he at last knew where home was. And then the foul weather that had almost prevented him leaving Russia, and the complicated journey, a series of trains and buses and ships and pony-traps.

'The War,' said Harold, suddenly looking up from the manuscript. 'You've written about the War.'

Daniel ran his fingers through his untidy hair. 'As I said, it wasn't what I'd intended to write. But I'd started having dreams again – awful dreams. Being buried alive, that sort of thing. And what I was trying to write just wouldn't work. Every sentence was an effort. I was getting pretty bloody desperate, so I thought, I'll write about what happened to me – like a diary, almost, but in retrospect. Anything to get the words flowing again. And I found that I was writing about the War. Once I started, it was obvious that I had to go on – had to get it out of my system. I was afraid it might make me feel worse, but it didn't. The dreams went, and they haven't come back.'

' "Grief brought to numbers",' muttered Harold, still flicking through the pages.

' "He tames it, that fetters it in verse". I know. It took three months to fetter it in verse, Harold. Four hundred pages of manuscript in three months.'

Each day during those three months Daniel had started to write at dawn. Often, he had forgotten to eat. Heaped with blankets and furs, his room lit only by candlelight, he had stared out at the snowy Moscow streets and had seen only the endless mud-fields of the Somme.

'You're not the only one,' said Harold. 'There's several other books of War memoirs in the pipeline. Siegfried Sassoon and Edmund Blunden have both got things underway.'

'We've grown up at last,' said Daniel. 'We're beginning to be able to face the past.'

'And the future looks brighter, don't you think? Pacifism has become almost respectable.'

The Kellogg–Briand Pact had been drawn up at the beginning of 1928: state after state signing the agreement to outlaw aggressive war. Daniel did not voice out loud his reservations – that the Pact failed to specify what action might be taken against those that broke the agreement.

But he had told the truth, Daniel thought. Shut away in that little room in Moscow, he had done what Thomasine had told him to, and told the truth. He had explained how it had been: the reality of war, not the myth. The reality had been poison gas and lice and rats and mutilation. It had been an intolerable fear, and a sickness of the soul so great that lives would be deformed for decades after the signing of the Armistice. Writing, he had shown that clouds of glory did not cling to twentieth-century war: those skies had darkened, perhaps for ever.

He had written his story with the clarity of expression that was, perhaps, his greatest asset. He had not exaggerated, had not embroidered. Every page was unemotional, factual, almost uninvolved. He had not directly expressed his own opinion on the folly of war, on the dynastic jealousies that had led to war, on the incompetence of the Old Men who had run the War at a safe distance from the Front. He had not needed to. He had known that his story had spoken for itself.

Harold touched his shoulder. 'You look like you haven't had a decent meal for months, old chap. All that bortsch and braised liver. Let me take you to my club. They do a jolly nice roast beef and Yorkshire pud, with jam roly-poly to follow. That'll put something on your bones.'

Daniel rose to his feet. Harold shuffled into his greatcoat, clamped a bowler hat on his head and wound a scarlet muffler round his neck. 'Oh –' He began to search inside a cupboard.

'Letters, dear boy – from your nearest and dearest, I should imagine. Would have forwarded them, but you didn't send an address after the first month. You can cast your eye over them at lunch.'

They ate three courses, washed down with a smooth claret. Over coffee, while Harold was smoking his inevitable cigar, Daniel drew out the bundle of letters.

'Do you mind . . .?'

'Not at all. In fact, I'll just have a quick word with old Freddy Bright, if you will excuse me.' Harold rose to his feet and crossed to the far corner of the dining-room.

Daniel had already quickly checked that there was no letter from Thomasine. He had not expected one: the absence of a letter meant only that Lally still lived, that Thomasine and William were still at Drakesden. What he had to say to her must be said face to face.

The letters were mostly bills, plus a missive from the landlord of his flat, and bulletins from various political and literary associations. A letter from Nell, telling him about the birth of her first child, his first nephew, and something from Harry Dockerill. Harry's letter was quite long, covering several pages. Daniel drank his coffee as he read it.

When he had finished, he folded the papers and stuffed them in his pocket. For the first time, he noticed the ceaseless rain, the angry wind. His Channel-crossing the previous day had been vile – five hours, with the waves battering furiously against the side of the boat. Uneasily, Daniel stared out of the window. Amongst other things, Harry had written to him about the results of the previous year's Royal Commission of Enquiry into the condition of the Fens. The Commission's conclusion had been disturbing: that due to a shortage of funds, the South Level was undefended against serious flooding.

'Bad news?' Harold had returned to the table.

Daniel grimaced. 'I'm not sure ...' He glanced out of the window again. 'Harold – how long has the weather been like this?'

Harold blinked. 'Not sure, dear boy. Never notice that sort of thing. Um ... damned wind broke my brolly a day or two ago, I recall.'

Daniel had risen from his seat. His unease, festering, was beginning to turn into anxiety. 'Harold,' he said. 'Can I borrow your motor-car?'

For the first few days of her illness Thomasine felt extremely unwell. A severe headache, aching and trembling limbs and the terrible itchy rash. William climbed into the bed with her and together they scratched and coughed and sniffed. When they needed water she had to crawl downstairs, too shaky to trust herself on the narrow, winding cottage steps. She was thankful of the rain: it filled the water-butt so that she had, at least, no need to pump water from the well. She left the hens to their fate, hoping that they had food enough to survive these few, awful days, and threw the pig some peelings and scraps from the bread bin. The ducks would have to fend for themselves. She could no more have walked to the pond to feed them than she could have flown to the moon.

William fed himself a peculiar diet of biscuits and apples and porridge and honey. When Thomasine stood at the stove, stirring the oats and water together, her stomach heaved and her forehead broke out in a sweat. Although the weather was very cold she plodded round the kitchen in a sleeveless silk dress. A remnant of grander times, bought in Harrods, encrusted with tiny beads. Anything heavier irritated her skin unbearably. 'That's a pretty dress, Mummy,' said William approvingly, and she almost laughed, looking down at the thin spotty limbs that stuck out from the oyster-coloured silk.

After the first day, Eddie did not reappear. Thomasine concluded that Eddie's family, too, had been struck by illness. He had left piles of wood in the outhouse, however, and somehow she managed to keep the range burning. She knew that though she might not feel the cold, William, now that his temperature had returned to normal, would.

Eventually she began to feel a little better. The angry scarlet of the rash began to fade and her head did not ache quite so badly. She made William and herself a cup of tea, shuffling round the kitchen in her tea-gown and slippers, her movements old, weary, jerky with exhaustion. They had bought no milk for days, so the tea was black, made very sweet with three teaspoonfuls of sugar. We've survived, Thomasine thought, looking at her son and feeling, just for a moment, immensely proud.

She recalled then for the first time in days that there was a world beyond the cottage and the island. She had lost all track of time. She no longer knew which day of the week it was. When she fumbled with the dials of Nicholas's wireless, no sound came out. 'The battery's flat,' she said. Or the aerial had blown down. Outside, the wind howled like a hungry wolf.

William nodded sagely. 'We'll have to buy a new one.'

'Yes.' She thought that, if they walked slowly, they might go to the shops the following morning. She could buy milk and butter and perhaps a cake to tempt William's fitful appetite. She could discover whether Annie Dockerill had given birth to her new baby, and whether the rest of Drakesden had survived the epidemic.

Thomasine put William to bed at seven o'clock and went up herself only an hour later. Exhausted, she hardly noticed the wind that shrieked round the chimney nor the rain that filled the nearby dyke, so that the black water rose closer and closer to the rim of the bank.

The River Wissey, that flowed between Downham Market and Southery, broke its banks in the early hours of the morning. The dykes and drainage ditches, waterlogged by the heavy rains of the last fortnight, had failed to provide a safety valve for the swelling river. Taxed beyond their capacity, the pumps and steam-driven windmills were overwhelmed by the force of the gales that swept through the Fens that night. Although men worked desperately to shore up the defences with sandbags, the banks of the rivers and dykes, which had fallen into poor repair throughout years of neglect, broke like fragile eggshells. Water poured through the breeches, flooding the lower-lying farmlands. What the Dutchman Vermuyden had begun in the seventeenth century, what had been the product of years of ingenuity and perseverance, was destroyed within a few hours. Water roared out of the rivers and dykes and glazed the rich soil of the fields with shining black. In that part of the South Level, the land returned to what it had been a thousand years before. Nature put paid to man's impertinent ambition in the course of a single night.

Her dreams were vivid and confused. There was a great gale, and the crack in the wall of Drakesden Abbey was widening.

Within the black fissure Thomasine could see people struggling to free themselves, hands reaching out, faces white and fleeting. Recognizing the faces, she cried out to Nicholas and Lally and Daniel, but they could not hear her. Instead the noise of the gale was overwhelmed by a new and terrible sound. A repeated booming, like the howl of some terrible marsh-creature. With every pulse of sound the crack in the house split wider.

Thomasine woke up, but the noise did not cease. Boom . . . boom . . . boom . . . threaded through with the shriek of the wind, the battering of the rain. She realized then that the church bells were ringing, and she could not for the moment think why. It was Sunday, perhaps. But on Sunday they pealed the bells, they did not ring out that awful monotonous clamour. They rang the church bells like that when someone had died.

Fumbling in the dark for matches, she lit her candle. When she pressed her face against the window she could not tell whether the great bulk of Drakesden Abbey still stood. The church bells still chimed. Far too many peals, surely, for even the oldest person in the village. And why were they ringing at night?

Then, suddenly, she knew, and she stared for a moment at the wildly beating rain and heard with new understanding the howl of the wind. Barefoot, clad in her nightdress, Thomasine grabbed her candle and ran out of the bedroom and down the stairs.

She almost fell into it. The water licked at the walls and stairs of the cottage, making the polished wood slippery. She heard her own gasp of horror, and when she held out the candle, she could see the water surging blackly round the kitchen. The windows and door had been forced open so that the cottage now stood in the floodwaters from the dyke. It was like a living creature, greedy and invasive. Some of their possessions swirled in it, incongruous in their domesticity, caught up in the dark vortex. A tea-towel, a teddy-bear, a wicker basket.

Driving from London to the Fens, Daniel told himself that it was all right, they'd be safe, that his anxiety was irrational. The defences would hold out – they'd held out for years, after all – and even if they didn't, then Thomasine would have noticed the rising water-level and would have left the cottage for the greater height and security of Drakesden Abbey. Dammit, even if she'd decamped to the potting-shed or the boiler-house she'd be safe, out of harm's way.

But he kept his foot pressed hard on the accelerator, and drove faster than he'd ever driven in his life. In London, getting ready for this journey, he had switched on the wireless. The BBC had warned of flooding in eastern England – which was why Daniel broke the twenty mile an hour speed limit every time he drove through a village.

Visibility was awful, the condition of the roads foul. He had set out from London just after two o'clock, and it had taken him until midnight to reach Cambridge. The car skidded, but he managed to right it, his heart pounding. Water filled every ditch and gathered in great puddles at the sides of the road. Daniel slowed his speed slightly, and cleared the windscreen yet again.

In the back seat of Harold's motor-car, he had placed a torch, ropes, waterproofs, blankets, food and first-aid equipment. Packing, he had almost laughed at himself for such measures. But the worm of unease that Harry Dockerill's letter had awoken still coiled and curved inside him. The conviction with which he had, over the years, predicted this sort of disaster in the South Level, taunted him with horrid prescience.

Conviction hardened as he drove out of Cambridge into the Fens. When the headlamps of the motor-car lit the drainage ditches beside the road, Daniel could see that every one was almost overflowing. The rain seemed harder here, the wind fiercer. The road led him up through Landbeach and Stretham towards Ely. In Ely, rounding a tight corner, he had to jam his foot on the brake to avoid hitting a pedestrian.

He saw that the pedestrian was a policeman. Daniel cursed

under his breath, leaned his head out of the window and put on his best accent.

'Frightfully sorry, sergeant. Didn't see you in this weather.'

The policeman glared at him. 'Driving a bit fast, aren't we, sir?'

'The thing is, sergeant,' said Daniel quickly, 'that I'm rather worried about a friend of mine. Do you know whether the river-banks are holding up?'

'The Wissey went a couple of hours ago, sir, and the men are trying to shore up the Lark.'

'I have to get to Drakesden. Is the Prickwillow road still passable?'

'It was a while ago, sir. Though whether it is now –'

Daniel pressed his foot down on the accelerator. The remainder of the policeman's sentence and his injunctions to drive carefully were lost in the roar of the engine, the howl of the wind.

As he headed north-east down the slope of the Isle of Ely, it seemed to Daniel that he was driving into the heart of the storm. Rain lashed at the motor-car, seeping in through the cracks between windscreen and roof. Visibility was appalling: he could see no more than ten yards ahead. He kept his speed down now, knowing the ease with which he could skid off the road and into a ditch. His conviction that Thomasine was in danger intensified the closer he drove to Drakesden. Daniel slowed from thirty miles an hour, to twenty, and then to ten. Rain glazed the road, and mud churned in the ditches. He could hear, through the rain and the wind, the chiming of bells.

Then, as the road rounded a gentle corner, the motor-car lurched sideways. Wrestling with the steering-wheel, Daniel managed to bring the vehicle to a screeching halt horizontally across the road.

He climbed out and looked around him. The headlamps of Harold's motor-car lit the water that covered the muddy surface of the road. Not rainwater, floodwater. It was like a new sea.

The chiming of the church bells was clear now; he must be within half a mile of Drakesden. The wheels of the car were clogged with mud, and Daniel realized that it was pointless trying to drive any further. He stood for a moment, trying to work out his bearings. He knew every inch of this land. He knew, most importantly, the slope of the land, the fields and paths which would first be inundated and those which would remain above water the longest.

Slinging the rope across his shoulder, stuffing the rest of his equipment into a haversack, Daniel began to make his way across the fields towards Drakesden.

The water in the kitchen was already too deep to wade through. Thomasine, holding out her candle and shining it down the stairs, could see neither the sink nor the table. The water churned and swirled like an angry whirlpool: alone, to swim to safety would have been dangerous. With William, she knew that it would be impossible.

She ran back to her bedroom, and with the stub of the candle lit her oil-lamp. The wick flared and then dimmed as she adjusted it, a comforting gleam in the darkness. Rapidly, Thomasine pulled on trousers and a thick jumper. Her waterproofs were downstairs in the lobby. As she ran to William's room, she shone the lamp down the stairs. Ten minutes ago, the water had covered the fifth stair. Now it lapped halfway up the sixth.

She found William's warmest clothes and then woke him as gently as she dared. 'You have to get dressed, darling. Just sit still, and Mummy will dress you.'

William's eyes were blank, sleep-ridden. 'Is it morning?'

'Not yet, sweetheart. But we may have to leave the cottage tonight.'

She dressed him quickly, thinking all the time. The cottage stood, as Daniel had pointed out the previous summer, at the foot of the slope of Drakesden island. She should have noticed the severity of the weather; she should have returned to the

Abbey for a night or two. But self-recrimination was futile. Just now, she was responsible for saving not only her own life, but William's also.

The extent of the flood would depend on where the dyke had burst its banks. If the defences had collapsed near Littleport then she might not yet be completely surrounded by water. Or the water might, in some places, be shallow enough to wade through. If the banks had burst at Drakesden . . .

'Shall I take Rabbit?' William was looking up at her, confused yet trusting.

'Yes, darling. Yes, you'd better.'

Drawing the curtains, she opened William's window and looked out. The floodwater on this side of the cottage was only a couple of feet from the bottom of the upper storey window-sill. Thomasine grabbed William's hand, and took him to her own bedroom.

'Mummy,' whispered William as they passed the stairs, 'there's water in the *kitchen*.'

She could think of nothing comforting to say. In her bedroom Thomasine opened the window and swung the oil-lamp outside. The reflection of the lamp in the waters told her that her worst fears had been realized: they were surrounded on every side by rapidly rising water.

The entire geography of the land Daniel had known since a boy had been altered within the space of a few hours. The church bell still boomed, echoing over the floodwater and marshes, helping to draw him towards the comparative safety of the hamlet. He was soaked to the skin, his boots heavy with mud, the torch providing only a feeble light in the stormy darkness. Reaching the outskirts of Drakesden, Daniel thought quickly. The church. They would be in the church.

As he ran through the main street, a few villagers were still loading possessions on to handcarts, ready to transport them to the safety of the higher ground. Daniel passed them, heading towards the churchyard. Inside, the church was filled with women and children. The men, of course, would be out there in the darkness, trying to shore up banks that had not yet given way, or attempting to ensure that the pumps continued to function. Daniel looked wildly through the sodden congregation, searching every face.

All the faces were familiar, but the one Daniel had longed to see was absent. None of these women was red-haired, none of them looked round at him with those great sea-green eyes. The bell echoed the anxious pattern of Daniel's heart. Catching sight of the Reverend Fanshawe in the vestry, he pushed through the crowds.

'Daniel!' The rector looked up at him, surprised.

There were two women in the vestry: Anna Fanshawe, spooning sugar into cups of tea, and the Fanshawes' maid, cutting bread.

Daniel did not waste time with pleasantries. 'Where's Thomasine? She's not out there with the other women.'

'Miss Thorne . . . I had forgotten . . . Are you sure she's not there, Daniel?' The rector frowned. 'The bells have been ringing since midnight –'

'She's not there, I tell you!'

'Then she'll have gone to the Big House. Yes – I'm sure that's where she'll be.'

From behind him someone said, 'My Eddie says they was both sick, Rector. Missus and the little 'un.' Turning, Daniel recognized the wide, fleshy features of Bessie Readman, Eddie Readman's mother.

'There has been a severe epidemic of the measles –' began the Reverend Fanshawe.

'But the Dockerills – Harry and Annie – Harry would have made sure that Thomasine and William were safe –'

For the first time, the rector began to look worried. 'The Dockerills left for Soham a fortnight ago to stay with Annie's mother. Annie is expecting another child, you see, Daniel, and

Harry's chest was bad again. Harry left the farm animals in the care of his mother.'

'*Jesus!*' blasphemed Daniel furiously. Then he pushed his way out of the vestry, out of the church and up the incline of the island, towards Drakesden Abbey.

Quite coldly, quite calmly, Thomasine made plans. If the water reached the penultimate stair and showed no signs of ebbing, then she and William would climb on to the roof. There was a hatch to the attic over the landing. She had already placed a chair beneath the hatch and removed the cover.

Thomasine tried not to think too much about the possibility that the cottage, lacking foundations to clamp it firmly to the ground, would be swept away by the force of the water. She opened all the upstairs windows, so that the wind blew through the house, rather than against it. She kept close to William all the time, and watched for the smallest movement of wall or floor. If they were to drown, then they would drown together.

Eventually, when she looked down from the landing once more, she saw that floodwater lapped the bottom of the penultimate stair. Back in the bedroom, she buttoned William's coat.

'We'll put Rabbit in here.' The cuddly toy was tucked securely between William's jumper and coat. 'Then he'll be nice and warm and safe.'

'Where are we going, Mummy?' William's voice was small, and his eyes were frightened.

'We're going on to the roof. Then we'll be a long way away from the water. And if we wave the lantern, then someone is bound to see us and come and rescue us.' Thomasine's voice was calm and confident.

She checked the level of the oil in the lamp and made sure the glass sleeve was secure. From the landing she could see that, in the few minutes it had taken to get ready, the water had risen halfway up the penultimate stair. Standing on the chair, she reached up and placed the lantern in the attic.

'Now, I'm going to lift you up, William. When you're in the attic, just sit still on one of the rafters and wait for me. Don't touch the lamp, and you'll be quite safe.'

Bending down, she took William in her arms. Though not an overweight child, he was still heavy. 'You'll have to climb on to my shoulders. That's it — I'm holding you. Don't be frightened — good boy.'

The weight left her shoulders, and when Thomasine looked up she could see the small face looking down at her. Then she balanced her own palms on the edge of the hatchway and hauled herself up after William.

There was only plaster between the rafters of the attic . . . she must be very careful where she trod. Thomasine thanked God that the Blythes had built their farm manager's cottage of brick and tile, and not of clunch and reeds. Clunch would have been swept away already, leaving only the supporting wooden framework to be plundered by the waters at will.

There must come a point, though, she knew, when the cottage, weakened by the incessant battering of wind and water, simply crumbled away. Which was why she dared not remain here in the comparative comfort and safety of the attic. The oil-lamp was her only hope: the possibility that someone might spot that tiny pinpoint of light in the darkness was their best prospect of survival.

'Sit still, William — I'm going to open the roof-light.'

On the roof, they must wedge themselves between the chimney and the sloping tiles. Even if the walls collapsed, the chimney-stack might stand a little longer. And while the house stood, the stack would offer some protection from the gale.

'We're going to climb on to the roof now. Step very carefully on the rafters, sweetheart — I'll catch you if you trip over.' With Thomasine clutching the hood of William's coat, they shuffled across the attic to the open roof-light.

She mustn't drop the oil-lamp, and she had to keep hold of William. In the end, she hooked the hanger of the lamp around her wrist, and climbed out on to the roof first. The wind and rain hit her with ice-cold violence, but Thomasine managed to keep her balance. She did not look down to where the waters waited greedily for a careless footfall or a fatal· loss of concentration. Using her scarf, she attached the oil-lamp to the chimney-pot, then she crouched down and pulled William up through the aperture in the roof.

She wedged him safely in the sharp angle between roof and chimney-stack, a small confused bundle of jumpers and scarf and coat. Then, leaning against the stack, she stood up and looked out.

Behind her lay the ruined dyke. To the east were fields; to the west, Drakesden village. And to the north, up the island, Drakesden Abbey. Thomasine could see none of these familiar landmarks. The lantern illuminated only the floodwater, but she stared northwards nevertheless, waiting.

The great front door of Drakesden Abbey was locked, so Daniel smashed a pane and opened a window from the inside. When he shone his torch around the room, he could see the white ghostly shapes of the furniture, swathed in sheets. He ran from room to room, calling Thomasine's name. Yet he knew that the house was deserted. The melancholy sense of abandonment was all-pervading, and the rooms were damp, ice-cold, dirty.

Still he searched, not quite trusting his instincts. Upstairs, he pulled aside a moth-eaten curtain and stared outside. The lawn was now bereft of the great trees that had once dominated it. Beyond were the paddock and the farm manager's cottage. A light was flickering where Daniel thought the cottage was.

He thought at first that he had imagined the light. Or that it was a will-o'-the-wisp, false fire, a firedrake . . . But the tiny light remained, swaying slightly in the darkness, and he seized his torch and ran outside.

Halfway down the island the rising waters licked at his feet. When he looked up he saw the light again, closer now, and around it the dim outline of a roof and chimney. He knew then that she was alive. The cottage was half-submerged in water, but Thomasine was alive. Daniel's heart leapt with joy. He thought wildly of swimming, but he knew that he could not save both Thomasine and the child. And the waters were strong, storm-ridden.

Joy turned to fear. He feared that he had come so close, had crossed continents for her, only to be condemned to watch her drown. He knew that she must be cold and exhausted, that the cottage itself might collapse and the waters sweep her away at any moment. That she might slip and tumble down the treacherous roof. He called her name, and knew that his voice was lost in the wind and the rain. He was overcome by a sense of outrage – that Thomasine might drown, as Fay had drowned . . .

Then he began to think clearly again. He recalled the Blythe children, Gerald and Nicholas and Marjorie, playing in a boat. A rowing-boat. The Blythes had owned a rowing-boat. It would be here somewhere.

He ran to the garages. He had to force the lock, and then he was inside, sweeping the torch around the darkness. There was no motor-car now, only a collection of tyres and petrol-cans and tools. And at the back of it all, propped against the wall, a rowing-boat.

The oars were stowed neatly inside. Daniel thanked heaven for methodical, organized people like the Blythes. Then he dragged the boat out of the garage and hauled it down the slope of the island.

Pulling out into the inland sea that the shattered dyke had made, the rain battered against his face and the wind tossed the tiny craft like a cockleshell. Unable to handle both rudder and oars, Daniel had to steer with the oars alone. His arms ached. He was exhausted before he had travelled twenty yards. Yet of his many journeys, he knew that no journey had ever mattered quite as much as this brief one. It held the difference between the possibility of happiness, and the certainty of terrible grief. Daniel, his mouth set in a grim line, dragged himself ever closer and closer to the cottage, and Thomasine.

Hunched against the chimney-pot, Thomasine knew that she could not endure much more. Although, to begin with, her fear for William's safety had given her strength, the effort of climbing on to the roof had sapped that strength, leaving her weak with exhaustion. Her limbs had locked with cold and the rain had seeped through to her skin. She could no longer swing the oil-lamp to and fro in the hope of catching someone's attention. She had tied it back on to the chimney-stack. If it went out now, the matches would be too wet to relight it.

William, still wedged between the chimney-stack and the roof, slept. Thomasine was glad of that – sleeping, he could not be frightened. As for herself, she had grown almost too tired for fear. A part of her was aware that she was not that far from the point when she might let herself slide off the roof and into the restful embrace of the waters. So she remained standing upright, forcing herself to keep awake, her hands cradled for warmth around the glass sleeve of the oil-lamp.

The rain beat against her face. Slowly her awareness of the cold and the rain was fading away, and Thomasine felt herself slipping into a hazy warmth, retreating from a reality she had fought against, but had ultimately been beaten by. The rooftop seemed to have become almost peaceful . . . even the sound of the storm was ebbing. She hoped that Nicholas too had known some sort of peace before he died. When she half-shut her eyes Thomasine remembered climbing the beech tree with Daniel and looking down to the bluebells. Only now, when she looked, the bluebells were black except for a single light bobbing through the darkness . . .

Abruptly, she snapped out of her half-dream. Fully awake now, her gaze fixed on the light. As she narrowed her eyes, shading them from the rain, the light illuminated the area around it and she could see the boat.

She heard her own insane crow of laughter. Afraid that it might dissolve back into the darkness, she did not take her eyes from the boat for a moment. It was now within a few yards of the half-submerged cottage. Thomasine called out and seized the lantern, swinging it violently. When the solitary rower looked up she recognized Daniel.

She knew then that they were safe. That Daniel — strong, practical Daniel — would rescue them from this place and take them to safety. Thomasine felt herself fall back against the slope of the roof, her legs weak with relief. Daniel was edging the boat round parallel to the house.

'Thomasine!' His voice cut through the sounds of wind and water. 'Are you all right? Is William safe?'

'I'm fine, and William's here!' she yelled, pointing at the chimney-stack. 'Oh, Daniel — thank God you've come —'

He was crouching in the boat, uncoiling a rope. 'I'm going to throw this to you, Thomasine. Try and catch it.'

She nodded, and the rope snaked through the air towards her. Reaching out a hand, she touched it for the briefest moment, but then it slipped through her cold fingers and slithered back down the roof.

'I'm sorry —'

'Don't worry. We'll try again.' He was winding the rope back round his arm. The boat joggled to and fro. Again, the rope was thrown towards her, and this time she caught it.

'Can you tie it round the chimney-stack?'

She realized what he intended to do. Carefully she looped the rope around the square brick chimney, winding it round several times. Her fingers were ice-cold and stiff; to tie a knot was agony.

'Knot the other end around William's waist and lower him towards me.'

Gently, she woke William. 'Mr Gillory has come for us in a boat, William. It's all right. We're going to be all right.' She managed to wind the rope around the little boy's waist, tying two knots for safety. Then she helped him crawl to the side of the chimney-stack.

'Mummy, I'm *scared –*'

'I know, sweetheart. But the boat's not that far away, really. Think of being high up on Fancy's back. You're not scared then, are you?'

William shook his head, his teeth pressed into his lower lip.

'Now – just sit and slide down the roof towards Mr Gillory. I'm holding the rope, so you can't fall.'

From behind the chimney-stack, the rope taut in her hands, Thomasine watched her son's slow descent down the slope of the roof towards the eaves. She could see Daniel poised in the boat below, waiting to catch him. Her hands were still numb, and all her muscles hurt as she took the child's weight. Her heart fluttered and missed a beat as William slid from the edge of the eaves and plunged down towards the water.

Daniel caught him. Thomasine sank back on to the tiles, overwhelmed with exhaustion and relief. When Daniel threw the rope back to her, she couldn't grip it. Her fingers grappled against the soaking tiles; her descent was an unco-ordinated rush. And then she too was in the boat, and Daniel's arms were around her and he was kissing her over and over again.

They took refuge in the broken shell of Drakesden Abbey. Daniel built fires to keep them warm, made food for them, wrapped them in blankets.

Thomasine swallowed the tea and aspirins that Daniel gave her, and watched him feed pieces of broken banister to the fire. She felt the load of responsibility slip a little from her shoulders for the first time in years. All she had to do was to keep warm, to rest and regain her strength. It was good, for a while, to be looked after, to be cherished.

The floodwater had washed clean the bare bones of field and island. When she looked out of the window, Thomasine could see a new world, reborn from the old, clean and cold and silver and glistening. Alone, she walked down the slope of the island. The cottage in which she and William had lived was a mud-stained, empty shell. Shallow puddles pocked the grass of the paddock. The breech in the shattered wall of the dyke had been made good with sandbags, the mud and reeds that had impeded the flow of the water for years had been scoured away by the force of the flood. The sky was an immense, clouded dome, protecting everything. When sunlight pierced through the cloud, it gave an illusion of summer to the bleak winter skies. It was as though, just for a moment, time itself had slipped out of joint, so that she stood in what was not just another season, but another year.

Another decade, another life. The last golden summer, the summer before the War. The whispering wind conjured up voices. The rays of sun, before the clouds swallowed them up again, gently touched the two dark heads, the golden-brown, the copper-coloured. Then the light faded, and the ghosts were gone, and the sun lingered for a final moment on the grass, conjuring jewels from the soaked earth.

One of the jewels seemed to shine a little brighter, a little more intensely than the rest. Thomasine stared at it for a long moment. From the far side of the paddock, a single bright winking eye seemed to catch the fading sun and steal its light.

Walking across the black muddy field, her heart began to pound a little faster. She did not yet believe what she thought she saw. It was an illusion: the sun made jewels out of the receding floodwater, and at any moment, as the cloud covered the face of the sun, the transient light would be gone.

Yet she crouched on her knees in the grass and her bare fingers dug away at the mud. And when she unearthed her treasure she knelt there for a moment, unable to move, cradling it in her hands. Its magic was tarnished now, smeared with grass and mud, yet that yellow eye still glinted and the mouth still gaped hungrily.

There were footsteps behind her. Thomasine rose to her feet.

'What is it?'

She realized that Daniel had never seen it before. 'It's the Firedrake.'

With her handkerchief she cleaned the patina of dirt from the ancient jewels. One of the topazes was missing . . . time had loosened some of the other clasps and replaced the precious stones with mud.

'The floodwater must have washed it up.' She glanced at Daniel. 'Lally took it. Did you know?'

'I guessed,' he said slowly. 'Oh – a while ago. There was something she said to me at the time . . . and then there was Fay . . .'

'Lally hid it in the paddock. It must have lain there all these years. She told me about it when I went to visit her in the sanatorium.'

She passed the jewel to him and watched him examine it. His eyes were lidded, his expression unreadable. He said, 'Was that why you sold the land to Harry?'

She touched his hand. 'It was right, Daniel. We were all hurt, but you were hurt the most. You lost everything. I had to . . . to try and put things right.'

When he looked up at her, she read on his face not hurt pride, but love and acceptance. He said hesitantly, 'We could fit together quite well, don't you think? You've got the market garden, and I've my writing. It'd be unconventional, but –'

There was a question in his eyes. She understood the question, but could not yet answer it. She said, looking around her, 'It's changing, Daniel – can't you feel it? Even Drakesden is changing.'

His hazel eyes narrowed as he glanced towards the horizon. 'I used to be jealous of Nicholas,' he said. 'Of the Blythes. Of all this. But their time's gone, hasn't it, Thomasine? It's all been washed away.'

She acknowledged silently that he was right. Even her son,

the last of the Blythes, would not follow the pattern of his forebears. She had refused Marjorie's offer to pay for William to go to public school. William would attend local schools, would be brought up in Drakesden, would belong to Drakesden. Everything was changing, and it was right that her son's life should reflect that change.

The Firedrake was still cradled in Daniel's palm. Thomasine focused on that single rancorous yellow eye, and thought how it had watched from its hiding-place and blighted all their lives.

Her voice was low, little more than a whisper. 'I am going to throw it away. Into the deepest dyke . . . or out to sea. *Nicholas,*' she said, staring at the brooch, 'Fay . . . even Lally . . . we were all hurt.'

'It was the War that hurt us,' said Daniel gently. He put his arm around her shoulders. 'The War hurt Nicholas more than it did me because he'd been brought up to think that it would be glorious. That he had to be a hero. Whereas I was just looking for something that would give me a few regular meals.' He drew her to him. 'But we're all right, Thomasine, aren't we? We've survived, haven't we?'

She let herself be encircled by his arms. Kissing him, she found that Lally was right, that it didn't matter. She slipped the Firedrake into her pocket, a useless and tarnished bauble. They had survived, and so had Nicholas's son, and so had Drakesden, after a fashion.

When eventually they drew apart, Daniel said again, 'It could work, couldn't it, Thomasine? Us, I mean.'

'What would the villagers think?' She was teasing him. 'Me driving the plough and you working at your books? Just think what everyone would say.'

His eyes glinted. 'I could lift the odd bale of hay, I suppose. And I'm a dab hand at hoeing turnips.'

'And when you're famous and invited to all the literary parties, everyone will wonder why you married that funny woman with straw in her hair and mud under her fingernails –'

He pulled her to him again. 'No, they won't,' he said. 'They'll be sick with jealousy.' He took her two hands in his, and said again, 'It'll work, won't it, Thomasine?'

She looked up at him. She was smiling. 'Yes. I think that it might.'

In Harold Markham's motor-car they drove to the coast. William sat in the back seat, the picnic basket beside him. The spring weather was fine, the fields almost clear of floodwater.

When they reached the coast, they walked together along the shingly beach. Daniel described to Thomasine the new house he would build for the three of them on the higher land that had once belonged to the Blythes. They picnicked on the sea-strand, wrapped in coats and scarves to protect them from the east coast's sharp wind. The high tide had cast up pink shells and brown ribbons of seaweed, and enough starfish to make a constellation. After they had eaten, they walked hand in hand along the sea-wall that jutted out into the waves. When she threw the Firedrake up into the sky, it seemed to Thomasine to pause for a moment in the parabola of its final flight, its colours glowing more brightly than ever before. And then it was gone, submerged for ever by the pounding waves.